GEMMA BURGESS

Brooklyn GIRLS

ANGIE

Quercus

First published in the US in 2014 by St. Martin's Press,
175 Fifth Avenue, New York, N.Y. 10010

This edition published in Great Britain in 2014 by

Quercus Editions Ltd
55 Baker Street
7th Floor, South Block
London
W1U 8EW

Copyright © Gemma Burgess 2014

The moral right of Gemma Burgess to be
identified as the author of this work has been
asserted in accordance with the Copyright,
Designs and Patents Act, 1988.

All rights reserved. No part of this publication
may be reproduced or transmitted in any form
or by any means, electronic or mechanical,
including photocopy, recording, or any
information storage and retrieval system,
without permission in writing from the publisher.

A CIP catalogue reference for this book is available
from the British Library

ISBN 978 1 78206 736 8

This book is a work of fiction. Names, characters,
businesses, organizations, places and events are
either the product of the author's imagination
or are used fictitiously. Any resemblance to
actual persons, living or dead, events or
locales is entirely coincidental.

1 3 5 7 9 10 8 6 4 2

Printed and bound in Great Britain by Clays Ltd, St Ives plc.

www.quercusbooks.co.uk

FIFE CULTURAL TRUST

HJ438037

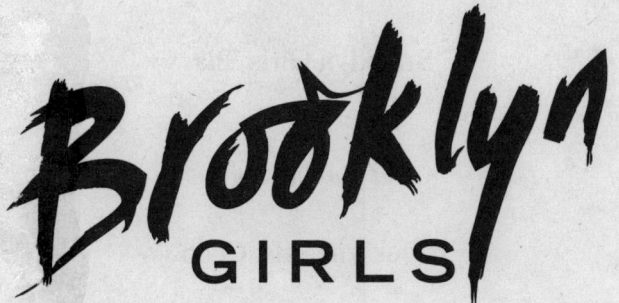

Also by Gemma Burgess

Brooklyn Girls: Pia

And coming soon

Brooklyn Girls: Coco

FIFE COUNCIL LIBRARIES	
HJ438037	
Askews & Holts	30-Oct-2015
AF	£6.99
GEN	KY

FOR US

CHAPTER 1

I was really going to be somebody by the time I was twenty-three.

Have a career. Be good at something. Be happy.

But here I am, less than two months before my twenty-third birth-day, "catching up" with my mother Annabel over waffles and fruit juice in a tiny café called Rock Dog, because I am unemployed and have nothing better to do on a random weekday morning.

The waffles are organic, by the way, and the juice is organic lingon-berry, a ridiculous Scandinavian fruit famed for its antioxidants. This is Brooklyn, where the higher the obscurity, the higher the cred. Personally, I haven't got a problem with SunnyD or good old full-fat Coca-Cola, but whatever fries your burger, right?

And of course the waiter—whom Annabel has already quasi-yelled at twice—rushes up with the jug for a refill, trips, and *boom*. Lingonberry juice all over me. So now I'm soaked. The punch line to an already (not so) delightful morning.

He's mortified. "Oh my! I am so sorry, let me clean that up—"

"You can forget about the tip!" My mother is furious.

"Don't overreact," I interrupt her. "It was an accident."

"But your top is ruined!"

"I was sick of it anyway."

"I don't know why you insist on coming to these ridiculous places." God, she's in a bad mood. Her phone rings. "Bethany! . . . No, darling, I'm still with Angelique. Somewhere in Brooklyn. I know, I know—"

The waiter has tears in his eyes, he's blotting frantically and whispering, "I'm so sorry. I keep spilling things because I'm so nervous. This is my first job waiting tables."

"Dude, it's not a problem," I whisper back. "Never cry over anything that won't cry over you."

He brightens. "That is such a good life philosophy! Can I take that?"

"It's yours. Get some T-shirts printed. Or a bumper sticker. Knock yourself out."

He starts giggling. "You are hilarious, girl! I'm Adrian."

"Angie."

Annabel hangs up and blinks at me till Adrian leaves. She blinks when she's annoyed. Making friends with the waiter is just the kind of thing that would irritate her. "Well. I have some news. Your father and I are divorcing."

What?

That's why she came all the way from Boston to see me? I'm so shocked that I can't actually say anything. I just stare at her, a half-chewed bite of waffle in my mouth.

"It's been arranged." She examines her glass for kiss marks. "The papers are signed, everything is done."

I finally swallow. "You're . . . divorcing?"

"It's not a huge surprise, is it? Given what he's been up to over the years? And you're too old to be Daddy's little girl anymore, so I don't see why you'd be upset."

"Right on." I take out a cigarette and place it, unlit, in the corner of my mouth. I find cigarettes comforting. (Yes, I know, they're bad for you.) "You're divorcing. Gnarly."

My mother blinks at me again. Princess Diana had a formative influence on her maquillage philosophy: heavy on the navy eyeliner. *They're divorcing* is playing on a loop in my head. Why didn't my father tell me?

Annabel clears her throat. "You broke up with Mani, I take it? Single again?"

I don't answer. Last year I told her about the guy I thought I was in love with in an unguarded moment of total fucking stupidity. Just before he dumped me.

"Unlucky in love, that's you and me," she continues blithely. "Perhaps we can go on the prowl, hmm? How's darling Pia? Why don't we all get together and have a girls' night out?"

I stare at her for several long seconds. She's out of her fucking mind.

The minute she goes to the bathroom I make eye contact with Adrian and mime the international pen-scribble sign for "Check, please."

He hurries over. "I am so sorry again! It's on me, I really—"

"Don't be crazy," I say, handing over a fifty-dollar bill as I stand up and put my coat on. "No change. The tip is all for you."

"Oh, Angie, thank you!" Adrian looks like he's about to cry again, but then stares at me in concern. "Wait, are you okay?"

I nod, but I can't even look at him, or I swear to God I'll lose it. I need to be alone.

While my mother is still in the bathroom, I leave. She'll find her way back to her hotel in Manhattan somehow. My mother is British, she lives in Boston most of the time, and her only experience in New York was the year they lived here, on the Upper East Side, when she gave birth to me. She got so fat during pregnancy that she wouldn't leave the apartment after I was born in case she saw someone she knew. So apparently I didn't see the sun till I was five months old and she'd lost the weight. And that, my friends, sums up Annabel's whole approach to motherhood.

The moment I get outside, I light my cigarette. That's better. It's late February, and goddamn cold outside, but I'm toasty. I'm wearing my dead grandmother's fur coat that I turned inside out and hand-sewed into an old army surplus jacket when I was sixteen.

They're divorcing.

Well, finally, I guess, right? Dad hasn't exactly been the best husband. Not that she knows about any of that stuff. I wonder if he'll tell her now. Probably not. Why rock a boat that's already sinking, or whatever that saying is. For a second, I consider calling him. But what will I say— congratulations? Commiserations? Better to wait for him to call me.

But how does this work? Like, where will we spend Christmas next year? How does divorce work when your kid is an adult? It's not like they can have visitation rights or custody battles or whatever, right? Will we simply cease to exist as a family?

When I was little, we spent every Christmas at my grandmother's house in Boston. I always emptied my Christmas stocking on my parents' bed. I sat in between them while they had coffee and I had hot chocolate and we shared bites of buttery raisin toast. I'd take each present out of my stocking, one by one. They'd get all excited with me and we'd wonder how Santa knew exactly what I wanted and how he got to every house in the world in just one night. Pretty standard stuff, I bet, but a happy warmth washes over me thinking about it. It just felt . . . good. I can still remember that sense of security and togetherness.

Now I can't imagine ever having it again. There's a hollowness in my stomach where that feeling used to belong.

Maybe I should grow the hell up. Our family hasn't felt good for a long time. Plus, I'm nearly twenty-three, the age that, to me at least, has always been the marker of true adulthood. It's the end of the carefree-unbrushed-hair-forgot-my-bra-I'm-a-grad-winging-it early twenties, and the start of the matching-lingerie-health-insurance-real-career-serious-boyfriend mid-twenties. And I'm nowhere near any of those things.

They're divorcing.

I take out my phone and call Stef. He's this guy I know, a trust-fund baby with a lot of bad friends and nice drugs. He's always doing something fun. But today he's not answering.

I live with four other girls in an old brownstone called Rookhaven, in Carroll Gardens, an area of Brooklyn in New York City. I'd love to live in Manhattan, but I can't afford it, and my best friend Pia hooked me up with a cheap room here after graduation.

I didn't think I'd stick around long, but it's the sort of place where you get cozy, fast. Décor-wise, it's a cheesy time capsule, but I've been living here since last August, and now I even like that about it. What bad things can possibly happen in a kitchen that has smelled like vanilla and cinnamon forever?

I let myself in and head up the stairs to my room. "Is anyone home?"

No answer. No surprise. Everyone's at work. Until a few weeks ago I was working as a sort of freelance PA to Cornelia Pace, the spoiled daughter of some socialite my mother knows. Basically, I ran errands (dry-cleaning, tailoring, Xanax prescriptions) for her and she handed me cash when she remembered. Cornelia's in Europe skiing for the next, like, month. She said she'd call me when she gets back. I've got enough cash to survive until then. I hope.

And no, I don't take handouts. My folks paid my rent when I first moved in last year, and always gave me a generous allowance, but between you and me, they don't have the money anymore. A few investments went sour over the past few years, and my dad told me at Christmas that they were basically broke, which totally freaked me out. I'd never seen him look that defeated, and I can't be a financial burden on him anymore. Especially with the bombshell my mother just dropped. *They're divorcing.* . . .

Do you think that an empty, cold, gray house at 2:00 P.M. in February, with nothing to do and no dude to text, might be one of the most depressing things in the history of the fucking universe? Because I do. I feel like my toes have been cold forever.

Oh God, I need a vacation. I want sandy feet and clear blue skies and hot sun on my skin and that blissed-out exalted tingly-scalp feeling you get when you dive into the ocean and the cool seawater hits the top of your head. I crave it. We had the best vacations when I was little. My dad taught me how to sail and fish, and Annabel would stop wearing makeup and not worry about her hair for a few weeks. It was the closest to perfect we came as a family.

I flop down on my bed and look around my bedroom. Closet, drawers, a bookshelf with back issues of *Women's Wear Daily* and Italian *Vogue,* an old wooden desk with my sewing machine and drawings and photos that I never get around to organizing, and clothes on every surface. Particularly the floor.

Clothes are my life, but not in a pretentious-label-whore kind of way.

I honestly love H&M as much as Hermès (and my only Hermès was a present from an ex, anyway). Making clothes—or styling clothes or thinking about clothes or mentally planning how I could pick apart and resew my existing clothes, my future clothes, my friends' clothes, and sometimes, to be honest, total strangers' clothes—is my favorite pastime. I can lose hours just staring into space, thinking about it.

Apparently, this sartorial daydreaming gives my face a sort of detached "fuck-off" expression.

I wonder how many of my problems have been created by the fact that I look like an über-bitch when I'm really just thinking about something else?

Sighing, I reach into my nightstand where there's always my latest Harlequin, M&M's, cigarettes, and Belvedere vodka. I read a lot of romance novels; they're my secret vice. But they're not going to be enough today. All I want—no, all I *need*—is to forget about everything that's wrong with my life. I need to escape.

And I know exactly how to do it.

Cheers to me.

CHAPTER **2**

"What's up, ladybitches?" I stride into the kitchen and do a twirl hello.

It's just past 7:00 P.M., and everyone's home from work. They've all assumed their usual kitchen places: Pia's texting her boyfriend, Madeleine's reading *The New York Times*, Julia is answering e-mails on her BlackBerry and eating pasta, and Coco is baking. How productive. La-di-dah.

"Angelface!" exclaims Julia. "You're just in time. Deal me in."

Julia's the loud, sporty, high-fiving, hardworking banking trainee, former-leader-of-the-debate-team type, you know the kind of girl I mean? I think her hair automatically springs into a jaunty ponytail every time she gets out of bed. We didn't get along that well at first, but actually, I think she's pretty fucking cool. She really makes me laugh.

Maybe it just takes me a long time to get to know people. Or for them to get to know me.

"Oh, I'll deal you in," I say, picking up the cards I always keep over the fridge. "I'll deal you in real good, just the way you like it."

Julia snorts with laughter. "You make everything sound dirty."

"Everything is dirty," I reply. "If it's done right."

"What's on your top?"

"Lingonberry juice. Duh."

"Have you been drinking?" asks Pia, looking up.

Pia's my best friend, and she used to be a reliable party girl, a high-maintenance and hilarious drama queen lurching from meltdown to meltdown, but then she went and got her shit together. Now she has a serious career in food trucks and a serious boyfriend named Aidan. She even looks after his dog when he's away, that's how serious it is. Serious, serious, serious. I'm happy for her—no, I really am. I've known Pia forever, she's so smart and funny and she deserves to be happy. But I miss her. Even when she's right here, it sort of feels like she's not really here. If that makes sense.

Pia stares at me now. She's absolutely gorgeous: mixed Swiss-Indian heritage, green eyes, and long dark hair. "Seriously, ladybitch. Have you?"

"No! . . . Okay, that's a lie. Yes, I've been drinkin'. Actually, I've been drinkin' and sewin'," I say, shuffling the cards so fast they look like a ribbon.

Drinkin' and sewin' was actually kind of fun. One part of my brain was focusing on the sewing, the other part was skipping around my subconscious, thinking about movies and books and Mani—the fuckpuppet who dumped me last year—and what my grandmother taught me about pattern cutting and wondering when my father would call.

"Angie, it's a school night," says Pia. She's wearing her version of corporate attire: skinny jeans, heeled boots, and a very chic jacket that— wait a second, that's *my* very chic jacket. "Don't you have to work for Cornelia in the morning?"

"Cornelia doesn't exactly need me to be firing on all cylinders," I say. "Or any cylinders." I haven't gone into details about my current job situation with the girls. "Nice jacket, by the way."

"Thanks. I asked your permission this morning, but you were sleeping at the time."

"I think I'll take the rest of this lasagne down to Vic later," says Coco. Vic's our ancient downstairs neighbor who has lived in the garden-level apartment for longer than I've been alive.

"Good idea, Cuckoo," says Julia.

Coco beams. Such an approval junkie. Coco is Julia's baby sister, and a total sweetheart. She's a preschool assistant, and whenever I think of her, I think of Miss Honey from that Roald Dahl book *Matilda*.

I take a swig of my drink and look around. How is it I can still feel alone in a room full of people? "How were your days at the office, dears?"

"Shit," say Julia and Madeleine at the same moment Pia says, "Awesome!"

"I'm on a project so boring, I may turn into an Excel spreadsheet," says Madeleine. She's kind of an enigma. (Wrapped in a mystery. Hidden in a paradox. Or whatever that saying is.) Accountant, Chinese-Irish heritage, smart, snarky, does a lot of running and yoga and shit like that. Pia once described her as "nice but tricky." Recently Madeleine joined a band, as a singer, but she hasn't let us see them live yet. Who the fuck wants to be a singer but doesn't want anyone to actually hear them sing?

"At least your work environment isn't hostile. I sit next to a total douche who stares at my boobs all day," says Julia.

"To be fair, your rack is enormous," I point out. Julia frowns at me. Oops. That comment might have pissed her off. Oh well, if you can't laugh at your own norks, what can you laugh at, right?

"Well, I'm happy. SkinnyWheels Miami has doubled profits in under a month," says Pia. SkinnyWheels is a food truck empire she started a few months ago. You know the drill: tasty food that won't make you fat. Sometimes I think Pia has literally replaced our friendship with a truck. Well, a truck and a hot British dude who has his own place, so she practically lives there. But it's not like I can beg her to be my best friend again, right? I'm a grown-up. Adult. Whatever. The point is, we're not fucking twelve.

"Actually, I'm happy, too. My boss said 'great job' again today. That's the second time this year!" Julia looks insanely proud, and spills pasta sauce on her suit jacket. "Fuck! Every fucking time!"

"Does anyone want herbal tea?" says Madeleine, standing up.

I raise my glass. "Could you dunk the tea bag in my vodka?"

Madeleine gazes at me. "Is that a withering look?" I say. "Because it needs practice. You just look a bit lost and constipated. Maybe you should—Oh, no, wait. Now *that's* withering."

Madeleine ignores me.

"How about you, Coconut?" I look over at Coco. "Good day shaping young hearts and minds?"

She grins at me, all freckles and blond bob and oven mitts, and her usual layers and layers of dark "hide me!" clothes. "I got peed on."

"Someone took a *piss* on you?" I pause. "People pay good money for that."

"Ew! Gross! He is four years old! And it was a mistake. I hope."

No one asks me how my day was, and they all go back to their own things, so I get up and open the freezer, where I always keep a spare bottle of Belvedere, and fix myself another three-finger vodka on the rocks, with a slice of cucumber and a few crumbs of sea salt. My dad taught me this drink; we drank it together at the Minetta Tavern last time he was in Manhattan, about a month ago. But he didn't say anything about a divorce.

Cheers to me.

Several swigs later, I take a cigarette out of my pack and prop it in the corner of my mouth, and look around at the girls, so calm and happy together, so sure of one another and their place in the world. I can't remember the last time I felt like that. Is there anything worse than feeling alone when you're surrounded by your friends?

My phone buzzes. Finally! A text from Stef. *Just woke up. Making a plan. xoxo*

It's weird the way he ends texts with *xoxo*, I think, making myself another drink. He's like a chick.

"Oh, Angie, there's mail for you." Julia points at some packages on the sideboard. "What the hell do you keep ordering?"

"Stuff." I start opening them. Buttons from a little store in Savannah, a bolt of yellow cotton from a dress shop in Jersey, and a gorgeous 1930s ivory lace wedding dress that I bought for two hundred dollars on eBay when I was drunk last weekend.

Julia screws her face up at the dress. "Wow. That is fucking disgusting."

This riles me up for some reason, though the shoulder pads and puffed sleeves *are* a little Anne of Green Gables meets *Dynasty*. "This lace is exquisite," I snap. "And the bodice structure is divine, so I'm gonna take the sleeves off and make a little top."

"Good luck with that," says Julia, with a laugh in her voice, which annoys me more.

"I'm not taking fashion advice from someone who wears a double-breasted green pantsuit to work."

"This pantsuit is from Macy's! And who died and made you Karla Lagerfeld?"

"You mean Karl Lagerfeld."

"I know that! I was making a joke."

"Really? What was the punch line?"

"Kids, play nice," says Pia, a warning in her voice.

"I am nice," says Julia. "Angie's the one living in a vodka-fueled dream world. I can't even remember the last time I saw her sober."

"That is a total lie! I was sober when I saw you this morning! As you headed out the door with your pantsuit and gym bag and laptop like the one percent banker drone that you are!"

"Okay, that's enough!" Pia says. "Both of you say you're sorry and make up."

I stand up. "Fuck that. I'm out of here."

I slug my vodka, run upstairs, throw on my sexiest white dress from Isabel Marant, some extremely high heels, my fur/army coat, take a moment to smear on some more black eyeliner, and stomp down to the front door. I love wearing white. It makes me feel clean and pure, like nothing can touch me.

I can hear the girls talking happily again in the kitchen, ruffles smoothed over, conversation ebbing and flowing the way it should. Without me.

For a second, just as I close the front door, I'm overwhelmed by the urge to run back and apologize for being a drunk brat. To find my place as part of the group, with all the ease and laughter and fun that entails . . . But I don't fit with them. Not really. Pia was my only tie to them, and she doesn't even act like she likes me these days. Though I don't like me much these days, either.

Anyway, I already said I was leaving. I need to stick to my word.

I call Stef from the cab. This time, he answers.

"My angel. Got a secret bar for you. Corner of Tenth Avenue and Forty-sixth Street. Go into a café called Westies and through the red door at the back."

He always knows the best places.

I quickly check my outfit in the cab; this is a great dress. Short, white, with a sort of punk-hipster-Parisian attitude. I tried to copy it last week but failed; I can't get the arms quite right.

And by the way, I tried to get a job in fashion when I first got to New York. I sent my résumé and photos of the stuff I've made and some designs I'd been sketching to all my favorite New York fashion designers. No response. So then I sent all the same stuff to my second-favorite designers. Then my third favorites. And so on. No one even replied. I don't have a fashion degree—my parents wanted me to get (I quote) a "normal" education first—and I don't have any direct fashion experience at all. I thought maybe I could leapfrog over from my job with the food photographer I worked for last year, but then she fired me. (Well, I quit. But she would have fired me anyway.)

The problem is that when you're starting out, there's nowhere to start. And there are thousands—maybe tens of thousands—of twenty-two-year-old girls who want to work in fashion in New York. Girls who do little fashion illustrations and take photos and love clothes. I'm a total cliché. And I hate that. I feel . . . *different*. I can't explain it, I'm just sure I am.

So I never talk about my secret fashion career dream. It's easier that way. Secretly wanting something and not getting it is one thing. I can handle that; I'm good at it. But talking about wanting it, putting it out there, making it real . . . and then not getting it? I couldn't deal with that much failure.

The café, Westies, is in Hell's Kitchen, an area of Manhattan I'm not that familiar with, but it seems appropriate today. The streets are freezing and empty, heaped with filthy, blackened snow. Manhattan looks mean in February.

Stef's car is parked outside. Predictably, it's his pride and joy, a red Ferrari 308 GTS. It's a gorgeous car, I admit. A little "look at me!" for my taste, but he loves it.

I stride into the empty café—past greasy counters and scabby cup-

cakes on a dirty cake stand—to the back wall, open the red door, walk
down some stairs that smell strangely like cabbage and yeast, past a
dark red velvet curtain, and find myself in a warm, dark little room.

There's a ladder against a wall, where someone's been putting up dark
red wallpaper. A handful of small round tables, a mirrored bar, candles,
and the Ramones playing in the background. The perfect secret after-
hours bar.

Stef's the only person in here, and he's sitting at the bar. He's cute,
though a little simian for my liking. Overconfident and overintense
with the eye contact. You know the type.

"What's up?" I greet him with a triple cheek kiss, the way Stef always
does.

"Nothing, my angel," he says, running his hand through his hair and
lighting a cigarette. Wow, this must be a secret bar if they let you smoke
inside. "How's life with Cornie? It's so cute that you work for her. Does
she say *yoo-hoo* every morning when she sees you?"

"She's away." Stef is part of that Upper East Side Manhattan rich kid
crowd that all know one another, always have and always will, and so is
Cornelia. "I need to make some money, fast."

"You wanna split an Adderall?"

"Sure." I look around. "So who do I have to blow to get a drink
around here?"

"You're funny. This is my buddy's place. It's not open to the public
yet, but the bar's fully stocked. Help yourself." Stef takes out his wallet,
looking for his pills. He has a sort of cracked drawl, so he sounds permanently amused and slightly stoned. He probably is. "Fix me something while you're at it. I'm going to the bathroom."

Two dirty vodka martinis and half an Adderall later, the world is a
lot smoother.

I like Stef, I really do. I think he's a nice guy underneath the
slightly sleazy exterior. There's nothing between us, either, which is so
refreshing.

And he's been good for meeting guys. That's how I met Mani last
year. He's the one who bought me this dress, actually. He liked shopping. He also dumped me without a second thought or a follow-up
phone call. I really thought we were in a serious relationship, so I guess

I was, um, stunned by that. The previous guy, Marc, had been married, and messed me around for a long time, but I thought Mani was the real thing. He wasn't. I sort of partied my way through November to get over it. Then just before Christmas I began sort-of seeing another friend of Stef's called Jessop, from L.A. But he only called me when he was in New York, which was rarely, and it fizzled out.

My love life is like a cheap match. Lots of sparks but the flame never catches. I pretend I don't care, of course. Even when I'm dying inside, I just put a cigarette in my mouth and say something stupid and flippant, and no one can ever tell. Well, Pia can. Or used to.

"You are very good at making dirty martinis, Angie," says Stef, taking another sip of his drink.

"One of my not-so-hidden talents," I reply. Alcohol always makes me cocky.

"I'll just bet."

"Hey guys," says a voice as two guys, one heavy and one skinny, walk into the bar.

"Angie, this is Busey and Emmett. Emmett is the owner of this particular establishment."

"Hey," I say. "Love the place. Does it have a name?"

"Not yet," says Emmett, the skinnier guy, fixing himself a drink in that self-consciously arrogant way that guys who own bars always do. "Why? Got any ideas?"

"Name it after me," I say. "The Angie."

The guys laugh. "Fuck it, why not?" Emmett smiles, holding my gaze just a fraction too long. "Maybe I will."

"Emmett, a word in my office?" says Busey. I look over. He's racking up lines on one of the little round tables. Ugh, I am so over coke.

"Angie? Ladies first."

"Not for me," I say. "Not my bag."

"I'm good for now, buddy," Stef takes out a little leather purse. "Let's have a smoke, and then I've got a couple of parties for us."

"Okay," I say. "What are we smoking?" It doesn't look like plain old weed.

"That's for me to know and you to enjoy."

For a second, I wonder if I should. I've been drinking since, what, 2:00 P.M.? And Adderall sometimes makes me a little crazy.

Then I think about why I started drinking. And about the fact that my father still hasn't called. I don't want to feel alone right now.

"My folks are splitting up," I say to Stef, accepting the joint.

"Mazel tov! Welcome to the club. Let's celebrate."

CHAPTER 3

I wake up naked. And alone.

The first thing I think is: forty-one days till I turn twenty-three.

The second thing I think is: something is wrong.

I'm not sleeping on my pillow. I always have the same pillow. It fits my head perfectly. This pillow is higher, firmer.

I open my eyes and sit up real fast, my heart hammering with panic. Where the hell am I? Big bed, square windows, taupe blinds, huge TV, desk, one of those weird phones with the Line 1 and Line 2 buttons.

A hotel room. NakedinahotelroomIamnakedinahotelroom.

Okay, breathe, Angie, breathe . . .

On the nightstand there's a little notepad with SOHO GRAND printed on it. I know that hotel. It's in downtown Manhattan. And the clock says it's 10:00 A.M.

Fuck.

What am I doing here?

I try to remember last night.

We hung out in the bar with no name for a while, drank more, then we met some friends of his—an Italian guy? And was the chick Croatian? Something like that. Then we were in some new bar on Lafayette, or maybe it was Hudson? Or did we get a cab uptown?

Nothing. I remember nothing.

With a sick thud somewhere deep inside me, I see the indent of a head in the other pillow. I didn't sleep here alone.

Maybe the pillow just does that. Or maybe I started the night sleeping on that side.

I head to the bathroom to pee. The wallpaper has cool little cartoon drawings of birds. Nice. It'd make a cute fabric print actually.

Then, with an even sicker thud than before, I see something in the bottom of the toilet bowl.

A discarded condom.

Stef, probably. We've had sex before. It was years ago, at a house party in Boston, and it was not pleasant, but shit happens. At least we used a condom.

Goddamnit. I always end up sleeping with my male friends. A couple of drinks, I think maybe I have feelings for them, they give me that *look* and then . . . boom. It's totally wrong, I know. But I always seem to do it. I always think that this time it'll be different. I'm a sexual optimist.

I quickly shower, lathering soap all over my body to obliterate the sticky drunk-sex-morning-after feeling, and use the hotel shampoo and conditioner. My hair is pale blond, almost white, and very long, and it responds well to almost any hair product. As does my liver with almost any booze. Ha.

I wish I had a toothbrush. I look like shit, but I can make a quasi–smoky eye by rubbing yesterday's mascara and eyeliner around my eyelid. Part panda, part rock groupie. Fine.

It's when I'm getting dressed that I notice it, right over on the TV cabinet.

My cell phone, propped carefully over a Soho Grand envelope with "A xx" written on the front.

First I pick up my phone. Two missed calls and a text from Pia wondering where I am. She didn't even bother to get in touch until this morning. Thanks a lot, ladybitch. If she left the house drunk and upset, I'd sure as hell chase her. Though she wouldn't do that, of course. Not anymore.

Then I open the envelope.

It's full of hundred-dollar bills. Thirty of them.

Three thousand fucking dollars.

I count it again quickly, my skin burning strangely at the sight of so much cash. It's such a tiny stack of notes, but just imagine what I could buy with it. . . . Holy shit, that's a lot of money. That's more than Cornelia gave me every month. When she remembered.

Three thousand dollars.

I pause, looking out the hotel window over SoHo. I can see over the downtown rooftops, some with those funny Manhattan water thingies on top, and a bit of West Broadway, and people walking and shopping and going to Felix for brunch and leading ordinary days that probably didn't start naked, alone, and confused in a hotel room.

Why would Stef give me three thousand dollars?

Then my phone buzzes again.

It's Stef.

Hey kitten! Great night. Sorry for bailing, but hope you two had fun. . . . ;-) Heading to a party in Turks tomorrow if you want to come. xoxo

What does he mean "hope you two had fun"? Two who? Who two? And he bailed? So I didn't sleep with him? And the money isn't from him? Who is it from? Who the fuck did I sleep with?

I turn the envelope over again. No signature. Nothing else.

I feel sick.

I don't want to think about it, so I quickly throw my white dress back on, tie my wet hair into a tight little knot and secure it with the Soho Grand pencil, put the "A xx" envelope in my fur/army coat, and leave the room. I hope I don't see Mani. He used to hang out in the lobby here a lot. He was so—Urgh, *why* am I thinking about my ex-boyfriend at a time like this?

Five-inch heels before noon: not cool. The Soho Grand lobby, at least, is kind of sexy and dusky, so I don't feel too out of place, but once I'm outside, the freezing white glare of the February morning is horrific.

I feel like everyone is looking at me and thinking, *Slut.* I try my usual walk-of-shame trick of dialing up the attitude and pretending I'm too gnarly for this shit, but it doesn't work.

Deep inside my body I'm nauseous . . . in my soul, or heart, or brain, or something. Cold and itchy.

I always do the wrong thing. Always.

It's always an accident.

But it's always wrong.

A tall doorman with kind eyes puts me in a taxi, and I say, "Union Street, Brooklyn, please."

And then as the cab starts driving, I lean forward, bury my face in my knees so the driver can't see me, and cry.

CHAPTER 4

When I get home, I throw my dress and shoes in the very back of my closet so I don't have to think about them again. Then I put on my favorite old jeans and a pale gray rowing sweater that belonged to my dad when he was at Princeton. I saved it from being thrown out in one of Annabel's house purges years ago, and I wear it on special occasions, when my soul is cold and anxious and I really need comforting. It's like sartorial Xanax.

Three thousand dollars. Three thousand dollars.

Grabbing my latest romance novel, *Heart Crossing*, I glance at the back.

Angry, petulant Ivy hated the imperious Captain Drummond almost as much as she hated love. When the only way to save her invalid aunt is to marry the captain, she thinks she knows what to expect. But she didn't know she was about to meet her match. . . .

They always meet their match in the blurbs, have you ever noticed?

Yeah, I know it's seriously uncool to read romance novels, and yeah, I know that it's lame that the dude is always a rich guy and the chick is always a secretary and all that. I don't care. A good romance novel is simple, predictable, and makes me smile. Perfect escapism.

Except today, it's not helping me escape. I keep starting paragraphs and halfway through, I've already forgotten what I've read.

Three thousand dollars.

I can't bear to be alone with my thoughts today. And there's only one solution.

Cheers to me.

Swigging vodka periodically and smoking out my window when the urge takes me, I play around with some vintage silky scarves covered in faded gold Art Deco prints that I picked up last week at Brownstone Treasures, this little place on Court Street, and sew them into a cool little clutch bag.

I have to pick the bag apart and resew it four times, but by about 6:00 P.M. and after the rest of the vodka, it's just how I want it. Perfectly sized to fit my phone, keys, cigarettes, money, and lipstick, with a little flat handle so it sort of hugs my hand just right, and padded with extra layers of scarves so it scrunches softly. The rain is hammering down outside, it's freezing cold and dark and endlessly, endlessly February. But right now I don't care. I'm sewing something out of almost nothing, making the dreams in my head into reality, creating something new and real and lovely.

My phone rings. I glance at it and quickly press "Ignore." Annabel. My mother. Probably calling to give me shit for leaving the other day. I don't want to talk to her until my dad calls me. I haven't heard from him yet, but maybe he's waiting until we can talk in person. He usually comes to New York about once a month for work.

The combination of hangover and vodka suddenly has me starving. So I smile at my handiwork once more, and then head down to the kitchen for some raisin toast with extra butter, cinnamon, and brown sugar (one of the best things in the whole world, by the way).

Three thousand dollars. Three thousand dollars.

It's not like I'm a bad person just for blacking out, right?

My vodka stash in the freezer has run out, so I open a bottle of Merlot that someone brought home. It's pretty nasty—very acidic, which Merlot shouldn't be (I know I sound like a wine fuckwit, and I'm at peace with that). But it's wet and alcoholic and that is what I need to survive the rest of the day. I'll buy another to replace it. As I'm pulling out the cork, I notice that the old green curtains above the kitchen window are torn. Like, seriously torn. I could fix them! That would be a good peace offering for Julia. Maybe she'd like me again.

So I climb on the kitchen counter, slightly unsteadily, carefully take down the curtains, pick up my toast and wine, and with the curtains tucked under my arm, head back upstairs.

La-di-dah! Thank hell for booze, right? I bet it would be easy to make new curtains for my bedroom, too. Maybe I could—Oh . . . shit.

I tripped and spilled wine *everywhere*. All over the curtains, and the carpet and wallpaper outside Julia's and Pia's rooms. It's all one big, red stain.

I'll just hand wash the old curtains now and then fix them and then deal with the other cleanup later. The curtains probably need cleaning anyway, right? They're like a hundred years old!

I try to wash them. I really do. But the stain won't come out.

Wait! Brain wave! I'll make curtains out of that new yellow cotton I just ordered instead. It'd be an even better peace offering for Julia, and yellow would look great in the kitchen! Yes!

I should always drink and sew.

Because then, an hour later, when I head back down to the kitchen to hang our brand-new, beautiful yellow curtains, I feel warm and loose and absogoddamnlutely peachy keen.

I climb up onto the counter, wobbling slightly. The kitchen so looks different from up here! And I carefully reach up to rehang the curtains.

BANG!

The front door slams, surprising me. I lose my balance and instinctively grab at the curtains as I fall backward off the counter and *whoomp* hit my head on a chair or the table or something, ripping down the entire curtain rail off the window frame at the same time. I land hard on my back, plaster and paint and wood chips showering over my body like confetti.

The pain is immediate.

Like the shrieking.

Julia. Of course. "What the fuck are you doing!? You've destroyed my fucking kitchen!"

I can't move, so I just lie on the floor and close my eyes, my head *bangbangbanging*. It really hurts. I can feel the throbbing reverberating in my cheekbones, the shock of the fall bringing a painful lump to my throat and tears to my eyes. What kind of person cries after she falls over? What am I, some kind of sissy?

God, I feel so detached from myself. It's like I'm watching myself lying prostrate and alone on the kitchen floor. Alone. Always, always alone.

I wonder when my dad will call.

"You're drunk again," Julia says. "And you reek of cigarettes."

I move my arms up, slowly, over my head, so that I'm hiding my face in the crook of both elbows. Maybe if I lie here long enough she'll go away. I wish I wasn't here.

Then I hear the front door bang again. It's Pia. On the phone with Aidan, as usual.

"No, you pick a restaurant. Why? Because I am not the goddess of food! . . . Ha, you are a sweet talker. . . ." I hear her footsteps approach the kitchen. "Oh . . . *merde*. Aidan? I'll call you back."

Julia: "She's drunk."

Pia: "Angie, are you okay?"

Julia: "She's fine! She's like one of those alcoholics who survive tornados!"

Julia leaves the room; I can hear her *stompstompstomping* up the stairs. "Sort it out, Pia! This is your goddamn problem!"

I'm not Pia's problem. I'm not anyone's problem except my own.

"Ladybitch?" Pia says softly. But I don't reply. I don't even move. I can't. I just lie still, in my bubble of aloneness, my arms still covering my face, and listen to the *whompthump* of the pain in my head, and a weird rocking feeling in the base of my throat. A tear escapes my right eye and runs down to my ear. "Angie? Do you want to talk?"

Something warm and sticky is running down behind my ear, different from the silky tickle of tears. Blood.

"JESUS CHRIST!" Julia shouts. "The landing is trashed! What the hell is *that*?"

Oh God. The wine. I forgot to clean it up.

"This won't come out! It's dried on the carpet. And the wallpaper is stained. How dare that fucking ice queen treat my home like this!"

"Calm down, Jules," says Pia. I hear her open the cabinet under the sink and pull out cleaning products. "Angie, I love you, but you're going to have to start talking to me. *Now*."

Right. Because she'd totally listen right now. And stick around more than five minutes after I stopped talking. What's the point of ever sharing problems with anyone? People always just leave, and then they have your secrets, and you can never get them back.

"Angie. I mean it."

I ignore her, my arms still hiding my face. When she leaves, I slowly roll over to my tummy and feel my head to figure out where the blood is coming from. A little graze to the temple, that's all. The kitchen linoleum is cold against my face. From this weird angle I can see that it's gritty with dirt, it needs sweeping or Swiffering or mopping or something, and it's probably my turn. I haven't even looked at the stupid chore sheet in weeks.

Three thousand dollars.

Don't think about it.

"She's a fucking liability, Pia," I can hear Jules saying upstairs. "She's unreliable, she's selfish, she just does whatever the hell she wants to do and everyone else can go fuck themselves. I can't take living with her much longer."

"Would you give it a rest, Jules? She's been my best friend since we were born."

"And she's always drunk. She's got a problem, Pia."

"She is *not* always drunk. Sheesh! And you call me a drama queen. She's just . . . tough to get to know."

"Tough as nails and cold as ice, you mean."

I don't want to be here anymore.

I stand up, steadying myself against the counter. Woo! Head rush.

I grab a kitchen towel, hold it to my bleeding temple, and rush upstairs as quickly as I can—past the first floor landing where Jules and Pia are cleaning the carpet and wallpaper—to my room. I grab my big duffel and swiftly throw in my clutch, bikinis, summer dresses, heels, travel toiletry kit, makeup bag, and passport. At the last minute I add two packs of Marlboro Lights, take one cigarette out and put it in the corner of my lips, and grab my open bottle of wine. Then I change out of my dad's Princeton sweater and pull on a white cashmere sweater, my fur/army coat, and sunglasses.

Duffel over my shoulder, I head downstairs, lighting my cigarette as I go.

"Where are you going?" snaps Julia.

I exhale my cigarette smoke and take a swig of the wine, my face twitching with the effort of a cold smile. "I'm going to the fucking beach."

CHAPTER 5

Good decision.

Coming to Turks and Caicos was a good decision.

Right?

Yes.

I called Stef the moment I left the house.

It sounded like he was in a bathroom. "Babe! Hosting a gathering at my place. And my friend Hal is throwing a party tomorrow. He's dying to meet you!"

I wanted to ask him who I slept with at the Soho Grand. I wanted to ask him if he knew why someone would give me three thousand dollars for no reason. But I didn't. I just shut up, drank my wine straight from the bottle, gave the driver a twenty to let me smoke in his cab, and tried not to think about it. Tried very, very hard.

Stef greeted me with a handful of pills and a bottle of Grey Goose. The next few hours became a blur. A party, a car, an airport, a plane charter, people laughing and shrieking. I just kept my sunglasses on and tried to look in control.

For a split second, as we boarded the plane, I wanted to turn around and run back to Rookhaven.

But I said I was going to the beach. And I hate going back on my word.

I sat in a corner and zoned out while everyone else partied, and next thing I knew, we'd landed. Everything had the glow of early dawn, and I could smell the ocean. We were finally in Turks and Caicos, a tiny, rustic, decidedly un–New York group of islands somewhere in the Caribbean. Sunshine and bare feet. Exactly what I need.

Forty days till I turn twenty-three.

Within minutes of landing, we're in open-top jeeps on the way to the party. I'm in the back of the smaller jeep, next to some Swedish guy called Lars, but he's been on the phone most of the time. Stef's sitting up front. He's hungover, I think, and very quiet underneath his straw boater hat. ("It's ironic!" he said, when I raised an eyebrow at it. "If you have to explain that it's ironic, it's probably not," I replied.)

I love—*love*—the Caribbean. I love sandy roadsides and paint-chipped houses and blue skies that look like they stretch forever. I love the big, strange blocky buildings that pop up now and again by the side of the highway, banks and hospitals and supermarkets, with parking lots that could fit hundreds, as though they're expecting a population boom any minute now. I love the eye-achingly bright light and the way the air feels so pure and warm when you breathe. . . .

I'm so fucking over New York.

And I'm *really* over Brooklyn.

The hot sun on my bare skin right this second is possibly the best thing I've ever felt. I'm sitting on my fur/army coat, wearing a little white sundress that I put on when we landed, and my studded Converse because I forgot to pack my flip-flops. With every breath of warm salty air, I can feel my bones thaw, my jaw relax, and the cold anxiety in my soul ease, for the first time in weeks.

When we arrive at Turtle Cove Marina, it's shiny and new and weirdly out of place in the shabby warmth of the rest of the island. Three young men wearing white polo T-shirts, shorts, and knee-high white socks—the kind of crew uniform that tends to indicate someone's working on a very, very, *very* big boat—come and grab our bags.

Everyone surges ahead, racing down the pier as though there's a prize at the end. There are eight of us in total: four other girls, all about my age, all gorgeous, all acting like best friends but ignoring me, all constantly reglossing suspiciously plump lips. Plus Swedish Lars, some guy called Beecher who kept cracking unfunny jokes about the mile high club while we were taking off in New York, and, of course, Stef. And me.

Three thousand dollars.

Don't think about it.

I look ahead and see a worryingly shitty-looking speedboat onto which our luggage is being loaded by the boat boys. The girls start squealing.

"Where the fuck did you find them?" I murmur to Stef.

"Old friends, babe, old friends."

Stef looks like shit. Pale and blotchy, with cracked skin in the corners of his mouth. It hits me that I've never seen him in daylight before. And I've known him for six years.

Wow. The realization stops me for a moment.

What am I doing here? Taking a vacation with Stef, the Jovial Medicated Playboy, and a cast of strangers?

Standing still, trying to gather whatever wits I have left, I watch everyone else surge ahead. The girls step from the pier into the speedboat, all squealing with excitement or fear or both, even though the boat is barely rocking at all and the boat boys are on hand to help them. One is offering them glasses of champagne.

But where are they taking us?

And where is the host? Hal, or whatever his name is?

Is getting on a tiny speedboat with people I don't really know the worst idea ever? Or the best, given my reality right now?

To stall for thinking time, I light a cigarette.

"Hey, you can't smoke on the marina," shouts a voice. I look over. One of the boat boys. Tall, tan, clean-cut, blond, ridiculously chiseled, as though he was bioengineered as an example of perfect all-American manhood. "Fire hazard. Gas spills."

I look around. The pier is totally dry beneath my studded Converse.

He reads my mind. "I know, it's not likely. I'm just saying, it's against the rules. You'll get a fine."

"The *rules*? Whose rules? What are you, some kind of nautical Nazi Youth?"

He raises his eyebrows in surprise, and then assumes the professional all-American mask again. "Something like that."

I take one last drag of my cigarette, stub it out, and walk toward the speedboat, ignoring him. How bad can a yacht party be when some angel-faced boat boy is freaking out about a stupid cigarette? This is just another rich guy's folly. Some loaded, insecure friend of Stef who wants to impress his friends and a bunch of girls by showing them a good time in the Caribbean sunshine. Bet you twenty bucks this Hal guy wears his shirt undone to midchest and says things like "island time, mon."

Once on board the speedboat, I grab a glass of champagne. Cheers to me.

And like I say, it's a good decision. Because the minute we clear the marina, the yacht—sorry, the superyacht—we're about to board comes into view. It's stunning, like something out of a movie, over 250 feet long, with three tiers stacked up like a wedding cake.

"A staff of eighteen for the comfort of up to twelve guests." A rote speech from one of the boat boys. I look around for my clean-cut goody-two-shoes. He's up front, staring into the wind. "Equipped with a swimming pool and a helipad, the *Hamartia* also boasts nine staterooms, including an indoor cinema and a fully equipped gymnasium with two state-of-the-art Pilates reformers."

"Oh, gnarly. I can work on my core," I say, to no one in particular. Which is good, because no one is listening.

"I am *literally* freaking out, you guys!" one of the girls squeals. "*Literally*. This is me, *literally* freaking out."

We pull up to the *Hamartia* and go on board. It's even bigger up close: shiny, white, and immaculately clean, like a bathroom turned inside out.

The other girls are squeaking and clapping their hands, and then accept yet more champagne from another boat boy. The crew is all men, I notice. And the host is nowhere in sight.

Something isn't right.

I turn to Stef. "What are we really doing here?"

He smiles, looking as unattractive as I've ever seen him. "Just good fun, babe."

Hmm.

Thinking, I gaze out at the view. We're a long way from shore. I can just make out the luxury hotels along Grace Bay beach, some with cabanas set up out front. People lined up working on their tans, or their marriages, or whatever people go on vacation to do.

There are three other yachts within swimming distance, and I can see a family running around on one, the daddy showing his kids how to do the mainsail, or some shit like that. My father taught me to sail, too. He taught me to sail but can't bother to call and tell me about the divorce.

My parents are divorcing. Wow. Every now and again it hits me, however much I try to ignore it. He hasn't called, and I haven't called my mother back. . . . It's like our family died or something.

I suddenly have a thumping headache that the champagne won't help. Caffeine. I need caffeine. And sugar.

"Could I please get some Coke?" I ask the boat boy offering the champagne, a short guy with a terrible cliché of a goatee.

"Si." Goatee draws a little one-inch-square plastic packet of white powder from his pocket and drops it into my hand. I stare at it for a second.

"No, um, a Coca-Cola," I say, staring at it. Cocaine. Fuck me, the crew is actually handing out drugs?

"I'll take that for later," says Stef, smoothly pocketing it. He swings an arm around my back. It's annoyingly ownership-like, but reassuringly protective at the same time. "I'm going to bed with Dr. Ambien and Dr. Dramamine, babe. See you in eight hours."

"Uh—okay—" I say, suddenly feeling panicky. Stef is my only link to quasi-normality.

"Just enjoy yourself, hon," Stef gives my waist a little squeeze and heads belowdecks.

I look over and see that clean-cut boat boy staring at me again, but I ignore him. I am in control of this situation. I can handle this. I can handle anything.

"I'll take you to your cabins," says Goatee, and we all follow him, the girls shrieking all the way down.

The décor below deck is sort of pan-Asian, with dim, sexy lighting, Chinese illustrations, Thai sculptures, and Japanese blossom prints on the bed. Interior decorators don't always care about the cultural sanctity of their creations, I've noticed.

The girls pair off to sleep in doubles together. I'm given my own room, a single with a tiny en suite. Three bottles of Coca-Cola are already waiting in a bucket of ice on my dresser. Wow. That's good service.

With the door shut and locked, I lie down on the bed, still wearing my Converse and sunglasses. I have that numb thoughtless inertia that I always get after a heavy night of meds and booze. I should really stop doing it. I will, I will stop . . .

The yacht is rocking gently, the bed is soft and clean and . . . I'll just close my eyes.

CHAPTER 6

I wake up alone to the sound of happy shrieks outside my cabin window (porthole, whatever). I can see a speedboat going around, trailing two of the girls in one of those blow-up donut things.

Man, I am going to get seriously sick of hearing those chicks squeal.

It's just past 3:00 P.M. I should let Pia know where I am . . . but I don't have cell reception out here on the goddamn ocean. And she probably doesn't want to talk to me after my behavior last night. She's at work right now anyway. And I'm all the way down here in the Caribbean. Weird. The world is so big. It's easy to get lost.

I drink one of the Coca-Colas, take a long shower, French braid my hair and tie a red ribbon on the end just for fun, and throw on my white bikini, sunglasses, and my white sundress. I forgot to bring sunscreen, which is a drag. (My skin is so white it's nearly translucent. I swear to

God, I can't even fake tan, it's like my epidermis rejects it.) I have a little blister from wearing my Converse for too long without socks, and I have a feeling that heels are not appropriate on deck, so I go barefoot.

I look at myself in the mirror one last time before I leave my cabin.

"No drugs, and no meds," I say sternly to my reflection. Angie in the mirror nods back obediently.

When I get upstairs, the party is in full swing. Beecher is making out with one of the girls, Lars is drinking margaritas with another, and the squealers are back from their donut excitement, self-consciously wringing out their hair in the sunshine so they can dry off their personal-trainer-and-surgeon-sculpted bodies without resorting to something as unsexy as a towel. Stef isn't here. No one even looks up when I arrive.

"Could I get a margarita, please?" I say to the guy manning the bar. "Where is the host?" I ask. "Hal, isn't it?"

"I'm right here," says a voice. I turn around and am greeted by the sight of a swarthy dude wearing huge wraparound shades, white pants, and a white linen shirt (undone to midchest, ha, I knew it!). He's hotter than I imagined. "Angie, right? Finally, we meet. I'm so glad we both dressed to match."

I flash him my best smile. "Virginal white. That's totally my thing."

"I'll bet it is." Hal looks around. "Lars! Take it easy, my friend! Beecher, whoa there, big fella. Get a cabin."

He's normal! Well, rich-kid normal.

I can relax. It's just a bored, insecure rich kid's party. I can play this scene like a fucking guitar. (Well, okay, I can't play a guitar. Like a harmonica. Whatever.)

My margarita and I follow Hal down to a shaded lounging area where mellow trance music is softly playing.

"This music is seriously annoying," I say.

"What do you want to hear, Angie?" Hal grins lazily at me. He's definitely cute.

"I'm going through a nineties electro dance phase." I look him straight in the eye and play with my hair in the unaffected-yet-sexy-I-hope way that I always do when I like a guy.

"The Prodigy okay? Hey! Carlos!" Hal shouts up to the drug-dealing goatee boat boy. "Put The Prodigy on! And can we get a couple more drinks? What is this, island time, mon?"

Two for two.

We both light cigarettes, lie back, and look at the view. It's stunning: the calming blue of the sky and sea meeting in a perfect line far, far into the horizon, and sunshine that floods your brain with feel-good endorphins. I'm glad I came to this party. I pick up my margarita, smiling. Cheers to me.

"I love being by the ocean," Hal says. "When I'm away from it too long, I physically crave it. I have no idea how those people in the Midwest survive. Like farmers and cowboys."

"Yeah, I bet farmers and cowboys wake up every day and crave the ocean."

"The prettiest girl on the yacht is funny, too, huh?"

"I'm the whole package."

Gradually, everyone else from the party, except Stef, comes and sits around us. We're the center of attention for some reason. Even the girls who ignored me the entire flight are suddenly trying to start conversations. All of their sentences end in exclamation marks. Including the questions.

"How do you French braid your own hair!" asks one excitedly. "I find it, like, totally hard to see the back of my head!"

"I just close my eyes and feel my way around it," I say.

"That's totally my motto in life," says Hal, stretching out one arm behind my neck.

I turn my head to make eye contact with him, and we smirk at each other for a moment. Boo and ya. It is in the bag, baby. (Isn't that the most awesomely arrogant thing to say about a dude? Pia and I used to say it a lot as teenagers, and then normally had way too much fun just being with each other to bother with said dude. Damn, she was fun to be around. I miss her.)

Hal is lightly stroking one finger up and down the top of my arm. I think he's trying to be sexy, but it's just making me shiver uncomfortably. . . . Maybe we could go out for dinner or something, back in New York. Or maybe we'll make out later. Nothing more than that though, I've had enough meaningless-sex remorse for one week. (Urgh, don't think about it.)

I love kissing. Actually, no, you know what I really love? I love that moment right before you kiss, when the guy looks into your eyes, you know, and you feel that *spark*. That funny tingle, all over your body, when you know you're just seconds away from touching lips. It's so romantic, so mind-blowingly perfect. . . .

It's the prekiss. The moment when you know you're really, truly connecting with the guy. And it's almost always better than the kiss itself.

"What's your sign, Angie?" asks one of the girls, a sweet-faced brunette wearing last season's DVF.

"Aries," I say.

"Fire sign," says Hal. I find it weird when guys are into horoscopes, don't you? "And it's your birthday soon. How old are you turning?"

"Twenty-three."

"You don't look it!" chorus two of the other girls in unison.

"Wow, thanks," I say. "I'm going for the preteen look right now. Like a tween, you know, but stacked."

The girls are not sure if I'm joking.

Ignoring their confused looks, I take a cigarette out and Hal lights it for me. I stare up at him while he does it. Ah, flirting.

"Another margarita?" asks the goateed bartender a few minutes later. It's the same one who offered me cocaine. He's been bringing the drinks out fast, potent as hell. I should probably eat something. Then, as if someone's reading my mind, great platters of food arrive, and a giant jug of iced water.

"Conch fritters, a local speciality." It's that pain-in-the-ass clean-cut boat boy again. "And snapper sandwiches."

"Thank you! I am starving!" I grab a plate. The conch is kind of weird, but the sandwiches are amazing: soft bread, salty butter, and hot, crispy fish. None of the other girls are eating. I always wonder if girls like them don't eat in front of guys so that they'll think they don't have a digestive system and never poop or something. Not me. I'm an eater. And I poop. Deal with it.

I look up, halfway through my third sandwich, and catch the clean-cut boat boy's eye again. He's staring at me intensely, kind of disapprovingly. Unused to seeing girls eat, I bet.

So I take the rest of the sandwich and jam it into my mouth, all at once, edging it past my molars on either side, and look back at the boat boy, my cheeks stuffed with sandwich, my face bulging like a cartoon. Then I blink a few times like Bambi. His entire face lights up with an ear-to-ear grin. Ha! I snort with laughter, crumbs blowing out of my mouth, and the boat boy ducks his head and turns away to hide the fact that he's cracking up.

"Wow, *that* is attractive," says Hal, looking at me. Like the others, he's barely picked at a couple of conch fritters. He's on coke, I suddenly realize, chewing through the half-sandwich in my mouth. They all are. That's why they're not eating. And actually, Beecher and two of the girls have disappeared belowdecks. Oh, well. All the more food for me.

When my mouth is finally clear of sandwich, I take a slug of water and smile at Hal. "I have an appetite. Is that a problem?"

He grins. "Absogoddamnlutely not."

Another margarita or two and more Euro trance music later, and the sun begins to set. Lars and another one of the girls disappear, and the other girl passes out on one of the daybeds. They're all kind of strange, and I'm used to Stef's freak-show friends. I can't even figure out how everyone knows one another.

Hal turns to me. "You should come check out my cabin. It's ridiculous. There's a bar and everything."

"Really," I deadpan. Wow, is he really going to be that obvious? It's so transparent, it's almost adorable. "Are you going to make me a cocktail?"

"Yes," he says, grinning at me. "Yes, I am."

We get down to his cabin, the blast of the air-conditioning assaulting my sun-warmed skin. As you'd expect on a megayacht, it's ridiculously big and glossily immaculate, with a gigantic bed, a full sofa area with a bar, and even a diving terrace.

"Wow," I say. "What a dump."

Immediately, Hal disappears into the en suite. You know, I don't think I will make out with him after all. He's clearly more interested in taking drugs than talking to me.

Maybe I'll wake Stef and find out when we're leaving tomorrow. Brooklyn suddenly seems really far away, and not in a good way. This whole yacht scene feels a little . . . I don't know, creepy. And I really do want to make up with Julia. And everyone else, too. Now that I've relaxed a bit, the situation at Rookhaven doesn't seem so dire. Everything will be fine. It has to be. Right?

Hal shuffles out of the bathroom, wiping under his nostrils.

"How was the powder room, dear?"

"You want?" he says, pointing his thumb in the direction of the en suite.

I shake my head. "I'm gonna go find Stef."

"Make me a martini first? Stef tells me you do a great dirty martini."

"Um, sure. Why not."

I walk over to the bar and am reaching up to get the martini glasses from the top shelf when WHAM, I'm slammed up hard against the counter, Hal nuzzling the back of my neck.

"Whoa, dude, slow down," I say, trying to push him off me. I hate it when guys mistake force for passion. "Stop it. I mean it."

"I've got a surprise for you," he whispers, slowly turning me around so I'm facing him.

I look down.

Hal's penis.

Is out.

In his hand.

Small, pink, and erect.

Oh. My. God.

Hal smiles at me, and then at his penis. "Do you want to touch him? He likes you."

I laugh out loud. "No!"

"No?"

"No . . . thank you?" How do you refuse an erect penis politely? "Sweet of you to offer, but, uh, no. Let's get back to the party."

Hal tucks his penis back into his pants, thank fuck, but as I go to push past him he grabs me, hoists me up so I'm sitting on the bar, pushes my knees apart, and pulls up my dress.

"Stop," I snap, but he's pinning me down, kissing my neck, his hands grabbing at my thighs and this isn't funny anymore, but he's not even looking me in the eye, he's just dryhumping like a fucking crazed teenager. "Hal, stop. Now. Stop it!"

I shove him away, get down from the bar, and push past him. I'm out of here.

"Sorry!" he says. "Listen, Angie, I'm sorry, I really am."

I pause in the middle of the room. "You should be. Jesus."

Hal sniffs. "Listen, let's just be totally open, okay? We're grown-ups. Maybe I went about it the wrong way. You're different."

I frown at him. What does he mean? Different from what?

"Let's set the boundaries now, and open a bottle of Veuve, go to the diving terrace, and figure it out from there."

"What boundaries?"

"Three thousand, right? Full sex, and I want head first."

I stare at him. If I was a cartoon, there would be a little exclamation mark above my head.

"What?" Hal looks surprised at my reaction. "Fuck, do I have that wrong? Is it four thousand? Stef said—"

In that moment, everything becomes crystal clear.

I'm suddenly sober.

And.

I.

Am.

Angry.

CHAPTER 7

I turn around, stalk out of Hal's cabin, and storm through the yacht. I'm so furious, I feel like sparks are exploding from my body.

"STEF!" I scream. "STEF, YOU PREPPY PIECE OF SHIT! WAKE THE FUCK UP!"

I get to the first sleeping cabin and kick it open. Lars and another girl, doing coke.

"STEF! WHERE THE FUCK ARE YOU?"

I kick in the next cabin door. Beecher and two girls, naked.

"STEF! SHOW YOURSELF!"

I kick open the next cabin door. Empty. But I can see Stef's ridiculous little hat. This was his room. Which means he's up.

My fists are clenched so hard that my nails are cutting into my palms. On my way up the last set of stairs I run into that clean-cut boat boy again.

He frowns at me. "Are you okay?"

"No. I am not okay!" I push past him angrily.

"Can I do anything?"

"Yes. Stay the fuck away from me."

I stomp above deck, look around wildly, and see him. Stef. Sitting at the bar, looking completely normal, the goateed drug-dealing boat boy serving him a chilled glass of rosé. I walk right up to him.

"Why the fuck did you bring me here?" My voice is suddenly shaking. "Hal thinks I'm a fucking hooker, Stef!"

"Labels are very ugly, Angie." Stef's drawl is even more pronounced than usual.

"You told him I'm a hooker?"

"You need cash. Hal needs a girl. Maybe he upset you by being too up-front, but c'mon. You must have been expecting it."

"I was *not* fucking expecting it," I hiss. "How dare you. I asked you what we were doing here, you said, 'Just good fun, babe.' You LIAR! I thought—"

"Mani took you shopping, right?" Stef interrupts. My ex? Why is he bringing him up? Stef introduced us, but—"Did you get an extra-nice present after the first time you fucked him? I bet you did. How about Jessop? A weekend in Aspen and a charge card for a couple of grand at Bergdorf Goodman, right?"

"That was . . . he said it was a freebie from his work, he said—" I'm stuttering now.

"Sex in exchange for what you want."

"No." Suddenly I can't breathe. "That's different."

"Is it? And does it even matter?"

"It matters to me. They were just . . . generous . . ." My voice trails off as I realize how ridiculous I sound.

"And you woke up yesterday morning in some hotel room with a stack of cash next to the bed, I'm guessing." Stef's voice grows eerily controlled. "Come on, tough girl. You're smart. You really think you're here for your conversational skills? Hal needs a girlfriend for the weekend. You told me you needed to make some money. Everybody wins."

"No—" My voice is a whisper.

Stef's eyes are glinting with controlled fury, and he's talking super-low, through gritted teeth. "Just sit the fuck down and play nice. I went to a lot of effort to make this party happen for my friend Hal. You're embarrassing me."

Total silence.

We stare at each other.

Suddenly, I'm very, very scared.

I don't know Stef, not really. I don't know what he's capable of doing to me. And I'm alone. Completely alone.

Panic rises like bile in my stomach. I stumble backward away from Stef and look around wildly.

The sun is setting, and the other yachts that surrounded us earlier have left. They're just gone, swoosh, vamoosed. I didn't even notice! Or did we sail somewhere? I wasn't paying attention, have we been sailing into the middle of the fucking ocean? I turn again, desperately trying to see land.

It's there. Thank God. Off the stern, I can see the long white beach of Grace Bay, and, in the soft dusk light, the twinkling lights of all the hotels. How far is it? A mile? Half a mile?

I look back at Stef for a second. He stands up and opens his mouth to say something.

Before he can speak, I look him in the eye. "Go fuck yourself, Stef."

Then I turn around, run toward the back of the yacht, take a deep breath, and dive.

CHAPTER 8

The moment the water hits my head, I have a weird flashback to my wish the other day. When I thought I was so miserable, back in freezing gray Brooklyn, and all I craved was the blissed-out feeling of diving into seawater.

Be careful what you wish for.

My dress is wrapping around my legs, making it hard to swim, so I quickly remove it. Then, wearing nothing but my bikini, I start swimming toward the shore.

"Angie!" I can hear Stef screaming at me from the yacht. "Get the fuck back here, you crazy bitch!"

There's no point in shouting back—I need to save my breath—so I tread water for a moment, and without turning around, raise my arms out of the water to give him the finger from both hands.

Then I keep swimming.

Fuck you, Stef, I think, with every single stroke. *I'm going to pay you back for this.*

I'm not exactly the running-around-the-soccer-field type, and the years of compulsory team sports in school just stressed me out because I was really uncoordinated and dreamy and forgot things like which direction to run if I ever actually got the ball. Swimming, however, is the perfect exercise for creative loners. And I'm pretty good at it.

Every few breaths I look up to make sure I'm still heading in the right direction. I think I am, but it's hard to tell. The land is a lot farther away than I thought. All I want is to get back on land, and then somehow I'll find my way to Brooklyn. I want my home.

Five, or maybe ten minutes later—I can't tell—I hear a voice.

"Hey you!"

I turn around. It's that fucking boat boy again, the clean-cut one who was watching me all day. He's in a tiny blow-up dinghy. They've sent him to collect me.

"Go the fuck away," I shout. "I'm not going back there."

"I'm not going to take you back to the *Hamartia*," he calls. "I'll take you to shore. I promise."

For a split second I consider it. But then reality hits: how many times do I have to be screwed over before I realize that everyone lies?

"I'm not going to trust some boat boy from a fucking superyacht," I say. "Go back and tell them I've drowned."

He laughs. "They don't know I'm here."

"Why the hell should I believe you?" I say. "I'm flying back to New York tonight. Leave me alone."

"There is no flight to New York tonight."

"Then I'll fly to Chicago and catch a fucking bus."

Before he can reply, I take a deep breath and keep swimming. Talking is making me breathless, and it's a waste of time.

A few minutes later I glance back again. He's still behind me. Just floating in that stupid little dinghy, using the oars to keep pace.

Whatever.

My arms and legs ache, but I don't stop. I figure this pain is my punishment for being such a moron. For trusting a guy with the morals of a vulture. For not realizing there's no such thing as a free lunch. (Or dress. Or trip to Aspen. Or charge card at Bergdorfs. Or . . . anything.) At one point, thinking about everything I've done, by accident and on purpose, but always with total stupidity, tears build up behind my eyes.

The last three men I slept with—Mani, Jessop, and whoever I was with at the Soho Grand—thought I was a hooker. Or something close to it.

But I thought they liked me. I really did. I thought I was just unlucky in love.

What would my parents think? What if my dad knew? How could I be so *stupid*?

I start sobbing, and my mouth fills with water, so I have to tread water for a second, making dramatic strangled choking sounds.

The boat boy stalker is right behind me. "Listen, it's Angie, right? My name is Sam, and I—"

"Please fuck off, Sam!" I am trying as hard as I can to sound normal and tough.

Stop crying, I tell myself sternly. *You can get through this. Just get away. Keep swimming.*

And so that's what I do. I swim, and breathe, and force every other thought out of my head.

"Angie?" Sam the boat boy calls out again. "Are you okay?"

"What are you going to do about it if I'm not, Sam?" I call over my shoulder. "Save me? I don't need to be saved. I just need to get home."

About two hundred feet from shore, just as the sun has finally set, swimming suddenly gets easier. It feels like the tide is helping me. I'm aiming for one of the smaller hotels, which I'm hoping will mean it's an exclusive luxury-type place, where everyone keeps to themselves and you tend to not know the other guests. My arms and legs are almost cramping now, and I am exhausted, but I won't stop. I'm determined to make it.

Finally, my feet hit sand. I turn around and see Sam, the boat boy, still twenty feet behind me in his stupid dinghy. God, what is he going for, some kind of Mr. Perfect medal or something?

"You can go now, Sam," I call. "I'm safe and sound."

"I don't think you're ever safe."

Ignoring him, I keep swimming until I can easily stand up, my body more than half out of the water. Then I walk out of the sea. When I'm on the beach, I look back. Sam has finally left, already halfway back to the *Hamartia*. Sayonara, annoying boat boy.

It's at that moment that I remember my passport, clothes, shoes, and money—the three thousand dollars—are in my cabin on the yacht. Oh shit, my phone! How could I have left everything behind without a second thought?

Fuck it. I'll manage. I can't go back now. I'll figure something out.

With as much dignity as I can fake, I walk across the sand toward the hotel. I'm wearing my white bikini and nothing else, but it's a beach resort, so it's not like I'm out of place, right?

In front of the hotel is a faux-shabby beach bar, with reggae playing quietly. It's a chill scene that stinks of money. The guests are predictably self-satisfied: the men are a little bit too sunburned, with the ubiquitous fat guy ostentatiously smoking an expensive cigar. The women are all wearing quasi-Ibizan tunic tops and deep conditioning their sea-and-chlorine-fried hair, pretending they're going for the slicked-back look.

And they're all gazing out, with restless boredom, at the ocean, at the pale twilight sky and the only yacht in sight. The *Hamartia*. It's so weird looking back at it, like it's a toy. A tiny, stupid toy.

Trying to look like I know exactly what I'm doing, I walk up to the bar. "I'll have a Coke, uh, a Coca-Cola, please," I say. "And I'll start a tab."

"Room number?"

"Um, I forgot!" I laugh gaily, trying to look dumb and charming. "My boyfriend will be down any second."

The bartender nods, and serves it up in a huge chilled plastic cup.

Taking big frantic gulps—ah, sweet sugar rush!—I glance around, hoping I look like I belong. I need Internet access so I can e-mail Pia, beg her to get me on a flight home, maybe help me get an emergency passport. . . . God, I wish I'd talked to her more lately. She's my best friend, but I never tell her what's going on with me. I don't even know why. I just always keep everything secret.

"Hey, can I buy you a drink?"

I turn around. Older guy, early thirties, accent. South American, maybe Spanish. Supermacho, in that almost pretty way Spanish guys often are, with dark brown eyes, ridiculously thick eyelashes, and perma-stubble.

"All good here." I hold up my drink.

"Shame," he says. "All I've wanted to do since I got here was meet a blond girl in a white bikini, and buy her a drink." He makes a sad puppy face.

"Oh, okay. I'll have another Coca-Cola." And maybe he'll pick up my tab.

"I'll have the same." The guy nods at the bartender. "I'm Gabriel," he says.

"Angie."

"I'd love to ask you out for dinner, Angie. But I have to go back to New York tonight. My sisters have to be back in the city for some school thing."

I turn around. Two petulant-looking teenage girls are sitting on the sofas behind us. Both have long, swishy brown hair, deeply tanned skin, and are texting furiously.

Then I remember something.

"I thought there were no flights to New York tonight?"

"Ah," he says, picking up his drink. "Well, I have my own airplane."

CHAPTER 9

A few hours later, I'm sitting on board a Gulfstream, halfway back to New York.

For some reason, taking a stowaway back to New York isn't fazing this family at all. I borrowed a pair of jeans and a sweater from Gabriel and a pair of fluffy slippers from his sister Lucia. I look baggy and weird, but it'll keep me from freezing until I get back to Rookhaven. Gabriel has been on the phone for the past half hour, and his sisters and I are tucked up in the corner under blankets, all cozy with gossip magazines, herbal tea, and plates of peanut butter cookies. Being around the girls, and listening to their chatter, has put me at ease for the first time all day. It's almost like being at Rookhaven.

"I am completely over Bieber," says Amada. She's twelve, wears braces, and though she says things with total self-importance, her eyes dart around nervously when she talks. It's adorable.

"Bullcrap. Bieber was practically your first word! You cried at his concerts!" says Lucia, who's fourteen. She's incredibly shy, and talks to Gabriel and Amada loudly and sarcastically to, I think, impress me. I admired her customized jean jacket earlier—she layered a vintage Jordache sleeveless denim vest over a leather jacket, and the result is unbelievably stylish—and she blushed for about ten minutes. God, I would not go back to being a teenager for anything.

Then again, being twenty-two isn't exactly working out that great for me, either. My birthday is coming up way too soon. I really thought I'd have a real career and a serious boyfriend by now. A life, in other words. A life that didn't include being invited to parties and paid to sleep with the host.

Ugh. Don't think about it.

"Where are your things?" asks Gabriel, coming over to talk to me for the first time since takeoff. "How can anyone travel in just a swimsuit?"

If you ever get the chance to hear someone from Madrid say "swimsuit," I highly recommend it. I shrug and try to act nonchalant.

"I'm just that kind of girl, I guess."

"Cool, calm, and collected."

"Mm-hmm." If he only knew the chaos inside me. I turn back to my magazine. "Wow, does anyone actually like Angelina Jolie? Because I just do not get that whole thing."

"She is a goddess, a statue," says Gabriel, looking over my shoulder. "For worshipping. Not for loving."

How can Spanish guys get away with saying stuff like that?

Oh, here's the downlow on Gabriel. I got it all before we left the hotel. He's thirty-four, Spanish, never married, no kids of his own, sold his first tech company when he was twenty-five, works between New York and Silicon Valley, and has an apartment on Columbus Circle. Basically, he's your average run-of-the-mill very rich guy. The girls are his half sisters from his dad's second marriage to an American woman. I get the feeling they're growing up with wealth, and he had to make his own.

Gabriel sits down and picks up Us magazine and, for a few minutes, we all read quietly.

"Are you hungry?" he asks.

"Almost always."

"The hotel made me these. Not quite as nice as the avocado and prawn salad I usually get to go when I'm at Eden Rock on St. Barts, but not bad."

Gabriel pulls out some sandwiches that the hotel must have made for him. Freshly cooked fish sandwiches on soft, buttered white bread. Like the ones I ate just a few hours ago on the *Hamartia*.

Suddenly, I've lost my appetite. But I take a sandwich anyway and force myself to eat it. The girls are chattering away.

"St. Barts is boring. I like Turks way more."

"I liked Antigua the best."

"No way!"

Eventually, they calm down and go back to their magazines, and Gabriel turns to me with a little grin. I smile back. His hair is still messy, probably from being on the beach all day, and he has a nice face, if a little pouty-pretty for my taste.

"So, we have to work out what you owe me for this trip."

A cold fear spikes through me. "What?"

"I fly you to New York, smuggle you through passport control, and you think it's all for free?"

My heart is beating in my mouth. Holy shit, not again. . . .

"In return, you have to buy me dinner sometime."

Oh. That's all he meant.

I smile glassily up at Gabriel, trying to look composed, my mind racing.

What *was* I doing, really, walking into a hotel bar in a bikini like a goddamn Bond Girl, confident that somehow, I'd find a way home? I'd just swum God knows how far, all the while thinking how stupid I was for walking into such a horrific situation, how clever I was to not trust that goddamn boat boy who followed me . . . but how stupid was it to trust the next total stranger I met? Just because Gabriel had his sisters with him, just because he seemed nice and polite, I decided to get on his private jet? What the fuck is *wrong* with me?

I keep making the same mistakes. That's why I'm stuck in this ridiculous, destructive holding pattern. I make the wrong choice. Every single time.

I glance up at Gabriel. If it was this time a week ago, I'd date him until he dumped me. I know I would. But that's not what I want anymore. And it's definitely not what I need.

"I'm sorry, Gabriel. I didn't mean to give you the wrong impression. I'm not . . . looking for anything. Uh, romantic." Interesting choice of words.

"Okay," he says, with an "easy come, easy go" shrug. "So you just want to get back to New York and say good-bye, is that it?"

I feel bad. Why do I feel bad? Like I owe him dinner. Like he gets to be with me in exchange for giving me a ride home. Why the fuck am I thinking like that? Sex in exchange for what I want. That's what Stef said. Is that how I think? It's not, it's really not. I accepted those gifts because I never had much spending money and the guys always did. Because I like clothes and nice things, and they liked buying them for me. Because I thought they liked me and I really, really liked them, especially Mani. And most of all, because I thought that when they gave me something, it meant that I was worth being with.

I was wrong.

That's it. My life has been all about guys for far too long.

I want my life to be about me.

I want to be single. I want my home. I want a real job. I want my friends.

And by the time I turn twenty-three, I want to be doing something that *means* something. Either I have a life that I can be proud of, that I earned on my own merits, or . . . or . . . or I don't know what.

Twenty-three is my deadline.

"You sure that's what you want?" repeats Gabriel.

I look up. "I am."

CHAPTER **10**

When we land, Gabriel offers me a ride home in their car. He gives me his business card, though I have no intention of calling him, and I thank him and his sisters profusely for being such Good Samaritans. They drop me at the corner of Smith and Union before continuing on to his apartment on Columbus Circle and, shivering from the cold, I walk down the street to Rookhaven.

It's past midnight. Everyone is asleep, and for a moment, as I walk up the stoop of my house in the darker than dark, freezing-cold February night, it feels like the whole sun-filled superyacht experience was just a dream. Or a nightmare.

With the hidden spare key, I open the front door and inhale the warm, comforting Rookhaven smell. Vanilla and cinnamon from the kitchen, the wood polish Coco uses on the furniture, all mixed with everyone's shampoo and perfumes and a sort of papery scent that I always think of as old wallpaper.

I have never been as happy to be in Rookhaven as I am right this second.

Minutes later, I'm tearing through my bedroom like that Tasmanian devil cartoon. Wrenching dresses off hangers, taking jewelry out of drawers, grabbing shoes and underwear, every gift from an ex-boyfriend, ex-flings, ex . . . whatevers. All my labels, all my most expensive clothes . . . Touching them, knowing now why I got them, gives me a cold, scared feeling in the pit of my stomach.

I'm so stupid. How could I have ever thought they actually liked me for me?

I will never trust a man again. Ever. They all lie. They lie and lie and lie. My father lies, Stef lies, Mani and Jessop and Marc and, oh God, all of them. Liars.

Now all that's left in my closet is stuff from H&M and Urban Outfitters and other cheapish places, stuff I borrowed from Annabel and never gave back, and secondhand pieces found in vintage stores and flea markets that I customized to suit just me. I bundle all the designer clothing in a bag to take to Goodwill tomorrow.

But I can't even bear to have the white dress from the Soho Grand night in the house anymore. It was from Mani, the guy I really thought I might be in love with, the guy who took me out for dinner and talked to me like he *cared*. . . . The dress was bought with bullshit.

So I grab it, head downstairs, out the front door, down the stoop, and throw the dress in the garbage.

"Watch out there, girlie, you'll break the lid," says a voice. I turn around. It's Vic, the old guy who lives in the downstairs apartment. I haven't seen him in ages.

"Vic! Hey! What are you doing out here so late?"

"Just sitting." He's all bundled up in an old coat and scarf and hat, perched comfortably on the chair outside his apartment. I can hardly see him, his voice is just rumbling out of the darkness as though it came from Rookhaven itself. "Sometimes I like to get some air. What about you?"

"Um, yeah, air." I don't even know why, but suddenly, I want to tell him everything. "I've made a mistake, Vic. A few actually, really huge mistakes, and I, um, I don't know if I can ever forgive myself."

God, I sound dramatic. Pia would be proud.

"What mistakes?"

"I don't . . ." I take a deep breath. "I don't want to talk about them. Ever. To anyone. But I don't know if I can deal with them alone, either."

"I understand that." Vic and I both sigh into the silence. My breath is coming out all misty, and I'm not even smoking. I'm so tired of being cold. I'm so tired of winter.

Then Vic pipes up again. "Regret . . . it'll kill you. Out of all the negative emotions, regret is the one that will get its claws into your soul."

My throat suddenly aches with the desire to sob, and tears well up behind my eyes. I blink them away quickly. I never cry in front of people. Ever.

"You tried talking to your friends? Your parents?"

"No," I say. "No way."

"You gotta let it go, girlie. Otherwise you'll spend your whole life thinking about it. Trust me. I know. And it's much easier to let go of problems when you share them with the people you love."

"But what if they judge me? What if they hate me for it?"

"Friends don't judge. Friends just listen."

The crying feeling threatens to engulf me again. "But I feel like . . . like this thing . . . this will never leave me. Like there's a permanent mark on my record. A stain on my soul."

"Nothing is permanent. Everything changes. You can choose to let that comfort you, or depress you. Once an event is in the past, it's just a memory."

"A bad memory."

"Sure, sometimes it's a bad memory. You can choose to remember it and hold on to it forever, or you can forget it, and it's like it never happened. You're in control."

"I'm never in control." I start laughing, though the lump of tears in my throat is so big and square it hurts. "I am, by nature, out of control."

"That's your choice, girlie." Vic stands up. "Night night. Sweet dreams."

CHAPTER 11

"Stef is an evil cockmonkey," announces Pia. "I hope he rots in hell."

"I hope he gets an STD!" says Coco.

"I hope Hal gets an STD," says Julia.

"I can't believe Hal told you his *dick* liked you," says Madeleine.

"Diving into the sea was the best idea ever," says Pia.

"You're so lucky that guy had a private plane!" says Coco.

"And your parents will have a much better relationship now," says Pia.

"Totally. No more fighting, no more problems. Divorce is great!" says Madeleine.

"I wish my parents would divorce!" says Pia.

"Being single is the best! Most of the time," says Julia.

"And you'll get a job in fashion in a heartbeat. Who wouldn't want to hire you?" says Coco.

Don't you just love girls? It's so simple: I walked into the kitchen two hours ago, apologized profusely for being such a nightmare, confessed everything, and received total acceptance, affection, and absolution in return. It surprised me, but this is how they've always treated one another, so it's how they're treating me. I'm part of the group. That probably shouldn't be a surprise, but it is.

Well, I didn't confess *everything*.

I didn't tell them about waking up in the Soho Grand with three thousand dollars in an envelope. I just can't. I told them about the yacht, that Hal had assumed I was, erm, someone who'd take money for sex, that Stef had set me up, that it was a one-off, the culmination of bad luck and bad decisions. They are shocked enough at that. If they knew I've accidentally been playing the part of the happy hooker for the past few months with Mani, Jessop, and whoever the dude was from the hotel room . . . well, I don't want to think about their reaction. How could they not judge me? *I* judge me.

I told them about my parents divorcing. And about being unemployed and my money issues, i.e., that I don't have any.

"And I am sorry for going so wild with the vodka," I said, looking each of them in the eye. "I know I've been, um, unreliable, and unpredictable. And a bad roommate. And I'm sorry. I was feeling crazy, I guess, and I acted accordingly. I'll be different now. I swear."

And then they all started talking at once. It was an orgy of emotional support, a total validation binge.

Just like Vic told me last night, the moment I shared my problems, I felt better. That cold, itchy feeling in my soul started to thaw and ease. I felt lighter, as if the weight that had been pressing down on me, keeping me from laughing or even smiling for the last few weeks, had magically disappeared. Secure is the word, I guess. I felt secure.

Who knew sharing felt so good? I mean, I hated all those late-night compulsory deep and meaningful heart-to-hearts at school, remember them? When all the girls eat junk food and one girl talks about her parents and another talks about her abusive ex-boyfriend and another talks about her body issues and another talks about whatthefuckever and at the end everyone has a Care Bears hug and then the bulimic sneaks off to puke. I wasn't really invited to those talks, mind you. But I was in the dorm when they happened.

Anyway. During my confession, Coco got tears in her eyes, Madeleine frowned, Pia gasped, and Julia clenched her fists and muttered "*Those fuckers*" a lot.

It should have been the easiest to confide in Pia. I've known her, literally, since I was born. But somehow, I felt most scared about her reaction. Maybe because she was always having her own crises, maybe because my parents aren't exactly the pull-up-a-pew types, but I've never really burdened her with my problems before. I always kept everything to myself. Sharing things felt, I don't know, like complaining, like asking for help, like saying I couldn't handle life, like I was weak. Keeping my secrets to myself felt like the only thing I could do . . . well, keeping my secrets, drinking, and falling for the wrong men.

Letting my friendship with Pia drift is just as much my fault as hers, I'm finally realizing. Maybe more my fault. How can she be around for me if I never tell her I need her?

"So that's that," I say finally. "From today, I'm just going to stay single and concentrate on my career. Get a damn job."

"No you're not," says Julia. "It's Saturday. You can get a damn job on Monday. Today you're making up for the whole curtain thing by coming with us to Smorgasburg."

"You're all going?" I don't want to be alone, not when I've got so much to think about. And to try not to think about. "Pia? Even you?"

"Yep. Aidan's in San Francisco till tonight, he had some work thing," says Pia. "It's a special presummer preview event. I'm going as a corporate spy."

"She means she's checking out the competition," Julia explains to a confused Coco. "We're going for the dudes."

"Smorgasburg doesn't worship at the altar of SkinnyWheels?" says Madeleine, making a pretend sad face. SkinnyWheels is Pia's food-truck business.

"Apparently my salads don't cut the Zeitgeist gourmet hand-cut mustard," Pia says sarcastically, but I can tell she's genuinely kind of pissed about it. "So let's go eat quail's egg quiche and banana-cheddar spring rolls and fig-studded mozzarella balls and crazy shit like that."

"And meet some dudes!" Julia cheers. "It's Meet a Dude Day! Angie, are you in? High-five me! Fivies! Come on!"

I'm not the high-fiving type, but Julia grabs my hand and forces me to high-five her.

"There. Doesn't that feel good? Next we'll work on hugs."

At that, I laugh out loud, and suddenly feel happy endorphins flooding my body. Laughing! Who knew it felt so good? Fuck it, why not go with the girls and help them meet dudes? It'll take my mind off . . . everything.

Smorgasburg is a weekly open-air festival of unique foods that grew out of the Brooklyn Flea. By midday, in the interest of getting as many tastes as possible, we've shared fried anchovies, spicy beef noodles, chicken and waffles, chili mozzarella balls, a caramelized-onion-smothered hot dog, a buttery porchetta sandwich, a lobster roll, teriyaki shrimp balls, and a basil-and-raspberry popsicle. Yeah. There's some funky food here, all right.

Julia and I are by far the most enthusiastic eaters. Madeleine is picky and sniffs everything distrustfully before taking a tiny bite, and Coco is staring at the food longingly and talking about it a lot, but hardly touching it. (Between you and me, I think she might have a guilty-secret-eater thing going on, based on the number of times I've come home to find her scarfing Cheerios at midnight.) And Pia is frowning thoughtfully with every bite, taking notes. Apparently it's called "competitor analysis."

"I could do something with basil and raspberries, if they're really going to be the next big thing," she's muttering to herself. "But, *merde,* I need some protein in there, too. With what? Low-fat feta, maybe? Ricotta? Would chicken be too overpowering?"

"Remember when Pia used to be fun?" Julia says to me, handing over a gigantic maple-frosted bacon donut.

"I think I do," I say, taking a bite. "Da-yam, that's good. . . . Was that the Pia who applied Captain Morgan topically to all of life's woes? The same Pia who is now permanently attached to her iPhone and says shit like, 'Let's action that'?"

"Yes! And 'Get back to me by EOP!' "

"What the fuck is EOP?"

"Exactly!"

"So now you're bonding over making fun of me?" says Pia, arching an eyebrow. "Whatever. I don't care, as long as you're getting along."

"Are we getting along?" asks Julia. "Ladybitch? Can I call you that?"

I arch an eyebrow at her. "That's *Sir* Ladybitch to you."

Julia giggles and chokes on some frosting, making a strange quacky-bark sound, and I crack up.

"What are you laughing at?" Pia sounds annoyed. Like Julia and I shouldn't be allowed to have private jokes.

"At Julia," I gasp. "She gagged on some frosting."

"That sounds like a euphemism," says Julia.

"What, like . . . he frosted my mouth?" I say. "Mmm. Glaze me, you stud. . . ."

Julia shrieks with laughter. Pia rolls her eyes.

"Exsqueeze me, but there are no *guys* here," says Coco, looking around plaintively.

Oh, yeah. I nearly forgot. It's Meet a Dude Day.

I do a quick survey of the area. There are hundreds, probably thousands of people here, but she's right. Hipstery girls, young families, older parental types, and bewildered tourists. This is not a target-rich environment for the single girl. You need two or three guys, alone, who are up for some flirty conversation over a drink. Or in this case, an artisan farm-reared slow-pulled-pork organic-sourdough sandwich.

"You could talk to the food dudes," I suggest.

Madeleine laughs. "Ugh, they'd be all obsessed with their work like all food people in Brooklyn."

I glance over at Pia to see if she heard, but she's too busy making notes. What is with Madeleine and the snide comments?

"That guy over there is gorgeous," says Jules. "See him? Next to the chick in the hat?" We all look over. "Don't look now! Jeez, you guys! Oh, shit, he just kissed her. What a dick."

We all sigh in supportive disappointment.

"I think the flaw in the Meet a Dude Day plan is that you need an excuse to talk to guys," says Madeleine. "Like, you know, an activity, a conversation starter. Maybe you should take a cooking course or something."

"Yeah. All hot single guys just love a cooking course," says Pia, deadpan.

"I'm not a joiner. And the flaw in Meet a Dude Day is that we're treating this like an excursion to the dude zoo," I say. "They're not wild animals waiting to be observed."

"No, the Meet a Dude Day flaw is that it's practically impossible to pick up a guy sober," says Pia. "You know, unless you work with him, or you're, like, religious or something."

"So true. Alcohol is a social lubricant," I say. "It makes everything slip just that little bit easier."

"Ew, gross." Madeleine wrinkles her nose.

"You're a sensitive little flower, aren't you?" I say. And a raging bitch, I don't add.

My phone rings. I glance at it quickly. It's Annabel, my mother. But I'm not talking to her until Dad calls me and tells me the full story. So I quickly press silent.

"Excuse me?" asks a voice. We all turn around. A dude! Slightly chubby, has not quite mastered the art of the clean shave, but a dude nonetheless. "I was wondering if you've seen the headcheese? One of my Twitter followers said it was going to be here, but we can't find it."

"Headcheese?" I repeat. "That sounds . . ."

"Fucking disgusting," finishes Julia. "What is it?"

"It's kind of like meatloaf made from the parts of a pig no one else wants to eat. The face, the feet. Sometimes the heart."

We all gaze at him in total horror.

"I think I might be sick," I whisper to Julia.

"I hope I will be," she whispers back. "That shrimp is really repeating on me."

Coco is fascinated. "Wow! Are you a chef?"

"No, I run a food blog called the Hungry Geeksters! You gotta meet my cobloggers, hang on—"

We all turn around as two guys—one tall and flabby, one short and squat—come over. They're not bad-looking, and they seem friendly. For a second, it looks like Meet a Dude Day might actually work out.

Then they start to talk.

Normally, I kind of like geeks. I hung out with them a lot at boarding school. They're easy to make blush, they're smart, they let you sit with them at breakfast. But these geeks are a different breed. Big-city geeks. Boring know-it-alls with superiority complexes who aren't making eye contact and just talking to one another *around* us, if that makes sense. Maybe they have a touch of Asperger's—hey, it's not unlikely, let's be honest—or maybe they just never hung out with people with real live breasts before. Whatever. It's boring me.

"...and remember that time you ate jellied eel, Gary?"

"That was great! It tasted like river trout cooked in Vaseline."

"You're such a gourmand! That was still our most successful post ever."

After a minute or two Coco is the only one still smiling at them hopefully. Madeleine surreptitiously started texting someone. Pia muttered something about making notes and wandered away. Julia is giving me "get me the fuck out of here" eyes. (You know the look: a stare, into a sort of eye-widening glare, back into a stare.)

Time to take charge. I clap my hands together, hoping it makes me look authoritative. "Well, boys, it's been great, but it's time for us to get home before we turn into pumpkins."

"It's two-thirty in the afternoon," says the chubby geek.

"And I believe that it was Cinderella's coach that turned into a pumpkin, not Cinderella herself," says the spectacled geek.

"Right on." I put a cigarette between my lips and walk away. The other girls follow me. "Why do I always have to play the bitch?" I mutter.

"Well, it just seems to come naturally to you," says Julia, and we both start laughing again.

I think Coco and Madeleine have that slightly dejected feeling you get when you were hoping something would be the highlight of your weekend and it turns out to be totally not. But as we walk home through the frosty afternoon, Jules and I are actually having a good time.

"You have such a cool walk, you know that? You sort of swagger like a cowboy," says Julia.

I arch an eyebrow. "Like I have a dick?"

She cracks up. "No! You just . . . look like you own the world."

"Ha." Yet another thing about my outside that doesn't match my inside. "I'm sorry Meet a Dude Day didn't work out, Jules."

She shrugs. "I haven't met any guys in forever. You know what we need? Some platonic male friends who can introduce us to a continuous flow of new single men," says Julia thoughtfully. "Only dudes know dudes."

"Like a dude dealer?" I say.

"Yes! Exactly like a dude dealer. Or a pimp."

I flinch. Fuck. Stef is a pimp, I guess. A casual rich-kid high-end pimp with a "he needs a girl, you need money" mentality, and hopefully without a switchblade and a sideline dealing meth, but essentially a pimp nonetheless. All day, I've been trying not to think about how I was on the boat this time yesterday, or what was happening to me. . . .

"Sorry," whispers Julia. "I was only messing around."

I turn to her and smile. Man, she's a nice person. "It's okay," I say. And all of a sudden, it is. Just like Vic said: it happened, now it's in the past. I have to let it go. Or at least try.

Coco skips up next to us. "Why did we leave? I liked them!"

"You liked the fact that they were male, Coco. Aim higher," says Julia.

"Harsh," I say, seeing Coco's face fall, before she plasters on her usual "everything's great!" smile.

"Is it? I don't mean to be harsh. Coco, honey, next time you decide you truly like someone, I swear we will all be one hundred percent behind you. Right, Angie?"

"For sure," I say. "I'll get his name printed on a T-shirt with an 'I heart' in front of it."

Coco is trying to act flippant. "Well, I will never meet anyone. I work in a preschool. My job is the least guy-friendly job in the world."

"What about all those hot dads?" Pia finally tunes in to the conversation, though she's still texting someone. Aidan, I bet.

"Are you *serious*? They're old. And married."

"Can you imagine being a wife and having, like, children?" says Julia. "Right now I think it would be easier to learn Russian."

"I could learn Russian in six weeks if I tried hard enough," I say. "But find a dude who might like me for *me* in six weeks? Not a chance."

"Aw, do you have low self-esteem?" Julia pulls my ponytail affectionately.

"No, I really don't," I say. "I just know what guys see in me. And it's never . . . me."

Julia is quiet for a moment, suddenly serious. "I know exactly what you mean. Sometimes I would kick a puppy just to have an interesting conversation with a good-looking guy who also happened to find me attractive."

We stroll along in silence, Julia's words echoing in my head.

An interesting conversation with a guy.

You know, I can't even remember the last time I actually talked to a guy. Like, really *talked*.

Take any of the guys I've dated (please! *Boom, tish*). Mani, Marc, Jessop, Hugh, the guys I met at college, in bars, on vacation . . . My entire life, it's always the same.

They talk, I listen. They joke, I smirk. I never reveal anything about myself, I never trust them enough to show them who I really am or how I really feel, so it's just chase, flirt, party . . . and then sex. Which is always shit, anyway, the kind of sex where afterward I feel inexplicably like crying, and I go to the bathroom alone and look in the mirror and wonder what the hell I'm doing and why I feel empty inside. (Urgh, sorry. Drama, I know. But it's true.)

And then in the morning I always wake up next to them and feel more alone than ever. But I stick around in the hope that next time, they'll try to see past the tough shell I've built over the years. That they'll suddenly *know* me, and I'd understand them and feel a connection. A real connection.

It never happens, of course. Why would a guy bother to get to know me? So I act flippant and cool and tough, and eventually they dump me, and I never hear from them again. They even defriend me on Facebook. Like there is no point in keeping in touch. Like I am disposable.

No wonder I've always liked that moment before the first kiss so much. The prekiss. That is the moment when there is still a chance that this time, it will mean something. Like I might meet someone worth trusting, someone to whom I can show my true self. Like there might be a happy ending.

Never again. Never, ever again. I'm staying single. Forever. I'm staying away from all dudes. Especially rich kids and liars.

And I'm going to get a job in fashion.

CHAPTER 12

I'm never going to get a job in fashion.

In the past week, I've tried everything. I've scoured *WWD*, talked to the few recruitment agencies that specialize in fashion, searched Craigslist and every fashion website and blog. I e-mailed my resume to all my favorite Manhattan-based designers yet again, just in case the last time I sent it last August, when I first got to New York, it was misplaced. I told them I loved creating clothes; I asked if they needed a junior designer, an assistant, a receptionist, a coffee flunky, shoe polisher, anything.

Nothing.

I called everyone nice who I met via my old boss The Bitch food photographer; I phoned Cornelia's contacts that I used to call to pull samples when she was on her way to some gala. I Facebooked, I IM'd, I tweeted. I called back and back and back.

Nothing.

I asked about internships, but they're booked up months or even years in advance, and the problem is that they don't pay anything and I need *money*. I guess this means that every intern in New York either still lives with their parents, or has an enormous salary-type allowance that enables them to pay for a New York apartment and, you know, eat. Which means that only rich kids get fashion internships, and therefore, are first in line and the most qualified for the best jobs. Doesn't that seem fucking stupid to you, by the way? Shouldn't it be the hardest working and most talented people who get the best jobs? Sometimes it seems like being in your early twenties in New York is not survival of the fittest, it's survival of the richest.

So I applied for sales positions in my favorite designers' stores. If you work in a Marc Jacobs store, you've got to meet him at some point, right? I spent all day yesterday going to all the best stores. I filled out forms and left my perfect Julia-approved résumé and smiled so much that my face ached.

Nothing.

Getting a job is the only thing I've thought about, the only thing I've focused on in the past week. When my thoughts slip back to Stef, and Hal, and the yacht, and everything else, I force them forward. *Get a job. Get a life.*

But I'm not getting anywhere. I'm failing.

New York City is rejecting me.

Today it was cold and rainy, a typical March day, so I hid in my bedroom, reading romances and drawing and sewing little bits and pieces. Throwing out all my high-end clothes the other night also ripped a hole in my wardrobe, and obviously I can't afford to go shopping right now, so I decided to take my cheap-ass basics and make them more interesting. For example, I ripped the sleeves off all my shirts and T-shirts. Yes, it's still cold as hell outside. Yes, I should have thought it through a bit more.

Anyway, when Julia found me moping in my room earlier ("Are you sick? I have never, ever seen you in the house on a Saturday night before"), she suggested I get the girls together to "brainstorm a solution." Pia isn't here, of course. She's with Aidan.

But that's okay. I'm in the warm, cozy kitchen at Rookhaven, eating pizza from Bartolo's and drinking wine while it rains outside.

"What the hell is this? I asked for triple pepperoni, this is, like, double at the most," says Julia, peering at her pizza.

"I think there's more than enough processed pig on there," says Madeleine through a mouthful of spinach and ricotta.

Julia sighs. "I guess." She looks up at me. "Pepperoni, Angelface?"

I grin at her and take a slice. There's nowhere else in the world that I'd rather be right now than right here.

"I don't know when I started drinking wine, but I like it," comments Julia. "It just tastes so fucking sophisticated."

"I started drinking wine about the time I got my first period," I say.

Julia cracks up. "You know, I would think you were joking, but I know you too well now. I was drinking Malibu and milk until I was, like—"

"Twenty-two," interrupts Madeleine. Julia flicks her the bird.

"I was allowed watered-down wine at dinner," I say. "Annabel thought it was the mature, European thing to do."

"Well, I'm glad that didn't backfire on her," Madeleine says snarkily. I'm not sure what she means by that, but I'm pretty sure it's not nice.

"Okay. What's the latest with the job search?" asks Julia.

The others look up, waiting for my response. It feels weird—but kind of nice—to be the center of attention in the group. In the past, that's always been Julia, the loud one, or Pia, the drama queen. (I'm probably the one sitting on the sidelines with a drink and a cigarette making comments.)

"Helmut Lang, A.P.C., 3.1 Phillip Lim, Opening Ceremony, Rag & Bone, Acne, Maje, Sandro, Alexander Wang, Marc Jacobs, Steven Alan, Intermix, Scoop . . ." I tick off all the names on my fingers as I chew my third slice of pizza. "I have applied for retail jobs with all of them. Not even a design job, just *retail*! But they still want someone with retail or fashion experience."

"So, plan B," says Julia.

"That was plan B! Plan A was getting a job with the actual designers! Plan B was to be humble. Start from the ground up . . ." I sigh, and look around the table at the girls. "I'm not even eligible for the ground. I'm somewhere below sea level."

"Just keep trying," says Julia. "Madeleine, if you don't man up and finish that fucking pizza I will never talk to you again."

Madeleine picks up her half-eaten slice and takes a tiny nibble. "Look, Angie, it's not like you're the only person looking for a career. The job market is a nightmare right now. Remember that *Newsweek* article? We're Generation Screwed."

"What happens to us, then? What will happen to Generation Screwed? The grads that can't get a job?" I look around the table. "Like, seriously. What if we *never* get jobs? Will we all become homeless? Destitute?"

"What does destitute even mean, anyway?" says Coco.

"It means to not have the basic necessities of life," says Julia. "None of us are in any danger of that."

"So you'll ask your parents for money," says Madeleine.

"Like fuck I will." The words come out far more vehemently than I want them to. The girls all look at me in shock. I mumble out an explanation. "My dad lost a lot of money, you know, in the last few years, the economy and everything . . . and with the divorce, I just, um, I don't want to make his life more difficult."

Everyone is quiet for a moment. No one wants to ask if I've heard from my father. They probably guess that the answer is no. Annabel, meanwhile, has called at least three more times. I still haven't answered. I'll call her back after I speak to my dad.

"What about volunteering at New York Fashion Week?" says Julia. "I just read something about girls who do that to get started in fashion. They dress the models and assemble gift bags, stuff like that."

"New York Fashion Week just finished," I reply. "The next one is months away. Plus, I can't volunteer, I need to earn money."

"Bartolo's is looking for a bartender. Jonah wants to cut his hours back because he got a part on that big lawyer show," says Coco. Jonah is one of Pia's friends, a Williamsburg acting/bartending/beekeeping hipster, you know the type. I think Coco has a crush on him.

"But I want *something* to do with fashion. I need to learn."

And I do. During the interviews last week, store managers kept asking me questions using all these fashion terms I didn't understand. I mean, I know the difference between a bugle bead and a seed bead—I've been reading *Vogue* since I was eight, you pick that shit up—but there's a whole world of other stuff I don't know. Sales terms, merchandising terms, industry acronyms . . . I panicked and bought a bunch of fashion business books. Probably not the best use of my credit limit right now. Oops.

Madeleine speaks up. "What did you study at college again? You were at UCLA, right?"

"Um, yes," I say. "I went to the University of Pennsylvania first, but I transferred because it was too cold in the winter."

"You left an *Ivy League college* for *sunshine*?" Madeleine is stunned.

"Yeah, but . . . it was really cold."

Actually, I left because I thought I was in love with a guy I knew from Boston who went to UCLA, but when I got to L.A. he just dated me—i.e., slept with me—for a few weeks and then didn't talk to me again. But I don't want to tell the girls that right now, not on top of everything else. They'd just feel sorry for me . . . and just because I've been dumped by every guy I've ever been with doesn't make me a loser. (Right?)

"What's this?" says an icy voice, and we all look up. It's Pia. "Having a house meeting without me?"

"It's just an impromptu pizza night!" says Julia.

Pia looks from Julia to me and purses her lips. "Right."

I suddenly realize that Pia is threatened by Julia and me becoming friends. God, I never thought she was that the jealous type. Then again, I don't think she's ever had two of her best friends independently make real friends without her, either. I would know: I've been her best friend forever, and I sure as hell never made an effort with anyone else before Julia.

"Pia, I'm so glad you're here," I say. Pia looks at me with a little more warmth. "I'm having a total career crisis, you know—"

"A lack-of-career crisis," interrupts Julia.

"Totally," I say. "And I really, really need your advice."

"Okay!" Pia sits down happily and grabs the bottle of wine and a slice. Quick to forgive, that's my Pia. But wait a minute—

"Why are you here? Why aren't you with Aidan?" Julia asks the question the same moment I think of it.

"He has a work thing," Pia says, through a mouthful of pizza. "I don't like his coworkers. They're all, like, forty. They patronize me like I'm just a stupid little girl. I'd rather be with you guys."

"Good. We'd rather you were here with us, too." Julia turns to me. "Angie. Let's start with education. What was your major?"

"Anthropology at Penn," I say. "And theater at UCLA."

"Theater!" exclaims Coco excitedly. "I could totally see you as an actress."

"They were cliquey asshats," I say. "I just kept to myself and took as many of the design-led things as I could. I barely passed. Then I applied to the Fashion Institute of Design and Merchandising and to the Art Institute of California. I didn't get in."

"You never told me that." Pia is always shocked when she discovers things I haven't told her. But it's not personal. I never tell anyone anything.

So I just smile. "Rejection is not a good look for me."

"What about *Project Runway*?" exclaims Coco excitedly.

"Like hell."

"I think you should go back to college," Madeleine says. "Apply to FIT or Parsons or something. If this is really what you want, and there are no jobs out there right now, then study more so you can get the advantage over every other fashion wannabe."

"I agree, but I can't," I say. "College costs money."

"No shit," says Pia. "Have you heard from Stef?"

"No," I say. "Hopefully the yacht capsized."

"Do you want to get revenge?" asks Julia hopefully.

I shake my head. "I just want to forget about it. Sweep it under the rug, pretend it never happened. That's the way I was brought up." I'm kidding, kind of, but no one laughs, so I get up to grab my sea salt caramels from the fridge and toss two to Julia. I found out this week that she shares my sea salt obsession. "Anyway, I have bigger things to think about. Like my career. Or lack thereof."

"You should start a blog," says Julia. "A fashion blog."

"Everyone has a fucking blog," I reply, through a mouthful of caramels. "I want a *job*. I want something I can feel passionate about."

I flush slightly, embarrassed to hear myself talk so emotionally about wanting something. Being this open isn't really my style.

"You should start your own line," says Pia, reaching over for a caramel.

"My own line of what?"

"Accessories," she says thoughtfully. "Leather bags, or bracelets, or something like that. Something that's one size fits all, right? So you don't need to worry about fitting models and stuff like that, and women of all body types can buy them."

"You are a terminal entrepreneur." Another snide remark from Madeleine.

"All I'm saying is, every woman wants at least one new bag every season," says Pia.

"I don't," says Julia.

"It's a great idea, ladybitch, but I don't know how to do leatherwork," I say. "I wish I did. I wonder if I could take a class . . . Wait, that would cost money. So would materials to start my own line. And I still need to pay rent, remember? And have a life."

It always comes back to money.

"Anyway, I don't want to run a business," I add. "I just want a job." Silence. I guess my career crisis talk is over. And we didn't find a solution. I take a cigarette out and prop it in the corner of my mouth. "Well, thanks again for listening, you guys. I'm not sure how the whole group-hug thing works but let's just pretend I instigated one."

"Poker time!" says Julia, throwing me the deck of cards we always keep in the kitchen. "Shuffle up, Angelface. I'm gonna wipe the floor with you guys. That's why they call me the Swiffer."

"I think you mean they call *us* the Swiffer," I say. "If we're the ones you're wiping the floor with, you know? If you're *doing* the wiping, we should call you the maid or something."

Julia snorts. "The maid. Hilarious."

Coco leans over and gives me a huge hug.

"Thanks," I say.

"You don't have to thank people for hugs," says Julia. "You just have to hug them back."

"Oh, my God, I've got it," says Madeleine. "Look."

She throws *New York* magazine open on the table in front of me.

It's an ad. For salespeople.

At the Gap.

There's silence.

I stare at Madeleine in slight disbelief, my cigarette wilting in the corner of my mouth. She stares back, a sunny "isn't this hilarious" smile on her face.

Suddenly, I don't want to play poker anymore.

"I'm going upstairs."

I stomp up to my room, flop down on my bed, and stare at the ceiling, trying to fight the tears pooling in my eyes. Hello again, empty gray bedroom. Hello again, empty gray life.

I'm so lost.

I automatically reach into my nightstand, shove aside my Harlequin and M&M's. There's no vodka, but then miracle of miracles, at the very back, I find half a bottle of Wild Turkey I'd totally forgotten was there. It's not my favorite tipple, but it does in a pinch. Guaranteed escapism.

As I'm unscrewing the lid, cigarette propped in the corner of my mouth, it suddenly hits me.

This is the moment that everything always goes wrong for me.

The moment that I walk—or dive—away from my problems. That I leave the restaurant, bar, house, car, party, conversation, or, let's not forget, yacht. The moment that I press the self-destruct button and bury myself in booze, or drugs, or men, in order to pretend that I'm feeling better than I am. That I'm not alone.

I swivel up to sitting, placing my feet on the floor with a thump, and put the alcohol back in the nightstand, the cigarette back in the pack.

At that moment, the doorbell rings.

Then there's a *thumpthumpthump* of Coco running up the stairs, screaming my name.

"Angie! Angie, it's a guy, he says he wants to see you, something about the yacht, I didn't ask him in, I didn't know if you'd want me to—"

Hal? Stef? Heart hammering in fear, I jump up and run out of the bedroom and downstairs, almost before Coco has finished talking.

The guy waiting politely outside the front door in the freezing cold is so bundled up in a huge coat, boots, and hat that you can barely see his face. But I recognize him immediately.

It's the tall, annoying dude with the intense frown. The clean-cut one who laughed when I was stuffing my face with sandwiches and followed me in the dinghy all the way to shore.

It's the boat boy.

Sam.

CHAPTER 13

"What do you want?"

"I . . . Wow, really? That's how you say hi?"

I take a deep breath. *Calm, Angie, calm.* . . . What the hell is Sam the boat boy doing at my house in Brooklyn? Thousands of miles away from Turks and goddamn Caicos?

I look up at Sam and try to maintain eye contact. He's at least six foot four. I hate the way men being taller than us automatically puts us at a conversational power disadvantage, don't you? But I can feel the girls hovering protectively behind me in the hall, which gives me the confidence to just talk normally rather than slam the door in his face. "Hi. What do you want?"

Sam smiles, all perfect teeth and effortless confidence. "I've got your stuff. Your weird coat. Your bag. Your—"

"My stuff!" I'm delighted. "Thank you thank you thank you! Ahh!" My fur/army coat! My makeup! My passport! The clutch that I made out of vintage silk scarves! I already replaced my old phone, but I got to keep my number, thank God.

"Also I wanted to see . . . see if you were okay." He frowns, as if not sure how to say it.

I frown back. "I'm just peachy."

"Really? That was pretty wild."

This guy is a living reminder of a memory I'd do anything to erase. I just want to get rid of him, though I can feel the burning curiosity of everyone in the hall.

"Yes, thank you." I affect my coldest voice. "It was a difficult situation, but—"

"From what I could see, you handled yourself perfectly."

"I screamed a lot and dived into the sea."

"Exactly. By the way, we weren't formally introduced. I'm Sam Carter," he says, holding out a hand. "And you're Angie James."

"Yep." I open the door wide, so he can see the girls, or more to the point, so they can see him. "And these are my roommates. Julia, Pia, Coco, and Madeleine." I turn to them to explain. "He was working on the yacht. For the dude. Hal. The party guy—"

"Really!" Julia struts to the door. "Listen up, buddy. You tell your coke-addled cockmonkey boss—"

"He's not my boss," interrupts Sam. "He just chartered the yacht for a week. Like a rental. He's gone, and the crew guy, Carlos, who was supplying the drugs for the—cockmonkey, did you say?—to get addled with, he's gone, too."

"This is the guy who followed me in the dinghy," I say to them. "The boat boy."

"Oh! Hi!" The girls are delighted. They loved that part of the story.

"Aren't you gonna ask him in?" says Pia.

"You should totally come in," agrees Julia.

Madeleine and Coco pipe up in unison. "Totally!"

I look around at them in surprise, then back at Sam. Oh. They've decided he's hot. He does look pretty good, I guess. Tan and healthy and rested, a novelty at the end of an extra-long New York winter when everyone else looks like an anemic sneeze.

But I'm not interested in dudes right now. And I'm definitely not interested in him. I don't like blond guys, I don't like outdoorsy guys, and I never, ever like guys who saw me being treated like a . . . well, you know. In fact, I'd like to never see him again. Effective immediately.

"Sam has to go home." The girls make disappointed noises, so I turn around to give them a "quit it" face. Then I turn back to Sam. "Thanks again, man. Sayonara—"

"May I trouble you to use your restroom?" Goddamn, is this the politest dude in the world? "I walked all the way here from the place I'm crashing in Fort Greene, it was farther than I thought, and—"

"Oh, my God, you must be freezing!" exclaims Julia, before I can say no. "Come on in!"

And boom, next thing I know, Sam's coat is off, Coco's handing him hot chocolate, Julia's leading him into the living room, Pia's grinning at the whole spectacle like it's the Rookhaven puppet show, and even Madeleine, who I've *never* seen act gaga over a guy, is putting on some French Nouvelle Vague music.

"I was singing this song, last night, uh, I've been singing with this band? You should come see us. . . ." Madeleine is saying. She and Julia have sandwiched him down between them on the sofa. Real cozy.

"I've got to call Aidan." Pia heads upstairs, leaving the single girls to their prey.

"So, um, Sam? You're a sailor?" asks Coco, blushing pink. She's hovering around the bookcase, trying to look busy.

"I am." Sam seems remarkably unperturbed by all of this. "Some people call us boat boys." He glances at me with a smirk. "We call ourselves crew."

I roll my eyes. *Some people.* I heard someone call them boat boys once, how was I to know?

Coco is impressed. "And working on yachts is your, like, career?"

"Looks that way. Though I'm looking for a new job right now."

"We're having a party next Saturday," Julia blurts out. "You should totally come."

I stare at her. "We are?"

"Yes! The dinner party, remember? For . . ."

"For Pia's twenty-third birthday!" says Coco quickly.

"Yes! It's a surprise dinner party. Right, Angie?"

I arch an eyebrow. "Right. Because who doesn't want a surprise dinner party." The fact that I share the same birthday as Pia, and that it's not for weeks, hasn't crossed anyone's mind.

"It's going to be sick," Julia adds. "And, and, and Madeleine's gonna sing!"

"I am? I am!" says Madeleine.

"And um, and Coco's gonna cook—Coco, what are you going to cook?"

We all turn to Coco, who is pink under the pressure of having to lie on the spot. ". . . Food?"

"Right, Coco's cooking food and I'm making this awesome punch."

"Sure," says Sam. "Sounds great. I'm crashing at my buddy's house, but he's away right now. Is it okay if I come alone?"

"You're new here? Oh, my God! Then you have to come!"

Please, God, don't let Julia hump his leg.

"I'd love to. What time should I be here?"

"Oh, seven-thirty. No! Eight. Yeah. Eight o'clock."

"Sweet," I say. "Can't wait. A dinner party. Right on. Well, Sam, thanks for stopping by—"

"Guess I should get going." Sam stands up, to the obvious disappointment of everyone else.

"And thank you, again, so much, for bringing back my stuff," I say, opening the front door for him as he puts on his coat. Then something occurs to me. "How did you know where I live?"

"Easy," he says. "I waited until that Stef guy was totally out of it, then I asked him. He would have told me anything."

"Wow. Crafty."

"Yeah. Weird thing, though. That same night, his phone and his wallet and passport fell overboard." Sam puts his hat on, his gray eyes looking very serious. "He doesn't remember what happened. He said he had them one minute, the next . . ." Sam mimes throwing something really far away.

"You didn't."

Sam grins and then turns and walks down the stoop. "It seemed like the right thing to do. See you Saturday."

When I get back upstairs, I remember.

The three thousand dollars. That envelope of cash that, though I hate its existence and the quasi-mystery of its origins, would come in pretty handy right now for paying for rent and, you know, life.

I reach into the inside pocket of my fur/army coat.

It's gone.

There's nothing in there but a little note, folded up.

Go fuck yourself, Angie.

Stef.

CHAPTER 14

Thirty-one days before I turn twenty-three.

I'm in a Starbucks on Seventh Avenue, just off Thirty-seventh. The throbbing heart of the Fashion District of New York City. Not that you'd know it by the streetscape: it's pretty fucking depressing, especially on a rainy March day like today. A lot of cheap bead shops. Everything is happening off the street, in the offices upstairs. That's where the production facilities and showrooms are for most big designers.

I'm (sort of) reading today's issue of *WWD,* the fashion industry newspaper, and (mostly) looking out the window.

My plan is to sit here, make my coffee last as long as possible, and look like I work in fashion.

Maybe a fashion person will come to Starbucks and we'll start talking about my semi-ironic Hello Kitty umbrella and that will lead to a job. Maybe I'll be reading about someone in *WWD* and look up and, boom, there they'll be and I'll be like "wow!" and they'll be like "aw shucks" and that will lead to a job. Maybe I'll meet someone, and they'll know someone, and they'll know someone, and that will lead to a job. You know the six degrees of separation, the theory that you're only six people away from anyone else in the whole world? It's just like that: I'm six degrees away from getting a job.

Where did this crazy hopefulness come from? Rookhaven, I guess, particularly Julia and Pia. They're so fucking can-do and optimistic, it's worn away my natural cynicism.

A young guy in a fedora, carrying a huge white umbrella, wheels seven dressmaker's dress forms tied together past on the street—you know, the headless, limbless soft mannequins that you pin dresses to—and my heart jumps. I wonder where he's going! I bet he's wheeling them somewhere for a designer. Maybe Anna Sui or Michael Kors is going to be touching those dress forms in, like, five seconds. My grandmother had one of those dress forms. She called it Elsie.

Suddenly, the rope breaks, and the dress forms spill out from the plastic sheet covering them, careening all over the sidewalk. I can see him panicking, so I jump up, grab my stuff, and run outside.

"I'll help you!" I say.

"Thank you!"

Most stayed under the plastic sheet and are damage-free, but one dress form rolled straight off the sidewalk into a huge black puddle. As I pull it out, fumbling with my Hello Kitty umbrella and my bag at the same time, I notice a shard of glass has somehow embedded itself in the side, and the wire frame at the bottom is bent.

"Oh noooooo!" The fedora guy is freaking out.

"Drowned and then stabbed," I say. "Fashion kills, huh?"

"Shitballs! What am I gonna do? She's destroyed!"

"She's fine!" I say. "You could spray and soak the mud off. Good as new!"

He's really freaking out. "Don't touch her! She's revolting!"

"It's just a little mud!"

"No! She's only fit for the garbage now. My boss is going to *kill* me! Fuck it, I'll throw her in the Dumpster."

He reaches out, but I snatch the dress form away from him. "No, don't, I'll take her!"

"You will?" he says, smiling and tilting his head to one side. "Who are you? And what do you do?"

"Angie James," I say, holding out my hand. "I'm a fashion designer."

That's the first time I've ever said those words. They feel good coming off my tongue. Even though, strictly speaking, I don't think they're true. Yet.

"Philly Meyer," he replies. "I'm a milliner and DJ, but I'm interning right now for Sarah Drake."

"Nice," I respond, smiling. Sarah Drake! I know about her. She was a protégé of Narciso Rodriguez and then they had some sort of huge bust-up. She just started her own label creating one-off pieces that are more like avant-garde art than fashion.

"Yeah. She's a stickler for time, so I have to run."

Before I can say anything, he turns and herds the six remaining dress forms around the corner.

Quickly I write his name down. *Philly Meyer.* Wow. One degree of separation from Sarah Drake, two degrees from Narciso Rodriguez. I'm so going to Facebook him later.

I turn and look at the dress form. She's pretty high-end: the kind you can make bigger or smaller, thinner or fatter, so you can fit whatever you're making to any specific size. She's covered in a rough cream canvas—though now, of course, it's stained with filthy New York puddle water, and the gash in her side is fairly unsightly, too.

But I can fix her. Underneath all the stains, she's still good.

I walk back into Starbucks, wheeling the dress form as I go, and as I'm lining up for another coffee I notice the woman in front of me.

Candie Stokes.

She was a stylist, got lucky with an Oscar winner a few years ago, and now runs a website called *What to Wear Now*. It's one of those fashion blogs that somehow rode the first blog success wave and just got bigger and bigger. Last time I checked, she was working with Neiman Marcus and Piperlime to create some über-fashion-blog empire. She looks a little tan-and-smoke-addled, and she's the size of, like, an elf, but damn! She's a fashion person! I knew my plan would work!

Okay. So what do I say?

Let's just go with the old reliable.

"Candie Stokes!" I am too nervous to sound anything but hyper. "I'm a huge fan!"

She turns, sees my muddy dress form, and instantly smiles. Heavy makeup and four-inch heels. "I don't think we've—"

"Angie James. I'm a fashion designer." It's getting easier and easier to say that. "I'm also an illustrator and photographer." Where did that come from? Well, it's true. Kind of. I draw. I take photos. Sometimes.

Candie's smile disappears. "Really. Ever been paid to design clothes?"

"Um, no."

"Ever been paid for an illustration?"

". . . No."

"And your photography? Ever been paid for that?"

I can hardly get the word out. "No."

Candie's eyes flick up and down. I'm wearing jeans, white studded Converse, layered sweaters, my fur/army coat, and an old trapper hat. My face is smeared with yesterday's eyeliner, because I forgot to take it off and left the house without bothering to do anything about it, and my hair is dirty and gathered in a topknot. I thought I looked kind of punk and tough, but now I wonder if I look like someone you see drinking cans of beer outside a train station.

"What, exactly, do you design?"

"Um, I'm just starting out. I want to work in fashion though, and I, um, I would love to talk to you sometime." I try to sound professional and enthusiastic, like Pia would. I grab my Moleskine sketchbook. "You can see my ideas—"

"No," she says decisively, picking up her coffee.

"Could we maybe swap numbers, or I could Facebook you—"

"No." She walks away, then pauses, and comes back, lowering her sunglasses, her bloodshot eyes staring hard at me. "You ever see that movie *Working Girl*? Melanie Griffith? Before your time, I bet. Well, there's a line in it. 'Sometimes I sing and dance around the house in my underwear. Doesn't make me Madonna. Never will.' Think about it."

She puts her sunglasses back on and walks away.

"Bitch," I say under my breath, in an attempt to master the panicky fear inside me. She treated me like I was nothing. Like I was totally worthless.

I'm never going to get a job.

I turn and face the barista, just as he hands over my black coffee.

He smiles, whispering loudly, "I'm launching a Navajo-inspired jewelry line in the fall! You should check out my blog! We could collaborate on something!"

Suddenly I just want to go home.

I wheel my dress form out of Starbucks. She looks as dejected as I feel. I'm going to call her Drakey. As a reminder to myself that the Sarah Drakes of the world probably didn't get their first job hanging out in Starbucks.

I walk toward the subway along Seventh, along the Fashion Walk of Fame. Do you know it? It's like that Hollywood thing, only instead of dead movie stars, each star honors American design legends. From Mainbocher to Diane von Furstenberg to Donna Karan to Norma Kamali. They've all walked this exact sidewalk. They all started out with nothing more than a love for fashion and a desire to create clothes, just like me. And they all made their lives happen.

Just like I can't.

CHAPTER 15

"SURPRISE!"

"Pia's not here yet. More to the point, Sam's not here yet."

"I'm practicing, and I'm, I'm—Oh, gotta go. Nervous pee."

I'm sitting on the sofa reading an old issue of *W*—because I can't afford the new one right now—while Jules and Coco snipe at each other in an affectionate sisterly way and put the last touches on the dining table for Pia's so-called surprise dinner party.

Pia's birthday is the same day as mine, and it's not for ages. Our mothers met in the maternity ward, for Pete's sake; they became friends so we became friends. But I'm glad everyone's forgotten. I don't want a big deal about a birthday that I always thought would be a huge milestone of adulthood and is turning out to be a reminder that I'm failing my twenties.

Madeleine screams from upstairs. "The freaking hot water is gone again!"

"Give it twenty minutes!" Julia shouts back.

"I don't have twenty minutes!"

Coco skips back into the room. Her face is unusually flushed.

"Are you okay?" I say to her.

"I'm great!" she exclaims. "I'm so excited. I asked this guy Ethan I met at my friend from work's birthday drinks? He's her roommate's friend from college's coworker? He's nice! He's said yes."

"Have you been drinking already?" I look at her closely.

"I pregamed!" She stands up and does a twirl. "WOO!"

I think the pressure of throwing a party is getting to all of us, but we've managed to prepare perfectly. Coco has been cooking individual chicken pot pies all day. I picked up some cheeses from Stinky. Pia bought Brooklyn Blackout from Steve's Ice Cream. Madeleine has been cleaning all day, including vacuuming the inside corners of the sofa and Q-tipping the fridge. Julia bought a bunch of early hydrangeas, her favorite flower, to put on the side table in the front hall. And we've invited one "date" each, to make it seem "totally normal."

"Like a trash-or-treasure party!" Julia said. "Bring a dude you haven't ever been involved with, and he might be perfect for someone else!"

Coco defied Julia's trash-or-treasure rules and invited this Ethan guy she's crushing on, Madeleine asked Heff, a guitar player from the band she sings with, and Jules asked Lev, some coworker from the bank. I literally could not think of a single man to bring that I haven't ever been involved with. (How depressing is that?) So I just decided my contribution is Sam. Whoever wants him can take him.

Julia is frantically polishing the wineglasses. "These things are re-fuckingvolting! How do you clean ancient glass? This one has lipstick marks from, like, before I was born."

"Baking soda and vinegar!" says Coco, running out of the room again. "Soak and scrub!"

"That seems like a lot of work." Julia puts the glass down.

I look over at her for the first time tonight. "What the *what* are you wearing? Those pants are wrong on, like, eight levels. Were you drunk when you bought them?"

"No! I was fifteen. Fuck! What should I wear then, fucking fashion guru of awesomeness? I hate all my clothes."

"Come on. I'll find you something."

Julia stomps behind me, up to my room. God, she's tense. She must really like Sam. Is he genuinely that good-looking?

I open my closet and frown as I skim the racks. "Let's see, you're bigger than me in the boob department—"

"And the ass department—"

"This is killer." I pull out a little black dress that I got from the Brooklyn Flea. "Black tights, borrow these shoes. And take your hair out of that damn ponytail."

Julia takes the clothes obediently. "Turn around. I don't do the public nudity thing like you and Pia. And I like my ponytail. I get a headache when I take it out."

"That's your hair follicles going, ooo, finally! We can stretch!" With my back to Julia while she changes, I do an imitation of hair follicles stretching, and she cracks up.

"You are not the cool bitch I always thought you were, Angie James."

"And you're totally the tactless sweetheart I always thought you were, Julia Russotti."

"Okay, you can turn around now. Is this right?" She's trying to tie the dress, but she's doing it all wrong. I take over. "Thanks," she says, suddenly relaxing a tiny bit. "I'm not good with the whole fashion thing. I fear change. You won't believe me, but I wore the same jeans every single day in high school. I washed them at night."

"I believe you, trust me. . . . So who's this Lev guy?" I ask, arranging Julia as though she were a doll.

"Lev? No one. I mean, he's my friend, kind of. I sit next to him at work. I like him, but I don't *like* like him. . . . Apart from him, I don't like any of the guys I work with at all. There are twenty guys on my team, and all of them except Lev treat me like I'm invisible and don't have a voice, like nothing I say is worth listening to." She's babbling now, her nerves kicking in. "Do you know what it's like to say something and have everyone act like no one has spoken? It fucks with your mind. Um, but I like Sam, I really do. In fact, he's the first guy I've liked since Mason, remember him?" I don't, but I nod anyway. "Sam is so fucking gorgeous, don't you think?"

I shrug. "He's a bit . . . clean-cut, isn't he? You know. Preppy. Square."

"Classic, you mean! He's like a Ralph Lauren model. Or Abercrombie & Fitch."

"Julia, Abercrombie & Fitch models are like, twelve years old."

"Well, whatever. He won't like me, I know he won't, they never do. I'm going to be single forever and I will never get any action ever again. My sugar is never going to see another wang."

"First, if you call them wangs and sugars, then, fucking hell yes, you're never going to get any action."

"May I call them both junk? Just generically?"

"No, you may not. Let's start with penis and vagina and take it from there. Or you can say dick and p—"

"Don't say that word! I hate that word."

"Fine. Second, of course he'll like you! Just be yourself."

Pretty rich coming from me since I've always found my personality at the bottom of a vodka bottle, but whatever.

"Really?" she says. "I just, ugh, it's so weird. . . . Putting myself out there is totally out of my comfort zone."

She's never talked to me like this before. In the past I would have assumed it's because her go-to confidante, Pia, isn't around much, but actually, I know that's not true anymore. Julia and I are friends now. Real friends.

"I haven't liked anyone like this in ages. What if he doesn't like me back?"

"Of course he'll like you back!" I say. "Sit down. You need eyeliner. When you look tough, you'll feel tough."

"Is that your secret to success?" she says, sitting down and closing her eyes.

I take out my eyeliner bag. "Right on. My success."

Julia glances down. "Whoa. You have, like, sixteen black eyeliners?"

"Yeah. It really depends on my mood. Gel, cake, liquid, pencil . . ."

"Just make me pretty. Prettier, anyway."

"You have amazing eyelashes."

"Why do chicks always say that to each other?"

For a minute or two, while I draw punk-yet-pretty eyeliner around Julia's eyes, we sit in silence. I'm good at eyeliner. The secret is getting it right into the lashes and waterline, and if you mess it up, just smudge it a bit. Perfect eyeliner is too amateur makeup blogger, you know?

"Look up. Okay, close your eyes."

"How's the job stuff going?" asks Julia.

"Hashtag fail. I have officially been rejected by every fashionista in New York City. Okay, open your eyes, look up."

"You can always get a job at the Gap."

"Double ha," I say.

"Madeleine was just kidding, you know," says Julia. "She thinks you're still pissed at her."

"I am, a little," I say. "That Gap comment the other day was so bitchy and demeaning."

"She's lovely, she really is. You just have to get to know her, that's all."

"I don't want to get to know her. She says that shit and it just . . . it cuts."

Julia looks at me funny.

"What?" I say.

"Pia told you," she says in a low voice.

"Told me what?"

"About Madeleine and the . . . Oh. She didn't."

"What?" I cast my mind back. What did I just say? "Cuts? Madeleine *cuts* herself?"

"Not anymore," says Julia quickly. "Please, forget I said anything."

I can't believe Pia didn't tell me something so big. . . . Though really, it figures, it's not like she talks to me lately anyway. But if Madeleine doesn't do it anymore, then it's not a problem, right? And why should I worry? She's not even nice to me. She's always so goddamn standoffish and sarcastic. I guess I can be, too, but . . . never mind.

"Look! Beautiful!" I say, handing Julia a mirror.

She takes a moment to gaze at herself. "Wow. If I could press a 'Like' button, I would. Thank you, Angelface."

"You're welcome, Ju . . . Ju . . ." I try to think of something cute to do with her name. "Juicy Fruit?"

She wrinkles her nose at me.

"Don't make that face or you'll never get laid."

At that moment the doorbell rings. Coco whizzes past my door heading upstairs.

"Oh, my god! It's Ethan! I know it is! Sugar! I'll be back in a minute!"

"What if it's Sam? I need to brush my teeth!" Julia runs to the bathroom.

I walk downstairs just as Madeleine opens the front door. It's Sam and Madeleine's date, Heff the musician guy. He's hot, in a skinny, put-the-crack-pipe-down-and-eat-a-fucking-burger kind of way.

"Mad!"

"Heffy!"

Madeleine and Heff hug, leaving Sam and me awkwardly not hugging.

"Sam."

"Angie."

Sam leans down to kiss me hello on the cheek. I'm not expecting it, so I sort of jump, and then frown because goddamnit, I am cooler than that.

"Don't you look all cute when you make an effort," I say. Sam is all stubbly and scruffy, very different from my first impression of the Nazi Youth, slick, boat-boy (sorry, crew) hair.

"I was just thinking the same about you," he says.

Yeah, right. I am not looking my best. I'm wearing a secondhand blouse I customized by cutting the sleeves off, the only cheap-ass jeans I could find that weren't too wrinkled to wear, and Converse, and I braided my hair instead of washing it.

Compared to all my roommates in heels and shiny blowouts, I look boring as hell. Which is new for me. And kind of nice. I realized today that I used to make clothes do the talking for me. I let my leather pants or four-hundred-dollar jeans tell people that I was a tough, important bitch they'd better not fuck with. But for the way I'm feeling at the moment, I don't want to be noticed at all.

And I don't own any four-hundred-dollar jeans anymore, anyway.

Sam hands over two bottles of wine just as Coco and Julia bounce downstairs, flushed with excitement, and immediately attack Sam with giggles and bashful questions. I look over at Madeleine, who is talking to Heff about some new band in Williamsburg, but he's one of those cool types who talks in a low monotone drawl so no one farther than fifteen inches away can hear a goddamn word.

God, where is Pia already? She's one of those people who makes a party work. She's the ultimate mixer, like tonic and lemon. I usually hide in the corner at parties, ignore everyone, and drink until I find my personality and/or a guy chats me up. But not tonight.

Julia claps her hands like a headmistress. "Right! Who's thirsty?"

We dole out Julia's punch—vodka, canned peach juice, sparkling white wine, and crème de cassis. Sam takes one sip, chokes slightly, and wordlessly accepts the beer I slip him.

Coco is positively flying. "Woo! This punch is punchy! Am I right?"

The doorbell rings, and she leaps to get it.

"Hiiiiiiiiiiiiiiiiiiiii!"

Coco leads Ethan into the room like a proud owner at a dog show.

"Everyone, this is my date!"

"I'm Ethan," he says in a Kermit the Frog voice. *"Enchanté."*

Ethan is a short, stocky guy wearing a blue plaid shirt and red plaid trousers. Without irony. (You always need to check for sartorial irony, especially in Brooklyn, but trust me, I know this guy is not being ironic.)

And his conversation is worse than his fashion sense. "So I thought, well, I'll take the L train, and descended a stairway that led me to a train heading in the wrong direction! I had to ascend to street level and cross to find the train that would take me to the correct destination! Now, take it from a Chicago man: there's a flaw in the system! In fact, as I was—"

That's it. I'm having a smoke to kill some time. I sneak out to the front hallway, pull on my fur/army coat, and head outside to the stoop. I can almost-but-not-quite feel the thaw in the March air. Time to lose the fur/army coat soon. Yay. I mentally start going through my jackets and blazers. . . . Ah, clothes. Always a comfort, especially when I'm feeling alone.

"You know, smoking is bad for you."

I glance over. It's Sam, standing next to me, looking out at the night.

"I heard that." I take a drag and frown. "I don't actually like cigarettes that much unless I'm drinking."

"You're not drinking?"

"Not really. I mean, I haven't officially 'quit' drinking or anything. I hate it when people do that."

"Yeah, it's so annoying."

"I'm just dialing it down for the foreseeable future. Vodka applies pressure to my self-destruct button."

"Good to know."

Sam glances over at me, a tiny smile on his face. He's very self-assured, but not arrogant. An unusual combination, at least in the dudes I've known. His nose is ridiculously straight. Like something from a coin. Regal. Or whatever you call noses you see on coins.

At that moment we see Pia and Aidan walking up Union Street toward us, gesturing intensely. Pia looks upset. They're fighting?

"I can't believe you'd do this to us—" she's saying, then glances up. "Angie?"

"Um, hi!" We have to continue the surprise party charade. "Pia, pretend to be shocked, okay? Just count to thirty, come in, and be like, 'Holy shit!' Dial up the drama, okay?"

"What? A surprise party? It's not my birthday!"

Before she can say anything else, I stub out my cigarette on the stoop, grab Sam's arm, and pull him back into the house. Pia and Aidan might be fighting, but I'll find out more later.

Sam raises an eyebrow. "It's not her birthday? This is a *pretend* surprise party?"

I smile at him and shrug, just as Julia lurches around the corner and pounces on Sam. "There you are! Would you like some more punch?" Then she cocks her head. "I hear them! Everyone hide! Hide!"

We all scramble to our assigned hiding places. Julia's date, the guy she works with, hasn't even turned up yet, I realize. Not that she's noticed. Sam and I are both behind the sofa. Our eyes meet, and he gives an incredibly dorky pretend-excited face. I try not to laugh and make a bursting sound.

"Angie!" hisses Julia.

Sam shakes his head at me and makes a "shh!" sound.

A few seconds later, as we're all crouched in the dark, Pia and Aidan walk into the living room.

"SURPRISE!"

"OH, MY GOD!" Pia screams, jumping up and down in pretend shock.

"Great acting skills," says Sam under his breath, as Julia and Coco yell and clap in delight.

"You should see her do an anxiety attack, seriously," I reply.

"She's a faker?"

"Oh, no," I say. "I think her emotions are real. I'm just saying that she really lets you know what she's feeling. She's highly expressive."

"Jeez, I could be collapsing inside and my face would look just the same to everyone around me," says Sam.

"Me too," I say. "It's my curse."

Sam's perma-frown turns into a grin, just as Julia walks up to us and downs her punch in one gulp. "Let's eat!"

Coco's face falls. "Oh, my god, the pies."

At that moment the smoke alarm goes off.

CHAPTER 16

Okay, the kitchen stinks of smoke, the house is now freezing because we opened all the windows for fresh air, and the pies are charred beyond saving. But the party is going strong. There was a team decision to have ice cream and cheese for dinner, and as a result, everyone is shitfaced and acting—to use a phrase I was fond of in my teens—totally wack.

Pia is ignoring Aidan. This never happens, they're usually sparkling at each other all night like two little birthday candles. I am waiting for the right time to ask her if she's okay, but right now, she's ranting at Madeleine and Heff, who are so stoned they can't respond. That never *ever* happens. I'd bet money Madeleine's experience of drugs up to now doesn't even extend as far as Midol PM.

Julia has stopped talking entirely and is just staring at Sam like he's television.

And Coco is hopping around like a big-boobed fairy on ecstasy, dancing to one of her favorite CDs (Will Smith's *Greatest Hits,* of all god-damn things), turned up to eleven. Sam and Aidan are the only people actually talking: they're discussing some scandal involving a Yankee or a Jet or something.

"What do you think of Ethan?" Coco whispers, hiccupping into my ear. "I asked Jonah? But he said no, he said no."

"He was probably just busy," I whisper back.

"No, he doesn't like me." Coco suddenly looks incredibly sad.

The doorbell rings. I head out to answer it.

It's a tall guy wearing a human-size Mighty Mouse outfit. What the?

"Tricksh and treatsh?" Ah. He's drunk out of his skull.

"Dude, it's March," I say, closing the door.

"I'm Lev." His eyes are crossing with the effort of getting the words out. "I'm here for a party dinner?"

"Dinner party."

"There was a party bachelor last night? In City Atlantic? So I'm . . . late. Where am I? You're pretty. You're so pretty. Are you my date?"

"No."

"Will you go out with me?"

"No."

I lead him into the living room.

"Jules. Your date is here."

"He's not my date! He's, he's just my friend from work, uh, a colleague, um, Lev, this is—"

Julia introduces him to everyone, but Lev ignores her, sits on the sofa, and goes straight to sleep.

"Get up, Lev!" Julia is freaking out. "You're missing a totally sick party!"

"Julia is shouting again," mumbles Lev. "I'm telling HR."

Sam catches my eye again and does his ducking-head laughing thing.

"Have you tried the Oregon Blue? I'm something of a cheese aficionado," says a froggy voice at my elbow. It's Ethan, Coco's date. "I once spent a summer making cheddar in Wisconsin."

"That must have been so exciting for you," I say.

"It was, it was," he says. He's very drunk. "You see, the secret with cheddar is the rennet—"

Ethan the Cheesemaker works for the Department of Health, but so far tonight has revealed himself to be "something of an aficionado" of wine, bicycles, fly-fishing, yachting, James Bond movies, headphones, the Battle of Brooklyn, typography, hip-hop, and Gothic architecture. He's the kind of guy who likes to teach people things, i.e., a dick. Worse? Coco thinks he's amazing.

"Wow!" Coco says now, suddenly standing next to us. "I never knew that about cheese, did you Angie? Did you? Hey! We should get matching tattoos! Saying 'Rookhaven Forever'! Because we are super awesome!"

If I didn't know better, I'd think she was on something.

"Lev!" Julia is prodding Lev. "Wake up!" She looks at Sam and smiles nervously. "He's really a nice guy, usually."

Lev opens his eyes. "Julia, can you go to the vending machine for me? Hey? Is that Ruthy?" he says, looking at Sam. "Ruthy! Ruthy!" And then he rests his head back, collapsing again.

Across the room, I see Aidan whispering to Pia.

"No, Aidan, we cannot talk about it!" she snaps. "You're moving to San Francisco. What more is there to say? Fucking awesome, dude. Awesome!"

"You're being a baby," says Aidan.

"You're being a baby," she mimics.

"Call me when you want to talk about this," he says in a low voice, and turns and walks out of the room. The front door slams.

With a loud sob, Pia gets up off the sofa and runs after him. "Aidan! Wait, oh God, wait!" The front door slams again.

Julia runs after Pia. Julia comes from the-more-the-merrier school of drama.

"Bad idea," I call. "She wants to be alone with him!"

"Pia is a princess," says Madeleine loudly.

I narrow my eyes at her. Madeleine and Pia have never been that close, but no one bad-mouths my best friend. "She is *not* a fucking princess, she's just a bit of a drama queen, and it's adorable."

"Adorable?" Madeleine snorts.

Before I can administer the verbal bitch slap I'd like to, Sam is at my side.

"So, Angie, what do you do?"

"What do I do? What DO I do, hmm, let's see. Well, I am unemployed, Sam. I am trying to get a job and I am failing." I pause and take a sip of punch. "Miserably. Any advice for me?"

Sam shrugs. "Find a passion, talk your way in, then impress the boss."

"Talk my way in? Like how?"

"Well . . . okay, I'm about to talk about me here, so, sorry if it's boring—"

"Apology accepted."

"Oh, thanks. So . . . I never sailed, you know, growing up, but I'd always wanted to. And I didn't have any other burning ambitions and I really wanted to, uh, get away for a while. My life was kind of . . . imploding. So I bought a one-way ticket to Trinidad, made some friends at bars the sailing crews all hung out in, and talked my way onto a yacht that was being delivered to the Bahamas. I just copied everyone else and learned on the job. Then, the new owner liked me, and that was that. Three years at sea and counting."

"And you love it?"

Sam thinks for a second, his gray eyes staring into the distance. "When I am sailing, I wake up looking forward to the day."

"Huh," I respond thoughtfully, frowning.

"You frown a lot."

"So do you! You're gonna need Botox by thirty."

"That's so sweet of you to say." He pauses and takes a sip of beer. "This whole thing is to set me up with Julia, right?"

"No. Maybe." Pause. "Yes."

He laughs, his face lighting up. "Really? I was only kidding. The entire night? Just for me?"

"Not exactly," I lie, suddenly feeling disloyal to Julia. "It really is Pia's birthday. Soon. Ish."

He raises an eyebrow at me. I raise mine back.

"There's something I've been wanting to ask you," says Sam. "How did you end up with that crowd, on that yacht, at that party? You didn't exactly fit in."

I smile, but my face suddenly feels locked with tension. Didn't fit in with a bunch of girls who tread the fine line between fun and fuck-for-money.

Even thinking about it makes me shudder.

"You okay? You look like you're about to ralph."

"I'm fine. . . . Do people still say 'ralph'?"

"Oh yeah. All the time. . . . Seriously, though, what were you doing there? Right from the start I knew something wasn't right. You swagger up, looking hungover and lost and pissed as hell, smoking a cigarette and wearing studded Converse. Unlike the other girls, you had no fake tan, no fake breasts, no fake teeth. . . . Are they your friends?"

"Hell no, I'd never met them before. It just sort of happened. I've known Stef a long time, I trusted him, I shouldn't have. End of story." I take a swig of my drink, hoping Sam will say something. He doesn't. And for some goddamn reason, I find myself gabbling. "So from now on, I'm avoiding rich kids forever. You know, they're all entitled assholes who just lie to get what they want. Um, enough about me. Where are you from, Sam?"

I know nothing about him. Except that he works on yachts and is living on a friend's floor in Fort Greene, broke and between jobs.

"Ohio."

"Ohio? Are you serious? Tell me more."

"Do you really need details? I'm Sam. Just Sam."

"And I'm Angie. Just Angie."

"So, how about I set you up on a blind date dinner party with one of my buddies, Just Angie? See how you like it."

"Oh . . . no. I'm not dating right now, Just Sam. I have made too many bad decisions with, uh, the dudes."

"If you can't date anyone nice, don't date anyone at all, is that it?"

"Something like that. I want to be single. But I totally think you should ask Julia for a drink or something. She's really hilarious." I pause and see Julia on the other side of the living room shouting "Fivies!" and forcing Heff to high-five her.

"She seems great, but really, uh, I'm not looking for anything, either. I just broke up with someone."

"Details, please."

"Her name's Katie. We went to college together and sort of did a long-distance thing, but it got complicated, you know. It's hard to stay in touch when you're at sea for weeks on end. . . . She's in Paris right now. Studying."

He shows me a photo on his phone.

I'm impressed. "Her friends are all doing that duckface-kiss pose but she's just smiling normally. She looks like the kind of girl I could have a drink with."

When it's his real smile, Sam's entire face is taken over by it, like a little kid's drawing. I grin back, and get the strangest, nicest, warmest feeling. I like this guy, I realize. As a friend. Purely as a friend. Which has never happened before in my entire life.

What a novelty.

"Do you want to be friends?" I say, the words out before I can assess how weird I sound. "I mean, seriously. Let's just not do that whole sexual-tension thing. No drunk kissing, no one-night regrets, no Dawson Does Joey. Let's just be friends."

"Friends?"

"Friends. Tomorrow, you should come over here and we'll have a *Freaks and Geeks* marathon or something."

"I love that show," Sam says, his face totally serious. "It was a travesty they canceled it. . . . Are you asking me out on a friend date? Is this what grown-ups do?"

"Yeah," I say. "I guess I am. And I guess it is."

I look around at everyone. Madeleine and Heff are lying on the floor giggling helplessly at Julia, who is doing the worm dance move, Ethan the Cheesemaker has passed out on the sofa next to a still-sleeping Lev, Pia and Aidan are missing, presumably fighting, and Coco is standing on a chair, singing and prancing like a pony on speed.

"They're usually not like this," I say to Sam. "Someone must have spiked the ice."

At that moment Coco shouts "WOO!" jumps off the chair, and falls on the floor.

That's a strange dance move.

Then she starts convulsing, throwing her head back violently, her entire body going rigid like she's being electrocuted, and starts making choking sounds.

Holy shit. Coco is overdosing.

CHAPTER 17

We all stare in shock for a few seconds until Sam takes charge. "Call 911. Now."

He crouches down next to her while I kneel, get out my phone, and dial 911. I put my hand on her forehead: her skin is boiling hot and damp with perspiration.

Julia is freaking out. "Coco! Coco! Oh my God ohmygodohmygod . . ."

"Calm down," says Sam. "She's fine, she'll be fine. Coco? Can you hear me?"

He puts his ear to her mouth, then feels her neck for a pulse.

The operator answers. "We need an ambulance—" I start talking her through what just happened. The operator instructs me to put Coco in the recovery position, which Sam has already done, and then check her vitals.

"She's, uh, she's breathing, but she's not a great color, and she's still unconscious," I say, as Sam instructs me. He seems to know exactly what to do.

"What has she taken?" asks the operator.

"I don't know," I say. "She's been acting weird tonight, but I've only seen her drinking alcohol—"

Coco starts convulsing again, puke bubbling out of her mouth. Sam turns her on her side, and, still unconscious, she retches a foamy mess of booze and cheese and crackers.

"Jesus," I murmur.

Sam rolls her back and puts his ear to her mouth again, trying to hear or feel her breath.

"She's breathing, but she's out cold," he says. "And her pulse is racing."

I'm talking to the operator calmly on the outside, but inside, I'm freaking out. This is my fault. I've been totally neglecting Coco. And I haven't talked about it before now because, well, it's her business, not mine, and I never tell other people's secrets, but she had an abortion a few months ago and confided in Pia and me. We helped her go to Planned Parenthood, the whole thing. She was sort of quiet and sad over the winter, but hell, everyone's quiet and sad over the winter, right? And she had an abortion, I mean, that'll make you feel pretty goddamn sad for a while. I've had one, too. About eight years ago. The guy was a bartender from a vacation I took with Pia and her family. I try not to think about it, ever. I guess I figured Coco would be the same.

"I need to know what she's taken," says the operator.

How the hell would I know? I never have any idea what's really going on with anybody else!

But maybe I should have asked, I realize, looking at Coco's little body lying on the floor. She's younger than me, she's infinitely more naive and inexperienced, she's just a baby, really. . . . We should be looking after her better.

We should all be looking after one another better.

Suddenly, Coco opens her eyes, convulses, and starts puking again. Sam quickly turns her on her side.

The operator is talking again. *"Ma'am? Drugs, alcohol, prescription medication?"*

"Um, I don't know, I'll find out, I'll find out." I hand the phone to Sam and stand up. "I'm going to search her room."

He nods, wiping away her puke, and turns to Julia. "Get me a wet towel."

Julia nods frantically and runs away, completely freaking out the way that über-bossy people always do in a genuine emergency. Madeleine and Heff are staring at Coco in stoned shock. Ethan the Cheesemaker is passed out on the sofa, totally useless, next to a still-sleeping Lev. And I guess Pia is still outside fighting with Aidan. The only people here who can really help are Sam and me. Fuck.

I hurry up to Coco's room, taking the stairs three at a time. It's an adorable room: all sloping ceilings and book-lined windowsills. Feeling like a thief, I open the drawers to her nightstand: books, lip balm, tissues, an old keychain, photos of her mom (she passed away when Coco was nine or something). Then I try her desk drawers. Pencils, pens, scissors . . . nothing else.

I look around. If I were Coco, where would I hide drugs? I wouldn't have drugs, comes the answer right back. Unless they were prescription. And I'd think of them as medicine, so I'd keep them with my Band-Aids and cough medicine.

Where the hell are her toiletries? I look around and finally see that hanging on the back of Coco's bedroom door is one of those plastic shoe storage things, you know the kind? With all the little pockets? But she's using it for toiletries, not shoes. I go through each pocket one by one. Moisturizer, face scrub, razors, deodorant, hairbrush, hair bands, sunscreen . . . and finally, pills.

Demerol and Xanax.

Of course.

I grab the pills and head back downstairs. The paramedics have arrived; they're in the living room asking Sam questions. Coco's eyes are open now, and her skin is a pale gray-blue, like someone has bled the color out of her with some faulty Photoshop app.

"I'll go to the hospital with her," I say to Sam.

"I'll come, too," he says.

"I'm going, too!" says Julia. "She's my sister."

So, somehow, the three of us end up in the ER.

Coco is put straight into a hospital bed, and the three of us sit around her, curtains drawn. Doctors come in and out, calm and preoccupied, concerned and cold. She's having palpitations, so they want to monitor her heart. And she's still not breathing properly, so they've attached an oxygen mask to her face, plus a drip in her arm to replenish her fluids. She's conscious again, but the oxygen mask means she can't talk. Her eyes look even bigger and more blue than usual, and tears are running down her face and pooling around the edge of the mask.

I've never been in an ER before. It's not like on TV and in movies: a lot quieter, more mundane. No gunshot wounds, no stabbings. Just ordinary, run-of-the-mill people who hurt themselves. I can hear the family at the next bed whispering to one another in Spanish, and an old lady talking in Russian down the hall. How scary it must be to be in a hospital speaking a foreign language.

The three of us are sitting in silence, sipping the sweet, metallic-tasting hospital coffee Sam bought, murmuring to one another in that intimate shorthand you use in the wake of an emergency. Strange how a crisis can fast-forward a friendship. Right now, I feel like Sam is one of us.

I take out the bottles of Demerol and Xanax that I found in Coco's room.

"Xanax?" says Julia. She hadn't noticed it before. "Oh God, poor Coco, this is my fault, it's my fault, it's my fault. . . ."

Sam reaches out and grabs Julia by the shoulder. "It's not your fault. These things happen. Drink your coffee."

Julia obediently picks up her coffee and takes a sip.

"Good girl," says Sam.

"Don't 'good girl' me, my friend," says Julia. "I'm twenty-fucking-three-years old."

"Good . . . woman?"

"That's more like it."

We sit there in silence a while longer.

"I hate hospitals," says Julia finally.

"Me too," says Sam. "I think everyone does."

"No, I really hate them. My mom died in a hospital. They wouldn't release her, even though she really wanted to go home for the last few days. Isn't that mean? It was so mean." Julia is talking in the tiniest voice

I've ever heard from her, and her breath catches. "I think about it all the time."

Sam pauses. "How . . ."

"Breast cancer."

"I'm really sorry," he says, and rather than sounding rote or formulaic the way those words usually do, it sounds real. Then, in a strangely paternal gesture, he reaches over, pulling Julia into a half hug, their little plastic hospital chairs clanging together. Like a daddy owl pulling a baby owl under his wing. "But you know Coco will be fine."

Julia looks over at Coco, now sleeping quietly. "Why would she need a prescription painkiller?"

Oh, my God. Coco never told her sister about the abortion. I never even thought about it, really. I was too busy thinking about Mani, who'd just broken up with me, and partying every minute that I could to obliterate all the emotions I didn't want to deal with. . . . Coco and Julia are incredibly close, how could she not tell her only sister something so important?

Because Coco thought she wouldn't understand. That she'd disapprove, and judge, and make Coco feel even worse. It's Coco's secret. Of all people, I can understand that.

So I just shrug. "Who knows? They hand those things out like candy. Didn't she get her wisdom teeth out last year?"

"Uh, yeah, I guess." Julia frowns. She doesn't seem surprised about the Xanax. She must have known about that.

Then a doctor comes back in and checks on Coco again. They decide to keep her overnight, for observation.

"What's really scary is that she was so out of it," says Julia to the doctor. "What if we hadn't been there? What if she'd been doing that with a bunch of people she didn't know? Anything could have happened to her!"

Three thousand dollars. The Soho Grand hotel. And I still don't know what happened that night. I shake my head, as if to clear it, getting a strange look from Sam.

"About a quarter of our admissions are related to alcohol and prescription abuse," says the doctor. "Sometimes more. With your permission, I'll dispose of those leftover pills safely. If she doesn't need them, it's best not to have them in the house."

Julia hands over the pills and the doctor leaves. Then she turns to us.

"You guys should go home, get some sleep. Thank you so much, Sam. Thank you."

Sam leans forward and gives Julia another hug, rumpling her hair as he does it. Her face changes from stress to bliss when she's in his arms. Wow, she really likes him. I hope he does ask her out.

"You sure you want to stay here by yourself?" I say to Julia.

"Totally," she says, and surprises me by grabbing me for a hug, too. I'm a non-hugger, I come from a long line of non-huggers—but I hug her back out of instinct. It's like putting on warm socks straight out of the dryer. A sort of *ahhhh* feeling.

"Angie, I'll escort you home," Sam says, as we're walking out of the hospital.

"Dude, I'm fine. I don't need a chaperone."

"That wasn't really my point. We're outside a hospital in the middle of the night, in one of the not-so-nice areas of Brooklyn. You'd probably get home fine, but you might not. Why take a risk?"

I sigh. "Fine. Have it your way. Jesus, do you do everything right? And how do you know what's nice and not nice in Brooklyn? You've been here, like, a week." Sam makes a snorting sound and doesn't answer.

The air outside is cold and crisp, but sort of sweet. A nice change after the stale chemical smell of the hospital. I pull my fur/army coat tighter around me.

"So, talk me through your friends," says Sam as we walk. "Coco's younger than the rest of you, right?"

"Yep," I say. "She's twenty-one, Jules is twenty-three. They're from upstate New York."

"Julia is the overprotective big sister. Coco is the little one looking for approval, huh?"

"More or less. God, I hope she's okay."

"She will be," says Sam. "She just made a mistake, that's all."

"Do you have any brothers or sisters?"

"One brother. And Pia's your best friend? The drama queen?"

"Um, yeah. Our moms met in the hospital when they were having us, we have the same birthday."

"The same birthday . . . that was not the reason for tonight's surprise party. Because I was that reason." He pauses. "I feel so important."

I start to giggle. "Um, well, yeah, so, Pia and I both turn twenty-three in April. And Madeleine is . . . I don't know, actually. We're not that close. She's hard to talk to. Unfriendly. Sometimes downright bitchy."

"I thought she was just shy," he says. "Whenever someone is sort of cold and controlled like that, making weird little comments, I figure they're shy and awkward. Trying to impress people."

This idea surprises me. "You might be right. I assume that what you see is what you get."

"That's a nice theory. But it can backfire in all sorts of ways."

I think about Stef, and the yacht, and all the mistakes I've made in the past by not bothering to look below the surface of anything, by not getting to know guys before I . . . Well, by not getting to know guys. That will never happen again.

"I'll keep that in mind."

"You do that, missy."

I smile at him, feeling that same easy warmth I felt with Julia before. The warm-sock *ahhh* feeling. Security and friendship. This guy is a good guy.

"They're a great group, anyway. Most of my friends are all over the country right now, some studying, some working. . . . You really fell on your feet in Brooklyn, huh?"

"Yeppers," I say. Actually, that's not exactly true, but I don't want to tell him everything about me.

"Did you just say 'yeppers'? What are you, nine?"

"Yes. I am nine"—I pause—"kinds of *awesome*."

Sam cracks up. I don't even know why I said that. It's the kind of dumb shit I would say if I was hanging out with just Pia.

"Do you have your favorite childhood toy hidden somewhere in your bedroom back at Union Street?"

I frown at him. How did he guess? "I have six of them," I say finally. "Big Ted, Little Ted, Grace, Rose, Ralph, and Pinky."

Sam laughs out loud again. "Six! Are you an excessive person by nature?"

"Shut up! Don't laugh at my toys!"

"I'm not laughing at them! I have one toy that I take everywhere with me. I just hide him in the bottom of my toiletry case."

"*Him?* Name, please?"

"Panda . . . He's, uh, he's a panda."

"You were obviously a highly inventive child."

"I was indeed." Sam pauses and smiles at me. "It's nice. Having Panda with me. It's a link to the past, you know? A nice one."

"I know what you mean. I guess I just like knowing that they're around," I say.

We smile at each other, and again I get that warm-sock feeling. A male friend I'm not going to sleep with. How bizarre.

When we get to Rookhaven, Sam turns to me. "Well, good night. Don't try to kiss me or anything, okay? It'd just be awkward, because of how I only like you as a friend."

I start laughing and punch him lightly in the arm. "Thank you for everything with Coco tonight. You kind of saved her life."

"Hey, it was nothing. And it's part of the platonic friend code, right? It's in the fine print: *save roommates from overdosing.*"

"Right on. So . . . I'll call you. About our friend date."

"You better."

When I get inside, Pia and Madeleine are sitting on the living room floor, around the wet shadow of a recently cleaned puke stain. The guys have all disappeared.

Pia looks up. "Angie, we need to talk."

CHAPTER 18

This is weird. Pia, my best friend in the house who I've grown apart from recently, with Madeleine, her former frenemy and my least favorite person in the house, sitting down and enjoying a 2:00 A.M. bottle of Malbec.

"What do you want to talk about?" I ask, suddenly feeling exhausted.

"Well, first, tell us about Coco," says Pia.

"How is she?" Madeleine pulls her sleeves down over her hands, looking at me anxiously. She's permanently covered up. Suddenly, I remember what Julia told me earlier. About the cutting. Maybe she is still doing it. Or maybe she has scars. Now probably isn't the time to ask. "That was so awful. . . . I've never seen someone collapse before."

"She's fine," I say. I tell them what happened. "It was a stupid mistake. She just didn't know not to combine them with alcohol."

"Where the heck did she even get those drugs?" says Madeleine. "Seriously. Coco is as straight as they come."

Pia and I exchange a look. I don't think we should tell her. It's not our place.

"She had an abortion," says Pia. "About three months ago."

Clearly Pia disagrees.

Madeleine sighs but doesn't seem shocked, which, though it sounds strange, sort of shocks me. I thought she'd be the judgmental anti-abortion type. "Poor, poor Coco. I thought she'd been a little withdrawn lately. I bet she hasn't told Julia, either."

"Nope." Pia shakes her head. "And you can't tell her, either, okay? If Coco wants to tell her, she will. . . . Anyway, so, the Demerol came from there. The Xanax . . . I don't know."

"How did you find out?" asks Madeleine.

"Angie found her crying in the kitchen one day, when she thought she was alone in the house."

I nod, remembering that day back in December. I thought Coco was just reading another goddamn Nicholas Sparks book. She's always crying over something like that. But she was sobbing—this scared, sort of intense, desperate sobbing—and I knew something was really, seriously wrong. I didn't know what to do, so I called Pia. She was on her way to see Aidan but came straight over. She guessed immediately. I think she'd suspected for a while. Then Coco told us everything.

Madeleine sighs again. "That's so awful. Of all the people for it to happen to . . . Who was the dude?"

"That guy Eric." Pia wrinkles her nose up with distaste. "The little fuckwipe."

"Urgh," says Madeleine.

We all sit in silence for a moment.

"Well, Coco will be home tomorrow, good as new, right? And it was a mistake!" I say. "I think we should just . . . let her forget about it. Not bring it up. That's what I would want."

"Coco might be different," Pia points out. "Maybe she'll want to talk about it."

"Well, if she does, then we'll listen," I say. "We'll be here for Coco if she wants to talk about it. But she's probably really embarrassed, you know. She'll be ashamed, because it's not like she does it all the time, it was an accident. She didn't really know what she was doing, it's not like she's a bad person! It was a weird situation, and it just sort of snowballed, and next thing you know, boom! She had no control over what was going on, she didn't know what was happening, but it was a mistake, a one-off, it won't happen again! You know?"

Pia and Madeleine stare at me. I try to catch my breath. Was I ranting?

Finally, Pia speaks. "Are we talking about Coco or you?"

I've nervously torn a tissue into tiny little pieces in my hand while rambling. I jump up and put it in the trash.

Time to change the subject. "Anyway, what happened with Aidan?"

Pia sighs, tears automatically springing to her eyes. "He's got a work project. In San Francisco. He might be there awhile. . . . Like, a year. Or longer. And I just, I, um . . . I don't know what to do."

"You'll be fine!" says Madeleine.

"He'll be back every weekend!" I echo. "You work so hard anyway, you'll just have more time to spend here at Rookhaven. With us."

"No, he won't be back," she says. "He's subletting his place here. He's taking his dog, Angie. His *dog*." She pauses dramatically, letting the dog factor sink in. "He's basically . . . he's leaving. And he didn't even discuss it with me. He didn't ask me what I thought, he just took the project. I thought we were about to move in together and he was just thinking about his job! What does that say about our relationship?"

"Nothing!" Madeleine and I say in supportive unison.

"He's career-focused! So are you!"

"And it's not like you're married!" I add. "You practically just got together!"

"You can do the long-distance thing. You can text and IM and Skype and FaceTime and—"

"No!" Pia shakes her head adamantly. "The long-distance thing never, ever works. You both know it as well as I do. It's like couples that take a trial separation, or a 'break.' What's the fucking point? It's just the beginning of the end. He's the first guy I've ever truly, truly loved, but I'm just trying to be a realist here. I think . . ." Her eyes well up again. "I think we're going to break up."

"Don't plan for a breakup before it happens." Madeleine pauses.

"Listen to me, giving relationship advice. I've never even been in love. Not really."

"What about that dude at Brown? The math major?"

"Sebastian? Pia, that was three years ago."

"What about Heffy? The guy from the band tonight?"

Madeleine shakes her head. "The same total disconnect I've felt with every guy I've ever known. Heff said he's got a girl back in Florida but he'd be happy for a 'casual bang' now and again. I was so stoned I didn't even know what to say. I just stared at him."

Pia cracks up. "I was hoping you'd bring that up! Dude, I *literally* never thought I'd see you stoned."

"I thought maybe it would give me a reason to laugh," says Madeleine. She looks up and meets our eyes. "Wow, how pathetic does that sound?"

At that we all crack up and laugh for such a long time that Madeleine starts drooling. Which makes us laugh more. I have an endorphin rush from laughing; I feel heady and good all over. I actually like Madeleine right now. Amazing what a crisis and a lot of booze will do.

Later on, I'm lying in bed thinking how I've never had a conversation that long with Madeleine before. Ever. And I've been living with her since August last year. I never thought about her at all, really. I never really thought about Coco, or how she was dealing with her problems after Eric and the abortion. I never thought about how Julia felt about her job. I never thought about how Pia and Aidan's relationship was going or if they'd move in together. I never thought about anybody else.

I only thought about me. My relationships, my problems, my life.

From now on, I'm not going to be the loner in the corner, smoking cigarettes and drinking vodka and shuffling cards. I'm going to be a good friend, I really am. To Pia and Julia and Coco. Even to Madeleine. I'm going to be single, always, no matter what. And I'm going to get a job.

(This time, I mean it.)

CHAPTER 19

I'm trying again.

That's how success works, right? You get knocked down, then you get up, dust yourself off, and try again. That's what Pia's always saying, anyway. And that chick had some knocks from hell last year.

There's a fashion PR agency called Maven in SoHo. They are my (new) ideal employer (if I can't work with a designer, then work with people who talk about those designers all day, right?). Their accounts are my favorite labels, they have satellite offices in London and Paris (Paris!), and they have a really cool website. I sent them my résumé by e-mail and snail mail, I tried to start conversations with them on Twitter, Facebook, and LinkedIn, and I've called. Every day. For weeks now.

Nothing.

So now I'm trying it the old-fashioned way.

Bribery.

Sam is helping me out. He texted to see what I was doing a couple of days after the dinner party, and I replied "seeking gainful employment." There's less than a month now till I turn twenty-three, so time is running out. Anyway, he offered to help.

And that's how we ended up standing outside the Maven office building on Broome Street. I'm holding twenty coffees on a tray and shouting, "Free nonfat lattes with every CV!"

My aim? Just to make someone look at me twice as a potential employee. If they even gave me one chance, just one day of work, I *know* I could prove myself to them. (Well, I don't really know that for sure. But I'm not going to show my self-doubt now, right?)

Sam is next to me, holding twenty copies of my CV, which has been written, edited, and proofed to within an inch of its life by everyone at Rookhaven. So far, the only people to take a latte have been the doorman and someone who I'm pretty sure was going to a different company entirely. (No one wearing Crocs works in fashion, it's just a fact.)

"Free latte with every CV!" I say, as a guy takes a latte, who almost-but-not-quite looks a bit like that famous sleazy British photographer who makes everyone look slutty.

"The latte is free! The CV'll cost ya!" shouts Sam.

"No ad-libbing," I hiss.

"Not helping? Okay. I'll shut up now. How about I stand on the lower step, like I'm your personal assistant."

Sam smiles winningly at me. He's dressed up in a very sharp suit and a crisply ironed shirt. He's lost that annoyingly innocent clean-cut look that was my first impression of him and instead looks sort of aloof and sharp, like a young Wall Street bloodsucker. He's been getting a lot of attention from passing women.

"Nice shoes," I comment. "J. M. Westons, right? My father wears them. How the hell did you afford them?"

"My roommate is the same size as me, he works in finance. Where did you get those sexy little things?"

I look down at my feet. Manolos that once belonged to Annabel. "My mother."

A stunning woman saunters past. She has perfect caramel-highlighted hair trailing over one shoulder and long, long legs in tight jeans, and stares at Sam so hard I think she might trip.

"You are getting some serious eye fucks, Samuel," I comment. "You should dress well more often."

"Eye fucks? Oh, that's nice. That's real nice. Well, you're getting a lot of stares, too, Angela."

"My full name is Angelique, bitch. I hate being called Angela."

"Yes, ma'am."

I stepped it up today, after my grungy errors with Candie Stokes. I'm wearing white Theory pants that I bought for my job interview with a photographer last year, a white turtleneck, and a little slim-sleeved leather jacket that came from Zara but could be designer. (I hope.) Plus that gold clutch I made from secondhand scarves, and my usual out-for-the-day oversize white tote with everything I own in it. There are girls like me all over New York, all lugging sofa-size bags with our lives inside, like glossy little snails.

Finally, around 9:30 A.M., the fashion girls start arriving. I can spot them a mile off: they're wearing some of the hottest items from the last five seasons with casual "this old thing?" aplomb, as though they were wearing something from Gap. Acne, Lanvin, Equipment, Alexander Wang, Current/Elliott, A.P.C., and a lot of Rick Owens. I even see four women carrying the Proenza Schouler PS1 satchels, which go for a couple of grand a pop, minimum. But I also see recognizable pieces from H&M, Topshop, J.Crew, and American Apparel. Real fashion people mix high and low. Only wannabes do head-to-toe labels.

Sartorial observances aside, I can see that the arrival schedule demonstrates the hierarchy. The younger ones come first. Mostly my age, mostly smoking, mostly gorgeous, as though they could have been models but something tiny—a too-long chin, a too-snub nose, or a too-traditional prettiness—kept them from achieving supermodel success. They're mostly in flats, and some pause at the front door and throw on a pair of heels.

"Take a latte!" I exclaim, while they're shoeless and defenseless. "My name is Angie James. If you need an intern or assistant or someone to fetch you coffee, please remember me!"

"This latte is cold," says a chic, pointy-faced girl about my age, wearing one of the Marni for H&M skirts from a few years ago.

"Well, put some ice in it and pretend it's summer," I say.

She grins, revealing a snaggletooth. "I wish." Why does imperfect dentistry always make someone seem more likeable?

"Great skirt," I say quickly. "Marni for H&M, right?"

"Right," she says, looking surprised. "I slept outside the store overnight to get it. I'm obsessed with Marni."

"I missed the best pieces from the Marni collaboration, but I got the jacket from the Versace one," I say. "I'm obsessed with Versace, like, 1990 to 1992."

"Oh, me too! Hey, *love* the clutch, whose is that?" Her phone beeps. "Shit, I gotta run. Good luck!"

I turn back to Sam, who gives me the thumbs-up.

Then the midlevel women come, most of them intimidatingly glossy-haired, some shouting on the phone, some quietly texting. All too busy to stop and talk, though three of them take a latte and a CV. One, a brunette with a dark bob, says "Thank you," and actually appears to read over my CV as she walks into the building.

And finally, a town car pulls up, and out steps a black-haired woman wearing Lanvin (I think)—and a mink coat. It's the owner and director of Maven PR, Cynthia Maven. (I Googled her.)

"Ms. Maven, I have a latte for you?" I say, with my best and brightest smile. "It's free with my CV!"

Her head moves slightly toward me and she takes a latte and a CV, barely breaking stride, and disappears into the building.

I turn to Sam and sigh.

"Well, so much for that idea. I am never going to get a job."

"Of course you are."

"No, I'm really not, Sam. I'm underqualified, underexperienced, and probably underdressed. I just . . . I can't compete."

"You think that now, but then, one day, you'll get your break. And that's when your future begins."

"Wow. That is some serious Hallmark card shit right there."

"Thanks. Now it's my turn," he says. "Do you know how the subway system works? I need to get downtown."

"You don't know Manhattan at all?"

"I prefer Brooklyn."

"God, really? I only live in Brooklyn because I can't afford Manhattan," I say. "Manhattan is way more glamorous."

Sam laughs. "You think? Well, from what I've seen, Brooklyn is kinder. Manhattan can be a total bitch. Come on, help me out. I gotta go see a man about a crew job."

"A blow job?"

"A *crew* job. I'm straight, Angie. You know that."

"Do I?" I say. "You suit up pretty well for a straight dude. And you're still refusing to ask Julia out."

"Dude, you've got to get over the Julia thing. Not gonna happen."

"Why not? Give me one good reason."

"Maybe I'm still hung up on Katie."

"Your ex? She's in Paris! One date! What's the difference? Come on. Grow a pair."

"This from the girl who has sworn off relationships."

I ignore him, and we take the subway downtown. Then, as we're sitting side by side, and I'm looking at everyone around me and wondering why fluorescent lighting was invented when it's just so uglifying, Sam turns to me.

"So what happened with the last guy you fell in love with?"

"What?"

"Just making conversation, Angela. Wondering why you don't trust men."

"What?" I say. "What kind of a dude talks about love, Samuel? You're like a chick. Why don't we just make some fucking s'mores and swap our traveling pants?"

"I was wondering why you seem a little bitter."

"Ouch."

"Just tell me. I mean—" Sam checks himself, as if wary of being too arrogant. "If you want to talk about it."

I pause. Fuck it. For once I do feel like sharing. "The last guy I thought I was in love with was named Mani. But he was just using me. I think maybe . . . dudes have always used me. But it's my fault."

"How is it your fault?"

"Um, because I choose to let them treat me that way. I just sit back and hope everything will be perfect and real and lasting if I behave just right." I take a deep breath. I don't know why I'm confessing all to Sam, but I can't help it. "I make the wrong choices. I put myself in situations where . . . where these guys treat me like nothing, you know, like shit. But I'm not shit." I suddenly hear a break in my voice. "I'm *not* nothing." Stop talking, Angie, Jesus.

Sam turns and looks me right in the eye. "It's never your fault if someone is an asshole and treats you . . . in a way that you don't want to be treated. It sucks, but it's not your fault. It's theirs. Fuck those people. Okay? You just . . . shake it off, pretend they don't exist, and move on."

This is a slight variation of Vic's "let regrets go" speech, but somehow, I'm not sure I agree with the fine print in Sam's approach.

"Pretend people don't exist? Isn't that kind of harsh?"

Sam stares into space. "Probably."

It occurs to me that I'm basically pretending my mother doesn't exist. And my dad still hasn't called me either. Sam's approach suddenly isn't looking that out-of-the-ordinary.

We're both silent the rest of the journey, and fifteen minutes later we're on the very edge of downtown Manhattan, at North Cove Marina. It's a square-cut marina for just a handful of incredible yachts, all nestled peacefully together, surrounded by the architectural beauty and chaos of the Financial District.

"It's totally surreal to see a yacht next to a skyscraper. Looks like drunk Photoshopping," I say.

"I know," says Sam. "But they balance each other perfectly, don't you think? I never even knew this place existed until recently."

"Why would you? You're from Ohio."

"Right. Anyway, there was a job I saw on CrewFile, the guy said he was interviewing in person down here today," Sam says, as we walk along the pier. "It's a six-man crew, sailing from here to Greece next month. So I need to make a really good impression."

"Wow, these are some amazing boats," I say.

"They're not boats. They're yachts. Never boats."

"Sheesh, touchy. Which one is the one you're interviewing for?"

"She's over there."

"She? Oh . . . right."

Sam points to a long yacht, easily the biggest in the marina, at the end of the pier. It—sorry, she—is truly beautiful, like something out of an old movie. Black body, white detailing, and immaculately clean and shiny, with masts reaching far into the sky. When we get to the end of the pier, I see her name. *Peripety.*

Why are real sailing yachts so romantic? I don't know why, they just are. Way better than the money-monster megayachts favored by sleazy types like Hal.

"She was built in the 1950s as an ocean racer," says Sam. "See how she's made from wood, not aluminum alloy? It makes for a smoother ride. Really old-school."

"How big is she? Is it okay that she's so old? I mean . . . is she safe?"

"She's one hundred and four feet. And she was restored a couple of years ago, she's in perfect condition. She's got the most amazing history, she's a work of art, really, she's . . ." Sam trails off, running his hands through his hair, suddenly nervous. "I really want this chance, Angie. It's all I've wanted for a long time."

"You'll get it," I say, trying not to show how surprised I am to see Sam shaken out of his customary cool. "That job is totally yours."

He nods, his voice low and intense. "This is the yacht, Angie. This is the one."

"You'll be fine!" I say. "Go get 'em, tiger. This job is your bitch and you are its daddy."

Sam's too tense to even smile.

"Okay," he says. "I'm gonna go talk to the guy. Back in twenty."

CHAPTER 20

While Sam is away, I play Let's Pretend with the boats. I wonder what it's like to be able to afford a yacht of your very own. To just have it here, waiting for you, whenever you feel like getting out on the open sea.

Pretty goddamn great, I bet.

I bet someone saying "you're hired" would feel pretty good right now, too.

Sighing, I sit down at the end of the marina and check my e-mail. Nothing, nothing, nothing. I've e-mailed hundreds of people about jobs, and I haven't had one single reply. Since when are job applications spam? And why is everything good in life so hard to get?

I get a text from Julia: *Yoo-hoo. Fashion Guru. Should I get green or purple panties? Ordering online.*

I grin to myself. Julia has been saying "yoo-hoo" a lot, ever since I told her it was my old boss Cornelia's favorite saying.

I reply: *Black.*

She replies: *Black feels kinda whorish.*

I smirk to myself. Jules is hilarious, and I never knew it before. I reply: *Maybe that means there's a chance you'll get some action.*

She replies: *BOOM. Okay. You win. Black panties it is.*

Julia is fast becoming one of my favorite people. I've barely seen Pia in days; she and Aidan are deep in crisis talks. I'm getting used to her not being around, to the point where I feel almost awkward when I *do* see her. Don't get me wrong; I still totally love her and everything, but it's a bit weird right now. Female friendship is so much more complicated than any dude relationship.

I pull out my latest romance novel, *Secrets of the Sahara.*

After being jilted at the altar, Suzanne goes on her honeymoon alone to Africa, attracting the attentions of big game hunters: arrogant, hateful Ty Hunter and his flirtatious brother, Rock. At first, her romantic preferences are clear, but soon Suzanne's feelings become tangled, and when their plane crashes in the desert, there's a choice she'll have to make. . . .

I admit, this one is pretty goddamn lame. But it is still somehow calming, you know? When I open a romance novel the real world, all my real world problems just disappear.

Sam comes back after about twenty minutes. I quickly hide my book.

"Fucking washout," he says angrily, walking down the pier. "It's always who you know, who you are. Where you goddamn come from."

"You didn't get it?"

"No. I didn't fucking get it." Sam is striding so fast I have to run after him.

"There are more boat jobs, right?" I say.

"That's not the point! I wanted *that* job!" Wow, Sam has a temper.

"Calm down. Why don't you just fly to fucking Nassau, or whatever, and bullshit your way into a crew again? I would totally employ you as my boat boy."

Sam stops and turns to smile at me, his face softening slightly. "You have such a way with words. *Boat boy.* Jeez."

"Crew member. Whatever."

"Yeah, whatever." Sam's all laid-back cool again, his anger passing like a storm.

Calling Sam a boat boy immediately reminds me of Turks, and I get a sick sour feeling in my stomach so fast that I feel dizzy. I wish I could take a scalpel and cut those memories out of my brain. Or swap them to find out what happened to me at the Soho Grand that night. I wince at the thought and turn to Sam to clear my head.

"Why do you want it so badly?"

Sam sighs. "I started from nothing, you know? No sailing experience, no training, no contacts, nothing. So if I were to get picked for the crew on something like the *Peripety* . . . I'd know I did it all on my own. Sailing across the Atlantic, forging my way on the open sea . . ." Sam smiles at me. "Like it when I wax a little lyrical for you?"

"Okay, so then you'll be like, oh, yay, I sailed around the world, woo for me. What the hell do you do after that?"

Sam gazes at me for a few seconds. "That's the big question."

I frown at him. "There's something you're not telling me." He doesn't respond. "You are a stubborn bastard, anyone ever tell you that?"

"Actually, yes," says Sam. "I'm hungry. Let's go to the Village and drink beer and eat burgers."

"I'm eating pasta and Cheerios for, like, every meal this week," I say. "We're both unemployed, remember? Why waste the cash?"

Across the street, I see a Duane Reade.

"Quick pit stop, Sammy," I say. "Tampons."

"Dude . . ."

"Oh, grow a pair. Girls get periods. It's not exactly breaking news. You're coming with me." I grab Sam's arm and pull him into the drugstore. "Hey! Where are the tampons, please?" I ask a Duane Reade guy stacking shelves.

He doesn't bother to turn around. "Back of the store to your right."

"Back of the store. Great. Well, it's not like fifty percent of your customers need them once a month, so why make it easy for them?" I mutter as I stride through the store, a deeply reluctant Sam beside me. "And while we're there, why not make it fucking expensive, too? Yeah. Nine bucks for a box of tampons. That seems reasonable. Asshats."

I grab the tampons off the shelf. Sam raises an eyebrow.

"Super plus?"

"Damn straight, super plus. Girls only buy regular tampons so guys will think they have teeny tiny vaginas," I snap over my shoulder as I stride toward the cash register.

Sam laughs so hard he stops walking for a moment and leans over with his hands on his knees.

"I'll pick up the new *Us* magazine for Coco, too," I say. "She's been a bit down after her dinner party meltdown. It might cheer her up. Oh, and some hand soap for the bathrooms; we're running out. And one for the kitchen; I hate getting food on my hands and just rinsing them, don't you? Oh, and body moisturizer. My legs are so dry and cracked right now. Nivea? What do you think?"

"When we met, I thought you were the tough, silent type," says Sam, as we line up to pay. "Now I know you have heavy flow and your legs are like the floor of an old church."

I feel the giggles coming on. "I am tough and silent, Samuel! You just bring out the chatterbox in me."

"That comes to $52.96," says the woman behind the counter.

Yikes. That's more than I expected. Giggles canceled.

I take out my credit card and zip it through the machine.

It makes a BA! sound.

I try again.

"It's not working, ma'am. May I see the card?"

She types in the numbers. Waits a few seconds, shakes her head.

"I'm sorry."

Burning with shame, I quickly take my card back and look through my purse. I thought I had some cash in here, but there's nothing. Just coins and one-dollar bills. I also thought I was nowhere near my overdraft limit.

"I'll pay," says Sam. "I have cash."

"No!" I exclaim. "No, no. I don't want your money. I don't want you to pay for me. Ever."

"Angie, don't be crazy. I have it right here—"

"No," I say, suddenly fighting the urge to cry. "I'll . . . I'll have to come back," I say quickly to the woman behind the register.

She sighs with annoyance and picks up my shopping bag, putting it on a counter behind her.

The thing is, I really do need the tampons. I can see them through the cheap plastic of the Duane Reade bag. I could probably afford them if I scraped together all my change. But I'm too embarrassed. Who pays for tampons with fucking quarters?

Sam and I take the train back to Brooklyn in silence. God, the journey to Brooklyn is depressing on a cold weekday afternoon. I'm broke. I'm unemployed. I'm too broke to buy tampons. I'm unworthy of anything except, apparently, something I really don't want to do. The kind of job that starts with a night out with friends and ends with an envelope of cash on the dresser.

We get out at Carroll Gardens, both eye the Momofuku Milk Bar with hunger but don't even bother to stop since we can't afford it, and silently trudge toward Union Street and Rookhaven. Wait, why is Sam still here?

"You're coming to my place?"

Sam looks embarrassed. "Is that cool? I like Rookhaven. . . . My friend's place isn't as cozy."

"His place is a disgusting shithole, you mean. How long is he going to let you sleep on his floor like some kind of vagrant bum, hmm?"

Sam laughs. "We're pretty close. I don't think he'll kick me out anytime soon."

"How do you know him again?"

"Old friends," Sam says.

I can tell he's being evasive, but before I can interrogate, we run into Vic, my downstairs neighbor.

"Well, hello, girlie." Vic's face creases into a craggy smile.

"Hi, Vic!"

I introduce them quickly. Sam shakes Vic's hand with a sort of earnest intensity. Such a goddamn Boy Scout.

"Where you kids heading?"

"We've been job-hunting," I say. "I want to work in fashion; Sam wants to work on a yacht."

"On a yacht!" Vic looks impressed. "That's hard work."

"Yes, sir," says Sam. Such a kiss-ass. I guess they teach good manners in Ohio.

"Brooklyn was a huge naval center, for decades," says Vic.

"Really?"

"Mm-hmm. When I was young, everyone worked on the docks. But manufacturing dropped, the factories closed, and that was that." Vic sighs. "There's a yacht club out in Sheepshead Bay, you know it?"

"Yes, sir, I do."

"We used to go out there sometimes." Vic stares into space for a while, his eyes looking sort of watery. Then he blinks and looks at us, as though only just remembering we're still here. "Never mind. Say, Sammy, I don't suppose you'd like to earn a little extra cash? I wanna knock through the wall between my sister's old room and my room. And re-paint the kitchen and update the bathroom. I'm tired of looking at the same damn tiles every day. What do you say?"

"Sounds great, sir!"

Vic starts walking toward Union Street. "No time like the present. Let's go."

Sam follows obediently. "I've done a little grouting before, and I can do basic plumbing. I also spent a couple of months helping a buddy build a bar on Canouan Island. It was pretty basic stuff, but I'm a fast learner, sir."

Vic turns and looks at him. "I can see that. And don't call me sir. Call me boss."

Now everyone's got a job but me.

CHAPTER **21**

Being broke has a way of fucking with your mind.

The night after the Duane Reade incident I dreamed that I called Stef. Asked him for a couple of grand in exchange for a night of, you know, partying.

In my dream, I knew what I was doing. I felt guilty. And sick. And I tried to stop myself, I tried to tell myself it was the wrong thing to do, but part of me—in my dream, a *big* part of me—felt relieved to know that I'd have cash. That I could survive another month in New York.

The next day I found two hundred dollars in an old purse. Enough to tide me over until I find a real job. In the week since then, I've only spent seventy-five dollars. It's amazing how little you can spend if you do absolutely nothing except hang out with Sam. He's been working for Vic, but that's only three or four hours in the mornings. The rest of the day, we mooch around Rookhaven, watching TV and playing cards and eating pasta. If it's nice out we go for walks around Brooklyn and try to find the bars that offer free food with a two-dollar can of PBR.

It's fun, it's an easy way to spend the day, and I feel like I've known Sam forever. . . . But somehow, I still lie in bed every night feeling tense and worried about the future and sort of, I don't know, unsatisfied. Like I'm still hungry and I don't know what for.

In the past, when I felt this way, I'd drink or sew or both. But I'm pretty sure that drinking myself into obliteration isn't the answer anymore, and I think I've lost my sewing mojo. Last night I dressed Drakey the Dress Form in a 1990s silk slip dress that I picked up from the Brooklyn Flea and stared at her for an hour. And I could not think of anything to do with it.

Tonight, while Madeleine's band is writing songs in the living room (and Pia is with Aidan and Julia's working late and Coco is seeing Ethan the Cheesemaker), we're lounging in my bedroom, reading magazines that Sam brought over as a special treat (magazines are one of the first things to go when you're broke), surfing TV, and generally being silly.

"Pass the M&M's, *Angela*."

"I think you've had enough, *Samuel*. You're getting jowly. I'm doing you a favor."

Sam reaches over and grabs the bowl off of me. I try to stop him, and a tug of war ensues, followed by the inevitable bowl upheaval and M&M explosion.

"See what you did?" Sam sighs with pretend annoyance.

"You're cleaning that up, sonny. I'm not sleeping on M&M's all night," I say, surfing the channels.

"I'm a guest. How dare you ask me to clean up? That is shocking."

"Oh, shut it."

"No, *you* shut it."

"Oh, gnarly. *Reality Bites*." I stop flipping.

Reality Bites is an awesome movie from the '90s. Though, slightly depressingly, the Janeane Garofalo character has to get a job at the Gap.

At one point, Winona Ryder tells Ethan Hawke, "I was really gonna be something by the age of twenty-three." I raise my eyebrow to myself and make a little snorting sound. I'll be twenty-three in less than two weeks, and I'm nobody. Sam glances at me and I quickly try to look normal again.

And I know what you're thinking. But there's nothing between me and Sam. Nothing. I swear. It's purely platonic. There's no frisson, no spark, none of that bubbly-tingly sexual tension, just a funny insta-friend easy intimacy. You know? It's like I've known him for years, not weeks.

I've never had a platonic male friend before. We never really talk about our personal problems, or our families, or anything like that. We just hang out. I can be myself with him—be relaxed and silly and loud and bitchy—the way I never am with actual boyfriends. It's incredibly nice. He's like Pia. But with a penis. And he doesn't borrow my clothes.

Right now he's wearing one of the two fleeces he wears constantly. One is navy, one is dark gray. The gray one looks nice with his eyes. But that's not the point. They're fleece. They're fucking disgusting.

"You need to buy some new clothes. No one is ever going to date you when you're wearing a fleece."

"This fleece is thermal insulated for optimal warmth!"

"That is all the more reason not to wear it."

"I should have never followed you when you jumped off that yacht." Sam crunches another M&M. "Should have let the sharks eat you. Lesson learned." He closes his eyes and nods reverently to himself. "Lesson learned."

I laugh until my attention is stolen by a feature in *Vogue* on the latest Rodarte collection. "God, those girls are amazingly talented," I comment enviously. "The Rodarte sisters."

Sam glances up. "Show me?" I hold up the magazine. "You could do that. Your drawings are better than that, the stuff you make is better than that."

I smile at him and shake my head. "How do you know? You haven't even seen my stuff."

"That dress on the doll thingy is nice," he says. "Sexy."

I look at Drakey the Dress Form, still wearing the black vintage silky slip dress. "I didn't make that. I haven't touched it."

Sam cracks up. "Oh. But still, I've seen the stuff you wear, you never look like everybody else. You don't really believe in yourself, that's your problem."

"Thank you for diagnosing my problem, Doctor Sam."

While Sam stretches his long legs out across my bed and grabs the latest issue of *New York* magazine, I check him out over my *Vogue*. His hair is growing out of the goody-two-shoes crew cut, and he's stopped shaving, so his cheeks are all stubbly. He looks scruffier. Older. And kind of sexy.

"Hey, Sam?"

"Yes?"

"I think you should ask Julia out."

"No."

"One date! Would it kill you?"

Julia keeps asking, with shy hope in her voice, if Sam ever talks about her. Given my newfound friendship with her, I would really like to make her happy. Anyway, why shouldn't they date, right? She's the clean-cut wholesome type, she's sporty, she's funny, she frowns a lot. She's just like him. She even wears fleece sometimes.

I take another M&M, peering into the bowl. I always eat the yellow ones first, I don't know why. So I take out five and line them up on my thigh, like little planes ready for takeoff. Then I zoom one up toward my mouth.

I look up and see Sam looking at me with a little grin on his face.

"What?" I say.

"You're so different from how you . . . seem on the outside."

"You thought I looked like a bitch?" I say, sighing. "I get that a lot. It's just because I'm thinking about something else. And, you know, it doesn't tend to be the person in front of me."

Sam cracks up again.

After *Reality Bites,* we flip channels till *Kramer vs. Kramer* comes on.

Sam is thrilled. "The young Meryl Streep. Totally my perfect woman. Icy-cool on the outside, dynamite within."

"Oh, God. Seriously? Okay, move over, let's watch it."

Sitting side by side—though Sam's shoulders are so wide I have to arrange my pillows around him and lean on his arm so that I'm not totally falling off the bed—we watch the movie. I haven't seen it before, so I have no idea what it's about, but basically it's about divorce and families.

At the very end, just when Dustin Hoffman and Meryl Streep are getting back in the elevator to tell their little kid that he doesn't have to leave his home and his daddy, and Dustin tells Meryl she looks terrific, I find myself crying hysterically, tears streaming down my face.

"Angie?" Sam asks. "Are you okay?"

I try to talk, to stop crying, but I can't even breathe. I'm just wailing and hiccuping, snot and tears covering my face, my chest shuddering with misery. I can't stop, I can't control myself, and I'm so embarrassed, so I curl up, burying my face in a pillow and hiding in my long hair.

"Angie, shhh . . ." Sam strokes my head and makes some slightly awkward mothering sounds, which makes me giggle through my tears. "I can't believe I'm saying this, but . . . do you want to talk about it?"

It all chokes out in a rush. "My parents—my parents are divorcing. My mother told me last month, and I haven't spoken to her since." I'm crying even harder now. I can hardly get the words out. "And my dad, we're really close, or we were, anyway, and, he, he hasn't even called me."

"That's terrible. You must feel like shit."

The fact that Sam is agreeing it's terrible, rather than the proactive hey-girl-high-five-sing-it-sister-you're-amazing-positive-thinking diatribe I've been getting about it from the girls, shocks me out of my incipient hysteria.

"You are not good at this supportive friend stuff, dude."

"Sorry." Sam frowns, propping his elbow on the pillow next to me, resting his head on his hand. "I just meant, uh, that's a shitty situation. And you must feel . . . sad."

"I do," I say, rolling over on the bed to face him. "I feel so sad. I try to ignore it and cover it in other thoughts, you know, but I can't. And when I think about talking to them about it, especially my dad, I just feel, um, scared." I exhale, feeling a strange, painful relief, like I'm stretching out parts of me that have been tight forever. "I ignore all my mother's calls, and my dad hasn't even tried to get in touch. They don't want to be a family anymore, they don't want—they don't want what we had. Even though what we had wasn't exactly the fucking Waltons, you know? It wasn't perfect."

Sam nods. I get the strangest feeling he understands exactly what I mean. "Why wasn't it perfect?"

"I saw my dad making out with his secretary." The words are out before I can stop them. I've never told anyone about this, ever, not Pia, not anyone. "When I was twelve. Her name was Alyssa. He made me promise not to tell Annabel—that's my mother—because it would hurt her feelings. I think he broke up with Alyssa, but then I became his alibi. . . . He'd tell me to tell Annabel that he'd been visiting me at boarding school when he was obviously with other women."

"Wow. What an asshole."

"He's not! He's not, he's . . ." I stop, trying to think how to describe my dad. "He's charming and funny, he dresses immaculately, he knows all about wine and history and the world. He always took my side against Annabel in fights and treated me like I was a grown-up and said I could go out without a curfew. In exchange, I helped him keep his affairs secret. . . . But maybe he is an asshole. A lying, cheating asshole, who just used me to lie to my mother and get what he wanted."

And boom, the tears start again, and with them an ache deep inside that I'd almost forgotten. . . . Whenever my dad asked me to lie for him, I felt nauseous, with strange blunt pains in my torso, like something was pressing on me, stopping me from breathing properly. It was stress, I guess. What kind of a kid gets stress pains?

Sam reaches over and grabs a Kleenex for me. "Are you close to your mom? You never wanted to tell her?"

"I guess I thought I had to keep his secrets." I'm now getting a strange heady feeling from crying so much. "And she should have guessed. It made me so angry that she never figured it out! He was so obvious sometimes!"

Sam frowns. "Maybe she was ignoring it. You can't tell what's going on in a marriage from the outside. Even the kids can't tell."

"Maybe."

A new thought occurs to me. What if she knew I knew about the affairs and that I never told her? It's almost the worst idea of all.

"Was she happy?"

The idea is so strange that for a moment I just stare at Sam in total surprise. "I don't know." How can I never have wondered that before? I try to think. "She wasn't around much. She just hung out with her rich friends, even though we're not rich like them. I mean, don't get me wrong, I know I grew up, um, privileged, but we were never crazy rich, and my dad lost a lot of money in investments in the past few years. I always worry about them being broke, isn't that nuts?" My face is wet with tears, my thoughts zigzagging erratically around my brain, finding everything about my parents that makes me unhappy. "But I bet Annabel still acts like she's loaded. And I hate that. I hate . . . that pretension. I hate rich people. They just use people to get what they want."

"I know," Sam whispers. "I hate that, too."

Everything is silent for a moment. We're both laying on our sides on the bed now, heads on pillows, facing each other. Sam is staring at me so intensely, it's like he can see right into me.

"So these days, Annabel and I don't really get along. I mean, we don't fight, you know, we just don't . . . we don't talk. I haven't answered her calls in weeks. Oh, and she sent me to boarding school without consulting me about it."

"She sent you to boarding school against your will?"

"No! I mean, it was fine, I sure as hell wanted to get out of the house, you know. Dad was never around, and I was avoiding her because it was so hard to keep those secrets from her, she's my *mother*, you know?" Tears threaten to overwhelm me again. "She just didn't ask me. I had no say over what happened in *my* life."

"That'll make anyone angry," Sam says. "Everyone wants control over their destiny."

"She sent me to this expensive all-girls school that all her friends' daughters went to, it was really sporty and outdoorsy and there was only a tiny art faculty. It was totally cliquey. I didn't fit in. And Pia's parents sent her to different schools, um, I think my mother convinced them that we'd be a bad influence on each other or something. But I needed her. And I think she needed me, too. I was alone all the time. Even in the middle of a crowded dining hall, I was alone. I was so alone, it was like I could *taste* it."

"Not fitting in somewhere makes you stronger," says Sam, leaning over to push a strand of hair out of my eyes. It's stuck to my skin with tears, and it takes him a few tries to get it off. The feeling of his fingertips on my skin is surprisingly lovely.

"That's true," I say. "I became tougher and more independent. I decided that if I was going to be alone, I was gonna look like I enjoyed it. I'm alone because I choose to be, you know? But then sometimes I think I can't break out of feeling alone, like I'm in a perma-bubble of alone-ness."

"Don't you mean loneliness?"

"No. I don't feel lonely. I like my own company, most of the time, I like drawing and sewing and being by myself. I just feel . . . *alone*. Like I can't rely on anyone. Like the world and I speak a different language."

I sigh deeply, breathing out all my sadness and worry. I've never told anyone this stuff. God, talking really does make me feel better. Even better than when I confessed to the girls. Why have I always kept everything to myself?

As I look into Sam's eyes, I realize something. Right now, right this exact second, for the first time that I can remember, I don't feel alone.

Instead, I feel like I belong right here with Sam. Together.

Sam gazes at me across the pillows, his gray eyes steady and sure. "Angie, I'm sure your folks are dying to hear from you. Both of them."

I want to believe him more than anything. "Would you contact them if you were me?"

Sam doesn't say anything.

"I'm just so sick of their lies, you know?" I say in a tiny voice. "I don't want to give them the opportunity to lie to me more. It seems sometimes like everyone lies. Everyone lies, and everyone's got secrets. I hate it."

"There's a difference between secrets and lies, Angie," says Sam.

"Is there?" I say. "It seems to me like they're interchangeable."

"Mmm." Sam doesn't agree, but he's too well-mannered to argue.

"I just, um, I want life to be . . . simpler."

Sam nods slowly. "I completely agree. My life before I took off was complicated. Sometimes I felt like it was overwhelming me. More than I could handle."

"Exactly," I whisper.

We're still lying on the pillows; our faces are just inches away from each other.

For a few seconds, there's total silence, the only sound our breathing.

My heart is beating so fast that I'm trembling, and I close my eyes for a few seconds, a fizzy tingle in my stomach.

Then I open my eyes again. Sam is still staring at me. He's so close that I can see his individual eyelashes, brown at the roots but white at the tips from sun, the tiny tan-free mark on his nose from wearing sunglasses, the fledgling stubble on his chin. He's staring at me, too, and it's making me self-conscious. I don't know what to do with my lips, I wonder if I have eye snot, if I look stupid, if . . .

Then Sam locks eyes with me again.

We're going to kiss.

I know it. I can feel it, that prekiss moment, the tingly tension, that almost unbearably sweet torture of anticipation. I can imagine the feeling of his lips on my lips so strongly it's like I'm craving the taste and feel and touch and smell of him, like he's the only thing that will satisfy me right now.

Sam leans in a tiny fraction, oh, my God, we're actually going—

No!

I jerk my head away and turn over to break the moment while my mind races. No! No. It's wrong. Sam's my friend. I can't fuck up this friendship by giving in to a base impulse that is the reason I've never had a male friend longer than two weeks. I only like him as a friend. I'm sure of it. Being friends is safer and easier. Take a deep breath. Yes. Another one. Good.

This is transitory sexual tension that is inevitable when you put two people of the opposite sex on a bed and give one of them a crisis. Right? Right. Friends. Safe.

So I get up, go over to my window, open it up, and light a cigarette. For a minute, neither of us says a word.

"My parents divorced when I was twenty-one," Sam says finally. "Then my mom decided she wanted to move to New Mexico and live on a ranch, and my dad, uh, he didn't. Boom. Family over."

I'm so surprised Sam is being so open with me, instead of his usual cryptic self, that all I can think to say is: "Where does your dad live?"

Sam doesn't answer, or doesn't hear me. He's just gazing into space, quiet and serious. "The thing is, it's just another change. You know? Not an ending, just a change. Everything changes, all the time, you move on, your life changes. You graduate from school, boom, change. Go to college, boom, change. You date, you break up, you move in with your buddies, people get sick and die, change change change. So divorce is just another change in life, which is constantly changing anyway."

"But what if you don't like what life changes into?"

"Then you do something to make it change again. Life has to change. If it didn't, then what would be the point? You'd always know what was going to happen next."

"That's pretty good," I say. "You should be a therapist."

"That's what my therapist says."

"You're in therapy? I thought you didn't like talking about yourself."

"Ha." He pauses, and then it all comes out in a rush. "I'm not in therapy anymore, I was in therapy, um, I was kind of angry about the divorce and stuff that happened around that time. . . . You know. And it was such a fucking waste of time, all that anger, people are just gonna do what they're gonna do, you know, you can't change them, not really, you just have to accept them and love them for who they are. I shouldn't have . . . Some of the stuff I did, I was kind of a dick. I wish . . ." He shakes his head, as if to clear it. "Sorry, we're not talking about me."

"We can talk about you if you want to."

"I don't want to. I just want to watch TV and not talk. That's my prerogative, as a dude."

"Where are you from?"

"Ohio. I told you."

"Ohio? I kind of thought you were joking about that. You just don't seem very . . . Ohio-like."

Sam makes a "huh" sound. "I really don't want to talk about it, Angie."

"Too bad, tiger, I do. Is your dad still in Ohio?"

A long pause. "My dad is dead."

"Oh, God, I'm so sorry."

"Don't be."

"Where'd you go to college?"

"New England. I dropped out."

"What did you study?"

"That's all for today."

"Talk," I say, poking him with my toe.

"Nope."

"Talk!" I poke him again.

"Don't poke the bear, Angie, or I will tickle you so hard you will yelp."

"Tickling is just an excuse for teenage boys to accidentally-on-purpose get some tit," I say. "And did you just refer to yourself in the third person as 'the bear'?"

"Did *you* just say 'get some tit'? Wow, you are some lady."

I giggle, overwhelmed with relief that the whole sexual-tension thing is over. He doesn't like me as anything more than a friend. Everything is back to normal.

"I call it like I see it," I shrug.

"Fine. I won't touch you. Not even if you beg me. Can we just watch the next goddamn movie?"

He flicks channels until we find another movie. It's *Rear Window,* an old Hitchcock movie with Grace Kelly and Jimmy Stewart. The sexual tension seems to have been broken, and I feel safe getting back on the bed now. We're just friends. Yes. It's fine.

"God, I love Jimmy Stewart," I say, snuggling down on my pillow.

"Yeah? I thought he'd be a little straight for you."

"Nah. He's perfect. . . . I'm getting under the covers. You can join me if you want, but no funny business."

"Yes, ma'am."

And so, side by side, snuggled up together in a purely platonic way, Sam and I watch the movie. And pretty soon I'm so warm and cozy and comfortable that I fall asleep.

CHAPTER 22

I'm in bed with Sam.

No, not like that, we really did just fall asleep while watching *Rear Window*.

But I'm all curled up into a little ball on my side, with my head over Sam's arm, and he's nestled into me.

We're fucking *spooning*.

For a few minutes I just lie here, listening to Sam breathing. . . . He still smells like soap, even after a night of junk food and no teeth brushing. What is that about?

And why is it so different, sharing a bed with a dude, even if he's just your friend? I'm fully dressed, and Sam's wearing a T-shirt and jeans, it's not like we're indecent. Pia and I have shared a bed a gazillion times, after nights out or on vacation, and during a weird period when this fuckpuppet Eddie broke her heart and I had to carry her home every night, shitfaced and weeping. She always puts her freezing feet on me and snores, I tell her it's goddamn annoying, she says it's freakish that I sleep either starfished out and facedown, or curled up into a tiny ball like a little porcupine. That kind of sleepover is funny and silly.

But with Sam, it's different. I'm so aware of his body next to mine, it's all I can think about. I'm conscious of his feet sticking over the end of my bed, of his deep, even breathing, of the size and strength of him.

There's such a vulnerability and sweetness to sharing a bed with a man, too. Awake, Sam always looks like he's got something very serious on his mind. Asleep, he seems, I don't know, peaceful.

And between you and me, well, sharing a bed with Sam is kind of sexy. Sam is so big, like a giant bear, heat is radiating out from his body, enveloping mine. I'm conscious of the warm, smooth strength of his arm I'm using as a pillow, I can feel the rest of his body pressed against mine all the way down to his feet, and I can see one of his hands: tan, very clean nails, big calloused fingers and palm. He's missing his little fingernail entirely; it was ripped off during a regatta last year. Right now, even that looks kind of sexy. Goddamnit. Why am I having these thoughts about Sam?

And then Sam puts his other arm around me and pulls me in closer against him. He's still asleep, his breathing hasn't changed, he's just hugging me tightly, like it's the most natural thing in the world.

"Angie," he mumbles.

I grin to myself. Sam's talking in his sleep.

"Yes, Sam?"

No response.

Hmm.

I'll try a trick my mother once told me about. Ask people questions when they're sleeptalking, and sometimes their subconscious will understand and respond. Apparently they'll tell you all kinds of stuff. So I wriggle around, still wrapped in his arms, until I'm facing him.

"Hey, Sam," I whisper, pulling my head back so I can see his face. "Sam, what do you think of Angie?"

He smiles in his sleep. "Angel . . ."

I find myself relaxing into him. God, this is lovely. I can't remember the last time I snuggled like this. And yeah, I just used the word snuggle. There's no other way to say it. Sam is wrapping me into him tightly, I can smell his neck, I feel warm and comfortable and safe and just a teensy bit tingly. . . . It's bliss.

Suddenly, Sam takes a deep breath and holds it, for what feels like forever but is probably only about ten seconds. Then he exhales, holding me even more tightly. I fit perfectly into him. I can hear his heart beating. For a second I lie there, listening to it.

Then I try again, craning my head back so I can see his face. "*Angie*. Tell me about Angie. Do you think she's funnier than you are? I bet you do."

Sam gives that little half-sleep smile again and, in one swift move, shifts his arms tighter around me and rolls onto his back, pulling me with him, so that I'm lying almost on top of him and my face is right over his. Holy shit, if Sam was awake right now, we'd be an inch from kissing, literally a *moment* from it. . . .

If I just turned my head a fraction of an inch, I could—

No.

For the second time in twelve hours I pull away from Sam almost violently, half jumping, half falling out of bed in my hurry to escape. This is wrong, this is all wrong.

I'll shower and dress, and then this whole weird intimate sleepover thing will be finished and we can go back to just being normal plain old friends. Right? Right.

I take a long time in the bathroom, washing and scrubbing and conditioning and shaving and moisturizing. I actually love shaving my legs, it's an art form to get each swoop perfect. And the money I used to spend on waxing! What's the point? I'm blond, I'm not exactly hairy, and that whole growing-back-thicker thing is a myth made up by the wax union. (Yes. They have a union.)

Then I shuffle back to my bedroom and check quickly to see that Sam is still asleep. I throw on some very comfortable old jeans, and, after reflection, my dad's Princeton sweater. So what if he hasn't called me in forever? It's still a good goddamn sweater, though it has a couple of small bloodstains from that night I fell off the kitchen counter. That feels like a very long time ago.

Then I turn around, see Sam smiling at me, and let out a little shriek.

"What the hell!? Were you watching me change the whole time?"

"No." Sam looks guilty. "Okay, yes. But I didn't see anything, like, R-rated. Just the beautiful PG parts of you."

"Really." I avoid his eyes. Let's get this conversation back to friend territory. And get the hell out of my bedroom. "How about some breakfast?"

"Buttermilk Channel? Or Café Luluc?"

"I don't have any money, Sam. And no, you're not paying for me. You must be broke by now."

"Right, sorry. Well, I can make you breakfast, how about that? I owe little Coco about sixty meals, too, she keeps feeding me. She's like a very young and innocent grandma. . . . I'll do it for the whole house. I'll fry up some bacon, eggs, pancakes. . . ."

"That would be great!" I say. "But can you grill the bacon, not fry it? I don't like it too oily."

"Oh, really?" Sam says. "I thought you'd like oil."

"What? Why would you think that?"

"Well, you like oil tycoons!" Sam grins widely, and brings out from underneath his pillow . . . *Her Secret Desire*! My latest romance novel!

"Give that back!"

Grinning, Sam leans away from me and starts reading the blurb on the back. *"Shy Millicent had always been unlucky in love. But when oil tycoon Rod Rockson moved to town, she thought her luck was changing. Till she discovered his secret past. . . .* I wonder what his secret past could be?"

"Shut it!" I jump on the bed and reach for the book, just miss it, and find myself straddling Sam, furiously trying to grab the book back. "Give that to me! That's fucking private! I'm not kidding! Sam! I mean it!"

"Now, Angela! Play nice!"

"My name isn't fucking Angela!"

I finally snatch it out of his hands, jump off the bed, and throw it under Drakey the Dress Form.

I'm so upset, I can't even look at Sam, so I pretend to be looking for something in my closet. I'm mortified to be caught reading something so uncool. I feel even more embarrassed than I did last night after my *Kramer vs. Kramer* meltdown! God! And why can't I read whatever I want? Who cares if it's cool? Why do I have to pretend to be tough all the time? Why is it so important to be cynical and unromantic, to not like happy endings and kisses and people saying I love you? Why?

Sam stands up, looking very apologetic, his hair sticking up at crazy angles.

"I'm so sorry, it was under my pillow, Angie. I just thought it was funny—"

"Well, it wasn't." I open my sock drawer and rifle through it pointlessly. He must think I'm such an idiot. "You know what, I've got shit to do," I say over my shoulder. "You should go home."

"You want me to leave?"

"Yes."

There's a long pause while I stare at my socks. Where the fuck do socks come from, I ask you? I don't remember ever buying any in my entire goddamn life.

Sam clears his throat.

"Angie, I'm really sorry, okay? I was just fooling around."

"Yeah?" I finally turn to face him. "Well, I'm sick of fooling around. I don't want to waste my life hanging out like this anymore. It's fucking depressing. I need to get a job. That's what I'm doing today. I'm gonna get a job."

Sam nods. "Right."

I stand up and head for the door, my face still burning from the shame of being busted as a romance reader, and pause quickly to snap at him over my shoulder.

"See yourself out."

CHAPTER **23**

Less than a week before I turn twenty-three.

And I could not be further away from having the adult life I always imagined I'd have by now.

I'm working at the Gap.

Stop laughing.

I need money. I need to pay rent. I need a job, something to focus on, a reason to get out of bed in the morning. Especially since I haven't seen Sam since the whole romance novel sleepover fiasco last week.

He texted the next day: *I'm sorry . . . Forgive me?*

I replied: *Totally. Not a problem.*

And he hasn't tried to get in touch since. I haven't called him, either. I'm too embarrassed; I still feel a hot flush of mortification when I think about him holding up the book with glee. He probably thinks I'm such a romantic. A total cockeyed optimist loser. I hate that. It makes me feel weak. I don't know why, but it does. And I was already feeling so exposed after telling him all that stuff about my parents. . . .

You know what? We became such close friends so fast, it was too intense. I needed space. That's all.

And a full-time job at the Gap has certainly provided it.

In some ways, the Gap isn't all that bad: it turns out my folding skills are kind of gnarly. Who knew? (I never folded anything of my own before; I just pretended the wrinkles were part of my unique style.)

But the hours are long, the salary is terrible, I'm getting blisters from being on my feet all day, and wow, it's boring. I'm so bored I almost can't keep my eyes from closing. Sometimes I fantasize about making a bed out of T-shirts in the changing rooms and curling up for a nap, like a little puppy.

Also, people never look you in the eye when you work in retail. Don't they realize it's my job to ask them if they need help finding anything? It's what I am paid to *do*. And one of the managers, Shania, has told me off twice for not having a "pleasant expression." I can't help it if I look bitchy when I'm preoccupied. She looks bitchy because she's a bitch.

But the best part? The clothes. Gap isn't exactly my style, but I genuinely like helping customers choose the right clothes. Sometimes someone asks me what style of jeans would suit them, or if this shirt will go with that skirt, and I get to style them. The smile when that person comes out of the changing room and sees they're looking better than they expected . . . I *love* that. I never upsell, either. I make sure that they stay in their budget. And I've pointed a few people in the direction of Urban Outfitters or Zara, to pick up something that will just make their outfit. (Usually a bright belt, clutch, or pair of shoes. Pretty textbook stuff.)

But no matter what, my mind still paces back and forth, trying to think of ways to get out of here, get a real job in fashion. . . . I know I can't be a designer, that dream is just that—a dream. It's out of reach. Impossible. But I could be an assistant, right? Or a receptionist, I could work for a fashion label or a PR company or a stylist.

I am sure I could do *something* better than this, if only someone would give me a chance.

But no one will.

Goddamn, I'm lost.

Right now, it's nearly the end of the day in this soulless part of Midtown Manhattan, and there's a particularly bleak cross section of society in the store. Sticky little whiners in strollers who just want to be home playing with toys, backpacked tourists shell-shocked from a day sightseeing, overweight solo shoppers eyeing merchandise like a potential foe. . . .

Humanity. Urgh. Pia always says how much she loves working with people; she gets energized by it. I'd rather just be in a quiet corner thinking about clothes. But not my parents. Or my future.

My phone vibrates in my pocket, and I immediately duck to the floor, pretending to rearrange some sweaters so I can check it. A text from Julia.

Just letting you know that my boss just invited everyone except me to a strip club tonight to celebrate a deal. My job is worse than yours.

I grin to myself and reply.

This morning, I found a shit in the mens' changing rooms. Not a dog shit, not a kiddie shit. A man. Took a shit. In the middle of the changing room. My job is worse than yours.

I get a reply a moment later.

You win.

Ha. Jules and I are still texting a lot. Mostly competing to see who has the worse job. It's so cute that she's even pretending working at an investment bank is anywhere near as terrible as working at the Gap. Pia was right all this time: Julia is kind of awesome. I'm so glad we've become real friends. I don't think Pia is jealous anymore. . . . Though, to be honest, Pia hasn't been around to be jealous. She's spending every minute she can with Aidan before he leaves for San Francisco. They've decided to give the long-distance thing a try.

I'm surreptitiously stretching out my hamstrings—why they're so tight from just standing around all day doing nothing, I don't know—when an older lady comes over and starts scanning the wall of jeans.

"Hello! May I help you find anything in particular?"

She nods. "I want a pair of jeans that don't make me look like a hoochie mama."

I grin. "Right . . . hooch-free denim. Well, this pair is really well cut around the thighs, so they're supportive but not too snug. They've got a ten-inch rise, which is so much more comfortable around your tummy area, and the dark shade is classic, no hoochie whiskering or wash. . . . It's almost like a pair of pants, but with the comfort and ease of denim."

"Wow. You're good."

"Thank you," I say, taking down the jeans. "I love clothes. Here, just for comparison, you should try on this pair and this pair, too."

"Thank you. . . . I used to love clothes. Now I just wear them." She takes the jeans I offer her and frowns. "This is my size. How did you know?"

"That's why they pay me the big bucks. Can I put them in a changing room for you?"

"I'll take them myself." She takes the jeans off to the changing area.

Suddenly, I'm in a much better mood. I *do* like this job! And I'm good at it! I helped that lady find jeans and she'll look *great* in them, I know she will, and it'll make her happy all day. All because of me. An old Rihanna song comes on over the music system, and without even thinking about it, I start bobbing my head and singing along, then do a teeny tiny twirl on the spot.

At that moment Derek, one of the guys who usually works the register, walks past. He frowns at me and shakes his head.

"This isn't a nightclub, Angela."

He's gone before I can reply "It's Angie, dickface," so I just flip him the bird behind his back. Real mature, but that's what retail does to you.

At that moment, I hear a familiar drawl behind me.

"What the fuck are we doing here, Blythe? You know my rules: no moms, no hugs, no chain stores."

I freeze, my heart suddenly hammering in my chest. I'd know that voice anywhere.

It's Stef.

The Blythe person giggles.

"Stef, baby, I told you, I need some tanks and Gap ones fit me best."

"Can't we go to James Perse or Splendid or, fuck, somewhere decent? I'll pay."

"Maybe later. I have to hit Intermix."

Their voices are getting louder and louder. Keeping my head down, I drop to the floor, pretending to adjust the chinos on the bottom level. No chinos have ever been this perfectly symmetrical in the history of casual pants. I look for an error, anything that will give me something to do. . . . Aha! A size six in the size eights! My face still turned away from their voices, I pull out the entire stack and start realigning them, very slowly, praying that Stef just walks away, that—

"Well, look at this," says a soft voice. Suddenly, inches from me on the floor, I spot Stef's shoes. John Lobb. Of course. "If it isn't the infamous Angie."

I slowly stand up, feeling a strange combination of fear and fury. "Stef."

Our eyes meet. He's looking his standard privileged, oily self.

At that moment the Blythe girl comes over. She's one of those tall, expensive brunettes that the Upper East Side breeds in litters. She's wearing DVF shoes, dress, bag, and coat. Style by numbers.

"What's this?" She cocks her head to one side, looking at me like I was a funny little painting.

"This is Angie," says Stef. "An old friend."

Blythe gives me a little fake smile. "How sweet." She saunters away.

"I'm not your friend," I hiss at Stef. "And I'll never forgive you for what you did to me."

"What I *did*? Chill out, Angie. You love rich guys. I just introduced you to some of them. Your behavior on the boat was really uncool. You totally overreacted."

My fists clench. I want to slap him. I want to scream and make a scene and quit this stupid job and run away and drink vodka and laugh all night and pretend everything is perfect. I crave it so badly, I can almost taste the joy of that escape.

But I'm not going to do it.

I'm not running away from my problems anymore.

Because I can't make them go away like that. Not really.

"You're a worthless scumbag." My voice is shaking with the effort of keeping it low. "Stay away from me. And get out of my store."

Blythe has sauntered back toward us and overhears me.

"I don't believe this! Where is your manager?" snaps Blythe. She looks around, her voice high and demanding and Upper East Side-y. "I need a manager here!"

"No, Blythe, leave it." Stef is staring at me, a half smile on his face. "I have a feeling I'll be hearing from her soon enough. When reality hits, a night of fun in the Soho Grand won't seem so bad."

I can't meet his eyes, so I stare at his nose instead (an old trick my dad taught me when I was little). *A night of fun in the Soho Grand . . .* What the fuck happened that night? I feel sick.

For a few seconds, there's total silence.

Then, I smile at them both. "Can I help you with anything? No? Then please excuse me. I have work to do."

Trembling, I walk away and start refolding T-shirts, following their progress through the store out of the corner of my eye. Stef stares at me, till Blythe starts sniping at him. He snaps back. She immediately shuts up, and they leave.

And I don't run away. I don't give in. I just focus on getting through the day.

That night, on the subway home to Rookhaven, the sick feeling slowly subsiding in my stomach, I can't help staring at every other worker drone, all of us jammed in side by side on the way home from our shit jobs, and everyone is doing something to distract their brains from reality. They're either listening to music with their eyes closed, or reading the *New York Post,* or staring at BlackBerrys or iPhones, thumbs frantically tapping away.

I always thought people did that stuff when they were bored and trying to kill time. But now I know it's because they're all trying to forget whatever it is they had to do that day to earn a living. Because it probably sucked.

This can't be what my life is meant to be like. It just . . . it *can't* be.

But I don't want my old life, either.

So I guess I'm stuck here. And suddenly, I know that the only thing in the world that will cheer me up is my friends. Pia, Coco, Julia, and Madeleine. And Sam. I miss Sam. It's only been a few days since I spoke to him, but it seems like forever. I don't care that he knows I read romance novels. I don't care if he thinks I'm a loser. I just miss him.

When I get off the subway at Carroll Gardens, I take out my phone and call him.

"Are we friends again?" he says, instead of hello.

"Affirmative. I'm sorry I kicked you out."

"I'm sorry I made fun of your book. Do you know that I love Harry Potter? I do. I'm crazy about that little wizard geek."

I can't help cracking up. "Okay, we're officially friends again."

"Our first fight! Man, I feel special. Do you feel special?"

"I feel hungry."

"I'm at Vic's, finishing off the bathroom. We're heading up to Bartolo's for pizza. You want in?"

"Yes."

"Where have you been, anyway, lady? I knocked on your front door, like, four times this week."

"Uh, I got a job."

"Oh yeah? That's awesome! Where?"

"If I tell you, will you promise not to laugh?"

"Yes."

"The Gap."

CHAPTER 24

Sam is still laughing when I get to Bartolo's. It's a real old-school Brooklyn Italian joint, the kind of place with mismatched plates and menus that haven't changed in forever. Vic's family started it decades ago, and it's still run by one of his nephews. It has that family feeling, you know? At least half the tables have kids, and tonight, most have kids, parents, and grandparents. I gaze around at them. Real live happy families. I wonder how my dad is.

"Okay, Angie, what'll it be?" asks Vic, interrupting my reverie.

I don't even look at my menu. "The margherita pizza, please."

Sam looks over at me and cracks up again.

"Shut it!" I say. "Vic, Sam's picking on me. Just because I got a job."

Vic grins at me, his face all gnarled and happy. "I think it's great, girlie. Work gives life meaning. Makes you feel fulfilled."

Working at the Gap is supposed to give my life meaning and make me feel fulfilled? The idea is so insanely depressing that for a moment I can't say anything. Then the bartender, Jonah, comes over with our drinks. A beer for Sam, a club soda for Vic, and a vodka on the rocks for me.

"You sure you want straight vodka, honeybunny?" asks Jonah.

"I'm sure, sugarnuts, I'm sure," I say.

Jonah winks at me and walks away. I grin after him. Cute guy. Not so bright.

Then I look back and see Sam staring at me with a strange look on his face.

"What?" I say. "He's a friend of Pia's! She worked here for about four and a half seconds last year."

"Right," says Sam. "So tell us about the Gap."

So I do, a bit. And then Vic tells us about a department store that his sister used to work at in Park Slope. It was called Germaine's.

"She hated it," Vic says. "Especially during the holiday season. She'd come home with dozens of mismatched gloves, you know. People would drop them on the ground when they were shopping. I didn't wear a matching set of gloves until I got married." Vic cracks up, and it's so weird and nice hearing him laugh like that that Sam and I crack up, too.

When our food arrives, we get lost in chewing and appreciative eating noises. I love margherita pizza. I like the constancy of it: you always know what you're getting, each bite is exactly like the last, no nasty surprises. And eating with Sam and Vic feels natural, like we're family. I think Sam's thinking the same thing. This is just so happy and peaceful.

I wonder who Vic eats with these days. His sister passed away last year, his wife died a long time ago. He must feel very alone.

"We should do this more often," I say. "Dinner, here, I mean. Every Thursday! Would you like that, Vic?"

"Me? Sure." Vic goes to take another leisurely bite of pizza, then stops, as though a thought just occurred to him. "You think I'm a lonely old man, Angie?"

"No," I say, slightly defensively.

"I never feel lonely," he says. "I'm very busy. I got my bocce ball, I got my social club, I got a million goddamn nieces always calling up and nagging me, I got cable now and that HBO is a whole lotta fun, I can tell you. . . . I got things to look forward to. Keep your life full of things to look forward to, and you'll never feel alone."

"Roger that," I say. More pearls of wisdom from Vic. We should start a goddamn blog.

The thing is, he always does make sense. It's just that it's never the answer I really want to hear. I don't think working full-time at the Gap qualifies as having a fulfilling life. But I know that's my problem. A lot of people probably love working at the Gap.

I look down at my little gold clutch. It's been the most incredibly useful purse. I usually get sick of bags and change every two or three days, but I love this one. I might make one with a long shoulder strap or a wrist strap, and a larger size for days when I need to take more with me but don't want the full snail-tote. I'm sure I have about fifteen more of those secondhand Art Deco scarves stashed away somewhere. And I've been tailoring that slip dress that Sam liked to suit me, too. (Four inches off the hem, natch.)

Suddenly, even just thinking about sewing makes me feel happy, awake, and excited, like I have something to look forward to. If I can just pretend sewing is my job, then my life does have meaning.

I look up at Vic and grin. "You are absolutely right."

At that moment my phone beeps.

A text from Pia: *Where are you? EMERGENCY.*

Bartolo's, I respond.

Ten minutes later, just as we've finished eating, there's a screech of brakes outside. A huge pink food truck has parked in the middle of the sidewalk. Pia.

She strides into Bartolo's, banging the door behind her dramatically, sees us, and comes straight over.

"Oh God, Vic, Angie, Sam, help me! Aidan and I broke up." She bursts into noisy sobs and throws herself down next to me. "We're not doing the long-distance thing, we're not even going to try. He just flew out tonight. It's over, it's really, seriously over." Pia is crying so hard that I can barely make out the words, and I automatically pull her into me, into Sam's baby owl hug where she's nestled under my wing, drenching me with her tears.

I look up at the waiter. "Check, please."

Pia drives me back to Rookhaven, wailing the whole way. There's nothing I can do except be a good friend and listen right now, so I try to make out words among the wails and hope like hell we don't crash. Sam and Vic decided to walk back, ostensibly to get some air but clearly to avoid Pia's crisis. She *does* cry pretty loudly. It scares men and small animals.

Coco and Madeleine are in the kitchen eating stir-fry chicken and broccoli, and Pia stops sobbing long enough to tell us all the whole story.

"We started breaking up last night, and then we went to sleep, and then we had, like, four A.M. sex—"

"Overshare," mutters Madeleine.

"—and then we woke up and didn't discuss it, you know. Like if we just drank our coffee and ate our bagels it would just be like any other day. And then we met up after work and broke up for real. We have done nothing but talk about it for weeks, you know, and the thing is, we were going to do long-distance but we know it'll never work! It's like a slow death rather than, uh, a swift stab to the heart." Nice. "And now Aidan's on a plane to California, and I can't believe it's over. . . . But my life is going this way, his life is going that way, and neither of us should sacrifice our careers for each other, right?"

"Right!" Coco and I say firmly.

"What if I end up old and alone? Choosing my career ahead of love! I'll be that woman with cats! I fucking hate cats!"

"Ladybitch, you're not even twenty-three yet. You don't have to worry about being old and alone."

"I'm gonna miss him so much!" Pia isn't listening to anyone. "Our relationship is like that movie *Dead Man Walking*!"

Madeleine frowns. "Uh, I'm not sure that—"

"I can't believe it's over! It's over." Pia stares into space, whispering, "It's really over."

"It's not over!" says Coco. "It's not like you've been fighting or fallen out of love, you're just forced apart by, um, by unforeseen circumstances, that's all! He'll be back one day!"

"Yeah!" I say. "And in the meantime, you can date!"

"No! Do you know how hard it is for me to meet guys who really, truly *get* me? With whom I have a genuine connection? It's just . . . it's impossible."

For a second, tears spring to my eyes. I try to imagine what it would be like to finally fall in love, *real* love, and then have it ripped away from me. It would be like a bitch slap from the universe, that's what.

Pia's ranting now. "Guys always think I'm weird, or stupid, or both. They think my upbringing is strange, that moving so much must mean I'm a basket case, or that being Swiss-Indian means I eat nothing but fucking cuckoo clocks and curry!"

I start laughing at this. "Ladybitch, calm down. . . ."

But Pia isn't listening. "And they think I'm great for a good time, but not for conversation, not for anything real. I am really good at talking, goddamnit! I could talk for hours if you wanted me to! Now I'll be single forever! And ever and ever! Oh God! I'm going to have a panic attack!" Pia closes her eyes and makes a sound that can only be described as "WAHHHH."

At that moment, Julia walks in the kitchen, still in her suit from work, little gym bag glued to her shoulders, as always.

"What the fu—?"

"Pia and Aidan broke up," says Madeleine.

"Holy shit!" says Julia. "I thought you guys would get married for sure. And we'd all be your bridesmaids."

That sets Pia off again, naturally. Five minutes later, she's still crying, and we've run out of calming platitudes.

So I put on my strictest voice, the one that has worked with a hysterical Pia in the past.

"Pia! Stop wailing and breathe," I say. "Now. I mean it. You're making yourself sick." Pia closes her mouth, her chest still shaking from hysteria. "If Aidan is the man you are meant to be with, then you'll get back together in the future. In the meantime, you get to enjoy your life. You love your job, you love Rookhaven. . . ."

"I love drinking," she says, sniffing. "Let's go out Saturday and get really shitfaced. I need attention from pretty boys. That will make me feel better."

"Um, I can't," says Julia, turning pink.

"Why not? Hot date?"

Julia looks around the room, a coy smile on her face, until she has all of our attention exclusively on her. "Well, yes actually. I just ran into

Sam on my way in, he was outside Vic's place . . . and he asked me out!"

"Woo!" shouts Madeleine. "How did that happen?"

Julia is pink with pleasure. "We were talking about Bartolo's, and I said it's my favorite place in Brooklyn, then he said his favorite Brooklyn restaurant was this Mexican place near his house, and then I said, 'Oh, my God I totally love Mexican,' and then he said, 'We should go sometime,' and I said, 'How's Saturday?'" She turns to me with a huge grin. "Isn't it awesome, Angie?"

Oh. My. God. Julia is going out with Sam.

CHAPTER 25

Five days until my birthday.

And another boring day at the Gap.

Fact: being bored changes the space-time continuum. As in, space starts to close in on you, and time stops moving. It seems like a month since I got up this morning. I can't even remember what I ate for breakfast. Or what I had for dinner last night.

Wait. Yes I can. I ate pizza at Bartolo's with Sam and Vic.

And then Sam asked Julia out.

I'm still so surprised. I'm like a little Angie cartoon with an exclamation mark above her head.

I'm also annoyed at myself for being surprised. Julia really likes him, and I've been bugging him to ask her out for weeks. It's just what I wanted, right? It's totally fine!

Well, whatever. I'm trying not to think about it. It's only weird because he's my friend, and we've been spending so much damn time together. We had that strange sleepover, though nothing happened, and, you know, it's just one of those friendships that you make sometimes when you're between relationships. I usually end said friendships by sleeping with the guy, and then find out that we weren't actually friends at all. But that won't happen this time.

Because he's going out with Julia Saturday.

So that's that.

And in thirty-two minutes, I can leave for the day.

(And then go home and put salve on my blisters and eat and sleep and get up and come in here and do it all over again. Argh.)

Suddenly, there's a tap on my shoulder.

"Angie! It's me!" Coco jumps up and down with delight. "Surprise!"

"Hey! What are you doing here?"

"I was in the neighborhood, um, going to the Museum of Modern Art."

We hug hello quickly.

Weird, I don't think I've ever been alone with Coco outside of Rookhaven. With Pia and Coco together, yes, but never just the two of us. I look around, trying to think of something to talk about, and see my coworkers Derek the dickface and Shania the bitch staring at me.

"Want to try on some clothes?"

"Sure!"

"You should wear blue." I have been dying to get Coco out of those baggy, faded black threads ever since we met. "Pale blue. To bring out your eyes. And gray. And white. Sharper shoulders, tighter waists, no more high-neck sweaters. . . . How much money do you want to spend? I'll buy it all for you and use my fifty-percent-off employee discount, and you can pay me back. It's kind of bending the rules, so we have to be real sneaky about it."

Coco's eyes light up. "Your job is so cool!"

I guess it is pretty cool. Kind of.

Coco and I spend the next half an hour enjoying a full-on makeover montage. All that's missing is the eighties music. By the time my shift ends, she's bought three pairs of jeans, four tops, an actual dress (I have *never* seen Coco in a dress before), and a really cool trench coat that's perfect for spring. I've managed to get her out of her oversize, baggy, hide-me look. She has enormous boobs so unless she wears something really fitted, she can look a little frumpy.

"Wow, Angie, thank you so much. This is going to be so great for my next date with Ethan."

"You're seeing that guy again?" I say, the words out of my mouth before I can stop myself.

She pauses. "Yeah . . . I mean, I thought I would. Why? You don't like him?"

"Of course I like him! Anyway, it doesn't matter if I like him. What matters is if *you* like him." God, I hate it when people say that shit, and here I am, saying it anyway.

"I think I do. . . ." She pauses. "Can we grab a coffee after this and talk?"

"Let's get a drink instead. Go to P. J. Clarke's on the corner of Fifty-fifth and Third, and I'll finish my shift, buy these clothes, and meet you in fifteen minutes."

P. J. Clarke's is an old bar with a Sinatra-Rat-Pack pedigree, but I like it because you can sit at the bar, eat tiny burgers called sliders, and drink martinis. I don't have the cash for sliders and martinis, of course, but I got my paycheck today, so I can totally afford a couple of beers for Coco and me. (I wonder if I'll ever be able to make social plans without mentally going through my bank balance.)

On the way, I call Pia quickly. She answers, but all I can hear is snuffling.

"Ladybitch. It's me."

A small choking sound comes out.

"I'm having a drink with Coco near your office in Midtown. You wanna join?"

"No." Pia's voice is barely a croak. "I have to work late. I'm way behind because of all this fucking crying. It's really hard to read a computer screen with tears in your eyes, you know?"

"Love you, ladybitch," I say, surprising myself. I never say shit like that.

"Love you, too."

When I get to P. J. Clarke's, Coco is sitting at the far end of the bar, drinking a cosmopolitan and staring at her phone, looking incredibly self-conscious. The rest of the bar is filled with the usual Friday night happy-hour crowd: suits, tourists, and some nervous daters.

"Voilà. Fashion delivery," I say, handing over the Gap shopping bag.

"Thank you! Wow. This is really so awesome of you!"

"Do you want another cocktail?" I ask Coco, praying she'll say no because I can't afford it.

"No, it's kind of nasty," she says, wrinkling her nose.

I nod. "Cosmopolitans taste like crap. That's the weird thing about them." I catch the bartender's eye. He's a huge hulk of a guy, in a perfectly pressed shirt and tie. "Two Heinekens, please."

The first sip of a supercold beer is always the sweetest. I take a sip and sigh. What a long, boring day. My blisters are throbbing, but I guess it would be kind of gross to apply fresh blister thingies right here at the bar.

Coco has started tearing pieces of her beer's label off with her fingernails. Nerves? I never have any idea how she's really feeling, since she's always sweetly smiling. Maybe it's time I found out.

"Do you want to talk about the dinner party med meltdown, Coco?"

"No," she says, and then looks at me and forces a little laugh out. "I just had a headache before the party, you know? So I took the Demerol they gave me at the clinic back in December."

"Have you told Julia about it?"

"She would never understand," Coco mumbles.

"Okay. Where did you get the Xanax? Was it prescribed to you?" I feel like a school counselor.

"I found it," she says carefully, ripping off another tiny shard of her beer label. "I just found it lying around."

Well, that's obviously not true. But I won't push her. "So why did you take it?"

"I thought it might make me less nervous," she says. "It's an anti-anxiety med, right? And I was feeling very anxious before the dinner party, about the cooking, and about Jonah, you know, because I asked him to be my date and he said no, and then I felt nervous about Ethan."

"Right. Ethan."

"My therapist thinks he sounds like he'd be very positive for me," she says, slightly defensively.

"You're in therapy?"

"Yeah. Um, they offered it, so I said yes," she says in a very low voice.

"Do you want to talk about it?"

"No."

"Are you sure?" Vic's words of advice from the night I got back to Rookhaven spill out of my mouth. "It's much easier to let go of your worries when you share them with the people you love."

Coco looks at me, her eyes filling with tears, and she puts her face in her hands. As usual, when faced with a crying friend, I'm not sure what to do, and particularly not in the middle of a crowded Midtown Manhattan bar. I get her a big wad of cocktail napkins from the bartender, who doesn't seem fazed to have a girl crying hysterically in his bar, and then stroke her arm in what I hope is a comforting manner. After a few minutes, she dries her eyes.

"Sorry," she says. "Sorry, Angie, you must think I'm such a freaking loser."

"Trust me. I don't."

A slick, suited guy is suddenly standing almost on top of us. "Ladies! Don't cry, I'm here now."

I stare at him, hoping he can read the fuck-off message in my eyes.

Apparently he can't.

"I was thinking—"

"No."

"You haven't even heard what I—"

"No."

His smile drops. "What's your fucking problem?"

"My problem is that my friend and I are not in the market for a date rape tonight, thank you."

"What the fuck? Are you getting your fucking period or something? I—"

"That's enough, buddy," calls the bartender. "Leave the ladies alone."

He slinks off, and I wink at Coco. She is giggling helplessly. "I can't believe you just said that."

"I know," I say. "Sometimes I open my mouth and shit like that just comes out. Are you okay?"

"Yes . . . no . . . I mean, yes, I'm fine like, right this second, but when I'm alone, I don't feel okay . . . and I've been having trouble sleeping, and it's so hard to feel happy when you're tired all the time, and I know it's a process, it's a process, my therapist keeps saying it's a process, but you know, I just . . . can't imagine . . . feeling normal again."

"Of course you will!"

"I've been thinking about antidepressants, what do you think about that?" Before I can say anything, she continues quickly. "I went on them after my mom died, but then they made me gain weight and gave me crazy dreams, which kind of made me more depressed, though I guess I could try another kind, you know?"

"Um . . . so you just keep trying different kinds until you find one that fits, like Goldilocks and the Three Medicated Bears?"

But Coco isn't listening. "My dad says everyone needs to feel sad sometimes, that it's part of being human, you know? He says that all great art and literature is created by people who feel things deeply, who experience love and hate and heartbreak and jealousy and loneliness and, you know, everything, so people taking antidepressants are cutting themselves off from real human emotions. They're making themselves, like, nonhuman. That's why I went to MoMA tonight, I thought maybe art would make me feel better. . . ."

"Did it?"

"A little. But then I think about the future, I think about going home for another sleepless night, and getting up tomorrow and going to work again surrounded by children and having no adult conversations, and I feel so alone and so exhausted." Coco takes a deep breath. "I don't want to keep feeling this way. I want to feel *better*."

I chew my lip, hesitating. Fuck it. "I had one, you know. An abortion."

"You did? Why didn't you tell me?"

"I don't know why I didn't tell you before. I guess, um, oh, I don't know." I pause, not wanting to tell her the truth: that sharing secrets, or problems, or issues, has always made me feel weak. "He was the first guy I slept with. A bartender while I was on vacation with Pia and her parents. I didn't plan on having sex with him, you know. I was really drunk and feeling sort of crazy. I don't even remember it really."

"Why were you feeling crazy?"

"I'd gone home at the start of the summer and my dad had moved out. Annabel—that's my mother—she kept saying he was away on business, but I didn't believe her, and he wouldn't answer my calls." I stare into space, remembering. "And then she sent me on vacation with Pia and her folks without asking me. I felt . . . I don't know. Crazy. I wanted to go completely out of control because I had no control over anything in my life, you know?"

"But your parents stayed together."

"Dad came to see me at school the next semester and told me everything was fine, and by the next vacation he was back in the house."

"And you got an abortion. . . ."

"In a town near my boarding school," I say. "I had a fake ID so they thought I was twenty-one. It wasn't hard."

"That makes me feel so much better, is that weird? Did you feel bad afterward?"

"I felt sad, but it was the right choice for me," I say. "Mostly I was relieved."

"I did some reading online, and I got so upset—"

"Never read about anything controversial online, Coco," I say. "That's where all the freaks come out to play. It's your body, it's your choice. If they spent half as much energy helping people in need as they do condemning them, the world would be a better place."

Coco nods. But she doesn't look convinced. "Abstinence is the only form of birth control that works," she says, clearly repeating something she's read.

"Abstinence is a myth," I say. "Humans fuck, Coco. It's the way the world works. We always have, we always will. And women have always tried to prevent conception. . . . Ancient Egyptians, Romans, Greeks, people in the Middle Ages, in Shakespeare's time, they all had birth control, and when it failed, they had abortions, though they were incredibly dangerous and women died, like, all the time." I put a cigarette in the corner of my mouth. "It's part of human nature. We fuck."

"Oh," Coco says in a tiny voice. She looks slightly shocked. I need to tone down the swearing.

"Sorry, honey. I'm just saying . . . sex is sex. The urge to do it is what has kept the human species alive for millions of years. But now we have the right and the ability to choose when and where we have babies. We're not animals."

Coco nods. "That makes sense. I guess."

Then I remember something else Vic said. "You've got to let regrets and worries go, honey. Otherwise you'll spend your whole life thinking about them."

"But *how* do I let them go?" Coco stares at me, willing me to have an answer. *"How?"*

I don't want to disappoint her, but I don't want to lie, either. So I shrug. "I wish I knew."

Coco sighs and picks up her beer. We clink a little silent cheers.

"So, are you gonna see Ethan the Chees—I mean, Ethan again?"

"I hope so!" She smiles. "He's so smart and nice! And my therapist says I have, um, self-esteem issues, so he'd be great for me."

"We all have self-esteem issues," I say. "They come with tits."

"You don't. You're gorgeous. Men always look at you. Right now, I can see, like, seven guys in this bar looking at you."

Sam pops into my head. Sam asked Julia out. Weird.

I force myself back to the present and shake my head. "They don't like me. They just like . . . my outside. They like my shell."

"How many times have you been in love?"

"Oh, Coconut. I don't know. A dozen times . . . and also never."

Coco stares at me. "I don't understand what you mean."

I take a sip of my drink, thinking. "I mean . . . I always think I'm in love . . . but if you're in love, you should be happy, right? I wasn't. I was always trying to please these guys who could never be pleased. I was always stressed, always putting them first, and doing anything I could to make them not break up with me, but trying to act really cool about it all. It was exhausting. That can't be love. Sometimes I even felt . . . a little psycho. And I don't even know if I was myself around them, not really. I don't think any of them ever really knew me at all."

Coco nods thoughtfully. "I don't think Eric knew me, either. Or Jonah . . . Maybe Ethan does, or will. . . . I think you need to be friends first, like Julia and Sam!" she says. "I hope they fall in love. Julia really wants a relationship."

"Yeah, totally, me too," I say, staring at my drink. Julia and Sam. Sam and Julia.

"I'm so glad you and Julia have gotten to know each other better," says Coco. "You're both so cool. You're the leaders of the house, you know?"

I laugh out loud. "I am not the leader of anything!"

"Yes you are," she says insistently. "Pia is never around anymore. But you and Jules are the ones who make everyone laugh. Plus, you're the cool one."

I smile. Only Coco would see the world in terms of cool and not cool.

"And you're really good for Julia. You know, the makeover stuff, and introducing her to Sam. You're a good friend."

"Really?"

"Really."

Coco's uncomplicated approval, and the idea of me being a good friend, makes me feel happier than I have in a long, long time. "Let's go home," I say.

"Okay!" She hops off her stool obediently. "Thanks, Angie. You really made me feel better about everything."

"Anytime, ladybitch."

"You've never called me that before!" Coco is beaming. "I love it . . . ladybitch."

On the subway home, I reflect on the ever-been-in-love question. I don't think I've ever been truly, madly, deeply in love. Or in a real relationship, one that really meant something, one that made me truly happy. Maybe I'm simply not capable of it. Which just makes me thank God, yet again, that I've decided to be single now.

So I'm glad Sam's going out with Julia.

I hope they'll be very happy together.

CHAPTER 26

"When can we see your band?"

"Never." Madeleine calmly looks at her cards. "I get stage fright when people I know are watching."

"Maybe we should blindfold you."

"Maybe we should gag *you*."

Julia takes a slug of wine. "Angie, are you sure I look okay?"

I glance at her. "Perfect."

It's Saturday night, and we're all in the kitchen at Rookhaven, having wine and playing poker before our Celebrate Pia's Singledom Night Out (subtitled Make Her Stop Crying Just for a Few Goddamn Hours for Fuck's Sake).

Well, almost all of us.

Julia is going on her date with Sam instead.

"I'm not nervous." Julia flicks her perfect blowout-by-Coco.

Madeleine smirks. "That's why you made Angie spend four hours shopping in SoHo with you for the right outfit?"

"I liked it," I say. Which is mostly true.

The shopping part was fine. And Jules bought me lunch at Café Habana to say thank you. But then she kept asking me questions about Sam. And really, all I know is he's from Ohio, he dropped out of college, he learned how to sail on the job, he's currently sleeping on his buddy's floor, he's my friend, and I've been avoiding his calls ever since he asked Julia out. But I don't own him! He can do whatever he wants. Right?

The rest of today, I've just been sewing and trying not to think about him. I altered Drakey's little slip dress, the one Sam liked, and I'm wearing it tonight. It felt so good to *do* something again, to be creating things, to take myself outside my head . . . The only time I've felt at peace in days is when I've been sewing. Just like Vic said.

"I feel . . ." Julia takes a deep breath, waiting for everyone to pay attention to her again. "I feel certain, in my soul, that it's going to be good. That's probably a sign, right? They say when you know, you know."

At this, Pia, who has barely spoken all day, makes a gulping sound, her huge brown eyes filling with tears. Any mention of romance, men, or breakups, and she loses her shit. Seriously, it's like every dramatic soap opera meltdown you've ever seen, in one woman. She came into my bedroom at 4:00 A.M., weeping, saying that she couldn't sleep alone, that the universe was against her, that she'd never love again. She was asleep and snoring within six seconds. Even Sam didn't snore . . . argh. Don't think about Sam.

"Oh God! My makeup . . ." Pia tilts her head back to stop the tears from ruining her eyeliner. "Damn you, Aidan, for breaking my heart," she whispers at the ceiling. "Damn you to hell."

"Have you talked to him today?" asks Madeleine.

"He keeps calling. I keep not answering." Pia slaps her palm on the table. "Fuck Aidan! Tonight is about my ego-driven, God-given right to drink hard spirits while enjoying the restorative power of the male gaze."

"Hey, you guys. Look at this," says Julia, pinging the leg of her black tights. A cloud of dust, or skin cells, or something, billows out.

Madeleine looks like she might puke. "Julia! That is disgusting!"

"I know!" Julia looks fascinated and does it again. "It's like a scab. I can't stop picking at it."

"You pick at scabs?"

"Everyone picks at scabs." Julia waves her hands dismissively. "Anyone who says they don't is lying. That's my whole philosophy on life."

"I don't *get* scabs," says Pia, shocked out of her Aidan-induced misery. "Do I look okay, too, ladybitch? No post-breakup sartorial errors?"

"You look perfect, too," I say. She's wearing supertight jeans and an extremely cool silk top.

Me? I'm wearing my newly altered slip dress with my Zara leather jacket and mean-looking boots. It's April, so it's a little chilly out, but I'm bare-legged anyway. Amazing how subversive bare skin can seem after months of bitter winter. All in all, I look like no one should fuck with me. Which is kind of how I feel right now.

Still haven't heard a word from Annabel. Or my dad. Maybe he'll call me on my birthday in a few days. No one forgets their only child's birthday, outside of a goddamn John Hughes movie, right?

Pia turns to Julia. "Where's your date with Sam, by the way?"

"Some Mexican joint in Fort Greene," Julia opens her purse and shows us a toothbrush, toothpaste, floss, and perfume. "But I will *not* smell—or taste—like quesadillas." She looks at her watch. "Oh, my god! I gotta run! I'm meeting him in twenty minutes! Wish me luck!"

"Ah, young love," Pia says with a weary sigh, as the front door slams. "So full of hopes and dreams. But it never lasts." She takes another dramatic slug of wine. "Ever. Love just rots and dies. Like a dog. In a ditch."

Two hours later, the four of us are at Pijiu, a bar in Williamsburg. It's one of those places that looks paint-peelingly nondescript from the outside during the day, but sparkles with attitude at night. One wall is taken up with a long wooden bar and, at the back, a stage is lit by hundreds of little red Chinese lanterns. The rest of the space is littered with old brown sofas covered in seventies-style plastic and a cluster of secondhand mahjong tables with mismatched chairs. Sort of Beijing disco farmhouse.

There's live music later, an up-and-coming Brooklyn band called Spector that Madeleine wants to check out. But for now, a vintage 1950s jukebox is playing Guns N' Roses, and the crowd is the usual mix of hipsters, yupsters, and normal people (i.e., us).

Since we're without Julia, who, whatever Coco thinks, is the real linchpin of Rookhaven, and since anything personal is off-limits due to Pia's propensity for breakup-related hysteria, we've turned to a subject that not-quite-perfect social gatherings employ to kick-start engaging conversations all over the world. Yep. We're talking about blow jobs.

"Use your hand to cup the balls," says Pia. "The balls are totally the secret."

"I also like to use one hand to work this bit—" I start miming.

"Stop it! Stop it!" Madeleine is scandalized.

Coco, surprisingly, is fascinated. "What do you mean? The helmet-y bit?"

"No, the helmet-y bit is in your, um, okay. Look—" I start drawing on a napkin. "See, there's that bit, and that's the shaft. That's a vein, by the way—"

"No! No cock diagrams! Jesus!" Madeleine snatches the napkin from me and rips it up into little pieces as Pia and Coco and I collapse into giggles.

"This is just what I needed," says Pia, after we calm down. "I've been weeping—weeping!—about Aidan for days, and the bastard is probably having sex with some Californian bimbo right now."

"Of course he's not, ladybitch," I say, placing a comforting hand on her arm. "California is three hours behind. He wouldn't screw a bimbo in the midafternoon. He's probably just masturbating now."

Coco collapses into hysterics again.

Pia rolls her eyes. "Too far, Angie. I swear you're like a dude sometimes."

"A dude with a great rack, you mean."

Actually, I'm feeling weird and wired. Alcohol, instead of calming me down, is stirring me up. And acting crass and drawing cock diagrams helps me pretend that I'm okay. The truth is, I'm worried about my birthday, I'm worried my parents will contact me and even more worried that they won't, I'm worried about what Stef might do after our meeting in the Gap the other day, I'm worried about my job and my future. And most of all, I'm worried about Sam and Julia's date and whether it will go well. Though I know it's none of my business.

Sigh.

I have enough cash for another two rounds of drinks, and then I'll go home. (I worked out that it's all I can afford on my salary from the Gap once I take out what I need to pay rent and kitty, till I get paid again on Monday. I know, how fucking responsible am I? Seriously. High-five me.)

I tune back in to the conversation.

"Of course you should text him," Pia is saying. "If you want to. Are you sure he's the guy for you though, honey?"

"Yup," says Coco. "All I want right now is someone who is kind and stable and smart."

"You make him sound like a horse you're investing in," says Madeleine.

"It is an investment!" says Coco. "I went with my heart with Eric, and that backfired. So this time, I'm going with my head."

It strikes me that boring little know-it-all Ethan the Cheesemaker isn't the right choice for her heart *or* head, but none of us will say that, of course.

Madeleine stands up and calls to someone on the other side of the bar. "Heff! Over here!"

It's her date from the dinner party, the perma-stoned musician. He ambles over, all beaten-up clothes and overgrown eyebrows.

"I'm having a fucking nightmare, man." Wow, Heff is unusually lucid tonight. "I'm filling in on bass for my friend Amy's band, but her lead singer has flaked."

I turn to check out the band. They're setting up, and a tall girl with pink hair is shouting into her cell phone. She looks pretty tense. For someone with pink hair.

"Amy is freaking. This is the first time Spector has played here, they won't book her again."

Madeleine looks over at the girl. "Okay. I'll do it."

"You will? Fuck, I was too scared to even ask you! That's totes rad, man!"

"You were scared of me?" Madeleine is stunned.

"*Everyone* is scared of you." Heff swings an arm around her shoulders as they walk away. "Everyone."

We all turn to watch Heff introduce her to Amy with the white and pink hair.

"I'm a bit scared of Madeleine," says Coco.

"Me too, sometimes," says Pia.

"I'm not," I say.

Coco sighs. "Yeah, but you're not scared of anything."

I snort. Right. I'm not scared of anything. Except for my past and my future.

"My round," I say, to change the subject. "Same again?"

"Make mine a double!" says Pia, taking a photo of the stage, one eye squinting shut to help her focus. "I am totally Facebooking this so Aidan can see what an awesome life I am having without him."

The bar is packed three-deep with young Billyburg hipsters all drinking Yuengling or PBR and talking passionately about their socially engaged graphic design skateboard business or urban farming co-op or karmic slam poetry or whatever. So not my bag, you know? I appreciate a bit of alternative entrepreneurship as much as the next girl, but come the fuck on. "What's your order?" the waitress asks, one of those short henna types with a lot of tattoos.

"Uh, four gin and tonics."

She slams them on the bar and I pay, just moments before the drunk hipster next to me stands up and knocks over one of the drinks.

"Whoopsh," he says, waffle crumbs in his beard, and wanders off.

"Sorry!" His friend stands up, a tall guy with gravity-defying hair and an air of pharmaceutical confidence. "I'll buy you another."

I want to say don't worry about it, but it's also a waste of my limited cash to replace them myself. So instead, I try to smile. Is there anything worse than worrying about money?

"Thanks. Gin and tonic."

"Any particular gin?"

"No, any gin will do. You know, your garden-variety, bathtub-produced, boring, ordinary old gin."

"Mediocre gin, got it. Something . . . unimpressive. Just my style."

Cute response. I focus on his hands. Long fingers, square nails, lots of little leather and fabric bracelets. Sam's hands are like ancient gardening gloves, all worn and battered from sailing.

Argh! Don't think about Sam.

"Here you go," Square Nails says, handing me the drink. "I didn't slip anything in it, I swear."

"Actually, I roofie myself these days, it saves time," I say.

He doesn't laugh. One of those arrogant pseudo-easygoing dudes who doesn't expect a woman to be funny. Instead he pats the vacant stool next to him, expecting me to sit on it. I don't sit down. He starts talking anyway.

"Let me ask you a question. So, my buddy and I are creating a morning coffee delivery service around Williamsburg and Brooklyn Heights. It's like a bespoke food truck service. Your cup of joe, however you like it, whatever time you like it, and you order it online the night before." While he's monologuing, I take a cigarette out of my purse and place it between my lips and stare at him. "Naturally, it's all free-trade organic coffee that's hand grown by farmers we know personally in Colombia. And you can choose from organic milk from our buddy's farm upstate, or non-GM unsweetened soy or almond milk. It's called MyJoe."

"So what's the question you wanted to ask me?"

"Would you use it?"

"I usually get coffee on my way to work."

"Oh yeah? Where do you work?"

I pluck the cigarette out of my mouth. "The Gap."

His jaw drops. I think he would be less horrified if I told him I made kitten porn.

"Thanks for the drink, big guy. Check you later."

I stride away, drop off Madeleine's drink at the stage—where she's going through the set list with Amy and Heff and looking extremely stressed out—and then walk back to Coco and Pia.

Pia is in full five-drinks-and-this-is-what-I-think-about-everything-goddamnit mode. "Fuck Aidan! And fuck California! I'm gonna start fucking dating as soon as I fucking can. Rip that fucking Band-Aid right off and get right the fuck back up on that fucking horse."

"That's a lot of fucks," comments Coco.

I raise my hand as if to ask a question. "By 'horse,' you mean 'penis,' right?"

Coco cracks up, sputtering her drink everywhere.

"Here are my new dating rules." Pia ignores us. "If they're rude to the waitress, walk away. If they order before me, walk away. If they leave their phone on the table during dinner, walk away. If they would rather live in California than New York City, walk the fuck away."

"Wow, that rules out, like, every dude I've ever met," I say, and Coco cracks up again, slapping the table with her hand. She's pretty tipsy. Her phone vibrates, and she grabs it, shutting one eye slightly to read a text, and then smiles a secret little smile.

"Is it Ethan?" I say. "Do you want to share something with the rest of the class, Coco?"

She smirks and ignores me to reply, and Pia continues her Aidan rant.

"Fuck love. You know? Fuck it! Fuck men! They're all just fucking cock-monkeys. I'm just gonna use and abuse from now on. Abuseorama." She tries, unsuccessfully, to hide a tiny belch. "What about you, ladybitch?"

"I am not using or abusing anyone," I say.

"What's your ideal man?" asks Coco.

I stare at her, my mind a blank. My ideal man? Does that even exist? "I don't know. Every guy I'm ever attracted to just ends up a lying, cheating sack of shit out for whatever he can get."

There's a pause.

"Wow. You want a little lemon to go with that bitter?" says Pia. "I thought I was fucked up, but seriously, dude . . ."

I shrug. "I call it like I see it."

"You guys, Ethan and I haven't even kissed," says Coco worriedly. "Do you think I should make the first move? Oh, shush, don't answer! He just walked in! I invited him along, is that okay?"

Pia and I exchange looks. Even without having talked about Ethan the Cheesemaker with her, I know we have the same opinion: he's a dick. And then when I see his sweaty face, I almost flinch with dislike. I can't help it. But that's bad, right? It's Coco's decision. Not mine.

"Ethan!" exclaims Coco. "Hi!" She leans in to give him a big hug.

"Do I have a story for you!" Ethan says. "Prepare for a twist in the tale that will shock and surprise! Now—"

Oh God. Ethan doesn't converse, he lectures. Thank hell Coco accompanies him to the bar, and I turn to Pia.

"Looks like it's you and me, ladybitch."

But it's not.

Because at that exact moment, Pia's jaw drops, her eyes filling with tears, and she stands up, unsteadily clutching the back of her chair, staring toward the front of the bar.

I turn to follow her gaze.

Aidan.

Jesus, is everyone's fucking love life turning up at this bar tonight or what?

Aidan strides right over to our table, carrying a huge duffel bag, as though he came straight from the airport, staring right over me at Pia like a man possessed. "Pia, I love you. I can't live without you."

"Oh, Aidan, I can't live without you either!"

Fucking drama queens.

And boom, they start to kiss, squishing my head between them. I have to duck down and crawl under the table to get away. I pause under the table for a moment. It's so quiet and calm. I just want to hide here. Forever.

CHAPTER **27**

But I don't. Of course. I just get up and find another chair like a normal person.

Then, while Pia and Aidan continue to kiss passionately and tearfully like the last scene of a romantic comedy, and Coco listens eagerly to Ethan at the bar, Madeleine steps up to the microphone, and one of the shaggy-faced bartenders introduces the band.

"Ladies and gentlemen, may I present . . . Spector!"

The music starts, and within a few bars, I realize it's a metal-pop cover version of a 1960s song by The Ronettes, "Be My Baby." They're playing it very rough and sultry, with a lot of angry guitar. Heff is on base, pink-haired Amy is on lead guitar, and some dude with a ringletty beard is on drums.

Then Madeleine starts singing. God, I forgot how good she is.

"The night we met, I knew I . . . needed you so . . ."

Somehow, her voice is whispery and husky at the same time, and every word sounds sad but sort of sexy. Like she's promising you something.

"And if I had the chance, I'd . . . never let you go . . ."

Pia and Aidan are kissing so hard there's a fighting chance one might collapse from oxygen deprivation.

"Get a room, you two!" says Ethan the Cheesemaker, coming back from the bar with a glass of red wine. He didn't bother to get anyone else a drink.

Coco giggles, skipping behind him. "Yeah! Ooh! Aidan! Hi! Madeleine's singing! Yay!"

Pia and Aidan stop kissing, and he whispers in her ear. She nods, then turns back to our table quickly, grabs her bag, and smiles at me, her face lit up with happiness.

"He flew back last night. He's been trying to find me all day but I've been ignoring his calls, then he saw my Facebook update that I was here." She smiles, happy tears filling her eyes. "God, I love Facebook. We're out of here. Tell Maddy I'll make it up to her. Love you, ladybitch."

And boom, just like that, I'm left with Coco and Ethan the Cheesemaker.

Ethan clears his throat loudly. "Angie, do tell me all about your family. I understand your mother is British? Now, the British healthcare system is fascinating, deeply flawed, but some would say, better than our own. Or it was. These days—"

And off he goes. I can get away with ignoring him, if I gaze at the stage. "Be My Baby" finishes and the bands starts playing "The Wanderer" by Dion.

"Well, I'm the type of guy who'll never settle down . . ."

Madeleine has such a beautiful voice, but she lacks confidence onstage. Her eyes are almost shut; she's practically singing to the floor. And the rest of the band is thinking the same thing: Heff is exchanging looks with Amy, and the ringlet-haired drummer is hitting the shit out of his drums in an attempt, I think, to make Madeleine give the song a little more energy.

"I gotta go to the little girls' room! Excuse me!" whispers Coco, hurrying off with her head down, as though we were in a movie theater.

I don't want to talk to Ethan the Cheesemaker, so I pretend to be enthralled with the band. Actually, I don't have to pretend: they are really good. If only Madeleine would give it a little oomph. . . . If only she'd smile. Watching someone not-really-enjoying singing is kind of excruciating.

A minute later, I feel a warm, slimy hand on my bare knee.

Ethan!

He's touching me!

"Angie . . ." he says, his voice low and froggy.

I instinctively jerk my knee away, look into his little eyes, and just have time to hiss "*Don't touch me*" before Coco returns from the bathroom, smiling happily.

"The bar snacks here look great! I got us each a menu!" She sits down, oblivious to the tension at the table.

Oh God, why, *why* does she like Ethan the Cheesemaker—hereafter known as Ethan Wonderslime—so much? In her current vulnerable state, she really doesn't need to fall for a fuckwit who will inevitably disappoint her. On the other hand, he seems to make her happy right now, and maybe that's more important. On the other hand (uh . . . the third hand), he just came on to me.

Ignoring them, I stare at the stage, where Spector is now playing a pretty awesome cover of "Peggy Sue" by Buddy Holly.

The ringlet drummer dude is really enjoying his little drum solos in this song, but Madeleine still looks nervous and uncomfortable as hell. If she wasn't onstage, if I didn't feel like she might need my support, I'd leave. Run away from this whole messy Coco-Ethan thing, from annoying know-it-all hipsters. But I know that impulse, that almost overwhelming urge to escape that I always get, isn't the answer.

Instead, I put myself in Madeleine's shoes: a bar full of strangers, songs she's not sure about and maybe doesn't even know that well, no one smiling, no one applauding, no one even dancing. . . .

Hang on. Why *don't* people dance in bars anymore? They should. Right? Why the hell is everyone here too cool to dance?

Without even thinking about it, I stand up and walk to the bar, where the Square Nails hipster coffee business dude is still sitting.

"Would you like to dance?"

"Say what?"

I stare at him. "You heard me. Let's go."

Square Nails gazes at me for a second before standing up. "Okay."

I hold my hand out and pull him toward the space in front of the band, suddenly very aware of everyone in the entire bar looking at us.

We start dancing, doing those semi-twist-n-shout moves that you do when you're too self-conscious and not drunk enough (pretty much the same thing in my book). Dancing wasn't my strongest talent, even in my vodka-fueled days of yore—a lot of nonchalant nodding, a lot of shoulder shapes—but right now, I give this dance floor everything I've got.

"You're a great dancer," says Square Nails.

"Thanks. I was professional when I was younger, but I had to give it up. Steroids, you know?"

Square Nails stares at me for a few seconds, confused. Sigh. My kingdom for a dude who thinks I'm funny. (Yeah, I totally have a kingdom.)

The song finishes, and the band segues straight into "Then He Kissed Me" by The Crystals.

I look up at Madeleine and wink, and she returns the most brilliantly huge smile I've ever seen. And then, something magic happens: her voice is louder, her words are clearer. Madeleine is shining.

More people join us on the dance floor, and within thirty seconds, it's a churning mass of twisting, turning, jiving couples. Halfway through the song, I glance back at the table where Coco and Ethan Wonderslime are sitting and suddenly, behind them, I see Julia and Sam walk in just as Square Nails grabs my hand and spins me out in the other direction.

"Dipping you!" he exclaims, and I make the involuntary "whoop!" sound that I always do when I'm dipped. I'm such a cliché.

Then he twirls me again.

Mid-twirl I glance over to our table and see, through the crowd, Julia and Sam.

Kissing.

A split second later, he spins me back into him, but I can hardly see where I'm going and land against his body with a bang.

Julia and Sam are kissing.

Julia is kissing my Sam. I mean, my *friend* Sam. That's weird. Why is that weird? It's normal! They were on a date! I quickly try to arrange my face into some kind of happy serenity and keep smiling as Square Nails pings me around the dance floor. He's getting pretty confident with the dips and turns.

But my brain is racing. Julia and Sam. Julia . . . and *Sam*. All I can see is that image of them kissing, like a snapshot that's been burned into the back of my eyelids. I feel strange, as if I've been punched, or winded, like when you're a little kid on the monkey bars in the playground and you fall off and land hard on your ass. Yeah, that's how I feel. Like the breath has been whacked out of me.

Julia and Sam were kissing.

By the time the song has ended, I've pulled myself together. It's totally normal to feel weird when your friends kiss. Right? Right. But it's only a thing if I make it a thing. It's totally fine for my friends to like each other! They went on a date! What did I expect? I don't want to be one of those people who won't share friends, or who gets jealous when their friends start a new relationship. It's fine. It's so fine.

I walk back to our table, smiling as wide as I can, focusing on nothing.

"Hey!" I say, trying to sound supernormal and happy. "How are you guys? How was dinner? Was it great? That's great!"

"Hey, stranger," says Sam. "You lose your phone or something?"

I haven't returned his calls since he asked Julia out. I mean, it's no big deal, I just had nothing to say. "No, just busy, you know, working. . . ." I can't even look him in the eye; instead I pretend to be really interested in the dance floor.

"Hey, you're wearing the dress!" Sam says. "The Drakey dress. It looks great!"

Turning around so I can avoid replying, I notice that Square Nails has followed me to our table. I turn to face him. "Thanks for the dance. You can go now."

Looking shocked, he walks away.

Julia and Sam are laughing.

"You're right! She is so goddamn harsh!" exclaims Sam.

"Told ya," says Julia. "She goes through men like water."

"That sentence doesn't mean anything," I say. Since when do Julia and Sam talk about me?

"We were wondering where you guys were so I texted Maddy, and she told me about her surprise gig," says Julia. "She's amazing!"

"She is," I agree. I don't know where to look. If I focus on Julia's smiley face I feel angry and guilty about feeling angry, and I can't even look at Sam.

I think I might cry if I see how happy he is with Julia.

I guess it's just because he won't be my friend now. Now that he's dating Julia. I mean, we won't be unfriends or anything . . . but it won't be the same.

And that makes me want to cry even more.

Thank God for the band. I turn to face them, trying to look serene and tough and normal and conceal the chaos inside me, just as they start playing "Do You Wanna Dance?" by Bobby Freeman.

"WOO! Madeleine, you ROCK!" screams Julia.

"Let's dance!" says Coco. "Me and Ethan, and you and Sam!"

"Yeah!" shouts Julia.

"Oh, no . . ." says Sam. "Angie, help . . ."

But I ignore him, and Julia grabs his hand and pulls him after her like a recalcitrant child, followed by Coco and Ethan. They're quickly swallowed up by a mass of churning couples on the dance floor.

And here I am. Alone at the table. I wonder again if I can just crawl under it and hide.

This is why people don't dance in bars. Because being the only person not on the dance floor makes you feel like a fucking loser.

I'm out of here.

I grab my bag and head for the exit without turning back. Sam didn't even think about the fact that I'd be left all alone at the table when he went off to dance with Julia and Coco and Ethan Wonderslime. Even though Sam and I have been practically inseparable for weeks. What ever happened to bros before hos? Not that Julia is a ho, exactly, but you know what I mean. . . . Does everyone just dump their friends when they fall in love or what? Fuck!

Once I'm outside, I angrily light a cigarette and take out my phone. There must be someone I can call, no not Stef, no one like that, but someone to distract me from everything . . .

Gabriel.

The nice guy from Turks. The one with the plane.

Done.

I tap out a quick text.

I think I owe you a dinner for the plane ride. How about a hot dog and a beer?

CHAPTER 28

Back at work. The Gap.

Back at work. The Gap.

Thegapthegapthegapthegapthegap.

You wouldn't think it, in a city the size of New York, but the entire store has literally been vacant since I got here. Midtown Manhattan is not shopping central on a rainy Monday morning. So I've been counting the seconds while arranging and folding and generally trying to look busy whenever a manager cruises by.

I have *literally* been counting the seconds, that's not a figure of speech. I count to sixty, and then hold out one finger behind my back. Then I count to sixty again and hold out another finger behind my back. Every time I use up all my fingers, I move location and try to look busy again.

It's seems like such a long time since I walked out of Pijiu on Saturday night, and yet nothing has happened. On Sunday morning I got up extra early—6:00 A.M.—and got out of the house, and then had a long, silent breakfast alone down at the New Apollo Diner. Great pancakes, bad coffee.

I tried to read the Style section of *The New York Times,* but the words just swam in front of me. So then I stared into space, wondering if Sam had slept over and whether it upset me more to imagine them having sex or to imagine them just kissing and whispering and giggling together in bed, and then getting annoyed with myself for caring when it's none of my business, and then thanking God that I wasn't at home to run into him as he walked out of Julia's room. Because it would be weird. Why? Because it just would, that's why. My thoughts ran around and around and around. I tried to ignore them, but they chased me.

Then I took the subway to work and stared into space and felt my blisters throbbing and tried not to think about anything.

I'm so stupid! Sam and I were always just friends. I know that. I guess I just haven't had a platonic male friend before, so I don't know how to handle it. Of course he's going to date. And Julia has liked him for ages. I need to get a grip. And not think about my twenty-third birthday tomorrow. *Bonjour,* adulthood.

I haven't seen any of the other girls since Saturday night, which has to be a record. Pia texted this morning that she and Aidan commenced some kind of sex marathon after he showed up at the bar, and both took today off work as a "personal day" so they can "try to come up with a solution" (i.e., have more sex). And no one else has been in touch. I guess Coco's been with Ethan and Madeleine's been with Heff. And Julia's clearly been with Sam.

Whatever. I'm not really feeling that social, anyway. I'm just going to meet up with Gabriel tonight for a hot dog, go to bed early, wake up tomorrow, avoid everyone, and pretend it's not my birthday. And work at the Gap.

Argh.

"Excuse me, blondie!" says a voice, and I turn around. It's a gorgeous spike-haired guy wearing such skinny jeans that he absolutely has to be gay.

"How may I be of assistance, sir?"

"I need help with sizes. We need to get my boyfriend, Adrian, a pair of white jeans for a Euro-trash party, and his budget is forcing us here! No offense!"

"None taken. So, what size is Adrian?"

"I'm a twenty-eight regular!" says a voice. I turn around. It's the little hipster waiter from Rock Dog, who spilled lingonberry juice all over me!

"Don't I know you?" Adrian frowns, cocking his head to one side.

"Rock Dog!" I say. "Lingonberry juice!"

"Oh my Lord!" Adrian looks like he's never been so happy to see anyone in his entire life, and quickly introduces me to his boyfriend, Edward. "This is the girl! The girl who gave me that amazing tip on my first day! Wow, honey, you shouldn't be giving out tips like that if you work here."

"I kinda fell on hard times just after that."

"Ugh, retail is *such* hell," says Edward sympathetically. "I worked at Urban Outfitters when I first moved to New York, and it was the longest three months of my life. I nearly got fat because the only joy in my life was Dunkin' Donuts. I am not even kidding."

"Okay, so how about these?" asks Adrian, holding up some white jeans that will be six sizes too big for him.

I look over. "They're good, but I'd recommend trying these and these, too. You never know the perfect fit till you're in it, you know?"

"That is totally my motto in life," deadpans Edward, and Adrian cracks up.

"Okay, boys, come with me. . . ."

Half an hour later, they're both overjoyed. Adrian found four pairs of jeans that fit him perfectly, and Edward got jealous and started shopping, too, and has two pairs of pants and three blazers.

"It's been so much fun helping you guys," I say.

"I never knew I'd love it here so much!" says Edward joyfully. "The fit is totally amazing!"

"So much for coming to the Gap to save money," says Adrian, combing worriedly through the price tags.

"Listen," I say, lowering my voice, "I can get you fifty-percent off if you just hang around twenty minutes. It's coming up on my break, so I'll buy this stuff for you with my employee discount and meet you at the deli on the corner. Sound good?"

"Oh, honey, is that allowed?" Adrian makes an anguished face.

"He's so naive! Of course it is," hisses Edward. "We did it all the time at Urban Outfitters!"

"This feels wrong. . . ." says Adrian.

"No! It's perfect! Angie, honeybun, we'll see you at the deli on the corner in half an hour, okay?"

They head off, and I try to look busy until my break. Then I grab their clothes, head to the register, and flash my employee card.

That dickface Derek is behind the counter.

"This is for you?"

"Affirmative," I say.

"Men's clothes."

"Yep. I'm going to customize them. Make a fabulous long patchwork denim skirt. It'll be sister wife meets Amish wife. A sort of Utah-Pennsylvania hybrid." I give him my smarmiest grin.

He remains uncharmed. "I don't believe you. I think you're buying this with your employee discount and selling it for a personal profit to those two men who were in here before." He pauses dramatically. "You're stealing from the Gap."

"What?! I am not!" I'm genuinely shocked. I mean, yeah, I'm buying this stuff for someone else using my employee discount, but I wouldn't even think about charging them and making money off it. I'm just doing them a favor! I'm bending the rules, not breaking them! "I'm not stealing! I swear to God! I'm not!"

Dickface Derek smiles, revealing very yellow teeth. "I think you are. I've called Shania."

A moment later, Shania, my manager, walks over, flanked by two security guards.

I decide the best defense is offense. "This is outrageous! How dare you suggest I would sell these for a personal profit! I wouldn't do that! How could you accuse me of that?"

She narrows her eyes. "We've had complaints about you from customers, so security has been keeping an eye on you. We were willing to overlook this the other day with your blond friend, but you were clearly cavorting with those two men today."

She must mean Coco. And the complaints could only have come from Stef. Or his bitchy girlfriend, Blythe.

But *cavorting*? Sheesh.

"Shania, I promise," I say, looking her right in the eye. "I swear I wasn't going to sell them for a profit. I was just, I was trying to help them out—"

"By abusing your employee privileges," she interrupts, with an evil little smile. "Angie, I'm going to have to let you go. Employee discount abuse is illegal. It's theft. You're a thief. I could have you arrested."

"I am not!" I respond angrily, and they all just stare at me. Judging me. Ready—no, *wanting*—to believe the worst.

And that's the moment I snap.

"I did nothing wrong! I didn't! I swear! Fucking hell! I wasn't stealing! What the fuck is with the universe? When the fuck am I gonna get a break? THIS IS BULLSHIT!"

CHAPTER 29

A few minutes later, I'm escorted off the premises.

I go straight to the deli to meet the guys, trying not to weep with shock and shame. I fight the tears back, and they all ball up in a lump in my throat. Ah, unshed tears. I wish I knew how to quit you. And of course it's freezing cold, windy, and raining, which just increases my misery. The media has been talking about a superstorm all week, but ever since Hurricane Sandy, they like to freak out about the weather. A little rain does not equal a fucking hurricane, you know?

Edward and Adrian are waiting for me.

"Those bastards," says Edward. "I'm totally boycotting them now. And I hate their ads."

"I am so sorry," Adrian keeps saying. "This is all my fault. I'm, like, your bad luck charm."

"No, no, you're not," I say, my voice unnaturally high, the lump in my throat aching. "I hated working there anyway. I really did. But I just . . . I need money." To try to fake the toughness I don't feel inside, I take a cigarette out of the pack and prop it in my mouth. The perfect accessory to a bad mood. "I'm so fucked."

"Angie!" Adrian claps his hands to get my attention. "First, come work at Rock Dog with me. Screw Gap! Rock Dog is totally fun, you can eat all day for free, and you could still job-hunt for something in fashion. They always let me have time off for auditions."

"You're an actor?"

"You think I'd waste a face this pretty on anything else? And second, I bet Edward can help you network. He's a floral event designer for the biggest names in fashion! You know Donna Karan? Diane von Furstenberg? Candie Stokes?"

I look up. "That bitch?"

Edward cackles. "She is *such* a bitch! But she spends so much on flowers, it's almost sinful. I'm, like, best friends with all her assistants now. They fucking hate her."

"She was so mean to me." I tell them about the day I talked to her in Starbucks and realized, to her, I was nothing, nobody.

My throat-lump dissolves into tears again. That feels like so long ago, and I still don't have a job. I'll never get a job. I really won't. I look down, blinking hard to get the tears to go away.

"Well, good for you for trying, girl!" says Adrian. "Now, I have a piece of advice for you." He takes a deep breath. "Never cry over anything that won't cry over you."

I smile, remembering that day, the bombshell Annabel dropped, everything that happened afterward. . . . God, that feels like so long ago. That was the moment that my life began spiraling out of control.

Oh, let's face it. It's never been in control.

"I know," I say eventually. "I'm just so tired of trying and failing. I'll never get a job in fashion. Never. I'm . . . I'm nothing."

"You are *never* nothing!" Adrian grabs both my hands. "Never, never say that! I'm deeply psychic, and I can tell that you're very kind and honest and loyal and talented. Your future is bright, okay? You just need to hang on. Just hang on, keep trying, and everything will be okay."

I really do start crying at this, but quickly pull myself together. Jeez, I hardly know these guys, but I can't help it. I feel like I've been so close to crying for days, like I'm a cup full of tears and this was just the little prod I needed to tip over. . . .

"Sorry," I say, wiping my face. "I'm such a loser. I can't do anything right."

"You are *not*. Just one break, that's all you need," adds Edward.

"I've been here since last summer!" I exclaim. "And I don't want my life to be like this anymore. I've made too many mistakes here. . . . I want to start over."

They look at each other and sigh.

"You can never start over," says Edward.

"Never," agrees Adrian. "No matter where you are, your problems follow you, so you may as well deal with them. Take it from a man who spent the first five years of his twenties running from city to city, looking for the meaning of life in empty hookups. God, I was such a little slut."

"*Plus ça change*," says Edward, raising his eyes to the ceiling.

"My tip? Hang on to your friends," says Adrian dramatically. "The only thing that will give your life meaning is the people around you. Create a circle of support that will keep you afloat when you feel like you might drown. A life raft. That's what your friends are. A life raft."

"And remember, you may feel like no one will give you a chance right now, but your dream job is out there, so keep trying," says Edward. "When you're intellectually and creatively stimulated by your work, the world is a different place. You feel valued. And valuable. Not just in terms of money, but in terms of what you're contributing to the universe."

"Oh my God! Oscar speech! Goose bumps!" says Adrian.

I nod slowly. Everything he says makes sense. But I don't know if I can keep trying.

Somehow, Adrian and Edward know I don't want to talk about it anymore, and they start chatting about accessories for the Euro-trash party. (Loafers with snaffle-bits and fake tans.) I'm numb as their conversation washes over me.

I was just fired.

From the Gap.

The day before my twenty-third birthday.

Reality really does bite.

No matter how you cut it, this is rock bottom. After we finish our coffee, we exchange numbers and air-kisses, and I head for the subway.

On the way, I automatically take out my phone to call Sam. Weird, right? In just a few weeks he's gone from being an annoying boat boy to being my go-to phone call after I get fired. . . . But I don't want to hear about how the date with Julia went or how much he likes her. I just . . . I don't want to hear it. It shouldn't bug me, but it does.

Then, as I'm sitting on the subway back to Brooklyn, it hits me.

I'm not going to make it in this city. I'll be chewed up and spit out like every other loser who tries to create a life here and doesn't have what it takes. It's obvious. It's so obvious, I can't believe I didn't see it before now.

So why waste any more time?

Next thing you know, I'll be in my late twenties, and then I'll be fucking thirty. Thirty!

I don't know what else is out there in the world, but I know it's got to be better than getting fired from the Gap and living in Brooklyn where everyone I know is happy, in love, and going somewhere with their lives.

Tonight, I'll see Gabriel, just so I can get out of Rookhaven and avoid everyone for one more night.

And to celebrate my birthday tomorrow, I'll book a flight to L.A. I know people there from college; I can crash with them until I get a job. They have the Gap there, right? (That's a joke.) (Kind of.)

And I know what you're thinking. But I'm not running away.

I'm moving on.

CHAPTER 30

"See? Best hot dog in the city," I say. "It's a New York classic."

Gabriel takes a tiny bite of his hot dog and chews like it might have thorns.

"This is not good." He looks around for a napkin, spits his half-chewed hot dog into it. "Not. Good."

We're at Gray's Papaya, a legendary hot dog joint, on the corner of Sixth Avenue and Eighth Street in Manhattan. You can't really sit down here, which means that when we finish our hot dogs in about five bites, this will have been the fastest date in the history of dates. I think that might be a good thing. Gabriel is not quite the guy I remember, and tonight might not be the easy killing-time exercise I thought it would. Gabriel is acting all sorts of precious. He could barely contain his horror when he saw where we were eating and keeps grabbing paper napkins to wipe everything down before he touches it. I mean . . . grow a pair.

Worse? Outside there is torrential rain. Not April showers, but dude-where's-my-ark rain. The kind of rain that makes you want to hide in a dark bar and drink wine and eat cheese and then have crazy dreams all night. But I'm not on a red-wine-and-cheese budget. I'm on a hot-dog-and-papaya-juice budget. So here we are.

And I'm just here for the food. I made it clear to Gabriel this wouldn't be the start of anything romantic or sexual or whatever, plus I'm wearing flats, so it's clearly not a *date*-date. I'm obviously not capable of having a functional relationship, just like I'm not capable of having a functional career. Fuck. What am I going to do with my life?

"What's the deal with the papaya juice?" says Gabriel. He pronounces it "pappa-yah."

"Pa-PIE-ya," I correct him. "It's traditional to have it with hot dogs. I don't know why." I take another bite. God, I love hot dogs. "You didn't put mustard on it," I say. "That's your problem."

"The mustard is not my problem," says Gabriel. "The hot dog is my problem." He looks so serious that I crack up.

Gabriel waits for me to stop giggling, pouting slightly. He doesn't have much of a sense of humor.

"Sorry," I say finally. "Sorry. I know. The mustard is not your problem."

"Okay, that's enough," says Gabriel, throwing his hot dog-filled napkin down. "I take charge now. We go to Minetta Tavern."

"You don't like the dog?"

"I don't like the dog." How to piss off a European dude: don't take dinner seriously. "I want wine and steak and a chair on which to sit. *Sí?*"

"*Sí, señor.*"

"You, stay here."

Gabriel pulls out a mammoth black umbrella and goes to hail a taxi while I wait inside. I think he might be a control freak. He tucked a napkin into his shirt to protect it from ketchup, and then tried to get me to do the same. Um, no. I'm pretty good at not getting food on my clothes since I stopped being able to afford dry-cleaning.

"Angie!" shouts Gabriel. "I have one!"

He runs back with his umbrella to escort me to the taxi.

"Man, it is insane out there!" I say, looking out over the street. The water is running up the gutters and over the sidewalk, and coming down so hard that you can hardly see out the front window.

"Helluva rainstorm," says the driver. "This storm is hitting the whole Eastern Seaboard. They're predicting serious flooding all over the city. We've had three inches of rain in the last two hours."

Gabriel's phone rings. "My sister," he says apologetically. "Lucia? *Qué pasa?*"

I wish I'd paid more attention to Spanish in school. My French is pretty good. Well, my dirty French is pretty good. To kill time, I check my phone. I've been texting some of my friends in L.A., hoping one of them has a place I can crash until I get on my feet.

But it's a text from Sam. It's the first time I've heard from him since Saturday night.

The text reads: *So are we talking yet or what?*

What the hell is that supposed to mean? I reply: *Why wouldn't we be talking?*

He replies: *Aren't you pissed at me about Julia?*

Wow, that's direct. How does he know how I'm feeling? I reply: *Dude, I'm the one who set it up. I'm delighted it went so well.*

He replies: *Uh, have you spoken to Julia?*

I reply: *I've been working.*

He replies: *The night was a total bust.*

I reply: *I saw you kissing in the bar. Didn't look like a bust.*

Sam replies: *Put the crack pipe down. That did not happen.*

Why the fuck is he lying to me? I reply: *Sam, you don't have to lie. I saw it.*

Sam replies: *Angie, we didn't kiss. She whispered in my ear at one point— telling me that guy Ethan is a dick. But we did not kiss. Pinkie swear.*

I frown. Why would he lie about something like that? But I didn't imagine it. Did I?

He sends another text: *Talk to Julia. Total fiasco. We have nothing in common. I figured you were giving me the silent treatment because she was pissed about what a bad night she had.*

The strangest, sweetest feeling of relief floods through me, and I look out the window at the rainstorm, smiling so hard I think my face might crack.

Sam doesn't like Julia. He didn't ditch me. He can still be my friend exclusively. Totally immature, I know, but hey, that's me.

"Angie, we are here." Gabriel nudges me, bringing me back to reality.

Yes! Dinner! Totally!

I shake my head to clear it of thoughts and put my phone back into my bag, just as we pull up to a corner on MacDougal Street.

Gabriel gets out first and walks around the cab to hold up the umbrella for me, though the wind-rain combination means I'm covered in an icy spray in seconds anyway.

Then he pulls open a heavy door and I push past a curtain, into the Minetta Tavern.

CHAPTER **31**

"Now *this* is a New York classic," says Gabriel.

It's true. The Minetta Tavern is how Hollywood would imagine classic New York décor: a long bar, black-and-white-checkerboard floors, dark red leather booths, hundreds of frames on the wall, and the sort of yellowy sepia lighting that makes all the beautiful people glow just a little more beautifully. This is one of my dad's favorite places when he's in New York. He took me here back in January.

And hasn't called since.

Whatever.

Even though it's not yet 7:00 P.M., Minetta Tavern is packed with patrons talking, eating, drinking: all with the kind of animated, joyful gusto that you only see in people who have made a success of their lives. The place is throbbing with self-satisfaction. I don't belong here.

But I want to be successful. I want to get a job. I want to stay in New York. And I want Sam—

Stop! Where did that little voice come from? No, I don't. I want to leave. I want to start fresh in California. I want to get a job in a place that doesn't chew up and spit out its young. I want to go somewhere where I don't feel completely worthless, useless, and restless. Where my life isn't just me, always by myself, ricocheting off everything around me like a tiny pinball trying to hit the jackpot. And Sam has nothing to do with anything.

"Angie!" a voice calls from across the bar, as we're following the maître d' to our table. "Yoo-hoo!"

Only one person I know says *yoo-hoo*. . . . I turn around and see Cornelia, my old sort-of employer, standing at the bar, glass of champagne in hand.

"Cornie!" I immediately assume my perfect fake Upper East Side face.

We air-kiss three times, *mwah-mwah-mwah,* to show how Euro we are. Cornie is a SoHo transplant from the Upper East Side: skinny, blond, pale to the point of translucent, and overly groomed. She models herself on Gwyneth Paltrow, not that she'd ever admit it.

"The notorious Angie!" she says, tilting her head slightly, showing her small white teeth in a tight little smile. "Up to no good, as usual?"

"*Moi?* Straight and narrow, darling," I reply.

The man she's with, a much older silver-fox-type gentleman, smiles at me. He has cold gray eyes and perfectly capped teeth. "I'm Roger Rutherford," he says. "Clearly, Cornie won't introduce us. She's the jealous-in-advance type."

I give my best "how charming" smile and quickly introduce Gabriel.

"Haven't we met before?" says Cornelia, narrowing her eyes. "That fund-raiser at the Boathouse last year?"

"Ah, yes," says Gabriel politely. "We did. I go every year."

Cornelia, Gabriel, and Roger make small talk about the fund-raiser for a moment, while I replay Cornelia's greeting in my brain. Up to no good? What's *that* supposed to mean? I was never late to work for her. I was the model personal assistant. And she said she would call me when she got back to NYC from skiing!

"So good to see you again, sweetie," says Cornelia. She leans in to kiss me on the cheek, and whispers, "Well done on catching such a big fish! Clever girl!"

So I smile and say all the right things and then follow Gabriel through to our table. *Well done on catching such a big fish. Clever girl.* I'm clever for dating a rich guy? If I were really clever, wouldn't I be making my own money?

We sit down at the table and look over the menu. Suddenly, I feel like an imposter. I would never come to the Minetta Tavern if I were the one paying. I can't afford it.

"I'm really not hungry," I say.

"I thought you were always hungry," says Gabriel. "You must order something."

God, I hate being told what to do. But I don't want to cause a scene, not with Cornie nearby.

"Bone marrow," I say. "Followed by the burger. Not the Black Label one, the normal one."

I had the burger here in January with my dad. Maybe I'll just call him when I get to California. He's obviously been too embarrassed to get in touch. And maybe I'll call Annabel back, too. She's been calling me at least three times a week. I know I need to do something about my relationship with my parents . . . I just don't know what that something is.

Gabriel is in a fantastic mood now that he's gotten his own way. He starts waxing nostalgic about the first time he ever came to New York, about what he thinks about the American restaurant scene, about the restaurant his cousin owns in Madrid, about his favorite hotels in the world.

He's is a total name-dropper, but not in the star-fucker sense. He drops names of restaurants and hotels he's been to as if he's qualifying for a Rich Guy Experiences Championship. Per Se, Babbo, Cipriani Downtown, Daniel, Mr. Chow, Hotel Arts in Barcelona, Ushuaia in Ibiza, the Capri Palace in Capri, the Hôtel de Crillon in Paris, the Hôtel du Cap on the French Riviera, Le Club 55 in St. Tropez. Does he ever truly enjoy anything, or does he just do certain things because it's the *thing* to do? A way to show the world that he's made it?

You know, now that I think about it, this aspect of his personality was evident from the start. He missed the salad from his favorite hotel in St. Barts, he had a private plane, an apartment overlooking Central Park . . . I just missed the signs. Or ignored them. Another self-involved rich guy. Well done, Angie.

I glance at his watch. It's a Patek Philippe, i.e., costs more than most people earn in a lifetime. He's wearing a gold signet pinkie ring that I don't remember noticing on the plane, and his clothes—a navy jacket, a white shirt, slim oatmeal jeans—have a casual Euro-fied pressed perfection, topped off by an Hermès belt. His cuticles are flawless, his hair is slicked back with studied nonchalance, his skin is suspiciously supple, even his eyebrows are freshly trimmed.

Money, money, money.

The real question is: why is Gabriel here with me? He never asks me anything about myself; he doesn't know what I want to do with my life. I've never been funny or interesting or, hell, anything around him. He doesn't *know* me. So why would he like me?

He doesn't like me, is the answer. He just likes my shell. A nearly-twenty-three-year-old blond girl in a dress that you hopefully can't tell that I made myself, and a face that looks okay when I've smeared black eyeliner over half of it.

I can't believe I'm in this situation again.

Why did I think he was different from every other guy I've dated? Because he was nice to his sisters?

I don't want to be here.

But I don't want to cause a scene, either.

So what do I do?

My cocktail arrives—a vodka martini with four olives—and I take a massive slug.

"Easy, tiger," says Gabriel, laughing as though he just made the funniest joke in the world.

My phone beeps again. I look quickly: it's Pia.

We need to talk. I'm moving to San Francisco.

I look back up at Gabriel. "Would you excuse me?"

I walk through the restaurant, to the tiny ladies room in the very back, and call Pia. There's no answer: either she's screening and she thinks I'll be too upset to talk to right now, or she's having sex (ew), or—most likely—she texted Julia at the same time and Jules called her first.

I leave a quick message.

"Ladybitch, call me. I think—I mean, I *am*—I'm leaving, too. I'm leaving New York. I guess that's the end of Rookhaven. . . ." I feel a stab of sadness. No more Rookhaven? No more *us*? I clear my throat and force myself to keep talking. "Um, see you later? Maybe?"

Then I get another text, from Sam.

Being ignored makes Sam sad.

I reply quickly. *Not ignoring you I swear. Am on a date with a guy who I think might be a pompous fuckpuppet.*

Sam replies immediately.

Name, vital stats?

At that moment, Cornelia walks into the bathroom.

"Angie, what a surprise," she says archly, quickly looking around to make sure we're alone. "Are you holding? Let's be naughty."

"Am I—What? No. Sorry," I say, quickly realizing she means cocaine.

"Don't worry. My guy is on the way. I need it to get through a night with the Rog."

"He seems nice," I say. Considering he's at least thirty years older than you.

"He'll do. He's divorced, knows *everyone,* and is richer than God, so all those bitches from Spence will be impressed." Cornelia shrugs, her gaze falling to my gold clutch. It's the soft, perfect, hand-hugging one I made all those weeks ago from secondhand Art Deco scarves. "Love, love, *love* the clutch. Who is it?"

"It's, um, it's me," I say. "I made it."

"Bullshit."

"No bullshit. Look, no label. Uh, I need to get back to my date."

"Of course you must. Duty calls!"

She turns her head. I'm dismissed again.

I head back to our table, where great sticks of bone marrow are waiting for me. They really are bones, I realize, slightly belatedly. I sort of thought they'd scoop the marrow bits out of the bone for me and make them pretty. Apparently not. I'm supposed to do it myself.

"Ah, Angie, you're back," says Gabriel, who ordered a very boring goat cheese salad. "Bon appétit."

I smile at Gabriel, take my fork, and look at the great sticks of yellowy bone stretching out in front of me on the plate. What animal is this again?

I don't want to eat it, but I don't want to look like I didn't know what I was getting myself into, either. I ordered it; I'm damn well going to eat every bite.

Then I'm gonna get the fuck out of here, go back to Rookhaven, and start packing.

So I dig out the marrow with my fork, smear it on my buttered bread, sprinkle some salt on it, and chow down. It's a strange, strong, meaty taste. Sort of rich and fatty. I take a slug of martini to cleanse my palate.

"Taste the wine." Gabriel is way too bossy. Who cares? Just get through the meal and go home.

So I take a sip of wine. It's delicious, a pretty standard Châteauneuf-du-Pape. My dad knows a lot about French wine, and somehow, I picked it up. It dawns on me that practically everything I know came from my dad. Except for how to sew.

"It's great," I say.

"Can you taste the earth? The berries? There is a chocolaty edge in this particular year, I always wonder why, and I always order it when I come here. . . . I keep studying wine, and I love it. But I will never truly understand it."

Oh for fuck's sake. Who *says* shit like that?

At that moment, Gabriel reaches across the table and places his hand over mine. I stare at it, unsure whether to snatch my arm away or just let my fingers go limp in the hope he gets the picture.

Then he starts talking.

"Angie, I know you said no romance, nothing serious. But I have to tell you . . . I've been thinking about you ever since we met."

"No kidding." I haven't thought about him. Not once. Not until I needed a distraction. An escape from reality.

"My last girlfriend was very . . . challenging," he starts talking again. "She was Spanish. Passionate, beautiful—"

Gabriel goes on about how amazing his ex was for a few *really* long minutes while the waiter clears our dishes.

"So, Angie. Tell me about you," he says finally.

I blink. Did he really just ask me about myself? That's the first time tonight.

"Um, you know. I'm . . . me. I'm trying to get a job in fashion, I work in, uh, in retail, I live in Brooklyn. . . ." How typical that the moment someone actually asks me about myself, I have nothing to say. "Your average twentysomething struggling to make ends meet in New York."

"You need money?" he says.

"Everyone needs money," I reply, taking another slug of wine. "You can't survive in this city without it."

"Where do you work?"

"The Gap. Well, I did. I was fired yesterday." I look him right in the eye, daring him to judge me.

"That did not pay very well."

"Nope."

Our burgers arrive, and I concentrate on salting my fries and arranging my burger.

I'm feeling kind of *woo* from the wine. Red wine always makes me feel a little funky. The heavy ones make me feel like going to sleep. Something to do with the histamines. And I had the worst insomnia last night. I kept thinking about Julia and Sam. How silly I was to be so jealous! Of course he's still my friend. They just had a friendly meal together, that's all. It's no big deal.

Gabriel clears his throat. "Angie? What are you doing?"

"I'm arranging my burger so the first bite is perfect," I explain, looking up at him. "It's really important. The first bite is like the first kiss, you know? It's everything that the rest of the meal will be."

Gabriel smiles at me. "You are a romantic."

"I am."

"I am a pragmatist."

"Really."

I take a big bite of burger, just as Gabriel reaches in his pocket, pulls out a card, and puts it next to my wineglass.

"This is my financial manager. He'll have ten thousand dollars waiting to transfer to your account on Monday."

"What?" My mouth is full of burger, but suddenly, I've forgotten how to chew.

"You shouldn't have to suffer without money. Life in New York is hard enough already. It is a gift. From me to you."

I swallow my food and stare at Gabriel.

Ten thousand dollars. That would mean I wouldn't have to leave Rookhaven. I wouldn't have to get another job in retail hell. With ten thousand dollars, I could try to get unpaid internships in fashion without worrying about rent and money, I could take a course in fashion design, I could survive for months, I could—I could—

But I can't. I can't do it. I can't take money from a guy in exchange for . . . whatever this would be in exchange for. I can't knowingly walk into a life that exists on the fine line between a girlfriend with spending money and a girlfriend for hire.

I look at Gabriel as he takes a bite of his trout, totally unconcerned. As if he hadn't just tried to buy me. He glances up. "My sisters would love to see you, by the way. Would you like to come to our house upstate this weekend?"

I take a deep breath. "No."

"You have plans? You can change them. It's Lucia's birthday, we're having a family party—"

"No."

I push my chair away from the table, stand up, drink all of the wine in my glass, grab my clutch and coat, and hand him back his financial manager's business card.

"Thank you for dinner. I don't want your money. Good-bye."

And with that, I stride out of the restaurant, past Cornelia and her ancient suitor, past all the crowds of beautiful people at the bar, feeling a sort of sick euphoria.

I just walked away from ten thousand dollars.

I could have solved all my problems; I could have made my life easy. But I didn't.

I did the right thing, instead.

Then, just as the door to the restaurant closes behind me, I bump into a couple sheltering from the rainstorm.

Oh. My. God.

My father.

And a woman I've never seen before. Thirtysomething, brunette, slim.

They're kissing.

CHAPTER 32

"What the fuck is this?" I say.

My father's face lights up. "Angelique? Sweetheart! I didn't—"

"Didn't know I'm living in New York now? Didn't know you were going to run into me? Didn't know that maybe you should call your daughter to tell her you're getting a divorce?"

Suddenly I'm furious, really truly spitting with anger that my father could be passionately kissing some strange woman outside a New York restaurant, sheltering from the rain like something out of *Breakfast at* fucking *Tiffany's*.

"And who's this? Some slut you picked up in a bar? Or does she work for you like all the others?"

The woman recoils as if I've slapped her. She's dressed very Midtown chic, you know, not quite flawless enough for Uptown, nowhere near edgy enough for Downtown.

My dad stares at me in shock. "Now, wait just a minute—"

"Annabel told me you were getting a divorce weeks and weeks ago," I interrupt him. "And I heard nothing from you. Not a word. After everything I did for you, after keeping all your fucking secrets for all those years—"

"Your mother told me you wanted to be alone—"

"Bullshit!" I snarl. "You didn't need me anymore, so you didn't bother. Do you even remember that today is my birthday?"

"Oh, God!" My father looks dismayed. "Honey, I swear—"

"Stop LYING!" I scream as loud as I can, and everything around us goes very still and silent.

My father stares at me, mouth open, unable to say anything. I thought he looked like George Clooney when I was little. I don't anymore. I think he looks like a fucking circus showman.

"It's true, your mother told him you didn't want to hear from him," says the slut. "I was there when we all met up to discuss arrangements."

"And who the fuck are you?"

"I'm—I'm Veronica," she says, her eyes suddenly wary. "I thought you knew—"

"Knew what?"

My father puts his arm around her and smiles proudly. "Veronica's pregnant. We're getting married."

I don't really know what happens next.

I think I scream, because my ears are ringing and my throat is raw and I can't breathe and I start running away from them, but they don't follow me anyway, then I'm running and running into the black night. There are no cabs and I don't know where I am but I keep going anyway, through the storm, through the rain and the wind that feels like it might blow me away entirely. My brain can't hang onto any thoughts, and I think I'm hysterical but I don't know because I feel, I honestly feel like I might be losing my mind, like I want to run away, out of myself, out of my life.

I wonder if my mother knows, and how she feels about it, and if she's upset, and I think back to those Christmases when the three of us opened my stocking in bed together with raisin toast and cuddles and everything was warm and good and simple.

I miss simple.

I fall down at one point, into a giant filthy gutter puddle, and force myself up and walk and walk until I don't know where I am. The rain is so heavy I can hardly see across the street. Store awnings are banging in the wind, the gutters are thick furious rivers, there's not a single other person on the street, and it's so dark and crazy, it feels like the end of the world.

My head hurts and my stomach hurts and I have these weird blunt pains in my chest. Oh God, where am I?

Eventually I'm too tired and wet to walk anymore. I sit on a little children's climbing frame in a playground, in the freezing darkness and pouring rain, shaking from the cold and crying because my life is fucked. I'm lost and cold and I don't have a job or any money or any future or any family.

I have nothing. Nothing.

At that moment, my phone rings. It's Sam.

"Hey! How's the date?"

"Sam—Sam—" I can hardly speak. Immediately his voice changes.

"Where are you? What happened? Angie. Stop crying. Tell me where you are and I'll come and get you. You shouldn't be out in this storm—"

I look around, trying to see a street sign. "The corner of Spring and Mulberry, in the playground. I'm fine, I'm fine, it's just, my dad—he's getting married again, he's having another baby, I know, I'm a fucking loser for crying, I can't—"

"Stay there. I'm coming."

I don't know what to do with myself, so I stay here, in the playground, feeling every last inch of me get soaked all the way through. Right this second New York feels empty, totally empty, and I am completely alone.

Then minutes—or hours—later, Sam turns up, jumping out of a black town car, and I stand up and look across the playground.

Our eyes meet, the rain still hurtling down, like a million tiny shooting stars lit by the streetlights.

And in that split second, everything becomes clear.

I love Sam.

I loved him from the moment I saw him on the pier in Turks and Caicos. I loved him when he followed me all the way to shore, I loved him when he brought back my stuff, I loved him when he saved Coco's life at the surprise party, I loved him when he helped me hand out lattes and CVs, I loved him when he comforted me after my *Kramer vs. Kramer* meltdown, I loved him when I woke up in his arms, and I loved him when he walked into the bar after his dinner with Julia. I love everything that he does and everything that he is. He's honest and real and true. He's everything I want to be.

For several long seconds, we stare at each other through the rain.

Then I run over to him, to my Sam, my gorgeous Sam with his perfect frown. Everything about him that I know so well. Everything that I love. And I know, *I know*, that he loves me, too.

"Sam—"

I tilt my face up to his. Our lips are nearly touching, so close that even the rain isn't coming between us. It feels, for a second, as the storm rages around us, that the wind is buffeting us together, like we're the only people in the universe.

"Angie—"

I shake my head. "Shut it. Just . . . just shut it."

He grins down at me, and we stare at each other.

This is the prekiss.

This is the moment that I always wish could last forever.

And for several very long seconds, I think it might.

But I want to know what happens next. So I reach my arms around his neck and pull him toward me, and our lips finally touch.

And *bang*. My brain is empty, but I feel like I'm going to burst, and everything bad that's happened to me, everything bad I've done, everything I'm always worried about, just disappears. Like magic.

We kiss and kiss and kiss. Then I pull back and I cover his face in frantic kisses, as though I'm trying to blot up the rain with my lips, until Sam grabs me, kissing me properly again. Oh God, our mouths were made for each other, and we're sort of giggling into each other's faces, laughing and shivering, and his lips are so warm, and his cheeks are so cold, and he smells just *right*. Like rain and soap and sugar and coffee and everything I like most in the world.

I pull back, gaze at him again for a second, and out of nowhere, I say it.

"I love you."

"You do?"

I pause for a second, shocked at myself. I said it out loud. But I *know* it. I know it's true. I've never felt this sure about anything in my life. I've never loved anyone, ever, like I love Sam. I had to tell him.

"Yes. I love you."

"I love you, too."

"You do?"

"I promise. Cross my heart."

Sam smiles at me, the kind of smile I've never, ever seen on him before. And I feel a funny bursting feeling in my chest. I love Sam, Sam loves me. The world makes sense.

He pulls me to him and we kiss again, kiss and kiss and kiss, until my lips are chattering so hard that it's no longer possible.

"You're freezing. Let's get out of here."

"Your place," I say. "Not Rookhaven." I only want to be with him tonight. Not the noise and drama of Rookhaven. Pia is leaving, I'm leaving, the entire house is imploding . . . but I'll deal with that tomorrow.

Sam leads me out to the street, where the car is waiting for us.

Such a strange sensation: I'm holding Sam's hand. But everything about this just feels *right*. Exciting, safe, and lovely. Like Christmas morning.

He opens the door for me. It's a high-end town car, little Evian bottles in the back, Kleenex, magazines, the whole deal.

"How can you afford this?"

He shrugs. "My roommate, Pete, has an account. Don't worry, he's away."

"How thoughtful of him."

Before climbing into the car, Sam looks back at the playground quickly and sees something.

"Just a second," he says.

Then he runs over to the climbing frame, picks something up, and runs back to the car. It's my gold clutch. I must have dropped it. It's soaked through, but it's still good.

"My clutch! Thank you!"

Sam closes the door. "Back to Fort Greene, please," he says to the driver. Then he turns to me, and I think, for the hundredth time in the past minute, *I love you.*

I lean in and we start kissing again, but I'm shivering from the cold, and my clothes are heavy with rain, so Sam helps me take off my sodden coat. Then he leans back to take off his soaking-wet fleece, and as he pulls it up I get a flash of his brown, muscled torso and my stomach buckles with lust. Holy shit, he's sexy. I grab him and we kiss more, as the car speeds through the storm, shivering with cold and excitement and lust, the rain and wind battering the roof, kissing all the way, until finally the car pulls up outside a nondescript ten-story building. It's the kind of place you wouldn't look at twice from the outside.

Once we get into Sam's building, it's a different story: expensive-looking high-gloss interior, and an elevator that requires a key to take you to your floor.

Sam inserts a key and presses the top button.

As the elevator whooshes up, I turn to him and frown. "Your friend lives in the penthouse?"

He takes a deep breath and nods. "Come on in."

CHAPTER **33**

"The penthouse?" I repeat. "Seriously?"

Sam just shrugs and smiles.

The elevator opens straight into the apartment, and my jaw drops. A huge loft-like space with wall-to-wall windows looking out over Brooklyn and Manhattan and the raging storm.

And it's decorated with the kind of understated, comfortably masculine touches that you only get from a professional interior designer. This is one hell of a place to sleep on the floor while you're trying to find a job. Why did Sam want to spend so much time with me at crummy old Rookhaven when he could have been hanging out here?

"Holy shit. What is your friend? A captain of goddamn industry?"

I look up at Sam to see if he's laughing, but he's suddenly frowning at me so intensely that my stomach drops and my heart races and oh, God, every cliché I've ever read in any romance novel, ever, and he's just so sexy and this is really happening, he really loves me, too, he wants me, too. . . . I want to kiss him again, but I feel paralyzed with, I don't know, shyness, or fear, or something.

Then Sam pulls me in to him and kisses me again.

And so we kiss. We kiss, standing up, against the closed elevator door. Then take a step toward the sofa, then stop, kissing more, then one more step again. My clothes are drenched and I'm freezing, but all I can feel is Sam's warm lips on mine and his arms around me, all I can hear is our breathing and the storm outside. This is perfect.

When we finally get to the sofa, there's a clap of thunder so loud that we both startle, and pause to look at the awesomely violent storm currently at play over the city. The thunder is making the entire building shake every few minutes, and the rain is coming down in hard, angry sheets hitting the windows with an audible *crackcrackcrack*. The strangest thing of all is that the clouds over New York City are purple and gray, furious-looking and illuminated every few seconds by lightning. It looks almost like CGI.

"Crazy . . ." I murmur. "This must be the best view in the city."

"It is," says Sam, and I look up and see he's looking only at me.

"Cheesy," I say.

"Yeah. That was a little cheesy." Sam kisses me again.

"It's like that hurricane," I say. "Sandy. The one that lasted all night and gave half of New York a blackout for days."

"Actually, this is a derecho, rather than a hurricane," Sam says. "A derecho is a series of storms. All of them pounding across New York City."

"Tell me more about the weather," I say. "You're so interesting."

"And you're such a smartass." Sam grabs me and I give a little involuntary shriek, and we get lost in kissing again, till another clap of thunder draws our attention back to the storm. There are over a dozen lightning storms right now over different patches of the city, like tiny rain gods are fighting wars in the clouds.

"Why did you ask Julia out?" I say, out of nowhere. "I mean . . . seriously. I was so shocked."

"I didn't ask her out." Sam looks surprised. "I thought you knew. She asked me out. We were talking about this Mexican place and I said 'We should go sometime.' I meant all of your roommates, especially you. . . ."

He leans forward and kisses me again. "Next thing I knew, she was texting me about what time she could meet me and that I should pick her up and that she was having first-date nerves and all this stuff, and I just . . . didn't know what to do."

"Oh . . ." I say.

"I tried to call you about it, but you weren't answering your phone. So I just went to the dinner. It wasn't romantic, at all. And the moment we finished our burritos, we came to find you. Trust me, Julia doesn't have any feelings for me. We're just friends."

Sam looks so serious, and so honest, and so fucking gorgeous, that all I can think about is how much I want to kiss him again. We kiss for a few more minutes, until a gunshot-like crack of thunder interrupts us and we both flinch.

"Man, that was loud," I say.

"Did you know you can count how many miles away a storm is by counting between the lightning and thunder?" says Sam.

"Is that true? I thought that was one of those mythical things. Like Santa Claus. And the Tooth Fairy."

"Yeah, right. Like the Tooth Fairy is a myth."

At that moment, lightning whites out the sky, and our eyes lock on each other as we both count silently. Eleven seconds later, a deafening clap of thunder makes me jump, even though I knew it was coming.

"Eleven miles," says Sam.

"It feels like Armageddon," I say. "Not the Bruce Willis one. The biblical one. Hey, Sam?"

"Yes?"

"Kiss me again."

We kiss more, stopping only when I start shivering so violently in my wet clothes that I can't kiss anymore.

Sam gives me a T-shirt with RUTHERFORD written across the front and a pair of green Dartmouth sweatpants. I go to the bathroom to change, but my skin is so cold and drenched with rain that I'm shivering too hard to dress, so instead I decide to take a quick, very hot shower. I wash my hair with his roommate's shampoo and conditioner (Aveda, nice) and wipe away the last inevitable residue of mascara and eyeliner with spit and toilet paper.

Then I look in the mirror. My lips are chapped and swollen, my chin is red and raw with stubble burn, my hair is wet and draggly, I'm not wearing any makeup, and I'm in boy's clothes. I'm a total mess and I don't care. It doesn't matter, because Sam knows who I am no matter what I look like. And he loves me.

I am so happy right now.

I look down and see an open toiletry case. Sticking out the side is an ancient, battered panda toy. Sam's Panda. I smile, thinking about the night he told me about Panda, on the walk back from the hospital after the dinner party. It feels like so long ago.

Holding Panda, I pad back to the sofa and pause for a second, gazing at Sam. He's changed into dry jeans and a long-sleeved T-shirt and is stretched out along the long leather sofa, eyes closed, arms crossed behind his head, a happy smirk on his face. God, he's gorgeous. (And may I just say, his guns are sick.)

Then lightning flashes around the night sky, and I count in my head. One . . . two . . . three . . . four . . . five . . .

"Five miles," says Sam, opening his eyes.

We stare at each other for a few long, silent seconds.

"Is there room for two more?" I hold up Panda.

"Panda! Oh, my God, he's been dying to meet you."

I leap onto the sofa and attack him with kisses, feeling like I'm, literally, physically craving him, like I want to lick and nibble and taste his lips for hours, and even then I won't be satiated. Kissing Sam again, after a period of just a few minutes, feels like coming home. Like every bit of his face and lips and neck and jaw belong to me.

"We should move Panda. He's really too young to see this sort of thing," murmurs Sam.

I grin and place Panda on the coffee table, facing away from us.

"We kiss extremely well together," I murmur.

"I know. Thank God. Imagine if you'd done that whole I-love-you speech in the rain and then I'd discovered you were all tongue or something."

This feels different from any make-out session I've ever had, and I think I know why. He's not grinding an angry hard-on against me. Or frantically clawing at my top or grabbing my ass. I know he's turned on, and I sure as hell am. But unlike every other dude I've ever been with, I don't have the feeling that he's racing against the clock in the endless battle to get laid.

"Why aren't you pawing at me like an oversexed puppy?" I ask at one point.

"Uh . . . do you *want* me to paw at you like an oversexed puppy? And how sexed should puppies be, anyway?"

I laugh, and then think for a second. "I guess not. I'm enjoying the kissing."

"Me too." Sam frowns for a second, as if deciding whether to say anything. "Don't get me wrong, I'd love to do . . . all kinds of things with you. And I will. But I always told myself that if I were ever lucky enough to kiss you, I'd enjoy it as long as I could. Before sex. Before anything else."

"You've thought about kissing me? Since when?"

"Oh, Angie." Sam looks at me and smiles. "Since always. Since you stubbed out your cigarette, called me a nautical Nazi Youth, and swaggered onto the speedboat."

I grin. "That's so . . ."

"Romantic?"

"Sad, actually. Really tragic. Like, what is this, a YA novel or something?"

Sam narrows his eyes in mock annoyance. "You're gonna pay for that."

And boom, we're kissing again, but this time he's trying to torture me. Kissing my neck slowly, so slowly, until I shiver uncontrollably, his bristles scratching my collarbone. Running the tip of his tongue behind my earlobe. Kissing just my top lip, then only my bottom lip, nibbling along my jaw. . . .

It's the sexiest, most excruciatingly divine thing that's ever happened to me, and I find myself gasping, genuinely gasping for air. At one point I actually moan, running my hands through his hair, until I realize I look and sound like something out of one of my goddamn romances, and I shut the hell up.

"Everything about you feels good," Sam murmurs a little while later. "You're just right."

"That's just what I was thinking about you," I say.

"I wanted to kiss you so badly that night we were in your bed. . . . God, I couldn't sleep. I just lay there, listening to you sleep-grunt all night like a baby hippo."

"I do not sleep-grunt! And you nearly did kiss me! The next morning . . . we were snuggling."

"We snuggled? God, and I slept through it? I will never forgive myself." Sam kisses me again. "I love your bottom lip. It's pouty and demanding, did you know that? It never wants to be left out of anything. But then, ah, your top lip, it's all innocent and hopeful. . . . It's so hard to choose my favorite."

"You really shouldn't play favorites. It's not fair."

"I know. And God knows what I'll do when I get to your perfect breasts, it'll be like a sexual *Sophie's Choice*. Okay, are you hungry? Wait, what am I asking. Of course you are. Come on, let's eat."

We head to the kitchen, holding hands. I don't think I've ever felt so happy. I feel like I must be glowing like the goddamn sun.

As Sam riffles through the big steel refrigerator, I take a moment to gaze out at the storm still raging outside, and around the apartment again. It's not at all what I expected from a couple of twentysomething guys sharing an apartment in Fort Greene. I figured it'd be some studio dump, all beaten-up bedbuggy Ikea sofas and dust bunnies. You know, dirty magazines and empty toilet paper roll in the bathroom and a crusty bottle of ketchup in the fridge. But it's serene, stylish, and very clean.

"This place is totally incredible," I say. "Is your friend Pete gay?"

"No, he's not, he just likes to do everything right," says Sam. He looks over his shoulder at me and grins. "How do you feel about grilled cheese?"

"I feel amazing about it."

Sam pulls out a loaf of sourdough bread, some cheddar cheese, and a huge block of butter. Then he takes a big frying pan out of a drawer and turns on the stove.

"This is going to blow your mind," he says, so intensely that I crack up. "Laugh it up, sweetface. Just you wait. I showed Vic how to do this the other day. He said it was the best grilled cheese he'd ever had, and he's been eating grilled cheese since before television was invented. First, we brown the butter."

"You want to burn the butter?"

"*Brown* it. Over low heat. You culinary philistine." Sam leans over to kiss me. "I take it back. You're not a culinary philistine." Then he looks at the pan, bubbling with three giant blobs of butter. "You need to keep stirring it while it bubbles till it turns brown and you can smell . . . ah. Perfect. Now, the bread." He puts four slices in the pan. "We let them hang out in there for a while. Come here again." I grin and lean in. God, I don't think I will ever get tired of kissing him.

After a few minutes, Sam leans back and looks at the pan. "Now we salt them, sea salt only, of course, I know how you feel about sea salt. Add some nice thick slices of cheese to two of the slices, flip the other two over as lids, and put the lid on the pan to let the cheese melt."

"And when do we kiss again?"

"We kiss . . . again . . . now."

Being with Sam is so sexy and giggly and easy. It feels just the way you always hope kissing will feel when you're growing up, you know? Effortless and intimate and romantic. It's just right.

There's a flash of lightning, and three seconds later the thunder claps louder than ever, like a gunshot going off, echoing around the apartment. I jump at the noise and pull Sam even closer to me.

"The storm is getting nearer," I murmur into Sam's lips.

"Are you scared?" he murmurs back.

"Right now, I'm not scared of anything."

Sam shifts his body slightly so he's leaning fully into me against the kitchen counter, and something changes. He's so much taller than me that I can barely reach up and around his shoulders. Isn't it so weird how guys are always taller than you think they're going to be? Or maybe I just think I'm a lot taller than I really am. I don't know . . . oh man, the kissing is good.

After a few minutes, I get the inevitable crick in my neck, and I hoist myself up so I'm sitting on the kitchen counter and we're kissing face-to-face. With my body pressed hard against his, I wrap my legs around Sam's waist and nuzzle his neck until I feel his breath coming out all shaky. I shiver inside with joy at the idea that I'm the person making him feel so excited.

Eventually, he can't take it anymore and pulls me hard against him with a little growl, kissing me even more passionately. This is different kissing now, it's kissing with intent, serious kissing, kissing that's going somewhere, and I know where it's going and I want it so much but I'm scared, though I don't even know why, and I run my hands under his T-shirt and wrap my legs around him tighter and let myself imagine what it would be like to be naked with him, what this would be like if we were in bed, what it would be like to—

Then Sam pulls back and looks me in the eye.

"I really do love you, Angie James."

"I really do love you, too, Sam Carter."

"Now we eat."

So, somehow, we peel ourselves apart, take our grilled cheese sandwiches, and head back to the sofa. Then we eat, sitting sideways with our legs up and layered over each other like two inward-facing bookends. I'm sure he's feeling as tingly with desire and excitement as I am. Wanting someone this much is the sweetest torture in the world.

All I can think is, *God, you're gorgeous. You're absolutely perfect and I love you and know you and trust you, inside and out.*

And looking into his eyes, I know he's thinking exactly the same thing.

I smile and take another bite of grilled cheese sandwich, as a crack of thunder makes the building shake again.

"This is the best thing I have ever tasted in my damn life."

"Yeah," Sam says. "Told ya."

Suddenly, I have a flashback to eating grilled cheese sandwiches with a babysitter when I was a kid. My parents came home early from a party that night, fighting, and I heard my mother saying, "Angelique doesn't need to know!" and my father replying, "You're overreacting! She's a tough little thing!" and my mother yelling, "No! I mean it!" She told me the next day about boarding school, so I figured the fight was about that.

But, maybe it wasn't. Maybe she found out I knew about his affair with his secretary. And didn't want him to make me keep it a secret anymore.

When she told me about the divorce all those weeks ago, she said that I shouldn't be surprised "given what he's been up to over the years." I figured he'd finally come clean about his affairs, or finally gotten busted. But maybe she always knew about them and was trying to protect me from having to know, too. Because a child shouldn't have to keep secrets for—or from—her parents.

Boarding school was the first time I ran away from my problems. Though involuntary, it started a chain reaction of running away that never stopped. Something goes wrong, something's not working, and I leave. Get out. Walk away. Run. Always.

And now I'm running away from Brooklyn.

Is it the right thing to do? Or is it just what I've programmed myself to do as a knee-jerk reaction to every situation? Do I even want to leave now that I've realized how I feel about Sam? And what does he want? All he's talked about since I met him was getting out of here, getting on a yacht and sailing away. So what happens now? Are we a couple? I mean, we are, right? But I can't ask him. We just said I love you, but we also only kissed for the first time like an hour ago. I don't want to sound needy, or psycho, and most of all I don't want to break the weird spell that seems to have been cast over us tonight. The we're-the-only-people-in-the-universe spell.

I look back at Sam and find him staring at me, that familiar intense frown on his face.

"What are you thinking about?" I say.

"Just . . . happy we're being open with each other, finally," he says. "I feel like we have a lot to talk about. I need to tell you some things."

"Sounds gnarly. Okay. I gotta take a leak."

"Oh, wow. You are one classy lady."

I flick him the bird, and he pulls me across the sofa and on top of him for more kisses, until we're interrupted by another clap of thunder.

"Really. When you gotta go, you gotta go," I say.

"Is that from *Annie*?"

"I love that you know that," I say, and lean in to kiss him again before peeling myself off the sofa, as the apartment flashes white again and the walls practically shake with thunder. The storm must be nearly on top of us. Thank God we're safe inside.

On my way back from the bathroom, I notice that my feet are cold. So I duck into the room Sam went into earlier to get me the T-shirt and sweatpants. It's a large bedroom with a desk in one corner and a stack of clean clothes folded perfectly in a laundry basket on the bed. I pick a pair of socks from the top, and sit on the bed to put them on.

As I go to put the second sock on my foot, it drops to the floor, and when I bend down to pick it up I see a picture frame sticking out from under the bed. Probably a picture of Katie, his ex-girlfriend, I think to myself with a stab of jealousy.

I pull the frame out so I can take a good look at her, just as the thunder and lightning finally unite, shaking the entire building with their force.

You've gotta hand it to Mother Nature. She has a hell of a sense of timing.

Because it's not Katie in the frame.

It's a photo of Sam's college graduation.

He's standing next to an older couple who must be his parents. Sam looks younger, yet somehow tired and unhappy. His mom has a kind-but-sad face, very tan with a white-blond bob. And his dad has the same steady gray eyes as Sam, with silvery-white hair, and—

Wait a second.

Sam said he never graduated, he said his dad was dead. But that's clearly his father; the similarity is undeniable.

Suddenly, I realize I know that guy. It's the rich old guy that Cornelia was with at Minetta Tavern just a few hours ago. Roger Rutherford.

What the hell?

Then I look at the T-shirt Sam gave me to wear. It says Rutherford. It's his team T-shirt. Sam's last name is Rutherford. His dad isn't dead and buried in Ohio; Cornelia said he's one of the richest men in New York. This is Sam's penthouse apartment, not some mythical roommate, and Sam isn't a poor college dropout from Ohio slumming it as a boat boy, borrowing clothes from his roommate and trying to get to Europe on the cheap. He's another fucking spoiled New York rich kid with no sense of right or wrong.

And he's been lying to me. Ever since we met.

CHAPTER **34**

I walk out of the bedroom, still holding the picture, my hands shaking, my heart beating painfully, my chest aching with a pain that I know is only just beginning.

"Sam Rutherford." My voice sounds surprisingly strong and calm.

Sam looks over and I hold up the picture, just as the entire building shakes again. Outside the wind is shrieking and the rain is violently hammering against the window. But all I can see is Sam.

Our eyes meet.

And I know it's all true.

He lied. He lied about who he is, where he was from. He lied about everything.

After everything that's happened to me, you'd think I'd have learned that what you see is almost never what you get. That when it comes to instincts, mine can't be trusted. That I'm always, *always* wrong.

But I haven't. And realizing it again breaks me.

"LIAR!"

I throw the picture frame as hard as I can so it breaks, splaying across the floor in pieces.

Sam leaps up from the sofa. "No, Angie—"

I need to get out of here. For once, running away is the right thing to do.

Tears running down my face, I grab my purse, pull on my cardigan, coat, and shoes over the sweatpants and T-shirt, and stuff my dress and scarf in my coat pockets. I feel so hot and sick, I might pass out. Sam is now standing in front of me, desperately trying to explain.

"Angie, wait, I didn't, Angie! No, listen, you're overreacting, please look at me, I didn't want to talk about that stuff, about my family—"

"Fuck you!" I push past him. "I told you things I've never told anyone. Ever. I was so fucking honest with you! And you just . . . you lied and lied and lied!" My voice breaks.

"But no, Angie, I didn't lie. My parents are divorced, my mom is in New Mexico—"

"And your dad? He's dead, is he? How was it, dropping out of college?" I say, jabbing the button for the elevator. "Sam *Carter*! You even lied about your name!"

"No, Angie, it's my middle name—"

"And you pretended you didn't know New York. You grew up here! You probably know it better than anyone! You're not living on your buddy's floor; this is *your* apartment! That was *your* car service! And all that time we spent, counting our pennies, talking about how broke we were, what we'd buy if we could only get jobs—for what? All just to get laid? Just to trick me into bed? Or do you just like fucking with people?"

"No! Angie, it's not like that—"

"Bullshit!" I stab at the elevator button again violently. "More bullshit!"

"This is my brother's apartment, really, it is, I swear, but yeah, I do sort of live here, now, but I haven't lived in the city in a long time and my dad and I haven't spoken in years, I never—"

"Stop fucking talking!" I scream, putting my hands over my ears. "I trusted you! I am so sick of people lying and bullshitting me and just using me to get what they want!"

Sam looks like he's about to cry. "No, darling, no—"

Finally, the elevator arrives. I step in, ignoring Sam's pleas, and press the button for the first floor a dozen times. He tries to get in with me, but I shove him out of the elevator as hard as I can.

"Fuck off! Just fuck off and leave me alone! I never want to see you again."

As the elevator doors close, I see Sam's face crumple with misery. But I don't care. I mean it.

I will never see him again.

Then I collapse against the elevator wall, sobbing. If this is heartbreak, it's not a figure of speech: I'm in real, physical pain. Something inside me has broken and will never heal. My heart, no, my whole *body* hurts.

I finally get to the lobby and look through the glass doors. The storm is raging wildly, the wind howling, the rain coming down so hard and fast that I can hardly see out of the building, let alone across the street. I've never seen a storm like this.

But I have to get home.

So I take a deep breath and push the doors open.

The moment I leave the building the ice-cold rain hits me, like a solid wall of water.

The trees are whipping back and forth, almost touching the ground, and above the screams and moans of the storm, I can hear sirens and strange cracking sounds. Half the streetlamps are out, giving the whole street an eerie gap-toothed look, and the night sky has changed from gray-purple to a scary green-gray. There are no cabs, not a person in sight. . . .

Oh God, I don't think it's safe to be outside. But I need to get home to Rookhaven.

I need my friends.

I start running. The wind makes it feel like I'm being held back by invisible hands, and the wall of rain is sleeting down so hard it actually hurts.

At the corner I hear a strange squealing sound, turn and look behind me, and—in a split second so surreal that it's almost like I'm dreaming—I see an enormous tree fall over, with an agonizing lurch, across the street, crushing a car. Holy shit.

My heart beating with fear and adrenaline, I push on, ignoring the instinct that's telling me to get the fuck to shelter, listening only to the crazed voice inside me screaming, *Run away, run away.* . . .

Then the hail starts. Chunks of ice smashing down to the ground, but also hitting me sideways, and whipping straight from left to right, like pebbles in a blender, pinging off cars with an audible cracking sound. What the hell?

The sky is now flashing yellow and gray, debris whipping in circles, and the wind is shrieking all around me. . . .

Oh, my God. I'm in a tornado.

CHAPTER 35

I saw a documentary once about tornadoes in big cities. Everyone thinks they only happen in the Midwest, with old farmhouses getting ripped up and landing on witches, cows whipping around looking mildly surprised, all that sort of thing. But they can happen anywhere. And the tornadoes in a city like New York are, in a way, the most dangerous. Because everything—*everything*—becomes a weapon of destruction. Street signs, garbage cans, trees, cars . . . You name it, and the tornado will use it to kill you.

So I do the only thing I can think of: I run right back up the street to Sam's apartment building, around the side, and down a driveway ramp slick with rainwater to the underground garage. It's inch-deep in water already, freezing cold and pitch-black, but it feels about as safe as I can imagine.

I climb on top of a Hummer—a car I've been known to climb on before, funnily enough—and sit there shivering, listening to the storm rage outside.

My cell has no reception, so I'll just stay here until it's over. I lie back, staring at the concrete ceiling as tears stream down my face. They haven't stopped since I left the apartment. *Sam lied.*

I hear cracks and creaks and shrieks and thuds. My imagination quickly goes wild picturing all of Manhattan and Brooklyn flattened, every building smashed to smithereens, every tree uprooted, like something out of a movie—something that matches how I feel inside. *Sam lied to me. He lied and lied and lied. . . .*

I think back to every conversation we ever had, every chance he had to tell me he was a rich boy just like Stef's gang. Instead he said he was from Ohio, that he'd dropped out of college, that his dad was dead. . . . Why? *Why?*

Then, just like that, everything goes quiet. The storm is over. The rain has stopped. But the ramp leading down here has become a fast-flowing river of water and leaves and garbage and—

Holy shit! I'm moving. The Hummer is floating across the garage. I look around wildly. The garage is flooding! Then again, of course it's flooding. It's a fucking basement. It's the first thing that floods. Thank God my bedroom is on the third—

Oh no.

Vic.

The moment I realize Vic could be in danger I climb down from the car, splash my way through the dirty storm water, trudge up the ramp to the street, and run as fast as I can toward Union Street.

Brooklyn is battered. Every single tree has been stripped of any early spring leaves, some ripped out of the earth and thrown across sidewalks and cars; skylights and chunks of roofs and iron gates are lying, bent and twisted, in the middle of the road; car windows are smashed in by hail . . . It's like a war zone.

It takes me forever to reach Carroll Gardens, but I don't even notice the wet sweatpants flapping around my shoes, or how numb with cold my hands are, or the storm-created chaos I pass along the way. I don't think about Sam, or my life, or my problems.

All I think about is Vic.

He's all alone. What if he fell? What if he's trapped inside? People drown all the time in flash floods. He's old; he's probably frailer than he looks.

Finally, I reach Union Street.

"Are the basements flooded?" I ask a woman coming out of her brownstone, just a few doors up from Rookhaven.

She stares at me, her eyes lit up in panic. "Boerum Hill is flooding! The storm drains gave way, it's three feet deep in water! My sister lives up there, and—"

"But what about our street?" I interrupt her. "What about *our* basements?"

She turns and looks back at her brownstone. "Oh . . . shit."

Immediately, the woman turns and runs toward her basement, and with a thud of dread, I sprint the last thirty feet to Rookhaven, going straight to the door underneath our stoop.

"Vic? Vic! Vic!" I pound my hands against his front door, slapping them so hard my skin hurts.

No response. I hold my ear against the door: I can't hear anything inside, but I'm suddenly sure, totally sure, that he's in there.

"VIC!" I scream at the top of my lungs, and then listen again. . . . I think I hear a knocking sound, but I'm not sure.

So I turn and run up the stoop, two steps at a time, fumbling in my clutch for my keys, and let myself into Rookhaven.

"Is anyone home?" I yell.

No response.

I run through the house to the kitchen and out onto our back deck, which is covered in broken branches and still-frozen chunks of hail. From the railing, I can see Vic's backyard: a swirling, churning mass of brown water, lit from our kitchen window. And it's surging toward his apartment.

Holy shit.

Rookhaven really is flooding.

Without pausing to even think about it, I take off my sodden coat and climb down over the fire escape railings, dangle for a few petrifying seconds, and land with a splash in the backyard. The dark, dank water comes up almost to my knees and is freezing cold and flowing fast. I wade, with difficulty, to the door leading to Vic's kitchen. I can see the water pressure changing as I get near the house and feel the pull on my legs: it's swirling, seeping in underneath the glass door, but still rising. . . .

I cup my hands over the glass door and try to look in: nothing but darkness, but again, I'm overwhelmed by the strongest feeling that he's in there. I knock frantically, screaming, "Vic? Are you in there? Vic! It's me, Angie! I'm coming in!"

I try to open the door; naturally it's locked. I look around for something to use to break it open and see an old flowerpot outside the kitchen windowsill. The flowers in it are destroyed by the storm anyway, so I pick it up and smash it hard against the glass of the back door.

The flowerpot shatters. The glass is intact. You've got to be fucking kidding me.

I look around again and see a little wood-and-metal stool that Vic sits on sometimes, floating in the dark water. I pick it up and, with all my strength, swing it as hard as I can against the back door window. It smashes clean through. Then I take off my cardigan and use it to pluck out the broken shards of glass, until there's a hole big enough to reach in and unlock the door from the inside.

As I open it, I'm swept into the pitch-black apartment so fast I fall over, landing face-first in the revolting floodwater. Oh, God, I hope no sewage pipes have burst; it stinks, this water *stinks*. Fighting panic, I push myself up, leaning against the wall to stand up.

"Vic?" I yell. "Vic?"

Nothing. I've never even been in Vic's apartment before, so I don't know where I'm going. I'm going to have to feel my way through the apartment inch by inch and find a light switch.

"Vic? Are you in here? It's Angie! I'm coming!"

Rookhaven is unusually wide for a brownstone, but also long, and from the back of the house to the front is a long way. Especially in the pitch dark. And even more especially in knee-high freezing floodwater.

Calling Vic's name the whole way, I edge through the kitchen, my hands groping wildly in the darkness. I can feel the edge of the counter, a fridge, a sink, and then a door. The water swirls around me, pulling and pushing me, rising by the second.

I wade through the doorway and down a hall. There is a room immediately to my left, and I shout Vic's name again. The hollow echo makes
me sure it's the bathroom, the one that Sam's been helping Vic renovate,
and Vic's not in there. *Sam.* My heart aches for a moment. But I need to
find Vic. Nothing is important right now except saving Vic.

I continue slowly making my way down the hall, smoothing my
hands up and down the walls looking for a light switch. Nothing! Where
are the light switches in this damn house?

Then a space opens up in front of my arms. Thanks to light coming
in the windows on the far wall, I can just see that I'm in the living room
and can barely make out a door on the far right wall. The bedroom. He
must be in there.

"Vic? Vic!"

It feels like forever, but I make it to the doorway and hear a funny
buzzing sound that starts, stops, and starts and stops again. *Bzzz. Bzzz.
Bzzz. . . .*

I peer around, trying to make out the shapes in the room. I think I
can see a bed, and a person lying on it.

Suddenly, I hear a moan.

"Vic?" I say. "Vic, is that you? Are you okay?"

There's definitely someone here. The buzzing sound has stopped, and
I put my hands out to the wall for the light switch.

Found it.

Just as I'm about to turn the switch on the buzzing starts again,
and with it, a strange, tiny spark. For a brief moment the room lights up,
and I can make out a bed, with Vic lying on it. The spark came from the
base of an old lamp on a nightstand that's almost covered in the murky
floodwater.

Oh, my God.

I snatch my hand off the light switch. I'm standing in three feet of
fast-rising water that's about to touch live electricity.

I could be killed at any second.

CHAPTER 36

I do the only thing I can think of.

I reach out to the nearest piece of furniture, a tall dressing table, and climb on it. My clothes are wet and heavy, but the adrenaline is rushing through me and I don't even notice.

"Vic? Vic, it's Angie. Are you okay?"

"Girlie?" I can hear Vic's voice, soft and breathy. "I was fixing the lamp. I was—"

"Did you get an electric shock?"

Vic tries to reply, I think, but all that comes out is a sort of wheezy sound. Fuck! Does he have asthma? The water is about to cover his bed, too. If it does, he'll be killed.

My mind is racing. Could an electric shock cause a heart attack? Does Vic have a pacemaker that could have short-circuited or something? I don't even know. He's about eighty years old; an electric shock probably isn't the best thing that could happen to him no matter what other health conditions he might have.

"Where can I turn off the electricity, Vic? Where's the fuse box?"

"Kitchen," he wheezes. "Above the icebox."

I jump off the dresser, landing with a splash in the still-rising flood-water. It's midthigh now; in just a minute or two it'll cover his bed!

With agonizingly slow progress, I swim-jog down the hallway back to the pitch-darkness of the kitchen. There, I find the refrigerator, and the fuse box above it. I open the door and feel my way along the little switches. What am I doing? I can't remember doing this ever before, in my whole goddamn life . . . but I remember seeing my dad doing it once, when the Christmas tree lights blew out all the electricity in the living room at my grandmother's house. He just flicked the one switch that was facing the wrong way back to the same side as the others.

So, since all these fuses are turned on, and all the switches are facing the same way, all I need to do is turn them back the other way in order to turn them off. Right? Right.

I quickly flip each switch one by one with a satisfying click. When I'm all done, of course, nothing happens.

But now I'm less likely to be electrocuted. So let's call that a plus.

I make my back to Vic's room, my heart pounding with cold and adrenaline and fear.

He's still breathing but now seems to be unconscious. "Vic! Please wake up!" I shake his shoulders, my voice high with panic. "Vic! *Please!*"

I try to pick him up, but I can't budge him. He's over a foot taller than me, and though he's skinny, he still weighs a ton. If I got him off the bed into the water, I could never support him, he'd just sink through the water to the floor. He would probably drown. But I can't leave him here, either. He needs medical help. God! What am I going to do?

He doesn't stir. I put my ear to his mouth—the way Sam did to Coco when she overdosed—to see if he's still breathing. But I'm trembling so hard from the cold I can't feel anything.

Shit. I don't know what to do. I just . . . I don't know what to do.

At that moment I hear a voice at the door. "Vic? Vic! It's Julia, are you okay?"

"Julia! Help me!"

Another voice. "Vic? It's me, Sam!"

What the fuck is Sam doing here?

"Angie?" Julia's voice is high with stress and panic. "Where are you? Where's Vic?"

"He's in here, in the bedroom!" I call. "He's unconscious; I think he was electrocuted or something!"

"How did you get in?"

"I broke in the back door when I saw the flooding, but listen, you need to call an ambulance, okay? Vic's in bad shape and the water's still rising in here."

"I'll call 911!" shouts Julia.

Then I hear Sam's voice, but louder, and I can see the shaky whiteness of a flashlight in the living room. "Angie? Where are you?"

Seconds later, Sam wades into the bedroom. The flashlight is so bright that I shield my eyes. "How long have you been here? Are you okay?"

"I don't know, a few minutes? Vic was conscious before; he told me he was fixing the lamp. I think a lightning strike caused a surge of electricity or something." I ignore Sam's second question.

"Angie, we have to talk—"

"Now really isn't the fucking time, Sam," I snap. "We have to help Vic."

"I was so worried about you out in the storm, I've been combing the fucking streets—"

"Not now! Help me carry Vic out of here!"

In silence, we carry Vic through the floodwater to the front door, where there are two steps up to street level. Thank God Sam is here: Julia and I could never have supported the weight of Vic alone. Outside, the water hasn't even risen as far as our stoop. Rookhaven—our part of Rookhaven—is fine.

We gently place Vic on the sidewalk, lying flat, his head resting on Sam's coat, and I crouch next to him and hold his hand.

Sam checks his pulse and his breath, the way I did earlier.

"I did that already, he's breathing," I say. "But I think it's getting weaker."

Sam checks Vic's hands. "Does he have any injuries? Electric shocks can burn the skin. Can you smell anything? You should be able to smell the burn."

"No," I say. People get *cooked* by electric shocks?

Julia comes bounding back down the stoop.

"Oh, Sam, you are the best, thank you."

"Are you okay?" I ask her.

"Fine, I just got home from work and ran into Sam, he came to check on Vic, and Vic gave me a spare set of keys for emergencies. . . . I was stranded in the office all evening watching the storm. It was insane! I've never seen anything like it! Where were you?"

I can feel Sam looking at me and purposely don't glance up or reply. Instead, I just keep stroking Vic's hand. He stirs, his eyes opening slightly.

"Vic, it's me, Angie, I'm here with Julia—"

"Uncle Vic!" Julia kneels down, clasping his other hand.

"Little Julia? And Sammy?"

"I'm right here, boss," says Sam. "There's an ambulance on the way."

"That's good news." Vic smiles weakly. "Damn electricity."

He closes his eyes and sighs deeply, his exhale coming out in shaky gasps.

"How did you know Vic was in danger, Sam?" asks Julia. "I mean, it's nice to see you! I was just, um—"

"I've been working for Vic for weeks, remember?" says Sam. "Once I saw the floodwater, I wanted to check up on him."

"Wow, that's so good of you!"

A voice interrupts. "Are you okay? Oh, my God, Vic?" I look up, and there's Pia standing with Coco and Madeleine.

"He's fine, I think, we don't know. . . ." I say. "Where have you guys been?"

"We just got back," says Pia. "We were stuck in Manhattan."

"I was with Ethan," says Coco, sounding tearful. "Oh, gosh, poor Vic."

The girls crouch down and start whispering to Vic, but my attention is on Julia and Sam. Something's just not adding up.

"So, um, anyway, Sam?" says Julia. "Is your friend's place damaged? It's in Fort Greene, right?"

"It's fine," says Sam, checking his phone. "Have you checked the rest of Rookhaven?"

"A few broken windows, but that's about it. So, uh, aside from biblical weather, how was the rest of your day? What have you been up to?"

I turn away. I can't look at Sam, that lying scumbag, or see Julia treating him like he's a friend, like she likes him. . . .

Wait a second.

I thought their date on Saturday night was a total bust. So why is Julia still sounding so happy and sort of, I don't know, excited to talk to him? Does she still have a thing for him, after all that Sam said about the date being terrible? Well, I can put a stop to that.

"He's not who you think he is," I snap, looking up at Julia. "He's not Sam Carter. He's a liar."

Julia looks at me, confused. "What do you—"

"He's from New York, not Ohio. He's not some poor college dropout, he graduated from Dartmouth and his family is loaded. And his name is Sam Rutherford."

Julia looks from me to Sam a few times. "I don't—"

"I tried to explain," says Sam. "Carter is my mother's maiden name, and—"

"Oh, my God," says Julia, putting her hand to her mouth and backing away from Vic and Sam. *"Rutherford."* She's staring at me. At what I'm wearing. The Rutherford T-shirt that is obviously way too big for me. And she knows me well enough to know I've never worn sweatpants in my life.

Julia backs away. I follow her, unable to say anything, feeling a desperate sense of panic and shame.

"You've been with him—How could you—You knew how I felt—" Julia is staring at me in total shock, almost whispering. No one else can hear us.

"No, no, it's not what it looks like, I mean, please, Jules, listen!" There's a note of desperation in my voice I've never heard before. Then I say the three little words said by treacherous friends everywhere. "I can explain—"

At that moment, the ambulance arrives, and we're distracted by paramedics running out to treat Vic. We try to comfort him as they load him on the stretcher.

"You'll be fine, Vic, everything will be fine," I say, covering his hand with both of my own.

"This is overkill," Vic grumbles as they slip an oxygen mask over his head.

"I'm going with Vic." Sam jumps in the ambulance, oblivious to the drama between Julia and me. "I'll call his family on the way to the hospital."

Seconds later, they're gone.

Julia turns to me again, her face blank and pale, the words coming out slowly, as though every new thought gives her pain.

"You knew how I felt about Sam. You *knew*. But you've been with him for the past three days. That's why you haven't been home. That's why I haven't heard from him. . . . Oh, my God, I bet he left to meet you on Saturday night. He left the bar just after you, you must have texted him."

"No, Julia, that's not what happened. I—"

But she's not listening. "You knew he was the first guy I've liked in so long, and you ruined it. Just to spite me. Of all the evil, bitchy, mean things to do—"

"No, that's not true, Jules, I promise! It just, oh God, it just happened tonight, I thought I had feelings for him, but I don't, he's just a liar, and he told me your date was a total failure, he said that there was nothing between you, I thought you didn't like him anymore, and—"

"And you didn't even think to talk to me about it? I thought you were my *friend*!" Tears fill Julia's eyes, and she turns and runs into the house.

I turn to Pia and Coco, trying not to sound hysterical. "What the fuck? Sam said nothing happened between them. Was that a lie, too?"

"They didn't kiss or anything," says Pia guardedly. "But . . ."

"She likes him, Angie." Coco is distraught. "She's liked him for weeks. How could you *do* this to her?"

And Coco runs up the stoop. I stare after her.

And the front door to Rookhaven slams shut.

Today I've been fired from the Gap, propositioned by a multimillionaire, found out my father's getting remarried and starting a new family, run through New York in a rainstorm, fallen in love with the guy I thought was my best friend, discovered he was a liar, had my heart broken, survived a tornado, saved a man's life, and accidentally betrayed one of my best friends.

But it's the shocked disappointment of Coco, the sweetest person I've ever known, that truly destroys me. I want to collapse right here, into a tiny ball, and never get up again.

I am a bad person.

I sit down on the stoop, my hands shaking with cold and shame, my breath coming out in hiccup-y gasps. I am too overwhelmed to even cry. Pia sits down next to me and sighs, then puts her arm around my shoulders. Her unspoken loyalty to me right now, even though we've barely crossed paths in weeks, is the only good thing in my entire existence. I rest my head on her shoulder and she kisses my forehead, a motherly gesture that is so tender and loving, it actually makes me feel worse. I don't deserve it.

Everything is fucked.

Then I remember.

"What time is it?" I ask Pia.

She looks at her phone. "Just past midnight."

"Happy birthday."

"Happy birthday."

CHAPTER **37**

"So, you're really moving out?" I ask Pia at 7:00 the next morning.

She nods. "I think so. I mean . . . yes. I am. I want to be with Aidan. I'm going to talk to my boss today, ask if I can work from San Francisco; we have an office out there. . . . But I haven't told the girls yet, so don't say anything, okay?"

Pia and I are in the sunlit kitchen having coffee. Lots of it. I didn't sleep last night. Not because of Sam, or my dad, or even the big black future-shaped hole in my life, but because when I close my eyes, all I can see is Julia looking at me like I'd just stabbed her in the heart.

Oh God, I feel so bad.

Guilt is different from heartbreak. Like heartbreak, guilt is inescapable, it's pervasive, it takes over your every thought. But where heartbreak makes you ache with tears, guilt just makes you, I don't know, *itchy* inside with shame and regret. And it feels like it will never go away.

"I'm leaving, too," I say. "I'm going to L.A. That whole Julia and Sam thing just gives me all the more reason to leave. I've totally fucked up everything here, you know? And I think I should start over. Today's my twenty-third birthday, and it's time I grew up."

Pia nods. "I understand. L.A. isn't that far from San Francisco. We can still meet up on weekends and stuff."

"Come on. You and Aidan won't be living in some couple-tastic dreamworld? Taking long weekends in Napa, going to Lake fucking Tahoe to waterski? Hiking? I'm pretty sure hiking is compulsory if you live in California."

Pia grins and covers my hand with her hand. "Ladybitch, I promise you. I will never hike."

"Doesn't it scare you? Leaving everything you know to move in with a guy?" I ask.

"Scare me? No . . . I love Aidan. Love isn't scary."

Yes it is, I think, but don't say aloud. Instead, my voice comes out in a tiny mumble. "But what if he changes his mind?"

"You think Aidan will change his mind?"

"No, no . . . I just mean, you know. Theoretically. This whole love thing . . . it can just go away, just like that. One minute you're safe and happy, the next minute it's over and you trusted someone you shouldn't have."

Pia stares at me, but I can't meet her eyes. I feel quiet and cold inside.

"You can't be scared of that," Pia says softly. "You have to just . . . hope."

Hope is for innocents and losers. I think of my mother, always hoping things would get better with my father, hoping he'd stop lying to her and come home. . . . How naive can you get? But then I think of Pia, who took so many huge risks last year, always hoping that the perfect combination of optimism, hard work, and luck would see her through. And it did.

Oh God, I don't know. If I try to figure out the world by looking at people in my life, I just get more confused.

I take another sip of my coffee and glance over at Pia. "I'm going to miss you, ladybitch."

"You are?"

"Of course I am," I say. "I'm happy that you're happy, of course, and

Aidan is great and everything, but . . . I mean, I really missed you the last few months when you were hanging out with him all the time. Imagine how much I'll miss you when you're living in a whole other city."

"You did?"

"You're surprised?"

"It's just that . . . you never act like you need me. You never act like you need anyone."

I'm stunned. "Pia, you saved my life when I jumped out of a taxi on the Brooklyn Bridge. You saved my life every time you invited me on vacation with your parents, because mine were such fuckups, and I felt so safe with you guys." I take a deep breath. "And you saved my life when you got me into Rookhaven. You just always save me. You're like . . . my life preserver."

Pia reaches out and gives me a huge hug. "I love you."

"I love you, too."

"God, we are lame," she says, tears in her eyes.

"I know," I say, that familiar painful lump forming in my throat. I'll probably never live with Pia again. And I didn't even really make the most of it while I could. I just got drunk and did whatever I wanted and acted like I didn't care about anything or anyone.

I'm such an asshat.

Pia seems lost in her own thoughts. "Sheesh, I don't know. I should be happy I get to be with Aidan all the time once I move. . . . So why do I feel so depressed?"

"Birthday blues."

"Yeah. I fucking hate birthday blues."

It's strange to have the same birthday as your best friend. Pia and I are so similar. We both act before we think, have a history of bad decisions with men, same silly sense of humor. But we're so different, too. She's a people person, a charming drama queen, a gung-ho-we-can-do-it type, a caring and loud and loyal friend. I'm a loner, I'm tougher, I'm more stubborn, I internalize everything, I'm dreamy and quiet.

And I'm clearly not a loyal friend.

I hate that about myself.

I haven't seen Julia this morning. I think she went into work before I got up. Coco came into the kitchen briefly to pack her lunch, but wouldn't even make eye contact with me, and Madeleine headed off for her morning jog half an hour ago without saying anything, either.

I guess I deserve it.

When I think about how everything in my life seemed complete and certain and perfect for just a few minutes last night, and how I was wrong *again,* and how everything about Sam—the guy I thought I loved!—was a huge lie, I feel a dry, empty sadness deep inside. My friendship with Sam didn't ever truly exist. My heart aches so much, I can't imagine ever feeling good again.

Then I think about how Julia looked at me when she found out I'd been with him, and Coco's reaction, and I am overwhelmed with a tidal wave of guilt and regret. I betrayed my friend.

And that feels worse than heartache.

"I need to make it up to Julia," I say to Pia. "I need to show her how sorry I am."

Pia sighs. "Look ladybitch, it only just happened. She'll get over it. Give her time."

"But I'm leaving for L.A.! I don't have time!"

"You did the crime, you do the time," says a voice, and Madeleine walks in from her jog, pink with sweat and health and exercise and all those things I will never care about.

"Thanks for your support," I snap. "I didn't know she liked him that much. He said nothing happened. I didn't *know.*"

My voice cracks, and I bury my head in my hands. Please, God, don't let me cry in front of the girls.

"Oh, waaaaaah," says Madeleine, stretching against the kitchen counter.

"Stop it, Maddy," says Pia. "It's not funny."

"Sorry," she says, and sits down at the table. "Angie, don't cry, okay? I'm sorry."

"You're so goddamn bitchy all the time," I say, trying hard to control my goddamn tears.

"I was just trying to be cute," she says. "You always make snarky little comments like that."

I look up. "I do? I don't mean to. I'm not thinking about what I say to other people most of the time. I'm just sort of, I don't know, trapped in my head."

"Me too," says Madeleine. "It's a living hell."

This statement is so dramatic and at odds with Madeleine's usual understated manner that Pia starts laughing. I try to smile, but my face feels like it's made of concrete. Heavy and gray.

"How is Vic?" asks Madeleine.

"Fine," says Pia. "Julia texted me. He's staying in the hospital for a few more days."

"Oh, hey! Happy birthday!" says Madeleine. Pia and I both make "let's not talk about it" headshakes. "Sheesh. Okay." Then she turns to me and clears her throat. "Angie, um, I haven't thanked you for what you did at the bar on Saturday night. For starting the dancing, when I was singing? I was so nervous, you know, and self-conscious, but once I saw you dancing, it was like . . . like I remembered how to enjoy myself."

"You're an amazing singer," I say. "Really. You're so talented. Plus, you know, I wanted to show off my amazing dancing skills. I mean, skillz. With a *Z*."

"Actually, you're a pretty terrible dancer." Madeleine grins. "But a good person."

And boom, tears rush to my eyes again. "I am not . . . I'm not a good person." My voice is all shaky. "Everything I do is always wrong. I'm bad, I do the wrong thing, I'm a bad friend, I'm such a bad friend. . . ."

I hold my hands over my face, fighting back tears and regret and misery. Pia puts her arm around me, but this time, I pull away. I can't bear to lean on her. I don't deserve her support.

"Stop with the self-pity," says Madeleine firmly. "Just fix the situation. It's within your control to fix it. Apologize."

"But what do I say?" My voice is croaky with misery. "I'm sorry I kissed that guy you like? This goes deeper than that for her. You know it does. This confirms everything bad she's ever thought about me."

"Just open your mouth and say how you feel," says Pia.

I stare at the kitchen table so long that it starts swimming in front of my eyes.

"I feel like I need a grand gesture or something," I say. "Like, I don't know, I need to show up at Julia's work with a balloon saying 'I'm sorry.'"

"Hell no, don't do that," says Madeleine. "She works in an investment bank, that shit will get her killed. . . . Oh, my God, is that the time? I have to get to work!"

"So do I," says Pia. "I want to stop in and see Vic at the hospital first, too." She turns to me. "See you at home tonight, ladybitch? Maybe you should try to brainstorm some ideas about how to make up with Julia!"

"Brainstorming. For fuck's sake. Such a corporate whore," I say.

Pia winks and flicks me the bird. "Later, ladybitch."

After the girls leave, I try to do just that. I sit at the table and try to make a list of ways to let Julia know I didn't betray her, that I really do value her friendship so highly, that I'm sorry I hurt her.

But I can't think of anything.

So instead, I make a list of things that I wish I could change about my life. In no particular order:

Not talking to my mother
Dad's marriage and baby
Lack of career
Lack of money
No idea what to do with my life
Everything that happened on the yacht
Soho Grand night (??)
The fight with Sam
Hurting Julia

As far as I can see, it's only in my control right now to change two of those things. The first. And the last.

So I pick up my phone and call my mother's cell phone. She answers on the second ring.

"Angelique?"

"Hey, um, yeah, it's me."

"Oh honey! Happy birthday, darling! I was just about to call you, but I didn't know if you'd—I mean, I am so happy to hear from you!"

I don't know what to say. . . . What was it Pia told me? *Just open your mouth and say how you feel.*

"I'm so sorry I walked out on you that day, when you told me about the divorce," I say. "It was a rash and, um, immature reaction. I should have stuck around to talk to you about it. And I'm sorry I've been ignoring your calls."

"Oh, darling ..." My mother's voice is soft with emotion. "I understand. I should have broken it to you more gently, and not in public. Your father had just called me that morning and, well, I was in shock, you see—" She takes a deep breath.

"He's getting married. And she's pregnant." My voice is totally flat. "I know. I ran into him last night." Was the Minetta Tavern just last night? It feels like so long ago.

"I was hoping he'd call you to tell you. . . . I've been so worried about it. I should just have told you."

"No, it's okay. You shouldn't have to do his dirty work for him." And neither should I. "How do you feel about it, Mom? Are you okay?" I can't remember the last time I said that word. *Mom*. I always called her Annabel. I de-Mommed her. Like a punishment. What a brat I was.

"I am. I really am!" Her voice suddenly brightens. "We were finished a very long time ago. . . . And my life is good. I've decided to stay in Boston, all my friends are here and he doesn't own the city, does he? I'm renting the most darling little apartment and I fill it with flowers twice a week, because who can be miserable when they're surrounded by flowers? And I've been so busy with volunteer work. We're throwing a domino party for charity!" She starts laughing with glee. "Can you imagine? Isn't it wild?"

"Sounds killer . . . but why are you friends with those women?" I ask. "The rich bitchy socialite women."

"Honestly, darling? I like them because they're always *doing* something. I know an awful lot of women my age who just do nothing with their lives. They just watch TV and gossip. It's depressing. And, well, they pay me very well to help organize their functions. I'm not relying on your father ever again, in any way, shape, or form. It feels wonderful."

My mother likes to work. Revelation.

"Now, I didn't know what you wanted for your birthday, so I simply transferred fifteen hundred dollars to your account. A little birthday surprise."

"No, no, I don't need that," I say quickly. "Really, Mom, I swear—"

"Too late, it's all done! Come on, if there's one thing I remember about being twenty-three it's that I never had enough money. . . . So what else is new with you, darling? How's Pia?"

And boom, we start talking, *really* talking, for the first time in years.

I tell her all about Rookhaven, and my roommates, about how I've been trying to get a job and working at the Gap. . . .

"And boys?"

I sigh. "I'm failing there, too."

"It's not called failing, darling. It's called living. Just keep trying. It's the trying that makes it fun. If you want to go to L.A., I think it's a wonderful idea. The most important thing to me is that you're happy."

I think about that for a moment. . . . Okay, maybe she shouldn't have sent me away to school without asking, but she thought she was doing the right thing. She was only trying to make me happy.

While I did everything I could to make her unhappy. But I know I can't fix that in one phone call. It'll take time.

She continues. "I'm so glad you rang. I didn't know whether you wanted to hear from me; I've been thinking about you so much."

"Me too, Mom." I pause. "Maybe you could come out to L.A. to see me. Or I'll come to Boston and see you."

"Of course! I would love that! Anytime. I love you."

"I love you, too, Mom."

As I hang up, I'm smiling.

Who can be miserable when they're surrounded by flowers. . . .

I have an idea.

CHAPTER **38**

"I can't *believe* you get to live in that brownstone." Edward claps his hand over his mouth in disbelief. "Do you have any idea how lucky you are?"

I look up at Rookhaven. "It's nice, huh?"

"Nice? Amazing is what it is. You're brand-new to the city and you land a place like that? Do you know what my first apartment here looked like, before I met Adrian? It had bloodstains in the bathtub, Angie, and the remnants of chalk body outlines on the floor."

I crack up. "I know, I know. I was lucky."

"And you're talking about leaving," Edward says, opening the back of his truck. "You're out of your cotton-picking mind."

I'm standing outside Rookhaven with Adrian's boyfriend, Edward, the guy I met in the Gap, next to his floral delivery van. His second van is right behind us.

And we're going to fill Rookhaven with flowers for Julia.

The moment I got off the phone with my mother this morning, I texted Adrian to get Edward's number, then called him and explained the situation. Together, we tracked down every hydrangea—Julia's favorite flower—in New York City. Enough to fill the hallway and living room and every bedroom in Rookhaven. And every other place I could think of.

It cost over half my birthday money, even though Edward got me a serious discount. Never underestimate the cost-cutting power of a florist on a mission. But it was worth it. It's going to look *amazing*.

Edward's even loaning me vases. And two of his delivery boys to help unload and arrange the flowers. He won't take any extra payment for his help, either.

"It's for a good cause," he scoffed, when I tried to protest. "I told you that you need your friends to survive in this city! You do whatever you can to hang on to them. Anyway, I owe you. We got you fired from the Gap, remember?"

Even with four people, it's backbreaking work to unload and arrange all the flowers and vases perfectly. Every time I climb the stoop, I glance down to Vic's apartment. The front door is open. I hear occasional thumps and shouts, and there's a big generator outside, with hoses going in and out. I guess they're pumping all the water out. I wonder if Sam is in there, helping to fix everything. But if he is, he's avoiding the front door.

Well, good. I don't want to see him anyway.

An hour later I'm sweaty and pink, and Rookhaven is transformed. Huge pots bursting with hydrangeas line the stoop, and inside, every room is overrun with gorgeous blooms, nestling in vases of every height and size. After the longest, coldest winter I can remember, it's like the house exploded with spring.

And when Julia gets home from work tonight, she'll see her favorite flowers everywhere she looks.

Maybe that will help her to consider forgiving me for being such a bad friend.

"Thank you," I tell Edward, when the place is done. "I could not have done this without you."

"Not a problem, sweetface," he says, triple-cheek-kissing me good-bye. "By the way, my heartbreak radar is going bananas around you. You wanna talk about it?"

I gaze at him. My body is so tired of making tears that I can't even muster up a throat-lump. "I think if I started talking about it, I would break into little pieces."

"Oh, honey." Edward sighs and gives me a huge hug. Man, I am really into the hugging thing these days. It's so goddamn nice.

I head upstairs to take a long shower and dress. Later, when Coco gets back to Rookhaven from her preschool, I can hear her mewing with delight as she walks up the stoop. When she walks into the front hall, her jaw drops. "Wowsers! Oh, my God! This is so awesome! Who did this?"

"I did," I say, from my vantage point by the kitchen door.

Coco's smile drops when she sees me. Sisterly loyalty trumps friendship. Every time.

"It's for Julia," I say quickly. "I want to tell her that I'm sorry about Sam, I'm sorry that I hurt her. You know, he told me they were just friends, that the date was terrible. And I had this crazy evening, um, anyway, no excuses, but I thought I had feelings for him. And we didn't sleep together, we just kissed."

Coco looks at me for a few seconds, narrowing her eyes suspiciously. "I always wondered why you didn't *like* like him. You get along so well, and he's so, you know, gorgeous."

"We were just friends. I swear. Last night, I thought that maybe there was something more there. . . . But I was wrong. He's a total sociopath. He said he was Joe Normal working on yachts to make ends meet, and it turns out he's just the kind of rich, entitled, lying fuckpuppet I've been trying to avoid."

"Why?"

"What?"

"Why did he lie?"

"Because that's what people do. People keep secrets and people lie."

"No, I mean . . . why would he lie to you? He's been working on yachts for years, right? It's not like he was doing it just so he could lie if he ever met a girl called Angie who hates rich boys."

I stare at Coco, trying to cover up my genuine surprise. "Are you telling me that everything isn't all about me?"

She giggles.

I take that as a sign of forgiveness. "Coco, I swear I would never try to hurt Julia. . . . I'm going to write her a little note, okay? Can you give it to her when she gets home?"

"Where are you going?"

"I'm going to visit Vic at the hospital."

Plus, I want Julia to see the flowers, read the note, and then decide if she forgives me without me being there. When you're angry at someone, sometimes just seeing them is enough to make you blow up. This is like sneaking in the side door and asking for forgiveness.

It takes me a while to write the note. I'm just not used to expressing how I feel. But finally, it's just right. I hope.

> *Julia,*
>
> *I'm so sorry about Sam. I don't know how much you want to know, but this is the truth: he told me that you and he had a bad date, that you were just friends. I'd just found out some stuff about my dad. I was upset, he was there, we kissed. I thought I had feelings for him. I was wrong.*
>
> *I would never, ever intentionally hurt you, and I hate that I caused you misery. Our friendship is the only thing I'm proud of since coming to New York. I really hope it isn't over.*
>
> *I'm sorry.*
>
> *A x*

Then I pick up my little gold clutch, the one I made all those weeks ago, and walk to the hospital. It feels good in my hand, this clutch. I guess I have to leave Drakey and my sewing machine behind when I leave. . . . I hate that. But I can just get new ones in L.A., right?

Today is the first time in ages that I can remember the afternoon sky being blue, truly blue. Like the storm ushered winter out and washed everything clean. It felt like the cold would last forever this year, but it never does. Spring always arrives eventually. I should really stop being surprised by that.

"Knock knock . . ." I whisper, at the entrance to Vic's hospital room. Vic is lying in bed with the *New York Times* crossword, wearing pale blue pajamas. "Why are you doing the crossword?" I ask. "What, you like being stressed out?"

"Girlie! Hiya . . . What, you mean this?" He gestures to the newspaper. "It reminds me of my wife. Eleanor did it every day, from 1942 when it started, and she was just a teenager, until the day she died. So every day I try to do it, just like she would, and I say to myself, damnit, Eleanor always knew how to make my head spin."

"She sounds smart."

"She was smart. And difficult and wonderful." He folds the paper up and puts it on his little sliding hospital table. "Like all the best things. Take a seat."

"How are you feeling?" I ask. It's weird seeing Vic in pajamas. He looks almost more vulnerable than he did when he was lying unconscious, fully dressed and soaked with floodwater, outside Rookhaven last night.

"I'm fine," he says. "Enough voltage went through me to start a car, can you believe that? From that damn lamp. I was paralyzed. . . . It threw me onto the bed. Next thing I know, you were there. My little guardian Angie."

I laugh. "No one's ever called me that before."

"You ever been electrocuted?"

"Nope."

"It's strange." Vic's voice is suddenly hoarse. "For a few seconds, the entire world flips. I knew what was happening, but I couldn't move, I couldn't do anything about it. . . . I feel like I'm still catching my breath."

There's an impatient knock on the door. A nurse. "Excuse me, visiting hours are over."

"This is my granddaughter."

"She signed herself in as a friend."

"Well, we're a friendly family. I have five granddaughters. They're very important to me."

I turn to Vic and he winks at me. But he does look tired.

"I should go, anyway," I say. "You rest. Will you be coming home tomorrow?"

"I promise." Vic smiles at me, his craggy old face creasing up. "You be good to that boy of yours, you hear me? He's a keeper. One of the good ones. He stayed with me in the hospital all night, you know that?"

"He did?" I'm surprised, though I shouldn't be. That's just the kind of thing Sam would do.

But he's not my boy.

"Didn't leave my side until my niece turned up this morning. You know, I've never seen a storm like that in Brooklyn. People could have been killed. I'm just glad luck was on our side."

I walk out of the hospital, Vic's words ringing in my ear. *One of the good ones.*

Ha.

For a few seconds the other night, my entire world flipped, too. For a brief moment, I loved Sam and Sam loved me, and everything made sense. I thought it was real. The kind of easy, warm, true love you always read about in romance novels. (Well, I always do, anyway.) For the first time in my life I felt . . . full. Complete.

And why *did* Sam make up all those lies? He must have a reason. I could find out right now. I could talk to him, I could let him explain. . . .

But I won't. First, it would upset Julia, and second, I have to go buy a plane ticket to L.A. with the rest of the money from my mom. It's time to start over. I won't have any spare cash, but I'll get a job as soon as I land—at the goddamn Gap if I have to—and figure it out from there. Life *will* change.

My phone is ringing. I look at it: Cornelia? What does she want?

"Hello?"

"Angie! Sweetie. Emergency! I need you. The Met Ball is tonight, and I picked up this fucking douchebag PA in France who just left me high and dry, the hairy bitch. I'll pay you twice the usual; I just need you to organize the car and things like that. How quickly can you get here?"

I look at the time. It's 5:00 P.M. "I'm in Brooklyn. I'll be there in thirty minutes."

"I am so fucking sick of everyone living in Brooklyn. Make it faster!"

And click, she hangs up.

CHAPTER 39

Cornelia lives in a loft apartment in the West Village. It's all boutiques and trees and tiny cafés, the kind of picture-perfect Manhattan neighborhood that makes you feel a mixture of longing and resentment.

She's also going through her "downtown intellectual slum" phase, or at least that's what her mother told my mother. (Cornelia's mother is a Boston society doyenne who married Cornelia's much older and very rich father, moved to New York, and had Cornelia and her brother. She moved back to Beacon Hill in Boston two years ago, about a minute after he died.)

The loft was professionally decorated, naturally, and it's perfectly disheveled arty chic. Piles of books (that she hasn't read) everywhere, lots of bijou Paris flea-market finds resting on $15,000 side tables, thick plush carpets and big fat sofas, you know the drill. Slightly overstuffed with things, slightly too impeccable, and all with that immaculate sparkle you only get with a full-time housekeeper.

I'm buzzed in and arrive to find the loft in a state of uproar.

"FUCK!" I can hear Cornelia screaming from her bedroom. "This is a FUCKING nightmare! Why does this shit always happen to me?"

"Hi, Cornie!" I call. "It's me! Angie!"

I quickly kiss her makeup artist hello. His name is Keith. We bonded last year during the holiday season, when Cornie went out every single goddamn night and I was the idiot running around picking up the right shoes and trying to help her borrow the right jewelry and making sure she had spare Spanx and extra MAC Face and Body Foundation and ugh, *everything*.

But the pressure of that is nothing compared to tonight. The Met Ball is a $25,000-a-seat gala held every year to celebrate the opening of the Metropolitan Museum's fashion exhibit at the Costume Institute. For the fashion world, it's like the Oscars plus Christmas plus New Year's Eve combined, and everyone who is anyone attends, from designers to *Vogue* editors to models to fashion-aware celebrities, and even sports stars, all wearing the most exquisite, glamorous dresses you've ever seen in your goddamn life. If you're into fashion, the Met Ball is your mecca.

"Hi, sweetie," Keith whispers. "We're in for a *rough* night."

"Angie!" screams Cornie. "Come here! Fuck!"

I run through the living room and down the tapestry-lined hallway into the pristine white-on-white master bedroom, through a walk-in closet (which, honestly, is bigger than my bedroom and would make you cry with envy) to the dressing room, where Cornie is staring at herself in the mirror while getting her hair blow-dried by Bibi, her personal hairdresser.

"Bibi, stop," she orders, clicking her fingers. "Angie. Lauren just texted me. That bitch Olivia is wearing the same Zac that I was going to wear. Little whore. I need to speak to Zac about it. Get him on the phone."

"Um, okay—" I walk back out to Keith. "I need Zac Posen's number."

"Well, only *Cornelia* has *that*." Keith has a habit of speaking in italics. "She's *freaking out*. She *only* got a ticket because this *Rutherford guy* is on the *board* or some shit." He lowers his voice. "This is *way* out of her league."

"Angie!" Cornelia is screaming. "Do you have Zac yet?"

Suddenly, I understand why she's hysterical. Cornelia's been swimming around the lower echelons of the socialite food chain for a couple of years. She's rich, but not superrich. She has a car service but not a permanent driver, a hairdresser but not a stylist. She's ambitious: she wants to be a Page Six name, have a purse named after her, open a lifestyle boutique in the Hamptons, and launch a makeup line in Japan. Tonight is her chance to climb up the society ladder. This is a job interview.

I march back into Cornelia's dressing room and try to sound authoritative and like I'm not lying. "Can you give me his new number? I only have his old one."

"Get with the now, Angie, he changed it, like, six months ago." Still gazing at herself in the mirror, Cornelia hands me her cell. "Tell him if Olivia is wearing the pink then I need to know, because I have it in the yellow, and tell him to tell me if Lauren is lying to me because I will fucking cut that bitch dead tonight."

I nod and back out of the room while it's ringing.

Finally, on the eleventh ring, it goes to voice mail.

"Hello, this is Angie James calling for Mr. Posen on behalf of Cornelia Pace. She has an urgent query about a dress for the Met Ball this evening. Can you please call me back?" I leave my number and hang up.

Who am I kidding? Zac Posen is never going to call me back. He doesn't care what Cornelia is wearing. She's not important enough.

Then I remember. Candie Stokes dresses all the top-tier socialites. And if she doesn't dress them, she'll still know what they're wearing, that's her job. And though she'd never answer a call from me, her third personal assistant sure as hell will.

So for the second time today, I call Edward.

"Edward!"

"Angie! Sweetface! Are the flowers okay?"

"They're perfect! So perfect! But, um . . . I need your help again. Can you please, please call the assistant you always speak to at Candie Stokes's office and find out who is wearing Zac Posen to the Met tonight? I know it sounds weird, but I'm with Cornelia Pace, and . . ."

"Ooh! I love a socialite emergency! Of course I will! But only if you promise not to move to L.A. I wanna be BFFs!"

Tears flood my eyes. He's so lovely. But I have to leave. The chaos of working for Cornelia is a great distraction, but I know that the minute I'm alone, thoughts of Sam will lurch back into my head and I'll just start crying again. It happened twice on the subway over here, and I looked like a total freak. I need a fresh start.

I can't say anything, but Edward doesn't notice. "I'll call you in three minutes! Stand by the phone!"

As promised, three minutes later he calls back. And the news isn't good.

I walk back into the dressing room, where Keith is now prepping Cornelia's skin with a lymphatic drainage massage. She's convinced it makes her cheekbones stand out.

"Cornelia, Olivia is wearing the pink. Natalie and Anna are wearing Zac, too. And I found out what all Candie Stokes's other clients are wearing tonight." I hand over the list. "Voilà."

"Oh, Angie, you are the best!" She reads the list and looks up, a note of panic in her voice. "Those bitches have taken everything. I have nothing! Oh, my GOD!"

She gets up off the chair and makes a bloodcurdling wail, then sinks to the floor, her hand clutching at her hair. "ARRRRRRRRRRRRRGHH!"

I exchange a glance with Bibi and Keith, who are their usual mute passive selves. Someone needs to take charge of this situation.

"Cornelia, calm down. We can come up with a solution," I say. "Okay, so all the big guns are gone. Let's call someone newer. A designer who is up-and-coming."

"I don't want to wear up-and-fucking-coming!" Cornelia is lying on the floor, screaming into the carpet. "I want to wear Oscar de la fucking Renta! Or Armani fucking Privé! Or Atelier fucking Versace! Or—"

"What about that guy who used to do the cutting for Vera Wang?" I interrupt her before she can insert "fuck" into every couture brand in existence. "I read in *Women's Wear Daily* that he just started out on his own."

"Vera and I had a fight when she wouldn't design my dress for junior prom the way I wanted it. I fucking hate that bitch and I hate everyone who works for her," says Cornelia, her voice muffled by the carpet.

"Okay . . ." I rack my brains for a second. There's someone else, I know there's someone else. "Wait! I know! Sarah Drake! She worked for Narciso Rodriguez, you know?"

"I love him." Cornelia flips over. "But he has those bitch actress groupies who always wear him."

Man, I am tired of Cornelia calling every other woman in the world a bitch. "Well, she started her own label, Drake, about six months ago. I met her intern Philly Meyer in Starbucks when I was, uh, interviewing in the Fashion District! We're Facebook friends! I can get in touch with her in ten minutes."

Cornelia looks up at me, her pale blue eyes shining with hope.

"Do it."

And it works. By 6:30 P.M., Philly Meyer is couriering three dresses straight from Sarah Drake's atelier on Thirty-seventh Street to Cornelia's apartment. The dresses are on loan, for free: it's good PR for Sarah Drake. Cornelia isn't exactly A-list or even B-list, but anyone going to the Met Ball has fashion cachet today.

Thank God Cornelia is sample size. I guess all that coke is good for something.

She tries each dress, one by one, and parades out in front of Bibi, Keith, and me.

The first dress is called, according to the Sarah Drake–branded name tag that came with the delivery, The Bettina. It's pale pink and strapless, making her look like an upside-down tulip, and not in a good way. It would be perfect on someone edgier, but not Cornelia. She's too white-bread.

"Amay-zing!" sing Bibi and Keith. Jeez. So not true.

"No. A bit garden-y," I say. Cornelia nods obediently and takes the dress off. She trusts my opinion? That's a surprise.

The second dress is called The Shadow. It's black, sleeveless, and divinely dramatic with a high neck, but her shoulders aren't broad enough to carry it off, so it just sort of hangs down from her face, making her look like a bat-nun hybrid.

"Ohmygod!" chorus Bibi and Keith.

"No good for photos," I say. "Drowns your body."

Again, Cornelia nods and obeys.

The third dress is called The Angel. And it's just right. It's an ivory column dress, extremely fitted with angular, slightly futuristic details, and elongates Cornelia's figure perfectly, giving her an elegance and class that, between you and me, she sure as hell doesn't possess in real life. She looks like Grace Kelly, if Grace Kelly was in *Blade Runner*.

"Wow! Like, wow!" Bibi and Keith are orgasmic with joy.

"That's stunning," I say. "Shoes?"

"I want to wear the Louboutins," Cornie says, looking at me slightly pleadingly, like I have to give her permission. I glance down: they're burnished gold and absolutely beautiful.

"Fine. Bag?"

Cornelia promptly opens drawers containing over fifty evening bags. But none of them work. They're all the wrong color, too big, too last season, too shiny, too tacky . . .

"I can run to Christian Louboutin," I say. "Give me ten minutes—"

"Your clutch!" Cornelia interrupts. "The gold clutch I saw you with in the Minetta Tavern. Where is that?"

"Next to my coat . . ." I say, confused. "You want to borrow my clutch?"

"Yes. It's perfect! It's a talking point! It's all soft and bunchy; it'll be perfect next to the angularity of the dress! And because it's not a big label, I'll look effortlessly eclectic and unassuming, like those bitches who always end up on the best-dressed lists . . . not like I've just thrown money at the whole thing, because that's so tacky, you know?" Cornelia does her best imploring face. "Please, Angie? Please?"

"Um, okay, sure." I grab my clutch and empty the contents into my coat pockets. "It's yours for the night. Now, we have thirty minutes until the car gets here. Keith, work your magic. Bibi, fix the hair. Cornelia, can I get you a Red Bull?"

"You're acting weird," Cornelia says a few minutes later, as she's having foundation painstakingly brushed into her pores.

"I am?" I say. I'm crouched on the floor next to her, rearranging the two rejected dresses in tissue paper so they can be returned crease-free. "How?"

"Maybe not weird. But you're . . . I don't know. Different. Confident. Kind of take-charge. I mean, you were confident before, but not like this. . . . Before, I was never sure if you'd do something I asked you to do, or just walk away."

"Ha," I say. Without any mirth whatsoever.

"I guess you should never underestimate the life-altering power of a little scandal, huh?" Cornelia raises an eyebrow at me knowingly, then glances at her phone as she gets a text. "Oh, for fuck's sake . . . It's Roger. Some family crisis. He's going to have to meet me there."

"Family problem?"

"His son." My heart stops for a second. Sam? "He's going for some big job at a bank. Roger wants to have a drink with the chairman, to try to win him the job."

That's pretty obnoxious. And she definitely can't mean Sam. So maybe he does have a brother.

"How old is his son?"

"Twenty-five, twenty-six, I don't know. His name is Pete," she says, then lowers her voice. "Rog actually has *two* sons, but the other isn't talking to him."

Sam! My Sam! I mean, not my Sam, but, oh never mind.

"No kidding. Why?"

"I don't know. Something to do with the ex-wife. She was a fucking hippie, apparently. Always taking the boys to South America or Africa or whatever to do volunteer work. So pretentious. Just throw a fundraiser, you know?"

"Right on . . ." I say, staring into space. So Sam is the product of a genuinely philanthropic mother and an overachieving, overbearing father. Huh. "Is, uh, the other kid a banker, too?"

"Nah. He's traveling the world, finding himself, or something ridiculous like that. I think he wanted to be a doctor, but Rog wanted him to go into finance or law, something normal, you know? So they had some big fight."

Who the fuck wouldn't want their kid to be a doctor?

Suddenly, I remember something Cornelia said before she started talking about Sam's father. Something that didn't make sense.

"What did you mean before? When you said 'the life-altering power of a little scandal'?"

"I just mean . . . you know, Angie." Cornelia lowers her voice, as though Keith weren't standing four inches away from her applying individual eyelashes to her eyelids. "The *bar*. The *tape*."

I look up at her, totally confused. "What bar? What tape? What are you talking about?"

"The tiny secret bar in Hell's Kitchen. It's called Angie's Secret. They play the sex tape in the bathroom the whole time. I heard about it from that little sleazebag, what's his name, that guy you hang around with? Steven, or Stef—"

But I'm not listening anymore. Instead, I've grabbed my coat and am heading straight for the door, every part of my brain and body and soul blazing with fury.

The Soho Grand night.

Now I know what happened.

CHAPTER 40

"That evil little fuckwit. We'll destroy it, okay? And cut his balls off. I'll be in Manhattan in half an hour. Don't kill anyone until I get there." Pia hangs up without waiting for a response.

Which is lucky, since I'm not sure I could say anything more right now. I just told Pia the truth about the Soho Grand night, about not remembering anything and waking up with three thousand dollars in an envelope. Pia, being Pia, didn't seem shocked at all. She just loaded her metaphorical shotgun and is coming with me to the bar to reclaim the tape.

I'm striding up Hudson, my face burning, my pulse racing, my stomach churning with an almost overwhelming need to vomit, or pass out, or scream.

There's a *sex tape* of me, taken when I was too out of it to know what the fuck I was doing.

Which means I had sex with—well, with someone—in the Soho Grand that night, and he taped me.

It's playing in that secret bar under the café in Hell's Kitchen.

They called the bar Angie's Secret in the end. After me.

Just like I asked them to.

I wonder who it was. Maybe it was one of the guys I met that night, one of the bar owners . . . Busey. Or Emmett.

Suddenly, I have a flashback to being in the back of a cab with Emmett. He gave me a keybump of coke. And then he kissed me. I remember tongue. Lots of tongue.

Yes. It was him.

Oh God. I am overcome with a sickening shame. I feel like I've lost something I can never get back. I wonder what I did on the tape, how bad it was . . . I mean, it shouldn't be a big deal, right? Everyone has sex! The existence of the human race is testament to the fact that everyone has sex. And every low-level celebrity and reality TV star has a sex tape. Hell, I'm pretty sure most of them make a sex tape to try to boost their fame quotient. They would probably just shrug this off. Or be proud of it, even.

But I'm not like that. I don't want fame. I don't want notoriety. I never did. I just want a job that will be the start of a real career and a life of which I can be proud. I'm fed up with people taking advantage of me, and yeah, maybe it's partly my fault for being immature and thoughtless and making so many stupid decisions.

But enough is enough.

As I argue with myself in my head, I'm marching through the West Village. The sky is getting dark, and this is postcard New York in April: beautiful buildings with yellowy lighting in the windows cut out against the dusk sky, trees kissing overhead, the twilight making everything magical. Everyone is walking home from work, thinking about their careers and love and sex and food and family and money and fashion and fun and all the things that New Yorkers are obsessed with. . . . God, I love it. I don't want to leave.

So what *do* I want? I keep walking until I reach the cobblestoned Meatpacking District, which reminds me of being in New York when I was about nineteen and dancing on chairs in those Sunday brunch places. I would so not do that now. I don't want that life. That's just not who I am anymore.

So who am I?

I feel like I'm still trying to find out.

My phone rings again. It's Pia.

"Where are you?"

I look up. "Thirteenth and Ninth?"

"Stay there."

A couple of minutes later, Pia comes zooming around the corner in Toto, her pale pink SkinnyWheels food truck, and screeches to a halt on the cobblestones in front of me.

Julia is next to her in the front seat. She opens the door and quickly climbs out of the truck.

Our eyes meet, and I feel, if it's possible, even sicker with apprehension. "Hi, Julia . . ."

"Angie, thank you for the flowers," Julia says. "I've never seen anything like it. I think it's the most romantic thing anyone's ever done for me."

I start laughing despite myself, feeling momentarily filled with relief. "Oh, Jules. I am so sorry I hurt you. I swear it wasn't deliberate."

"You didn't, not really," she says, leaning in for a hug. "Angie, the date with Sam *was* a total washout. There was no, I don't know, connection, no sexual tension; I knew it was a failure . . . but I wanted him to like me anyway. I wanted it so badly. I'm just tired of being single."

"I understand," I say. "I'm just tired of being me."

Julia smiles. "Let's go nail these assholes, shall we?"

"Yes," I say. "God, yes."

I climb into the truck, next to Pia, and Julia climbs in after me. Pia reaches back and knocks twice on the hatch behind her head. A double knock comes right back. I frown quizzically at her.

"Maddy and Coco," she says. "They're hiding back there. It's kind of illegal, but you know, they really wanted to help."

"Oh, my God, you guys are the best. I don't deserve this," I say. "Did Pia tell you? About the Soho Grand night? About the money?"

"I did," says Pia. "I hope that's okay."

"Of course it's okay," I say. "I don't want any more secrets from you guys. You must think—"

"We think you're our friend, and bad shit happens, and we're going to fix it," says Julia. "We're all in this together."

We smile at each other for a second, then she reaches down and turns on the radio. After a few seconds of loud static, it starts playing Blondie's "One Way or Another."

"Toto has such great taste in theme songs," says Pia, patting the steering wheel approvingly.

By the time we get to Westies, at the corner of Tenth and Forty-sixth, screaming along to the radio the whole way, I'm feeling better. I can do this. With the girls by my side, I can do anything.

We get out of Toto and stand in a group on the sidewalk for a moment.

"I can never thank you enough for this," I say. "You must think I'm an idiot."

"I promise we don't," says Madeleine. "And personally, I think you should question whether this was sex with consent."

"I don't think we'll know without watching the video," I say. "And I don't want to."

"We've all been drunk, and we've all had sex, we've all made mistakes," says Julia. "Could have been any one of us."

"It could easily have been you since you have, in fact, made a sex tape, and you weren't even drunk," points out Pia.

Everyone gasps, and Julia shrugs. "That was a long time ago, P-Dawg. My experimental phase. And I destroyed the evidence, anyway. It won't, like, pop up when I run for president."

Madeleine cracks up. "You had an experimental phase?"

"Enough!" says Pia. "Let's focus on the problem at hand."

"I'm focused." Coco makes a snarling sound. "Let's get these fuckers."

The five of us stalk into the café, all trying to look as angry and mean as we can, past the greasy counters and ancient cupcakes. I open the door at the back of the room and we march down the old cabbage-y stairwell, past the velvet curtain, and into the bar.

It's been weeks since I was last here, the night that started with a bad mood and a bad friend and ended in . . . blackout. But it feels like a lifetime ago.

The bar looks kind of like a stage set now, the way bars always do when they're empty, the lights are on, and you're sober. It's just the same as it was that time I met Stef here, with one change: above the bar, in a cursive script, is *ANGIE'S SECRET* spelled out in pink neon.

Looking at it makes me feel sick.

Leading the way, I walk straight to the back of the room, where there's a tiny unisex bathroom.

It's locked.

"Shit!" I say.

"Don't worry," says Madeleine. "I can pick locks."

"Where the fuck did you learn how to pick a lock?" asks Pia.

Madeleine arches an eyebrow. "You don't know everything about me, Pia. So it looks like a single-pin pick will do fine. Anyone got a bobby pin?"

Pia takes a pin out of her chignon.

"And I just need . . ." Madeleine runs to the bar, picks up a knife, throws it down, then grabs a corkscrew. "Aha!" She hurries back. "Give me two minutes."

But all she needs is thirty seconds. Click, click, click, the lock is done.

"Hurry," says Pia. "It's, like, 7:30. Even the latest of the late-night bars probably need someone in early to set up."

"Okay, okay." I open the door and look in the bathroom. It's just a communal sink with a huge mirror and two toilet stalls. I can't see a TV screen, or a DVD player, or even a laptop, anywhere.

The girls push past me. "Did you find it? Let's get out of here!"

"It's not here," I say, feeling a lump of desperation in my throat. "There's no screen, there's nothing. Anyway, what am I even thinking? They would have made copies of any tape. . . . It's digital, it's probably on the Internet. I can never destroy everything. There'll always be a copy somewhere. What were we thinking, driving up here like fucking vigilantes?"

Julia is frowning. "Something's weird about this room. . . . Look, why is the mirror angled up? Mirrors are usually angled down so that it's flattering to the person looking at their reflection, right?"

I gaze at the mirror. "So?"

"So . . . it's like it's designed to reflect something high on the opposite wall. You see?"

"What are you, Nancy fucking Drew?" says Madeleine.

Julia doesn't respond. Instead, she turns around and looks at the blank opposite wall, then swivels back to the mirror, and looks up.

And then I see it. There's a hole the size of a quarter in the wall above the mirror.

"It's next door," she says. "The camera. It's projecting the movie onto the wall and reflected in the mirror. So that when you're in the bathroom, you can see the movie, no matter which way you're facing."

We all file out of the tiny bathroom. Next door to it is another door . . . the janitor's closet.

"Hairpin! Hairpin!" says Madeleine, holding her hand out like a surgeon in an operating theater.

"Fuck the hairpin," Julia says, and kicks the lock on the door, very hard, with all her strength. On the third kick, I can hear wood splintering, and the door falls open.

Inside is a bucket full of cleaning products and a few crates of mixers. And when we look up, a tiny newly made shelf containing a vintage-looking movie camera.

"That's a Super 8 home movie camera," says Pia. "Aidan has a bunch of movies his folks made of him when he was a baby; it tapes and plays back from the same machine. . . . Super 8 has that grainy old-fashioned look, you know? It's totally popular again."

"Oh, good," I say. "So I was filmed having sex without my knowledge, but at least I look cool?"

"Well, it's unlikely that those losers bothered to transfer the film to digital, so that's a bonus."

"Get the fucking camera and let's go already," says Julia.

I reach up, knocking the camera off the shelf. It clatters to the floor.

"Oops. I think I broke it," I say, making a pretend-anguish face at the girls.

Julia grins and stamps on it so hard it breaks into three pieces. "Oops. I think I broke it more."

"Okay, can we do this back at Union Street?" Pia interrupts.

Everyone files out as I pick up the broken camera, and then they all turn around and walk back into the bar.

The other girls are frozen in front of me.

259

I look at them in confusion. "What are we waiting for? Let's go!"
Then I see why they're not moving.
Emmett, Busey, and Stef. Blocking the exit.
"Hello, Angie," says Stef. "Looks like you've discovered our secret."

CHAPTER **41**

"How could you *do* that to me?" I stride right up to Stef. "You *filmed* me! Having *sex*! Do you really fucking hate me that much? What did I ever do to you?"

"Hey, it wasn't me, babe!" He puts his hands up and takes a step back. "I was as surprised as you were. Well maybe not *as* surprised . . ."

"I don't believe you."

"I swear."

I turn to Emmett and Busey, feeling like I might collapse from stress and anger. "You evil assholes," I stammer. "I could have you arrested."

"You're overreacting," says Busey, his chubby cheeks wobbling with every word. "It's really a beautiful movie. Very sixties, very classic. You should be proud."

I gasp, feeling like I've been hit.

"I thought you were into it." Emmett looks bored. "I set the camera up while you were in the bathroom. You never even noticed. . . . You were pretty wild."

I try to speak, but only a choking sound comes out, and tears flow down my face. I can't bear this. I can't. I don't know what to do.

"You piece of shit," says Julia. "How *dare* you take advantage of Angie like that! How *dare* you show a sex tape in your disgusting bar, like she was some kind of porn star!"

Busey smirks. "If the shoe fits—"

"Shut the hell up," says Pia, her voice low and threatening. "Don't you dare say that shit about my best friend, you fat fuck."

"We're leaving," Madeleine adds. "And we're taking the camera."

"By the way," Coco says, "my boyfriend works for the Department of Health, in the Bureau of Food Safety and Community Sanitation. Bet you twenty bucks you'll lose your liquor license and be shut down within the month."

"What liquor license?" Stef says under his breath, then looks up and sees that we all heard.

Coco looks at him, then back at Busey and Emmett. "I'd say you're pretty screwed, assholes."

Coco is one tough broad when she wants to be.

Just as we reach the curtain, Julia stops, turns around, walks back to Stef, and slaps him, once, very hard across the face.

"Hey—"

"That's for everything you did to my friend. She's a good person. She didn't deserve it."

When we get up to the street, I feel a heady euphoria. Victory! But before I can celebrate, I need to do one thing.

With shaking hands, I find the latch and open the camera, slip my finger into the film, and pull it all out by hand. Ribbons upon ribbons of film come out, quickly spooling in a huge pile at my feet. I start jumping and stamping on it, and then all the girls join in, laughing with the sort of relieved hysteria that you get when you've just escaped a scary, ridiculous, weird situation.

"We're throwing this film off the Brooklyn Bridge," says Julia. "And then we're going home. I need a drink."

"We really shouldn't litter," says Coco. "We'll cut it into tiny pieces at home instead."

"Let's get pizza," says Pia. "My treat."

I know what she's thinking. It's confession time. Pia and I are leaving Rookhaven.

As I'm getting into Toto the food truck, I spot Stef's car parked just down the street. His red Ferrari 308 GTS. The thing that means the most to him in the entire world.

I have an idea.

Without pausing, I stride into the deli next to the café, buy a two-liter bottle of Coca-Cola, walk over to the car, open the gas cap, open the Coke bottle, and pour every last drop of sugary, engine-frying Coca-Cola into the gas tank. Glug, glug, glug.

"What the fuck are you doing?" shouts Pia from the truck.

I don't reply. When every last drop is in the tank, I turn around and walk back to the truck, smiling to myself. Stef's precious car is fried.

Revenge. Is. Awesome.

Then we drive back to Rookhaven, sit down at the kitchen table, order pizza from Bartolo's, open a bottle of wine, and attack the film with scissors.

"No vodka tonight, Angie?" Madeleine teases me, as she slices up frame after frame. "No cucumber, no sea salt? No cigarette tucked between your lips?"

I smirk at her. I finally understand Madeleine. She's trying to be funny. It just comes out as bitchy sometimes. "Not tonight. Tonight, I want to toast to you guys. Thank you. I could not have survived that without you."

We all raise our glasses and clink, with all the obligatory intense-eye-contact-or-seven-years-bad-sex stuff.

Then the pizza arrives, and after we all take our first bite, Pia and I exchange a glance. It's time to tell everyone.

"I'm moving to San Francisco to be with Aidan," she says.

"I'm moving to L.A. to be with myself." I raise an eyebrow. "God, that's depressing."

"What?" Julia, Madeleine, and Coco exclaim in unison.

"Why?" Coco is distraught. "You're leaving? Both of you?"

"I just . . . I'm miserable without him," says Pia. "If you love some-one, you want to be with them. Right?"

"What about your job?" asks Julia. "They're letting you work from San Francisco?"

"Um, no," says Pia. She looks up guiltily. "I asked my boss today. She said that she needed me here in New York, with the rest of the company."

"So you quit working at Carus?" Julia is horrified. "That's it?"

I'm stunned, too. Pia didn't tell me that her boss said no to the pro-posed San Francisco move. She'd walk away from her perfect career—when it's so impossible to find a job right now? Let alone one as amazing as hers?

"Not yet," Pia admits. "I couldn't bring myself to actually resign. After she said no to the move, I said, oh of course, I was just wondering if it was an option, yada yada. . . . But I will. Tomorrow."

"*How* could you quit the job that you worked so hard to get?" I slam my palm on the table so hard that everyone jumps. "You *earned* that job, Pia. You went through hell to get it."

"And we went through hell with you!" points out Madeleine.

"Oh man, I know, I know . . ." Pia looks at the ceiling in anguish. "I love my job. I mean, I *really* love it, and I've only just begun to realize my potential. . . . And I'm good at it! Finally, for once, I'm actually good at something. It's where I'm supposed to be, I'm sure of it . . . but I also feel like I'm supposed to be with Aidan. I love him."

"I guess you have to choose," says Madeleine. "Work or love?"

"I hate that!" says Pia. "Why should I be the one making sacrifices? Why can't he give up his stupid job to stay with me? What fucking de-cade are we living in?" She takes a slug of wine and sighs dramatically.

"And what about you, Angie?" Julia turns to me. "You're just going to fill Rookhaven with flowers and leave?"

"Just when we were finally getting to know you?" adds Madeleine.

"Come on, you guys," I say, looking at them uncomfortably. "You know I'm never going to make a life here. A real life. I can't get a job. And I can't keep working at places like the goddamn Gap or be a per-sonal slave to rich bitches like Cornelia or that psycho bitch photogra-pher, you know? I need to feel like I'm on the right track, like my life has direction, a purpose. And I don't."

There's silence. No one seems able to argue with me. This makes me crumble a little bit inside. I sort of hoped—half hoped, maybe—that one of them would tell me she didn't want me to go, that they simply wouldn't allow it. But why would they try to argue me out of anything? It's never worked before.

"What about Sam?" asks Julia.

"Sam is a liar." I stare at my plate. Talking about my emotions makes me feel so fucking awkward. "I have no feelings for him. I thought I did, and I was wrong, he's a liar. I was, you know, projecting." Yeah. That's a good word. I'm just not completely sure what it means.

"He's crazy about you, you know," says Julia.

I look up. "What?"

"On our date he kept mentioning you, or asking if I knew where you were, because he hadn't been able to get in touch with you. . . . I swear we only turned up at the bar because I said you were there and he insisted we go. Our date wasn't a real date; it was just dinner with a guy who happened to be into one of my friends."

"Oh," I say in a tiny voice, trying to process all this. "Well, he should have been up-front with you. Why did he go out with you, if he wasn't interested? He's still a bastard."

"He's not. I saw him when I got home from work tonight. He's been cleaning up Vic's place. He said he was sorry, that he thought we were on the same page with being more friends than anything else. He said he thought he'd be able to get you and his brother Pete to come to dinner, too. Make a happy little foursome. He was about to tell you all about his family stuff. He never liked me like that."

"Ouch," says Pia. "Jules, that bites."

"No, it's fine," says Julia, rubbing her temples and frowning. "He was so honest, I couldn't even be upset. . . . I don't even know if I liked him all that much, either. I just wanted to like *someone* so badly. . . ." She sighs. "I would really like a boyfriend. That's all."

There's a long pause.

"So, Sam has a brother?" Pia says finally. "Do they look alike?"

Jules cracks up. "I know! That was the first thing I thought, too!"

We all eat in thoughtful silence for a while. I'm thinking about Sam, trying to figure out how I feel and what I should do, but there are just too many emotions jumbled inside me. Too much has happened in the past twenty-four hours. I feel like I could get into bed and sleep for a week. And I still need a job. I need a real life, a life that's heading somewhere. That's the bottom line.

"God, I love Bartolo's," says Julia, when the pizza is all gone. "But it always leaves me in the mood for something sweet, you know?"

"I know!" says Madeleine. I frown at her. Madeleine practically never eats sugar. "I could really do with, hmm, let me think, something pink and white, with icing, and candles. . . ."

Suddenly I notice Coco is at the fridge, pulling out a cake. "Ta-da! For Pia and Angie! Birthday cake!"

"I thought I wouldn't get a cake this year!" Pia is delighted. "Happy twenty-third birthday to us!"

Coco lights the candles, everyone sings "Happy Birthday," and then Pia and I take deep breaths, close our eyes, and blow out the candles.

"Don't forget to make a wish!" shouts Julia.

I wish to create a life that will make me happy.

The wish comes, unbidden, into my head. If I'd had time to think about it, I would have wished for something more specific, like a job that pays $150,000 a year and a house with a private chef and a rooftop goddamn swimming pool.

Or even just a job. But that'll never happen in New York. So I guess my wish will take me to L.A.

Then I open my eyes and look around at the girls. They're my family now. I don't want to say good-bye to them.

This is what it all boils down to: I don't want to leave, but I feel like I have to.

What the hell am I going to do?

CHAPTER **42**

I barely slept last night.

Again.

I have that dull exhaustion faceache behind my eye sockets, you know the kind I mean? The kind that can only be relieved by about twenty-four hours of sleep and then a gallon of espresso. But it won't be happening here. Every time I closed my eyes last night, a kaleidoscope of images rushed through my brain. Everything that's happened, everything I wish I could erase, everything I wish I could ask Sam, everything...

A few things have become clear, in the restless thinkfest that was my night.

First, I was wrong.

(Again.)

Yes, Sam lied about who he was and where he was from.

But he obviously had reasons. His father, his mother . . . I don't know the full story. But I should have stuck around to find out. I should have given him the benefit of the doubt. Just like I should have stuck around with my mom that day she told me about the divorce, and I should have stuck around Rookhaven the night that Julia and I had the fight in the kitchen. But I didn't. My instincts said run.

So I ran.

I'm always led by instinct. Ruled by it, really. I always thought it was just who I was, I thought it was part of my personality. Unpredictable. Mercurial. Sometimes it's not such a bad idea, like getting away from the yacht in Turks. But sometimes—more often—it is.

So is it a bad idea, leaving Brooklyn, when I can't get a real job in New York? Or is it logical? I honestly can't tell what's rational and what's crazy anymore, or what's smart and what's stupid. There are too many choices. It's all too confusing, and I have this terrible fear, deep down inside, that I'll make the wrong choice and always regret it.

And now, it's Wednesday morning. Everyone else in the world is getting up, going to their jobs, earning money, having a life that's worth living.

Except me.

I need some air.

So I get out of bed, take a very quick shower, and pull on jeans, my studded Converse, and a white blouse. I got up at 3:00 A.M. and finished altering the neckline. It's so pretty. Maybe it'll bring me luck.

Then I grab my old Zara leather jacket, and throw my keys, money, phone, and lip balm in the pocket, since Cornelia still has my damn gold clutch, and leave Rookhaven without running into anyone else. I walk slowly down Union Street as the sun rises, getting that quiet buzz you feel when you're the only person awake and the world feels like your secret. Brooklyn seems fresh and clean and full of promise.

I walk down Smith Street and end up back on the corner of Smith and Atlantic Avenue, in the New Apollo Diner, the same diner I went to the morning after Pijiu, when I thought Julia and Sam had . . . well, you know.

That day I stared at my menu, thinking about Sam. I thought about the time we spent together, about bursting into tears in front of him after watching *Kramer vs.* goddamn *Kramer,* about him helping me hand out CVs and lattes. About how I was sure, totally sure, that we were about to kiss that time on my bed.

And I just kept telling myself, *No, he's just your friend.*

What would have happened if I had kissed him that night he slept over? Why did I decide that he had to be my friend and there was no alternative?

But I don't want to go.

There. I said it. (In my head, anyway.)

The events at Angie's Secret last night made me realize the girls are my family now. We're all in this together.

But if I don't go to L.A. and stay here, I'm right back where I started. No job, no career, no money, no options.

No Sam.

I have a huge urge to call Sam and ask him to forgive me for flipping out and charging into the storm like King Lear with tits. I want to ask him to explain his situation to me, why he didn't want to be honest about who he was and where he was from. I'm sure he had good reasons for lying. But I just can't. He hasn't even tried to contact me. And even though he lied, I can't judge him. I don't know his backstory, I don't know what it's like to be him. Just like no one knows what it's like to be me.

When did life get so complicated?

Though, when you think about it, has life ever been simple?

Finally my pancakes arrive, and I can't eat *and* think about life-changing decisions, so I pour maple syrup all over my plate, grab the *New York Post* that someone left on the table next to me, and stare at the cover as I stuff the first sweet bite into my mouth.

Oh, my God.

CHAPTER **43**

It's Cornelia. A mug shot. On the cover of the *New York Post*.

She was arrested. She's wearing The Angel dress and staring into the camera, looking spoiled and sullen.

Next to it, another shot of Cornelia in the dress, jumping on the back of an NYPD police officer, I guess just before she was arrested. She looks stunning. Crazy, obviously, but stunning. That dress rocks.

"CORN ON THE COP!" says the headline.

And then I see it. Down low, in the bottom corner of the front page, is a close-up photo of my clutch! My gold clutch! The one I made from the secondhand scarves I picked up months ago down at Brownstone Treasures. What the? I quickly read the story.

Blond, beautiful . . . and busted. Manhattan socialite Cornelia Archer—great-great-granddaughter of Randolph Archer, founder of Standard Oil—was arrested for smuggling two grams of cocaine into the Costume Institute Gala at the Metropolitan Museum last night.

Security guards noticed Archer's erratic behavior and called the NYPD, leading to a struggle in front of hundreds of shocked style stars, including Anna Wintour, Beyoncé, and Jennifer Lopez.

As Archer, wearing The Angel dress by Drake, was escorted from the gala, her Prada gold clutch was thrown to the floor in front of hundreds of waiting paparazzi, spilling its contents for all to see: lip gloss, cell phone . . . and two grams of cocaine.

Archer awaits sentencing today.

Oh. My. God.

They thought my bag was Prada.

Heart racing, I pick up my phone with trembling hands and call Pia.

"Ladybitch?"

"Cornelia, last night, my clutch, front page of the *Post,* oh, my God," I stammer.

"What? Slow down."

I can't sit still, so I get up and start pacing the diner while I explain.

"Wow," she says. "Your clutch is a drug mule!"

I pause for a second and crack up.

"Let's get practical," says Pia. "What do you want to do? I bet you could spin this to your advantage, you know, career-wise."

"Yes, um—" I'm trying to think. What do I want to do? Then I notice I have a call waiting from a withheld number. "Pia, I have to go, there's a call. . . ." I take the other call. "Hello?"

"Angie! This is Philly Meyer! From Drake!"

"Hey . . ."

He sounds slightly hysterical. "Cornelia Archer was arrested last night! And—"

"I know."

"We need The Angel back! The ivory column dress! It's the sample, it's the only one we have, and we've already had two requests for it, from *W* magazine and French *Vogue*. This is huge, you know? *Huge.* Everyone at the Met Ball saw the dress. It's the only thing anyone is talking about." Philly lowers his voice. "Sarah Drake is *freaking out.*"

"Okay . . ." My brain is spinning. "I can get it back. I'll call you back."

"Hurry!"

I quickly stuff half my pancakes in my mouth at once, throw down some money, and leave. How do I do this? I can't just show up at Manhattan Central Booking and demand the dress.

Think, Angie, think. . . .

When you're arrested, you call a lawyer. And Cornelia being the Upper East Side WASP that she is, she would have called a family lawyer. Someone she could trust. So that's probably the best way to contact her. If I can get in touch with her lawyer, I can get to the dress. And my clutch. Unless it's being held as evidence. (Poor innocent clutch.)

So I call my mother to get the cell number of Cornelia's mother, legendary socialite CC Archer. The cell she only gives out to friends.

"Are you sure CC will want to hear from you, darling?" asks my mother. "She can be a little . . . difficult. And if her daughter's in a scandal, well . . ."

"I can handle it, Mom, I promise, I'm just going to ask her one question," I say. "I'll call you later this week to explain everything."

Then I call Mrs. Archer, introduce myself, and ask if she can tell me the name of her daughter's attorney.

"Why?" CC says suspiciously.

"Because I need my clutch back," I say.

"This hardly seems important right now," she snaps. "This whole silly affair will just blow over soon enough, you can have it then. And Chester won't be taking any calls."

"Chester?"

That's a pretty obscure name for an attorney. Not to mention fucking ridiculous.

"Tell your mother not to hand out my private cell number. Using this number is a privilege, not a right. I am displeased."

I fight the urge to say, "Blow me," and instead put on my cheeriest voice and say, "I'll tell her you asked after her. Thanks so much!" and hang up.

I immediately Google "Chester attorney Manhattan" on my phone. I scroll down and click on a *New York Post* entry from a couple of years ago, when a certain Chester Newland defended one of the Kennedy clan against a drunk-driving charge. And got him off.

That's just the kind of pedigree that would impress the Archers.

I find his number and dial.

CHAPTER 44

Chester Newland's unusually chatty receptionist tells me he is currently at New York City Criminal Court. Getting Cornelia out as quickly as possible, I guess.

Next, I call Philly Meyer and tell him I'll be able to get the dress back this morning.

"I need it, like, *now*. Sarah is freaking. You better get it back," he says. "I'm not kidding."

Man, he's tense.

It's a quick twenty minutes to the criminal court in Chinatown. My guess is that they're posting bail right now, arguing that Cornelia has no prior record and all that jazz, and she'll be out in minutes.

And for once in my life, I'm right.

Just as I arrive at Centre Street, I see a gaggle of paparazzi going nuts.

It looks like a feeding frenzy you see on a nature show: they're running and jostling violently, shouting the same things over and over again.

"Cornelia! Here! Over here!"

"Cornie! Are you a drug addict, Cornie?"

"Cornelia! Are you out on bail?"

In the middle of the mass I catch glimpses of Cornelia, still wearing The Angel, with sunglasses she picked up from somewhere. She looks pale and tired but surprisingly dignified, carrying her gold heels and walking with the perfect posture of the terminally self-assured. She's flanked by two large bodyguard types in suits and a short bald guy in a suit. Chester Newland, I'll bet.

I can't see my clutch. . . . God, what if they had to keep it for evidence or something?

A black limo is waiting on the street, so I hurry to the car, ahead of the paparazzi.

"Cornie, it's me! Angie!" I say, over and over again, hoping she'll look up. But she's concentrating too hard on ignoring the jibes of the paparazzi while looking serenely beautiful.

Then the bodyguards shove me out of the way, the driver opens the limo door, and Cornelia gets in. The door slams after her, and thanks to black-tinted windows, I can't even see in! Shit!

The bodyguards are holding the paps back, and just as I'm sure that all is lost, that the limo is about to drive away with Cornelia and the dress and my clutch, the back window winds down one inch.

"Angie?"

"Yes! Cornie, it's me! I have to talk to you!"

"Oh, thank God!" Cornelia sounds like she's about to cry. "Chester! Get her in, get her in!"

And boom, like magic, the paparazzi are moved and the car door opens for me and I climb into the back.

Cornelia immediately leans forward and hugs me. I'm so surprised, and touched, that I simply hug her back. Imagine the trauma of being arrested for drugs. Imagine the embarrassment. I'd be so mortified; I'd be so—

"Isn't this amazing?!" Cornelia squeals, her eyes shining. "Keith and Bibi are waiting at my mother's house to sort this whole mess out." She gestures to her face. "And then I'm going to La Grenouille for lunch with my mother, so I can show the world I'm not guilty." She pauses and looks over at Chester. "You told the paps La Grenouille, right?"

She's not mortified at all. She's just thrilled to be the center of attention. How weird.

"Cornelia, I'm not here to—" says Chester.

"Did Roger call?" she interrupts. "No? Fuck him. He didn't even show last night. Asshole, putting his kids first. I can do better now, anyway. Angie, call Patrick, remember him? Tell him it's me and I need a date to Le Bernardin tonight."

"No," I say.

"What?" Cornelia looks at me in shock. "What do you mean, 'no'?"

"I can't be your PA today, Cornelia. I have to get that dress back to Sarah Drake, and I need my gold clutch back. Do you have it, or is it being used as evidence?"

"The case was dismissed due to police tampering with the evidence," says Chester, clearly relieved to have the conversation back on familiar ground. "Here." He pulls the gold clutch out of his bag. I grab it quickly. Thank God. My poor little drug mule. And "tampering"? Who'd they have to bribe to get *that*?

"No, Angie! I need you today!" says Cornelia. "You can courier the dress back later. I'll change at my mother's house. I can borrow one of her Chanel suits."

"Where does she live?"

"She lives at Seventy-ninth and Park." Cornelia sighs. "God, I miss our place on Fifth. Divorce is so selfish."

We're only just passing through the East Village now. It'll take me forever to get all the way up there, get the dress, do whatever else Cornelia orders me to do, and get back to the Fashion District to give The Angel to Sarah Drake.

"I can't do it, Cornelia." I try to sound as forceful-yet-polite as I can. "I have to get the dress back to Sarah Drake, now. Please, come with me to her atelier now. We can get you something else to wear, it'll be—"

"Be seen out in public again, in the middle of Manhattan, strolling around in this like some kind of trashed fucking starlet? I don't think so." With every block we get farther away from the courthouse,

Cornelia's officious attitude grows. "I need to wear it when I'm getting out at my mother's building, so the paps can see how close I am to my family, and then I need to change and go to lunch and let everyone see me."

Chester clears his throat. "Actually, Cornelia, I think you shouldn't be seen in public in that dress again. Period. Not at your mother's apartment, not anywhere. From now on, you need to look like the most innocent girl in the world."

Cornelia pouts. "So what the fuck am I supposed to do?"

And that's how I end up in my bra and panties in the back of a limo pulled over on East Thirty-fifth and Madison, while Chester and the bodyguards and driver stand outside the car and Cornelia and I swap clothes.

"This is a cute outfit." Cornie looks over the white top and jeans I hand her. "Where are these from?"

"Erm, I customized the top myself, and the jeans are just H&M," I say, shimmying into the dress.

Cornelia wrinkles her nose. "How adorably fiscally sensitive of you."

"Um . . . thanks."

Cornelia straps her sky-high gold shoes back on and opens the car door. "Okay, you can go now."

"Wait!" I say, struggling to cover my boobs before anyone outside the limo can see. "Can you zip me up?"

I step out of the limo, still wearing my white studded Converse and carrying my clutch and leather jacket, and start walking. The dress is a tight fit for me, and way too long, so I have to hitch it up with one hand.

Then I put my sunglasses on, hold my head high, and walk—or, let's face it, swagger—west along Thirty-fifth Street, in the dress that made the cover of the *New York Post* this morning.

No one even looks at me twice, of course. This is New York City. I could French kiss a rat while shooting up and no one would flinch.

Fifth Avenue, Sixth Avenue, Broadway . . . and then I'm in the Fashion District. They even call the stretch of Seventh between Thirty-fourth and Forty-second "Fashion Avenue," did you know that? I walk up it toward Thirty-seventh Street. Bizarrely, it's here that people start staring at me. Maybe recognizing the dress from the *Post,* maybe wondering why a girl would wear an evening dress that's so obviously worth thousands of dollars at 10:00 A.M., maybe just wondering who designed it. It *is* a stunning dress and an amazing piece of craftsmanship, after all.

I take out my phone and call Philly.

"What's the exact address?" I ask.

"220 West Thirty-seventh, seventh floor," he says. "I'll meet you in the lobby."

"Um, no, I'm going to have to come up," I say.

"Why?"

"You'll see."

I hang up and head to 220 West Thirty-seventh. A nondescript building, one that I'd usually walk past without even wondering what was upstairs. I walk past the security guard, dozing with a Dunkin' Donuts coffee by his side, and take the elevator to the seventh floor. I suddenly feel unaccountably nervous. I never got this far when I was actually applying for jobs. I'd send my résumé, e-mail, call . . . but I never got into the actual design studios.

The elevator opens on a shabby hallway, and I look around nervously. One door is labeled with the name of a Pilates studio, the other is blank. That must be her.

I knock.

About ten seconds later—such a long time to stare at a door!—it opens, revealing Philly Meyer, the intern slash DJ slash milliner I met at Starbucks that time, the guy who gave me Drakey. It's kind of strange to see him in person again; thanks to Facebook I know he's just gone through a breakup, sells his hats at the Brooklyn Flea, DJ'd last weekend at a bar in Washington Heights, and is totally obsessed with the crème brûlée donut at Doughnut Plant, but thinks it's making him fat. But I haven't seen him in person once since we met.

"Wow," Philly says, looking at me, and opens the door wider, so everyone in the studio can see me.

I glance around quickly. Two guys and a girl standing together over a cutting table, another guy on the phone, and in the corner, working at a huge architect-style desk, is Sarah Drake.

Thirtysomething, dark blond hair, glasses, no makeup. She looks impressive and intimidating, but somehow normal, like she needs coffee and maybe forgot to brush her hair this morning. It's kind of blowing my mind. I guess I've built up the idea of what someone who works in fashion would look like, you know. Not someone on the periphery, not trying to break in, not blogging about it, but someone *really* doing it. But she looks kind of normal. Smart and sharp and cool, yet normal.

Sarah looks up at me and for a second, it feels like everyone in the room stops breathing.

"The Angel," says Sarah finally.

I look down at the dress. The Angel dress. There's total silence.

"Well, that's one way to wear it."

I suddenly feel embarrassed. Who the hell am I to wear this dress with my dirty Converse and my Zara leather jacket? "I'm sorry, I didn't have any choice, Cornelia had nothing to change into; we swapped clothes in the limo—"

"And you walked it here from where?"

"Oh, just a couple of blocks, I didn't sweat in the dress or anything, but um, but otherwise it would have taken me another two hours; she wanted to wear it back to her mother's house on the Upper East Side. . . ." I trail off.

"I get it," Sarah says. "I appreciate the effort to get it to me on time. Punctuality is my thing."

"Punctuality!" chorus the boys at the cutting board. Everyone in the room grins, clearly this is an inside joke.

"Where's the clutch from?"

"From me," I say. "I mean, I made it. I was just playing with some old scarves."

Sarah walks over to me and takes the clutch. "Nice work. Where did you train?"

"I taught myself," I say. "I don't know much, I just, you know, I do what I like, I need to learn, really, I know I have so much to learn—"

"Okay." Bored of me, Sarah puts the clutch down and turns to Philly. "The Angel. Clean it, steam it, get it to *W*."

"But I have to run The Dahlia over to Julianne Moore!" Philly is panicking again. "Her PA just pulled it for a movie premiere tonight!"

"I can take care of The Angel!" I say quickly. "I know how to do that. I can do it. It's really no problem, I, um—"

Sarah narrows her eyes at me for a moment, thinking, then nods.

"Okay. That would be great. Thanks, Angie."

I clear my throat, feeling kind of foolish. "Can I, uh, can I get something to change into once I take the dress off?"

Sarah grins and throws me a gym bag from underneath her desk. "Hope you like spandex."

CHAPTER **45**

By the time the day is over, I feel like my world has shifted on its axis. Not a lot. Just a little. But enough to make me dizzy.

First I clean, steam, and courier the dress to *W*.

Then I help one of the other designers fold a particularly complicated dress for shipping to Japanese *Vogue*. (Say what you like about the Gap, but it sure as hell taught me how to fold.)

After that I offer to sort out the chaotic button drawers for another of the designers; answer phones; do a coffee run and stuff a sandwich in my face while on my way back; dust the shoe shelf; refold the samples because they were in total disarray; act as a fitting model for Sarah for a jacket she was tweaking; arrange three returns for dresses Sarah loaned out to other celebrities for the Met Ball; Google, print, and clip all the Sarah Drake press from last night; and silently kneel and help as Sarah fits a couture wedding dress for a private client, a Korean heiress.

It was, in other words, the best day of work—no, the best day, *period*—that I have ever, ever had. Everything just felt . . . right.

Being near clothes all day, seeing Sarah Drake's next collection taking shape, is magic. Her design style is sort of old Hollywood meets sci-fi, like if Hitchcock were directing *Alien*, angular and very glamorous. I adore it.

I only make one false move all day. When the wedding dress is being fitted, I notice the fabric has pulled, very slightly, around the sleeve. I point at it, silently, so Sarah can see without the Korean heiress noticing. She gives me a total death look and ignores me.

Apparently pointing out a flaw in the dress is a bad idea. Good to know.

My heart kind of sinks after that misstep. I wait till the Korean heiress has left and then go over to Sarah's desk, bobbing awkwardly, feeling a little bit sick with nervousness at what I'm about to ask.

But I have to do it. This is the first real opportunity I've ever had to get the job I want. I can't fail now.

"Um, Sarah? Thank you for letting me help out today."

"No problem, you've been great," she says, without looking up from her laptop.

I take a deep breath. "I know you already have one intern, but I was wondering if you could keep me in mind if you ever need a personal assistant, or anything like that—"

She looks up at me, a little smile on her lips. "We do. Judging by the press The Angel got last night, and the volume of e-mail I've received today, we're going to need another pair of hands, effective immediately."

"Okay," I reply coolly, trying not to clap my hands and jump up and down. "I mean, great! What, um—"

"I'll work out the money tonight and we can talk about it tomorrow morning. It won't be great, but being a junior assistant is better than being an intern, and whenever I ask you to get me lunch or a coffee, I'll pay for you to have the same, too. I don't do slavery."

"Wonderful!" God! I feel all hot and burny inside! "That's so amazing! Thank you!"

"Cool. See you here tomorrow at 9:00 A.M.," she says.

"I won't be late, I promise." I am grinning so hard my face hurts a little bit. "Punctuality!"

"Right," she says, her face breaking into a genuine, huge smile for the first time today.

"Oh! And I'll wash your gym clothes tonight and bring them back in the morning."

"Don't rush," she says, waving her hand. "Gives me an excuse not to work out. Where do you live, by the way?"

"Brooklyn," I say. "Carroll Gardens."

"Oh yeah? I'm in Boerum Hill. Brooklyn's the best, isn't it?"

I smile. "Without a doubt. The best."

I never understood what people meant when they said they *floated on air,* but now I do.

Because I float home to Rookhaven.

I feel like my body is moving without me having to think about it. I feel light and free and happy. So very, very, *very* happy. I want to skip and sing and punch the air and jump for joy and hug the people next to me. I have a job. Ajobajobajob.

It's just past seven o'clock when I get home to Union Street, still wearing Sarah's gym clothes with my studded Converse and leather jacket, smiling joyfully at everyone I see and noting, with delight, that almost everyone smiles back.

I run up the steps at Rookhaven, past the vases of hydrangeas blooming beautifully, into the flower-filled front hallway, and shout as loud as I can.

"I got a joooooooooob!"

Immediately, I hear four screams from all over Rookhaven as everyone rushes out to meet me. Coco from the kitchen, Pia and Julia from the living room, Madeleine from upstairs.

Pia: "What? What? What happened? I've been trying to call you all day!"

Julia: "Pia told us about the purse thing! In the newspaper!"

Madeleine: "Where are you working? What are you doing?"

Coco: "I'm so happy for you!"

So we go into the kitchen, and I tell them everything. About stalking Cornelia, about getting the dress back, about walking across Manhattan to Sarah Drake's design studio. And then I tell them about the job.

"It was just the best day," I say. "I mean, I wasn't doing anything important, you know, but she gave me a job, a real job, and she's going to pay me and everything. So I must have done something right!"

"That is so awesome, ladybitch," says Pia. "I am so proud of you."

"I'm proud of me, too!" I say. I take a cigarette out of the pack and try to prop it between my lips, but I'm smiling so hard it keeps falling out. I put it back in the pack. Then I remember. "Hey! Pia! Did you resign today?"

Pia bites her lip, pausing before her answer for as long as humanly possible. "No. I couldn't do it. My life is here. My job is here. I love New York, I love Brooklyn, and most of all I love Rookhaven. I realized it when we got back last night. Being with all of you guys is where I'm supposed to be right now. . . . I don't know what will happen with Aidan, but this is my home."

"Damn, woman, you give a good speech," says Julia.

"I thought you were allergic to the word home," says Madeleine.

"I had a slight intolerance. But I've grown out of it."

"I decided the same thing this morning," I say. "I realized I didn't want to leave Rookhaven, no matter what. Right about the same time that I saw the cover of the *New York Post*."

"Cornelia is a piece of work, huh?" says Julia. "I wonder if she got papped outside Le Grenouille just like she planned."

"I'll check," I say, taking out my iPhone. I Google "Cornelia Archer" and a couple of gossip site images immediately come up from her lunch with her mother. They're both wearing Chanel, two little peas in a pod. Well, I guess Cornelia got the job she wanted, too. She'll be a socialite wild child for a while. Until someone else comes along to replace her.

Then something farther down the Google results catches my eye. From Fashionista, a fashion industry news site.

EXCLUSIVE! Met Ball scandal clutch designer revealed!

What the hell?

I click on it, trying frantically to read the entire thing all at once, and then force myself to slow down so I don't miss a word.

Mistakenly identified as Prada, then Miu Miu, then Rodarte, the gold silk clutch at the center of socialite Cornelia Archer's Met Ball drug scandal is by up-and-coming designer Angie James.

The clutch, a hand-sewn gold silk palm-strap pochette, was dropped by socialite Cornelia Archer as security questioned her about her erratic behavior. Cue: two grams of cocaine spilling onto the floor in front of fashion's A-list, cementing Cornelia's position as fashion's newest bad girl, and the clutch as the most talked-about bag of the night.

But who is Angie James? Word has it she worked as muse to Dutch food photographer Anouk Brams, quit in an epic show-down at the end of last year, and has since gone underground. Our sources—and our instincts—tell us a collection is coming.

I read it again: once to myself, and then out loud to the girls.

"This is amazing. . . . Which one of you did this?" I say, staring at them. "Ladybitch? Is this you?"

"Nope," says Pia. "Swear to God."

"Julia? Maddy? Coco?"

"Like we would even know how to do something like that," says Julia.

Suddenly, a lightbulb goes on over my head. I can only think of one other person in the world knows I made that clutch.

It was Sam.

CHAPTER 46

Sam's not answering my calls.

So I'm going to him.

I march into Sam's Fort Greene apartment building, feeling a mixture of excitement and apprehension. I tell the doorman my name, and he picks up the phone.

"There's an Angie James here? . . . Okay."

He escorts me to the elevator and inserts his key to give me access to the top floor. At least Sam wants to see me, that's a good sign, right?

I take a second to check myself out in the elevator mirror. I changed out of Sarah Drake's gym gear, obviously, and quickly showered and put on what, I hope, is a perfect did-you-do-my-PR? outfit: a white silk top, my best jeans, my leather jacket, and boots. I was shaking so much, thinking about what I was about to do, that I could hardly even do my eyeliner right, and ended up wiping most of it off.

As I wait for the elevator to reach the penthouse, feeling breathless with nerves, I try to think, yet again, about what I'll say. I want to apologize for running away, I want to ask him why he lied to me, I want to thank him for telling the world the clutch was mine and find out how he did it, and I want . . . I want . . . I want to say something I'm too scared to even think.

In the end, I settle on four words.

Please, can we talk?

The elevator gets to the top, the doors open, I take a deep breath and prepare my best smile, and . . .

That's not Sam.

A guy who is not Sam, but who reminds me very much of him, is standing in front of me. Same blond hair as Sam, but pale blue eyes rather than gray, and slightly shorter.

"Angie. I'm Pete. I'm Sam's brother." He even sounds like Sam. Just a lot less friendly.

I step slowly into the apartment, looking around. We're the only ones here. "Where is Sam?"

"No idea. I just got home. All of Sam's stuff is gone, and he's not answering his phone. I figured you might know where he is."

I stare at Pete and realize he's wearing the same perfectly cut suit that Sam wore that day in SoHo when I was handing out lattes and CVs. And the same shoes: J.M. Westons.

So they were his roommate's shoes, just like he said. That wasn't a lie.

"This is your apartment," I say eventually.

"Yes," he says.

So that wasn't a lie either. It's not Sam's apartment.

"Can I ask you a few questions?"

"Knock yourself out," Pete says, looking at his phone.

"Sam's been sleeping on your floor."

"He has a bedroom. But he's been staying here, yes."

"Did he graduate from Dartmouth?"

"Yes. He majored in applied math." So *that* was a lie. Ha! "But he got into Dartmouth Medical School and then had to drop out before the semester started." Ah. So it wasn't a lie. Shit. "Why?"

"Just . . . trying to figure something out. And your dad . . ."

"Is coming here, now, to try to find Sam." Pete is very terse now, clearly warning me off the topic of the history of Sam and his dad. "So let's go find him."

Discovering that all of Sam's so-called lies were, in fact, not lies at all has left me reeling. They were just secrets.

What's the difference between a secret and a lie, anyway?

"I really don't know where he might be," I say, as we wait for the elevator. "Sam and I mostly hung out at my house, you know, we couldn't do much. . . . We were broke." Pete shoots me a funny look. Ah. He doesn't quite get the concept of broke.

"Where did you go most often when you did go out?"

"Wherever had free bar food that night."

Pete gives me that confused look again. He's never gone to a bar for free food.

"Wait!" I say. "I know where he might be! He was working for my neighbor. Vic."

"Vic? What does he do?"

"Uh, he's like, eighty-something years old. He does whatever the hell he wants."

"So what was Sam doing for him?"

"He fixed up his kitchen and bathroom; I think he helped knock through a bedroom wall. . . ."

Again, the look. Clearly Sam's old life didn't include helping Brooklyn octogenarians renovate their homes.

We get outside the building, and I glance up and down the street. "I think we can get a cab up that way, and if we can't, we can get a bus—"

Then a town car pulls up in front of us, and Pete opens the door for me. It's the same town car that Sam picked me up in at the playground in the rain that night. Of course. Pete has a permanent driver. This is Roger Rutherford's son, after all.

"Um, so, why do you live in Brooklyn?" I ask Pete, after giving the driver directions. "You do something finance-y, I'm guessing, a banker or something, so how come—"

"How come I don't live in Manhattan with all the other bankers?" he says, raising an eyebrow. "Don't judge a book by its cover, Angie."

"You're a book?"

Another death stare. Wow, Sam's brother is an arrogant fucker. Sam isn't exactly lacking in confidence, either, but somehow . . . somehow with him, it's an open, warm self-assurance. He's kind. And sexy. And funny and silly and gorgeous and everything I want and need and love. . . .

God, I miss him. I hope we can find him. I hope he hasn't just flown to some Caribbean island to get lost for another three years.

I stare out the window, trying to collect myself. I feel kind of panicky and wired. I was so nervous on the way up to the apartment in the elevator, all that adrenaline is still pulsing around my body, and this situation is so bizarre.

Then a new thought occurs to me.

What if he doesn't even want to see me?

I clear my throat. "Look, I don't know if I should come with you, okay? I don't know if Sam wants to see me. We kind of had a fight."

"I know," Pete says, flicking some fluff off his knee.

"You know?" I'm suddenly tired of Pete's clipped arrogance. "What the fuck do you know?"

"I know my brother told you he was broke because he didn't want to deal with all the inevitable Rutherford questions, and because it's just not part of who he is right now. I know he left a job because he wanted to see you again, and I know he stuck around in New York for way longer than he wanted to, just to be near you."

"Oh," I say in a small voice. "I didn't know that."

Pete looks over, frowning. "He's completely in love with you, Angie. Of course he wants to see you."

"Oh," I say again.

But inside, I'm exploding.

"Sam called in a couple of favors earlier today with a family friend who works at some fashion website. They called our father, who called me, wanting to know why I'd been keeping Sam a secret from him for the past few months."

"Why did your dad think that you'd know he was back?"

"Sam's my only brother, Angie. He's my best friend. Just because we're doing different shit doesn't mean we're not simpatico."

Simpatico. What a banker word to use. Sam would never use a word like that.

"Anyway," he continues. "We have to find Sam, now, before Rog does, and get him to leave the city."

"Leave?"

"My dad wants to kill him, Angie."

"You mean like . . ."

Pete looks over at me. "I mean like kill him."

CHAPTER **47**

"I haven't seen him," is the first thing Vic says when he opens his front door. If I weren't freaking out right now, I'd laugh: Vic is a terrible liar.

"I don't believe you," says Pete.

"I don't care." Vic tilts his head so that the few inches of height difference between them looks like a lot more. He looks at me. "You should know better than this."

"Vic, it's really important we find him," I say. "This is Sam's brother."

"You're Pete?" Vic's face changes, just a fraction of warmth creeping in. "Okay, come on in."

Pete and I walk into Vic's apartment. It's surreal being back in the room that was waist-deep in floodwater a few nights ago. There's no furniture, the carpet has been ripped up, and there's a muddy, chemical smell from whatever they are using to clean the place.

"I was just packing up some things. I'm going to Jersey to stay with my niece until the fix-up is finished," says Vic. He turns around and stares at Pete for a few seconds, then gives him a little nod. "So what do you want to know?"

"Where is Sam?"

"He got a job."

"Where?"

"Some yacht he was talking about, something going to Europe," says Vic. "One of the crew dropped out at the last minute, Sam got the call. He stopped by first to say good-bye."

"Why didn't he tell me?" Pete asks.

Vic shrugs. "Didn't want you to have to lie to your father."

Well, obviously Sam never had a problem confiding in Vic.

Once we're outside, I turn to face Pete. "Now we go to the North Cove Marina."

"Are you sure he's leaving from there?"

"I'd bet my life on it. No, better than that. I'd bet my job on it."

Pete looks at me funny again. I have the feeling he thinks I'm a little nuts.

The drive over the Brooklyn Bridge is largely silent. Pete doesn't bother to make conversation, he just keeps drumming his hands against his thighs, fidgeting, biting his thumbnail, putting the window down, then up, then down.

"Stop it! Just stop it!" I finally snap, just as we reach Manhattan. "You're so fucking tense!"

Pete looks at me, his jaw clenched. "I need. To find. My brother."

"You're being a total drama queen. I need to find him, too. Your dad isn't going to kill him."

"Really?" Pete pauses for a very long time, staring at me, and then seems to make a decision. "Look, Angie, because of Sam, our father had to fork over more than half his money to our mother in their divorce settlement. Sam had been spying on him, taking photos of Rog, uh, playing around. Gave them to our mom."

"So?" I say. "Your father cheated. Sam did the right thing." I wonder if that's what I should have done when my dad asked me to lie. Probably.

"Well it turned out she'd cheated on him, too," snaps Pete. "She'd been having an affair for years. So, actually, Angie, Sam did the wrong thing. He judged the situation before he knew the entire story."

"Oh."

"Dad found out. Epic fight. It got . . . it got pretty bad. So Sam dropped out of college, went a little wild, then took off and didn't come back. We're less than a year apart in age, we're best friends. But I only know half of what's going on with him. Sam always does what he thinks is right."

"Like keeping secrets from me? Even though I was supposedly the reason he came back to New York?"

"Yeah. Probably. He told me he thought he was busted one time. This guy we went to school with, Lev? He ran into him at some dinner party at your place."

"Lev? Julia's coworker? The guy who called Sam 'Ruthy' at the surprise party?"

"It's an old school nickname," says Pete, grinning to himself. Then he assumes his scowly-mean face again. "Anyway, thanks to you, my brother has been a fucking mess the past few days."

"Sam lied to me." I know I sound defensive, but I can't help it. "I told him everything about me, about who I was, and he lied."

"He didn't lie to you, Angie. He just didn't tell you everything. It's not the same as lying. He was trying to figure out the right time. . . . You don't get to know everything about everybody right away. None of us do."

I stare at him. Maybe that's true. I might never tell Sam or anyone else outside of Rookhaven the whole story about the Soho Grand night and everything that happened with Hal and Stef. It's my life, it's my past, and it belongs to me.

So by judging Sam for doing the same thing, does that make me a hypocrite?

Pete sighs. "Sam's problem was he never thought he did the wrong thing. Ever."

"He does now, I think. . . . He regrets doing that stuff," I say, thinking back to our conversation on my bed at our sleepover. "He told me something about your parents' divorce one time. . . . I think he regrets fighting with your dad."

"He said that?"

"He said he acted like a penis. No, wait, that wasn't it, not a penis—a dick."

Pete laughs for the first time tonight. "Yeah, that's pretty true. . . . Sam has always been the principled one, always the guy who did everything right. The ultimate good guy." Wow. The opposite of me. "But he could be kind of a dick sometimes, too. Self-righteous. And stubborn. If he decided to do something he had a hard time going back on his word." Okay, maybe not the total opposite of me. "What can I say? We were brought up to be arrogant."

"I wouldn't call him arrogant," I say. "Self-possessed, yes. Cool under pressure."

"I think the last three years have changed him. He used to care more about principles and less about people."

"He cares about people now!" I suddenly want Pete to know how amazing I think Sam is. "He looked after my roommate, Coco, and Vic, and, um, and me. . . ." A tear-lump swells in my throat and I can't say anything else. He did look after me. And I had stupid tantrums about romance novels and ignored his calls and sulked when he asked Julia out, and he still looked after me. He loved me.

Pete's too wrapped up in his own world to notice my tears. "Well, now he wants to start somewhere with nothing and end up sailing across the world." While we've been talking about Sam, Pete has stopped fidgeting, loosened his tie, and undone his top shirt button. He's calming down and warming up, and somehow, reminding me more of Sam. "It's symbolic. Or some shit like that. Whatever, I don't fucking get it. . . . And then he's going to apply for scholarships to medical school in the fall."

"Scholarships?"

"Yeah. He won't take money from either of our parents, and he won't take it from me, either, though I keep telling him there has to be some benefit to me becoming fucking mini-Dad." I glance at Pete, but he's not actually being bitter, he's just being honest.

God. I wish Sam had told me a tiny bit of this stuff. Though maybe the clues were there all along. I just didn't look. Too busy thinking about myself.

And now my brain is turning over and over, thinking about the difference between doing the right thing and the wrong thing, between being a good person or a bad person, between secrets and lies. It's so confusing....

The thing is, everyone thinks they're making the right decision when they're making it. It's only later that our mistakes become clear. And then we either make amends and fix those mistakes and deal with the aftermath, or we don't. Either way, life moves on.

Perspective is a bitch, but at least she's consistent.

We reach lower Manhattan. Endless skyscrapers light up the night sky. Millions of tiny twinkly lights, millions of people ... Goddamn, this city is big.

And then we're finally here.

North Cove Marina. The place where yachts meet skyscrapers, where Manhattan meets the deep blue sea.

Pete and I jump out of the car and hurry toward the pier, and as we get closer, I can just make out two figures. They're screaming at each other. And then I realize who they are, and suddenly, I forget how to breathe.

Sam.

And Roger Rutherford.

CHAPTER 48

At first, I can't make out any words. Just two extremely angry male voices shouting over each other. Even from twenty feet away I can see Sam is upset—oh God, I hate that. I feel almost sick at the idea of him being miserable.

Pete immediately charges between them and starts shouting, too, but I hang back, right at the end of the pier. It's horrible to watch, an almost violent fury between them. I can't imagine my father or mother ever screaming at me like that. It's like Sam's father really hates him. No wonder Sam wanted to leave.

"Don't you dare tell me you didn't know—"

"I was standing up for what I thought was right, goddamnit—"

"You were picking sides and being a pain in my ass—"

"I told you I never wanted to see you again, I meant it—"

"STOP IT!" Pete shouts so loudly that my ears hurt.

Sam and his father turn to Pete, their faces consumed with anger.

"Dad, back off, Jesus Christ!" says Pete. "What, you thought you'd come down here and bully Sam back into the family?"

"I thought I'd—"

"I'm still talking! And Sam, do you think maybe you could apologize to the old man for causing him so much trouble over the years?"

"I was doing what I thought—"

"But it wasn't right. It wasn't black or white, Sam, nothing ever is!"

"I don't need this! Fuck! This is why I left in the first place!"

Sam throws his arms up in the air, and then turns around, walking quickly away from his family, down the pier toward me. I've never seen him so worked up; he looks like he wants to cry and scream and run, all at once. I know that feeling; hell, that feeling has ruled me for years.

And then, when he's about fifteen feet away, Sam sees me and stops walking.

"Angie?"

I can't hang back anymore. I rush toward him, wrap my arms around him.

"I'm so sorry," we say in unison.

Then I lean back and kiss him, over and over again. My brain, my heart, my body is in free fall, and the only thought in my head is *Sam*.

Right this second, all I want is to make Sam's life easier and happier. I want to take away every sadness in his life, to make everything better for him, in every way possible.

It's the strangest feeling, this love. It's overwhelming. I want to protect him and be protected by him. I want to talk to him and listen to him. I want everything he wants to come true for him. It's not like anything I've ever felt before . . . it's whole. Complete. It will always be a part of me, it will never go away. But we don't have time to talk about it right now.

All we have time to do is kiss.

So in every kiss I try to tell him that I love him, that I hope he forgives me for running away, that I understand his past was his past and he didn't want to talk about it. I try to tell him that I know him so well, I love every inch of him, and that I know that I've only just breached the surface of him, of who he is and what he wants and what he's capable of doing with his life. I want to tell him that he's my best friend and my love, like no one else ever has been or will be again. And with every kiss, I feel like he's telling me the same thing.

"Oh, Angie, I'm so glad you're here, so glad," he whispers, leaning his forehead against mine. "I'm sorry. I should have told you everything."

"No, I'm sorry I wouldn't listen, I was wrong—"

"I wanted to tell you, it was killing me, really—"

And then I'm absorbed again by the warmth and sureness of his lips against mine, his lovely Sam-smelling skin, the truth and strength and *rightness* of him.

I pull back. "The clutch—it's all over the blogosphere. . . . That was you, right? You told the world it was mine."

"I pulled a favor with an old friend of my dad's."

"And that's what got you busted," I say, looking past him at Rog and Pete. "Helping me."

Sam smiles. "You're so talented, Angie, you just need one tiny break."

"I got one," I say. "I got a job today. A real one. In fashion." Even saying the words makes me smile so hard my cheeks hurt.

"Oh, Angie, that's amazing, I'm so happy for you—" Sam pulls me back in for more kisses.

Then I break away, glancing back at his father and brother, who are still talking angrily to each other. "You have to talk to them. You know you do. You don't want it to be like this."

Sam stares at me, smiles, and nods.

We kiss a couple more times, then once more for luck, then Sam takes my hand and leads me back down the pier. And for the first time in days, I feel quiet and calm inside.

"Angie James, this is my father, Roger, and my brother, Peter."

I nod at them, slightly awkwardly, given I know exactly who they are and that they have no goddamn interest in me right now.

Then Sam turns to his father. "Dad, I'm sorry I took those photos, I'm sorry I took sides. I just didn't like seeing Mom upset; I thought it was the right thing to do. I was wrong. I regret . . . everything."

Roger looks, immediately, like someone has pressed his deflate button, all that belligerent self-absorption disappears. "I understand, Sammy. I do. You've always been such a good kid, always sticking up for the little guy. . . . But what I don't understand is how you could not talk to me or your mother for three years. Three years, and nothing! Not a word!"

"I didn't think you'd want to hear from me. I thought you'd probably be happier without me around."

"Oh, Sammy . . . Never. I haven't been happy since you left. You're my *son*. No matter what else happens."

And just like that, the fight is over. Roger seems to have aged ten years in ten seconds and just looks like a sad old man, and Sam looks like, well, a sad young man. They stare at each other in silence.

"Your hair's turned gray," Sam says finally.

Roger grins. "I'd like to blame you for that, but I think your mother has the honor."

"Ha."

"Have you spoken to her?" asks Roger.

Sam shakes his head.

"I have," says Pete. Roger looks at him in surprise. "I didn't tell you, Dad. I knew you'd freak out."

"Well, I've been talking to her, too," says Roger eventually. "She's very happy out there, away from all this. . . ." He gestures to Manhattan, to the lights and sparkle and wealth towering over us. "She misses you, though, Sammy. She talks about you a lot, you know. She's been having some knee problems and been laid up a lot, so she's had a lot of time to think. . . . We started talking again because we were both so worried about you. Pete wouldn't tell us anything except that you were fine and figuring life out for yourself."

Sam looks away, and for a second, I think he's about to cry. Three years without even talking to your mother or father. And meanwhile, his parents are just getting older, and frailer, and lonelier. The minute that you think you don't need them anymore, that's when they need you.

"I'll call her," Sam says. "Tell her I think about her all the time. Tell her I'll call her, I don't know when I'll get phone access after tonight, but I'll call her."

Suddenly, from across the water, we hear a tiny speedboat approaching.

Sam turns his head. "That's my boss, we're about to go," he says, his face creasing in distress. "Dad, Pete . . ."

Pete leans forward to hug Sam, with a few back slaps for good measure.

Then Sam turns to his father. I don't think Rog is the physical affection type, but then he surprises me and leans forward, hugging Sam tightly. He whispers something in his ear, and Sam nods and then pulls away.

"I'll be in touch, okay? I promise."

Sam looks at Pete again and gives a funny little brotherly salute. Then he takes my hand, leading me down toward the end of the pier, where the *Peripety*—the yacht that will take him all the way to the other side of the world—is waiting for him.

We finally reach her, just as the little motorboat pulls up alongside and the captain jumps out carrying a box of supplies.

"Hey, Sam! This is the last of it. All good to go?"

"Yes. Good to go." Sam nods, his face assuming that professional crew member mask I remember from the day I met him. "Can I get two minutes?"

"You got it." The skipper climbs aboard the *Peripety* and disappears belowdecks.

The yacht that looked so big the first time I saw it now seems tiny. He can't sail across the ocean in this. It's not safe. I mean, she's not safe.

I turn to Sam. "Please, please be careful. Please. Nothing can happen to you, okay? I need you to be alive."

"I promise. If I could, I'd call you six times a day, but the cell reception on the Atlantic is really shit."

Sam pulls me to him and kisses me again. Then I pull away. I have so many questions.

"So you can't use a phone on board? What about e-mail? How long will it take you to get to Greece?"

"Three weeks, maybe four . . . The guy who owns the yacht won't be meeting us until June. Then we're sailing around the Greek Islands with him. Returning by September. I'm applying to schools. Some of them aren't that far away, Angie, we'll work it out—"

"Wow." Five months away. Five months is a long time. And then he won't even be living in Brooklyn anymore. Suddenly I feel a desperate panic in my chest. What if he forgets me? What if this is it?

There's a shout from the yacht. "Sammy! Let's go!"

"So no e-mails? No phone calls? Nothing?" I can't stop my voice from rising in distress. "I'll miss you so much."

"I'll miss you more." Sam kisses me again. "I'll be able to text sometimes, and whenever I get the chance to use the Internet somewhere, I'll e-mail you, okay?"

"The yacht doesn't have Wi-Fi?"

Sam laughs and kisses me again, and I try to empty my brain so all I think about is how this feels, this kiss, this feeling of his lips on mine and his arms around me, so I can have it at my mental fingertips to remember anytime I want, until the moment I see him again.

"This is for you, by the way. Happy birthday." Sam hands over a tiny gift-wrapped box. "I've had it for weeks. . . . I was going to give it to you for your birthday and tell you everything. Open it later."

I take the gift and smile at him. "I love you."

"I love you, too."

One tear runs down my cheek, and Sam wipes it away gently with his thumb. Then he gives me one last kiss, turns, and walks quickly away.

I'm overwhelmed with panic. Oh God, that's it. He's leaving.

A second later, Sam turns around and rushes back to me.

"One more," he says in a low voice, pressing his lips against mine. "Just one more, I couldn't let that be the last kiss. I couldn't take it." I start laughing and crying at the same time and kiss him back. Between kisses he whispers: "I'll stay. Say the word and I'll stay."

"No way," I say, tears running down my face. "This is yours. This is what you want now, it's what you need. You have to go. Just go."

And we kiss again, and then again. And then he turns around and, without looking back, walks to the end of the pier and climbs aboard the yacht. I watch for a few minutes as the skipper shouts instructions to him and the rest of the crew. Sam does everything quickly and confidently, with an air of intense concentration.

What feels like seconds later, the yacht finally pulls away into the darkness, and I watch the gap widening between me and him.

I stare after the yacht, my heart pounding, tears in my eyes, and a sadness deep in my stomach. But above all that, I know, I *know* this is the right thing. I need to stay here to find my future. He needs to leave to find his.

Please turn, Sam. Please look at me. Just one last time.

Then, just as I think that's it, I won't see his face again, Sam turns around and smiles at me, his face lit up by the flickering lights of the marina and the skyscrapers above us, and even from this distance, I can see he mouths "I love you."

I mouth it back. "I love you."

When the night has finally swallowed up the *Peripety,* I turn around, tears still wet on my face. I take a few deep breaths, looking up at the city above me.

I feel strangely okay and calm inside. Sam will be back.

And meanwhile, I have my own life to live.

I walk slowly back to Pete and Roger, a tiny smile on my face. When I get to them, Rog finally looks at me properly. "Haven't we met before?"

"I met you the other night at the Minetta Tavern," I say. "With Cornelia."

"Ah, Cornelia. The naughty yet ambitious socialite," Rog says, nodding. "I don't think I'll be hearing from her for a while. She's got bigger fish to fry."

"Dad, you wanna go grab a bite?" says Pete.

"I'd love that," says Roger. He turns to me. "Care to join us?"

"No, uh, thank you, I have to get home," I say. "I need my friends."

"Take my car service," says Pete. "I'll go with Dad."

"Oh no, I couldn't, really."

"Look, it's the least I can do, Angie," he says in a low voice, as Rog strides ahead. "You're the reason I found Sam. Without you, they'd have killed each other."

And so I say good-bye to the Rutherfords and get into the town car.

"Brooklyn, please. Union Street. Just up from Court."

The driver nods, and seconds later, we're heading across Manhattan toward the Brooklyn Bridge. Toward home.

Then I unwrap the little gift Sam gave me on the dock.

It's a tiny square box. Inside is a small pair of sapphire stud earrings. And a note.

*Happy Birthday, Angie. These earrings are the color of the
Caribbean sea you dived into the first day we met. You probably
hate them. Your taste in jewelry is just one in the long list of
things that I want to know about you, and don't . . . yet.*

I love you.

Sam

I put the earrings on and smile, feeling that happy warmth inside
again. Sam will be back.

There's just one thing I need to do. I take out my phone and quickly
text my dad. Despite the way he behaved, he's my father. And he probably needs me as much as I need him.

Let's meet up this weekend. I think we should talk. A x

Then my phone rings. A number I don't recognize.

"Hello?"

"Angie James?"

"Speaking . . ."

"Hi! This is Edie Jansen. We met a month or so ago, when you were
handing out your CV with a free latte outside Maven? That was you,
right?"

"Uh, yes?"

"I was the girl wearing Marni for H&M!"

"Oh! Hi!" The pointy-faced chic girl, the one who actually talked to me!

"Great! God, I have been looking everywhere for your CV, you would
not believe the day I had, but in the end Cynthia had it, isn't that amazing? She was impressed with your ingenuity and kept it this whole time!
Okay, so I saw on Fashionista that Cornelia Archer's clutch bag was designed by you, right? We want to know if you'd be interested in a hookup
with one of our clients. It's a tiny fast-fashion brand called Serafina; it's
only small-time now but it's—"

"Yes," I say. "I'm interested."

"Can you come in for a meeting tomorrow morning?"

"I'm working with Sarah Drake right now." I try to sound as official
and efficient as I can. "Can you do six forty-five P.M.?"

"Yes! *Love* Sarah Drake. We'll work around you. That would be perfect! Okay, *ciao!*"

I hang up and put my window down, looking out at the city night-scape as we drive over the Brooklyn Bridge. I feel more calm and sure than I ever have in my life.

I am exactly where I am supposed to be. I have a job. I have a passion. I have best friends. I have true love. I have a life. I have things to look forward to and people to care about. I am never alone. I am happy.

This is where everything begins.

ACKNOWLEDGMENTS

The problem with writing these acknowledgments pages is that everything I write sounds clichéd. So let's pretend it doesn't, okay? Okay. Good.

Thanks to Vicki Lame and Dan Weiss at St. Martin's Press, and my agents, Jill Grinberg and Laura Longrigg for—oh, everything.

Thanks to all my friends. And all those times you [insert meaningful friendship-related event HERE]. And Hawk, for giving me exact instructions on what would give Coco an overdose. He's one hell of a fun doctor.

Thanks to everyone who read *Brooklyn Girls* and e-mailed me to tell me you loved it. You guys are my spirit animals. (I don't really know what that means, but it sounds funny.)

And most of all, thanks to my lovely little family for being perfect. I love you.

READ ON TO FIND OUT WHERE IT ALL BEGAN

Out **NOW!**

www.quercusbooks.co.uk

CHAPTER 1

Never screw your roommate's brother.

A simple rule, but a good one. And I broke it last night. Twice.

Oopsh.

At least the party was awesome. I'll try that excuse if Julia is pissy. And if her house is trashed. Which I'm pretty sure it is.

I'm not exactly surprised. I like parties, I'm good at them, and it was August 26 yesterday. And on that date, I always drink to forget. This year, I did it with whips, chains, and bells on.

My bare ass keeps brushing against the wall as I squish away from Mike. Don't you hate that? Doesn't random hookup etiquette demand he face the other way? I wish he would just leave without me having to, like, talk to him.

I wonder what Madeleine, his sister, would say if she found out.

She'd probably ignore me, which is what she always does these days. I wish Julia hadn't asked her to move in.

Julia, my best friend from college, inherited this house when her aunt passed away. So Julia invited me, her little sister Coco, and Madeleine to move in. And then we needed a fifth, so I asked my friend Angie. We're a motley crew: Coco's the Betty Homemaker type, Angie's all fashi-tude, Julia's super-smart and ambitious, and Madeleine's uptight as hell. And me? I'm . . . well, it's impossible to describe yourself, isn't it? Let's call me a work-in-progress.

We moved in two weeks ago. It's a brownstone named Rookhaven, on Union Street in Carroll Gardens, a neighborhood in the borough of Brooklyn in New York City. None of us has properly lived in New York before.

Carroll Gardens is a weird mix of old people who've probably lived here forever, young professionals like us who—let's face it—can't afford to live in Manhattan, and a bunch of yupster couples with young kids. There's a real neighborhood village vibe with all these old, traditional Italian bakeries and restaurants next to stylish little bars.

I like stylish little bars.

I like my bedroom, too. I've had a lot of bedrooms in my life— twenty-seven, if you count every room change at boarding school and college—but never one quite like this. High ceilings, windows looking out over the front stoop, wall-to-wall mirrored closets. Okay, the mirrors are yellowed and the wallpaper is a faded rosebud print that looks like something out of an old movie. It just *feels* right. Like this is how it's supposed to look.

That's kind of Rookhaven all over. If I were feeling nice, I'd call the décor vintage and preloved. (Old and shabby.) I'm just happy to be in New York, far away from my parents, in the most exciting city in the world, with a job at a SoHo PR agency. My life is *finally* happening.

Can I be honest with you? I shouldn't have slept with Mike. Not when things are already, shall we say, complicated with Madeleine. Casual sex only works when it's with someone you can never see again. But, as I said, it was August 26 (also known as Eddie Memorial Day, or Never Again Day). And on August 26, shit happens.

What is that damn ringing sound?

"I think that's the doorbell."

Gah! Mike! Awake! Right here next to me. I peek through my eyelashes. Like Madeleine, he's ridiculously good-looking. I guess it's their Chinese-Irish DNA. Good combination.

"Erm . . . someone else will get it," I murmur. My breath smells like an open grave. Not that it matters. Because I don't like him like that. Even though last night I—ew. God. Bad thought. But hey! So what? So the whole sex thing was a bad idea. There is no reason to feel stupid Puritan guilt about one-night stands. I am a feminist. And all that shit.

The doorbell goes again.

"Pia . . . Come here, you crazy kitten," Mike says, pushing his arm under me.

"I better get the door. It could be someone important!" I say brightly, slithering down around him and falling onto the dark green carpet with a thump.

I wriggle into my panties, trying to look cool and unbothered as I put on the first T-shirt I see. It belonged to Smith, a guy I dated (well, slept with a few times) in college. The back says, "I brake for cheerleaders . . . HARD."

I pull on my favorite cutoff jean shorts and Elmo slippers and stuff my cell phone in my pocket.

"I'm glad you brake for cheerleaders," says Mike. "They're an endangered species."

"Um, yup, totally!" I say, and slam the door behind me, cutting him off. Mike! God! Nightmare!

I close my eyes, trying to remember last night. It's worryingly hard. I was feeling meh after Thompson (this cockmonkey I've been dating, well, sleeping with) ignored my text (*Hola. Bodacious party. Bring smokes if you can . . .* Good text, right? Ironic use of passé slang, trailing ellipses rather than a lame smiley face, etc.). And rejection is not a good look for me. Not on August 26.

So I drank more. And more. And then more.

I remember dancing. On a table, maybe? Yeah, that rings a bell. . . . And I think I was doing some '80s-aerobics-style dance moves. The grapevine. Definitely the grapevine. I was having fun, anyway. I don't usually worry about much when I'm having fun.

And Mike was doing one-handed push-ups, really badly, and making me laugh, and then I stumbled, and next thing I knew Mike's lips were on mine. Now I *love* kissing, I really do, and he is pretty good at it, and I was trashed, so I suggested we go to my room. And then . . . oh, God.

Nothing burns like hangover shame.

The person at the door is really dying to get in. *Dingdongdingdongdingdong.*

"Coming!" I shout, picking my way over the bottles and cigarette butts on the stairs.

I hope it's not the cops. I don't *think* there were drugs at the party, but you never know. Once time at my second boarding school I thought that my boyfriend Jack had OCD, which was why he arranged talcum powder in little lines, and as it turned out— Wait. Back to the nightmare.

I open the front door and sigh in relief.

It's just a very old man. His face is like a long raisin with pointy elf ears, on the top of a tall and skinny body.

"Young lady, where is your father?" he says in a strong Brooklyn accent. *Fadah.*

"Zurich," I say, then add, "Sir." (And they say I don't respect my elders.)

"Are you a relation of Julia's?"

"Fu— I mean, gosh, no."

"Well, that figures. I didn't think Pete remarried, and you're definitely a half-a-something."

Seriously? "I'm a whole person, not a half. My mother is Indian, my father is Swiss. Please come back later." I try to close the door, but he's blocking it.

"I need to speak with Miss Russotti."

"Which one? There are two. Russotti the elder, also known as Julia, and Russotti the younger, also known as Coco."

"Whichever is responsible for the very loud party that went on till 5:00 A.M. and caused the total cave-in of my kitchen ceiling."

I gasp. He must live in the garden-level apartment under our house. My mind starts racing. How can I fix this?

"Oh, I am so sorry, I can pay for the ceiling, sir, I—"

"I take it that there were no parents present?"

"I think my roommate Madeleine has babysitting experience, does that count?"

"Don't be smart with me."

"I've never been called smart before," I say, twisting my hair around my finger, trying to get him to laugh a little bit. No one can stay angry after they laugh, it's a fact.

His expression warms slightly, then falls as though pushing the crags and crevices into a new shape was too much effort. "Just get Julia."

"Yes, sir. Would you like to wait inside?"

"If you think I want to see what this house looks like this morning, you've got another think coming."

"Is it think or thing?"

"It's think."

"I'll go get Julia."

I run up the stairs, jumping over the leftover party mayhem, and knock on Julia's bedroom door.

"Juju?" I peer in.

No Julia, just Angie and some tall English lord guy she met in London at the Cartier Polo (yes, seriously). I saw them making out in the laundry room last night after a game of "truth or dare," which Angie renamed "dare or fuck off." Man, I hope they didn't screw on the washing machine. My laundry is in there. I keep forgetting to take it out, and it goes all funky with the heat, so then I have to wash it again and— Oh, sorry. Focus.

"*Angie!* Wake the hell up!"

I shake her, but she just gives a little snore and buries herself deeper into the bed. She looks like a fallen angel with a serious eyeliner habit. And she's *impossible* to wake after a night out.

Julia will lose her shit if she finds out about this. She and Angie haven't exactly bonded. My bad: I talked Julia into letting Angie move in before they'd even met, because Angie's folks got her a job as a PA to some food photographer woman in Chelsea and she needed a place to live, and Angie's been, like, my best friend since I was born. (Literally. Our moms met in the maternity ward.)

Then Angie walked in, said, "It's a dump, but it's retro, I can make it work," and lit a cigarette. Julia was not impressed.

"Angie! Get. The hell. Up."

"Pia?" She peers up at me through her long white-blond hair. "I had to sleep here, there was a threesome in my bed."

"Ew," I say, grimacing, as I pull Angie onto her feet. "Help me. Major crisis."

"You're such a fucking drama queen. Hugh. Dude. Get up."

Hugh climbs out behind her unsteadily. He has a very posh English accent. "Tremendous party." *Pah-teh*. He's very handsome, like a young Prince William, with more hair.

As soon as he leaves, Angie licks and smells her hand to check her morning breath. "Yep, pretty rank. What's wrong, ladybitch?"

"Everything. We have to find Julia."

"Roger that." Angie's still wearing her tiny party dress from last night and slips on a pair of snow boots from Julia's closet. "You have a hickey on your neck."

"How old school of me." I grab Julia's foundation to dab over it. "Ugh, why is she wearing this shade? It's completely wrong for her. Sorry, off topic."

We head upstairs. Angie stares at her closed bedroom door. "God, I hate threesomes."

"Totally. It's just showing off."

Angie smirks, then karate kicks her door in. "Show's over, bitches! Get the hell outta my house."

Two girls I've never seen before and a tall dark-haired guy I vaguely recognize from college saunter out of Angie's room.

"Pia, babe!" says the guy, putting on his shirt. "I tried to find you all night! Remember that party back in junior year? A little Vicodin, a little tequila . . ."

I shudder. Now I remember him.

"Leave," snaps Angie. "Now."

"Bitch," he calls, walking down the stairs.

"Blow me!" she calls back, then heads into her room. "Fuck! I'm gonna have to burn the sheets."

I hear a hinge squeak. It's Madeleine, coming out of the bathroom in a pristine white robe, her hair wrapped perfectly in a towel-turban.

"Morning!" I say, smiling as innocently as I can.

She pads to her bedroom and slams the door. Typical. Good thing I didn't add, *"By the way, your brother is naked in my bed."*

I trudge up the last flight of stairs, finally reach Coco's attic room, and knock. Julia must be in here. There's nowhere else to go.

"It's me . . ." I open the door slowly.

Julia is sitting on the bed, still wearing her clothes from last night yet sportily immaculate as ever, next to Coco, whose blond bob is bent over a plastic bucket and—oh, God. She's puking.

"Coco!" I say. "Are you sick?"

"Clap, clap, Sherlock," says Julia.

"I'm fine!" Coco's voice echoes nasally in the bucket. "So fine. Oh, God, not fine." Noisy, chokey barf sounds follow. "Wowsers! This is green! Oh, Julia, it's green, is that bad?"

"It's bile," says Julia, rubbing Coco's back and glaring at me. Furious and sisterly, all at once. "I need to talk to Pia. Try to stop vomiting, okay?" She has a deep, self-assured voice, particularly lately. It's like the moment she graduated, she decided it was time to *act adult at all costs.*

"Maybe I'll lose weight," Coco's voice echoes from the bucket.

I follow Julia to the tiny landing at the top of the stairs, closing Coco's bedroom door behind us. I feel sick. Confrontation and I really don't get along.

"I am sorry," I say immediately. "I guess you're angry about the party, and—"

"You sold it to me as a 'small housewarming,'" interrupts Julia. "This place was like Cancun on spring break, but less classy."

I hate being told off, too. It's not like I don't *know* when I've screwed up. Or like I do it on purpose. And I never know what to say, so I just gaze into space and wait for it to be over.

"I *said* no wild parties. When we all moved in, that was the rule." God, Julia is scary when she wants to be. "What the fuck were you *thinking,* Pia?"

"It just sort of, um, happened. . . ." I say, chewing my lip. "And I'm sorry about this, too, um, there's an old dude at the door? He said his ceiling caved in? I'll pay for it! I have the money and—"

"Vic?" says Julia in dismay. "I swear to God, Pia, I can't live with you if you're going to fucking act like this all the time. I mean it!"

She's going to kick me out of Rookhaven?

"I won't!" I exclaim. "I'm sorry! Don't overreact!"

"Start cleaning up!" she shouts, thundering down the stairs.

She's going to kick me out. I thought I finally had somewhere that I could call my own, somewhere that wasn't temporary, and somewhere I might actually not have to wear shower shoes. Yet again I am the master of my own demise. Mistress. Whatever.

I walk back into Coco's room. "Can I get you anything, sweetie? I've got rehydration salts somewhere."

"No," she croaks, smiling cherubically at me from the pillow. "I had fun last night. You were so funny."

"Oh, well, that's good." What the hell was I doing?

There are hundreds of books on Coco's floor. I think they're usually in the bookshelves in the living room. They're all old and tattered, with titles like *What Katy Did* by Susan Coolidge and *Are You There God? It's Me, Margaret* by Judy Blume. I loved *What Katy Did,* I remember. The sequel, *What Katy Did at School,* was one of the reasons I thought boarding school would be awesome. Stupid book.

"Why are these here?" I ask.

"I didn't want them to get, um, you know, trashed at the party," says Coco. "So I picked up all the ones that my mom loved the most and brought them up here."

"It must have taken you a while," I say.

"Every time I made a trip, I had a shot. . . ." Coco starts puking again.

"Hey, ladybitches," says Angie, sauntering in with an unlit cigarette propped in the side of her mouth.

"For you, Miss Coco." Somehow, Angie has found an icy-cold can of Coke.

"Wow, thanks! I normally drink Diet Coke, but—"

"Trust me, Diet Coke is bullshit. Okay kids, I am officially over this post-party chaos thing. Let's clean up."

At that moment, my phone rings. Unlisted number. I answer.

"Hello?"

"Pia, it's Benny Mansi."

Benny Mansi is the director of the PR agency where I work. My parents know his family somehow and got me the interview back in June. I started working there last week. Why would he call me on a Sunday? Is that normal? Perhaps it's a PR emergency!

I try to sound professional. "Hi! What's up?"

"Are you aware that there's a photo of you on Facebook, dancing on a table topless and drinking a bottle of Captain Morgan rum?"

WHAM. I feel like I just got punched.

"Um, I—"

"Pia, we're letting you go before your trial period is over."

WHAM. Another hit.

"You're firing me . . . for having a party?"

"Captain Morgan is one of our biggest clients," Benny says. "As my employee, you represent the agency. You're also Facebook friends with all your brand-new colleagues. You were tagged, they saw it. I applaud your convivial approach to interoffice relations, but that sort of behavior is just . . . it's unprofessional, and it's completely unacceptable, Pia."

"I know." A wash of sickly cold horror trickles through me, and I stare at the yellowed glow-in-the-dark stars on the sloping ceiling in Coco's room. They lost their glow long ago. . . . Oh, God, I can't be fired. I can't be fired after *one week*. "I'm so sorry, Benny." Silence. "Did you . . . tell my, um, father?"

He sighs. "I e-mailed him this morning. I didn't tell him why." I don't say anything, and his voice softens. "Look, Pia, it's complicated. We made some redundancies a few months ago. So hiring you, as a family friend, really upset a few people, and that photo . . . my hands are tied. I'm sorry."

He hangs up.

I can feel Coco and Angie staring at me, but I can't say anything.

I've lost my job. And I'm probably about to get kicked out of my house. After one week in New York.

My phone rings again. It's my parents. I stare at the phone for a few seconds, knowing what's on the other end, what's waiting for me.

I wonder if Coco would mind if I borrowed her puke bucket.

I need to be alone for what's about to happen, so I walk back out to the stairwell and sit down. I can hear Madeleine playing some angsty music in her room on the floor below, mixed with Julia's placating tones and Vic's grumbly ones from down in the front hall.

Then I answer, trying to sound like a good daughter.

"Hi, Daddy!"

"So you've lost your job already. What do you have to say for your-self?"

My voice is gone. This happens sometimes. Just when I need it most. In its place, a tiny squeaking sound comes out.

"Speak up!" snaps my father. He has a slightly scary Swiss accent despite twenty years living in the States.

"I'm . . . sorry. I'll get another job, I will, and—"

"Pia, we are so disappointed in you!" My mother is lurking on the extension. She has a slight Indian accent that only really comes out when she's pissed. Like now.

"You wanted the summer with Angie, so we paid for it. You wanted to work, so we got you a job. You said you had the perfect place to live, so we agreed to help pay rent, though God knows Brooklyn certainly wasn't the perfect place to live last time I was there—"

"You have no work ethic! You are a spoiled party girl! Are you sniff-ing the drugs again?"

They've really honed their double-pronged condemnation-barrage routine over the years.

"Work ethic. Your mother is right. Your total failure to keep a job . . . well. Let me tell you a story—"

I sink my head to my knees. My parents have the confidence-killing combination of high standards and low expectations.

They also twist everything so it looks terrible. They told me if I got good grades they'd pay for my vacation, and that I'd never find a job on my own, *and* they offered me an allowance, so of course I said yes! Wouldn't you?

". . . and that is how I met your father and then we got married and had you and then lived— What do you say? Happily ever after . . ."

Yeah, right. My parents hardly talk to each other. They distract themselves with work (my dad) and socializing (my mother). They met in New York, where they had me, then moved to Singapore, London, Tokyo, Zurich . . . I went to American International Schools until I was twelve, and then they started sending me to boarding school. Well, boarding school*s*.

"Life starts with a job, Pia. You think we will always pay for your mistakes, that life is just a party. We know you'll never have a career, but a job is—"

"A reason to get up in the morning!"

"And the only way to learn the value of money. Do you understand?"

I nod stupidly, staring at the wall next to me, at the ancient-looking rosebud wallpaper. At the bottom the paper has started to peel, curled up like a little pencil shaving. It's comforting.

"Pia!" my mother is shouting. "Why are you not listening? Do we have to do the Skype again?"

"No, no, I can't, my Skype is broken," I say quickly. I can't handle Skyping with my parents. It's so damn intense.

"We are stopping your allowance, effective immediately. No rent money, no credit card for emergencies. You're on your own."

"What? B-but it might take me a while to get another job!" I stammer in panic.

"Well, the Bank of Mom and Dad is closed unless you come live with us in Zurich and get a job here. That's the deal."

"No way!" I know I sound hysterical, but I can't help it. "My friends are here! My life is here!"

"We want you to be safe," says my mother, in a slightly gentler tone. Suddenly tears rush to my eyes. "We worry. And it seems like you're only safe when you're with us."

"I *am* safe."

"And we want you to be happy," she adds.

"I am happy!" My voice breaks.

My father interrupts. "This is the deal. We're vacationing in Palm Beach in exactly two months, via New York. If you're not in gainful employment by then, we're taking you back to Zurich with us. That's the best thing for you."

The tears escape my eyes. I know I've made some mistakes, but God, I've tried to make it up to them. I studied hard, I got into a great college. . . . It's never good enough.

How is it that no one in the world can make me feel as bad as my parents can?

"Okay, message received," I say. "I gotta go."

I hang up and stare at the curled-up rosebud wallpaper for a few more seconds. Then, almost without thinking, I lick my index finger and try to smooth it down, so it lies flat and perfect against the wall. It bounces right back up again.

With one party, I've destroyed my life in New York City. Before it even began.

CHAPTER 2

When Julia comes back upstairs moments later, pink with fury, my stomach flips over. I hate fighting. And Jules is really good at it. She should have been a lawyer.

"You destroyed our neighbor's ceiling," she snaps. "Destroyed. A piece of plaster fell on his sister's head this morning. She's eighty-six-fucking-years old, Pia!"

"Is she okay? Oh, my God, I can't—"

"She's fine," says Julia. "It was only a tiny piece. But Vic is *pissed*."

"I'll pay for it, I promise!" I say. "I have, like, sixteen hundred dollars. He can have all of it." It's all I have in the world, and the last of the money from my parents, but I need to convince Julia not to kick me out. "I'm sorry, Julia, I didn't know it'd get so out of control."

"What were you *thinking*?"

"I just . . . I thought it would be fun, that everyone would have a good time." I can't tell her that I was drinking because it was August 26. I never talk about Eddie to anyone. Only Angie knows the story, only Angie saw me that day. "Seriously, Juju, I never meant to hurt anyone . . . or destroy the old guy's, I mean Vic's, ceiling."

"Vic and Marie have been here *forever*. Since long before I was born, or my mom," says Julia. "They're like family, okay?"

Suddenly, I understand. Her mom grew up here, and she died of breast cancer about eight years ago. Her dad has cocooned himself in silent grief ever since, and then her Aunt Jo passed away, so I guess Vic and Marie—and Rookhaven—are sort of a last link to her mom. No wonder she feels so protective.

"I'll fix the floor damage," I say, reaching out for Julia's hand. She doesn't resist, which I take as a good sign. "And I'll get them flowers to say sorry. Today. And I will not let anything bad happen to this house again. I cross my heart."

Julia takes a deep breath and leans against the wall, closing her eyes. She looks exhausted, and it's not just from the party. Her job—trainee in an investment bank—starts at 6:00 A.M. every day, and she doesn't get home until past 7:00 P.M. every night. It's step one in her plan to take over the world. She's so exhausted, she's actually kind of gray. And she's not even hungover.

"I had fun last night, by the way."

"What?" I say.

She opens one eye, a tiny grin on her lips. "It was a great party. I had fun. Right up until Coco started to do a striptease in the kitchen."

I clap my hand over my mouth. "No way."

"I carried her up here. Anyway, don't tell her. She doesn't remember. I always think it's better that way."

"Oh, I know," I say. "You never flashed an entire bar your Spanx on Spring Weekend."

"Totally. Goddamnit, I wish I'd been wearing a thong that night."

We grin at each other for a second, remembering. That's the Julia I know and love. The girl who works hard and plays hard, too. And the girl who always wants to make everything right. But I can't tell her what happened with my job and parents just yet. I need to process it (uh, pretend it didn't happen).

"Hang on a moment." Julia narrows her eyes at me. "Bed hair. Panda eyes. And stubble rash. Peepee, you got action last night!" she exclaims.

"I did not! And don't call me Peepee!"

"Have we made up?" coos Angie, peering out from Coco's room. She wraps her bare leg around the door, lifting one snow boot–clad foot up and down like a meteorology-loving stripper. "Are we all friends again?"

"Those are my boots," says Julia. "Why are you wearing them?"

"Are you planning on skiing soon? I think not." Angie sashays past us down the stairs. "It's August. I'll return them in pristine condition as soon as the house is clear of party debris, okay, Mommy?"

Julia rolls her eyes and heads downstairs. "Start cleaning."

Angie flicks the finger at Julia's retreating back.

"Real mature, Angie."

"Suck my mature."

"I'm hungry."

"You're always hungry. Let's clean."

Somehow, being hungover and giggling with Angie cheers me up and helps squash my what-the-sweet-hell-am-I-going-to-do-now thoughts. She keeps making little moans of dismay at each new inch of party filth, and pretty soon we've both got the giggles.

"When I have my own place, there will be no carpets," I say. "Carpets are just asking for trouble."

"Did anyone lose a shoe? And why did we invite someone to our party who wears moccasins?"

"Is this red wine or blood? No. Wait. It's tomato sauce. Weird."

"You wanna talk me through the hickey, ladybitch?"

I catch Angie's eye and bite my index finger sheepishly.

"You had the sex? You little minx . . ."

"With her brother," I whisper, pointing at Madeleine's door. "Bit of an oopsh."

Oopsh is our word for a drunken mistake.

"Oopsh I kissed the wrong dude, or oopsh I tripped and his dick landed in my mouth?"

I crack up. No one does crass like Angie. She looks like a tiny Christmas angel and acts like a sailor on a Viagra kick. "Or was it more like, oopsh, I'm riding his face and—"

"Too far! That's too far."

"Sorry."

"Don't tell Jules, she'd just have to tell Maddy, and it'd be a whole thing."

"Absolute-leh, dah-leng," she says, in her best imitation of her mother's British accent. "You were totally kamikaze last night."

"It was August 26. That's International Pia Goes Kamikaze Day, remember? Crash and burn."

There's a pause. "Oh, dude, I'm sorry. I totally forgot. Eddie."

I can't bring myself to look at her. Only Angie saw me that day, only Angie knows how bad it was. She always calls me a drama queen, but she knows that misery was real. You don't fake that kind of breakdown.

"I don't want to talk about it," I say.

Angie keeps cleaning. "Fuck him, Pia. Okay? Fuck him! It's been four years!"

I nod, scrubbing as hard as I can. It has been four years since we broke up. And I really should be over it. Then, thank God, Angie changes the subject.

"So I'm gonna move out to L.A. after the holidays," she says. "I don't really belong here in Brooklyn, you know?"

This news just makes me feel even sadder. There's no point arguing with Angie. She does whatever she wants. Instead I scrub harder and, stair by stair, stain by stain, we make it downstairs. Angie puts on some music, and we clean to the post-party-appropriate strains of the Ramones. I can hear Julia and Coco throwing out empty bottles in the kitchen and, every now and again, shrieking when they find something nasty. Oh please, God, no drugs or used condoms. Just spare me that.

"What time did the party finish?" I ask Angie.

"About five. Lord Hugh and I saw out the last of the party people just as the sun was coming up."

"He seems . . . Lordesque."

"He's very Lordesque." She nods. "He also knows his way around a washer-dryer."

"Did you guys do a"—I pause and grin at her—"full load?"

"Just a half load. Then we rinsed. Very thoroughly. Oh, look. Half a spliff. How nice."

We make it to the first floor, and help Julia and Coco finish up the kitchen, which primarily involves de-stickying every surface. Nothing does sticky like forty-year-old linoleum.

"That was intense," says Julia, wiping her forehead with her arm. "The laundry room flooded. That's what made Vic's ceiling collapse."

"I'll fix it," I say again.

"Oh, I know you will."

"I cleaned the bathrooms," says an icy voice. I look up, and see Madeleine, carrying a mop and bucket. "They were absolutely revolting."

"Thanks, Moomoo," says Julia. Madeleine rolls her eyes at Julia's nickname for her—she professes to hate it—and pushes past us to the sink, giving Julia's ponytail an affectionate tug. She's so nice underneath that cold-and-controlled exterior, just not to me, not anymore.

Okay, the Madeleine story, in brief: we were friends once. Really good friends. In fact, she and Julia and I were pretty much inseparable for freshman year. We're all very different, but somehow we just . . . clicked, in an opposites-attract kind of way.

Then, suddenly, at the end of freshman year, Madeleine got crazy drunk for the first time ever and, out of nowhere, told me she hated me. I was holding her hair back so she could throw up, and she just said over and over again, "I hate you. I hate you, Pia, I hate you." Then she passed out. The next day, I tried to talk to her, she shut down, and we've been in a cold war ever since. And now her brother is naked in my bed.

Hmm.

Between you and me, I wouldn't have moved in if I'd known Madeleine was going to be here, too. Jules was probably hoping we'd make up, that the five of us will become best friends and start swapping traveling ya-ya pants, or whatever. I can't see that happening. Particularly given that Julia's now busy making her own little cold war with Angie.

An hour later, the whole of Rookhaven is clear of party fallout, not including hangovers.

"Perfect," says Julia, smiling as she looks around the living room.

"C'mon, Ol' Rusty hasn't been perfect since the Eisenhower administration," says Angie.

"Don't call this house Ol' Rusty," snaps Julia. "If you hate it so much, you can always leave."

"Who said anything about hating it?" says Angie.

"I like it just how it is," I say.

"I *love* it. And I love Brooklyn. I'm a lil' Brooklynista." Angie smiles sweetly at us all.

"Can we get some food, please?" I say to distract them from their almost-argument. "I'm starving."

"I'm making French toast!" That'd be Coco. She's been trying to force-feed us comfort food since we moved in. "Everyone in the kitchen!"

"I'll just be a minute," I say.

Time to deal with you-know-who.

"Hey." Mike is groggily stretching in my bed. He looks a lot better clean-shaven and in a pressed shirt. "Where've you been? You wanna snuggle?"

I laugh. "Snuggle?"

"All the cool kids are doing it. C'mon . . ."

I put on my aviators and take a deep breath. "Mike, your sister will kill me if she finds out about last night. Let's just pretend it didn't happen, okay?"

"Okay. Fine." Wow, he's bratty when things don't go his way.

"I'm serious. She doesn't like me as it is."

"She doesn't?"

"No . . ." Suddenly I realize that talking to Mike about his sister being a bitch isn't the smartest move. "Um, you know. I'm probably misinterpreting it."

"Maddy's pretty hard to read," he says. "She never lets her guard down. Even with me, and I'm family. I think it's insecurity."

I fight the urge to roll my eyes. I am so sick of people blaming everything on being insecure. It's not a get-out-of-jail-free card, you know?

"Whatever. We're all in the kitchen. Wait ten minutes and you can leave without being seen."

"Why don't I just climb out the window and shimmy down the drainpipe?"

"That would be perfect! Do you think you could?" I say, just to see his reaction. "Kidding. See ya."

Thank hell that's over with. I have more important things to worry about. Like being unemployed, broke, and cut off from the so-called

Bank of Mom and Dad (pay interest in guilt!) with the threat of being forced to leave New York in exactly eight weeks.

If a kitchen could be grandmotherly, then this one is. It's huge, yet also 1960s-sitcom-rerun cozy. The kind of kitchen in which cakes and cookies and pies are always baking, you know? My mother *never* baked.

As we're sitting around the kitchen table, listening to Lionel Richie and eating Coco's amazing French toast with bacon on the side, I finally tell the girls everything. About the Facebook photo, work, and even my parents.

"In a nutshell, I destroyed Rookhaven, and I'm unemployed, unemployable, and broke," I say, pushing my food around my plate miserably. "I don't know what to do. Who gets fired after one week? I'm such a fuck-up. . . . If I don't get a job, my parents will make me go live with them."

"You can't do that!" Somehow, Angie manages to look cool even talking through a mouthful of bacon. "You'd never survive! Your parents can't make you do anything."

"Yes, they can!" I say. "I've never stood up to them. I just do what they say, and then avoid them."

"Sounds healthy," Julia says.

I shrug. Is anyone's relationship with their parents healthy?

"I can't believe you were fired!" says Coco. "That must have been awful." She reaches over to give me a hug. For the second time today, I have to blink away tears. I swear I want to cry more when people are nice to me than when they're mean.

"Yuh," says Madeleine. "Who would have thought dancing topless at a party would backfire like that?"

"I was wearing a bra!"

"Pia, it was a sheer bra."

"Stop it, Maddy." Julia forks another piece of French toast onto her plate. I notice she hasn't said anything about not wanting me to move out.

"Listen, I have loads of cash, you won't go hungry . . . or thirsty." Angie picks up a piece of crispy bacon with her fingers and dips it in a pool of maple syrup, and then lowers her voice. "And I think the laundry room flooding might have been our, uh, my fault. I'll help pay for it."

"I can loan you money, too," says Julia quickly, her competitive nature kicking in.

"Don't be crazy." I can't accept charity. I won't. "If I need money that badly, I'll go to a bank. Get a loan."

"Are you crazy? Take a loan? You'd have some bananas interest rate, and the loan would just get bigger and bigger and you'd never be able to pay it back! So you'd have no credit rating! It would destroy your life!" Wow, Julia is really upset about the idea of a loan.

"Okay, jeez, I won't go to a bank," I say. "Anyway, that's really not the point. The point is, I need a job. And I just have no idea what I could do."

"What was your major?" asks Coco.

"Art history."

"Art . . . historian?"

Everyone at the table giggles.

"Yes, I chose a very impractical major. No, I don't know why."

"Probably because it sounded cool," says Angie, flashing me her best I'm-so-helpful smile.

I raise an eyebrow at her. "Not helping."

"I could see you working at a fashion magazine," says Coco, hopping off her chair. "Who wants more coffee?"

"Me please!" say Julia and Angie in unison, and frown at each other.

"I'm not a writer," I say. "Anyway, it would be all *Devil Wears Prada*–y. And the models would make me feel shitty."

"Besides, it's really hard to get a job in anything related to fashion," says Angie. For a second, I wonder if she knows that from personal experience. Before I can ask, she picks up her phone to read a text.

"And I need to earn money, *now*," I say. And, I add silently, it's a fact: the cooler the job, the worse the money. My salary at the PR agency—not even that cool compared to working in, like, fashion or TV or whatever—was thirty-five thousand a year, which, if you break it down and take out money for rent and bills, works out to about twenty-five dollars a day. I mean, a decent facial in New York is at least a hundred and fifty. How could anyone ever survive on that salary and still eat, let alone have a life?

Julia is in fix-it mode now. "Let's make a list of your skills and experience. What did you do at the PR agency last week?"

I think back. "I pretended not to spend all my time e-mailing my friends, sat in on meetings about things I didn't know anything about, and watched the clock obsessively. I swear I almost fell asleep, like, twenty times, right at my desk."

Everyone (except Madeleine) laughs at this, though, honestly, it was kind of depressing. Am I really meant to do that for the rest of my life?

"If you need fast cash, get a fast-cash job, girl," says Julia. "Waitressing. Bartending."

I blink at her. "Manual labor?"

Madeleine makes a snorting sound of suppressed laughter. I ignore her. I said it to be funny. Kind of.

"With that kind of princess attitude, you're screwed," says Julia.

"I want a real job. Something that will impress my parents, which means something in an office. Something with an official business e-mail address."

"So e-mail your résumé to PR recruitment agencies in Manhattan," says Julia. "Then wow them with how bright and smart and awesome you are. Any PR agency in Manhattan would be lucky to have you!"

"Okay." I love having a bossy best friend sometimes. It makes decision-making much easier.

'This scandalous read breaks all the rules'
Now Magazine

And coming soon . . .

Tower Hamlets College
Learning Centre

Withdrawn

131725

KT-466-696

Withdrawn

NUMBER FREAK

TOWER HAMLETS COLLEGE
POPLAR HIGH STREET
LONDON
E14 0AF

Withdrawn

Withdrawn

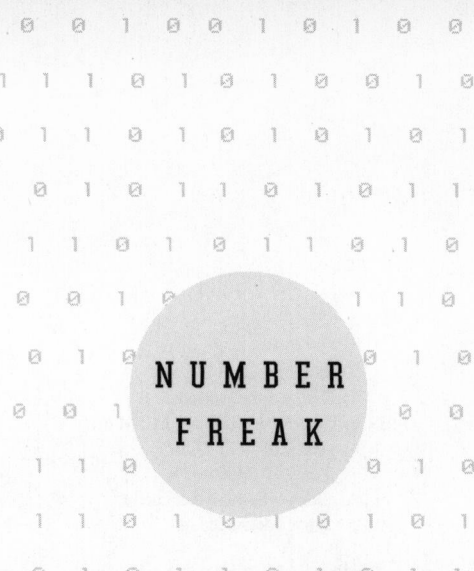

NUMBER FREAK

From 1 to 200
The Hidden Language of Numbers Revealed

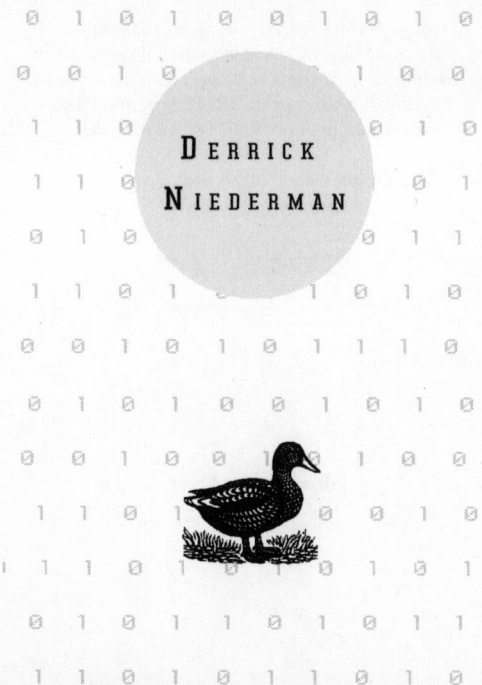

Derrick Niederman

First published in 2010 by
Duckworth Overlook
90-93 Cowcross Street, London EC1M 6BF
Tel: 020 7490 7300
Fax: 020 7490 0080
info@duckworth-publishers.co.uk
www.ducknet.co.uk

© 2009 by Derrick Niederman

First published in the USA in 2009 by
The Penguin Group

The moral right of the author has been asserted.

All rights reserved. No part of this publication
may be reproduced, stored in a retrieval system, or
transmitted, in any form or by any means, electronic,
mechanical, photocopying, recording or otherwise,
without the prior permission of the publisher.

A catalogue record for this book is available
from the British Library

ISBN 978 0 7156 3710 4

Printed in Great Britain

Order No:
Class: 510 NIE
Accession No: 131725
Type: L

NUMBER
FREAK

"**NUMBERS** make them number."

Those were the words of Eugene T. Maleska, former crossword editor of the *New York Times*. The year was 1981, and he had just accepted one of my efforts for publication. In doing so he inquired about my lot in life, and I replied that I was a graduate student in mathematics (at the moment making crossword puzzles instead of working on my thesis, but that's another story). He replied in turn that most word people aren't interested in mathematics, letting the quote above speak for itself.

Gene has long since left this world, but in a way this book is for people just like him—intellectually curious people intent on learning something new every day, but for whom numbers remain something of a mystery. People who have heard of a prime number but might not be able to define what it means.

As it happens, as I began writing this book, Gene's successor Will Shortz titled one of my later puzzles in a way that illustrates what this book is all about. The puzzle in question appeared in the *Times* in August 2006, and involved names and expressions such as H. L. Mencken, IQ test, MX missile, and C. S. Lewis. Will gave the puzzle the title $13 \times 2 = 26$, hoping to have dropped a big hint. The idea was that once solvers reminded themselves that the English alphabet contained 26 letters, they had a big head start in deciphering the puzzle's theme—13 entries, each beginning with a pair of letters as per the examples above, altogether representing every letter in the alphabet once and only once.

And that's what this book is about. Go to the nth page and you'll find out everything about the number n you ever wanted to know—its arithmetic, its geometry, and even its appearances in popular culture. We will discover that numbers have an individuality about them that you'd never see from afar. Just because 16 and 17 are close together, for example, doesn't mean they act the same. One is a perfect square, being 4×4, the other is prime, having no factors other than itself and 1. Sixteen is a wonderful number for a weekend tennis tournament, while seventeen stinks in that regard but excels at others. How many people are aware that there are precisely 17 symmetric wallpaper patterns?

I ended up tackling every number from 1 to 200, winnowing the discussions as I got to triple digits. I found that some numbers had enough going for them to be their own book, while others presented a struggle to find anything at all: 138, anybody? But I ended up being amazed at just how many numbers had a story to tell if you were willing to dig deep enough.

Now for a few true confessions. First, even though this book *feels* comprehensive, there are plenty of number properties that didn't quite make the cut for the simple reason that there had to be a cut. I don't think I mentioned that there are 13 witches in a coven, or that 200 is a common cutoff when assessing cholesterol readings. Sorry. And I could have written an entire book using only sports numbers, so you can imagine how many sports-related entries were moved aside to make room for others. Religious or otherwise sacred numbers could have made yet another separate book, again one that I chose not to write. This is a book about numbers, not a book about numerology, and there's a big difference. Yes, I dabbled in some numerological notions. I even observed that numbers such as 37 have built cult followings for their supposed mysticism. Even if I didn't share their particular zeal, I at least tried to show what the fuss is all about.

I also failed to give adequate explanations for expressions such as "the whole nine yards" or "23-skidoo," but in this case please don't blame me. In 95% of these cases, there's no single origin, but rather a list of theories of origin. I gave it my best shot with "86," as in "to jettison," but I found that it's tough to write when you're busy making disclaimers and caveats, so I left many if not most such numerical expressions alone. Frankly I was surprised at just how many number-related expressions had no definitive roots.

This book is stuffed with trivia, but it's also stuffed with the history of mathematics—and don't you dare equate the two! As tours to mathematical history go, this is about the most zigzagging one you can imagine. You will be in 1800 on one page and back to 200 BC on the next. But before you're done you'll encounter all the greats, from Euclid to Euler and on to modern day standouts of whom you may have never heard.

Part of me worries that I have occasionally done these great scholars a disservice. After all, there's a lot of just plain fun and silly stuff within the book, often rubbing right up against some important mathematics. Even worse, I won't necessarily tell you in advance which is which! Sometimes there is in fact a fine line between what we call "recreational mathematics" and areas in mathematics that have a wide range of useful applications. But the point is that most of the great names in the field have dabbled in both, because their curiosity wouldn't let them do otherwise. This book is ultimately about developing your mathematical mind, and there's more than one way to do it. If some of the basic mathematical terms remain foreign to you, I whipped up a glossary that should help keep you in the game.

And if you want to read the book with an eye for popular culture only, that's fine. The seven wonders of the ancient world are every bit as "sevenish" as the seven bridges of Konigsberg, and you don't need any graph theory to understand them. And you don't need me to tell you that there are seven days in a week, but I tried not to forget those everyday items as well.

The nature of this project made it a bottomless pit, but I'm almost sad that it had to come to an end. You, however, are just beginning, and I wish you well along your numerical journey.

—Derrick Niederman
Needham, MA

1

THE number 1 is both a logical and a lousy way to start this book. Logical because 1 comes first, and its omission would seem absurd. But also lousy, because this book is about special properties of whole numbers, and the number 1 just has too many special properties for its own good.

For starters, 1 is the "multiplicative identity"—if you multiply any number by 1, that number is left unchanged. In particular, 1 is its own square and cube, and in general 1 to the nth power equals 1 for any n. A probability of 1 is the same thing as certainty, and 1 is also the maximum value attained by the basic trigonometric functions sine and cosine. The number 1 is also a trivial solution to many equations that mathematicians study, so much so that it pretty much has to be exempted: Not only is it a perfect square and a perfect cube, it's a triangular, pentagonal, and hexagonal number, and so on. You see the problem?

The idea that the number 1 is everywhere has a specific foundation in the form of Benford's Law. Introduced in 1938 by physicist Frank Benford, the idea is that the digits found in a variety of naturally occurring datasets (molecular weights, population sizes, digits on the front pages of newspapers, to name a few of the thousands of sets studied by Benford) are not uniformly distributed. In particular, the leading digit of such numbers is 1 about three-tenths of the time, far above the one-in-nine frequency you might expect. (Sorry, but zeroes don't count in this context.)

The progenitor to Benford's Law was astronomer Simon Newcomb's 1881 discovery that within a book of logarithm tables, the pages containing logarithms beginning with 1 were much more likely to be worn around the edges. More recently, Benford's Law has been applied in the detection of tax and accounting fraud. The basic principle is that people who make up numbers are not familiar with Benford's Law, and the bogus datasets they generate stand out because they have far too few 1's in them.

▼

THE Greek philosopher Parmenides (fifth century BC) was of the view that "all is one." While I can't say I understand exactly what he meant, apparently it was Parmenides who inspired Zeno (which can be spelled with either a Z or an X, followed by *one* backward) to come up with his now famous set of paradoxes. Perhaps the best known of these paradoxes, known in the trade as Dichotomy, asserts that before you can ever reach a destination, you have to go halfway first. No problem there, except that from the halfway point you have to go halfway again, and so on, the paradox being that as long as you do so you'll never quite get to your destination. This line of reasoning confounded the thinkers of Zeno's day, but by the time Newton and Leibniz drafted the concepts of calculus in the late 1600s, the notion that an infinite series of numbers could converge to a finite number was no longer paradoxical. The specific series at hand is represented by the equation

$$1 = \frac{1}{2} + \frac{1}{4} + \frac{1}{8} + \frac{1}{16} + \frac{1}{32} + \ldots, \text{ or more compactly as } 1 = \sum_{n=1}^{\infty} \frac{1}{2^n}$$

▼

A more advanced type of paradox involving the number 1 came from the great French mathematician Henri Lebesgue (1875–1941). His Lebesgue measure (pronounced *le-bayg*, by the way) provided a means for measuring various subsets of Euclidean space. A simple example would be the interval [0,1] (namely, all real numbers between 0 and 1), which has a Lebesgue measure of 1. No problem so far, but it jars our intuition when we hear that the set of irrational numbers between 0 and 1 also has measure 1. In other words, the entire set of proper fractions, infinite though it may be, has a measure of zero, a stunning reminder that not all infinities are the same.

Lebesgue was apparently the last notable mathematician to think of 1 as a prime number. Yes, the late astronomer Carl Sagan included 1 as a prime in his 1985 book *Contact*, but nowadays most mathematicians would be more swayed by the views of longtime UCLA professor and Einstein protégé Ernst Gabor Straus, to whom is attributed the following quotation: "The primes are the building bricks of arithmetic, and 1 is just not a brick!" In that spirit, 1 is the only number in this volume that will not be designated at the top of its page as being either prime or composite; in the latter case, we will of course be kind enough to provide the factorization.

IN the world of music, *A Chorus Line* highlighted one as a singular sensation, but Harry Nilsson had already warned us that it is also the loneliest number. Three Dog Night's 1969 version of the Nilsson song "One" was that band's first gold record, although it did not reach number 1 on the Billboard charts.

IN chess, the number 1 is used to indicate victory, so a line-by-line recap of a chess game that ends with 1–0 indicates a victory by white, while $\frac{1}{2} - \frac{1}{2}$ indicates a draw and 0–1 indicates a black victory.

FINALLY, the phrase "We're number one" is by now a rather tedious refrain, especially when it comes from the other side of a football stadium, but the expression isn't about to be replaced, such is the power of one. Along those lines, it must be said that the expression "public enemy number one" simply isn't what it was in the days of Al Capone. Nor is the "identity parade," known to Capone and even law-abiding Americans as the "police lineup," whose popularity has fallen with the advent of computer databases and DNA technology. But even when lineups were in vogue, many police sta-

tions started their lineups with number 2, simply because the mighty number 1 was chosen disproportionately often, no matter where the guilty party happened to be standing. Frank Benford might have predicted as much.

2 [prime]

THE number 2 is the only even prime number. It is also the only prime number that lacks an *e* in its name, but that's because every odd number has an *e*.

▼

THE square root of 2, written $\sqrt{2}$, was the first number shown to be irrational, meaning that it cannot be written as the quotient of two whole numbers. The discovery of this fact is credited to Hippasus of Metapontum (circa 500 BC), and its proof is surprisingly easy. Just assume that $\sqrt{2} = \frac{p}{q}$, with p and q positive integers with no common factors. If we square both sides we get $2 = \frac{p^2}{q^2}$, or $2q^2 = p^2$. But it's not possible for one perfect square to be twice another. Specifically, note that p can't be odd in the above equation, because if it were, the right-hand side would be odd, whereas the left-hand side is clearly even. But if p is even it has a factor of 2, and there p^2 would be divisible by 4. But since $p^2 = 2q^2$, that would mean q is even, violating our assumption that p and q have no common factor. Hence the equation $2q^2 = p^2$ cannot ever hold.

Okay, maybe that wasn't as easy as you would have liked, but don't be jealous of Hippasus. Apparently the notion of irrational numbers was an affront to his fellow Pythagoreans, a group that thought the world revolved around nice simple ratios. Hippasus made his discovery while at sea, or so the legend goes, whereupon his shipmates threw him overboard. Nowadays we are more tolerant of mathematical discovery, although it should be said that those who demonstrate an early aptitude for mathematics are often the object of derision and ridicule in grade school. The irony of the Hippasus tale is that the set of irrational numbers turns out to be a higher-order infinity than the set of rational numbers, a fundamental fact that neither he nor his tormentors lived to discover.

▼

THE prefix *bi-* means two, as in bicycle, binoculars, biplane, bisect, and binary. Curiously, the word *biscuit* also applies, as it derives from the Italian biscotti, which literally means "twice cooked."

▼

IN geometry, the number 2 shows up in the famous saying "two points determine a line." This statement is emphatically true in planar geometry, but frequently abused in the real world, where two data points may be insufficient to determine an actual trend.

▼

IT is well-known that if a right triangle has legs a and b and hypotenuse c, then $a^2 + b^2 = c^2$. This equation, known to one and all as the Pythagorean Theorem, may not even be the most recognized equation involving c^2 (that title probably belongs to $E = mc^2$), but it is still way up there on the list of recognizable mathematical equations. And it's a mite easier to prove than Einstein's trademark equation, as the following diagram shows:

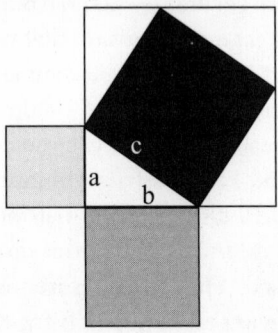

The largest square measures $a + b$ on each side, so its area equals $(a + b)^2$. But this square also consists of the square with side c coupled with four triangles each with area $\frac{ab}{2}$. Putting everything together, $(a + b)^2 = c^2 + 4(\frac{ab}{2})$. Multiplying out the left-hand side, $a^2 + 2ab + b^2 = c^2 + 2ab$, so $a^2 + b^2 = c^2$. In particular, if a and b both equal 1, c equals the square root of 2, and the exploration of what c could possibly be is apparently what got Hippasus his ticket to Davy Jones's locker. (It was fourth-century BC geometer Theaetetus who is credited with the more general result that the square root of any integer that is not a perfect square must be an irrational number.)

Note that the above proof required that the angle between a and b was a right angle, because otherwise the areas of the white triangles would have been more complicated to calculate. You should know that the Pythagorean Theorem works the other way around—if the legs of a triangle are such that $a^2 + b^2 = c^2$, then the triangle in question is a right triangle. That much was common knowledge in the time of Euclid (300 BC). Since Euclid's day there have been hundreds of published proofs of the Pythagorean Theorem. One of the most notable was devised in 1876 by James A. Garfield, who became president of the United States five years later. (Alas, nowadays anyone with such mathematical curiosity and competence would probably have it used against him in a national election.)

▼

THE Pythagorean Theorem generalizes to three dimensions, so if a, b, and c are the three sides of a rectangular prism (box) and d is its diagonal, you have the equation $a^2 + b^2 + c^2 = d^2$. And it even generalizes in two dimensions to triangles other than right triangles, yielding the law of cosines.

But the one thing you can't do to the Pythagorean Theorem is to take the 2 out of it. The celebrated Fermat's Last Theorem, proved by Princeton's Andrew Wiles in the mid-1990s after a 300-year wild-goose chase, declares that the equation $x^n + y^n = z^n$ has no solutions for any positive integer n other than 2. (Okay, I lied. That equation has infinitely many solutions when $n = 1$, proving the point made in **1** that 1 can be a nuisance, because so many mathematical truths "accidentally" include 1 as a completely trivial case.)

▼

FOR a final appearance of the number 2 in a geometric context, it shows up in a formula derived by the great Swiss mathematician Leonhard Euler (1707–1783), who noticed that in a three-dimensional shape known as a polyhedron, there is a fixed relationship between the number of edges, faces, and vertices.

To take a simple example, in the cube below there are 12 edges, 8 vertices, and 6 faces, and $8 + 6 - 12 = \mathbf{2}$.

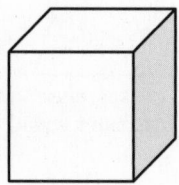

Euler showed that this formula holds for any polyhedron. Specifically, if the number of edges, vertices, and faces are denoted by e, v, and f, respectively, then $v + f - e = 2$.

(No, the e you see there isn't the e from a calculus course, though it is perhaps worth pointing out that the calculus e is named for Euler, whose extraordinary work will appear many times before this book is through.)

3 [prime]

THE "Three Legs of Man" has been the official symbol of the Isle of Man since the thirteenth century. A possible inspiration was the Sicilian flag, which features the head of Medusa surrounded by three legs. Many European flags, notably the French and Italian flags, consist of three vertical stripes.

JUST as two points determine a line, any three points that aren't in a straight line determine a plane. In particular, those three points can be joined to form a triangle, of which there are a few basic types:

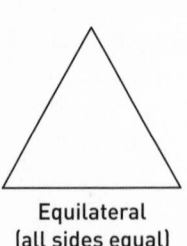

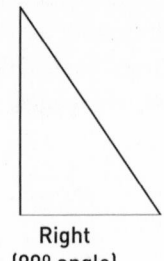

Equilateral
(all sides equal)

Isosceles
(two sides equal)

Right
(90° angle)

THREES IN GEOMETRY

IF three congruent circles intersect in a single point (the point P at right), the other three points of intersection must lie on a circle congruent to the first three. This result is known as Johnson's Theorem, having been discovered by Roger Johnson in 1913.

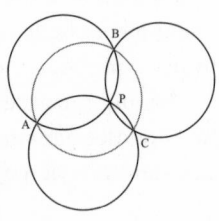

IF three equilateral triangles of different sizes are joined point-to-point (shown at right), their centers will form the vertices of a fourth equilateral triangle. This result is actually known as Napoleon's Theorem, in honor of its discoverer, an amateur mathematician named Napoleon Bonaparte. Napoleon's combination of intellect and, eventually, power, led the great astronomer and mathematician Pierre-Simon Laplace to dedicate his groundbreaking *Celestial Mechanics* to him. As legend has it, Napoleon thanked Laplace for this dedication and observed that the manuscript had

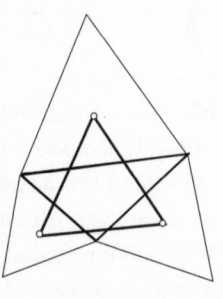

made no mention of God. To which Laplace replied, "Sire, I found I had no need of that hypothesis."

▼

IT is possible for a right triangle to be isosceles, but a right triangle can never be equilateral, as all angles of an equilateral triangle must be 60 degrees. A non-right triangle with three unequal sides is called scalene.

▼

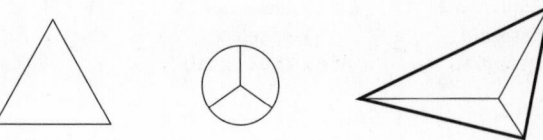

THERE is a nice relationship that unites a perfectly symmetric equilateral triangle (above left) with a perfectly asymmetric scalene triangle (above right). The figure between them looks quite a bit like a Mercedes logo, but for our purposes it is just a three-pointed star whose endpoints form an equilateral triangle. Now imagine taking that logo and placing it inside the scalene triangle such that each point of the logo is pointed directly at one of the vertices of the triangle—if it helps to envision yourself driving a Mercedes, so be it. Once you find this point, draw lines to the three vertices as in the right-hand diagram. Whether you realized it or not, you have created three line segments such that the angle between any two of them is precisely 120 degrees (always possible unless the triangle had an angle exceeding 120 degrees in the first place). That magical point in the interior of the triangle is known as the "Fermat point" and has the property that the sum of the distances to the three vertices is the smallest possible. Finding points such as these is of interest today if you're laying cable or constructing paths on semiconductors, but back in the 1600s it was a challenge given by Pierre de Fermat to Evangelista Torricelli. Torricelli apparently solved the problem and had time left over to invent the barometer.

▼

PERHAPS the best-known triangle of all is of infinite length, and that would be Pascal's Triangle, the first few rows of which are seen below. The sides of the triangle consist of 1's, while every number in the middle is obtained by adding the two numbers to the above-left and above-right.

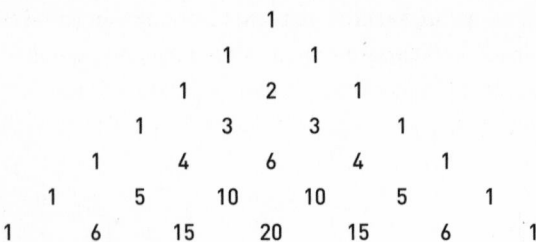

While simple in its construction, Pascal's Triangle contains a host of important patterns and rules. For example, in the bottom row above (usually referred to as the sixth row, with the single "1" on top treated as row zero), the third number from the left (15) is the number of ways of choosing a subset of three objects from an original set of 6 (6 ways of choosing the first one, multiplied by 5 ways of choosing the second, multiplied by 4 ways of choosing the third, divided by 6 ways of arranging the three objects you chose). In general, the kth entry of the nth row of Pascal's Triangle equals $\frac{n!}{k!\,(n-k)!}$ where ! is the factorial function (n factorial is the product of all positive integers less than or equal to n).

An alternative interpretation of the triangle can be seen by calculating an expression such as $(a + b)^6$, which equals $a^6 + 6a^5b + 15a^4b^2 + 20\,a^3b^3 + 15\,a^2b^4 + 6\,ab^5 + b^6$. Suddenly the sixth row of Pascal's Triangle emerges in the form of the numbers in front of the various expressions involving powers of a and b (more compactly, but more off-puttingly, known as "binomial coefficients").

ALTHOUGH much of mathematics is universal, the name of Pascal's Triangle is not, as it was studied in many places in the world long before the arrival of Blaise Pascal in the 1600s. In China, Pascal's Triangle is called Yang

Hui's Triangle after the thirteenth-century Chinese mathematician who studied it. In Iran it is known as Khayyam's Triangle, while in Italy it is known as Tartaglia's Triangle. All of which raises the question of why in the world we call it Pascal's Triangle, and the answer is that a fellow named Pierre Raymond de Montmort decided to name the triangle in Pascal's honor sometime in the early eighteenth century. Here's a relatively new puzzle arising from the triangle: Suppose that after creating any particular row of Pascal's Triangle, you calculated the ratio of odd numbers to even numbers. If you kept going, that ratio would approach a fixed limit. What is that limit? (See Answers.)

▼

THE expression "Two's company, three's a crowd" applies in all sorts of situations. To take a relatively benign example, while many games are designed for one-on-one play (chess and backgammon come quickly to mind), and while many more modern board games work perfectly well with multiple players (Sorry, Clue, Monopoly), it's rare for board games to be designed specifically for *three* players. Yet many TV games, including such stalwarts as *Jeopardy!* and *Wheel of Fortune*, are designed to accommodate three participants. And *Let's Make a Deal* often made contestants choose among curtains numbered 1, 2, and 3, a feature that eventually placed emcee Monty Hall in the middle of a mathematical paradox.

What became known as the Monty Hall Problem was actually formulated by Martin Gardner as the Three Prisoner Problem as far back as 1959. In the modern version, a contestant on *Let's Make a Deal* chooses one of the three curtains in hopes that a car—as opposed to, say, a goat—was behind it. Let's say that the contestant chooses curtain number 1. In the workings of the problem, though not in *Let's Make a Deal* itself, Monty Hall then opens one of the other two curtains, revealing a goat. The question is, assuming that curtain number 2 has now been revealed (and that Monty Hall is not being mischievous), does it make sense to switch your original guess from number 1 to number 3, or should you stay put?

This problem was posed by Marilyn vos Savant in *Parade* magazine in 1990, and the volume of reader mail was extraordinary. Thousands of respondents simply couldn't accept her claim that the contestant should indeed switch her choice from curtain number 1 to curtain number 3. Many prominent mathematicians apparently entered the debate—on the wrong side.

While it is counterintuitive to think that switching curtains improves your chances—after all, the only thing Monty Hall did was to reveal a curtain that did not have the car behind it, and you already knew that such a curtain existed—there's a way of seeing through the paradox. The key is to note that Hall's actions did not change the likelihood that curtain number 1 held the car; its chances were and remained one in three. But now that curtain number 2 has been ruled out altogether, the likelihood of the car being behind curtain number 3 must have risen from $\frac{1}{3}$ to $\frac{2}{3}$.

▼

A Koch snowflake is made by starting with an equilateral triangle, removing the middle third of each side, building three new equilateral triangles to fill in the missing thirds, and continuing the process. As the number of iterations grows, the perimeter of the snowflake grows without bound, but the area never exceeds $\frac{8}{5}$ the area of the original triangle. This phenomenon plays out in the real world in the form of coastlines. For example, the coastline of Alaska, full of

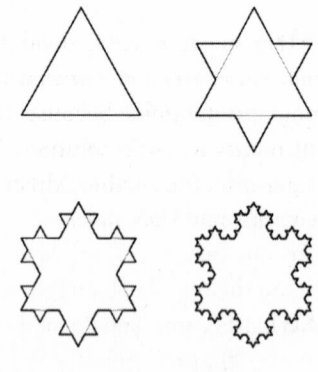

little jigs and jags, is 5,580 miles, almost as great as the 6,053 miles of coastline of the 48 contiguous states combined.

The Koch snowflake is an example of a fractal—a shape that can be split into smaller parts that mimic the whole. The father of fractals, Benoit Mandelbrot, would argue that the length of a coastline is in fact unbounded, limited only by the amount of natural detail that you wish to incorporate. Fractal-like objects occur frequently in nature and are as varied as mountain ranges, river networks, and ferns.

FAMOUS THREES

THE Big Three at Yalta were Churchill, FDR, and Stalin. A generation earlier, the Big Three would have been Lloyd George, Wilson, and Clemenceau at Versailles.

In American business, the Big Three either means the television networks ABC, CBS, and NBC or the automakers General Motors, Ford, and Chrysler. The term is applied the world over in various forms, from American colleges, as in Harvard, Yale, and Princeton, to Portuguese sports clubs, as in the *Os Três Grandes* SL Benfica, FC Porto, and Sporting CP.

THE DIVINE COMEDY

DANTE'S masterpiece is divided into three segments called *canticas*: *Inferno*, *Purgatorio*, and *Paradiso*. The three-act structure is standard in theatrical productions because it creates a natural sequence of setup, confrontation, and resolution. This same sequence appears even in four-act plays such as Arthur Miller's *The Crucible* and five-act plays such as Shakespeare's *Macbeth*.

GAUL

"ALL Gaul is divided into three parts." Julius Caesar's famous statement on Gaul was not always borne out by history: Gaul was home to many different cultural subdivisions before the fourth century AD, when the emergence of the Franks gave the country its current name and boundaries. Along these lines, the French Revolution was also characterized by *Liberte, Egalite, Fraternite*, a troika that to some is embodied by the French *tricolore* of red, white, and blue.

. . .

4 $\left[\, 2^2 \,\right]$

THE number 4 can be created by taking two to the second power, as above, or by multiplying two 2's, which boils down to the same thing, or by adding two 2's, which boils down to the same thing as that.

▼

COMBINING two 2's to make four is something of a quintessential truth: In George Orwell's *Nineteen Eighty-Four*, Winston Smith of the Ministry of Truth proclaimed, "Freedom is the freedom to say that two plus two make four. If that is granted, all else follows." Fyodor Dostoevsky preferred the multiplicative route, as in the following passage from his 1864 novel *Notes from Underground*: "Good heavens, gentlemen, what sort of free will is left when we come to tabulation and arithmetic, when it will all be a case of twice two make four? Twice two makes four without my will. As if free will meant that!"

▼

AS marvelous as the equation $4 = 2 + 2 = 2 \times 2 = 2^2$ is, it sometimes makes patterns more difficult to figure out. To wit, consider that there are precisely four subsets of a set of two elements, which we'll denote by {A,B}: Those subsets are {A}, {B}, {A,B} (the set itself), and Ø (the empty set). But what is the formula for the number of subsets of a set with n elements? Is it $2n$? Or maybe n^2? Anyone for 2^n? n^n? All those formulas work in the case where $n = 2$. As this is not *Suspense Theater*, let me reveal that the correct answer is 2^n: The principle here is one of binary inclusion/exclusion—each of the n elements is either in a particular subset or it isn't, and those two choices are multiplied by one another n times to produce the final result of 2^n.

▼

4 is the only number in the English language that contains the same number of letters as its name. But there's more going on here. Choose any number whatsoever and count the number of letters in its name to get a new number. Count the number of letters in the new number, and keep going. No matter what number you started with, you'll eventually end up with four. The proof is actually a little easier than you might think. Care to take a stab at it? (See Answers.)

THERE are said to be four fundamental forces in nature—gravity, electromagnetism, and weak and strong nuclear forces—so it is fitting that a whole bunch of things are divided into fourths:

Directions/points	north	south	east	west
Cards/suits	spades	hearts	diamonds	clubs
Orchestra/sections	brass	woodwind	percussion	string
Year/seasons	spring	summer	fall	winter

No doubt you can come up with a few quartets of your own, but you should be aware that the concept of groups of four dates back to the followers of Pythagoras, aptly named the Pythagoreans. We will encounter this quirky group a bit later on, but for now let's just say that they were apparently aware of the groupings below as far back as the fifth century BC:

Numbers	1	2	3	4
Magnitudes	point	line	surface	solid
Elements	fire	air	water	earth
Figures	pyramid	octahedron	icosahedron	cube
Living Things	seed	growth in length	in breadth	in thickness
Societies	man	village	city	nation
Faculties	reason	knowledge	opinion	sensation
Seasons	spring	summer	autumn	winter
Stages of life	infancy	youth	adulthood	old age

SPEAKING of groups of four, we owe another one to the Pythagoreans—the division of mathematics into four groups. The tree branches down as follows:

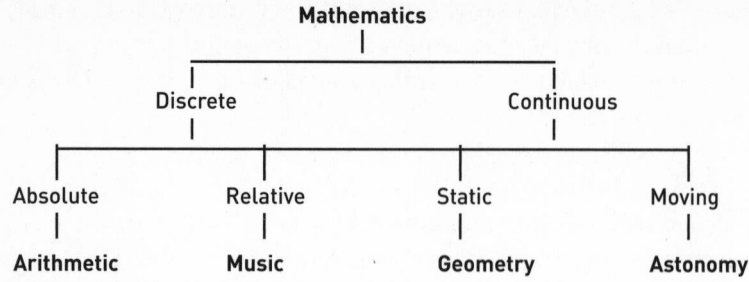

The base of the tree is the famous *Quadrivium*, the four subjects needed for a bachelor's degree in the Middle Ages.

▼

THE French mathematician and poet Claude-Gaspar Bachet de Méziriac (1581–1638) made a famous conjecture about the number 4. Having demonstrated that the numbers 1 through 120 could be written as the sum of four perfect squares, Bachet conjectured that it was possible to write *every* positive integer in this fashion. (For example, $120 = 64 + 36 + 16 + 4 = 8^2 + 6^2 + 4^2 + 2^2$. Note that the statement really means "four or fewer" squares, as you could substitute 10^2 for $8^2 + 6^2$ in the equation above.)

Pierre de Fermat (1601–1665) claimed to have a proof of Bachet's conjecture, but, in typical Fermat fashion, he never revealed it. The conjecture remained unresolved until 1770, when Joseph-Louis Lagrange published a proof.

▼

THE Four-Square Theorem falls in the category of existence theorems—although it proves that any positive integer can be written as the sum of four squares, it does not show how to get them. It takes a little poking and prodding to find out, for example, that $1,718 = 49 + 144 + 625 + 900 = 7^2 + 12^2 + 25^2 + 30^2$. And the representation doesn't have to be unique: 1,718 also equals $1,600 + 81 + 36 + 1 = 40^2 + 9^2 + 6^2 + 1^2$. Nor do the squares have to be distinct—for example, the only way to get to 15 is via $9 + 4 + 1 + 1$. As it happens, the number 15 is not achievable using three or fewer squares, and in fact it is possible to identify those integers requiring the full four squares.

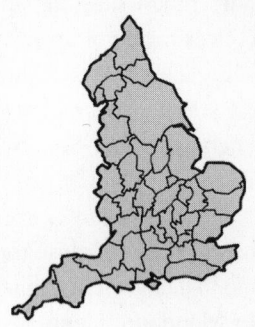

IN 1852, a young man named Francis Guthrie noticed that a map of the counties of England could be filled in using only four colors—while preserving the essential feature that no two adjacent counties (presumably, of the 39 historic counties, shown here in gray) be given the same color. Guthrie asked his brother Frederick if it was true that *any* map can be colored in this fashion. Frederick Guthrie then communicated the conjecture to his professor Augustus de Morgan (now known for the de Morgan rules of symbolic logic), and the battle was joined.

Like Fermat's Last Theorem, the Four-Color Theorem (or Four-Color Map Theorem) was called a theorem rather than a conjecture for many years. After a laborious process, and quite a few false starts, the theorem was finally proven—in 1977.

GERMAN mathematician Hermann Minkowski (1864–1909) is perhaps best-known for introducing the technique of using geometry to prove results in number theory, and he is associated with the number 4 in two completely different respects. One is that the four-dimensional concept sometimes referred to as "space-time" (ordinary Euclidean 3-space—the kind we live in—together with a time component), is officially called Minkowski space. The second can be explained by use of the following diagram:

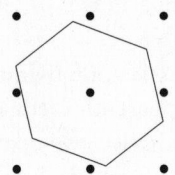

Assuming that the distance between any two adjacent dots (row or column) is 1, what can you say about the area of the hexagon? Well, it certainly appears that the area is less than the total area bounded by the dots, but Minkowski came up with a more tightly defined result: Any symmetric, convex region of area 4 must contain more than one lattice point. This result generalizes to n dimensions, and in the case of $n = 4$ it is possible to construct a special four-dimensional ball that leads to a quick proof of the Lagrange's Four-Square Theorem!

I don't mean to close this discussion on a down note, but honesty compels me to acknowledge that some societies don't like the number 4 very much. In Mandarin, Cantonese, and Japanese, the words for "four" and "death" are apparently pronounced nearly identically, and the result is a cultural phobia for the ages.

5 [prime]

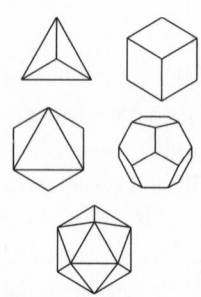

THERE are precisely five Platonic Solids—the name for a three-dimensional shape whose faces are all identical polygons. The most familiar Platonic Solid is the cube, whose faces are of course squares. The cube is joined by the tetrahedron, octahedron, and icosahedron (composed of equilateral triangles) and the dodecahedron (regular pentagons).

EUCLID noted in his Elements (circa 300 BC) that these five solids were the only ones possible, the proof apparently credited to Theaetetus (see **2**). But at least some of the solids themselves were known quite a bit before that, judging by the photograph below, which shows carved Scottish stones believed to date to around 2000 BC.

THE world's largest office building is in the shape of a pentagon and goes by that name. Not only does the Pentagon in Arlington, Virginia, have five sides on the outside, it consists of five concentric pentagons with an interior courtyard that measures five acres. The pentagonal shape was originally deemed essential because of the contours of the original site of the building, but the shape wasn't changed even when Franklin D. Roosevelt opted for an alternative site. Roosevelt apparently took great interest in its architecture, praising the pentagonal shape because it had never been done before.

According to the official Pentagon website, the building itself covers 29 acres, bringing up an interesting coincidence that may not be coincidental at all. It starts with the observation that if you start with a regular pentagon, you can always create another, smaller pentagon by connecting vertices like so:

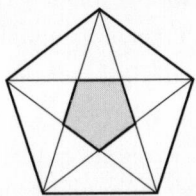

The length of a side of the inner pentagon turns out to be $\frac{(\sqrt{5}-1)^2}{4}$, or .038 times the length of a side of the outer pentagon, meaning that the inner area is $(0.38)^2 = 0.145$ times the area of the outer pentagon. Now, the five-acre courtyard inside the real, capital-p Pentagon is different in that it has the same orientation as the building itself, rather than the inverted orientation in the diagram. But the real-life relative area is $\frac{5}{(5+29)} = \frac{5}{34} = 0.147$, meaning that the real-life nested pentagons follow essentially the same proportions as the diagram we just drew.

IN yoga, the human body is often viewed as a pentagram, with the extremities defined by the head, two arms, and two legs. Positions such as the triangle pose involve five lines of energy. The number 5 also plays a role in less uplifting human processes, notably the Five Stages of Grief defined by nineteenth-century Swiss psychiatrist Elizabeth Kubler-Ross: (1) Denial and Isolation, (2) Anger, (3) Bargaining, (4) Depression, and (5) Acceptance.

IF you remember the quadratic formula from either your childhood or from the discussion in **2**, you know that an equation of the form $ax^2 + bx + c = 0$ has an explicit solution (or two), namely $x = \frac{(b \pm \sqrt{b^2 - 4ac})}{2a}$. The point is that the answer, x, is determined by the coefficients a, b, and c, as you'd expect. And there's a formula using radicals (i.e., square roots) for general cubic equations as well, though it's considerably more complicated than the quadratic formula. There's even a formula for the general quartic (fourth degree) equation, even though it takes that complexity several steps further. But there is no such formula for equations involving fifth powers. In other words, there is no way of writing down the solution(s) to the equation $ax^5 + bx^4 + cx^3 + dx^2 + ex + f = 0$ as a function of the numbers a, b, c, d, e, and f, using radicals. There's not even a hideously complicated way of approaching the problem. You just can't do it at all.

THE unsolvability of the general quintic equation is perhaps the most prominent conclusion that springs out of Galois theory, named for the Frenchman Evariste Galois (1811–1832). A quick look at Galois' entry and exit dates is a reminder of his precocity and of what might have been had he not taken up dueling at such a tender age. His final work wasn't published in full until 1846, fourteen years after his death at age 20. (The very first proof of the unsolvability of the quintic equation using radicals was accomplished in 1823 by the Norwegian mathematician Nils Henrik Abel. Abel was cursed in a different way, dying of tuberculosis at age 26.)

5 also serves as a limit for a completely different situation:

In the diagram above, checkers are placed below a line, with empty spaces above the line. Suppose you can advance the checkers above the line by leapfrogging over other checkers, as in the actual game of the same name. You can easily see that only two checkers and a single move are required to advance a man to the first rank above the line, as follows:

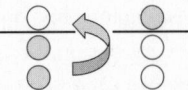

And you can advance a man to the second row if you had four originally, in the following three-move sequence:

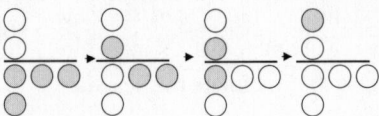

A little experimentation reveals that 8 men are sufficient to reach the third rank. If you've noticed the pattern so far (2^n men are required to reach the nth rank for $n = 1, 2, 3$) you might expect that 16 men will suffice for level 4, but in fact you need 20 men. The real surprise comes at level 5. No matter how many checkers you start with, you can *never* reach the fifth rank. This result is credited to John Conway, then of Cambridge University and now of Princeton.

SPEAKING of impossibility, it is appropriate to introduce the magic pentagram, which is basically a star. A standard five-pointed star has 10 vertices, each covered by a letter in the diagram. It would be aesthetically pleasing if you could replace each letter with a different number from 1 to 10 so that the sum of the numbers along each of the five lines was the same. But, as Charles Trigg first demonstrated in 1960, it just can't be done.

▼

WHEN you hear that the five Olympic rings represent the five regions of the world, it's easy to nod in agreement, but there are seven continents, not five, and only one of those (Antarctica) isn't represented at the Olympic Games. But the design is the brainchild of Pierre de Coubertin, founder of the modern Olympics, and it is apparently based on an old Greek artifact of similar shape.

The five regions of the world are Asia, Africa, Europe, the Americas, and Oceania. Although the colors of the rings—blue, black, yellow, green, and red—do not correspond to these regions in a one-to-one sense, each of these five colors is represented in every national flag in the world. Oceania doesn't have an Olympic team, but I would be remiss if I didn't mention a couple of nature's most marvelous pentagons: the sand dollar to the right and the sea star, or starfish. Five-fold radial symmetry is a characteristic of all echinoderms, a marine class that includes the sea star.

▼

SPEAKING of stars, my friend Norton Starr of Amherst College reminded me of one final appearance of the number 5 as a limit that I wanted to pass on. Consider a circle of radius 1, known in the trade as the unit circle. Because the area of a circle is given by the formula $A = \pi r^2$, the unit circle has area π. In three dimensions, the volume of a sphere is $(\frac{4}{3})\pi r^3$, so the unit sphere has volume $\frac{4\pi}{3}$. Although it is impossible to draw a unit sphere for n dimensions with $n > 3$, the concept is easily written down: Just as the unit circle is the set $\{x: x^2 \leq 1\}$, the general form for the unit sphere in n dimensions is the set of n numbers $\{x_1, x_2, \ldots, x_n\}$ such that $x_1^2 + \ldots + x_n^2 \leq 1$.

Our intuition tells us that the unit sphere keeps on growing in size, just as the unit box does—if only FedEx carried ten-dimensional boxes, we'd never have any trouble finding a box big enough for all our packages. But the punch line is not only that the volume of the n-dimensional unit sphere does not keep growing as n gets bigger. The real surprise is that this volume attains its maximum when $n = 5$, and steadily declines thereafter. In fact, the volume approaches *zero* as n heads to infinity.

6 [2 × 3   1 + 2 + 3   1 × 2 × 3]

6 is the third triangular number, as evidenced by the triangle formation of the Blue Angels flight team.

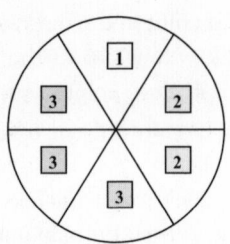

6 is also the first perfect number. A perfect number is a number that equals the sum of its proper divisors. In this case, $6 = 1 + 2 + 3$, or $\frac{1}{6} + \frac{2}{6} + \frac{3}{6} = 1$, as shown in the diagram. Perfect numbers are quite rare: 28 is the next one, followed by 496. To date, fewer than 50 such numbers have been identified.

AT sea, a depth of six feet is a fathom (derived from the Old English *faethm*, meaning outstretched arms). A fathom is likely associated with the expression "deep six," as in throw overboard. When on land, a depth of six feet is the traditional location of a casket, as in "six feet under."

▼

DRAW six points on the plane (shown at right), and begin connecting each pair of points with either a black line or a gray line. By the time each pair of points is connected in this fashion, there will be at least one triangle that is either all gray or all black.

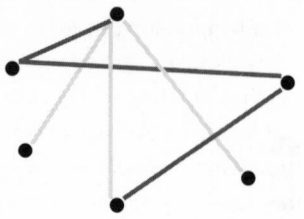

Note that the role of the number 6 is crucial. If you had only five points, no monochromatic triangle would be assured: For example, starting with a regular pentagon, you could color the perimeter gray and the interior diagonals black.

The proof of the above result doesn't require anything beyond simple arithmetic. Start by choosing any one of the six points. Consider the five line segments emanating from that point. Because there are only two colors, at least three of these lines must be the same color, say, gray. (As in the three gray lines from the top point in the diagram: The argument would be the same if they were black.) Now look at the points at the other end of these segments. If any two of these points were connected by a gray line, that line would complete a gray triangle. If not, they would all have to be black, creating a black triangle.

If this proof eluded you, don't worry. Back in 1953, an equivalent problem appeared in the William Lowell Putnam mathematics competition, an annual competition for math majors. The exact Putnam question was "Prove that in any group of six people there are either three mutual friends or three mutual strangers." Note that this problem is equivalent to the black and gray formulation above—for example, a black line connecting two points could represent friendship between two people.

▼

SPEAKING of interpersonal friendships, the idea behind the now-popular phrase "six degrees of separation" is that any two people on earth can be connected through a chain of mutual friends that has no more than six links. The concept dates back to a 1929 short story "Chains" by Hungarian writer Frigyes Karinthy, and is not as preposterous as it sounds: Each new interpersonal link opens up a vast number of new connections, creating exponential growth.

Karinthy's concept was put to the test by social psychologist Stanley Milgram in a famous 1967 experiment, wherein random Midwesterners were each given a package to send to Cambridge, Massachusetts, guided only by the name, occupation, and rough location of the intended recipient. Without Google or switchboard.com to guide them, the only available strategy was to relay the package to whomever among their acquaintances they felt was most likely to get them close to their goal, and so on down the chain. Not all of the packages were delivered, but the median number of intermediaries for those that did make it was just five.

The "small world" concept came of age with John Guare's 1990 play *Six Degrees of Separation*, which was followed by a 1993 movie by the same name starring Stockard Channing, Will Smith, and Donald Sutherland. The Internet then created a few new wrinkles, including various attempts to update Milgram's experiment, and, most memorably, a game called Six Degrees of Kevin Bacon.

Bacon Number	Number of Actors/Actresses
0	1
1	1,879
2	158,022
3	447,500
4	109,360
5	8,178
6	863
7	93
8	13

Not only was Bacon's full name a perfect melodic fit, he was in so many well-known movies that most actors and actresses could be traced to him using three or fewer links, where the "0" link is Bacon himself, the "1" consists of the 1,879 performers who have acted in a movie with Bacon (as of 2004), and so on. The three Hollywood stars mentioned in the previous paragraph have "Bacon numbers" of 2, 2, and 1, respectively, Sutherland having appeared opposite Bacon in *JFK*. The average Bacon number within a database of 800,000 actors was a stunningly low 2.95.

Of course, once movie databases could be harnessed to prove how centered Kevin Bacon was within the Hollywood universe, those same databases revealed over a thousand performers who were even *more* centered. The most-centered actor of all—connected throughout the database with an average of just 2.67 links—turned out to be Academy Award–winner Rod Steiger.

There's actually an analogue to Bacon numbers within higher mathematics. Anyone who ever wrote a paper in collaboration with the prolific Hungarian mathematician Paul Erdos is said to have an Erdos number of 1, and so on down the chain. As with Bacon numbers, virtually all mathematicians have an Erdos number, and in virtually all cases that number is a single digit.

The ultimate achievement is a low Erdos-Bacon number, obtained by adding your Erdos and Bacon numbers together as if they were factored placements in a figure skating competition. (Or something like that.) Actress Danica McKellar (Winnie on *The Wonder Years*) also has a degree in mathematics from UCLA and an Erdos-Bacon number of just $4 + 2 = 6$. But MIT professor Daniel Kleitman wrote a paper with Erdos and also appeared in *Good Will Hunting*, giving him an Erdos-Bacon number of just 3.

▼

THE great French mathematician Adrien-Marie Legendre (1752–1833), who developed among other things the *méthode des moindres carrés* (known in English-speaking statistics classes as the "least squares method" of linear regression/curve fitting), made a rare blunder by claiming that 6 could not be represented as the sum of the cubes of two rational numbers. (Obviously such a sum is impossible for two integers, and if irrational numbers were allowed you'd have trivial solutions such as 1 and the cube root of 5.) Legendre was no longer alive when Henry Dudeney, master British puzzlist of the late nineteenth and early twentieth century, found the surprisingly small counterexample of $6 = (\frac{17}{21})^3 + (\frac{37}{21})^3$.

SUPPOSE you had a map with a bunch of dots representing towns, and you drew lines connecting every dot with the closest dot to it. You might be surprised to hear that no town would have more than six lines emanating from it.

While the statement doesn't sound obvious, the proof is surprisingly easy and hinges on the simple fact that $\frac{360}{6} = 60$. Watch.

Suppose there were more than 6 lines coming from, say, Springfield. Then, since $\frac{360}{7} < 60$, two of those lines would have to meet at an angle less than 60 degrees, like so:

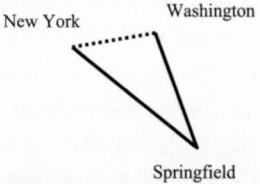

Now we have a triangle in which the angle at the Springfield vertex is less than 60 degrees. But if that's true, then at least one of the other angles is *greater* than 60 degrees, because the measures of the three angles of a triangle always sum to 180 degrees. In particular, the distance between New York and Washington would have to be less than the distance between either New York and Springfield or Washington and Springfield. (In the diagram, it's both.) But if New York and Washington are the closest together of the three, a line should join *them*, and the other lines shouldn't be there in the first place. The proof is now complete.

RELATED to the above discussion is the unique role played in the hexagon in two-dimensional tiling. Hexagonal tiling is actually quite familiar to us even if we've never heard the term, because it's the structure of chicken wire, honeycombs, and old-fashioned bathroom tiles.

BUT no regular polygon with more than six sides can possibly tile the plane. (Among regular polygons with *fewer* than six sides, equilateral triangles and squares easily tile the plane, but regular pentagons do not.) The key to tiling is found in the interior angles of the polygon. The interior angles of the equilateral triangle, square, and hexagon are 60, 90, and 120, respectively, and these numbers divide evenly into 360. In the diagram above, for example, three hexagons meet at each vertex, nicely filling the space and reminding us that $3 \times 120 = 360$. However, anything over six sides creates an angle measure of greater than 120 degrees, and the only proper divisor of 360 in this territory is 180, which is the angle measure of a line, not a shape. (The only other case is the pentagon, whose interior angles measure 108 degrees; again, it's impossible to shape a set of such angles around a vertex, so you're out of luck.)

▼

IF you take two equilateral triangles and put them together just so, you get a hexagram known as the Star of David. The symbol of Judaism, the Star of David has been in use since the Middle Ages and has appeared on the flag of Israel since its founding in 1948.

▼

IN mathematics, a Star of David Theorem refers to certain relationships within Pascal's Triangle (see **3**). Perhaps the simplest theorem to describe starts by surrounding one of the numbers in Pascal's Triangle with a tilted Star of David, as in the diagram.

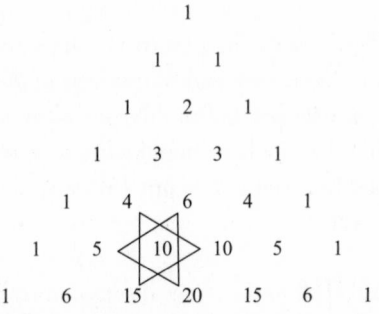

Each of the two triangles points to three different numbers. One of the triangles points to the numbers 5, 6, and 20, which have a product of 600. The other triangle points to the numbers 4, 10, and 15, whose product is also 600.

Yes, of course this always works. That's why it's a theorem. The results are even more remarkable-looking when you go farther down the triangle.

▼

EVERYONE knows that snowflakes are six-sided, but the first person to ruminate on the subject was Johannes Kepler. Legend has it that a snowflake fell on Kepler's overcoat as he was crossing a bridge over the Vltava river in 1611, and he decided to write a treatise on snowflakes as a gift to his patron. Kepler's view was that the abundance of sixes in nature, from flower petals to honeycombs to snowflakes, arose from deep-seated structural principles—which he dubbed *facultas formatrix*—associated with the efficiency of hexagonal packing. Apparently Kepler was something of a punster, as he wrote his treatise in Latin, in which the word for snowflake is *nix*, which in turn meant "nothing" in his native Lower German. The fact that his treatise cost nothing appealed to Kepler, chronically short of funds because of the stinginess of Emperor Rudolph II, to whom Kepler served as the imperial astronomer.

7 [prime]

THE number 7 isn't quite as easy to cope with as any number we have seen thus far, because the arithmetic of 7 isn't characterized by obvious patterns. That property actually makes 7 useful to neurologists: One of the basic tests for the onset of dementia is to have the patient successively subtract 7 from 100. The sequence runs 100, 93, 86, 79, 72, etc., and clearly provides more of a hurdle than using, say, five instead.

▼

ONE nice pattern produced by 7 that 5 cannot match is the fraction for $\frac{1}{7}$: 0.142587.

Get a load of the multiplication table for the repeating portion of the number:

142857 ×	
2	285714
3	428571
4	571428
5	714285
6	857142
7	999999

The number 142857 is called a cyclic number, because you obtain its successive multiples by beginning with one of its other digits and wrapping around, maintaining the same order. The key to the magic is that the repeating portion of the decimal expansion of $\frac{1}{7}$ has six digits. The next fraction to have this property is $\frac{1}{17}$, which equals 0.0588235294117647. (Note that the repeating portion now has 16 digits. In general, if the fraction $\frac{1}{p}$ has a decimal expansion with a repeating sequence of length $(p-1)$, that sequence forms a cyclic number.)

▼

THE Seven Bridges of Konigsberg is a topological problem (indeed, perhaps the *first* topological problem) studied by Leonhard Euler. The legend has it that Euler himself traipsed across the bridges of this old Prussian town (now a part of Russia and renamed Kaliningrad in 1946). The bridges connected various parts of the town separated by rivers, and the question of the day was whether it would be possible to walk across all seven bridges without retracing his steps.

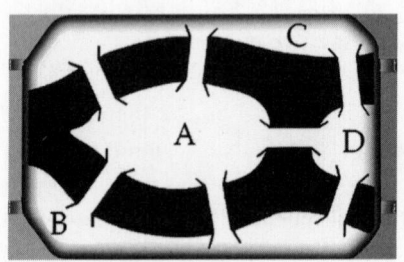

Euler eventually realized that such a crossing was impossible. The analysis of the problem is made easier by a diagram focusing on the bridge structure. The impossibility of an Eulerian path that encompasses all the bridges is found in the node structure of the bridges; namely, the number of entrances and exits from the points A, B, C, and D.

It turns out that an Eulerian path is only possible if there are exactly two or zero nodes of odd degree. In Konigsberg, however, all of the nodes had odd degree—five for region A and three for the other three. As mathematically important as Euler's walks through Konigsberg were, the daily walks of Konigsberg resident Immanuel Kant were memorable in a different way. Legend has it that Kant was so punctual in his appearances around town that locals learned to set their watches by him.

Seven Famous Sevens						
Continents	Days of the Week	Hills of Rome	Wonders of the Ancient World	Wonders of the Modern World	Colors of the Spectrum	Deadly Sins
Asia	Sunday	Aventine	The Great Pyramid of Giza	Empire State Building	Red	Lust
Europe	Monday	Caelian	The Hanging Gardens of Babylon	Itaipu Dam	Yellow	Gluttony
Africa	Tuesday	Capitoline	The Temple of Artemis at Ephesus	CN Tower	Blue	Greed
Australia	Wednesday	Esquiline	The Statue of Zeus at Olympia	Panama Canal	Green	Sloth
North America	Thursday	Palatine	The Mausoleum at Halicarnassus	Channel Tunnel	Indigo	Wrath
South America	Friday	Quirinal	The Colossus of Rhodes	Delta Works	Violet	Envy
Antarctica	Saturday	Viminal	The Pharos of Alexandria	Golden Gate Bridge	Orange	Pride

THE dots on opposite sides of an ordinary die must sum to 7. In cards, it is a commonly held belief that a series of 7 shuffles will result in a deck being fully randomized.

THE frieze design is characterized by repeated copies of a single pattern in one direction. Friezes are often seen in wallpaper borders or perhaps as part of an architectural flourish in an old building. Although we have all seen plenty of examples of friezes, the word itself is not universally known and more obscure still is the fact that there are fundamentally only seven different types of symmetries that a frieze can possess. Princeton's John Conway introduced footprints as a means of distinguishing among these seven "one-directional" symmetries, a practice we will follow in the list below:

1. **THE HOP** (a simple translation symmetry)

2. **THE STEP** (translation and glide reflection symmetries)

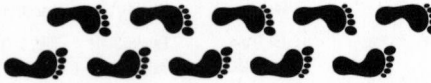

3. **THE SIDLE** (translation and vertical reflection symmetries)

4. **THE SPINNING HOP** (translation and half-turn rotational symmetries)

5. **THE SPINNING SIDLE** (translation, glide reflection, and half-turn rotation)

6. THE JUMP (translation and horizontal reflection)

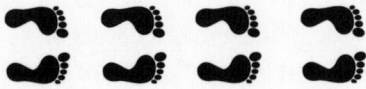

7. THE SPINNING JUMP (translation, horizontal and vertical reflection, and rotation)

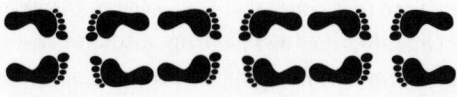

THE two diagrams to the right illustrate the Seven Circles Theorem. If you start with a circle and draw six circles tangent to that circle, six points of tangency are created. Remarkably, those six

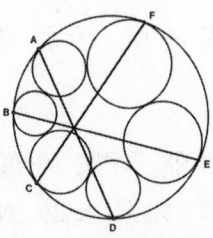 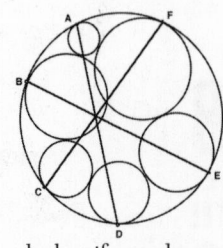

points can be separated into three pairs of two points such that if you draw a line connecting each of those three pairs, the three lines intersect in a single point. That's true regardless of what configuration happens to be involved.

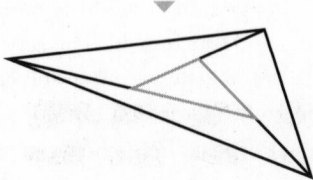

START with a triangle (above), and extend each of the three legs out until it is twice its original length. The result is a new triangle whose area is precisely seven times the area of the triangle you started with. This is because if you connect any vertex of a triangle at the midpoint of the opposite side, you have created two triangles of equal area. Drawing a few extra lines into the diagram enables us to create seven triangles, all of which have equal area, which is another way of saying that the center triangle is one-seventh the size of the large triangle.

▼

FINALLY, the diagram to the right is called a "seven segment display." Its name is not well-known but it is a standard means of displaying the ten digits 0 to 9 as well as the letters A, b, C, d, E, and F. Note that b and d are in lowercase, and that's because their capital forms can't be distinguished from 8 and 0 respectively. The seven segment display is often slanted to improve readability, but in this form it is in the shape of an 8, our very next subject.

8 $\left[\, 2^3 \,\right]$

THE number 8 owes many of its appearances to the fact that it is a power of two. For example, cutting a block in half along each of its three axes will produce eight smaller blocks. But 8 also appears within an entirely different formulation.

Consider the humble though famously fertile rabbit. Actually, start with a pair of rabbits, one male and one female. The reproductive ground rules are (1) any pair of rabbits becomes fertile after one month, and (2) the pair delivers another pair one month later, and every month after that. As long as the rabbits don't die, so to speak, here's how the generations proceed:

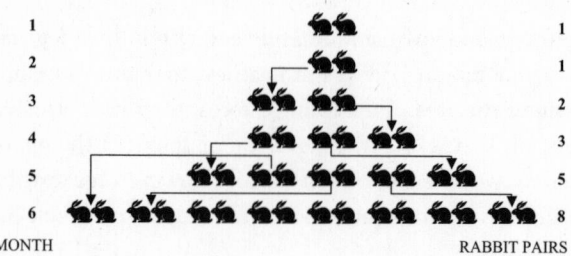

MONTH   RABBIT PAIRS

The numbers in the rightmost column form the famous Fibonacci sequence, named after Leonardo de Pisa (circa 1175–1250), aka Fibonacci, who was apparently the first person in the Western world to study the sequence and the one who is credited with originating the rabbit metaphor. The Fibonacci sequence turns out to have many other interpretations (the number of ways of climbing an n-step staircase using either one or two steps at a time, the number of coverings of a $2 \times n$ checkerboard by 2×1 dominoes, and so forth), but we don't need those or even the rabbit labyrinth to keep the sequence going, because we can see at a glance that any member of the Fibonacci sequence is the sum of the previous two members of the sequence. (In math talk, this is an example of a recursively defined sequence.)

If you are troubled by the inbreeding of the rabbits required to sustain the Fibonacci sequence, consider this paradox of sorts. When we scan our family tree past our two parents, four grandparents, and even our eight great-grandparents, we expect 16 in the generation before all of those, 32 in the one before that one, and so on. But you can't very well keep doubling your ancestors, can you? There are *more* people alive today than centuries ago, not fewer. In particular, if you figure that Fibonacci himself lived 30 generations ago, there is simply no way that we had 2^{30} (more than one billion) ancestors from that time, because there weren't that many humans on the planet. What's going on? The inescapable conclusion is that there were plenty of duplications among these 2^{30} forebears, so there was inbreeding, all right, not necessarily the scandalous kind of our rabbit model, but a bit closer to home.

You will have noticed by now that 8 is both a Fibonacci number and a perfect cube. Eight is actually the last cube in the Fibonacci sequence, the only other one being 1. What's more, 8 is the largest Fibonacci number that has a prime neighbor—namely, 7. (We will see more Fibonacci numbers before this book is through, and you can check out all of their neighbors to make sure a prime number doesn't show up.)

IN the United States, the stop sign has officially been an octagon since the 1920s, the idea being that motorists could recognize its distinctive shape even from the reverse side. Most of the English-speaking world uses the same construction.

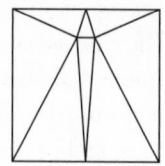

THE geometry of the number 8 goes well beyond octagons. For example, a square can be subdivided into 8 acute triangles (all angles less than 90 degrees), as in the diagram to the right. Seven triangles do not suffice.

SPEAKING of squares and the number 8, if you put an asymmetric diagram inside a square, you can produce precisely eight different images via rotations and reflections, as below. (The top-left figure is rotated by 90, 180, and 270 degrees to produce the three images to its left, and the top row is reflected from top to bottom to produce the bottom row.) In math-speak, the diagram is being acted upon by the dihedral group of order eight. In general, the dihedral group associated with a regular polygon of n sides has order $2n$.

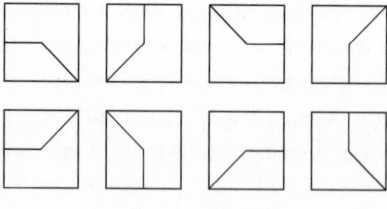

IT is commonly believed that seven shuffles are the right amount to produce a random order of 52 cards, but eight perfect riffle shuffles will return a 52-card deck to its original order.

SPIDERS have eight legs and, usually, eight eyes. But the eight-leg part is what distinguishes them from insects.

IF an octagon has eight sides, an octopus has eight legs, then surely October is the eighth month of the year. No, wait a minute, that's not right. October is the tenth month. What happened? The answer is that October was indeed the eighth month of the Roman calendar, but that was before January and February were officially christened to occupy what had been a monthless winter period.

▼

IN the sport of rowing, an "eight" typically refers to an eight-person crew (coxswain not included), but the number 8 figures into a wide range of other sports:

For example, running tracks and swimming pools typically have eight lanes. (In both cases, not all lanes are created equal; some positions are known to be more advantageous than others.)

The middle lanes were familiar territory to the USA's Michael Phelps as he swept to a record eight gold medals in the 2008 Summer Olympic Games. Those games, of course, began on 8/8/08, in keeping with the long-standing reverence for the number 8 in Chinese numerology.

The "figure eight" is commonly associated with figure skating, an eight being one of many different patterns that competitive skaters once had to trace with their blades. Fittingly, the last time that so-called compulsory figures were seen in the Winter Olympics was in '88. The very next year saw a rather quirky appearance of the number 8. At the conclusion of the 1989 Tour de France, after American Greg Lemond came from behind on the final day's time trial to win the Tour by a grand total of eight seconds, runner-up Laurent Fignon could be seen lying on the ground in exhaustion and disbelief. The wheels of his bicycle, lying beside him, formed a perfect 8.

▼

THE idea of a wheel with eight spokes goes back to the Dharmacakra, one of the eight auspicious symbols of Buddhism. And the idea of using two circles to represent the number 8 is best known in golf, giving rise to the colorful term *snowman* to represent an 8 on a particular hole—no better than a triple bogey.

9 $\left[\ 3^2\ \right]$

THE equation $9 = 3^2$ is a nice follow-up to $8 = 2^3$ and it's one of a kind. Never again will you find two consecutive numbers that are both perfect powers, much less perfect powers having the beautiful symmetry of 2^3 and 3^2.

▼

IN American sports, a "nine" is a baseball team, and the number is imbued throughout the game. When using an official scorecard to follow a game, for example, each defensive player is given a number, from 1 (the pitcher) to 9 (the right fielder). In any particular half inning, there are three outs, and given that three strikes make an out, it is possible for a half inning to consist of nine strikes and nothing else (a feat that has happened more than 40 times in the history of Major League Baseball). And if a team doesn't show up for a game, that game is forfeited, and in the official score the winner is given a number of runs equal to the number of innings in a game, also nine. That's right. A no-show in a major-league baseball game goes into the record books with the score 9–0.

▼

ONE of the most familiar depictions of 9 as three squared comes from a different game, tic-tac-toe, also known as noughts and crosses.

Tic-tac-toe is of course a very simple game. Unless you've never seen it before, you'll have no difficulty in achieving a draw no matter whom you're playing against. Or even what. Ginger the tic-tac-toe playing chicken was an instant hit when she reached Las Vegas in 2002, having apparently played for nine months at Atlantic City's Tropicana Hotel and only lost five times.

▼

A different expression of 9 as three 3's comes from "the nine Worthies," a group of historical/legendary figures designated in the Middle Ages. The Worthies were as follows:

Pagan	Jewish	Christian
Hector	Joshua	King Arthur
Alexander the Great	David	Charlemagne
Julius Caesar	Judas Maccabeus	Godfrey of Bouillon

Together, the nine Worthies supposedly represent all facets of a perfect warrior.

▼

SOME of the most important properties of the number 9 stem from its being just 1 less than 10, the base of the number system. Perhaps the best known of these properties is the test to determine whether or not a number is divisible by 9: Just add the digits of the number, and if the resulting sum is divisible by 9, so is the original number.

For example, if you add the digits of the number 176,328 you get $1 + 7 + 6 + 3 + 2 + 8 = 27$. Because 27 is divisible by 9 (you could repeat the process to get $2 + 7 = 9$, which certainly is divisible by 9), so is 176,328.

▼

THE technique of checking your arithmetic by "casting out the nines" is based on a similar idea. Suppose you've just performed the following addition:

$$\begin{array}{r} 1428 \\ + 5837 \\ \hline 7255 \end{array}$$

If you add the digits of 1428 and "cast out the nines," you're left with $1 + 4 + 2 + 8 - 9 = 6$. (In math talk, 6 is the "digital root" of 1428.) If you do the same with 5837 you get 5. And if you add 6 and 5 and cast out one final nine, you get 2. If you've done the addition properly, you should get the same result if you add the digits in your sum and cast out the nines. Unfortunately, that doesn't work here, because $7 + 2 + 5 + 5 - 9 - 9 = 1$. Something has gone wrong. Upon double-checking the original problem, we see that we made an error in the tens column, when the one wasn't carried from the sum $8 + 7 = 15$. The answer should have been 7265.

Note that "casting out the nines" cannot guarantee that your original arithmetic was correct. If you were wrong originally, however, the technique gives you a shortcut in discovering that an error was made.

▼

ALL this is rather tedious stuff, but consider that the number 9 and its digital roots are core building blocks for the likes of Arthur Benjamin—professor of mathematics at Harvey Mudd College during the day, mathemagician by night. Benjamin routinely fools his audiences with math "tricks" that involve nothing more than the basic properties of 9 and so-called digital roots in the spirit of casting out the nines. Example: Pick a four-digit number. Scramble its digits to form a new number, and subtract the smaller one from the larger one. From this new number, which we'll call N, take away a nonzero digit. Upon hearing the remaining digits, it's child's play to figure out the missing digit, because the digital root of N must be 9.

▼

LONG after teachers stopped advising students to cast out the nines, they were still telling students that there were nine planets: Mercury, Venus, Earth, Mars, Jupiter, Saturn, Uranus, Neptune, and Pluto. Unfortunately, as everyone knows by now, Pluto has been demoted to "dwarf planet" status, where it joined the likes of Ceres and Eris. Why the International Astronomical Union waited until August 2006 to officially define a planet in a way that excluded Pluto, I have no idea, but I suppose it was their way of casting out the ninth one.

▼

ONE group of nine that is not destined to change is the Nine Muses, together with their specialties:

Calliope: Epic poetry
Clio: History
Erato: Love
Euterpe: Music/lyric poetry
Melpomene: Tragedy

Polyhymnia: Sacred songs
Terpischore: Dance
Thalia: Comedy/bucolic poetry
Urania: Astronomy

ANOTHER more recent group of nine is the US Supreme Court, set at its current number in 1869. The group was referred to as the "nine old men" by Franklin Roosevelt, who went so far as to propose in 1937 that the president should be able to appoint an additional justice for every one over $70\frac{1}{2}$ years of age. The reason given for the change was to reduce the workload, but Roosevelt's thinly disguised aim was to pack the court with justices who were less likely to declare his various New Deal proposals unconstitutional. Despite making it the subject of the first of his nine fireside chats, FDR's court-packing plan went absolutely nowhere, but because his presidency was so long, he was able to appoint a total of eight justices to the court, the biggest number of appointments since George Washington.

WE'LL close with a magical appearance of 9 that may be less familiar. Start by drawing an acute triangle. (Others will do, but an acute triangle works out the best.)

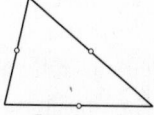 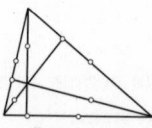 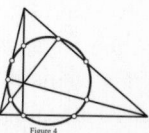

Figure 1   Figure 2   Figure 3   Figure 4

1. Mark the midpoints of each side (3 points). See Figure 1.
2. From each vertex, drop an altitude (a line that is perpendicular to the side opposite the vertex). Mark the points where the altitudes intersect the opposite side. See Figure 2.
3. Notice that the altitudes intersect at a common point. Mark the midpoint between each vertex and this common point. You have created a total of nine points. See Figure 3.

4. No matter what shape triangle you started with, these nine points all lie on a perfect circle! See Figure 4.

10 $\left[\, 2 \times 5 \,\right]$

WRITING about 10 is a little bit like writing about 1. It's everywhere, and what makes the number 10 special is kind of the same thing as what makes it less than special. We take it for granted.

The number 10 is best known as the base of our number system. The arithmetic of 10 is especially easy, in that $10^2 = 100$, $10^3 = 1000$, and in general 10^n equals a one with n zeroes after it. In particular, when we say that an estimate is off by an order of magnitude, technically that means it's off by a factor of 10, though real-life usage isn't always that exact. Although there are many other bases/number systems in life and in this book, 10 could be considered the base of any number system, in the sense that the number n, when written in base n, is always 10.

▼

THE sequence EOEREXNTEN ends with TEN. What does the sequence represent? (See Answers.)

▼

10 is a triangular number, as anyone who has ever bowled can tell you. But 10 is really, really triangular. Not only is it the sum of the first four integers, it is also $1 + 3 + 6$ – the sum of the first three triangular numbers. This last property makes 10 a tetrahedral number, meaning that you can build a tetrahedron by stacking 10 spheres—bowling balls, say—on three levels.

▼

THE figure below is not the familiar triangular arrangement of the ten bowling pins. It is the Tetraktys of the Pythagoreans, those spiritual followers of Pythagoras who were especially taken with the fact that $10 = 1 + 2 + 3 + 4$.

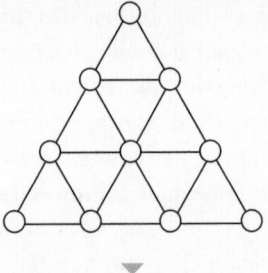

THE list below is another link between Pythagoras and the number 10:

The 10 Principles of Pythagoras	
(Also known as the table of the Opposites)	
limit	unlimited
odd	even
one	plurality
right	left
male	female
at rest	moving
straight	crooked
light	darkness
good	bad
square	oblong

So we see that the Top 10 list is an ancient concept. It seems, however, that the Pythagoreans weren't above a little shading and fudging to make their lists the right length: Said Aristotle, "They (the Pythagoreans) say that the bodies which move through the heavens are ten, but as the visible bodies are only nine, to meet this they invent a tenth—the 'counter-earth'" (*Metaphysics* 906a 10–12).

SPEAKING of triangles, the dissection to the right is the handiwork of William Gosper, a mathematician and programmer who is sometimes credited as being one of the original computer hackers. In this particular creation, a square is subdivided into 10 acute isosceles triangles (two sides equal), the minimum possible. (Compare **8**, the minimum number of acute triangles, not necessarily isosceles, into which a square can be subdivided.)

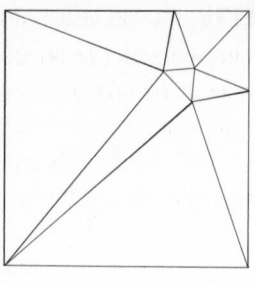

EVERYONE knows about the Ten Commandments, but less well-known is that there were only 10 original Rorschach inkblots, each with an unbounded number of possible interpretations.

THE prefix *dec-* means "10" in a whole range of contexts. A decagon has 10 sides, a decimal point refers to a place in our base 10 numbering system, a decathlon has 10 events, and so on. Less well-known is the word *decimate*, which is now used interchangeably with such words as *destroy* and *annihilate*, even though a quantity that has been decimated has, technically speaking, only been diminished by one-tenth of its original size. Apparently the word dates back to ancient Rome, when the punishment for mutiny was to kill one mutinous soldier out of ten. The fact that *decimate* has morphed into "utter destruction" suggests that the original policy of decimation had a powerful deterrent effect.

THE equation $10! = 6! \times 7!$ is a special one. While it is not too hard to construct an infinite family of factorials that are products of other factorials (in general, if $A = B!$, then $A! = (A-1)! \times B!$), you won't find any others where two *consecutive* factorials are being multiplied.

WE'LL close the discussion with an even more remarkable equation, one that represents any positive integer n using only the 10 digits 0 through 9, in order! (The number of square roots in the expression below equals n.) The formula is attributed to Verner Hoggatt Jr., a mathematician best known for his work on the Fibonacci series. Readers familiar with the definition of a logarithm are invited to ponder why the formula works.

$$\log_{(0+1+2+3+4)/5} \left(\log_{\sqrt{\sqrt{\ldots\sqrt{(-6+7+8)}}}} 9\right) = n$$

(See Answers.)

11 [prime]

J. J. SYLVESTER, the British-born founder of the *American Journal of Mathematics* and the onetime mentor of ace statistician turned nursing pioneer Florence Nightingale, proved in 1884 that the highest number that can't be created out of the numbers x and y equals $xy - x - y$. In particular, 11 is the highest number that cannot be attained as a score in rugby union using only drop goals (3) and converted tries (7), because $11 = 3 \times 7 - 3 - 7$. The same calculation applies to American football, using field goals and touchdowns with one-point conversions. That's only fair, as each team has 11 players on the field at any given time, the same as in soccer and cricket.

ONCE you've seen Sylvester's formula, you should be able to absorb the similar-looking formula $\frac{1}{2}(x-1)(y-1)$ as the total number of scores that cannot be attained using x and y. Sure enough, whether you're talking about rugby or football or just numbers, you can't get to 1, 2, 4, 5, 8, or 11 using combinations of 3 and 7, and that's a total of 6 numbers, just as the formula $\frac{1}{2}(2)(6) = 6$ predicted.

AN 11-sided figure is called a hendecagon. Surely the most famous hendecagon of all time is the one inscribed within the Susan B. Anthony dollar, first issued from 1979 through 1981 and then again in 1999. Originally, the coin itself was supposed to have been a regular hendecagon, but vending machine manufacturers never got around to ac-

commodating any shape other than round. Unfortunately, without an 11-sided exterior to set it apart, the Susan B. Anthony dollar was frequently mistaken for a quarter.

▼

THE number 11 provides some curiosities in the areas of multiplication and division. To begin with, the two-digit multiples of 11 are easy to spot, because they consist of repeated digits: 11, 22, 33, all the way up to 99. Three-digit multiples of 11 don't stand out quite as much, but they are surprisingly easy to generate. For example, start with 3 and 4. Add them to get 7. Put the seven in the middle of the 3 and 4 to form the three-digit number 374. That number is divisible by 11. In particular, 374 = 34 × 11. The appearance of the 7 is even more logical when you write out the multiplication in old-fashioned grammar school form and examine the middle column:

$$
\begin{array}{r}
34 \\
\times\ \underline{11} \\
34 \\
+\ \underline{340} \\
374
\end{array}
$$

The above procedure doesn't generate all three-digit multiples of 11, because it depends on the two chosen integers (3 and 4 above) not adding up to more than 9. If you started with 5 and 8 instead of 3 and 4 and followed the above rules literally, you'd get 5138, at which point you'd have to add the 5 and 1 to get the actual product of 638.

▼

THAT same principle of carrying extends to the following triangle:

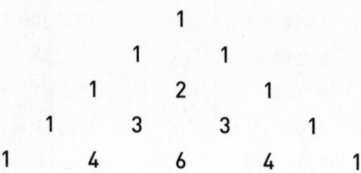

The five rows of the triangle happen to coincide with the first five powers of 11: $11^0 = 1$, $11^1 = 11$, $11^2 = 121$, $11^3 = 1331$, $11^4 = 14641$. But in fact this is the beginning of the famous Pascal's Triangle, in which 1's appear on the diagonal and each inner number is the sum of the two numbers above it, to the left and to the right. The next row of Pascal's Triangle is 1 5 10 10 5 1, not $11^5 = 161051$. Note that 11^5 is the first power of 11 that is not a palindrome.

THE general rule for divisibility by 11 works like this: Add up the digits of the number located in an odd position, then add the remaining digits. If the difference between these two sums is a multiple of 11, including 0, then the original number is divisible by 11. For example, the number 42,658 is divisible by 11 because $(4 + 6 + 8) - (2 + 5) = 18 - 7 = 11$.

NOW for a completely different multiplicative property that borders on the unbelievable. Take any number and multiply its digits together. Whatever number results, multiply *its* digits together, and keep going. Eventually, you'll get to a single-digit number. Sometimes the process is swift. For example, if the original number has a 0 in it you get to 0 immediately, while if the number has a 5 and any even digit you'll get to zero in two steps. But sometimes things take a bit longer. For example, though not by chance, if you start with the number 277,777,788,888,899 you get the following chain:

Step	Number	Product of Digits
1	277,777,788,888,899	4,996,238,671,872
2	4,996,238,671,872	438,939,648

Step	Number	Product of Digits
3	438,939,648	4,478,976
4	4,478,976	338,688
5	338,688	27,648
6	27,648	2,688
7	2,688	768
8	768	336
9	336	54
10	54	20
11	20	0

If you're thinking that 11 steps is a lot, you're on the right track. Remarkably, *no number* is known to require more than 11 steps, and it's not as if people haven't been looking. In 2001, Phil Carmody confirmed that all numbers less than 10^{233} have a "multiplicative persistence," as it is called, of less than or equal to 11. Our chosen number of 277,777,788,888,899 is the *smallest* number with a multiplicative persistence of 11.

▼

THE number 11 pops up behind the scenes in some clock problems. For example, start at 12:00 noon, when the hands of a clock are pointing in the same direction. Sixty-five and $\frac{5}{11}$ minutes later—in other words, one-eleventh the time between 12:00 noon and midnight—the hour and minute hands will again be pointing the same way.

▼

AN "Ask Marilyn" column (*Parade*, May 6, 2007) asked readers to fill in the time that is missing from the following sequence: 1:38, 2:44, 3:49, 4:55, ___, 7:05, 8:11, 9:16, 10:22, 11:27, 12:33. While it is tempting to look for patterns within the times themselves, once you notice that there are 11 times altogether, you'll shift to another tack.

The puzzle, called to Marilyn vos Savant's attention by Jacob Miller of Mount Joy, Pennsylvania, is a variation on an old theme. While the times don't appear to have anything to do with one another, that's just a casualty of the changeover from analog to digital watches (the bigger casualty being the heightened difficulty of being able to tell the time by catching a glance of someone else's wristwatch). The 11 times of day in the puzzle would stand out on an analog watch as being those occasions when the minute hand and hour hand point in precisely opposite directions. The missing time, obviously, is 6:00, which also happens to be the only time that comes already rounded off.

Let's look at this situation another way. Starting with and including 6:00, how many times will the hour and minute hands be precisely 180 degrees apart before the next 6:00? This obviously happens every hour, except that 6:00 is the only occurrence between 5:00 and 7:00. And clearly the time between any two successive occurrences is the same, because the phenomenon is a function of the relative speeds of the two hands, which never changes. Therefore you get a 180-degree spread every $\frac{12}{11}$ hours, or every one hour, five minutes, and $\frac{5}{11}$ seconds. (Sorry, but you just can't get rid of the 11 in the denominator. In particular, the times in the "Ask Marilyn" version are necessarily rounded off.)

▼

THE number 11 shows up in two geometric counting exercises. The 11 figures here represent the ways in which the edges of six squares can be connected so that the resulting two-dimensional shape can be folded into a cube. Six-squared figures of this type are called hexominoes, of which there are 35 altogether, assuming that reflections and inversions are not considered distinct. The 11 special ones are called the nets of the cube.

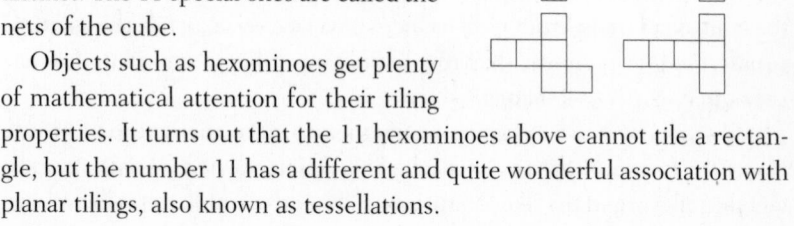

Objects such as hexominoes get plenty of mathematical attention for their tiling properties. It turns out that the 11 hexominoes above cannot tile a rectangle, but the number 11 has a different and quite wonderful association with planar tilings, also known as tessellations.

We have already seen that there are just three regular polygons (the hexagon, the square, and the equilateral triangle shown on the left below) that can tile the plane. But if you can mix *different* regular polygons, the number of tilings increases to 11. These 11, one of which appears in the middle below, are the so-called Archimedean tilings of the plane, though Archimedes himself didn't have a whole lot to do with them. They were apparently studied and classified by Johannes Kepler, who for the record lived some 1800 years after Archimedes' time. The Archimedean tiling found in the middle combines regular hexagons and equilateral triangles.

In what at first glance appears to be an extraordinary coincidence, there are also 11 fundamentally different tilings of the plane by identical, convex, symmetric polygons (there are a couple of other restrictions, but that's enough math jargon for a family publication). The right-most tiling, made up of identical irregular pentagons (recall that *regular* pentagons cannot tile the plane) belongs in that category:

 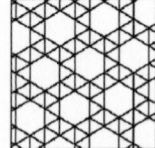 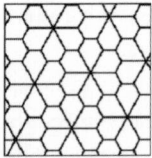

There is a simple one-to-one correspondence between the two sets of tessellations. If you start with an Archimedean tiling, mark the center of each polygon and then connect each dot to its neighbor(s), you obtain a tiling called the "dual" of the one you started with. In the layout on this page, the tessellation on the far right is the dual of the Archimedean tiling to its left. The dual tilings are called laves, or at least that's what I first thought. In fact they are Laves tilings, named after Swiss crystallographer Fritz Laves. Oh, well. Note that the standard hexagonal tiling is the dual of the equilateral triangle tiling shown here (and vice versa), while the standard square tiling (not shown) has the distinction of being self-dual, if I may sneak in one more mathematical term.

Although these various tilings justify their study by their intrinsic beauty alone, the Laves tilings are also studied in the science of materials: crystals, metallic alloys, and the like. Nature may abhor a vacuum, but it loves symmetries, and many of the designs on the previous page arise in many natural (though sometimes microscopic) contexts.

12 $\left[\, 2^2 \times 3 \,\right]$

THE number 12 is a favorite in many religions, what with the 12 days of Christmas, Twelfth Night, the 12 Apostles, the 12 feasts of Eastern Orthodoxy, and the 12 Tribes of Israel. These 12 tribes are associated with the 12 sons of Jacob, so it bears mention that the Norse god Odin also had 12 sons.

▼

THE concept of a dozen was also alive and well in Greek mythology, as evidenced by the 12 principal gods of the Greek pantheon atop Mount Olympus. These gods won't be listed here because their total number actually exceeded 12, but 12 was apparently the limit at any given time. However, we *can* list the twelve labors forced upon Hercules by King Eurystheus of Tiryns. Most involved killing some ghastly creature or another. One notable exception was labor number three, as the Cerynian Hind was actually a delicate deer, loved by Artemis, which Hercules had to stalk for a year before gently carting it away.

The Twelve Labors of Hercules
One: Kill the Nemean Lion
Two: Kill the Lernean Hydra
Three: Capture the Cerynian Hind
Four: Capture the Erymanthian Boar
Five: Clean the Augean Stables
Six: Kill the Stymphalian Birds
Seven: Capture the Cretan Bull
Eight: Capture the Horses of Diomedes
Nine: Take the Girdle of the Amazon Queen Hippolyte

Ten: Capture the Cattle of Geryon
Eleven: Take the Golden Apples of the Hesperides
Twelve: Capture Cerberus

▼

ON the other hand, whereas today it is standard for a jury to consist of 12 people, Ancient Greece had no such limit. The trial of Socrates involved 501 jurors.

▼

ONE reason for the prominence of the number 12 is that it is evenly divisible by 2, 3, 4, and 6, and is therefore convenient for all sorts of applications, from eggs to donuts to numbers on a clock to months in a year to signs of the zodiac.

▼

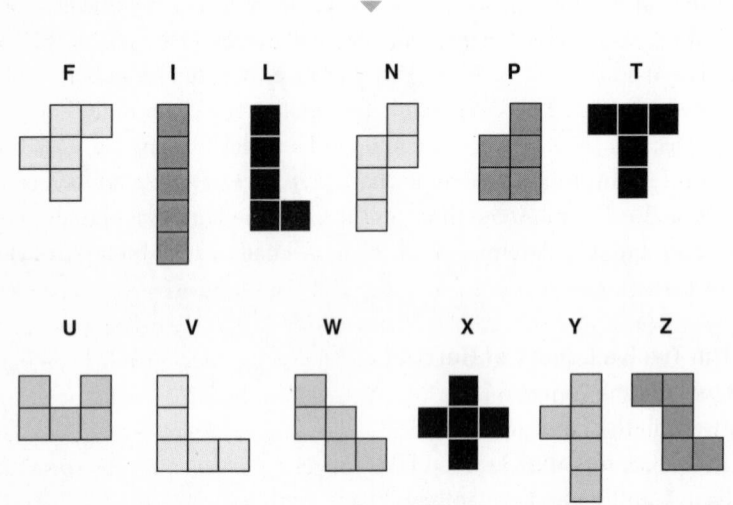

THERE are 12 different shapes that can be made out of five squares joined at the edges. Called pentominoes, these shapes are frequently labeled by the letters they most closely represent. Altogether, the 12 pentominoes account for 5 × 12 = 60 square units, and in fact it is possible to arrange the 12 pieces so as to make rectangles measuring 6 × 10, 5 × 12, 4 × 15, and

3 × 20. There is even a board-game variation in which players alternate placing pentominoes onto an 8 × 8 grid until someone (i.e., the loser of the game) cannot place a remaining pentomino without overlapping one that has already been played. Author and futurist Arthur C. Clarke was a big fan of pentominoes, and for *2001: A Space Odyssey* he worked in a scene that showed HAL the computer playing the 8 × 8 pentomino game. Unfortunately for fans of the game, the scene was cut in favor of a different 8 × 8 game: chess.

12 is also the "kissing number" in three dimensions. To see what this is all about, it might help to visit the two-dimensional case, in which the kissing number is defined as the number of circles of radius 1 that can simultaneously touch a given circle. That number is clearly 6, as suggested by the diagram at right.

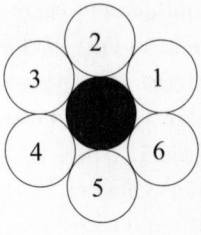

THE situation in three dimensions is necessarily more complex. When you put 12 spheres around a central sphere, there is substantial free space, and it is tempting to believe that there might be room for a thirteenth sphere.

Apparently the possibility of a thirteenth sphere arose in a conversation between Isaac Newton and Scottish astronomer David Gregory back in 1694. Although the precise nature of their disagreement has been lost to history (most accounts suggest that Newton was on the 12 side and Gregory on 13), there is no record of so much as a gentleman's wager on the subject and certainly no possibility of anyone collecting, as the question wasn't fully resolved until 1953.

SPEAKING of spheres, the traditional black pentagon/white hexagon Telstar soccer ball design was the official ball for the 1970 Mexico City World Cup and for several years thereafter. (1970 was the first year in which the

World Cup was televised, and the new ball was especially easy to follow on television.)

There are 12 pentagons and 20 hexagons on this ball. So why is this discussion being held under 12 rather than 20? Because the Telstar ball is actually a special case of a more general concept called a Buckyball, named for Buckminster Fuller of geodesic dome fame. (I say this rather sheepishly and ironically, as Buckminster Fuller was the speaker when I graduated from high school and I had never heard of him.) It turns out that many different sphere-like structures can be made from a combination of pentagons and hexagons, but whereas there is no limit on the number of hexagons, the number of pentagons must always be 12. (This follows from Euler's Theorem and the reader is invited to take a stab at a proof. See Answers.) In particular, it is possible for the number of hexagons to equal zero, in which case you're left with the regular dodecahedron, one of the five Platonic solids (see **5**). There is also a dodecahedron whose faces are all rhombi. Rhombic dodecahedra, as they are called, can, like cubes, be fitted together to fill three-dimensional space, in the same sense that rhombi—or squares, but not pentagons—can tile the plane. But a desk calendar can be made out of either form of dodecahedron, with each face getting a different month.

▼

AN alexandrine, found in French literature from Racine to Baudelaire, is a line of 12 syllables. Alexander Pope, alas, was not taken with this virtually eponymous form, as he writes:

A needless alexandrine ends the song
that like a wounded snake, drags its slow length along

▼

THE Necker cube is a 12-lined optical illusion that first appeared in 1832. Because the cube has no dotted lines, the figure produces (at least) two different interpretations.

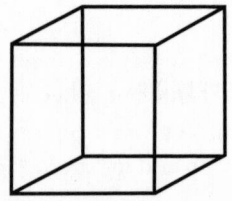

13 [prime]

THE number 13's biggest claim to fame is that it is considered exceedingly unlucky. There is no single reason why 13 is treated the way it is, but most explanations begin with the fact that it compares poorly with 12, its immediate predecessor. Twelve is nicely divisible by 2, 3, and 4, and shows up in months of the year, signs of the zodiac, and a whole range of other designations, as we have just seen. Thirteen, on the other hand, is prime and therefore quite a bit harder to love.

▼

THE fear of the number 13 is known as triskaidekaphobia. The fact that the Last Supper was attended by 13 people appears to have retrofitted to explain the fear. Ditto for the arrest of the Knights Templar on Friday, October 13, 1307. But it bears mention that it is *Tuesday* the 13th that is considered unlucky in Greece, Spain, and a few other cultures.

▼

FRANKLIN Delano Roosevelt was perhaps history's most prominent triskaidekaphobe. It is said that when luncheon or dinner parties numbered 13, he would ask his secretary to join the guests to make an even 14. Not that he invented that particular practice. In France there's even a word for it: A *quatorzieme* is a professional fourteenth guest. And legend has it that Mark Twain found out he was to be the thirteenth guest at a dinner party, at which point a friend told him not to go because it was bad luck. "It was bad luck," Twain later told the friend. "They only had food for 12." But FDR's fear of Friday the 13th—as opposed to, say, fear itself—knew no bounds. In April 1945, as everyone else in America geared up for the Friday the 13th of that month, Roosevelt managed to avoid the day altogether . . . by dying on Thursday the 12th.

▼

NOT every culture hates 13. The Egyptians regarded 13 as a sacred number, and despite FDR's phobia the number has a unique place in American history. Everyone knows about the original 13 colonies as represented by the 13 stars and stripes of the original flag.

But while the flag has undergone numerous revisions (ultimately leaving the number of stripes intact but not the number of stars), if you look at the back of a modern one-dollar bill, you will still find a bunch of thirteens:

- 13 stars above the eagle
- 13 steps on the Pyramid
- 13 letters in ANNUIT COEPTIS
- 13 letters in E PLURIBUS UNUM
- 13 vertical bars on the shield
- 13 horizontal stripes at the top of the shield
- 13 leaves on the olive branch
- 13 fruits
- 13 arrows

ELEVEN PLUS TWO = 13 = TWELVE PLUS ONE

NOT only is the above arithmetic accurate—the three-word expressions to either side of 13 are anagrams of one another.

THE numbers 12 and 13 are also linked by the equations below. The reversal of their squares is also the square of their reversals. (Eleven has this same property rather more trivially, but 13 is the best of all because no digits are duplicated in either the number or its square.)

$12^2 = 144$	$13^2 = 169$
$21^2 = 441$	$31^2 = 961$

THE soccer ball we encountered in **12** is one of 13 Archimedean solids: three-dimensional convex shapes built up of two or more types of regular polygons. Perhaps the most spectacular is the great rhombicosidodecahedron, which is built from 30 squares, 20 hexagons, and 12 decagons.

▾

THE movie *Apollo 13* chronicled the ill-fated 1970 flight of the spacecraft bearing that same name. Like many if not most feature films, *Apollo 13* made a handful of technical errors, including using a logo that didn't appear until 1976, misplacing the Sea of Tranquility, and apparently forgetting that propulsion jets do not make any noise in space. But the most amusing blunder for numbers people came when an engineer at mission control whipped out a slide rule to check the arithmetic of one of the astronauts. The audience laughed at the pure primitivity of it all, drowning out the fact that it was an *addition* problem. The whole point of a slide rule is that numbers are marked in proportion to their logarithms, facilitating multiplication and exponentiation, but not addition.

One postscript: When *Apollo 13* came out on DVD, its release had an unintended effect on the entire movie rental business. A young man named Reed Hastings rented the film and incurred some late fees upon returning it. Upset by what he felt was an unwarranted charge, Hastings founded Netflix, the first DVD-by-mail service.

14 $\left[2 \times 7 \right]$

007 × 2

IAN Fleming wrote a total of 14 James Bond novels, one per year from 1953 (the year of his debut with *Casino Royale*) through 1966 (the year of Fleming's death). Two of the 14 books (*Thunderball* and *Octopussy*) were actually collections of short stories.

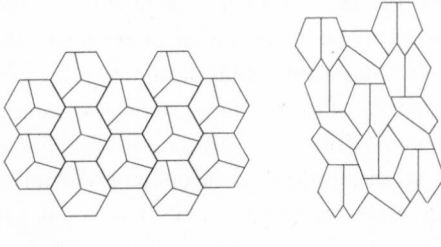

WE'VE seen that it is impossible to tile the plane with *regular* pentagons, but there are 14 known types of irregular convex pentagons that will tile the plane just fine. Two types are shown below: The first is just a hexagonal tiling with three lines drawn inside each hexagon, while the second, discovered in 1985 by German graduate student Rolf Stein, relies on specific relationships between the sides and angles of the convex pentagon. Stein's creation was the fourteenth pentagonal tiling. The discovery of a fifteenth type would rock the tiling world, but it's a possibility that has yet to be ruled out.

BACH is said to have been especially fond of the number 14, possibly because in the standard alphanumeric code, the letters in BACH add up to 2 + 1 + 3 + 8 = 14.

IN the old British system of weights and measures, a stone equaled 14 pounds avoirdupois.

A *fortnight* is a strange term for a two-week period, until you realize that the word is a contraction of "fourteen nights."

SPEAKING of days, nights, or whatever, there are 14 possible calendars, as January 1 can fall on seven different days, and leap year creates two different calendars for each of those seven choices.

▼

CARBON-14, the basis of the carbon dating technique, is a radioactive isotope whose nucleus consists of 6 protons and 8 neutrons. It occurs naturally and has a half-life of 5,730 years.

▼

IN 1949, the comic duo of Ma and Pa Kettle (Marjorie Main and Percy Kilbride) challenged a salesman's assertion that one-fifth of 25% was 5%, feeling that it was 14% instead. They started by dividing 5 into 25. Well, five won't go into 2, so you have to go to the 5. Five into 5 is 1, so Pa Kettle placed a 1 to the left. What's left when you subtract the 5 from 25 is 20, and 5 goes into 20 four times. Writing a 4 next to the one gave him 14, as he had predicted. And so on, and so on. (Alas, much better on their little chalkboard and washcloth than on the printed page, but their sheer butchery of the number 14 was too thorough not to mention.)

▼

A sonnet is a poem with 14 lines, written in iambic pentameter and separated into an octet and a sestet.

▼

AND let's not forget the Palimpsest. A strange name for a puzzle, but the other names it has picked up are no less strange: the Loculum of Archimedes, or simply the Stomachion. By any name, this is perhaps the world's oldest puzzle. It consists of 14 triangles and quadrilaterals that can be rearranged to form a variety of shapes. One of those shapes is a square, pretty much by definition, because the 14 pieces of the Stomachion (my preferred name, as it essentially means that the solver

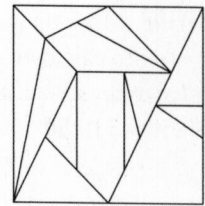

is going crazy) were originally made by cutting along line segments ending on the lattice points of a 12 × 12 square. Since the time of Archimedes (circa 200 BC), the biggest challenge surrounding the puzzle is to compute the total number of ways in which the 14 pieces can be configured to form a square. The answer—536—was not computed once and for all until 2003. And we thought Fermat's Last Theorem took a long time to solve.

15 $\left[\, 3 \times 5 \,\right]$

IN a game of backgammon, each player starts off with 15 pieces, arranged in columns of 2, 3, 5, and 5, as at left.

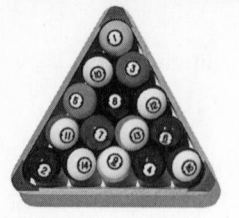

15 is the fifth triangular number, easily depicted by the pre-break arrangement of 15 billiard balls—in this case, held within the triangular wooden rack used in American eight ball.

GIVING a 15% tip is a common guideline when dining out. And it's a simple matter to calculate 15% tips in your head. Just take 10% of the price of the meal and add half again as much. A $70 check produces a tip of $7.00 + $3.50 = $10.50.

THE 15-letter word *uncopyrightable* is the longest word in the English language that does not repeat any letters.

▼

THE Fifteen Puzzle, supposedly of puzzlemaster Sam Loyd, was a puzzle craze of 1880, almost exactly 100 years before the introduction of Rubik's Cube. The puzzle features square blocks numbered 1 to 15, with the 14 and 15 reversed. The idea is to use the puzzle's one empty square to slide the blocks so as to place the 14 and 15 into their proper positions.

One of the pieces of lore surrounding this puzzle is that a Massachusetts dentist named Charles Pevey offered a reward of a $25 set of teeth (and, soon afterward, $100 in cash) for anyone who could solve the puzzle. Presumably Pevey knew that his money was safe, as no solution is possible. The impossibility of a solution involves what is called a parity argument: Curiously, no matter how the puzzle pieces are arranged, the sum of the number of pieces that are in reverse order plus the row number of the empty square does not change. Because a 14–15 switch would reduce this number by 1, it is unattainable.

Although Sam Loyd took credit for the invention of this puzzle, the actual inventor was apparently a New York postmaster named Noyes Chapman.

▼

8	1	6
3	5	7
4	9	2

THE above figure is said to be a magic square because every row, column, and diagonal sums to the same number. Fifteen is the magic constant for any 3 × 3 square, because the sum of 1 through 9 equals 45 and $\frac{45}{3} = 15$.

▼

IN the discussion in **4**, we saw that any positive integer can be written as the sum of four perfect squares. In other words, any positive integer can be written as $w^2 + x^2 + y^2 + z^2$ for some $w, x, y,$ and z, not necessarily distinct. The number 15 played a role in that discussion because it is the smallest number that requires the full four squares: $9 + 4 + 1 + 1$. But mathematicians can't let a theorem like Lagrange's Four-Square Theorem go without trying to generalize it. And what does such a generalization look like? Well, is it true, for example, that any positive integer can be expressed in the form $w^2 + 2x^2 + 3y^2 + 4z^2$? Let's try it out:

$1 = 1^2 + 2 \times 0^2 + 3 \times 0^2 + 4 \times 0^2$	$6 = 2^2 + 2 \times 1^2 + 3 \times 0^2 + 4 \times 0^2$	$11 = 0^2 + 2 \times 1^2 + 3 \times 1^2 + 4 \times 1^2$
$2 = 0^2 + 2 \times 1^2 + 3 \times 0^2 + 4 \times 0^2$	$7 = 2^2 + 2 \times 0^2 + 3 \times 1^2 + 4 \times 0^2$	$12 = 0^2 + 2 \times 0^2 + 3 \times 2^2 + 4 \times 0^2$
$3 = 1^2 + 2 \times 1^2 + 3 \times 0^2 + 4 \times 0^2$	$8 = 0^2 + 2 \times 2^2 + 3 \times 0^2 + 4 \times 0^2$	$13 = 1^2 + 2 \times 0^2 + 3 \times 2^2 + 4 \times 0^2$
$4 = 2^2 + 2 \times 0^2 + 3 \times 0^2 + 4 \times 0^2$	$9 = 3^2 + 2 \times 0^2 + 3 \times 0^2 + 4 \times 0^2$	$14 = 0^2 + 2 \times 1^2 + 3 \times 2^2 + 4 \times 0^2$
$5 = 1^2 + 2 \times 0^2 + 3 \times 0^2 + 4 \times 1^2$	$10 = 1^2 + 2 \times 1^2 + 3 \times 1^2 + 4 \times 1^2$	$15 = 1^2 + 2 \times 1^2 + 3 \times 2^2 + 4 \times 0^2$

I know this is getting awfully tedious, but, believe it or not, we don't have to go any further. According to an extraordinary 1993 theorem by John Conway and William Schneeberger, any positive-definite quadratic form that represents the first 15 integers will represent any integer whatsoever!

As it turns out, there are 54 expressions of the form $Aw^2 + Bx^2 + Cy^2 + Dz^2$ that represent all integers, ranging from $w^2 + x^2 + y^2 + z^2$ to $w^2 + 2x^2 + 5y^2 + 10z^2$. This list was first identified by the great Indian mathematician Ramanujan in the early twentieth century—that is, unassisted by computers. The only flaw in Ramanujan's work was that he included the form $w^2 + 2x^2 + 5y^2 + 5z^2$, which turns out not to be universal. In fact, the number 15 is the first (and only!) number that cannot be represented as $w^2 + 2x^2 + 5y^2 + 5z^2$ with w, x, y, and z integers.

▼

In the future, everyone will be world-famous for 15 minutes.
—Andy Warhol, 1968

16 $[2^4]$

BECAUSE 16 is a perfect square, it is possible to arrange 16 circles in a square, as follows:

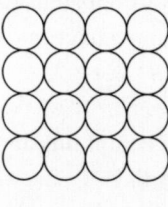

IT is also possible to arrange these same 16 circles in a different sort of square formation:

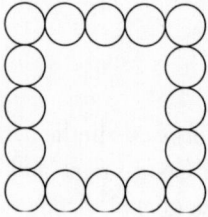

The above square works out because 16, in addition to being a square, is a difference of squares that are two apart, namely $5^2 - 3^2$ or $25 - 9$. (The second figure is just a 5×5 square with its 3×3 interior taken out.) No other number of circles (or whatever) can be configured as two squares in this fashion.

THE equation $16 = 2^4 = 4^2$ is unique. No other number can be represented in the form a^b and b^a with $a \neq b$.

THE fact that there are 16 ounces in a pound is related to 16 being a power of two, sort of. The word for ounce comes from the Latin *uncia*, or twelfth part, making it a cognate of *inch*. The Roman pound was indeed 12 ounces, a standard that remains today in the form of the Troy pound used in the measurement of gold. In between, it seems that seventeenth-century Scottish goldsmiths used a standard of 16 ounces per pound, and, more generally, merchants in the Middle Ages saw the advantage of a unit that could be halved repeatedly, and it was apparently on that basis that today's 16-ounce avoirdupois pound emerged once and for all.

THE hexadecimal base used in computing and other applications is nothing more than base 16, with digits 0, 1, 2, 3, 4, 5, 6, 7, 8, 9, A, B, C, D, E, and F. Because $16 = 2^4$, a hexadecimal bit essentially substitutes for four ordinary bits, making computer codes that much less cumbersome. In Boolean logic, there are 16 possible Boolean operations that can be performed on two variables P and Q: ZERO, P, NOT P, NOT Q, P AND Q, P AND (NOT Q), Q AND (NOT P), and so on.

THERE are 16 basic personality types in the Myers-Briggs classification system, devised by Katharine Cook Briggs and her daughter Isabel Briggs Myers in accordance with ideas published by Carl Jung in 1921. People are either introverted or extraverted (I or E), sensing or intuitive (S or N), thinking or feeling (T or F), and judging or perceiving (J or P). With four basic markers, each having two possibilities, the number of possible combinations is $2^4 = 16$. They are commonly referred to by a set of four letters, as in the following:

ISTJ	ISFJ	INFJ	INTJ
ISTP	ISFP	INFP	INTP
ESTP	ESFP	ENFP	ENTP
ESTJ	ESFJ	ENFJ	ENTJ

The most common personality type is ISFJ—introverted, sensing, feeling, and judging—which accounts for an estimated 13.8% of the population. The least common type, at an estimated 1.8% of the population, is ENTJ—extraverted, intuitive, thinking, and judging. Note that the most common and the rarest types are opposite in three, but not four, of the basic categories.

MOVING to a different type of identification process, for much of the twentieth century, fingerprint identification in the United Kingdom was based on 16 points of similarity. This standard was eventually abandoned because of technological improvements, but the delicious part of the story is that the paper on which the 16-point standard was originally based turned out to have been a forgery.

THIS arrangement of sixteen 0's and 1's is known as a de Bruijn cycle. If you start at the top center of the diagram, the four characters going clockwise form the set {0,0,0,0}. Starting at the next character to the right and going clockwise four spaces yields the set {0,0,0,1}, and so on. By the time you go around the whole circle you will have created each of the 16 possible arrangements of four binary (i.e., either 0 or 1) characters. The existence of de Bruijn cycles for any desired alphabet and cycle size can be proved 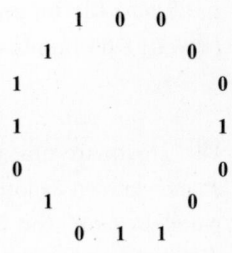 using graph theory, and these cycles are related to a problem known as universal coloring. This book doesn't happen to use four-color printing, but the related challenge to the above diagram, which you are free to ponder, would be to color each of the 16 positions with one of four colors in such a way that as you went around the circle, you'd come across each of the 16 possible ordered pairs of those four colors—that is, (red, blue), (blue, yellow), and so on.

SPEAKING of books, it isn't widely known that the traditional book assembly process uses "signatures" of length 16, which is why the total page count of so many books is something like 272, 288, or some other multiple of 16.

DEFINE two sets of numbers A and B as follows:

$$A = \{1, 4, 6, 7, 10, 11, 13, 16\}$$
$$B = \{2, 3, 5, 8, 9, 12, 14, 15\}$$

It is obvious at a glance that the sets A and B are (1) disjoint and (2) together account for every positive integer from 1 to 16. A second glance reveals that each of the eight pairs {1, 2} through {15, 16} has precisely one element in A and one in B, with four even numbers and four odd numbers in each set, so that the sum of the members of A equals the sum of the members of B. But what is considerably less obvious is that the sum of the *squares* of the elements of A equals the sum of the squares of the elements of B, and similarly for *cubes*. This construction is remarkable but turns out to be possible for any power of 2: a 32-number construction uses fourth powers, a 64-number construction incorporates fifth powers, and so on.

THE 16-square-unit diagram below shows how to create the geometrical shapes known as tangrams. The 7 tangrams—5 triangles, 1 square, and 1 parallelogram—can be combined to create a variety of shapes, including the 4 × 4 square from which they originated.

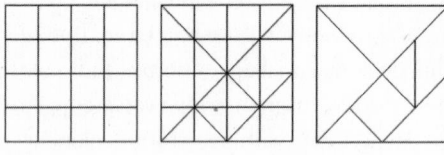

AS an exercise, try dividing the 16-square-unit figure below into the 7 tangram shapes:

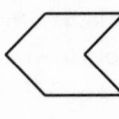

OUR final 16-square-unit diagram is the Bachet square, in which each row, column, and diagonal has one ace, one king, one queen, and one jack, with each of the four suits also represented once and only once. These squares were discovered by Claude Gaspar Bachet de Meziriac in the 1600s, and in 1624 he posed the question of how many different ones there were. The answer, 1152, is better recognized as 2 × 576 = 2 × (4!)^2, the idea being that once you fix the top row, there are only two Bachet squares associated with that row, and the rank and suit requirements each end up contributing 4! possible arrangements.

17 [prime]

THE Pythagoreans supposedly detested the number 17, feeling that it was no match for the symmetric beauty of 16 to the left and 18 to the right. They're entitled to their opinion, of course, but history has shown them to be rather foolish in a variety of areas and this one is no exception. Of all the numbers we will encounter in this book, the number 17 is perhaps the biggest surprise in terms of just how much it has going for it.

▼

GEORGE Balanchine had no difficulty finding symmetry in the number 17. That's the number of ballerinas who showed up for one particular class, and Balanchine responded by arranging them in the double-diamond formation, which became the opening for his signature ballet, *Serenade*.

▼

IN Italy, the number 17 takes on the role of bad luck and superstition that 13 occupies in other cultures. Alitalia has no seventeenth row, many Italian buildings do not have a seventeenth floor, and when the Renault R17 went to Italy, its name was changed to R117. This cultural aversion to 17 has long roots, apparently tracing to the anagrammatical relationship between the characters for XVII, the Roman numeral designation for 17, and the Latin word VIXI, whose translation "I lived" somehow morphed into "I am dead." (Note that VI + XI = 6 + 11 = 17.)

▼

THE number 17 is a threshold of sorts for consecutive number sequences. But we'll start at the beginning:

▼

ANY two consecutive integers, pretty much by definition, contain no common factor. They are, in math-speak, relatively prime. That doesn't have to be true of three consecutive numbers, as two of them may be even and thus both divisible by two. But the middle one must be relatively prime to the other two. And among four consecutive integers, one of the middle two must be odd, and is relatively prime to the other three.

How far can we go? You guessed it, any sequence of *fewer than* 17 consecutive integers must contain at least one number that is relatively prime to all the others. But if you look at the 17 consecutive numbers 2184, 2185, 2186 . . . 2199, 2200, you will see that each shares a factor in common with at least one other member of the sequence. In fact, if you choose any number $n \geq 17$, it is always possible to locate a sequence of n consecutive integers such that each shares a factor with at least one of the others. The sequence beginning with 2184 just happens to be the smallest sequence of its kind.

▼

IF you visit Braunschweig, Germany, the birthplace of Carl Friedrich Gauss, you just might come across a statue of Gauss atop a circular pedestal. But give that pedestal a second look. If you do, you'll see that it is not circular but instead forms a figure with 17 equal sides. The statue recognizes one of

Gauss's great early achievements—the creation of a regular 17-gon with only a ruler and a compass (the grade-school compass with a point on one end and a pencil on the other, not a compass that will tell you where the North Pole is).

Let's take a moment to ponder what such a construction is all about. If you were asked to construct an equilateral triangle using only a ruler and compass, you'd proceed as follows: Pick two points A and B. Digging your compass into point A, draw an arc that passes through point B. Now dig the compass into point B and draw an arc that passes through point A. If the arcs you drew are big enough, they intersect at a third point, which we'll cleverly label point C. Now you can finally use your ruler, drawing segments that connect A to B, B to C, and C to A. The result is an equilateral triangle.

While the 17-gon construction is necessarily complex, the diagram to the right gives a hint of its underlying methods.

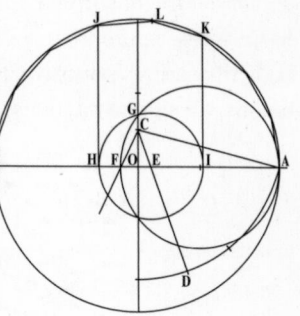

GAUSS didn't stop there—as well he shouldn't have, because he constructed the regular 17-gon when he was only 18 years old. He eventually gave an explicit categorization of those regular polygons that lent themselves to a ruler-and-compass construction, along the way proving that it was impossible to create a regular nonagon (9 sides) with such limited means.

THE Cincinnati Zoo has a display that looks much like a 17-gon, except that it displays the various broods of the 17-year cicada, an insect whose extraordinarily annoying chirping noises are made at least tolerable by the fact that they only appear in a given locale once every 17 years. The diagram begins with the appearance of one particular brood in 1987, and ends just before the reappearance of that same brood 17 years later, in 2004.

RECALL from **6** that if you join six dots with lines colored either red or blue, you will automatically create a monochromatic triangle—an all-red or all-blue triangle whose vertices are three of the six dots. If you up the ante to three colors, it turns out that 17 is the magic number.

▼

WE'VE all seen wallpaper patterns and taken note that they repeat in a symmetric fashion. While a wallpaper store or catalog will offer thousands of choices, it might surprise you to learn that any symmetric pattern is one of 17 basic types, appropriately called wallpaper groups. The designs below embody the various symmetry techniques, from translations to reflections to rotations, then on to rotations of different angles and combinations of the above.

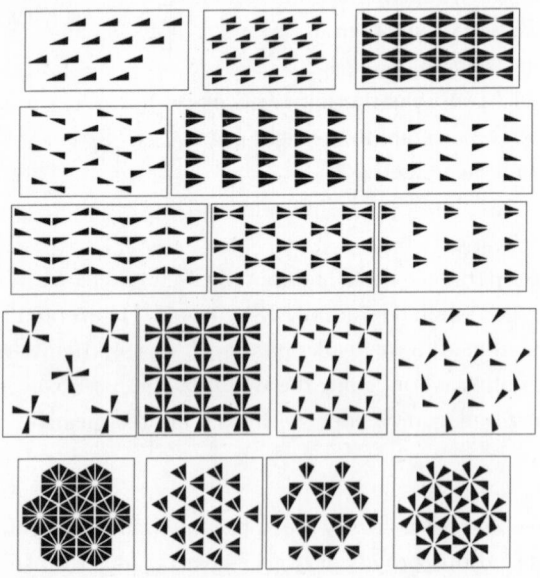

The proof that the number of planar symmetries is limited to 17 is somewhat outside the scope of this book, but there's a great proof in the book *The Symmetries of Things*, by John Conway, Heidi Burgiel, and Chaim Goodman-Strauss.

Scholars appear divided as to whether all 17 planar symmetries are present in the tilings of the Alhambra, the Moorish castle in Granada, Spain (a country that is itself divided into 17 so-called autonomous regions). A brief conversation with David Kelly of Hampshire College, the world's leading authority on the number 17 (no, I'm not kidding) suggests that the answer is yes, though there are some written accounts that are less sanguine. Whatever the final verdict on Alhambra tilings, their reputation inspired an obscure Dutch graphic artist named M. C. Escher to pay visits in both 1922 and 1936. These visits were the cornerstone of Escher's now-legendary pursuit of magical planar symmetries.

▼

FINALLY, consider the Sudoku puzzle below. You may have noticed that there are fewer starting numbers than your typical Sudoku. But if you're thinking that you've seen a published puzzle with fewer givens, there are a lot of mathematicians who'd like very much to talk to you. You see, this puzzle has precisely 17 givens, the minimum number ever achieved at this writing. In other words, no puzzle with 16 or fewer givens has ever been shown to produce a unique solution, and circumstantial evidence is building in favor of 17 remaining minimal, although there is currently no theorem to that effect. Surprisingly, this particular puzzle isn't all that hard. (See Answers.)

	1	4				8		
			2	7				
7	6						2	
			4					
2								
3	7			8				
			5			4		1
						5		

▼

I think I'll stop here as far as 17 is concerned. I'm not sure I've written anything that David Kelly didn't already know, but I trust I've shown enough to demonstrate that the Pythagoreans' dismissal of this wonderful number was woefully off the mark.

18 $\left[\, 2 \times 3^2 \,\right]$

A rectangle with a perimeter of $3 + 6 + 3 + 6 = 18$ has an area of $3 \times 6 = 18$. Other than a 4×4 square, this is the only rectangle whose area is numerically equal to its perimeter.

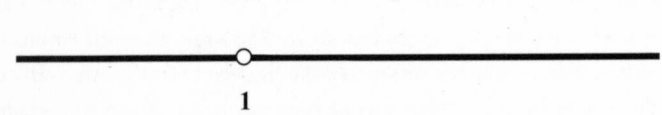

STARTING with a single dot placed somewhere on a line segment, it is a simple matter to place another dot so that each dot belongs to its own half of the segment, as below.

Now we place a third dot so that each of the three dots is in its own third. Oops, wait a minute. These two are already in the middle third of the segment. Let's start over.

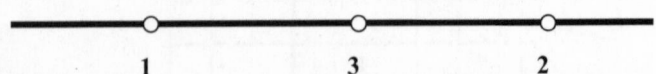

There, that was easy. The first two dots are in different halves, the three dots in different thirds. Can we keep going? Maybe, but only so far. In 1970, Elwyn Berlekamp and Ronald Graham proved the remarkable result that no matter how many times you start over, it is impossible to place 18 points in this manner.

THE 18-Point Theorem, as it is called, has an interesting application in the area of political representation, first written up in 1984 by Virginia Tech economics professor Amoz Kats. Professor Kats's thesis has particular resonance in such places as Israel and the Scandinavian countries, where a legislative body is elected using proportional representation: If a party receives $x\%$ of the votes, it gets $x\%$ of the legislature, with the seats filled in order from the party's list. The question is, can the various constituencies of a party always be represented? In Kats's construct, "A list truly represents the constituency of the party if whenever the first k members of it are elected, each of the k equally spaced sections of the party is represented in the elected body." There's no problem for small legislatures, but the 18-Point Theorem rears its head with larger ones: Kats's specific conclusion was that "a party can construct an *ordered* representative list . . . if and only if it contains not more than seventeen names." Fortunately, this condition is satisfied most of the time, whether or not the party pays homage to the 18-Point Theorem.

THE modern golf course has 18 holes. Volleyball is played on a court that is 18 meters long, with a ball that is divided into 18 sections.

THE number 18 is a standard of sorts for a completely different sport: barrel jumping. As in how many barrels can you jump over with a running start . . . on skates? In the 1960s, the ABC television program *Wide World of Sports* often featured barrel jumping competitions from the Grossinger's resort in the Catskills. The world record of 18 barrels (translating into 29 feet, 5 inches) was set by Yvan Jolin of Canada in 1981, and it's a record that could be around for a long, long time.

AND 18 forms a different barrier still in horse racing. At this writing, the Kentucky Derby winner with the longest name is the 16-letter champion of 2000,

Fusaichi Pegasus (in horse racing, spaces count). The Steven Spielberg co-owned Atswhatimtalknbout raced in 2003, finishing fourth but tying a record that will never be broken. There are 18 letters in Atswhatimtalknbout, and the official rules for the Kentucky Derby (and in many horse racing venues throughout the world) prohibit horse names from exceeding 18 letters.

19 [prime]

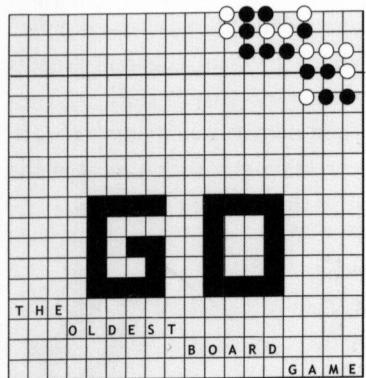

THE game Go features a 19 × 19 grid onto which players place white and black pieces in hopes of surrounding their opponent's pieces and thereby removing them from the board. Legends have it that the game dates back to 2000 BC or so.

COMPARED to Go, cribbage is a newcomer on the gaming scene. The invention of cribbage has been attributed to the English poet Sir John Suckling (1609–1642). The game consists of dealing and valuing hands of cards and then moving pegs around a board in accordance with the hand values. It turns out that 19 is an impossible score in the game of cribbage, and is the smallest number with that property. A 19 has come to mean a useless hand.

19 is a so-called centered hexagonal number, meaning that it is possible to place 19 dots in such a way as to form concentric hexagons, with one of the dots forming the center. In the figure below, the numbers 1 through 19 have been placed in the dots so that the sum of the three numbers in any leg of the six triangles is the same: 22. As it happens, there are many such solutions, with a variety of possible sums. The biggest possible sum is 31. Can you find a solution that yields it? (See Answers.)

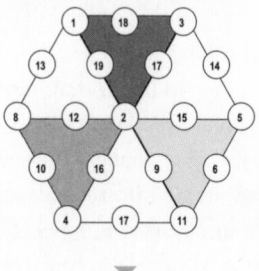

TAKE away the numbers from the above diagram and you're left with the 19-hole hexagonal pattern below, most commonly seen in sink or lavatory drains.

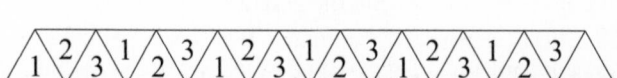

A different sort of association between the number 19 and hexagons starts with the figure above—19 equilateral triangles that can be colored and folded into a hexahexaflexagon. If each of the numbers 1, 2, and 3 is given a different color (and likewise for the back), it is possible by appropriate folding and manipulation to make hexagons of each of the six colors emerge, with none of the other colors visible.

KELLOGG'S Product 19 was introduced in 1967 as a competitive response to Total from General Mills. As the story goes, Kellogg's had trouble coming up with a name for the new product and eventually settled on Product 19, as it was the nineteenth product in company history, Corn Flakes being number1.

▼

THE philosopher Bertrand Russell once pondered the futility of identifying "the least integer not nameable in fewer than nineteen syllables." By way of comparison, 11 requires three syllables to name, either by saying "e-le-ven" or "eight plus three," and it is the smallest integer with that property. However, Russell was on a completely different wavelength. His point was that the description inside the quotation marks consists of 18 syllables, meaning that the least integer not nameable in fewer than 19 syllables can in fact be named in 18 syllables, a contradiction. Russell attributed this paradox to Oxford University librarian G. Berry. It survives in many different forms, but the basic idea is called the Berry paradox.

▼

QUICK: What does the equation below have to do with the number 19?

$$559 = 256 + 256 + 16 + 16 + 1 + 1 + 1 + 1 + 1 + 1 + 1 + 1 + 1 + 1 + 1 + 1 + 1 + 1 + 1$$

The answer is that there are 19 numbers (summands) on the right side. But there's more. We can rewrite the equation as:

$$559 = 4^4 + 4^4 + 2^4 + 2^4 + 1^4 + 1^4 + 1^4 + 1^4 + 1^4 + 1^4 + 1^4 + 1^4 + 1^4 + 1^4 + 1^4 + 1^4 + 1^4 + 1^4 + 1^4$$

In other words, the number 559 can be written as the sum of 19 fourth powers. But guess what? *Every single positive integer* can be written as the sum of at most 19 powers. Perhaps you remember our discussion in **4** concerning Lagrange's Theorem, which states that every positive integer can be written as the sum of four squares. Well, mathematicians didn't leave that one alone. In 1770, Oxford mathematician Edward Waring conjectured among other things that 19 fourth powers would suffice to represent any positive integer. The result was finally proved in 1986, by Balasubramanian, Deshouillers, and Dress. It turns out that only seven numbers (559 being the largest of the seven) require the full 19.

1	1	2	3	5	8	13	21	34	55	89	144	233	377	610	987	1597	2584	4181
F_1	F_2	F_3	F_4	F_5	F_6	F_7	F_8	F_9	F_{10}	F_{11}	F_{12}	F_{13}	F_{14}	F_{15}	F_{16}	F_{17}	F_{18}	F_{19}

ABOVE are the first 19 Fibonacci numbers, where $F_1 = F_2 = 1$ and each successive member of the sequence is obtained by summing the previous two. (See **5**, **8**, etc.) The entries that are highlighted in gray are those Fibonacci numbers with *prime* subscripts (not including F_2). The first six prime subscripts—3, 5, 7, 11, 13, and 17—each produce a Fibonacci number that is prime. There is no good reason why this pattern should continue, and in fact F_{19} is the first of infinitely many exceptions: F_{19} equals $4{,}181 = 37 \times 113$.

SPEAKING of divisibility, any number that is divisible by 19 will have the following peculiar property: If you multiply the last digit by 2 and add that number to the remaining digits, the resulting number will be divisible by 19. For example, 625632 is divisible by 19 because all of following results are divisible by 19: $(62563 + 4 = 62567)$; $(6256 + 14 = 6270)$; $(627 + 0 = 627)$; $(62 + 14 = 76)$; $(7 + 12 = 19)$; $(1 + 18 = 19)$. As a divisibility test, this procedure is relatively easy to describe, but it usually requires so many iterations that you may wonder why you didn't just divide by 19 in the first place. But don't take my word for it. If you like, you can try the process out with one of the most famous multiples of 19, the number 19181716151413121110987654321—formed by stringing together the first 19 integers in reverse order.

IN general, 19 divides a positive integer if and only if (abbreviated iff) 19 divides the number that results from adding twice the value of the last digit that results from stripping off this last digit. For example, $19|704836$ iff $19|70495$ iff $19|7059$ iff $19|723$ iff $19|78$ iff $19|23$ iff $19|8$. Since this last divisibility $19|8$ is obviously false, 19 does not divide evenly into 704836.

20 $\left[2^2 \times 5 \right]$

THERE are 20 possible first moves for either player in a game of chess: Any of the eight pawns can be moved forward either one or two squares, while either of the two knights can be moved two squares up and one square either to the left or to the right. (In standard chess notation, the possible moves for white are a3, a4, b3, b4, c3, c4, d3, d4, e3, e4, f3, f4, g3, g4, h3, h4, Na3, Nc3, Nf3, and Nh3. Four of the 20 possible moves are made by a knight—labeled N because K is already taken for king—while the other 16 moves are made by pawns, so lowly that modern notation doesn't even give them a letter.)

THE number 20 shows up elsewhere in the worlds of games and music, notably in 20 Questions.

WHILE Dungeons & Dragons uses a 20-sided die (an icosahedron) that everyone can see, the Magic 8-Ball, invented by Abe Bookman in 1946, relied on an icosahedron suspended in blue fluid inside the ball. You ask the ball a question, shake it up, and wait for the answer to emerge in the window on the ball. The 20 standard answers are as follows:

Signs point to yes.	Yes.
Reply hazy, try again.	Without a doubt.
My sources say no.	As I see it, yes.
You may rely on it.	Outlook not so good.

Concentrate and ask again.	It is decidedly so.
Better not tell you now.	Very doubtful.
Yes—definitely.	It is certain.
Cannot predict now.	Most likely.
Ask again later.	My reply is no.
Outlook good.	Don't count on it.

AN even sneakier icosahedral structure is at the heart of many viruses, as first conjectured in 1956 by Francis Crick and James Watson of DNA fame.

THE number 20 has always been considered a viable number for a numerical base, because it coincides with the total number of digits in the human body. In the former British currency system, 20 shillings made up a pound.

IN the non-metric world, 20/20 vision is the standard for normal vision, literally meaning that what you see at 20 feet is what you should normally see—as opposed to, say, 20/60 vision, in which you see at 20 feet what a person with normal eyesight sees at 60. In the metric world, this same concept is often described as 6/6 vision, where the 6 stands for meters.

As desirable as 20/20 vision is, someone described as applying 20/20 hindsight is seldom being lauded. Apparently to be a true visionary you have to make decisions before you know how they turn out.

21 $[3 \times 7]$

THE factorization of the number 21 into two prime factors was apparently not lost on Franklin Roosevelt. When Roosevelt took office in 1933, one of the president's regular tasks was to set the price of gold. Sounds weird, doesn't it? It sounds even weirder when you hear that on one occasion Roosevelt proposed raising the gold price by 21 cents . . . on the grounds that 21 was three times seven and therefore a lucky number. (One can presume that Roosevelt never raised the gold price by 13 cents, given his legendary fearfulness of that number. See **13**.) Actually, the number 21 really did turn out to be lucky within the Roosevelt administration, in the sense that the 21st Amendment to the Constitution, ratified in December 1933, repealed Prohibition. Today, of course, it is legal to drink alcohol in any of the 50 states—provided, of course, that you are at least 21.

THE game 21, otherwise known as blackjack, is so called because a gambler seeks to come as close to 21 points (an ace and a face card, for example) without going over. This same idea was used in the infamous 1950s game show *Twenty One*, in which participants would get points for answering questions, with the option of stopping if they felt they were closer to the magical total of 21 points than their opponent was. Some of the participants were prodigiously smart with their answers and uncannily accurate in playing the 21 game, but within a couple of years it was revealed that the entire show was staged, as were many other quiz shows during that era. The 1994 movie *Quiz Show* focused specifically on *Twenty One*. As for the movie *21*, well, that focused on blackjack and was based only in loose fashion on Ben Mezrich's book *Bringing Down the House*, the tale of some MIT undergraduates who took Las Vegas for a ride by using a card-counting system.

Quiz Show and *21* offer a pair of symmetric flubs to go with their symmetric background. In the former, the film shows Jack Barry as the emcee of *Twenty One* when the quiz-show scandals broke in the summer of 1958, but in fact the emcee that summer was none other than Monty Hall. Yes, that's the same Monty Hall of *Let's Make a Deal* fame, now immortalized mathematically by the Monty Hall paradox, which we introduced in **3**, and *21* showcased in its early stages, when the professor played by Kevin Spacey gave the problem to Ben Campbell, star student and future star gambler. While Ben got the paradox right, noting that the chance of winning had gone from 33.3% to 66.7% (see **3**), the awkward use of decimals and percentages felt like a director's decision to spare his audience the ickiness of fractions. In the words of David Boyum, coauthor with yours truly of the quantitative reasoning guide *What the Numbers Say*, "There is a 0.0% chance that an MIT math whiz would say 33.3% and 66.7% instead of the correct $\frac{1}{3}$ and $\frac{2}{3}$." At least *21* tried to redeem itself by putting the sequence 1, 1, 2, 3, 5, 8, 13, . . . on Ben's twenty-first birthday cake, well aware that 21 was the next number in the Fibonacci sequence.

THE number 21 shows up elsewhere in the world of games. A game of table tennis is won by the first player to 21 points. The same was true in horseshoes until 1982, when the 21-point game was officially shelved in favor of a 40-point game. Twenty-one is also the total number of dots on a standard die, being the sum of the numbers 1 through 6. In mathematical terms, 21 = T_6, the sixth triangular number.

IN any given year, the National Hurricane Center generates 21 official hurricane names for the storm season.

In general, people named Quentin, Upton, Xavier, Yvonne, and Zelda never have to worry about having a hurricane named for them, because they represent the five letters that the National Hurricane Center omits on the grounds that they don't generate enough names.

IT'S easy to subdivide a square into four smaller squares, but if you stipulate that no two smaller squares can be the same size, you need a minimum of 21 squares to accomplish the dissection. It turns out that there is only one such minimal dissection (subject to rotations and reflections), and that is the one given here. It was discovered by A. J. W. Duijvestijn in 1978.

22 $\left[\, 2 \times 11 \,\right]$

A representation of a positive integer as the sum of positive integers is known as a partition. The number 22 shows up in several places in partition theory. For example, there are exactly 22 partitions of the number 8, starting with $1 + 1 + 1 + 1 + 1 + 1 + 1 + 1$ and ending with 8 itself. Perhaps more interesting is the following pair of partitions of 22:

$$22 = 4 + 5 + 6 + 7$$
$$22 = 1 + 4 + 7 + 10$$

In the top line, the four numbers being added are one apart. In the lower addition, they are three apart. The number 22 is the smallest number that can be written as the sum of evenly spaced integers in two different ways.

Even more interesting is the following trio of partitions of 22:

$$22 = 3 + 3 + 4 + 12$$
$$22 = 2 + 5 + 5 + 12$$
$$22 = 2 + 4 + 8 + 8$$

In each case, the sum of the reciprocals of the members of the partition equals 1: $\frac{1}{3} + \frac{1}{3} + \frac{1}{4} + \frac{1}{12} = 1$, and similarly for the others. Partitions of this sort are sometimes called exact partitions, and 22 is the smallest number with more than one exact partition.

▼

ASIDE from number theory, partitions also play a role in the analysis of systems of particles. Energy levels for individual particles appear as exponents, which are then added when calculating the energy of a thermodynamically closed system. A "partition function" means something different in this context, but the underlying question can still be the representation of positive integers by a bunch of smaller ones.

▼

TURNING to different kinds of partitions, whereas Gaul was renowned for having precisely three parts, modern-day France is partitioned into 22 regions, from Alsace to Upper Normandy.

▼

AS it happens, 22 is also the maximum number of pieces that can be created out of six intersecting lines or five intersecting circles, as shown in the diagrams below. Somehow neither diagram looks much like France. It is inevitable in such constructions (at least, the ones I draw) that certain regions end up much bigger than others. Note that the twenty-second region of the right-hand drawing is the area *outside* all of the five circles. In general, n lines can divide the plane into as many as $\frac{1}{2}(n^2 + n + 2)$ parts, while n circles can divide the plane into as many as $n^2 - n + 2$ parts.

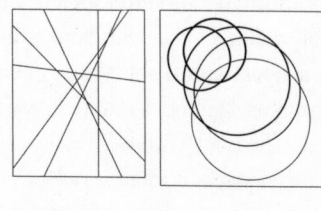

▼

IN elementary mathematics, the best-known appearance of the number 22 is as the numerator of $\frac{22}{7}$, the most commonly used approximation for π. But get a load of this: In the United States, a man's hat size of 7 actually corresponds to a woman's size of 22, because the size of a woman's hat is generally given as the circumference of the inner sweat band, while the size of a man's hat is the diameter of that band, if reconfigured to form a perfect circle. The correspondence of 22 and 7 is then to be expected, as π is by definition equal to the circumference of a circle divided by its diameter.

▼

THE diagram on the next page uses only the numbers 1 through 22 and has the remarkable property that the sum of any two numbers joined by a line segment equals a prime number.

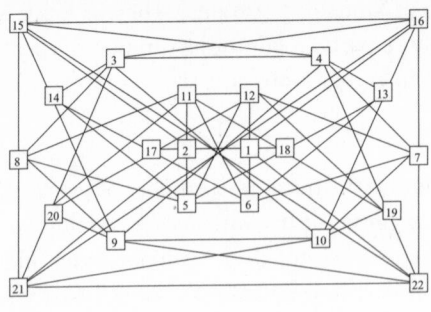

SINCE Joseph Heller's breakthrough novel of 1961, *Catch-22* may be the most recognizable use of the number 22 in modern culture. The expression *catch-22* is nonetheless disappointing for the utter lack of 22-ness to it. Apparently Heller's book was originally called *Catch-18* before being re-titled in deference to Leon Uris's *Mila 18*, a novel about the Warsaw Uprising that also came out in 1961. Numbers such as 11, and 14, and 17 were eventually proposed and rejected. No matter. In the book *Catch-22*, only crazy pilots had a chance to avoid certain combat missions, but mere awareness of the absurd dangers of those missions was considered the work of a rational mind, not craziness. Today we can use *catch-22* to describe a wide variety of no-win situations.

A cricket pitch measures 22 yards, the same as the length of a Gunter's chain (see **66**) and also one-tenth of a furlong. *Furlong* is a contraction of "furrow long," as these and other early measurements arose in the context of plowing through farmland. A strip of land measuring one furlong by one chain was known in olden days as a Saxon strip-acre, having the same square footage as a modern acre (43,560 square feet) but restricted to those specific rectangular dimensions.

A solid cube Greek cross is formed by putting together five cubes, or alternatively 22 squares.

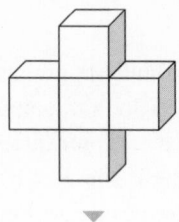

FINALLY, the product of the first 22 positive integers, written 22!, is the 22-digit number 1,124,000,727,777,607,680,000. It turns out that 22, 23, and 24 are the only positive integers n (aside from the trivial case $n = 1$) for which $n!$ has precisely n digits.

23 [prime $2^3 + 3^2 + 2 \times 3$]

THE number 23 was given an enduring place in the history of mathematics at the dawn of the twentieth century, when German mathematician David Hilbert presented 23 unsolved problems as a challenge to his peers. One measure of the difficulty of these 23 problems is that the easiest of the lot turned out to be this one: Given any two polyhedra of equal volume (such as the cube and tetrahedron below), is it possible to dissect the first into finitely many polyhedral pieces that can then be arranged to form the second?

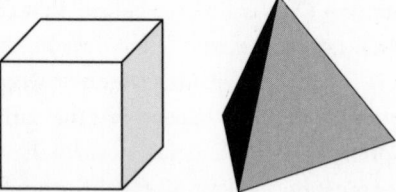

The answer, produced by Hilbert's student Max Dehn within a year, was no. Hilbert suspected this very result, but he was well-aware, as you are now, that such dissections and rearrangements are always possible for polygons—

that is, two-dimensional figures. (The Bolyai-Gerwein Theorem from the early nineteenth century.)

Perhaps the most famous of Hilbert's problems is number 2, which asked if the laws of arithmetic (i.e., Peano's axioms) could be proved to be internally consistent. An answer of sorts came in 1931 in the form of Gödel's Incompleteness Theorem, which shocked the mathematical world by concluding that no system of axioms for arithmetic can be complete. Unlike propositional logic (p implies q and all that), any arithmetical system built on axioms will always produce statements that are true according to those axioms but not provable using those same axioms. So if you want to prove Peano arithmetic consistent, good luck, but you can't do it within Peano arithmetic itself.

The proof of Gödel's Theorem (actually *theorems*, but we'll spare you the distinction among his various efforts) revolved around a coding system for mathematical notation and expressions (called Gödel numbers) and the creation of self-referential statements having paradoxical implications. The Berry Paradox in **19** gave a flavor of how such statements can work. We now consider a conundrum introduced by logician Raymond Smullyan in his Gödel's Incompleteness Theorems of the Oxford Logic Guide series:

Start by imagining an island of knights and knaves, in which knights only make true statements and knaves only make false ones. As Smullyan points out, "No inhabitant can claim that he is not a knight (since a knight would never make such a false claim and a knave would never make such a true claim)." And the plot thickens when a logician—who never believes anything that is false—visits the island and meets a native, who comes out with the surprising declaration, "You will never believe that I'm a knight." I'll let Smullyan tell you what happens next:

"If the native were a knave, then his statement would be false, which would mean that the logician *would* believe that the native is a knight, contrary to the assumption that the logician never believes anything false. Therefore, the native must be a knight. It, then, further follows that the native's statement was true and, hence, the logician can never believe that the native is a knight. Then, since the native really is a knight and the logician believes only true statements, he also will never believe that the native is a knave. And so the logician must remain forever undecided as to whether the native is a knight or a knave."

Gödel's Theorem is just confusing enough to have been misapplied by mathematicians, philosophers, and theologians alike. Swedish logician Torkel Franzen has chronicled and analyzed such nonsense as "Gödel's Theorems show that the Bible is either inconsistent or incomplete"; "By Gödel's Incompleteness Theorem, all information is innately incomplete and self-referential"; or even "By equating existence and consciousness, we can apply Gödel's Incompleteness Theorem to evolution." But Gödel's efforts also led mathematicians to concrete proofs of the undecidability of a variety of propositions in computing, set theory, and even algorithms for the solution of Diophantine equations.

▼

PERHAPS the most difficult of Hilbert's problems was the Riemann Hypothesis. Have you heard of this one? It's gotten some play in the popular press just for the daunting challenge it represents, but technically it's a conjecture about when a function of complex variables called the Riemann zeta function takes on the value zero: The first billion-plus "zeroes" have been shown to lie on a special line in two-dimensional space, but mathematicians won't be happy until a theorem emerges covering *all* zeroes. Although the Riemann Hypothesis is couched in terms of complex numbers (the so-called imaginary numbers of high school, those involving the dreaded $i = \sqrt{-1}$) its primary application is to refine our understanding about the distribution of *prime* numbers. Hilbert seemed to understand the problem's intrinsic thorniness when he uttered the memorable 23 words, "If I were to awaken after having slept for a thousand years, my first question would be: Has the Riemann Hypothesis been proven?"

And Hilbert wasn't alone in his wondering. Those who watched the movie *A Beautiful Mind* may recall a backyard scene in which the protagonist John Nash told a mathematical colleague/visitor that he was working on the Riemann Hypothesis. The camera followed the visitor's eyes to a notebook that contained only the random scribbles of a paranoid schizophrenic, and certainly nothing approaching a solution to one of the holy grails of higher mathematics. The visitor rolled his eyes, and the problem remains unsolved at this writing. Nash, as it happens, had a special fondness for the number 23. One of his most inspired delusions was that *Life* magazine had done a story on him in which he was disguised as Pope John XXIII, in whose pontificate (1958–1963) Nash's schizophrenia first emerged.

HERE'S an odd one: Because we are discussing it here, we know without counting that the following sequence contains 23 letters. But what does it represent? And why are three letters missing? (See Answers.)

ONE TWHRFUIVSXGLYDAMBQPC

AND here's an odder one: If you start with a square, you need 23 line segments of equal length in order to make that square rigid—imagine that the square is made of toothpicks, then surrounded by identical toothpicks until its movement is completely restricted. (The symmetry of the drawing is revealed if you rotate it 45 degrees.)

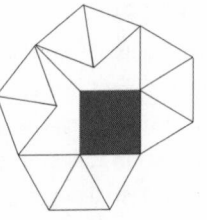

FINALLY, the number 23 plays a decisive role in the so-called birthday paradox. The paradox is the answer to a question: How many people would you have to assemble in order to assure that the probability of some shared birthday among those people is greater than one-half? The answer—just 23 people—seems impossibly small. After all, you'd need 367 people in a room before a shared birthday became 100% certain. (That's an easy application of the pigeonhole principle—see **37.**) The birthday paradox often remains counterintuitive even after an explanation, but I'll give it a try:

The reason that the number is so low is that you're not looking to match the birthdays of any two particular people, nor do you care on what date the shared birthday happens to fall. Any match will do. Imagine placing 23 objects into 365 boxes. There are a whole lot of ways of doing it so that no two objects are placed in the same box (365 × 364 × ... × 343). Yet there are also a whole lot of ways of placing the objects so that two or more *do* end up in the same box. Start by choosing any two of the objects at random and placing them in box 1, then distribute the remaining 21 objects in the other 363 boxes, and so on, and so on. When all is said and done, 23 objects are enough to create a 50% probability that some box has more than one object in it. The chart below demonstrates that a shared birthday crossed the 50% threshold at 23 and leads to virtual certainty within a group of 60 or more people.

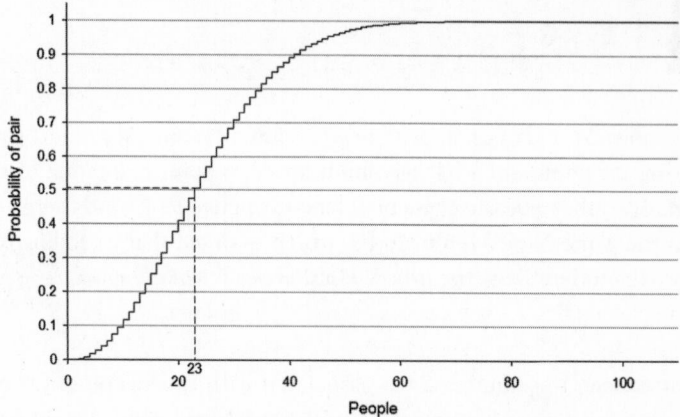

The last word on the birthday paradox belongs to Raymond Smullyan, just introduced as a logician but also skilled in other branches of mathematics. Here's a snippet of a correspondence I received from him while this book was in progress:

I was teaching a course in probability at Princeton, and at one point I told the class that if there are more than 23 people in a room, the chances are more than 50% that at least two of them have the same birthday. I then told them that since there were only 19 students in the room, the chances were extremely small that two of them had the same birthday. One student then said, "I'll bet you a quarter that two of us here have the same birthday!" I thought about this and said, "Oh, of course! You know the birthday of someone here other than your own!" He replied, "I can assure you that I do not know the birthday of anyone here other than my own. Nevertheless I'll bet you that at least two of us here have the same birthday." Well, I thought I would teach him the error of his ways and so I took the bet. I then asked one student after another his birthday, but at one point suddenly realized that two of them were identical twins! Boy, the class had a really good laugh! I then said, "This really shows the futility of pure theory when not backed by empirical observation!"

24 $\left[\ 2^3 \times 3\ \right]$

THE number 24 makes an appearance in some of mankind's oldest games. There are 24 points on a backgammon board, a point being one of those thin triangles that give the game board its distinctive look. And there are 24 dots in the game Nine Men's Morris, which is so old that its fading popularity was noted in Shakespeare's *A Midsummer Night's Dream*.

AND, of course, the number 24 is associated with timekeeping. Everyone knows that there are 24 hours in a day. Not everyone knows that 24 frames per second is a longtime standard in the movie industry.

WHEN you blend sports with timekeeping, you move inexorably to the 24-second clock, a fixture at NBA games since the 1954–55 season. The clock was the brainchild of Danny Biasone, onetime owner of the Syracuse Nationals franchise. The idea was to increase shooting and scoring. Biasone estimated that an average NBA game produced a total of 120 shots, or one shot every 24 seconds for 48 minutes. He was well aware that most possessions would not use up the full 24 seconds, so a 24-second clock would necessarily lead to more shooting and thus more scoring, and that's exactly what happened. The lowest scoring game since the adoption of the shot clock was that very same year—1955—when the Boston Celtics beat the Milwaukee Hawks, 62–57. Despite the emphasis on tight defense in the modern game, the advent of the 3-point shot makes it extremely unlikely that this record will be broken, much less the Pistons–Lakers all-time record of 19–18. (Fort Wayne over Minneapolis, that is, in 1950.)

▼

24 is the product of the first four positive integers, usually written 4! Admittedly, the exclamation point looks silly at the end of the sentence. It's a little bit like writing "Today I watched *Jeopardy!*" If the reader doesn't know that the exclamation point is part of the title, it looks as though you're just really, really excited about having watched a TV show. What I meant was 4!—read as "4 factorial" and meaning the product of the positive integers less than or equal to 4—equals 24.

For any n, n factorial is the product of all positive integers less than or equal to n, and it also happens to equal the number of ways of arranging n objects: n ways to place the first object, $n - 1$ ways to place the second, and so on. In particular, there are 24 ways of arranging 4 objects, illustrated below by using the letters O, P, S, and T. In the layout below, all six entries in the first column are words, and in fact no other choice of four letters will yield more than six words.

OPTS	OPST	OSTP	OSPT
POST	OTSP	OTPS	PSOT
POTS	PSTO	PTOS	PTSO
SPOT	SOPT	SOTP	SPTO
STOP	STPO	TOSP	TPOS
TOPS	TPSO	TSOP	TSPO

▼

THE concept of ordered sets of four letters can be taken a step further, leading to the plausible (but not dictionary-approved) word ANTITRINITARI-ANIST—someone who opposes the Christian doctrine of the Trinity. To see what makes this "word" special, note that "doctrine" contains the letters

TRIN in that order. "Trinity" starts with TRIN but also contains the sequences RINT and RNIT, though not consecutively. Well, if you look closely enough at ANTITRINITARIANIST, you will find *all 24* rearrangements of the letters I, N, R, and T imbedded somewhere inside.

The drawing above could never be considered antitrinitarianist. That 24 people are represented is no surprise. But what does the drawing depict? (See Answers.)

24 can be expressed as the product IV × VI, a Roman numeral palindrome.

TO arrive at one of the most remarkable properties of the number 24, start by adding one squared plus two squared. You should get $1 + 4 = 5$. Now add one squared through three squared. You get $1 + 4 + 9 = 14$. Note that neither 5 nor 14 are perfect squares, and there's no reason why they should be. Not until you add the first 24 perfect squares do you get a perfect square: $1^2 + 2^2 + \ldots + 23^2 + 24^2 = 4900 = 70^2$.

The situation above was commonly known in the mathematics literature as the cannonball problem. If you make a square consisting of 24 cannonballs on a side, then place atop those cannonballs an inner square consisting of 23 cannonballs on a side, you can keep going until you make a pyramid, and the total number of cannonballs in the pyramid is a perfect square. The beautiful part is that 24 is not only the first number (other than 1) that makes this construction possible; it is the last.

A cube has 24 rotations: four for each of the six faces. There are also precisely 24 jigsaw-like pieces that can be created by starting with a square and giving each side either a male or female connection or no connection at all.

The bi-sex are seven (one side). I am lucky to find four angles. Of all, these 24 pieces can be interlocked to form a 4 × 6 rectangle.

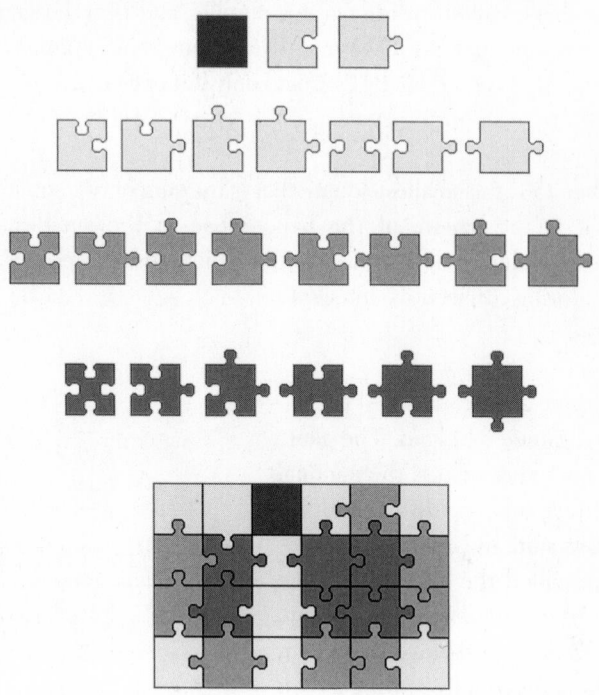

25 [5^2]

BECAUSE the expression 5^2 represents 25 using each of its digits precisely once, 25 is called a Friedman number, in honor of Erich Friedman of Stetson University in DeLand, Florida. All one-digit numbers are trivially Friedman numbers, but 25 is the smallest two-digit Friedman number. It has been conjectured that all powers of 5 are Friedman numbers.

▼

WHEN you take 25 to any power, the resulting number always ends in 25. Such a number is called an automorphic number, and 25 is the smallest two-digit automorphic number. (The one-digit automorphic numbers are 1, 5, and 6.) A number is divisible by 25 if and only if it ends in 25, 50, 75, or 00.

▼

THE number 25 is the smallest square that is the sum of two squares, meaning that it is the square of the hypotenuse in the smallest possible Pythagorean triple: (3, 4, 5). It is also the hypotenuse in another triple (7, 24, 25) featuring consecutive integers.

▼

THE card game 25 is considered the national card game of Ireland. The game Pachisi depicted at right is the national game of India, and *pachisi* is Hindi for "25." Players start and finish in the middle square called the Charkoni. Note that each of the four legs of the game board has 3 × 8 = 24 slots, so you get back to the Charkoni by moving a total of 25 spaces, which happens to be the maximum that can be produced by the 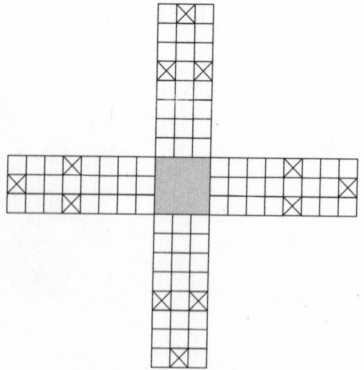 rolling of the cowrie shells used in a dice-like fashion (don't ask) to determine movement in the game.

▼

A standard Bingo card has 25 spaces, 24 of which are occupied by numbers.

26 $\left[\, 2 \times 13 \,\right]$

26 is better known for being half of something than something in its own right. Twenty-six weeks make up half a year, and 26 playing cards constitute half a deck, as you can see from the factorization above. Since there are 13 cards in each suit, any two suits together consist of $2 \times 13 = 26$ cards. Alternatively, in a game of bridge each side starts off with a total of 26 cards. It's still half a deck.

▼

THE equation $2 \times 13 = 26$ also shows up in croquet. The standard form of the game is played with two balls, each of which can generate 13 points: 12 hoops and the center peg. The winner of a game of croquet therefore has a total of 26 points.

▼

IF you subtract 1 from 26 you get 25, a perfect square. If you add 1 to 26 you get 27, a perfect cube. No other number is nested between a square and a cube in that fashion.

▼

SPEAKING of proximity, cards, and the number 26, take out a deck of cards. Now think of any two cards in the deck. What do you suppose the probability is that these two cards are next to one another? The question supposes that the cards are thoroughly shuffled, meaning that it's no fair to unwrap a new deck and choose the king and queen of diamonds. Assuming that the cards are in fact randomly distributed, the likelihood that your two cards will be next to one another turns out to be precisely one in 26.

▼

BECAUSE there are 26 letters in the alphabet, the number 26 plays an important role in cryptography. We'll start with an easy encryption to build our confidence. In the sentence below, each letter stands for a different letter of the alphabet:

SGE ZNK LUXIK HK COZN EUA

Unraveling this sort of gibberish becomes easier upon the revelation that the underlying code is an old-fashioned shift cipher, meaning that every letter in the original quotation is shifted ahead some constant number of spaces in the alphabet to produce the coded version. One of the weaknesses in shift ciphers is that the letter appearing most frequently—in this instance, K—is likely to be associated with the most common letter in the English language, namely E. Sure enough, that's the case here. The letter K is six spaces ahead of E in the alphabet, so to break the code you must take every letter back six spaces, obtaining the more familiar:

MAY THE FORCE BE WITH YOU

There's a teensy-weensy wrinkle in setting up the code, and that's where 26 enters the picture. To go from, say, M to S involves counting six spaces to the right (from position 13 in the alphabet to position 19). That's obvious enough. However, in order to go from Y to E (the first letter of the last word), you must wrap around from the twenty-fifth letter to the fifth. In mathematical terms, we are using modular arithmetic, a term that somehow complicates a process that is intuitively simple (especially when you're looking at the alphanumeric table below). In modular arithmetic, we say that $25 + 6 = 31$ is congruent to 5 (mod 26), because 31 gives a remainder of 5 upon division by 26. It's the same principle that makes three hours after 11:00 a.m. not 14:00 but 2:00 p.m. The only difference is that clock arithmetic uses a modulus of 12 rather than 26. Again, the use of words like "modulus" makes the process look messier than it really is. The bottom line is that the letter Y is encoded by using the letter E when using a shift of 6.

A	B	C	D	E	F	G	H	I	J	K	L	M	N	O	P	Q	R	S	T	U	V	W	X	Y	Z
1	2	3	4	5	6	7	8	9	10	11	12	13	14	15	16	17	18	19	20	21	22	23	24	25	26

The whole business of shift ciphers dates back to Julius Caesar, who apparently preferred a left-shift of three spaces—not terribly sophisticated militarily, but remember that the Roman Empire's prior key adversary had ridden elephants through the Alps. A shift cipher of 13 is perhaps the easiest to convey, because you just place the first half of the alphabet on top of the second and switch every vertically aligned pair. Note that under this construction the word VEX doesn't change much, as it is converted into IRE, and vice versa.

There are many different ways of using the above table to form a code. (It's worth pointing out that A is often given the value 0, with Z then equaling 25.) For example, using modular arithmetic, we could *multiply* the values in MAY THE FORCE BE WITH YOU by 3 to get the code MCW HXO RSBIO FO QAHX WSK. Note that M gets mapped into itself by this method, because $3 \times 13 = 39 = 13 \pmod{26}$. But multiplying by 2 wouldn't have worked, for several reasons. Why not? Well, suppose the letter N appears in the code. N has a numeric value of 14, which is 2×7, so it appears that N stands for the seventh letter, G. But why couldn't it stand for T instead? T is the twentieth letter, and multiplying 20 by 2 gives 40, which upon subtracting 26 for the wraparound yields 14, or N.

The general principle working here is that for multiplicative ciphers you can only multiply by numbers that have no common factor with 26, namely the following twelve numbers: 1, 3, 5, 7, 9, 11, 15, 17, 19, 21, 23, and 25. These numbers are said to be relatively prime with 26. (Admittedly, using 1 as a multiplier doesn't generate much of a code.) For a given integer n, the number of integers less than and relatively prime to n is given a name: $\phi(n)$ (read "phi of n"). Also called the totient function, $\phi(n)$ can be calculated by the formula $\phi(n) = (n)\pi(1 - \frac{1}{p})$, indicating a product where p takes on all distinct primes that divide into n. In the case of $n = 26$, 2 and 13 are the only prime factors, so $\phi(26) = 26(1 - \frac{1}{2})(1 - \frac{1}{13}) = 26(\frac{1}{2})(\frac{12}{13}) = 12$.

THERE are a few more English-language tie-ins for the number 26. One is that 26 is the maximum number of words you ever have to create in the game Word Whomp. Word Whomp is a downloadable online game in which players have a limited amount of time (2+ minutes) to create all possible words from a set of six letters, including at least one word using all six of those letters. Sometimes that six-letter word contains very few smaller words, but every word in the makeshift sentence STRONG MAYORS LOOSEN TENDER BOUGHS contains the 26-word maximum. (Perhaps "maximum" belongs in quotes there, as a Scrabble dictionary would surely generate different entries for many words.)

And it's impossible to resist including the sentence "Mr. Jock, TV quiz PhD, bags few lynx." Nonsensical, perhaps, but it's one of the best "sentences" that uses every letter of the alphabet precisely once.

27 $\left[\, 3^3 \,\right]$

THE number 27 is not only a perfect cube, but it also bears an unusual relationship with its own cube. Twenty-seven cubed equals 19,683, and if you add the digits in that number you get $1 + 9 + 6 + 8 + 3 = 27$. As it happens, 26 shares this same property, but no larger number does, and in fact the only numbers (other than 1) that do are 8, 17, 18, 26, and 27. How nice that this sequence begins and ends with a perfect cube.

▼

AND that's not the only thing perfect about the number 27. In a perfect game in baseball, a pitcher faces the minimum of 27 batters—3 per inning for 9 innings.

▼

A different sort of appearance of 27 in the world of fun and games is that a three-person game of Rock-Paper-Scissors has a total of 27 possible outcomes. This is of course just another way of saying that 27 equals 3 cubed.

▼

IN New Zealand, Australia, and the United Kingdom, housie cards are 3 × 9 rectangles, with the first column containing numbers between 0 and 9 and so on—the ninth column containing numbers between 80 and 89.

5			49		63	75	80
	28	34		52	66	77	
6	11			59	69		82

▼

IN snooker, the six non-red colored balls have point values 2, 3, 4, 5, 6, and 7 (yellow, green, brown, blue, pink, and black, respectively). Their combined point value is therefore the sum of the numbers 2 through 7: 27. Can you find another two-digit number that equals the sum of the numbers between its first and second digit, inclusive? (See Answers.)

▼

A 27-speed bicycle gets its name because it has three chain-rings and nine cogs, so theoretically you have 3 × 9 combinations. While that's technically true, these chain-ring/cog combinations overlap in terms of distance per crank-arm revolution, the figure that actually determines speed. In practice, a 27-speed bike has something like 15 discernibly different speeds. Credit for this observation goes to David Boyum, coauthor of the quantitative reasoning book *What the Numbers Say*.

▼

27 is the smallest number whose reciprocal has a three-digit repeating decimal: $\frac{1}{27} = 0.037037037\ldots$ Curiously, 37 is the next (and only other) number with this property, and $\frac{1}{37} = 0.027027027\ldots$ This relationship looks mystical, but all it means is that 27 × 37 = 999. In general, a number has an n-digit repeated decimal expansion if and only if it divides into a string of n 9's and no smaller such string.

28 $\left[\, 2^2 \times 7 \,\right]$

EVERYONE knows that February is the shortest month, with just 28 days in a non–leap year. One nicety of this length is that 28 days is precisely four weeks, meaning that the day of the week for a date in March will be the same as for the corresponding date in February. Not much of a convenience, but at least it's with us for that one particular month three out of every four years.

▼

HERE'S another nifty trick of the calendar, courtesy of the number 28. As a general rule, any two calendars that differ by 28 years must be identical: With 4 years between leap years and 7 days in a week, the calendar cycle automatically renews itself every $4 \times 7 = 28$ years. Yes, there are exceptions, so please don't write in. For example, T. S. Eliot was born on Wednesday, September 26, 1888, but his twenty-eighth birthday was on *Tuesday*, September 26, 1916, because the intervening century year of 1900 was not a leap year. Lacking the century irregularity, however, the patterns continued.

▼

FOR a breather, consider that the twenty-eight parrot, native to Australia, got its name because its call sounds like the number 28. Fortunately, its natural habitat is an English-speaking territory.

▼

BACK to math: 28 is the second perfect number. It equals the sum of its proper factors: $(1 + 2 + 4 + 7 + 14 = 28)$.

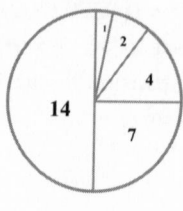

▼

NOTE that the first perfect number, 6, equals $2(2^2-1)$, while $28 = 2^2(2^3-1)$. The ancient Greeks were aware that perfect numbers could be constructed in this fashion, but it took until 1849—in a posthumous paper of Leonhard Euler's—to reveal that *all* even perfect numbers must follow this same template: Namely, if p is a prime such that $2^p - 1$ is prime, then the number $P^n = 2^{(p-1)}(2^p-1)$ is a perfect number. Primes of the form $2^p - 1$ are known as Mersenne primes, in honor of French monk Marin Mersenne (1588–1648). The first six Mersenne primes, together with the perfect numbers they generate, are listed below. Note that the perfect numbers get big awfully quickly, and it is not known whether the list is infinite. Nor has the existence of an *odd* perfect number ever been revealed or proved impossible. The hard part is the fact that any even perfect number has the form $2^{(p-1)}(2^p-1)$ for some p. But that's just $\frac{2^p(2^p-1)}{2}$, which is the sum of the first $2^p - 1$ positive integers and therefore triangular by definition.

n	P_n	P_n
1	2	6
2	3	28
3	5	496
4	7	8,128
5	13	33,550,336
6	17	8,589,869,056

28 is also the fourth hexagonal number. The term doesn't quite mean what you'd think it would mean, as it refers to the combined number of dots in a bunch of nested hexagons. The concept does lend itself to a surprisingly easy formula, however, as the nth hexagonal number is given by the formula $H_n = n(2n - 1)$. It turns out that every hexagonal number is triangular (but not vice versa), with $H_n = T_{2n-1}$. Below, the first four hexagonal numbers are converted into the first, third, fifth, and seventh triangular numbers, with $28 = T_7$. (Note that the perfect numbers 6 and 28 are both triangular: While it might seem naïve to conjecture that all even perfect numbers must be triangular, that conjecture turns out to be true, and isn't even very hard to prove.)

▼

TO see the triangularity of 28 in a different context, a set of standard double-six dominoes has precisely 28 pieces: Each of the seven possibilities (0 through 6 and blank) is paired with each of the others, including itself, for a total of $7 + 6 + 5 + 4 + 3 + 2 + 1 = 28$ dominoes.

29 $\left[\text{prime} \qquad (2 \times 9) + (2 + 9) \right]$

WHEN two primes differ by two, they are called twin primes, and 29 and 31 are the fifth such pair. The first five pairs of twin primes are $(3, 5)$, $(5, 7)$, $(11, 13)$, $(17, 19)$, and $(29, 31)$.

Twin primes have held fascination to number theorists for many centuries, but surprisingly little is known about them. The most important open question is whether there are infinitely many such pairs.

One small step in that direction was advanced in 1919 by Viggo Brun, who demonstrated that twin primes aren't especially common within the world of primes. Brun's Theorem states that the infinite series $\frac{1}{3} + \frac{1}{5} + \frac{1}{7} + \frac{1}{11} + \frac{1}{13} \cdots$, where each term is the reciprocal of a twin prime, is a convergent series, meaning that the sequence of partial sums $\frac{1}{3}, \frac{1}{3} + \frac{1}{5}, \frac{1}{3} + \frac{1}{5} + \frac{1}{7} \cdots$, approaches a fixed limit. (That limit, called Brun's constant, is a number in the neighborhood of 1.902.)

Brun's result might seem singularly unimpressive for those who have never seen the harmonic series $\frac{1}{2} + \frac{1}{3} + \frac{1}{4} + \frac{1}{5} + \dots$, formed by summing the reciprocals of every positive integer. The harmonic series *diverges*, meaning that the series of partial sums will exceed any fixed number if you go far enough out. In fact, even if you use only prime numbers, the sum $\frac{1}{2} + \frac{1}{3} + \frac{1}{5} + \frac{1}{7} \cdots$ is still unbounded. However, Brun showed that the partial sums of *twin* prime reciprocals converges—whether or not there are infinitely many of them!

Brun, being Norwegian, would have been very familiar with a 29-letter alphabet, made official in Norway in 1917 and now pretty much the standard throughout the rest of Scandinavia: the traditional 26-letter Latin alphabet plus three special vowels.

IF surveyor A. P. Green had been in charge, the city of Twentynine Palms, California, might have had a different name. In an 1858 survey, Green found only 26 palm trees surrounding what is now the Oasis of Mara, three short of the unconfirmed count of 1855. Today, Twentynine Palms is best known as the home of the world's largest marine base as well as Joshua Tree National Park, immortalized by U2's landmark album, *The Joshua Tree.*

THERE are 29 different pentacubes—objects created by joining five cubes at their faces. Whereas the 12 two-dimensional pentominoes (see **12**) can be arranged to create various rectangles, the 29 pentacubes cannot possibly form a three-dimensional block, or rectangular prism. Do you see why that's the case? (See Answers.)

THE Lebombo bone is considered by many to be history's oldest mathematical artifact. The bone, excavated from the Lebombo Mountains in Swaziland during the 1970s, is a baboon tibia into which 29 notches were carved circa 30,000 BC. Although the precise utility of the bone is a matter of dispute, it resembles the counting or calendar sticks used in many primitive cultures. Some archaeologists have conjectured that the markings relate to the lunar or menstrual cycle of 29 days.

FEBRUARY 29 is the leap day, and it occurs essentially once every four years. The concept of a leap year dates back to 45 BC, when Julius Caesar, acting on the advice of Alexandrian astronomer Sosigenes, mandated that the calendar adjust for the fact that the earth's journey around the sun takes 365.24 days. At the time, February was the last month of the year, so it made way for the extra day, though originally on the twenty-fourth of the month. February 29 became more and more entrenched as the centuries went by. According to a piece of Scottish folklore, that country's Parliament passed a law in 1288 establishing February 29 as the one time when a woman could propose marriage to a man. In Ireland, it has been said that St. Patrick refused a February 29 marriage offer from St. Bridget, although there is scant evidence for this claim. The modern leap-year standard was established in the 1500s by Pope Gregory XIII: In the Gregorian calendar, every year that is divisible by 4 is a leap year, except for century years such as 1900 that aren't divisible by 400 and—although it hasn't happened yet!—years divisible by 4000.

30 $\left[\,2 \times 3 \times 5\,\right]$

THE stacking game Pylos, made by the French game company Gigamic, consists of 30 wooden balls: 15 light and 15 dark. In playing the game, the balls are placed on four levels, beginning with the 4×4 array at the bottom and ending with the solitary ball at the top. In mathematical terms, 30 is a square pyramidal number, the name for any number that can be expressed as the sum of the first n squares for some value of n—in this case $n = 4$.

THERE are 360 degrees in a circle and 12 hours on a clock, and therefore $\frac{360}{12}$ = 30 degrees between any two adjacent hours. In three dimensions, however, things change. Because a complete rotation of planet Earth is 24 hours as opposed to a clock's 12, 30 degrees of longitude effectively represents *two* hours, not one.

IF one of the angles in a right triangle is 30 degrees, the side opposite that angle is half as long as the hypotenuse.

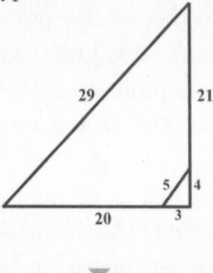

THERE are 30 distinct dice that can be created by arranging the numbers 1 through 6 on a cross-shaped figure and then folding along the lines to form a cube. The standard die, in which opposite faces sum to 7, is in gray, while the ninth cross reverses the position of 3 and 4.

ANY number that is less than 30 and relatively prime to 30 (sharing no common factors) must itself be prime. No number greater than 30 has this property—for example, 32 doesn't work, because 15 is less than 32 and shares no common factors, but 15 is not prime.

What makes 30 special is that it is the product of the first three primes. Note that the property doesn't extend to 210 (the product of the first four primes), because 210 exceeds products of primes such as 143 (11 × 13), which obviously have no factor in common with 210.

AT one time a 30 signified the end of a wire service story. The precise reason for this use of 30 is unknown, although it has been traced to the Roman numeral XXX as well as to *fertig* (a German word meaning "finished" or "ready").

30 is the sum of four consecutive numbers: 6, 7, 8 and 9. Not extraordinary perhaps, but to see this addition in action, check out the four sides of the Beatles' *White Album*, which consist of eight, nine, seven, and six songs respectively.

31 [prime]

AS we saw in **28**, a Mersenne prime is a prime of the form $2^p - 1$, with p prime. If $p = 5$, then $2^p - 1 = 31$, making 31 the third Mersenne prime, after 3 and 7.

Numbers of the form $2^n - 1$ crop up in solving the Tower of Hanoi puzzle, as depicted above. The puzzle was devised by famed mathematician Edouard Lucas in 1883, and the general form of the puzzle has three pegs and some number of discs sitting on one of the pegs, tapered so as to form a cone. The challenge is to move the discs one at a time to transfer the nested sequence onto another peg; the rub is that you cannot ever place a disc on top of a smaller one.

For the five-disc version shown here, a solution requires 31 moves. In general, for n discs, the minimum solution requires $2^n - 1$ moves. The more mathematically inclined will be interested to hear that solving the n-disc puzzle is equivalent to finding a Hamiltonian path on an n-hypercube.

THERE'S a different sort of puzzle, not quite as famous, that ends up highlighting the position of 31 as one less than a power of two. We start by choosing two points on the circumference of a circle and connecting them with a line segment. Obviously, that separates the circle into two parts. If we choose three points on the circle and connect every two of them, we separate the circle into four parts. If we continue, we get the following diagram, with the results summarized in the table below:

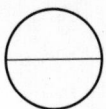 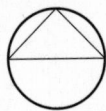  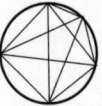

Number of points	Maximum number of pieces in circle
2	2
3	4
4	8
5	16

From the pattern thus far, choosing *six* points and connecting every possible pair with line segments seems destined to produce a total of 32 pieces, but in fact the maximum number of pieces is only 31. So close and yet so far. This unexpected result is only the beginning. Suppose the above situation arose in the context of a standardized exam, where you were asked to fill in the blank in the sequence 1, 2, 4, 8, 16, __ with one of the following choices:

A) 30   B) 31   C) 32   D) 33

Obviously if we choose anything other than C, we'll have some explaining to do. But *any* answer can work if you're creative enough. We have already seen that B can be justified by the points/lines/circles example. If you choose A, just tell the examiners that the sequence was the number of divisors of $n!$. (That's right: $1! = 1$ has one divisor, $2! = 2$ has two divisors, $3! = 6$ has four, $4! = 24$ has eight, $5! = 120$ has sixteen, and $6! = 720$ has thirty divisors.) And if you choose D, just say that you thought the sequence was the number of ways in which the first player gets killed in a five-player Russian roulette game using a gun having n chambers, where the number of bullets can equal anything from 1 to n, with no rotations of the cylinder allowed. That should give you extra credit.

IF you'd rather see this same principle in a puzzle than something out of a standardized exam, here's one from the late, great puzzle inventor Nob Yoshigahara. With the understanding that you can't always trust patterns, all you have to do is figure out what number belongs in the circle with the question mark.

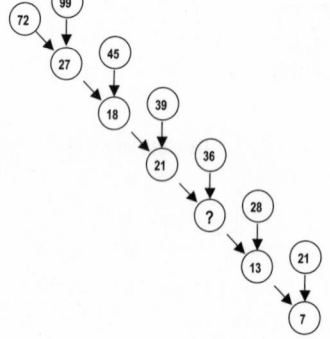

(See Answers.)

WE saw in **4** that any positive integer can be represented as the sum of at most four perfect squares, not necessarily distinct. Well, there are only 31 numbers that cannot be represented as the sum of *distinct* squares. With the observation that 31 is one of these numbers, here is the entire list:

2 3 6 7 8 11 12 15 18 19 22 23 24 27 28 31 32 33 43 44 47 48 60 67 72 76 92 96 108 112 128

Now consider the following list, again 31 numbers long:

1 2 3 5 6 7 9 10 11 13 15 17 18 19 22 23 25 27 31 33 34 37 43 47 55 58 67 73 82 97 103

I came across this list online, alongside the claim that any positive integer could be written as the sum of four distinct squares . . . except for these numbers and any power of four multiplied by any of these numbers.

Now wait a minute. What was going on? A different set of 31 numbers, also linked to sums of distinct squares but with a different conclusion? That was a little weird. The key to understanding the claim is to observe that 14 is the first number that is neither on the list nor a power of 4 times a number on the list. And look what we have here: $14 = 9 + 4 + 1 + 0$. Evidently this second list governs what numbers cannot be represented as the sum of *precisely* four distinct squares . . . including zero!

32 $\left[\, 2^5 \,\right]$

I have to confess that when I starting writing this book, the number 32 was the sort of number I expected to write about at great length. After all, 32 is a power of 2, 32° Fahrenheit is the freezing point of water at sea level, 32 ft/sec^2 is gravitational acceleration in the non-metric world, and 32 is a popular uniform number for professional athletes, among them Magic Johnson, Sandy Koufax, and Jim Brown. But I don't have all that much!

IN the world of sports and games, the number 32 isn't restricted to uniform numbers. The card game Skat uses a deck with no card lower than a 7, for 32 cards in all. In chess, there are 32 pieces on the board when the game begins, not to mention 32 white squares and 32 black squares. And, speaking of black and white, there are precisely 32 geometric shapes (12 pentagons and 20 hexagons) on a soccer ball. (See **12** for a more complete discussion of such shapes.)

▼

A compass rose indicates all 32 named directions—north, north by east, north-northeast, northeast by north, northeast, and so on clockwise around the circle. Because these various directions basically arise from bisecting a circle again and again, powers of two keep appearing, from the four basic directions N, E, S, and W all the way to the 32 directions represented.

33 $\left[\ 3 \times 11 \qquad 1! + 2! + 3! + 4! \ \right]$

THE UK version of peg solitaire is played on a board with 33 holes. A move consists of a jump, either horizontal or vertical, of one peg over another into an empty hole, at which point the jumped-over peg is removed. The objective is to continue in such a way that the final peg lands in the middle square.

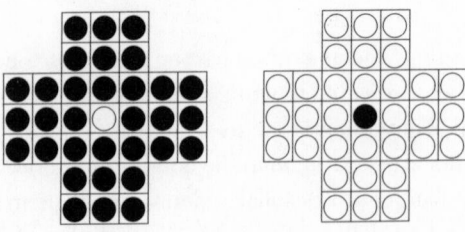

Because there are 32 pegs initially, a total of 31 jumps are required to go from the starting position to the winning position in the diagrams above. However, by combining jumps in a single move, as in draughts, only 18 moves are required to go from start to finish.

▼

IN the magic hexagram below, each arrow points to a set of five numbers adding up to 33.

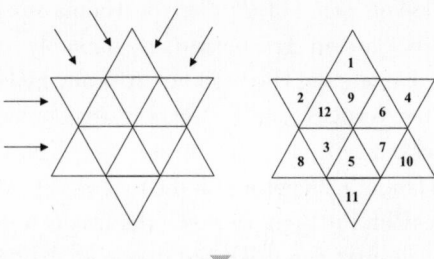

THE triangles in the picture above remind me that 33 is the largest number that cannot be represented as the sum of distinct triangular numbers. (After 33, we have 34 = 6 + 28, 35 = 1 + 6 + 28, 36 = 36, 37 = 1 + 36, 38 = 10 + 28, to name just a few.)

THE number 33 has found its way into cultures the world over. In Spanish, the phrase *"Diga treinta y tres"* ("Say 33") is used in the same way as is "Say cheese" in English. In Romania, doctors often ask their patients to say "33" (*"Treizeci si trei"*) when listening to their lungs with a stethoscope.

34 $\left[\, 2 \times 17 \,\right]$

THE figure to the right was created by join-ing 34 dots in a special way. What makes the graph special is (1) it cannot be traced, meaning that it is impossible to draw a path that visits each dot once and only once (what mathematicians call a Hamiltonian path), and (2) if you remove any one dot,

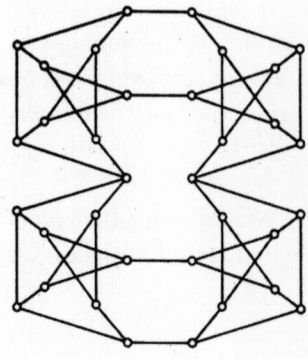

the resulting graph *can* be traced. Any graph with properties (1) and (2) is termed *hypotraceable*.

This construction on page 111 is called the Thomassen graph, after Danish mathematician Carsten Thomassen. Remarkably, it is the smallest known hypotraceable graph. (There do not exist any hypotraceable graphs with fewer than ten vertices, and for years it was conjectured that there weren't any, period.)

The theory of Hamiltonian paths is at the root of a classic problem called the Traveling Salesman Problem, in which the task is to find the cheapest route by which a salesman can make one stop in each of a set of cities and then return to the city in which he started. A more modern version of this problem arises in scheduling the route of a drill machine in manufacturing a printed circuit board. In robotic machining or drilling applications, the "cities" are parts to machine or holes (of different sizes) to drill, and the "cost of travel" includes time for retooling the robot (single machine job sequencing problem). As the number of holes (or cities) grows, the number of possible circuits becomes so vast that the computations cannot be handled by brute force, so a theoretical approach is required.

▼

THE most famous 4 × 4 magic square ever created is the one imbedded in Albrecht Durer's 1514 engraving, "Melancholia I." That square appears to the right.

Note that all rows, columns, and diagonals sum to 34. The number 34 is the magic constant for all 4 × 4 magic squares because the sum of the first 16 integers divided by 4 equals

16	3	2	13
5	10	11	8
9	6	7	12
4	15	14	1

$$\frac{\left(\frac{16(17)}{2}\right)}{4} = 2 \times 17 = 34.$$

Note also that the year of Durer's work is displayed in the middle of the bottom row of his magic square.

▼

A relative of the 4 × 4 magic square is the following simple piece of mathemagic. Select a number from the 16 numbered squares above. Say we start with 5. Now choose a number that is not in the same row or column as 5, say 15. Repeat this process once more, this time by choosing the number 2. (The third number cannot share a row or column with *either* of the first two choices.) There is one number left that is not in the same row or column as any of the first three choices, and that is 12. Add 5, 15, 2, and 12 together and what do you get? Thirty-four, of course.

1	2	3	4
5	6	7	8
9	10	11	12
13	14	15	16

The reason the trick works is that the square can be constructed as the sum of a row and a column, as below. Every white square is obtained by adding the gray square to its left and the gray square above it. Therefore, if you have four white squares that share no row or column, their sum must be the sum of all the gray, which is $1 + 2 + 3 + 4 + 0 + 4 + 8 + 12 = 34$.

	1	2	3	4
0	1	2	3	4
4	5	6	7	8
8	9	10	11	12
12	13	14	15	16

EVERY two years voters across America elect members of the Senate. There are 100 senators in all, each serving terms of six years. Because the elections are divided up as equally as possible, the theoretical maximum number of Senate contests in any particular election year is 34.

This particular subdivision of 100 goes all the way back to Dante's *Divine Comedy* (see **3**). Of the 100 cantos in his masterpiece, 33 were devoted to the Sky, another 33 to Purgatory, and 34 to the most famous segment of all, Hell, otherwise known as Dante's *Inferno*.

THE number 34 is the ninth Fibonacci number (the sum of 13 and 21, the previous two members of the sequence). Field daisies are sometimes used to illustrate the appearance of Fibonacci numbers in nature (a phenomenon known as Ludwig's Law), as they often have 34 petals. Because daisies are used in the classic game of "she loves me, she loves me not," an even number of petals is undesirable. Fortunately, nature isn't always exact in its proportions, and in any event there are plenty of 13-petal and 21-petal flowers to go around.

35 $\left[\begin{array}{cc} 5 \times 7 & (10-3)(10-5) \end{array}\right]$

A figure made up of six squares joined at their edges is called a hexomino, and there are 35 of these altogether, assuming that each shape is considered equivalent to those obtained by rotating it or flipping it over. (See **11**.)

▼

IT is possible to place a knight on a standard 8 × 8 chessboard and then move the knight 35 times without crossing over its own path. Care to find that sequence? (See Answers.)

▼

IF you add the first five triangular numbers, you get $1 + 3 + 6 + 10 + 15 = 35$. Geometrically, this means that if you place 15 billiard balls into their standard triangular rack, then place atop that triangle a triangle with four billiard balls on a side, and keep going, then the last of the 35 billiard balls will complete a triangular pyramid, or tetrahedron.

▼

LUDOLPH van Ceulen was a German mathematician who moved to the Netherlands and in 1600 became the first professor of mathematics at the

University of Leiden. When van Ceulen died in 1610, the number 3.14159265358979323846264338327950288, which you will recognize as π carried to 35 decimal places, was inscribed on his tombstone. Carrying out that calculation was van Ceulen's life's work.

Van Ceulen's approach was basically that of an obsessed Archimedes. The idea, in fact known to the Greeks of 200 BC, involved the inscription and circumscription of polygons in and around a circle. In English, we'll look at a simple case: the square.

In the diagram to the right, we assume that the diameter of the circle is 1. The diagonal of the inscribed square therefore has length 1, so the side of that square has length $\frac{\sqrt{2}}{2}$, for a perimeter of $2\sqrt{2}$. The sides of the outer square are each equal to the diameter, or 1, 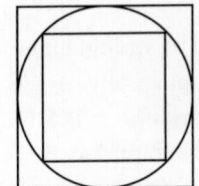 so the perimeter there is 4. The point is that the circumference of the circle must lie somewhere in between those two perimeters. Because π, by definition, equals the circumference of a circle divided by its diameter, we get that $2\sqrt{2} < \pi < 4$, a valid inequality but, alas, only a crude approximation. Obviously you can improve the approximation by inscribing and circumscribing a regular polygon having more sides than a mere square, and that's precisely what van Ceulen did. His 35-digit approximation of π used polygons having 2^{62} sides! (No, he couldn't draw them. But he could calculate their perimeters, and that's all he needed.)

▼

THE Pont du Gard, near Remoulins in the south of France, is a Roman-style aqueduct with several rows of arches. Its topmost row consists of 35 small arches.

By happy but meaningless coincidence, there are 35 bridges across the Seine in Paris, beginning with the Pont est du Boulevard périphérique and ending with the Pont ouest du Boulevard périphérique, of course.

▼

THE number 35 also makes an appearance in the world of weights and measures. There are 35 Imperial gallons in a barrel of oil, and 35mm film has been an industry standard since the days of Thomas Edison and George Eastman.

36 $\left[\, 2^2 \times 3^2 \,\right]$

THE world-famous Rockettes consist of precisely 36 dancers. This number apparently derives from how many dancers can comfortably fit onstage to perform a kick line. (On the road, away from spacious Radio City Music Hall, the troupe is smaller.)

As it turns out, 36 dancers can be arranged either as a 6 × 6 square or as a triangle with a height of 8. The triangle formation was adopted in the Rockettes' performance of Happy Feet, not to be confused with the 2006 penguin movie of the same name. (The triangularity of 36 also arises within the rituals of Hanukkah, because by Hillel tradition one Menorah candle is lit the first night, two the second night, and so on, yielding a total of $1 + 2 + 3 + 4 + 5 + 6 + 7 + 8 = 36$ separate lightings during the eight-day celebration.)

▼

36 is in fact the first number (not including the trivial 1) that is both square and triangular. The great Leonhard Euler demonstrated back in 1730 that there are infinitely many such numbers, but 36 is really the only one available to the Rockettes, as the next square triangular number is 1,225.

▼

SPEAKING of squares and triangles, the 6 × 6 square diagram on the next page displays the 36 possible outcomes of rolling a pair of dice. The gray circles contain the 21 distinct outcomes—not differentiating 2-5 (a 2 then a 5) from 5-2 (a 5 then a 2), and so on. The white circles contain the 15 repeated outcomes. By arranging the 36 possibilities in this fashion, we get a simple illustration of the fact that *any* perfect square can be written as the sum of two consecutive triangular numbers.

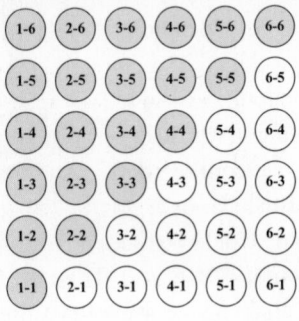

THE Lincoln Memorial in Washington, DC, has 36 columns—12 in the front and back, and 8 on each side. (Adding 12, 12, 8, and 8 together yields 40, not 36, but 4 must be subtracted from that total because each corner is counted twice.) The top of each column is inscribed with the name of one of the states of the union at the time of Lincoln's presidency; conveniently, the thirty-sixth state, Nevada, joined the union just days before Lincoln's reelection in 1864.

NOT far from the Lincoln Memorial, the Alexandria, Virginia-based game and puzzle company ThinkFun has found the number 36 just right on a couple of occasions. In 1996, they produced the 36 square-unit puzzle Rush Hour, devised by the inventor Nob Yoshigahara, whose diabolical number puzzle we encountered in **31**. The challenge in Rush Hour is to move surrounding cars and trucks so that

a red car can escape from a 6 × 6 grid. Then, in 2008, the company released 36 Cube, which challenges solvers to complete a solid cube out of 36 towers: six sets of towers, with each set consisting of six pieces of the same color but different heights. Labeled "The World's Most Challenging Puzzle," the median solving time has been estimated to be . . . never.

▼

THE 36 Officer Problem is an age-old conundrum that can be explained using this grid:

A	B	C	D	E	F
A	B	C	D	E	F
A	**B**	C	D	E	F
A	**B**	**C**	**D**	**E**	**F**
A	B	C	D	E	F
A	**B**	**C**	**D**	**E**	**F**

Note that we have placed six different versions of the letters A through F into a grid with 36 squares. The problem is to rearrange the letters so that no row or column contains two of the same letters or two of the same typeface. The grid below shows a solution for the 3 × 3 case. (The 2 × 2 case is easily seen to be unsolvable.)

A	C	B
C	**B**	A
B	A	**C**

The 36 Officer Problem gets its name because the problem was originally posed in terms of six regiments each containing six officers of different rank. Alas, the problem is unsolvable. That much was conjectured by Euler in 1780 or so, and was proved once and for all in 1901 by an amateur mathematician named Gaston Terry.

Euler had in fact speculated that so-called Graeco-Latin squares might be unsolvable for a wide range of square sizes, and it wasn't until 1959 that mathematicians discovered the astonishing truth that the *only* unsolvable squares are the trivial 2 × 2 case and the 6 × 6 case depicted on the previous page. That's right: A solution exists for any other square size whatsoever.

▼

THERE are 36 inches in a yard. As it happens, 36 inches is also the official height of the center of a tennis net (where the so-called center strap can be tightened or loosened to determine the overall height). In the days of wooden rackets, the height of a racket plus the width of the racket face came out to almost precisely 36 inches, and you'd often see players checking the net height that way. Once tennis rackets became oversized, however, that technique no longer worked. Today you seldom see the height of a net checked, even though having a simple yardstick on hand would serve that purpose.

▼

EACH angle of the five-pointed star below measures precisely 36 degrees. But you don't have to take my word for it.

Simply rearrange the five triangles as follows. Together, the tip angles sum to a half circle, or 180 degrees, so each one must measure $\frac{180}{5} = 36$ degrees.

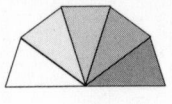

▼

BASE 36, sometimes called the alphadecimal system, is a convenient positional numeral system because it uses each of the 26 letters of the alphabet coupled with the digits 0 through 9 (A = 10, B = 11, . . . Z = 35). Although base 36 is most useful in the context of computer programming (it is used by many URL redirection systems), it can also be used to give a unique number for any word or name. For example, GO = 16 × 36 + 24 = 600: G and O have positional values of 16 and 24, respectively, so the word GO corresponds to 16 × 36 + 24 = 600.

Unfortunately, because each place in the number represents a power of 36, the base 10 numbers associated with base 36 words are rather large: As unwieldy as NIEDERMAN is, for example, I'm not about to jettison it for 66,327,368,641,439. Because the idea of a positional numerical base is credited to the Babylonians (their preferred base was 60), I should point out that Babylon nemesis XERXES translates into 2020201444, but it's too bad that the Persian king of 20 years (485–465 BC) wasn't XERXUS instead, as his base 10 equivalent would then have been the far more satisfying 2020202020.

▼

NINETEENTH-CENTURY French writer George Polti wrote a book called *The 36 Dramatic Situations*, an attempt to classify every story line that could possibly arise in a play or book: "Crime pursued by vengeance," "Fatal imprudence," "Mistaken jealousy," and so on. Polti admitted that the choice of 36 was somewhat arbitrary, but he might have been modeling his list on "The Thirty-Six Strategies," a collection of military strategies from ancient China. The military strategies are surely more colorful, ranging from "(3) Kill with a borrowed knife" to "(15) Entice the tiger to leave its mountain lair" to perhaps the most famous of them all, "(36) If all else fails, retreat."

37 [prime]

$$37 = \frac{666}{(6+6+6)} \qquad 123{,}456{,}790 \times 3 = 370{,}370{,}370$$

THE curiosity that underlies these and other multiplication formulas involving the number 37 is that $3 \times 37 = 111$.

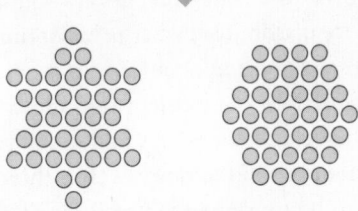

THE above arrangements show how 37 dots can be made into either a star or a hexagon. Note that a star of this type is constructed by first forming a hexagon, then adding six triangles of dots around the outside. Very few numbers can be represented as both a centered hexagon and a star—37 is the first number other than 1 to have this particular feature, and the next one doesn't come around until 1,261. The arrangement on the left is that of a French solitaire board, while the arrangement on the right corresponds to the dots on the mouthpieces of yesteryear's telephone handsets, or even the airholes of a bathroom vent on a Boeing 757.

IT is easy to see that 37 is the maximum number of points in a bridge hand. According to the standard point-count system, aces count as 4 points, kings 3, queens 2, and jacks count as one point. All told, the 16 honor cards yield a total of 40 high-card points for the whole deck, but a single hand can only accommodate 13 out of those 16 cards. Subtract three (one-point) jacks of your choice and you have your maximal 37-point hand—four aces, four kings, four queens, and a jack.

IF you've never seen the Sultan's Dowry Problem before, you're in for a treat. The setup is that a sultan has granted a commoner the chance to marry one of his hundred daughters. The commoner will be shown the daughters one at a time and will be told each daughter's dowry. The commoner has only one chance to accept or reject each daughter, meaning that he can't go back and choose one that he previously rejected. The catch is that the commoner may only marry the daughter who has the highest dowry of them all. Assuming that the commoner knows nothing in advance about the way the dowries are distributed, what is his optimal strategy to locate that special daughter?

Sounds kind of impossible, doesn't it? After all, the chance of any one daughter having the highest dowry is $\frac{1}{100}$, and nothing is known about the magnitudes and distributions of the dowries. But there is an optimal strategy, which turns out to be to wait until precisely 37 of the daughters and dowries have been shown, then to pick the next daughter whose dowry exceeds any of those seen thus far. Coincidentally, the chance of finding the highest dowry by following that strategy is about 37%.

▼

THE normal human body temperature, usually referenced as 98.6°F in the United States, is precisely 37° Celsius. At least, that's true if you follow the formula $F = (\frac{9}{5})C + 32$. But the original scientific work on human temperatures was conducted in the nineteenth century by the memorably named German physician Carl Reinhold August Wunderlich, who took the temperature readings of thousands of people for his statistical study. The figure 37°C is actually nothing more than Wunderlich's average temperature reading rounded off to the closest degree Celsius, meaning that our sacrosanct Fahrenheit equivalent of 98.6°F connotes far more accuracy than it is entitled to.

▼

WILLIAM Shakespeare wrote a total of 37 plays. Recall from our discussion in **36** that in the eyes of Georges Polti, there are precisely 36 dramatic situations. We can therefore state with 100% certainty what everyone already knows—that at least two of Shakespeare's plays must revolve around the same basic plot! Yes, I know—the multiple subplots yield even more repetition than that. But there's an important mathematical principle at work here, one that goes by the unassuming name of the pigeonhole principle (also known as the Dirichlet box principle). It basically states that if you have more than n objects (as in 37 plays) and you try to place them in n holes (as in 36 dramatic situations), at least one of the holes must have more than one object in it.

The great thing about the pigeonhole principle is that its applications run wide, even though the principle itself is completely obvious. Lest you think this is much ado about nothing, note that pigeonhole arguments can also be used to prove a wide variety of other results in the areas of geometry, elementary number theory, the game of bridge, and just plain common sense, including the following:

1. There are at least two people in Tokyo with the same number of hairs on their heads.
2. If you place five points inside an equilateral triangle that measures two inches on each side, you can always find a pair of points separated by no more than one inch.
3. If you choose any ten positive integers between 1 and 100, there will always be two disjoint subsets of those ten numbers (i.e., no elements in common) that have the same sum.

The pigeonhole questions got a little tougher, didn't they? Well, you are invited to take a crack at any or all of the above. (See Answers.)

38 $\left[\, 2 \times 19 \,\right]$

THE number 38 can be written as the sum of two odd numbers in ten different ways, as on the next page:

$$38 \quad = \quad 1 + \mathbf{37}$$
$$= \quad \mathbf{3} + 35$$
$$= \quad \mathbf{5} + 33$$
$$= \quad \mathbf{7} + \mathbf{31}$$
$$= \quad 9 + \mathbf{29}$$
$$= \quad \mathbf{11} + 27$$
$$= \quad \mathbf{13} + 25$$
$$= \quad 15 + \mathbf{23}$$
$$= \quad \mathbf{17} + 21$$
$$= \quad \mathbf{19} + \mathbf{19}$$

Observe that each of the ten pairs of odd numbers contains at least one prime number (shown in bold). In other words, 38 cannot be written as the sum of two *composite* odd numbers. In and of itself, that may not seem so remarkable, but it turns out that 38 is the *largest* even number with that property.

The above assertion isn't all that hard to prove. We start by noting that the first few even numbers greater than 38 can be written as the sum of two odd composite numbers: $40 = 15 + 25$, $42 = 15 + 27$, $44 = 35 + 9$, $46 = 25 + 21$, $48 = 15 + 33$. Obviously we can't keep going one even number at a time, but we don't have to. We can cover the numbers 50 through 58 simply by adding 10 to the first number in each of the above sums; for 60 through 68, we add 20, and so on. The reason this approach works is that any number ending in 5 (other than 5 itself) is composite. Admit it, that was easier than expected. Right?

By contrast, the assertion that any even number is the sum of two primes has proved extraordinarily difficult to prove. Prussian mathematician Christian Goldbach conjectured this result back in 1742 and it remains unsolved at this writing. At this point it is known that if an even number cannot be expressed as the sum of two primes it must be extraordinarily large, and it's fair to say that computers are working day and night in the search for a counterexample that no one other than the programmers themselves really wants to find.

THE number 38 is also at the end of a very different type of list. When written in Roman numerals, 38 is expressed as XXXVIII. It just so happens that if you wrote down all possible Roman numerals in alphabetical order, XXXVIII would be the very last number you'd write.

▼

AN American roulette wheel has 38 slots, consisting of the numbers 1 through 36 plus 0 and 00. The primary effect of the extra zero slot is to increase the house advantage, as the probability of a gambler winning a red or black bet is $\frac{18}{38}$, smaller than the $\frac{18}{37}$ chance of winning such a bet on a European wheel. (See **37**.)

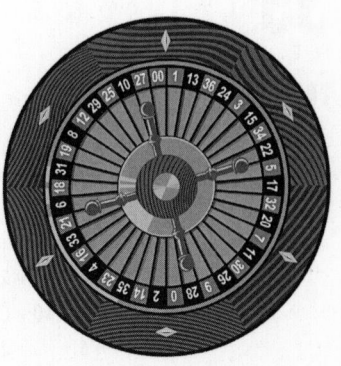

▼

THE figure to the right is a magic hexagon, in which the numbers in the five columns, five left-slanting rows and five right-slanting rows all add up to 38.

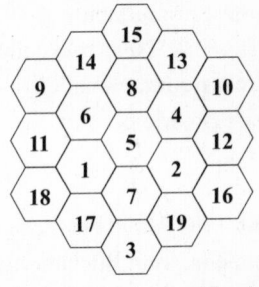

Legend has it that this hexagon was constructed by retired railroad clerk Clifford Adams, who then passed it on to Martin Gardner at *Scientific American*. Gardner in turn showed the construction to renowned recreational mathematician Charles Trigg, who confirmed that this magic hexagon is unique (any other solution of this size is a rotation/reflection of Adams's design).

Not only that, Trigg showed that the magic constant for a hexagon with n cells on each outside edge is given by the formula $\frac{9(n^4 - 2n^3 + 2n^2 - n)}{2(2n-1)}$. Without getting carried away in the particulars, this expression can only be an integer if $\frac{5}{(2n-1)}$ is an integer, which only happens for $n = 1$ and $n = 3$. In other words, Adams's creation is the only possible magic hexagon of any size, except for taking a single hexagon and sticking a "1" in it, and that's not so magical, is it?

39 $\left[3 \times 13 \right]$

THERE are three different partitions of 39 that multiply to the same product, and 39 is the smallest number with this property. This is the Christmas Ribbon Problem with $n = 3$: Find three different package sizes with the same ribbon length and volume (see **118**):

$$39 = 4 + 15 + 20 \quad : \quad 4 \times 15 \times 20 = 1200$$
$$39 = 5 + 10 + 24 \quad : \quad 5 \times 10 \times 24 = 1200$$
$$39 = 6 + \;\; 8 + 25 \quad : \quad 6 \times \;\; 8 \times 25 = 1200$$

If you list all the primes between the smallest prime factor of 39 and the largest prime factor of 39, you get 3, 5, 7, 11, and 13. And $3 + 5 + 7 + 11 + 13 = 39$. Neat trick, and it doesn't happen again until 155. (There's actually a number smaller than 39 with this same property. Can you find it?) (See Answers.)

▼

THE 1935 Alfred Hitchcock film *The 39 Steps* was based on a book by the same name by John Buchan. In the movie, the title refers to the name of a spy organization, while the book's title refers to a coastal site in Kent, where a path from a cliff to the water has precisely 39 steps. Along this latter line, perhaps it is worth noting that at the old Wembley Stadium, a winner had to ascend 39 steps in order to reach the Royal Box and receive the appropriate trophy.

▼

THE 39 Articles of Religion were established by the Anglican church in 1563 and even today form the basis for the Anglican faith. Somewhere in between, the United States of America declared its independence and wrote its own Constitution, which was ultimately signed by 39 men.

39 is the highest number on a standard Master combination lock.

A bowling lane consists of precisely 39 strips, usually made of wood, each measuring slightly more than an inch, for 42 inches altogether.

IN bridge, there are only 39 possible distributions, or hand patterns. The most common distribution is 4–4–3–2, meaning that the hand consists of four of one suit, four of another, three of a third suit, and two cards in the fourth suit.

40 $\left[\ 2^3 \times 5\ \right]$

RELIGION is replete with references to the number 40, from the 40 days of Lent to the traditional 40-day period of mourning in the Muslim faith. But the number 40 in the Bible sometimes refers to just a really, really big number, as opposed to a specific quantity, as in the 40 days and 40 nights of the Great Flood. Similarly, the use of 40 in the story "Ali Baba and the Forty Thieves" was less than literal, and the expression "40 winks" just meant a lot of sleep. It is a measure of societal inflation that the 40 of olden days has come to be today's "gazillion."

ONE surprisingly literal use of the number 40 is found in the word *quarantine*. The word looks suspiciously like *quarante*, the French word for "forty" and the original Roman *quarantine* is said to have kept ships isolated in the harbor for forty days.

TOWER HAMLETS COLLEGE
POPLAR HIGH STREET
LONDON
E14 0AF

THE expression "Life begins at forty" is an outgrowth of a 1932 book by Walter Pitkin and a 1937 song by Sophie Tucker. The expression certainly applied to Princeton mathematician Andrew Wiles, a native Brit who had just turned 40 years of age when he gave his famous "Modular Forms, Elliptic Curves, and Galois Representations" lecture at Cambridge University in 1993: This was the lecture in which Wiles proved Fermat's Last Theorem—the assertion that the equation $x^n + y^n = z^n$ has no solutions in positive integers for $n > 2$ (see **2**). Unfortunately for Wiles, the Fields medal, perhaps the most prestigious award in higher mathematics (and the one credited to Matt Damon's mentor in *Good Will Hunting*), is only given out to people under 40, and when his original proof was revealed to have a gap, Wiles was essentially out of the running for the Fields class of 1994 (the medal is bestowed every four years). However, the International Mathematical Union gave Wiles a special plaque concurrent with the Fields Medals of 1998, by which time the gap in Wiles's proof, and his place in mathematical history, had long been resolved.

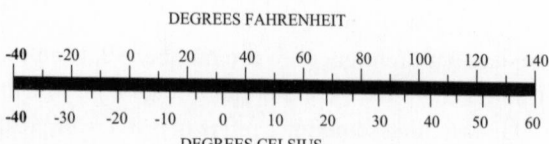

AS the drawing indicates, -40° Celsius is the same as -40° Fahrenheit, the only time the two temperature scales coincide. In general, the two scales are connected via the formula $F = (\frac{9}{5})C + 32$.

IN 1953, three scientists at the start-up Rocket Chemical Company were working on a compound to eliminate rust and corrosion on rockets and other metal parts, using a technique called water displacement. On their fortieth try, they succeeded and in so doing created their first commercial product. The company was renamed in 1969 to honor their flagship (and, at the time, only) product. The WD-40 Company finally expanded its product line through a series of acquisitions beginning in 1995. Within a few years, its offerings included such familiar consumer brands as 3-IN-ONE oil, Lava soap, 2000 Flushes, and Carpet Fresh.

▼

A B C D E F G H I J K◎M N O P Q ℝ S T U V W X Y Z

40 is the only number whose letters are in alphabetical order when written out in English.

41 [prime]

THE expression $x^2 - x + 41$ looks innocuous enough, but it has a remarkable property first noticed by Euler. Try plugging in some numbers for x, starting with 1, and see what the output looks like:

x	$x^2 - x + 41$
1	41
2	43
3	47
4	53
5	61
6	71
7	83
8	97
9	113
10	131

The first two numbers on the list, 41 and 43, form a set of twin primes—primes that differ by just two. Then you will note that the differences between successive terms go up by two with each step; $47 - 43 = 4$, $53 - 47 = 6$, and so on. But what makes this sequence remarkable is that *all* the numbers thus far are prime. In fact, if you kept going, you'd get a streak of *40* consecutive primes, ending with $40^2 + 40 + 41 = 1681$. (Note that you obviously get a composite result when $x = 41$, because $41^2 - 41 + 41$ equals 41^2.) While there are polynomial expressions that yield more than 41 consecutive primes, Christian Goldbach proved in 1752 that that no polynomial with integer coefficients can possibly yield a prime for all integer inputs x.

▼

A related sort of structure, known as a prime spiral, was apparently discovered by Polish mathematician Stanislaw Ulam while doodling during a boring meeting. His creation began by placing a 1 in the center of a grid and continuing outward with consecutive integers. He noticed that primes in such spirals often create interesting patterns. Had he started with the number 41 in the center, he would have come up with the following diagram, in which primes are shaded. Continuing this spiral would have produced a 40 × 40 square in which every element along this diagonal was prime—the very same primes doled out by Euler's quadratic!

45	44	43	
46	41	42	
47	48	49	50

▼

THE pattern to the right consists of 25 white squares and 16 black squares. A similar pattern can be created for any number that, like 41, is the sum of consecutive squares. But one nicety unique to 41 is that $41 = 4^2 + 5^2 = 1^2 + 2^2 + 6^2$, and the rightmost equality remains true even if the exponents are removed.

42 $\left[\, 2 \times 3 \times 7 \,\right]$

THERE are 42 eyes in a deck of cards: three two-eyed kings, one one-eyed king, four (all two-eyed) queens, two two-eyed jacks, and two one-eyed jacks makes a total of 21, and this number must be doubled because the images on the face cards appear twice on each card. (Speaking of games and doubling, we have seen that there are a total of 21 dots on a die, and therefore 42 dots on a pair of dice.)

CRICKET, whose regulations are entrusted to London's Marylebone Cricket Club, has 42 official laws, with Law 42 governing fair and unfair play. In America, 42 was the number worn by Jackie Robinson during his career with the Brooklyn Dodgers. Robinson's number was retired by the Dodgers in 1972, just months before he died at the age of 53, and it was retired by all of Major League Baseball in 1997, with a grandfather clause exempting those who were already wearing the number at that time. Longtime Yankee closer Mariano Rivera has continued to wear number 42 for over a decade. Another longtime relief pitcher—Bruce Sutter of the Cubs, Cardinals, and Braves—also wore number 42 and was the only other player to have it retired.

IN Douglas Adams's *Hitchhiker's Guide to the Galaxy*, the computer Deep Thought was asked to calculate the Ultimate Answer to the Great Question of Life, the Universe and Everything, and the answer was "42." The following memorable line was thereby uttered:

> "I checked it very thoroughly," said the computer, "and that quite definitely is the answer. I think the problem, to be quite honest with you, is that you've never actually known what the question is."

The Observer once called Adams "the Lewis Carroll of the twentieth century," perhaps unaware that the number 42 held special fascination for Carroll as well. The original *Alice in Wonderland* had 42 illustrations, the famous "All persons more than a mile high to leave the court" was Rule 42, and the Baker in "The Hunting of the Snark" had 42 boxes.

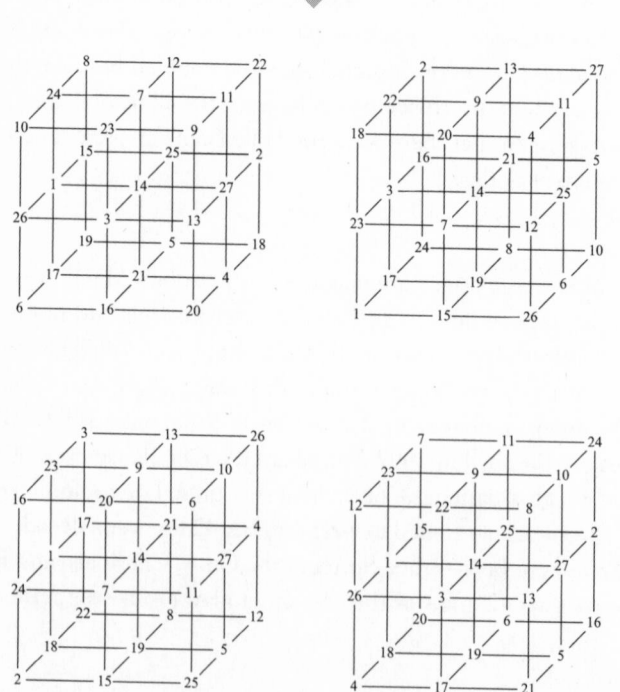

THE constructions above represent the four possible 3 × 3 magic cubes. (Technically they are called semi-perfect magic cubes or Andrews cubes, after early twentieth-century cube pioneer W. S. Andrews. All other 3×3 solutions are rotations or reflections of these four.) In each case the sum of the three numbers in any row or column equals 42, as does the sum of any three numbers occupying the same square in the three different sheets, as does the sum of any three numbers along a diagonal of the cube beginning and ending with one of the corners—but not the diagonal of any face. The magic constant of the magic cube is 42 because 42 equals the sum of the first 27 integers divided by 9. In general, the magic constant for an $n \times n$ magic cube equals $\frac{n(n^3 + 1)}{2}$. Note that $42 \div 3 = 14$ is the center number for all of the cubes.

The structure of the magic cube somehow reminds me that there were 42 prison cells in the infamous D Block at Alcatraz Prison, comprising 36 segregation cells and 6 solitary confinement cells. The D Block was the prison's maximum security area and was reserved for the worst offenders of the prison, which is saying a lot. The one redeeming feature of the cells was that they were bigger than found elsewhere in the prison. Block 42 was the longtime home of Robert Stroud, aka the Birdman of Alcatraz, who developed his interest in birds at Leavenworth Prison before entering the less ornithologically friendly confines of Alcatraz in—you guessed it—1942.

43 [prime]

BACK in the good old days, when Chicken McNuggets were available only in lots of 6, 9, 20, you could have asked the question "What is the largest number of McNuggets you *can't* buy?" The answer was 43. This type of problem has actually been around for some time, enabling mathematicians to call 43 the *Frobenius* number of the set {6, 9, 20}, thereby honoring German mathematician Ferdinand Georg Frobenius (1849–1917).

Strictly speaking, what's being sought is the highest number that isn't a linear combination of 6, 9, and 20—that is, cannot be expressed in the form $6a + 9b + 20c$, with a, b, and c all positive integers. The question makes sense only if the three numbers, as here, don't have a common factor. By way of contrast, if you combine a nickel, dime, and quarter, you'll always get a multiple of 5 cents.

Unfortunately, the introduction of a Happy Meal box of four Chicken McNuggets ruined everything. Once you could buy a box of four separately, the maximum number of McNuggets that can't be bought (using combinations of 4, 6, 9, and 20) is 11.

▼

WHICH reminds me: If you read our discussion in **11,** you know that there is an easy expression for Frobenius numbers for *two* variables: namely, the largest number that cannot be created using combinations of x and y equals $xy - x - y$. It turns out that having three (or more) numbers makes the problem substantially harder, and finding the Frobenius number is accomplished by use of an algorithm rather than a single formula, though there are formulas that work if the initial set of numbers is friendly enough. The problem is in fact difficult enough that certain classes of algorithms will always be inadequate because of the computer time required to implement them.

The general Frobenius Problem has applications far outside Chicken McNuggets. In economics, the question might be to gauge the possible outputs of a set of production or cost functions that take on integer values. In mass spectrometry (a technique to identify and/or quantify molecular compounds), the question might be to compute what types of molecular configurations might give rise to so-called peaks found in the data. All of which makes for interesting gatherings at Frobenius conferences.

▼

THERE'S one other appearance of 43 that's more of a curiosity than anything else. Recall that the Fibonacci sequence starts out 1, 1, 2, 3, 5 . . . with each successive term being the sum of the two that preceded it. From the same start, let's define a new sequence by making the sixth term equal to the sum of the squares of the first five terms, divided by the number $(5 - 1)$. We get $\frac{(1^2 + 1^2 + 2^2 + 3^2 + 5^2)}{4}$, which equals 10. (Note that the 2, 3, and 5 in the sequence are in fact generated by this same formula!) The seventh term equals $\frac{(1^2 + 1^2 + 2^2 + 3^2 + 5^2 + 10^2)}{5} = 28$, and so on. The sequence starts to grow quite rapidly starting with the tenth term. But because the creation of the sequence involves division, there's no reason in the world why the numbers produced should be integers. In fact, though, the first 43 members of the sequence are integers. I'd show you the first non-integral result, but it's too big to fit on this page—even if I had started at the top.

44 $\left[\, 2^2 \times 11 \,\right]$

AN Euler brick is a rectangular block in which the three sides a, b, and c are all integers, and the resulting diagonals d_{ab}, d_{ac}, and d_{bc} are also all integers. The smallest possible Euler brick has sides of length 44, 117, and 240, with diagonals of 125, 244, and 267. This

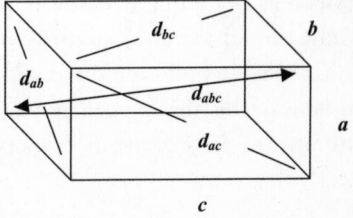

brick was discovered in 1719 by German mathematician Paul Halcke, but somehow Euler got his name on the whole concept even though he was only 12 years old at the time.

The diagram above actually has seven labeled lines, not six, the seventh being the "space diagonal" (with arrows) d_{abc}. Alas, the space diagonal in this diagram is the square root of 73,225, which is not a whole number. Remarkably, despite the long and storied history of the Euler Brick Problem, even today it is not known whether there exists *any* Euler brick whose space diagonal is an integer.

▼

ON Bastille Day of 1951, Frenchman A. Ferrier proudly announced that the 44-digit number $\frac{2^{148} + 1}{17}$ = 20,988,936,657,440,586,486,151,264,256, 610,222,593,863,921 was prime. Ferrier thus broke the 75-year record held by Edouard Lucas, who had checked the primality of $2^{127}-1$ by hand. Ferrier confirmed his number's primality by using only a desk calculator, and his discovery has the distinction of being the largest-known prime number calculated without any type of electronic computing device. Within a month of his announcement, a new age had dawned, and a 79-digit number was discovered by computer. As I began this book, the largest known prime (coincidentally, the forty-fourth Mersenne prime; see **28**) had 9,808,358 digits.

▼

IF you have five letters and five pre-addressed envelopes, in how many ways can you place the letters into the envelopes so that none of the letters is in the correct envelope? This problem was posed and solved by Pierre de Montmart in the early eighteenth century. De Montmart was a colleague of Nicholas Bernoulli, who solved the same problem using a set-counting formula called the inclusion-exclusion principle. De Montmart also knew Blaise Pascal and is credited with giving Pascal's Triangle its name. Permutations of this sort are called derangements, and the general formula for the number of derangements of n objects is given by the following formula:

$$n! \sum_{k=0}^{n} \frac{(-1)^k}{k!}$$

In particular, if $n = 5$, $n! = 120$, and the formula yields $120(1 - 1 + \frac{1}{2} - \frac{1}{6} + \frac{1}{24} - \frac{1}{120}) = 44$.

45 $\left[3^2 \times 5 \right]$

THE number 45 is triangular, being the sum of the numbers 1 through 9. In particular, 45 is the sum of the numbers in any row or column of a finished Sudoku grid. And, speaking of triangles, in an isosceles right triangle (where two legs of

equal length surround the 90-degree angle), both acute angles have a measure of 45 degrees.

▼

ANY triangular number is, by definition, the sum of the first n integers for some n. What makes 45 special is that it is the first number that can be represented as the sum of consecutive positive integers in six different ways. The representations are 45, 22 + 23, 14 + 15 + 16, 7 + 8 + 9 + 10 + 11, 5 + 6 + 7 + 8 + 9 + 10, and, finally, 1 + 2 + 3 + 4 + 5 + 6 + 7 + 8 + 9. It turns out that the number of representations of a number as the sum of consecutive integers is the same as the number of odd divisors of that number. For 45, we can enumerate the six expected divisors: 1, 3, 5, 9, 15, and 45 itself.

▼

ONE final item on the subject of numbers adding up to 45. Check out the square of numbers to the right. It is a magic square because every row, column, and diagonal adds up to the same number—45.

5	22	18
28	15	2
12	8	25

Of course, by itself that's nothing special. It's easy to generate magic squares with a constant of 45 because any genuine 3 × 3 magic square (using the numbers 1 through 9) will add up to 15 (see **15**), so you can just multiply every number by 3 to get 45. Of course, it's easy to see that the above square isn't of that sort. Actually, when you look further, this square doesn't look all that special in terms of the variety of the numbers, because every one of them ends in 2, 5, or 8. But check this out. Starting with the upper left, the number of letters in *five* is 4. The number of letters in *twenty-two* is 9. Look at the new square we create by continuing in this fashion:

4	9	8
11	7	3
6	5	10

The new square is itself a magic square, with magic constant 21. Words fail me.

▼

A 45-degree angle plays a theoretical role in the shot put and hammer throw events in track and field. In theory, a 45-degree landing angle is associated with the greatest distance for any release velocity. In real life, however, this figure is slightly reduced, for the simple reason that the objects are released several feet above ground level. And for events such as the discus and javelin, where aerodynamics play a more significant role, the 45-degree figure is all the more elusive.

▼

THE forty-fifth parallel is halfway between the North Pole and the equator, although the flattening of the Earth near the poles creates a slight error.

▼

THE number 45 can be broken into two parts that form its square, three parts that form its cube, and four parts that form its fourth power. No other number less than 400,000 has this property. (Numbers that have this property for any particular power n are known as Kaprekar numbers of order n.)

$$(20 + 25)^2 = 2025$$
$$(9 + 11 + 25)^3 = 91125$$
$$(4 + 10 + 06 + 25)^4 = 4100625$$

46 $\left[\ 2 \times 23\ \right]$

IN New York State, a "46er" is someone who has climbed all 46 of the Adirondack mountains. The peaks range from Mount Couchsachraga, at 3,820 feet, to Mount Marcy at 5,344 feet.

▼

THERE are 46 ways of using all 9 nonzero digits to create a fraction that equals precisely $\frac{1}{8}$. No other fraction of the form $\frac{1}{n}$ comes close to such a tally. In fact, these pandigital constructions for $\frac{1}{n}$ are impossible for all but a finite number of choices for n. (See **68**.)

▼

1. God is our refuge and strength, a very present help in trouble.
2. Therefore will not we fear, though the earth be removed, and though the mountains be carried into the midst of the sea;
3. Though the waters thereof roar and be troubled, though the mountains **shake** with the swelling thereof. Selah.
4. There is a river, the streams whereof shall make glad the city of God, the holy place of the tabernacles of the most High.
5. God is in the midst of her; she shall not be moved: God shall help her, and that right early.
6. The heathen raged, the kingdoms were moved: he uttered his voice, the earth melted.
7. The LORD of hosts is with us; the God of Jacob is our refuge. Selah.
8. Come, behold the works of the LORD, what desolations he hath made in the earth.
9. He maketh wars to cease unto the end of the earth; he breaketh the bow, and cutteth the **spear** in sunder; he burneth the chariot in the fire.
10. Be still, and know that I am God: I will be exalted among the heathen, I will be exalted in the earth.
11. The LORD of hosts is with us; the God of Jacob is our refuge. Selah.

Above is Psalm 46 from the King James Bible. In case you're wondering what it's doing here, the answer is that exhibits a Bible Code of a different sort from the one you may have read about. In Psalm 46, the forty-sixth word from the beginning is *shake* and the forty-sixth word from the end is *spear*. And in the year when the King James Bible came out—1610—William Shakespeare celebrated his forty-sixth birthday.

The above is nothing more than coincidence, but there is one age-old story involving 46 that happens to be true. Namely, 46 BC was the longest year in history, because that's when Julius Caesar adopted the Julian Calendar and in so doing created a year with 445 days.

▼

THIS diagram may look like a spiderweb, but it's actually the Tutte graph, a famous counterexample devised in 1946 by William Thomas Tutte, then a graduate student in mathematics at Cambridge University. By that time in his life, Tutte had already broken a vital German code system, altering for the better the course of the Allied invasion of Europe. The Tutte graph is a more humble sort of achievement. It is a graph with 46 vertices, each of which is connected to two other vertices, and with the property that any two vertices can be removed and still leave a connected graph (which means what you think it means). Peter Tait of the University of Edinburgh had conjectured in 1880 that any graph with these two properties must be Hamiltonian—that is, starting with any vertex, you can devise a path that takes you through each and every other vertex precisely once before returning to your starting point. The Tutte graph, which is not Hamiltonian, showed that Tait's conjecture was false. Too bad, because, in a great example of how different-looking pieces of mathematics are in fact intimately related, Tait's conjecture, if true, would have implied the Four-Color Map Theorem! (See **4**.)

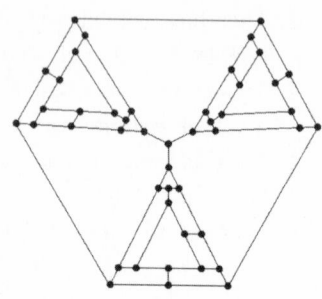

47 [prime]

A cube cannot be divided into 47 subcubes, and 47 is the largest number with that property. This funny-looking result was proved in 1977, resolving a 30-year-old problem that went under the name of the Hadwiger Problem, after Swiss mathematician Hugo Hadwiger (1908–1981).

Part of the proof isn't all that hard. It begins with the curious observation that it is possible to divide a cube into 1, 8, 20, 38, 49, 51, or even 54 sub-cubes, based on the following equations:

$$1^3 = 1^3 \qquad\qquad\qquad 1 = 1$$
$$2^3 = 8 \times 1^3 \qquad\qquad\qquad 8 = 8$$
$$3^3 = 2^3 + 19 \times 1^3 \qquad\qquad 1 + 19 = 20$$
$$4^3 = 3^3 + 37 \times 1^3 \qquad\qquad 1 + 37 = 38$$
$$6^3 = 4 \times 3^3 + 9 \times 2^3 + 36 \times 1^3 \qquad 4 + 9 + 36 = 49$$
$$6^3 = 5 \times 3^3 + 5 \times 2^3 + 41 \times 1^3 \qquad 5 + 5 + 41 = 51$$
$$8^3 = 6 \times 4^3 + 2 \times 3^3 + 4 \times 2^3 + 42 \times 1^3 \qquad 6 + 2 + 4 + 42 = 54$$

The next step, equally curious, is to note that if the numbers m and n have the property that a cube can be divided into m and n subcubes, then the number $m + n - 1$ must have the same property. Just divide the original cube into m subcubes, then divide one of the subcubes so obtained into n subcubes, for a total of $m + n - 1$ subcubes. (Strangely, it is never possible to cut a cube into subcubes that are all of different sizes—no matter how many subcubes are involved, at least two of them must be identical.)

What makes the initial set of numbers special is that by starting with {1, 8, 20, 38, 49, 51, 54} and applying the formula $m + n - 1$ successively, it turns out to be possible to create *any* number greater than 47—for example, $57 = 20 + 38 - 1$, and so on. I'll leave the proof of that fact to the reader, and likewise for the demonstration that 47 subcubes *can't* be attained. (Remember, all we showed is that any number > 47 *can* be attained.)

▼

IF you'd prefer an easier challenge, 47 smaller triangles are nested in this triangle. Identifying the 47 is painstaking but not that difficult. Tougher would be to count the strings on a concert pedal harp, though I will spare you the challenge by revealing that there are 47.

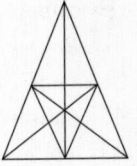

IN 1964, Pomona College professor Donald Bentley "proved" that all numbers are equal to 47, the beginning of a long association between the college and that particular number. Here is a sampling of some 47 trivia accumulated on the Pomona website:

> Pomona College is located off the San Bernardino Freeway. The sign reads: Claremont Colleges Next Right, Exit 47.
>
> Claremont McKenna College, named after Donald McKenna '29, was founded in 1947.
>
> There are 47 pipes in the top row of the Lyman Hall organ.
>
> The Declaration of Independence consists of 47 sentences.
>
> The Disney comedy *The Absent-Minded Professor* features a basketball game filmed at Pomona's old Renwick Gym. The final score: 47–46.
>
> Harwood Dormitory has rooms 45 and 49, but (mysteriously) no Room 47.
>
> In the film *The Towering Inferno*, actor Richard Chamberlain '56 was the 47th person in line to be rescued.
>
> The Pythagorean Theorem is Proposition 47 of Euclid's Elements.
>
> There are 47 letters in the dedication plaque on Mudd-Blaisdell Hall, which was completed in 1947.
>
> At the time of Pomona's first graduating class (in 1894), there were 47 students enrolled.
>
> If all this 47 trivia upsets your stomach, you'll be glad to know that Rolaids absorbs 47 times its weight in excess acid.

At risk of bursting Pomona's bubble, it is worth pointing out that pretty much any number is capable of producing a string of coincidences such as those above. But one area where the appearance of 47 is not a coincidence is in *Star Trek: The Next Generation*, where the crew stops at Sub-Space Relay Station 47, Data is unconscious for 47 seconds, a main character shrinks to 47 centimeters, there's a planet of 47 survivors, the crew discovers element 247, and many more. These selected mentions have the same feel as those on the Pomona website, but apparently they were instigated by Joe Menosky, a writer/coproducer of *Star Trek* whose handiwork has been continued by subsequent production teams. Menosky is a 1979 graduate of Pomona College.

48 $\left[\, 2^4 \times 3 \,\right]$

48 is the smallest number with ten divisors: 1, 2, 3, 4, 6, 8, 12, 16, 24, and 48 itself. (In general, $2^{n-1} \times 3$ is the smallest number with $2n$ divisors, as long as $n \geq 2$.)

48 is twice the total number of major and minor keys in Western tonal music (twenty-four), not counting enharmonic equivalents. Johann Sebastian Bach's *Well-Tempered Clavier* is informally known as *The Forty-Eight* because it consists of a prelude and a fugue in each major and minor key, for a total of 48 pieces.

WITH the addition of Arizona and New Mexico in 1912, the United States comprised 48 states, and the stars on the flag could be arranged in six rows of eight apiece. This configuration was maintained until Alaska joined the Union in 1959. Even today the continental United States is referred to as the "lower 48."

THIS rectangle contains 48 square units, half of which are gray and half of which are white. There is only one other rectangle that can be lined in this same fashion using an equal number of two different colors. Can you find it? (See Answers.)

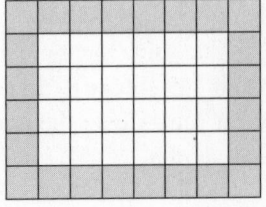

49 $\left[\ 7^2 = (11-4)^{(11-9)}\ \right]$

IT is possible to arrange 49 triangles (including the upside-down white ones) to form one big triangle of the same shape. But this construction can be done for *any* square number, not just 49. The principle here is that any perfect square can be written as the sum of two consecutive triangular numbers, as we saw in **36**. In this case 49 = 28 (gray) + 21 (white).

Alternatively, if you count the number of triangles (both white and gray) in each row, as you progress downward you get 49 = 1 + 3 + 5 + 7 + 9 + 11 + 13. In fact, *any* square can be written as the sum of consecutive odd numbers starting with 1.

But 49 is a very special square, as it is formed by joining two squares, 4 and 9, whose product is itself the perfect square 36.

▼

NOT only is 49 a square, it also has the peculiar property that if you put 48 in the middle you get another square, 4489. Repeating the process yields 444889, another square, and 44448889, yet another square.

▼

IN the standard game of lotto, six balls are drawn from a set that is numbered from 1 to 49. Given that the balls are not returned to the drum (in the probability world this is called "sampling without replacement"), the total number of choices equals $\frac{49!}{6!43!} = 13{,}983{,}816$. This quantity is written as either $_{49}C_6$ or, using the more old-fashioned notation $\binom{49}{6}$, pronounced, descriptively, "49 choose 6." In general, "n choose k" equals $\frac{n!}{k!(n-k)!}$ and means just what you'd think: the number of ways of choosing k objects from an original set of n.

▼

THERE were two gold rushes in the United States during the nineteenth century. The first of these—the California Gold Rush of 1849—led to the term *49er* to describe a miner, immortalized in the song "Oh My Darling, Clementine" and by the San Francisco football team of the same name. In the last few years of the nineteenth century, the gold rush turned to the Klondike River region of Alaska, which eventually became the forty-ninth state.

50 $\left[\ 2 \times 5^2 \quad (10 - 5)(10 - 0)\ \right]$

THE title of the hit TV show *Hawaii Five-O* derives from Hawaii being the fiftieth state. (Obvious, I know, but I have to confess that I never thought of that during the entire run of the series.) The US flag adopted its current configuration to accommodate the addition of Hawaii. The grid of 50 stars is essentially a 4×5 array nested inside a 5×6 array.

THERE have been a total of 27 different star configurations on US flags, ranging from the original 13 stars to today's 50 stars. There was actually a 49-star flag that followed the flag in **48**; although Alaska and Hawaii were both admitted to the Union in the same year (1959), their admission dates straddled July 4, and, according to an Act signed by President James Monroe in 1818, the flag officially gets updated on the July 4 following the admission of a new state. The 50-star version therefore became official on July 4, 1960, and on July 4, 2007, it became the longest-lived flag in US history.

THE book of Genesis contains 50 chapters.

IN darts, the bull's-eye (innermost circle known as the bull) is worth 50 points.

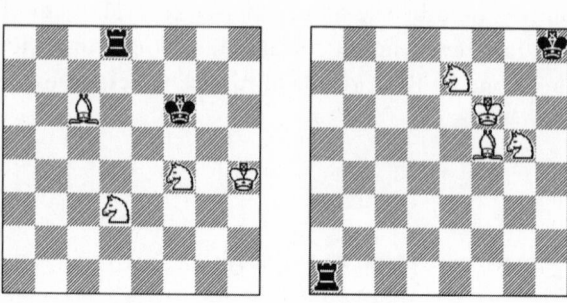

IN chess, a player can claim a draw if no piece has been captured and no pawn has been moved for the previous 50 moves. This rule was apparently first proposed in 1561 by Ruy Lopez, whose name now adorns a classic chess opening. Some 430 years later, Anatoly Karpov and Garry Kasparov battled for over 50 moves after reaching an end position in which Karpov held two knights and a bishop while Kasparov held just a rook (left). What made the game's conclusion especially fascinating is that Kasparov, perhaps unaware that the 50-Move Rule applied (a draw is not automatically granted—a player has to claim it), offered his rook as a sacrifice (two moves after the position on the right). But a draw was reached anyway. Had Karpov taken the rook, a stalemate would have resulted, while turning down the sacrifice would have reduced the end game to just two knights for Karpov, and it is impossible for a king and two knights to force checkmate!

IT is well-known that $50 = 1^2 + 7^2 = 5^2 + 5^2$ and is the smallest number that can be expressed as the sum of two squares in two different ways. But there's a geometric interpretation to this fact that isn't quite as familiar. Check out the following diagrams:

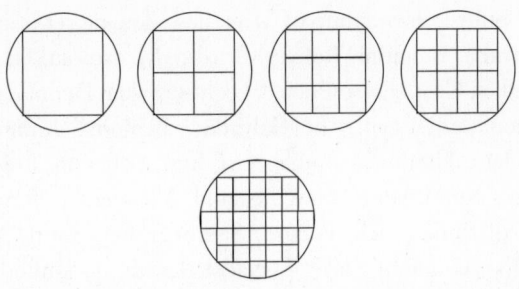

The top-left diagram shows a square inscribed within a circle. Obviously you can't insert any more squares of the same size. Ditto for the entire top row, ending with a 4 × 4 square. But when you circumscribe a 5 × 5 square with a circle, four more small squares fit inside the circle, as shown by the diagram in the bottom row. But that's just another way of saying that the hypotenuse of a right triangle with sides 1 and 7 is the same as the hypotenuse of the isosceles right triangle with sides 5 and 5, and that's what the equation $50 = 1^2 + 7^2 = 5^2 + 5^2$ is all about.

51 $\left[\, 3 \times 17 \,\right]$

THE number 1,979,339,339 is a prime number with the rare property that if you take any number of digits off the right-hand side, you're still left with a prime . . . as long as you consider 1 to be a prime. Such numbers are called right-truncatable primes or, more colorfully, Russian doll primes, presumably in recognition of those little nested wooden dolls that can be taken apart repeatedly only to reveal another, smaller doll inside.

Of course, you may be wondering what all this has to do with the number 51. The answer is that there are precisely 51 Russian doll primes, with 1,979,339,339 being the largest of the lot.

A somewhat better-known group of 51 is the following set of countries: Argentina, Australia, Belgium, Bolivia, Brazil, Byelorussia, Canada, Chile, China, Colombia, Costa Rica, Cuba, Czechoslovakia, Denmark, Dominican Republic, Ecuador, Egypt, El Salvador, Ethiopia, France, Greece, Guatemala, Haiti, Honduras, India, Iran, Iraq, Lebanon, Liberia, Luxembourg, Mexico, Netherlands, New Zealand, Nicaragua, Norway, Panama, Paraguay, Peru, Philippines, Poland, Saudi Arabia, South Africa, Syria, Turkey, Ukraine, Union of Soviet Socialist Republics, United Kingdom of Great Britain and Northern Ireland, United States of America, Uruguay, Venezuela, and Yugoslavia.

Perhaps you'd like to contemplate what these countries have in common. Or should I say *had* in common, as they're not all around today, or in some cases still around but under different names. (See Answers.)

AT the right is a path that starts at the origin and ends up six units to the right, with the only legal steps being one unit to the right, one unit up diagonally, or one unit down diagonally. There are a total of 51 such paths. In math jargon, 51 is the sixth Motzkin number, named for Berlin-born American mathematician Theodore Samuel Motzkin (1908–1970).

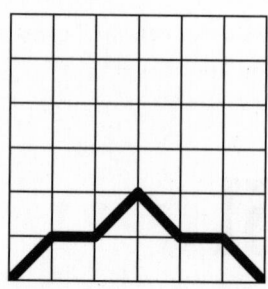

Motzkin numbers arise in a variety of contexts within the field of combinatorics, the snazzy word for "counting." For example, Motzkin numbers count how many expressions can be created by combining a letter with nested parentheses. In the case of 6 total characters, this gives us a more compact way of listing the 51 possibilities:

You can convert to paths using the scheme (= /, x = — , and) = \.

xxxxxx	xxxx()	xxx()x	xxx(x)	xx()xx	xx()()
xx(x)x	xx(xx)	xx(())	x()xxx	x()x()	x()()x
x()(x)	x(x)xx	x(x)()	x(xx)x	x(xxx)	x(x())
x(())x	x(()x)	x((x))	()xxxx	()xx()	()x()x

()x(x)	()()xx	()()()	()(x)x	()(xx)	()(())
(x)xxx	(x)x()	(x)()x	(x)(x)	(xx)xx	(xx)()
(xxx)x	(xxxx)	(xx())	(x())x	(x()x)	(x(x))
(())xx	(())()	(()x)x	(()xx)	(()())	((x))x
((x)x)	((xx))	((()))			

52 $\left[\ 2^2 \times 13\ \right]$

BESIDES being famous as the number of weeks in a year and the number of white keys on a piano, 52 shows up in all sorts of games. The most obvious connection is that there are 52 cards in a deck, consisting of 4 suits with 13 cards apiece. Today those suits are conventionally spades, hearts, diamonds, and clubs, but many other symbols have appeared over the centuries, among the earliest known being the polo sticks, coins, swords, and cups of the fourteenth century.

▼

LESS familiar, perhaps, is the legend surrounding Parker Brothers' initial rejection of Monopoly. As the story goes, game developer Charles Darrow was informed that his creation contained "52 fundamental errors," among them the complexity of the rules and the absurdly long playing time. The happy ending didn't occur until Darrow succeeded in selling the game at Wanamaker's Department Store in Philadelphia, whereupon Parker Brothers reconsidered and made Darrow the first person to become a millionaire via the game-invention route.

▼

THERE were 52 squares in the Aztec game Patolli. As it happens, the Aztec calendar, like the Mayan calendar, operated on a 52-year cycle, but that may be just coincidental, as Patolli predates the Aztec civilization. Patolli is said to have had religious significance. While avoiding the human sacrifice ascribed to the infamous Aztec ball game *ullamaliztli*, Patolli players could in theory wind up as indentured servants if they bet more than they can afford. (No doubt this would qualify as a "fundamental error" in the view of Parker Brothers.)

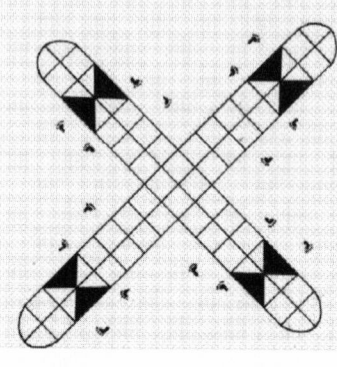

MOST people are familiar with the structure of a limerick: five lines, with the first one rhyming with the second, the third and fourth forming a different rhyming pair, and the fifth line rhyming with the first. This AABBA pattern is but one of 52 rhyme schemes that can be created from a poem of five lines. In the world of combinatorics, 52 is known as a Bell number, after Scottish-born mathematician and author Eric Temple Bell.

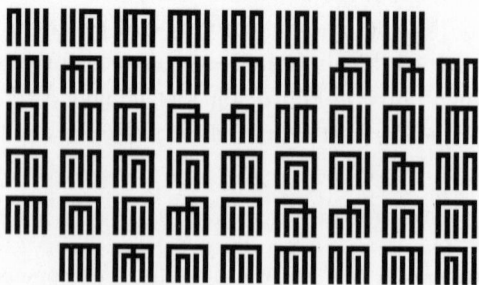

The Bell numbers, like the Motzkin numbers introduced in **51**, can be described in a number of different but equivalent ways. The figure above lists the 52 possible configurations of Genjiko, a Japanese art form whose icons consist of five columns joined by a horizontal bar at the top. If you think of a column as a line of poetry and a bar joining two columns as meaning that those lines rhyme, the 52 possible rhyme schemes for a five-line poem are thereby delineated.

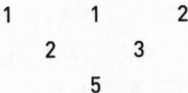

The list of Bell numbers can be created by a process that evokes both Pascal's Triangle and the Fibonacci numbers. Basically you start with the assumption that 1 is a Bell number, at which point you make a little triangle like so, adding the numbers of the top row to form the number below it. Since 1 + 1 = 2, you welcome 2 to the list.

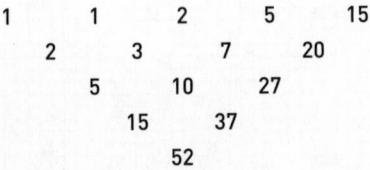

Now that 2 has joined the club of Bell numbers, it gets added to the top row and is now used to generate the next Bell number, 5, as follows:

1	1	2	5	15
2	3	7	20	
5	10	27		
15	37			
52				

Two more steps of this same process produce the triangle above, which identifies 52 as the fifth Bell number.

In math-speak, the nth Bell number is the number of partitions of a set of n objects or the number of ways in which n distinguishable balls can be placed into n indistinguishable urns. The nth Bell number is also the number of multiplicative partitions of a number with n distinct prime factors. In particular, the number $2310 = 2 \times 3 \times 5 \times 7 \times 11$ can be written as a product in precisely 52 ways.

IN 1917, British puzzlemaster Henry Dudeney introduced the No-Three-in-a-Line Problem, which asked how many dots could be placed on an $n \times n$ lattice without ever having three dots lying on the same straight line. It is not hard to see that the theoretical maximum for the $n \times n$ case is $2n$ dots, because anything beyond that would produce three dots in some row or column. For what values of n is the maximum of $2n$ actually achieved? Well, it has long been conjectured that for sufficiently large n, no solution exists. At this writing, the largest known solution, depicted below, is the 52-unit construction discovered in 1992 by the colorfully named German mathematician Achim Flammenkamp.

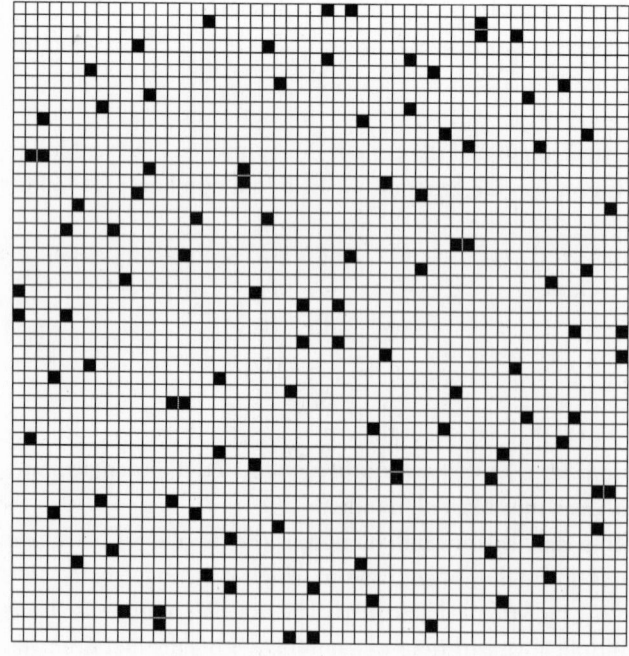

53 [prime]

53 = (3 × 16) + 5, so 53 = 35 in the hexadecimal system (base 16). No other two-digit number reverses itself upon hexadecimal conversion. But when you allow for more digits, reversals are spawned by 371 (= 173_{16}), 5141 (= 1415_{16}), and 99481 (= 18499_{16}), and all three of these numbers are multiples of 53.

▼

VENICE 53 was the name given to the gambling affliction that hit Italy in 2004, when the number 53 failed to appear in any of Venice's biweekly lotto drawings for an inordinate period of time (eventually over 180 drawings between May 2003 and February 2005). Gamblers lost over $2 billion betting on the reemergence of 53, apparently forgetting that despite 53's prolonged drought, its chances of coming up on any particular drawing were no greater than those of any other number.

▼

48 49 50 51 **52** 53 54 **55** 56 57 58

53 is the smallest prime whose five neighbors in either direction are all composite. (The next primes with this property are 89 and 157.)

The frequency of primes within the positive integers is a subject that has been explored for centuries. In the early 1800s, Carl Friedrich Gauss and French mathematician Adrien-Marie LeGendre (who had proved Fermat's Last Theorem for the single case $n = 5$), both conjectured that the number of primes less than n, denoted $\pi(n)$, was approximately $\frac{n}{\ln(n)}$, where $\ln(n)$ is the natural logarithm of n. This result, now known as the Prime Number Theorem, was proved independently by Hadamard and Vallee Poussin in 1896.

▼

LONGTIME baseball fans will recall that Don Drysdale wore number 53 for the Los Angeles Dodgers in the 1960s, but not many are aware that his number was intentionally passed on to Herbie, the Volkswagen Beetle that first appeared in the movie *The Love Bug*, by producer and Dodgers fan Bill Walsh.

54 $\left[\, 2 \times 3^3 \,\right]$

THE area of a regular pentagon equals $(\frac{5}{4})a^2\tan(54)$, where a is the length of a side. The 54 arises because the area is calculated by dividing the pentagon into five congruent isosceles triangles, each with angle measures of 54°, 54°, and 72°.

THE most famous disco of them all, Manhattan's Studio 54, was located at 254 West 54th Street.

THERE are a total of 6 × 9 = 54 faces on a Rubik's cube.

THE expression "54–40 or fight" was a campaign slogan of James K. Polk in 1844. The slogan's implicit threat was that Polk would go to war with Canada in order to set the northern border of Oregon at the parallel 54°40′. It didn't happen, and the border was officially set at 49° in 1846. The 54°40′ parallel lives on, however: It is the southernmost latitude of Alaska, and it is the patriotic and surprising name of a popular quilt pattern.

OFFICERS Gunther Toody and Francis Muldoon drove a red car in *Car 54,*

Where Are You? whereas actual police cars of the era were painted green. The car's distinctive coloring enabled it to be driven on location in New York City without creating confusion. The show's viewers never knew the difference, because *Car 54* (1961–63) was broadcast only in black and white.

▼

AT this writing, Africa has 54 countries, from Algeria to Zimbabwe.

▼

IN our discussion of quadratic forms in **15**, we mentioned that the great Indian mathematician Srinivasa Ramanujan identified 54 expressions of the form $aw^2 + bx^2 + cy^2 + dz^2$ that can generate all positive integers. The list is as follows:

(1,1,1,1)	(1,1,1,2)	(1,1,1,3)	(1,1,1,4)	(1,1,1,5)	(1,1,1,6)
(1,1,1,7)	(1,1,2,2)	(1,1,2,3)	(1,1,2,4)	(1,1,2,5)	(1,1,2,6)
(1,1,2,7)	(1,1,2,8)	(1,1,2,9)	(1,1,2,10)	(1,1,2,11)	(1,1,2,12)
(1,1,2,13)	(1,1,2,14)	(1,1,3,3)	(1,1,3,4)	(1,1,3,5)	(1,1,3,6)
(1,2,2,2)	(1,2,2,3)	(1,2,2,4)	(1,2,2,5)	(1,2,2,6)	(1,2,2,7)
(1,2,3,3)	(1,2,3,4)	(1,2,3,5)	(1,2,3,6)	(1,2,3,7)	(1,2,3,8)
(1,2,3,9)	(1,2,3,10)	(1,2,4,4)	(1,2,4,5)	(1,2,4,6)	(1,2,4,7)
(1,2,4,8)	(1,2,4,9)	(1,2,4,10)	(1,2,4,11)	(1,2,4,12)	(1,2,4,13)
(1,2,4,14)	(1,2,5,6)	(1,2,5,7)	(1,2,5,8)	(1,2,5,9)	(1,2,5,10)

A word on the notation seems appropriate. When we say that (1,2,3,8) is a universal quadratic form, we mean that any positive integer can be expressed in the form $w^2 + 2x^2 + 3y^2 + 8z^2$ for some choice of $w, x, y,$ and z, and similarly for the others. My personal favorites are (1,2,3,4) (the first four positive integers), (1,2,3,6) (the first three followed by their product or sum), (1,2,3,5) (Fibonacci numbers), and (1,1,2,6) (my birthday, if the first and third commas are removed and US birthday notation is used).

Ramanujan's list was remarkable given that he had no formal training in mathematics and no access to modern calculating tools. Ramanujan died in 1920 at the age of 32.

55 $\left[5 \times 11 \right]$

55 is the tenth Fibonacci number as well as the tenth triangular number and the largest number that is both Fibonacci and triangular.

▼

```
A B B A C A C B B A      A C A B C A C C A B
 C B C B B B A B C        B B C A B B C B C
  A A A B B C C A          B A B C B A A A
   A A C B A C B            C C A A C A A
    A B A C B A              C B A B B A
     C C B A C                A C C B C
      C A C B                  B C A A
       B B A                    A B A
        B C                      C C
         A                        C
```

THE two triangles above each contain 55 letters and are created by a method that yields some surprising results. To begin with, the letters A, B, and C are placed in the top row more or less arbitrarily. The second row is determined by the following rule: If two consecutive letters in the first row are different, the third letter is placed between them in the second row. If two consecutive letters are the same, that letter is repeated below. The process continues until you are left with a single letter in the tenth row.

Note that in the left-hand triangle, the first and last entries of the top row are the same, namely A, and the letter at the bottom is also an A. In the right-hand triangle, the top left and top right letters are different (A and B), and the letter at the bottom is the third one (C). Guess what? No matter how you place the letters in the top row, you will always get the same result! (This property turns out to be a function of the triangle's height: It works for any triangle whose height is an even number not divisible by 4.)

▼

THE number 55 also has an odd but logical significance within the game of basketball. Historically, 55 was the highest uniform number a player could have without special dispensation. Why? Check out the next time you see a referee call a personal foul. The ref must inform the scoring table who committed the foul, and the standard method to do that is to signal that player's uniform number by holding up the appropriate number of fingers on each hand. Until refs start growing extra fingers, the digits 6, 7, 8, and 9 are out of the question, so the biggest number they can comfortably signal is 55.

NOT only is 55 a triangular number, it is also square-pyramidal. What does that mean? Well, start with a 5 × 5 array of bowling balls. Using the spaces between the balls, place a 4 × 4 array on top of that, and so on. By the time you reach the single bowling ball at the top of the pyramid, you will have used a total of 25 + 16 + 9 + 4 + 1 = 55 bowling balls. (Otherwise stated, a 5 × 5 square grid forms a total of 55 squares along its lattice lines.)

WHAT'S with this peculiar shape?

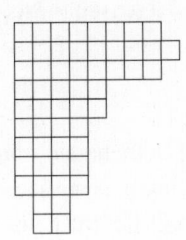

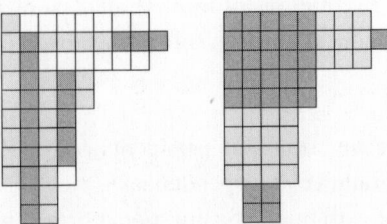

The answer is that the shape consists of 55 individual blocks and can be tiled either by using rectangles of sizes 1 × 1 through 1 × 10 or by using squares having sizes 1 × 1 through 5 × 5. This simultaneous tiling is a two-dimensional way of illustrating that 55 is both triangular and square pyramidal—a rare animal indeed, as we will discover in **91**.

56 $\left[\ 2^3 \times 7\ \right]$

IN the United States, the single biggest reason why the number 56 is part of the public consciousness has to be Joe DiMaggio's 56-game hitting streak. DiMaggio's achievement came in 1941 and is now widely viewed as unassailable, right up there with Cy Young's 511 wins, Sam Crawford's 312 triples, and, yes, Cy Young's 316 losses. No one has ever seriously challenged DiMaggio's mark, the best hitting streak since 1941 being Pete Rose's 44-game streak in 1978. John Allen Paulos has pointed out that the *a priori* likelihood of DiMaggio, a career .325 hitter, hitting safely in 56 straight games over the course of a season is exceedingly small—on the order of one in a hundred thousand.

▼

THE 56 Aubrey holes of Stonehenge would appear to be much longer-lived than DiMaggio's streak, but in some sense that's not the case. Stonehenge itself dates back to 3000 BC, but the holes weren't formally registered until antiquarian John Aubrey discovered them on a visit in 1666, and most weren't excavated until the twentieth century, if at all. The claim that the Aubrey holes have an astronomical function isn't backed by scientific consensus.

▼

THE names of how many future US presidents can be found among the 56 signers of the Declaration of Independence?

If you ever get hit with that trivia question, phrased just so, a quick scan of the list of signers indicates that the answer is four. Two of them (John Adams and Thomas Jefferson) actually became president. Another (Benjamin Harrison) was the father of William Henry Harrison, the ninth president, and shared a name with that Harrison's grandson, who became the twenty-third president. The fourth and final name is a bit of a stretch, but New Hampshire's Josiah Bartlett qualifies in some sense, as his name (minus one of the trailing *t*'s) was used in the television series *The West Wing* as that of the fictional president played by Martin Sheen.

1	2	3	4	5
2	3	4	5	1
3	4	5	1	2
4	5	1	2	3
5	1	2	3	4

THE above is the simplest possible example of a 5×5 Latin square. As we saw in **36**, a Latin square of order n is an $n \times n$ array, typically using the numbers 1 through n, such that no row or column repeats a number. Once you have created such a square, you can always rearrange the columns so that the first row consists of the numbers 1 through n in that order. And once you've done that, you can always rearrange the rows so that the first column is 1 through n reading down. The result is a called a reduced (or normalized) Latin square. The above square is kind of a self-working reduced square, but altogether there are 56 reduced squares, listed below in four groups of 14. The total number of 5×5 Latin squares equals $56 \times 5! \times 4! = 161,280$. In general, if R_n equals the number of reduced Latin squares of order n, the total number of Latin squares of order n equals $R_n \times n! \times (n-1)!$

12345 12345 12345 12345 12345 12345 12345 12345 12345 12345 12345 12345 12345 12345
23451 21453 21534 21534 21453 21453 21534 21534 23451 23451 23514 23514 23154 23154
34512 34512 34152 34251 35214 35214 35421 35412 31524 31524 31452 31452 34512 34521
45123 45231 45213 45123 43521 43521 43152 43251 45132 45213 45123 45231 45231 45213
51234 53124 53421 53412 54231 54132 54213 54123 54213 54132 54231 54123 51423 51432

12345 12345 12345 12345 12345 12345 12345 12345 12345 12345 12345 12345 12345 12345
21453 23514 23514 23514 23154 23154 23451 23451 23451 23514 24153 24513 24531 24531

34521 34152 34251 34251 35412 35421 35124 35214 35214 35421 31524 31254 31254 31452
45132 45231 45123 45132 41523 41532 41532 41523 41532 41253 45231 45132 45123 45123
53214 51423 51432 51423 54231 54213 54213 54132 54123 54132 53412 53421 53412 53214

12345 12345 12345 12345 12345 12345 12345 12345 12345 12345 12345 12345 12345 12345
24513 24531 24153 24153 24531 24531 24153 24153 24153 24513 24531 24513 25134 25413
31452 31452 35214 35421 35124 35412 35214 35412 35421 35124 35214 35421 31452 31254
45231 45213 41532 41532 41253 41253 43521 43521 43512 43251 43152 43152 43521 43521
53124 53124 53421 53214 53412 53124 51432 51234 51234 51432 51423 51234 54213 54132

12345 12345 12345 12345 12345 12345 12345 12345 12345 12345 12345 12345 12345 12345
25431 25413 25431 25413 25134 25134 25134 25431 25413 25431 25134 25134 25413 25413
31254 31524 31524 31524 34251 34512 34521 34152 34251 34512 34251 34512 34152 34512
43512 43152 43152 43251 41523 41253 41253 41523 41532 41253 43512 43251 43521 43152
54123 54231 54213 54132 53412 53421 53412 53214 53124 53124 51423 51423 51234 51234

57 $\left[\ 3 \times 19 \qquad 2^5 + 5^2\ \right]$

SHOWN at right is what is described as the most complex
Chinese character still in use. It apparently involves 57
separate pen strokes (though I confess I haven't counted)
and represents *biang*, as in biang-biang noodles.

IN the United States, the number 57 is better known in food circles through
H. J. Heinz's "57 varieties." The company actually had well more than 57 offerings when the slogan was introduced in 1896, but 57 lives on in their
corporate culture. The address of Heinz's world headquarters in Pittsburgh,
Pennsylvania is P.O. Box 57.

About the only way in which Heinz didn't exploit the number 57 was to
build an office building with 57 floors. That task was accomplished by F. W.

Woolworth in 1913, and the Woolworth Building was the world's tallest until surpassed in 1930 by both 40 Wall Street and the Chrysler Building.

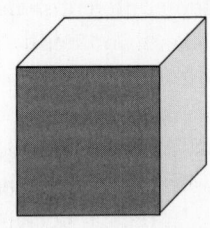

IF you had three different colors at your disposal and you had to paint each face of a cube with one of those three colors, you could create 57 distinct cubes, where *distinct* in this context means that no coloring could lead to another via rotation. In particular, the number of possible colorings using k colors (with $k = 1$ through 6) can be shown to equal $\frac{(k^6 + 3k^4 + 12k^3 + 8k^2)}{24}$, where 24 just might be recognizable as the number of possible rotations of the cube (six faces each rotated in one of four ways). Plugging in $k = 3$ yields the desired 57 colorings.

IN advanced trigonometry and calculus, angles are generally measured in radians rather than degrees. A radian is defined as the angle measure that makes an arc of a circle equal to its radius, as in the diagram: It turns out that one radian equals slightly more than 57 degrees. The exact number is $\frac{360}{(2\pi)}$, which to three decimal places equals 57.296.

58 $\left[\, 2 \times 29 \,\right]$

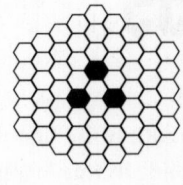

THE game Hexxagon, an online and/or arcade variation of Othello, is played on a hexagonal grid with three of the interior flattened hexagons blacked out, for a total of 58 usable spaces. (Game spaces are usually called squares, but that seemed inappropriate here.)

REGULAR polygons such as the hexagon can be extended to form different shapes, known as stellations of the original object, and a little time with stellations will produce another appearance of the number 58. We start with the observation that the hexagram to the right, usually thought of 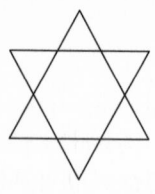 as an overlapping pair of equilateral triangles, is also just a regular hexagon with its edges extended until they meet:

A regular octagon (below left) has not one but two stellations, as the edges in the original extension (below middle) can themselves be extended to form the figure on the far right.

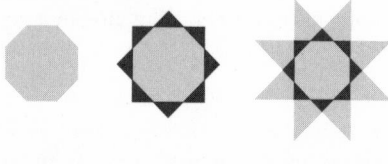

IN three dimensions, it is impossible to extend a tetrahedron or a cube, just as it is impossible to extend a triangle or square in two dimensions. However, each of the other five Platonic solids (see **5**) has at least one stellation. An octahedron (eight faces) has one stellation, known as the stella octangula. The dodecahedron (12 faces) has three distinct stellations. Finally, the icosahedron (20 faces) has a preposterous total of 58 stellations.

59 [prime]

IF you multiply the first two primes and add 1, you get 7, a prime. If you multiply the first three primes and add 1, you get 31, a prime. We can keep going in this manner:

$$2 \times 3 + 1 = 7 \qquad\qquad \text{prime}$$
$$2 \times 3 \times 5 + 1 = 31 \qquad\qquad \text{prime}$$
$$2 \times 3 \times 5 \times 7 + 1 = 211 \qquad\qquad \text{prime}$$
$$2 \times 3 \times 5 \times 7 \times 11 + 1 = 2311 \qquad\qquad \text{prime}$$

But if we went one more step, the pattern would come to a screeching halt, and the number 59 makes an appearance:

$$2 \times 3 \times 5 \times 7 \times 11 \times 13 + 1 = 30{,}031 = 59 \times 509$$

Of course, there's no earthly reason why the product of the first n primes plus 1 should itself be prime. However, this type of construction is historically important because a variant of it was used by Euclid, circa 300 BC, to show that there must be an infinite number of primes. To wit, suppose that there were only finitely many primes. Multiply those primes together and add 1. This new number may or may not be prime, but we know for certain that none of its prime factors could be in our supposedly complete list, because no number other than 1 divides evenly into two consecutive numbers. Therefore any finite set of primes cannot possibly be sufficient.

THE number 59 also produces an interesting chart when you start dividing it by small numbers, starting as small as possible.

When you divide 59 by	You get a remainder of
2	1
3	2
4	3
5	4
6	5

You will note that the above table works because 59 is one less than 60, the smallest number that is evenly divisible by 2, 3, 4, 5, and 6. (Divisibility by 6 of course follows from divisibility by 2 and 3.) With that in mind, you should be able to come up with a number that when substituted for 59 enables the table to be extended to include division by 7. (See Answers.)

60 $\left[\, 2^2 \times 3 \times 5 \,\right]$

THERE wasn't much to say about the numbers 58 or 59, but with 60 comes a wealth of connections. The key is divisibility. Whereas 58 had but two prime factors and 59 was prime, 60 is divisible by each of the first three primes and is in fact the smallest number divisible by each of the first six positive integers and the smallest number with 12 factors: 1, 2, 3, 4, 5, 6, 10, 12, 15, 20, 30, and 60 itself.

▼

EACH of the three angles of an equilateral triangle measures precisely 60 degrees.

▼

THERE are 60 seconds in a minute and 60 minutes in an hour. These properties are taken for granted today but they date back to Mesopotamian civilizations, which used 60 as the base for their number systems. The Babylonians had no symbol for zero, but they were able to generate the first 59 integers using only two basic symbols.

▼

HERE'S a slightly more technical property of the number 60. It starts with the observation that there are 120 permutations of five elements ($120 = 5!$ $= 5 \times 4 \times 3 \times 2$). Any permutation is built up of "transpositions," meaning the switching of two particular elements. For a given permutation, either an even or an odd number of transpositions will be required. (That sounds silly, but the point is that there is more than one way to build a permutation out of transpositions, but it is not possible for one way to involve an even number and the other an odd number.) Of the 120 total permutations of five elements, 60 are "even." The permutation shown to the right is even because it involves an even number (namely two) of

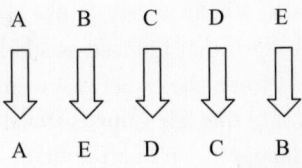

individual transpositions—B and E switch with one another, as do C and D.

Because a combination of even permutations is itself even, in mathematical terms the even permutations form a subgroup of the full "symmetric group" of permutations of five elements, denoted S_5. This subgroup, called A_5, is the smallest possible non-abelian simple group. The non-abelian part means that multiplying different permutations isn't commutative, while the simple part means that the group contains no proper normal subgroups other than the identity permutation.

If the foregoing didn't make sense, don't worry. It's just math talk, cleverly designed to scare people away. But as far as the math world is concerned, it's an important appearance of the number 60.

▼

TO close on a more understandable note, the diagram shown is the board for Bridg-It, a game devised by the late American mathematician and economist David Gale circa 1960. The board's 60 dots are raised and serve as landing places for pieces of two different colors (red and black in the actual game), the objective being to create an uninterrupted path

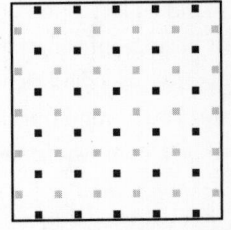

of your chosen color from one side of the board to the other. It is not possible for the game to end in a draw: one player or the other will always be able to create such a path. (By way of contrast, in the presidential election of 1960, John F. Kennedy won despite being unable to fashion either a north-south or east-west chain of states. He could have gone north-south had he been able to jump over Lake Michigan—but if that had been possible, Richard Nixon would have had an East-West chain to go with his multiple north-south "victories." In any event, no "jumping" is permissible in Bridg-It.)

▼

SOMEWHERE in my house there's an old game of Bridg-It that I played as a kid. (I was about 6 years old when the game was invented.) But I was never aware that the game is trivial from a mathematical standpoint, in that the first player can always force a win. The strategy, as deduced by Oliver Gross and communicated by Martin Gardner back in the '60s,

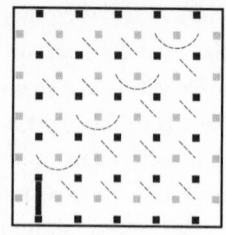

is for black to place his first move as shown below, and then to follow any move by his opponent with a move that touches the other end of the dotted line touched by the opponent's piece.

While the triviality of Bridg-It was no doubt a disappointment to its inventor and manufacturers (the small Rhode Island firm of Hassenfeld Brothers, now the not-so-small company called Hasbro), it is not unusual for certain classes of games to be "determined" in one way or another. The mathematician who did the seminal work in this field was Ernst Zermelo (1871–1953), also a giant in the world of set theory. Zermelo is credited with the 1913 theorem that in chess, either white can force a win or black can force a win or either player can force a draw. As game theory developed, so did its lingo, and now you can say that "finite two-person zero-sum games of perfect information" are strictly determined. Fortunately for chess players, the so-called tree for chess is so vast that the actual calculation will always be beyond the capacity of mankind. But the Bridg-It example happens to be a case where the winning strategy can be mapped out explicitly.

61 [prime]

IN the TV game show *Jeopardy!*, the Jeopardy! and Double Jeopardy! rounds each consist of six categories with five questions (or answers) apiece. Throw in Final Jeopardy! and that's a total of $6 \times 5 + 6 \times 5 + 1 = 61$ questions and answers, although in most games the contestants don't have quite enough time to use up all of them.

THAT'S not the only connection between *Jeopardy!* and the number 61: In 1961 (the only year in the twentieth century that reads the same right-side up and upside down), a young newscaster named Alex Trebek made his TV debut for CBC, the Canadian Broadcasting Company. Trebek moved to the United States in 1973 to become a game-show host, and his talents were rewarded in 1984, when he was named emcee for the revived version of *Jeopardy!*

SPEAKING of Canada, a hockey rink is 61 meters long, but with a catch. The 61 meters figure only applies to North American (i.e., National Hockey League) standards, and is an approximation, albeit a pretty good one, to the precise measurement of 200 feet. In the rest of the world, hockey rinks follow the metric system. Unfortunately for the number 61, the official length of international rinks is just 60 meters. But 61 has enduring significance in the world of hockey, as it represents the number of NHL scoring records owned or shared by the great Wayne Gretzky upon his retirement in 1999.

WORKING south from Canada, Highway 61 makes its way from the Canadian border all the way to New Orleans. Early in its path it passes through Hibbing, Minnesota, the birthplace of Bob Dylan, who immortalized the road in his 1965 album *Highway 61 Revisited*.

THE number 61 has served as an upper bound of sorts in US presidential elections, as no candidate has ever received more than 61% of the popular vote. At this writing, the top percentage vote getters in US election history were Warren Harding in 1920, Franklin Roosevelt in 1936, Lyndon Johnson in 1964, and Richard Nixon in 1972, with 60.5%, 60.6%, 60.6%, and 60.3% of the popular vote, respectively. Given that America begins and ends with an A, it is appropriate that A is the most common letter among the individual state names in the United States, with a total of 61 A's in the 50 state names. You may be wondering whether any presidential candidate has ever captured precisely those states with an A in them. The answer is no. Not even close.

A standard eye chart contains 61 letters distributed among 11 rows. Such a chart is called a Snellen chart, in honor of Dutch ophthalmologist Hermann Snellen, who invented the chart back in 1862.

62 $\left[\, 2 \times 31 \,\right]$

THE number 62 shows up in a well-known brainteaser. It starts with the figure below, which contains 62 squares.

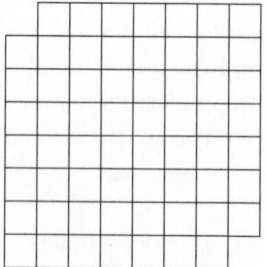

Now imagine that you have 31 dominoes, each measuring 1 × 2 squares, as follows:

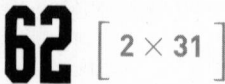

We know that 62 = 2 × 31, so the number of squares in the figure equals the total number of squares on the dominoes. The natural question, which you should feel free to tackle if you haven't seen it before, is whether it's possible to cover the entire 62-square region with the 31 dominoes. (See Answers.)

▼

SPEAKING of squares, 62 can be written as either $1^2 + 5^2 + 6^2$ or $2^2 + 3^2 + 7^2$. It is the smallest number with two different representations as the sum of distinct squares. And there are 62 different arrangements of five X's and four O's on a tic-tac-toe board that produce a win for X and X only.

63 $\left[3^2 \times 7 \right]$

DR. Subrahmanyam Karuturi has a long name. In fact, he has the longest name in the world. Not his own name, mind you, but the domain name below:

Iamtheproudownerofthelongestlongestlongestdomainnameinthisworld.com

If you take the time to count, you will discover 63 letters in the body of the URL. Dr. Karuturi's record cannot be broken (at least not without resorting to subdomain trickery), because 63 letters is the maximum allowable domain name with a .com extension.

THE board for the Game of Goose consists of a picture of a goose covered by 63 discs. The game, a precursor to an extended family of dice/chase games, was originally registered by John Wolfe in 1597. The classic version by Laurie first appeared in 1831. That very same year saw the passage of the Game Act, which classified the pheasant, partridge, and grouse as game birds and defined a hunting season for them, but made no mention of geese. Have geese ever had a better year?

25	16	80	104	90
115	98	4	1	97
42	111	85	2	75
66	72	27	102	48
67	18	119	106	5

91	77	71	6	70
52	64	117	69	13
30	118	21	123	23
26	39	92	44	114
116	17	14	73	95

47	61	45	76	86
107	43	38	33	94
89	68	63	58	37
32	93	88	83	19
40	50	81	65	79

31	53	112	109	10
12	82	34	87	100
103	3	105	8	96
113	57	9	62	74
56	120	55	49	35

121	108	7	20	59
29	28	122	125	11
51	15	41	124	84
78	54	99	24	60
36	110	46	22	101

PICTURED above are the five cross-sections of a 5 × 5 × 5 magic cube, in which the sums of every row, column, and diagonal are equal (to 315). Remarkably, the existence of a magic cube of order 5 wasn't proved until November 2003, when the pictured construction was revealed to the world by

Christian Boyer and Walter Trump. What *had* been known for some time that magic cubes of order 2, 3, and 4 were impossible, so a five-sided cube was the smallest possible nontrivial case. What also had been known was that if such a cube existed, its middle cube would have to be the number 63, the middle number in the string 1, 2, . . . 124, 125. Sure enough, that's the number in the center of Trump and Boyer's creation.

64 $\left[\, 2^6 \,\right]$

MANY of the special properties of the number 64 are the result of it being a power of two. In computing, where binary arithmetic is paramount, 64 bits is a well-established size for various data types. (The word *bit* is in fact shorthand for "binary digit.") And the 64 in *The $64,000 Question* was hardly a coincidence, as the number was attained by repeated doubling of a $1,000 wager, which itself was attained after successive doubling from $1 to $512 and then an approximate doubling to $1,000. (The proximity of 2 × 512 = 1,024 and 1,000 has caused confusion over the years in the computer world, where both numbers end up having a "K" attached to them, even though the former is a binary kilo and the latter a metric kilo.)

THERE being six faces on a cube, the numbers on the doubling cube in backgammon range from $2^1 = 2$ to $2^6 = 64$.

THE classic Chinese text *I Ching* (pronounced *e ching*) employs constructions called hexagrams, which are characters formed by stacking six bars, each row of which is either broken or unbroken (yin/yang). Those familiar with binary logic will at once recognize that there are $2^6 = 64$ possibilities altogether.

A better-known construction, though not widely known for its ties to the number 64, is Braille. There are 64 characters in Braille, each formed by placing a raised dot (or not) in one of six fixed locations. As with the *I Ching*, the result is 64 different possibilities, though there are different versions of Braille. Only 26 of the characters are devoted to letters, with the first ten letters doubling as digits, subject to yet another character that warns you a number is coming.

The picture below is one of many ingenious mosaics made by computer graphics pioneer Ken Knowlton. This particular mosaic uses 16 copies of each of the 64 Braille characters to form a likeness of Helen Keller.

THE Beatles introduced "When I'm 64" in 1967, at which time no one in the group had even turned 30. For the record, Ringo Starr turned 64 in July 2004, while Sir Paul McCartney came of age in June 2005.

CHESS champion Bobby Fischer (1943–2008) made it to age 64 but no further, a poetic lifespan in that a chessboard has 64 squares. The alternating black/white pattern of the chessboard actually provides a clue for the classic puzzle introduced in **62**.

65 $\begin{bmatrix} 5 \times 13 \end{bmatrix}$

IN some ways the number 65 is a relic of the twentieth century. For years it stood as the mandatory retirement age, but that was when people didn't live as long or work as long as they do today. And 65 miles per hour is perhaps the most familiar speed limit for seasoned drivers, but somehow it doesn't seem likely to survive the latest century and in fact has already fallen in a number of states. Fortunately, American society found a new way to honor the number 65 in 2001, when the NCAA basketball tournament was expanded from 64 to 65 teams. The idea was that a "play-in" game would be held during the week prior to the official tournament opening, thus reducing the field back to 64 again.

▼

MATHEMATICALLY speaking, the strange thing about the number 65 is that even though it is one away from being a square, several of its best-known properties revolve around squares. We'll get things rolling by the casual observation that 65 minus 56 (its reversal) equals 9, a square, while 65 plus 56 equals 121, also a square.

▼

BETTER known is the fact that 65 is the smallest number that can be represented as the sum of two squares in two different ways: $65 = 8^2 + 1^2 = 4^2 + 7^2$. Geometrically, this equation can be brought to life by the diagram on the next page, in which one line segment is the diagonal of a 1×8 rectangle and the other segment is the diagonal of a 7 × 4 rectangle. The two line segments appear to be about the same length, and any lingering doubt is removed by the Pythagorean Theorem, which shows that the length of each segment equals the square root of 65.

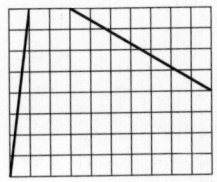

IN the same general area, sixty-five is the smallest number that can be a hypotenuse in four different ways, as shown by the identities $65^2 = 25^2 + 60^2 = 16^2 + 63^2 = 33^2 + 56^2 = 39^2 + 52^2$. The last of those four represents a right triangle with lengths 39, 52, and 65, which is just the famous 3-4-5 right triangle with each side multiplied by 13.

1	15	24	8	17
23	7	16	5	14
20	4	13	22	6
12	21	10	19	3
9	18	2	11	25

IN the magic square to the left, all rows, columns, and diagonals sum to 65. As we saw in our discussions of **15** and **34**, the magic constant for an $n × n$ magic square is obtained by adding the numbers 1 through n^2 together and dividing by n: In this case, the sum of the numbers 1 through 25 equals 325, and dividing by 5 yields 65.

The magic square above is actually of a special variety. Note that the sum of the four corners of the square, coupled with the center square, equals $1 + 17 + 9 + 25 + 13 = 65$. The fun doesn't stop there. If you take any 3 × 3 subsquare and sum its corners plus center, you also get 65: The 3 × 3 square in the lower right yields $13 + 6 + 2 + 25 + 19 = 65$, and so on. Quite cool, I'm sure you'll agree, but in official math lingo the magic square is described using the more clinical adjectives of pandiagonal, associative, complete, and self-similar.

PERHAPS it is fitting to close the discussion of 65 and squares with a classic puzzle that claims 65 = 64. We start with the rectangle on the next page, consisting of 5 × 13 = 65 square units.

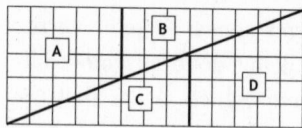

We now reassemble the four pieces to produce an 8 × 8 square—only 64 square units!

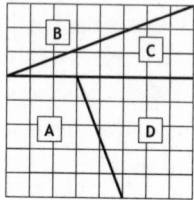

We know that some trickery is involved, being quite certain that 65 does not equal 64. The illusion results from the fact that the "diagonal" of the top rectangle is actually two line segments of different slopes. If we put the pieces of the square back into a rectangle, that rectangle would have a long, slivery hole in it of area 1.

▼

SPEAKING of holes, 8 × 8 boards, and the number 65, if you take an 8 × 8 chessboard and remove the middle 4 squares, you're left with 60 square units, exactly the number in a set of 12 pentominoes (see **12**). Back in 1958, Dana Scott of Princeton University showed that the 12 pentominoes could fill the chessboard-minus-hole space in precisely 65 different ways.

66 $\left[\, 2 \times 3 \times 11 \,\right]$

ROUTE 66 was once a major thoroughfare connecting Chicago with Los Angeles. The TV series of the same name was about the adventures of two men (Martin Milner and George Maharis) driving that route, which in essence represented the wide-open spaces of the western United States. The show was shot on location, but the locations seldom coincided with actual points on Route 66. (The Phillips 66 gas stations, named for the route, also showed up elsewhere.) As it happened, *Route 66* ran from 1960 to 1964, several years after the passage of the Interstate Highway Bill (1956) had already doomed the legendary road to oblivion.

▼

IN 6, we established that if you draw six dots on a piece of paper and connect every possible pair of dots with one of two colors, you are guaranteed to form a triangle whose sides are all the same color and whose vertices are at three of the dots. In **17**, we extended that concept to three colors. The extension to four colors gets a wee bit tricky, but it is possible to use the result from **17** to prove that if you connect all possible pairs from 66 dots with one of four colors, you are guaranteed to form at least one monochromatic triangle. The idea behind the proof is to connect 66 with 17, the magic number for three colors. So suppose you have a set of 66 dots such that every pair of dots connected with a line that is one of four colors: red, yellow, blue, or green. Pick a dot at random. There are 65 lines emanating from that dot, and since $65 > 16 + 16 + 16 + 16$, at least one of the four colors must appear 17 times. Without loss of generality we can assume that there are 17 red lines. Now consider the 17 dots at the other end of those red lines. If any two of them are joined by a red line, they must form a red triangle with the original dot as the third vertex. But if no pair is joined by a red line, then all the lines among those 17 dots must be blue, yellow, or green. But from the result of **17**, any set of 17 dots joined by line segments of three different colors must have a monochromatic triangle.

Note that the above proof doesn't demonstrate that 66 is the *minimal* number with the desired property. At this writing, that number is unknown, as is the case for the vast majority of higher-order Ramsey numbers, as they are called.

▼

THERE are 66 books in the Christian Bible. Tack on an extra 6, however, and everything changes: the number 666, also known as the number of the beast, is considered satanic.

▼

A surveyor's chain, also called a Gunter's chain or just a chain, measures exactly $\frac{1}{80}$ of a mile, or $\frac{5,280}{80} = 66$ feet. A patch of land one furlong in length and one chain in width measures precisely one acre. It is believed that the width of one chain corresponds to the width that could comfortably be plowed by a team of oxen. Though the measurement has declined in popularity, it can still be found today not so much as a width but as a length: A cricket pitch is 10 feet wide and 66 feet long.

67 [prime]

THE number 67 played a role in the Mansion of Happiness, America's very first board game. The game was manufactured by the W. & S.B. Ives Company, a stationer out of Salem, Massachusetts, beginning in 1843. Although the Puritan culture of the day frowned upon children wasting time with frivolous activities, Mansion of Happiness proved acceptable because of its moralistic overtones. Invented by clergyman's daughter Anne Abbott, the game encouraged good deeds as players worked their pieces through an inward spiral. Squares labeled charity, industry, and humanity represented rewards, while drunkenness and ingratitude were penalties. The objective of the game was to reach the Mansion of Happiness in the center of the board, square number 67.

▼

A pizza can be divided into 67 pieces using only 11 straight cuts. In general, n cuts will divide a pizza into a maximum of $1 + \frac{n(n+1)}{2}$ pieces, or 1 plus the nth triangular number. The reason triangular numbers arise is that after the initial piece (the whole pizza), each successive cut adds a maximum of one piece, two pieces, three pieces, and so on.

▼

WITHIN the US Senate, any amendment to the Constitution must be approved by a two-thirds majority—67 of 100 senators present and voting. This same number applies to any change of Senate rules. In particular, in 1975, when the number of senators required to override a filibuster was reduced from 67 to 60, that change required the approval of 67 senators.

▼

"QUESTIONS 67 and 68" was a song on Chicago's first album (the group was then called the Chicago Transit Authority). The peculiar title generated many theories about its origin, but the eventual explanation of Robert Lamm (keyboard and vocals) was disappointingly mundane: The song was apparently about a man (possibly Lamm himself) whose girlfriend had asked a lot of questions during the prior two years. The above-referenced album came out in 1969, and "Questions 67 and 68," the fourth song on the first side, peaked at number 71 on the Billboard charts.

68 $\left[\, 2^2 \times 17 \,\right]$

HOW many unit discs can be placed inside a standard 8 × 8 chessboard? Even though there are 64 squares and the diameter of each disc equals the length of a square, the maximum is not 64. By nesting the discs together as shown in the diagram, it is possible to fit five columns of 8 and four columns of 7, for a total of $(5 \times 8) + (4 \times 7) = 68$ discs.

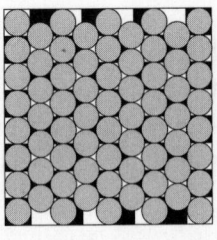

The packing of the discs in this manner is a hexagonal packing, much like the honeycomb found in **6**. The theoretical packing density of this pattern is approximately 90%, the most efficient packing using circles in the plane. The actual packing density in this case is $\frac{68\pi}{(4 \times 64)} \approx 83\%$, the lower figure arising because of the wasted space at the top and bottom of the board.

At this moment you're taking my word (and the suggestive drawing) that the nine columns actually fit inside the chessboard, but the fit isn't hard to prove. Note that the centers of the discs form the vertices of equilateral triangles spread across the grid. The total width of the discs equals the height of eight such triangles plus one (there is half a unit to the left and to the right of the triangles). An equilateral triangle whose sides are 1 has height equal to the square root of three (1.732) divided by two, so the total disc width is $1 + 4(1.732)$, or approximately 7.93—just barely under 8. In particular, no chessboard smaller than the standard 8×8 board would have accommodated the extra column.

▼

THE fraction $\frac{631,254}{314,526}$ equals 2 using octal (base 8) arithmetic. There are precisely 68 octal fractions in which the numerator and denominator consist of permutations of the digits 1 through 6 and whose quotient is an integer. Of perhaps more interest is that there are *no* solutions using the first five (or fewer) positive integers. The situation in base 10 is similar. If you take the first seven (or fewer) nonzero digits, there are no two permutations of those digits whose quotient is an integer. However, there are 2,338 solutions using eight digits, as in $\frac{86,314,572}{21,578,643} = 4$. Using all nine nonzero digits produces 24,603 distinct solutions.

▼

HOCKEY great Jaromir Jagr chose the uniform number 68 to honor the Prague Spring Rebellion of 1968, in which both of his grandfathers lost their lives. Jagr was the first Czechoslovakian player to be drafted by the NHL without first having to defect to the West.

69 $[\ 3 \times 23\ ]$

STARTING with the earliest days of programmable calculators, the number 69 provided a somewhat mysterious upper bound. To illustrate, the Texas Instruments TI-59 calculator, introduced in 1977, could calculate any factorial from 2 to 69. Why that particular limit? Well, it turns out that 69 factorial—the product of all the positive integers less than or equal to 69—is approximately 1.71×10^{98}. Multiplying that number by 70 would push you beyond 10^{100}, the cutoff point for the TI-59 as well as the ensuing generation of pocket calculators—you have to stop somewhere, right? The result is that 69 gained a little fame as the largest number whose factorial could be calculated by a pocket calculator.

THE number 69 also has the amusing property of being the only number whose square and cube contain all the numerals from zero to nine, once and only once.

$$69^2 = 4{,}761$$
$$69^3 = 328{,}509$$

AN even more remarkable property of 69 arises from the standard alphanumeric coding, in which A = 1, B = 2, C = 3, and so on. Using this code, which is commonly found in the pseudoscience of numerology, the value of any word or collection of letters is defined as the sum of the individual letter values. In particular, this code can be applied to Roman numerals. Where 69 fits in is that its Roman numeral representation is LXIX. The value of these four letters in the standard code is equal to $12 + 24 + 9 + 24 = 69$. Sixty-nine is one of only two numbers that are equal to their Roman numeral code values. Can you find the other (smaller) number? (See Answers.)

IN the United States, Channel 69 is the highest-numbered UHF channel. Its supremacy dates back to 1982, when the Federal Communications Commission allotted channels 70 through 82 for cellular telephones.

▼

69 equals 105 in base 8, while 105 equals 69 in hexadecimal (base 16). Although this reversal is uncommon, it is shared by the numbers 64 through 69.

▼

THE Gordian's Knot puzzle shown to the right is named after a conundrum faced by Alexander the Great in 333 BC. Alexander ended up "untying" a knot, either by cutting it or removing it from its pin, after which conquering much of Asia was child's play. No cutting is allowed for the Gordian's Knot, but solving the puzzle involves a minimum of 69 moves.

70 $\left[\, 2 \times 5 \times 7 \,\right]$

THE proper divisors of 70 are 1, 2, 5, 7, 10, 14, and 35. The sum of these seven numbers exceeds 70 (it equals 74, actually), yet no subset of them adds up to precisely 70. Believe it or not, 70 is the smallest number with this property—that is, the smallest number that is less than the sum of its proper factors but which cannot be represented as the sum of a subset of those factors. It's even harder to believe that there's a name for this kind of number: a weird number. So 70 is the smallest weird number.

▼

TAKE a square, and divide it into eight isosceles right triangles, as follows:

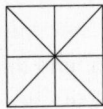

By coloring each triangle black or white (and disregarding the lines as necessary), it is possible to create designs such as the following:

THE Izzi puzzle, designed by Frank Nichols and introduced by Virginia-based puzzle company Binary Arts (now called ThinkFun) in 1992, is made up of designs of precisely this type. How many are there altogether? Because each of the 8 triangles can be one of two colors, binary logic suggests that there should be a total of $2^8 = 256$ possible designs. But by that reckoning two designs such as

and

are counted separately, even though one can be converted into the other via a simple 90-degree rotation. Given that any one shape can be rotated four times before returning to its original state, it's tempting to just divide 256 by 4 to get 64, but that's not quite right, either, because of symmetries. The all-black design above, for example, never changes upon rotation.

Counting the actual number of designs is made easier by a mathematical tool called Burnside's Lemma. (It is named for the prolific nineteenth-century group theorist William Burnside, even though he apparently had nothing to do with this particular insight, which dates back to Cauchy and Frobenius in the first half of that century.) Although Burnside's Lemma is usually phrased in terms of "orbits" of "groups," here the idea is that you start with the total number of designs (256), add the number of designs that are symmetric with respect to 180-degree rotations (16), and then add the number that are symmetric with respect to 90-degree rotations in either direction (4 + 4), for a total of 280. *Now* you can divide by 4 (again, the number of possible rotations) to get a grand total of 70 distinct designs.

The idea behind Izzi is to arrange the pieces into various 8 × 8 squares such that the colors on any two adjacent pieces match up, as in the following:

But wait a minute. An 8 × 8 square uses 64 designs, and we just went to a lot of trouble to show that there are 70 designs altogether. What happened is that the folks at Binary Arts picked out six designs that wouldn't be used in the final puzzle. Those six designs are the ones shown at the beginning of this discussion.

71 [prime]

THE equation $7! + 1 = 71^2$ is one of only three known equations of its kind, the others being $4! + 1 = 5^2$ and $5! + 1 = 11^2$.

Just to be clear what's going on, let's spell those equations out:

$$4 \times 3 \times 2 + 1 = 25 = 5^2$$
$$5 \times 4 \times 3 \times 2 + 1 = 121 = 11^2$$
$$7 \times 6 \times 5 \times 4 \times 3 \times 2 + 1 = 5041 = 71^2$$

In other words, 71 is the largest known number whose square is one more than a factorial. That it happens to be one more than 7 factorial adds the finishing touch of having 7 and 1 on each side of the equation.

Research has indicated that $n! + 1$ is not a square for n up to one billion, and it is widely believed that 4, 5, and 7 are the only values of n that work. Technically, though, the problem (known in the trade as Brocard's Problem) remains very much in need of a proof.

▼

RECENT visitors to Hong Kong may have come across a little place called Club 71. The number 71 has special significance on the island because July 1, 1997, marked the handover of Hong Kong from the British to the Chinese. The date July 1 goes by the delightful name of *chat yat* in Cantonese.

Because 71 and 73 are both primes, 71 is a twin prime. And because 71 and 17 are both primes, 71 is an EMIRP, the name given to any prime that is the reverse of a prime. But the prime connections don't stop there. If you add the prime numbers less than 71, you get $2 + 3 + 5 + 7 + 11 + 13 + 17 + 19 + 23 + 29 + 31 + 37 + 41 + 43 + 47 + 53 + 59 + 61 + 67 = 568 = 8 \times 71$. For a number to be a factor of the sum of the primes less than it isn't exactly an important property, but it's a rare one: The next number to have it is 3,691,119. The final prime-related property is that $71^3 = 357,911$, a number obtained by stringing together five consecutive prime numbers beginning with 3.

▼

THE number 71 played a relatively brief role in a problem called the Happy End Problem. We start by noting that if you place four points on a piece of paper, it is not necessarily possible to connect them so as to create a convex quadrilateral, as follows:

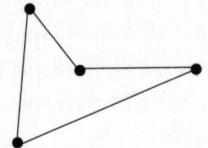

(*Convex* means that any line segment joining any two points inside the quadrilateral must lie entirely within the quadrilateral, so this particular figure doesn't qualify.)

However, if you add a fifth point, provided that no three of the points fall along the same line, it is always possible to connect four of the five points so as to create a convex quadrilateral.

The question obviously extends to polygons with more than four sides. Somewhere in this exploration, the legendary Paul Erdos demonstrated that 71 points will always be enough to guarantee the creation of a convex hexagon. His work actually proved that for any n, there is some number, called $g(n)$, such that $g(n)$ points would insure a convex polygon with n sides. He even gave an upper bound for $g(n)$ in a formula that yielded 71 when $n = 6$.

Precisely because Erdos's work was so general, other mathematicians had no trouble improving upon it, and today it is known that $17 \leq g(6) \leq 37$. But that's not the happy end. The reason this problem got its name is that two of Erdos's colleagues in working on the problem—Ester Klein and George Szekeres—became engaged during that process and eventually married.

72 $\left[2^3 \times 3^2 \right]$

THE Rule of 72 is a shortcut that answers the question "How long will it take my money to double?" Suppose, for example, that you expect your investments to grow at an annual rate of 8%. Dividing 72 by 8 gives 9, and you can therefore expect your money to double after 9 years.

As it happens, I've chosen a case where the Rule of 72 estimate is almost exactly equal to the actual doubling time. The estimate will be less precise for very small or very large rates of return, but gives adequate perspective for most rates of return that could be considered reasonable. Other numbers can be used (you will see references to the Rules of 70, 71, and even 69.3, depending on the nature of the compounding), but 72 has the advantage of being evenly divisible by a wide range of numbers, among them

2, 3, 4, 6, 8, 9, 12, and 18. Remember, we're looking for an estimate, not an exact answer, so we can use whatever number suits our purposes.

The reason why the rule works at all for numbers in this range is that the equation for doubling times involves the natural logarithm of 2, which is very close to 0.69. Of course, if you want to quadruple your money instead of merely doubling it, just double the number that the Rule of 72 gives you. (A simple point, perhaps, but often overlooked.)

Perhaps the most remarkable aspect of the Rule of 72 is its longevity. It appeared in *Summa de Arithmetica* by Fra Luca Pacioli, an occasional collaborator of Leonardo da Vinci. The year was 1494. If Pacioli had invested his life savings into a perpetual investment paying $\frac{1}{7}$th of a percent each year, the Rule of 72 suggests that his investment would have doubled by the start of the twenty-first century.

SPEAKING of da Vinci and Pacioli, the two also collaborated in the production of the 72-sided sphere, a popular geometric rendering of the period. This image, spurred by Leonardo's drawings, appeared in Fra Pacioli's 1509 book *The Divine Proportion*. By approximating a sphere with polyhedra—whose volumes could be calculated—the "sphere" con-

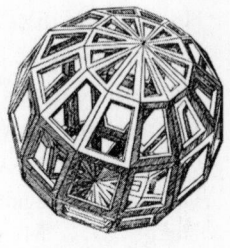

firmed a result, known since Euclid's time, that the volume of an actual sphere was proportional to the cube of its radius. Today, the invention of integral calculus now long behind us, even high school students can derive the formula $V = (\frac{4}{3})\pi r^3$.

IN many international archery competitions, including the ranking rounds of the Olympic Games, archers shoot a total of 72 arrows. Because the inner gold of the bull's-eye is worth 10 points, a maximum score is 720. Although archery appeared in the first several Olympics, confusion over stan-

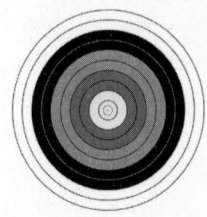

dardization knocked it out for many years. It returned for the Munich games of '72.

▼

WHEN *New York World* reporter Nellie Bly set off around the world on November 14, 1889, her goal was to match Phileas Fogg's fictional time of 80 days (see **80**). She did a bit better than that, as she returned to New York on January 21, 1890, 72 days and a few hours later.

▼

THE multiplicative properties of the number 72 plays a key role in a well-known puzzle that you are now invited to solve.

> A man in a bar is talking with the bartender. The bartender asks him if he has children and he replies that he has 3.
> He then asks their ages and the man responds that the product of their ages is 72.
> The bartender says, "That is not enough information."
> The man then says that the sum of their ages is on the front door of the bar.
> The bartender again says, "That is not enough information."
> The guy says, "My youngest likes ice cream."
> The bartender says, "In that case, I can figure out their ages."
> *What are the ages of the kids?* (See Answers.)

This puzzle is sometimes told using 36 instead of 72, but it is almost never told with the next number (after 72) that yields a solution. Care to guess what that number is? (See Answers.)

73 [prime]

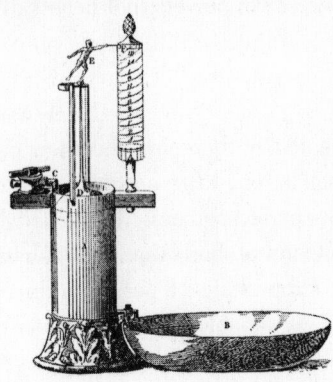

THE number 73 played a role in ancient clock making, a consequence of there being 365 days per year and the fact that $73 = \frac{365}{5}$. The clepsydra (water clock) pictured here is of the third century BC. Clocks with 5 water compartments and 73 teeth could create a 365-day cycle.

THE picture below demonstrates that 73 is a star number. There are a total of 73 dots in the star; the number of dots in the interior hexagon is 37, the reversal of 73.

THERE is an old puzzle that asks solvers to make various positive integers using four 4's, plus basic arithmetical operations, including decimal points, square roots, and factorials. For example, $1 = \frac{(4 + 4)}{(4 + 4)}$, $2 = \frac{4 \times 4}{(4 + 4)}$, and so on. Things get a bit more complicated for higher numbers, as you'd expect. For example, $70 = 44 + 4! + \sqrt{4}$, $71 = \frac{(4! + 4.4)}{.4}$, and $72 = 44 + 4! + 4$. But I didn't include a simple expression for 73 because there isn't any. That's right. The number 73 is the smallest number for which no simple expression exists.

IN the context of Waring's Theorem, it can be said that all positive integers can be written as the sum of no more than 73 sixth powers (not necessarily distinct).

THE number 73 also shows up in a relatively recent theorem concerning different types of representation of integers. Recall from **4** that any positive integer can be expressed as the sum of at most four perfect squares. More generally, the famous 15 Theorem of Princeton's John Conway shows that if a quadratic form represents the numbers 1 through 15, it represents all positive integers. (A quadratic form is any expression in which the variables have degree two: $a^2 + b^2 + c^2 + d^2$ is such a form, but so is $a^2 + 2b^2 + 3c^2 + 4d^2$ and so on.)

Manjul Bhargava was introduced to these subtleties while a graduate student at Princeton, and he did them one better. One of his extraordinary results is that if a quadratic form (a positive-definite, matrix-defined form, but that's another matter) represents all prime numbers through 73, then it represents *all* prime numbers.

74 [2 × 37]

FOR almost four centuries, the number 74 represented an unconfirmed limit for the three-dimensional sphere-packing problem. Johannes Kepler, in his famed 1611 treatise *Strena sue de nive sexangula* (on the six-cornered snowflake— see **6**), conjectured that no packing method is more efficient that the standard pyramidal (or hexagonal) stacking. The density of such a stacking is $\frac{\pi}{3}\sqrt{2}$, just a tad over 74%, and the longstanding question was

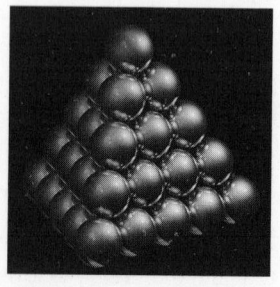

whether it was possible to find an alternative stacking method that occupied more than 74% of the available space.

In 1831, Carl Friedrich Gauss demonstrated that the Kepler conjecture was valid for *regular* lattices. Irregular lattices (it sort of means what you think it means) posed a problem for essentially two reasons. First, irregular packings are much more difficult to categorize than are regular packings. Second, it is in fact possible to construct asymmetrical arrangements that are denser than the hexagonal packing over a limited amount of space (the conjecture applied to the entirety of three-dimensional space).

Like the Four-Color Map Theorem, the Kepler conjecture went unresolved until the computer age provided the required analytical tools. University of Michigan's Thomas Hales issued a computer-driven verification in 1998. Kepler was apparently right all along.

It would have been fitting for Hales to have celebrated his achievement with a trip to Australia's Whitsunday Islands, located in the heart of the Great Barrier Reef. Though only seven of these islands are inhabited, they number 74 altogether.

▼

BACK in the Western Hemisphere, the Saffir-Simpson Hurricane Scale, developed by civil engineer Herbert Saffir and meteorologist Robert Simpson in the early 1970s, dictates that a storm doesn't officially get to be called a hurricane until its wind speed hits 74 miles per hour. This scale went into widespread use beginning in (you guessed it) 1974, when Simpson stepped down as director of the US National Hurricane Center.

75 $\left[\, 3 \times 5^2 \,\right]$

THERE are only 4! = 24 ways to rank four objects. However, if the ranking system allows for ties, that number increases all the way to 75. One way to list all 75 possibilities is to first list the standard 24 orderings of four objects, then group with brackets ties involving two players, then group ties involving three players, then strike through duplicates. The basic rule is that we remove any ordering in which the bracketed letters are not in alphabetical order. And, of course, we can't forget the seventy-fifth case—in which all four objects are tied. But something has gone wrong: the numbers in the columns don't add to 75 the way they should.

What possibilities have been left out? (See Answers.)

24

ABCD	ABDC	ACBD	ACDB	ADBC	ADCB
BACD	BADC	BCAD	BCDA	BDAC	BDCA
CABD	CADB	CBAD	CBDA	CDAB	CDBA
DABC	DACB	DBAC	DBCA	DCAB	DCBA

12

[AB]CD	[AB]DC	[AC]BD	[AC]DB	[AD]BC	[AD]CB
[BA]CD	[BA]DC	[BC]AD	[BC]DA	[BD]AC	[BD]CA
[CA]BD	[CA]DB	[CB]AD	[CB]DA	[CD]AB	[CD]BA
[DA]BC	[DA]CB	[DB]AC	[DB]CA	[DC]AB	[DC]BA

12

A[BC]D	A[BD]C	A[CB]D	A[CD]B	A[DB]C	A[DC]B
B[AC]D	B[AD]C	B[CA]D	B[CD]A	B[DA]C	B[DC]A
C[AB]D	C[AD]B	C[BA]D	C[BD]A	C[DA]B	C[DB]A
D[AB]C	D[AC]B	D[BA]C	D[BC]A	D[CA]B	D[CB]A

12

AB[CD]	AB[DC]	AC[BD]	AC[DB]	AD[BC]	AD[CB]
BA[CD]	BA[DC]	BC[AD]	BC[DA]	BD[AC]	BD[CA]
CA[BD]	CA[DB]	CB[AD]	CB[DA]	CD[AB]	CD[BA]
DA[BC]	DA[CB]	DB[AC]	DB[CA]	DC[AB]	DC[BA]

4

[ABC]D	[ABD]C	[ACB]D	[ACD]B	[ADB]C	[ADC]B
[BAC]D	[BAD]C	[BCA]D	[BCD]A	[BDA]C	[BDC]A
[CAB]D	[CAD]B	[CBA]D	[CBD]A	[CDA]B	[CDB]A
]DAB]C	[DAC]B	[DBA]C	[DBC]A	[DCA]B	[DCB]A

4

A[BCD]   ~~A[BDC]~~   ~~A[CBD]~~   ~~A[CDB]~~   ~~A[DBC]~~   ~~A[DCB]~~
B[ACD]   ~~B[ADC]~~   ~~B[CAD]~~   ~~B[CDA]~~   ~~B[DAC]~~   ~~B[DCA]~~
C[ABD]   ~~C[ADB]~~   ~~C[BAD]~~   ~~C[BDA]~~   ~~C[DAB]~~   ~~C[DBA]~~
D[ABC]   ~~D[ACB]~~   ~~D[BAC]~~   ~~D[BCA]~~   ~~D[CAB]~~   ~~D[CBA]~~

                        1

[ABCD]

TOTAL   **75?**

76 $\left[\, 2^2 \times 19 \,\right]$

IF you multiply 76 by itself, you get 5776, a number whose last two digits are 7 and 6. Obviously if you keep multiplying by 76, you always get a number that ends with 76. A number that is found at the end of all its powers is known as an automorphic number. Virtually all automorphic numbers end with either 25 or 76.

WE have discussed (see **22**) partitions of integers into smaller positive integers. Within that subject, number theorists look into partitions of integers into primes—specifically, partitions into distinct primes. It turns out that small numbers have relatively few such partitions: For example, the number 15 has only two partitions into distinct primes—13 + 2 and 7 + 5 + 3. Eventually, of course, the number of distinct prime partitions of a number becomes much bigger than the number itself. It just so happens that 76 is the crossover point. There are 76 partitions of the number 76 into distinct primes, and here they are:

31+17+11+7+5+3+2	37+13+11+7+5+3	41+17+11+5+2	43+23+7+3	71+3+2	73+3
29+19+11+7+5+3+2	31+19+11+7+5+3	37+29+5+3+2	43+19+11+3	67+7+2	71+5
29+17+13+7+5+3+2	31+17+13+7+5+3	37+23+11+3+2	43+17+13+3	61+13+2	59+17
23+19+17+7+5+3+2	29+19+13+7+5+3	37+19+13+5+2	43+17+11+7	43+31+2	53+23
23+19+13+11+5+3+2	23+19+13+11+7+3	37+19+11+7+2	41+23+7+5	47+29	
23+17+13+11+7+3+2	23+17+13+11+7+5	37+17+13+7+2			
	59+7+5+3+2	31+29+11+3+2			
	53+13+5+3+2	31+23+17+3+2			
	53+11+7+3+2	31+23+13+7+2			
47+19+5+3+2	31+19+17+7+2	41+19+13+3	37+19+17+3		
47+17+7+3+2	31+19+13+11+2	41+19+11+5	37+19+13+7		
47+13+11+3+2	29+23+19+3+2	41+17+13+5	31+29+13+3		
43+23+5+3+2	29+23+17+5+2	41+17+11+7	31+29+11+5		
43+19+7+5+2	61+7+5+3		31+23+19+3		
43+17+11+3+2	53+13+7+3		31+23+17+5		
43+13+11+7+2	53+11+7+5	37+31+5+3	29+23+19+5		
41+23+7+3+2	47+19+7+3	37+29+7+3	29+23+17+7		
41+19+11+3+2	47+17+7+5	37+23+13+3	29+23+13+11		
41+17+13+3+2	47+13+11+5	37+23+11+5	29+19+17+11		

77 $\left[\quad 7 \times 11 \qquad 4 \times 4 + 5 \times 5 + 6 \times 6 \quad \right]$

THE Group of 77 is a coalition of developing nations that was first organized by 77 founding nations in 1964 at Algiers. The group has since expanded considerably, but its original purpose remains: to further the economic well-being of its member states.

During World War II, at the Sweden/Norway border, "77" was used as a password because its tricky pronunciation in Swedish made it easy to determine whether the speaker was Swedish, Norwegian, or German.

PARTITIONS OF 77

77 is the smallest number of coins that cannot be combined into a dollar. Note that a solution with 76 coins is trivial—75 pennies plus 1 quarter: 75 coins can produce a dollar via 70 pennies, 4 nickels, and 1 dime, and so on down to a silver dollar.

$$77 = 3 + 4 + 5 + 5 + 60 \qquad \frac{1}{3} + \frac{1}{4} + \frac{1}{5} + \frac{1}{5} + \frac{1}{60} = 1$$

NOTE the duplication of 5 in the above sums: It turns out that 77 cannot be written as the sum of *distinct* numbers whose reciprocals add to 1, and it is the largest number with that property. (See **22** and **96**.) For example:

$$100 = 2 + 6 + 7 + 8 + 21 + 56 \qquad \frac{1}{2} + \frac{1}{6} + \frac{1}{7} + \frac{1}{8} + \frac{1}{21} + \frac{1}{56} = 1$$

THE Rose Bowl in Pasadena, California, is the regular-season home of the UCLA Bruins and host to a bowl game of the same name since 1923. A *bowl*, by definition, has an unbroken sequence of rows instead of different tiers (so from any seat you can see every other seat), and the Rose Bowl has 77 numbered rows of seats from top to bottom.

78 $\left[\, 2 \times 3 \times 13 \,\right]$

A typical 15 × 15 crossword grid (the size used by daily newspapers in the United States) contains 78 entries. The number of entries can be quite a bit smaller, but puzzles with more than 78 entries are usually rejected by the top puzzle editors.

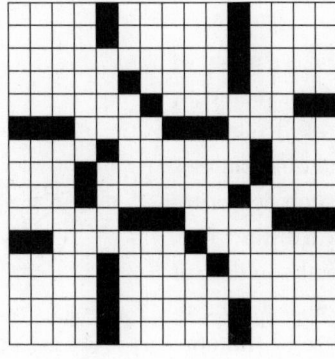

ELSEWHERE in the world of black squares, one of 35 possible heptominos (figures formed by joining seven squares at their edges) is shown below. Mathematicians take special interest in the tiling properties of such objects, and in 1989 Karl Dahlke proved the remarkable theorem that it takes at least 78 of the figures below to tile a rectangle.

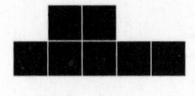

SPEAKING of rectangles, a tennis court measures 78 feet from baseline to baseline.

THERE are 78 tarot cards in a complete deck—22 of the major arcana, and 56 of the minor arcana.

78 is the twelfth triangular number, being the sum of the numbers 1 through 12. From which we can see that there are a total of 78 presents (not including repetitions) in the song "The Twelve Days of Christmas."

THE figure to the right is known as Metatron's Cube, and is created by joining the centers of 13 circles arranged in a "Flower of Life" pattern. If you consider each such center-to-center connection to be a distinct line, it follows that the total number of lines in the diagram equals 13 (number of starting points) × 12 (number of ending points), divided by 2 (to avoid double-counting) = 78. Metatron was an angel in Judaism, and Metatron's Cube has a rich history of applications in alchemy and religion. At one time it was used as a means of warding off satanic powers.

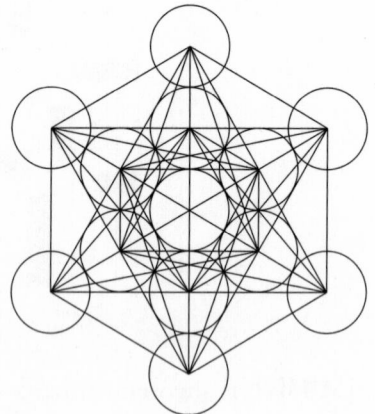

79 [prime $\quad 7 \times 9 + 7 + 9 \qquad 2^7 - 7^2$]

NOT only are 79 and its reversal, 97, both primes, they form the sums of the following addition table, in which all of the numbers are reversible primes:

$$79 = 11 + 31 + 37$$
$$97 = 11 + 13 + 79$$

$$79 = 4 \times 16 + 15 \times 1 = 4 \times 2^4 + 15 \times 1^4$$

That's kind of a strange equation, but all it says is that 79 can be written as the sum of 19 fourth powers: 4 of two to the fourth and 15 of one to the fourth. In and of itself, that says nothing, because one aspect of Waring's Theorem assures us that *every* number can be written as the sum of 19 fourth powers. What makes 79 unusual is that it *requires* 19 fourth powers, and is the smallest number to do so.

▼

HERE'S a well-known brainteaser:

Three thieves stole a bunch of coconuts and agreed to divide them up evenly the following morning, then retired for the night. After an hour passed, the first thief decided to take his third. After dividing the nuts evenly, he had one left over, which he gave to a monkey. An hour later, the second thief did the exact same thing with the remaining nuts, as did the third thief an hour after that: In other words, both of the thieves took one-third of the coconuts they saw, and handed the single leftover coconut to a monkey. In the morning, the thieves divided the remaining nuts evenly and had one left over, which they gave to the monkey. What was the smallest number of coconuts they could have started with and not had to deal with coconut parts?

Can you show that the answer is 79? (See Answers.)

80 $\left[\, 2^4 \times 5 \,\right]$

IN French, the number 80 is *quatre-vingts*, or literally four twenties. Perhaps the most celebrated appearance of this version of the number came in 1873, upon the publication of Jules Verne's *Le Tour de Monde en Quatre-vingts Jours*, otherwise known as *Around the World in Eighty Days*.

Technically, Phileas Fogg and his companion Passepartout didn't quite go "around the world." According to standards developed after Jules Verne's time, an official circumnavigation of the globe must pass through antipodal points—that is, two points that are completely opposite from one another. Here is Fogg's proposed itinerary:

London to Suez	rail and steamer	7 days
Suez to Bombay	steamer	13 days
Bombay to Calcutta	rail	3 days
Calcutta to Hong Kong	steamer	13 days
Hong Kong to Yokohama	steamer	6 days
Yokohama to San Francisco	steamer	22 days
San Francisco to New York	rail	7 days
New York to London	steamer	9 days
TOTAL		**80 days**

Of course, a series of unanticipated events derailed this schedule, but Fogg and Passepartout made it back to London almost a day early. The only problem was that they thought they were late: They had forgotten that by traveling west, they had crossed the international date line, and had therefore had picked up an extra day.

▼

ITALIAN economist Wilfredo Pareto (1848–1923) made the surprisingly powerful observation that 80% of his country's wealth was concentrated in 20% of the population. This phenomenon, dubbed Pareto's Law by legendary business thinker Joseph Juran, also goes under the name of the 80/20 Rule. Juran extended the rule to quality controls in manufacturing, where 80% of the problems could be attributed to 20% of the causes. The 80 and 20 aren't sacred, of course, but they form a useful guideline with plenty of applications. The table below contemporizes some of the old standbys. For a hypermodern version of Pareto's Law, one might use Woody Allen's famous observation: "Eighty percent of success is showing up."

THE 80/20 RULE, FILL-IN-THE-BLANKS STYLE

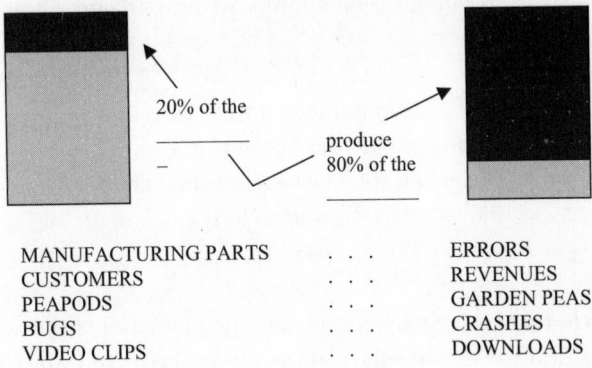

20% of the
_____

produce
80% of the
_____
–

MANUFACTURING PARTS	. . .	ERRORS
CUSTOMERS	. . .	REVENUES
PEAPODS	. . .	GARDEN PEAS
BUGS	. . .	CRASHES
VIDEO CLIPS	. . .	DOWNLOADS

81 [3⁴]

ALTHOUGH Sudoku puzzles come in many sizes and shapes, a standard Sudoku has 81 squares. This size implicitly takes advantage of the fact that 81 is both a perfect square and a perfect fourth power.

▼

ALTHOUGH similar-looking puzzles appeared in the French daily *La France* in the nineteenth century (*carre magique diabolique*), it is generally acknowledged that the modern version of these puzzles was invented in 1979 by retired Indiana architect Howard Garns. Although Garns's efforts were published back then by Dell Magazines (as *Number Place*), the Sudoku craze didn't arrive in earnest until 2005.

▼

ANY odd perfect square > 1 can generate a Pythagorean triple by first representing that square as the sum of two consecutive integers—in this case, $81 = 40 + 41$. The triple $(9, 40, 41)$—where 9 is the square root of 81— can be seen to satisfy the usual $a^2 + b^2 = c^2$ equation. Of course, there's a much better-known famous separation of 81 into 40 and 41, and it goes like this:

> Lizzie Borden took an axe
> And gave her mother forty whacks.
> And when she saw what she had done
> She gave her father forty-one.

▼

THE eighth letter of the alphabet is H, and the first letter of the alphabet is of course A. Put the two together and you have the reason why 81 is used as an insignia by the Hell's Angels motorcycle club.

▼

FOR any four positive numbers p, q, r, and s, the following relation holds:

$$(p^2 + p + 1)(q^2 + q + 1)(r^2 + r + 1)(s^2 + s + 1) / pqrs \geq 81$$

By rewriting the left-hand side in a suitable way, can you prove the inequality? (Note that if p, q, r, and s all equal 1, you get $3^4 \geq 81$, which is actually an equality in this case.) (See Answers.)

82 $\left[\,2 \times 41\,\right]$

THERE are 82 different shapes (called hexahexes) that can be created by joining six hexagons along their edges. This diagram uses these 82 shapes to form a giant hexagon plus some trim. Note the nice touch of taking the unique hexahex with a hole in the middle and placing it in the center of the construction.

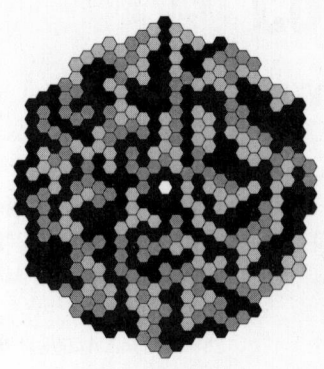

A standard dartboard has a total of 82 regions (20 wedges with four regions apiece, plus the inner and outer bull in the center). The numbers around the circumference provide the scores for the corresponding wedges, and the credit (or blame) for their peculiar arrangement is generally given to nineteenth-century British carpenter Brian Gamlin. By placing small numbers around the desired big numbers, Gamlin's system penalizes inaccuracy and therefore discourages risk-taking. On that latter note, the left side of the board is sometimes called the married man's side, as it is the better option for those who want to play it safe.

MOVING to winter sports in North America, the National Basketball Association and the National Hockey League both have regular seasons consisting of 82 games.

83 [prime]

WHAT property unites the following 83 five-digit numbers? (Commas within the numbers are deleted so as not to drive you batty.) (See Answers.)

0   11826, 12363, 12543, 14676, 15681, 15963, 18072, 19023, 19377, 19569, 19629, 20316, 22887, 23019, 23178, 23439, 24237, 24276, 24441, 24807, 25059, 25572, 25941, 26409, 26733, 27129, 27273, 29034, 29106, 30384

2   12586, 13343, 14098, 17816, 21397, 21901, 23728, 28256, 28346

5   10136, 13147, 13268, 16549, 20513, 21877, 25279, 26152, 27209, 28582

8   10124, 10214, 14743, 15353, 17252, 20089, 21439, 22175, 22456, 23113, 26351, 28171

9   10128, 10278, 12582, 13278, 13434, 13545, 13698, 14442, 14766, 16854, 17529, 17778, 20754, 21744, 21801, 23682, 23889, 24009, 27105, 27984, 28731, 29208

There is a huge hint to this puzzle elsewhere in this book. For now, though, your only hint—other than the left-hand marking numbers, whose meaning you'll have to figure out—is that the only numbers that could conceivably have this property must be between 10000 and 31622. But the numbers above are the only 83 that actually work.

▼

IF you list all the positive integers from 1 to 500,000,000, how many 1's appear altogether? And why is this question being asked here, on the page for the number 83? (See Answers.)

84 $\left[2^2 \times 3 \times 7 \right]$

ONE of history's oldest and best-known algebra problems goes by the name of Diophantus's Riddle, and it reads as follows:

"Here lies Diophantus," the wonder behold. Through art algebraic, the stone tells how old: "God gave him his boyhood one-sixth of his life, One-twelfth more as youth while whiskers grew rife; And then yet one-seventh ere marriage begun; In five years there came a bouncing new son. Alas, the dear child of master and sage, after attaining half the measure of his father's life chill fate took him. After consoling his fate by the science of numbers for four years, he ended his life."

How old was Diophantus when he died? The solution is readily obtained by converting the text into a simple algebraic equation with a single variable. If you let x = Diophantus's age, then, according to the text, $\frac{x}{6} + \frac{x}{12} + \frac{x}{7} + 5 + \frac{x}{2} + 4 = x$.

Note that the least common denominator of 6, 12, and 7 equals 84. Reworking the equation yields $14x + 7x + 12x + 42x + (84 \times 9) = 84x$, so $75x + (84 \times 9) = 84x$, therefore $84 \times 9 = 9x$ and therefore $x = 84$.

History did record that Diophantus had a son who died at age 42.

▼

ON the subject of old mathematical puzzles, the Rhind Papyrus of the Egyptian Middle Kingdom (circa 1650 BC) contained 84 mathematics problems of various sorts. Rhind was actually a Scotsman, not an Egyptian: He purchased the papyrus in 1858 in Luxor, Egypt, following its discovery there in what may have been illegal excavations. The papyrus measures about a foot wide and 18 feet long. It also goes by the name Ahmes Papyrus, in honor of the scribe who copied it down way back when.

In one of the problems, Ahmes appears to equate the area of a circular field whose diameter is nine units with the area of a square having a side of eight units. Such an inequality would imply that the ratio of the circumference of that circle to its diameter—a ratio we recognize immediately as the definition of π—would be $3\frac{1}{6}$, not exactly right but perhaps not bad by 1650 BC standards.

85 $\left[\, 5 \times 17 \,\right]$

"A well-tied tie is the first serious step in life."
—Oscar Wilde, c. 1880, *A Woman of No Importance*

IN Oscar Wilde's day, the traditional four-in-hand knot (shown above) was really the only thing going, at least for conventional neckties. The full and half Windsor knots didn't come until the 1930s, and the Pratt knot, invented by Jerry Pratt and popularized by news anchorman Don Shelby, took another fifty years to emerge. But necktie history was accelerated in 1999, when Cambridge University's Thomas Fink and Yong Mao determined through exhaustive study that there are precisely 85 ways of tying a necktie. Most of these 85 knots look absolutely terrible, but in addition to the four known knots, the two men uncovered another six knots deemed elegant enough for actual use.

Fink and Mao's methodology incorporated a basic set of six moves: R_I, R_O, C_I, C_O, L_I, and L_O, the letters denoting left to right, center, and right to left, and the subscripts denoting "out of the shirt" or "into the shirt." The ending move, or T, meant "through," as in through whatever loop had been created by the previous maneuvers. For any given number of three or more "half winds," denoted by an h, Fink and Mao computed the associated number of knots, $K(h)$, as equaling the expression $(\frac{1}{3})(2^{h-2} - (-1)^{h-2})$. The finite length of a tie, coupled with basic aesthetic principles, led Fink and Mao to limit the number of "half winds" to 9, so the total number of knots became:

$$K = \sum K(i) = 1 + 1 + 3 + 5 + 11 + 21 + 43 = 85$$

In other words, while the choice of 9 as a cutoff point had a small element of arbitrariness to it, the final result did not.

Knot sequences can be represented as random walks on a triangular/hexagonal lattice as depicted below, with the directions L, R, and C denoted by the arrows.

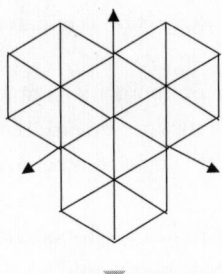

ON some old American cars, the speedometer did not exceed 85 miles per hour. Today, although speedometers uniformly allow for higher rates of speed, the posted speed limits do not.

Of course, lower speed limits are associated with fuel savings, and in that respect 85 mph does not qualify. But in certain areas of the United States, the number 85 does align itself with fuel savings, in the form of E-85, a mixture of 85% ethanol and 15% unleaded gasoline (the gasoline component promotes easier starting in cold weather, among other things). Most cars don't accept this mixture, although the development of E-85 fleets began in 1992.

ETHANOL derives from corn, and the number 85 makes a final appearance in the direct payment formula for farmers of corn and other commodities, the underlying assumption being that farmers use 85% of their "base" acreage:

$$DP_{corn} = (Payment\ rate)_{corn} \times (Payment\ yield)_{corn} \times [(Base\ acres)_{corn} \times 0.85]$$

86 $[\,2 \times 43\,]$

TO "eighty-six" something means to get rid of it. How, you may ask, did this usage come to be? The list of possible explanations sounds like a takeoff of *What's My Line?* or some other TV guessing game show. The following explanations suggest that the expression originated in New York City:

A. At New York's famous Delmonico's restaurant, the house steak was number 86 on the menu. Because the restaurant frequently ran out of this item, "86" came to mean something that was no longer available.

B. Article 86 of the New York state liquor code defined the conditions under which a customer would not be served alcoholic beverages.

C. Chumley's, a well-known New York speakeasy, was located at 86 Bedford Street.

D. The elevators at the Empire State Building stop at the eighty-sixth floor.

Alternative explanations include the observation that missing soldiers came to be known as "86'ed" because being AWOL was a violation of Subchapter X Article 86 of the Uniform Code of Military Justice. Finally, there is the theory that the expression is simply a variation of the phrase "deep six." Unfortunately, this last explanation, though the least colorful, is the choice of most etymologists. We close the discussion by noting that Agent 86, otherwise known as Maxwell Smart of *Get Smart* fame, apparently got his number for its suggestion of expendability. But as long as the public maintains its thirst for bogus explanations, I would point out that *Danger Man*, starring Patrick McGoohan (known as *Secret Agent* in the United States), ran for precisely 86 episodes and was created by a gentleman named Ralph Smart.

$2^{86} = 77{,}371{,}252{,}455{,}336{,}267{,}181{,}195{,}264$, a number with no zeroes. No larger power of 2 is known to be zero-free.

87 $\left[\, 3 \times 29 \,\right]$

THE number 87 is spoken as *quatre-vingts sept* in French—literally "four twenties and a seven." This construction was made famous in America by Abraham Lincoln's Gettysburg Address, which began "Fourscore and seven years ago," a recognition of the 87 years between the signing of the Declaration of Independence in 1776 and the Battle of Gettysburg in 1863.

THE word *decimoctoseptology* won't be found in any dictionary, but it means the study of the number 87, at least to a handful of practitioners who share the quirky view that 87 is the most random number.

IN Australian cricket, a score of 87 is considered unlucky. The superstition supposedly began in 1929 when superstar-to-be Keith Miller went to the Melbourne Cricket Ground to watch legendary batsman Don Bradman bat for New South Wales against Harry "Bull" Alexander of Victoria. Miller, who was but 10 years of age at the time, recalled that Bradman was on 87 when Alexander bowled him. When Miller came of age as a cricketeer, he and South Melbourne teammate Ian Johnson would apparently nudge each other when a batsman or opposing team reached 87, the idea being that an unusual number of batsmen were retired on that number.

Not surprisingly, the data don't support the idea that batsmen fall on 87 any more than on surrounding numbers. Even worse, Miller's memory seems to have failed him, as Bradman was actually on 89 when Alexander bowled him. Yet the reputation of 87 as the "devil's number" endures. The final straw came in 1993, when Bull Alexander died . . . at age 87.

CERTAINLY 87 isn't considered an unlucky number in hockey. Legendary Canadian junior player Sidney Crosby chose 87 as his uniform number because of his birthdate (8/7/87), and continued to wear the number upon entering the NHL in 2005.

▼

THERE are 87 numbers whose squares are a rearrangement of the ten digits 0, 1, 2, 3, 4, 5, 6, 7, 8, and 9 ($32043^2 = 1026753849$, and so on):

32043, 32286, 33144, 35172, 39147, 45624, 55446, 68763, 83919, 99066
35337, 35757, 35853, 37176, 37905, 38772, 39336, 40545, 42744, 43902,
44016, 45567, 46587, 48852, 49314, 49353, 50706, 53976, 54918, 55524,
55581, 55626, 56532, 57321, 58413, 58455, 58554, 59403, 60984, 61575,
61866, 62679, 62961, 63051, 63129, 65634, 65637, 66105, 66276, 67677,
68781, 69513, 71433, 72621, 75759, 76047, 76182, 77346, 78072, 78453,
80361, 80445, 81222, 81945, 84648, 85353, 85743, 85803, 86073, 87639,
88623, 89079, 89145, 89355, 89523, 90144, 90153, 90198, 91248, 91605,
92214, 94695, 95154, 96702, 97779, 98055, 98802

88 $\left[\, 2^3 \times 11 \,\right]$

A piano has 88 keys. There being 7 white keys and 5 black keys to an octave, the full keyboard consists of slightly more than 7 octaves.

▼

AN n-digit number is called "narcissistic" if the sum of the nth powers of its digits equals the number itself. All one-digit numbers are narcissistic by definition, but narcissism gets increasingly rare as the number of digits goes up. Altogether there are 88 narcissistic numbers, the largest being the 39-digit monstrosity 115,132,219,018,763,992,565,095,597,973,971,522,401.

That's right: $1^{39} + 1^{39} + 5^{39} + 1^{39} + 3^{39} + 2^{39} + 2^{39} + 1^{39} + 9^{39} + 0^{39} + 1^{39} + 8^{39} + 7^{39} + 6^{39} + 3^{39} + 9^{39} + 9^{39} + 2^{39} + 5^{39} + 6^{39} + 5^{39} + 0^{39} + 9^{39} + 5^{39} + 5^{39} + 9^{39} + 7^{39} + 9^{39} + 7^{39} + 3^{39} + 9^{39} + 7^{39} + 1^{39} + 5^{39} + 2^{39} + 2^{39} + 4^{39} + 0^{39} + 1^{39} = 115,132,219,018,763,992,565,095,597,973,971,522,401.$ (See **153**.)

THE number 88 reads as *ba ba* in Chinese and has come to mean "so long" in Chinese Internet shorthand.

THE bingo call for 88 is "two fat ladies." UK residents will recognize the term as the title of a late 1990s TV show starring Clarissa Dickson Wright and the late Jennifer Paterson. The two stars drove around the countryside on a Triumph Thunderbird with a sidecar: the motorcycle's plate number was N88TFL.

IF the two fat ladies happened to be driving at 60 miles per hour, they'd be going 88 feet per second, according to a standard conversion formula:

60 miles/hour × 5280 feet/mile ÷ 3600 seconds/hour = 88 feet/second

And even 88 *miles per hour* has some historical significance, it being the speed at which Michael J. Fox's DeLorean would enter into time-travel mode in the *Back to the Future* trilogy.

88 is the fourth "untouchable" number, by which it is meant a number that is not the sum of the proper divisors of any other number. (The first three untouchable numbers are 2, 5, and 52.) Paul Erdos demonstrated the existence of infinitely many untouchable numbers, but there is only one known odd untouchable number, namely 5. Are there others? Well, oddly enough, this question is tied to Goldbach's Conjecture, one of the most famous unsolved problems in number theory. Goldbach's Conjecture, first suggested by Prussian mathematician Christian Goldbach in 1742 and still unproven at this writing, is the simple-looking assertion that any even number is the sum of two primes. Suppose for a moment that this conjecture is true, and look at the odd number $2n + 1$. According to Goldbach's conjecture, we may write $2n = p + q$ for some primes p and q. But the sum of the proper factors of the number pq is therefore $1 + p + q = 2n + 1$, so the original odd number $2n + 1$ can't be untouchable.

89 [prime $8^1 + 9^2$]

89 is the only two-digit number that can be expressed as the sum of its digits raised to the consecutive powers 1 and 2—that is, the position of the digits from left to right. (See **135** and **175**.)

▼

89 is the eleventh Fibonacci number, and the reciprocal of 89 bears a curious relationship with the Fibonacci sequence. Create a triangle of numbers such that the rightmost digit of the *n*th Fibonacci number is in the *n+1st* decimal place.

.01
.001
.0002
.00003
.000005
.0000008
.00000013
.000000021
.0000000034
etc.

_____

The sum of these numbers = .01123595505618 . . . = $\frac{1}{89}$

Although this result is surprising, the proof is relatively straightforward. The idea is to let x equal the sum in question, and then use the fundamental Fibonacci relationship ($F_{n+1} = F_n + F_{n-1}$) to produce the equation $100x - 10x - x = 1$. Because the left side equals $89x$, you get $89x = 1$, or $x = \frac{1}{89}$. What makes 89 special in this equation is not so much that it is a Fibonacci number, but that it equals $100 - 10 - 1$.

▼

THE appearance of Fibonacci numbers in nature is well-known if not always exact. It seems that sunflowers often have 55 (F_{10}) clockwise spirals and 89 (F_{11}) counterclockwise spirals.

89 is a Sophie Germain prime, meaning that $2 \times 89 + 1$ is also prime. As it happens, starting with 89 and continuing in this fashion creates a sequence of six primes, given below. (The longest-known such chain contains 16 primes, starting with 810,433,818,265,726,529,159.)

89	2A + 1	2B + 1	2C + 1	2D + 1	2E + 1
89	179	359	719	1439	2879
A	B	C	D	E	F

In 1825, Sophie Germain proved that there is no solution to the equation $x^p + y^p = z^p$ if p is a Sophie Germain prime, one small step on the road to proving Fermat's Last Theorem.

THE definition of Sophie Germain primes and the magnitude of the largest known such prime were mentioned by the characters Hal and Catherine in the 2005 film *Proof*. Not long after the film came out (May 2006), an even larger Sophie Germain prime was discovered. It has 51,780 digits, a bit much for this page, but we can describe it more compactly as $p = 137211941292195 \times 2^{171960} - 1$.

90 $\left[\ 2 \times 3^2 \times 5 \qquad 9^1 + 9^2 \qquad (15 - 9) \times (15 - 0)\ \right]$

AN angle whose measure is 90 degrees is called a right angle. In radian measure, 90 degrees corresponds to $\frac{\pi}{2}$ radians.

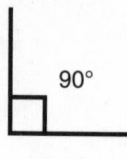

A baseball diamond not only has four right angles; it has 90 feet between bases. Said columnist Red Smith (1905–1982), "Ninety feet between home and first base is perhaps as close as man has ever come to perfection."

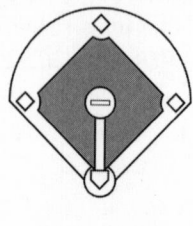

THE pattern below is a sample of dried-out mud. Although the pattern contains much curvature, the equilibrating pressures at intersecting lines create angles very close to 90 degrees.

IN *Gulliver's Travels*, the people of Laputa evidently lacked instruments such as the T-square, whose purpose is to create 90-degree angles. Wrote Swift, "Their houses are very ill built, the walls bevil, without one right angle in any apartment."

▼

THE number of primes less than 90 equals the number of integers less than 90 that are *relatively* prime to 90 (i.e., share no common factor with 90). There are only 7 numbers with this same property, and 90 is the largest of those seven. (The others are 2, 3, 4, 8, 14, and 20.) So, for example, there are six primes less than 14 (2, 3, 5, 7, 11, and 13) and six numbers less than 14 that are relatively prime to 14 (1, 3, 5, 9, 11, and 13).

91 $\left[\, 7 \times 13 \,\right]$

IN the card game Diamond Points, the diamond suit is separated from the rest of a deck of cards and is placed facedown in a stack. Players (two or three, ideally) are each given another suit. The diamonds are revealed one at a time and players vie for the points represented by the diamond (Ace = 1 . . . King = 13) by selecting a card from their given suit, the high card winning the "diamond points." In a two-player game, it is sufficient to win 46 points, because the total number of diamond points equals $1 + 2 + . . . + 13 = 91$. You will perhaps recognize this last equation as establishing 91 as the thirteenth triangular number.

▼

THE equation $91 = 1^2 + 2^2 + 3^2 + 4^2 + 5^2 + 6^2$ shows that 91 is the sum of the first six squares, so 91 is a square-pyramidal number, and is the first triangular and square-pyramidal number that we have encountered since 55. But that gap is stunningly small for such a mathematical rarity. The next number that is both triangular and square-pyramidal—208,335—is also the *last* number with both properties.

BY using negative numbers, we can write 91 as the sum of two cubes in two different ways, namely $91 = 4^3 + 3^3 = 6^3 + (-5)^3$.

We can also write $91 = 1 + 5 + 10 + 25 + 50$, so if you had every US coin short of a silver dollar, you'd have a total of 91 cents. Elsewhere in the world of US finance, the term "91-day T-bill" arises because 91 days represents one-quarter of a year. Bills that mature in 91 days are the shortest maturity securities issued by the US Treasury.

THE multiplication table for 91 yields a cute result. If you look at the three columns individually, they speak for themselves:

91	×	1	=	9 1
		2	=	1 8 2
		3	=	2 7 3
		4	=	3 6 4
		5	=	4 5 5
		6	=	5 4 6
		7	=	6 3 7
		8	=	7 2 8
		9	=	8 1 9

ONE classic version of the abacus consists of 13 columns, each with 7 disks, for a total of 91 disks. The Babylonians are credited with the earliest form of the abacus, and calculations using the abacus are referenced in the writings of Greek scholars such as Herodotus and

Demosthenes. The separation of the abacus into two zones is a Japanese innovation, and the instrument is of course associated with the Far East

to this day. Perhaps the greatest day in abacus history came in 1946, when abacus-wielding Kiyoshi Matsuzaki won a speed calculation contest against a US Army Private (T. N. Wood) equipped with a state-of-the-art mechanical calculator.

The worst day in abacus history, probably during the same era, came when an abacus salesman entered a restaurant in Brazil and challenged a customer to a calculating contest. Although the salesman proved to be the speedier one at addition and multiplication, he faltered upon upping the ante to *raios cubicos*, or cube roots. His specific undoing was in choosing 1729.03, a number that the customer recognized as just fractionally higher than 1728, or 12 cubed. Within seconds, the customer jotted down 12.002 as the cube root of 1729.03, an estimate that left the abacus salesman in the dust. The salesman left in disgrace, presumably never knowing that the man in the restaurant was none other than Richard Feynman, a Nobel laureate-to-be and one of the most sparkling minds of his generation.

92 $\left[\, 2^2 \times 23 \,\right]$

THERE are 92 ways of placing 8 queens on an 8 × 8 chessboard such that no queen is under attack from another. Below are the 12 basic solutions, which grow to 92 by suitable rotations and reflections (as long as you don't mind having a black square in the lower right-hand corner, contrary to the orientation of the board in an actual chess game):

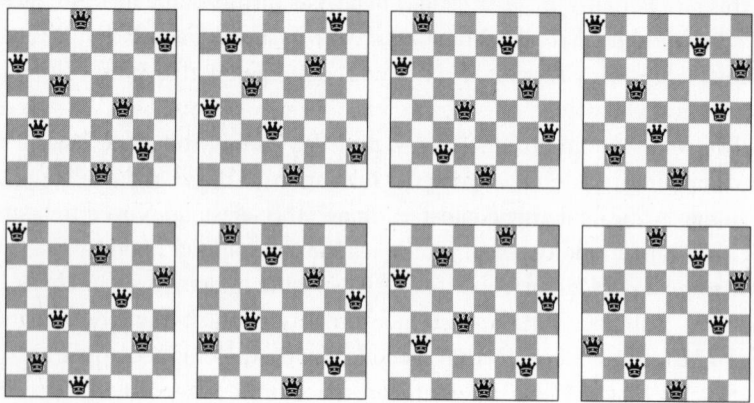

Let's think about that last sentence for just a minute. Exactly how do you go from 12 to 92? It's not obvious, is it? If you start with, say, the top-left image, you can rotate it in any of four ways (three 90-degree turns and another to return to the starting position) and you can reflect it in two ways (upside down or right-side up). Altogether that's $4 \times 2 = 8$ solutions out of that one image. If you followed the same procedure with each of the 12 images, you'd expect to generate $8 \times 12 = 96$ total solutions. But in real life you only get to 92, a number that isn't even divisible by 12. What gives?

The answer is that one of the 12 basic solutions doesn't quite carry its own weight. The rogue is the very last one, at the bottom right. Because the queens in that solution are placed symmetrically with respect to the center of the board, rotations and reflections only produce 4 solutions, not 8, so the total number is $8 \times 11 + 4 = 92$.

The 8-queens puzzle was introduced in 1848 by a chess player named Max Bezzel. The problem was solved in 1850 by Franz Nauck, who extended the problem to queens on an $n \times n$ chessboard, where n can take any value. For example, on a 24×24 board, the total number of solutions equals 2,275,141,71,973,736. It is unreasonable to ask that you produce all of these solutions, so here's an easier, somewhat related problem: What is the smallest number of queens that can be placed on an 8×8 chessboard so that every square is attacked by at least one of the queens? (See Answers.)

93 $\left[\, 3 \times 31 \,\right]$

THE first time a schoolchild is apt to encounter the number 93 is upon learning that the sun is, on average, 93 million miles from Earth. That distance is officially known as an astronomical unit. The defrocked planet Pluto, for example, is 39.5 AUs from the sun, plus or minus 9.8 depending on Pluto's position along its elliptical orbit. Progress in astronomy being what it was, the AU was in use as a relative measure long before scientists knew what its exact distance was.

▼

QUATREVINGT-TREIZE was Victor Hugo's final novel. The reference of the book's title is to 1793, the most horrific year of the French Revolution, and in particular the year in which Marie Antoinette of "Let them eat cake" fame was sent to the guillotine.

▼

OF course, had the French put the guillotine to a more benign use they would have discovered that it is possible to cut a cake into 93 pieces using only 8 straight cuts.

And we can generate that number by taking advantage of a tidy mathematical relationship between cutting in three dimensions versus just two.

Recall (see **22**) that in two dimensions the number of pieces of pizza that can be generated from n straight cuts equals $\frac{(n^2 + n + 2)}{2}$, or just 1 more than the nth triangular number. (The discussion there involved drawing straight lines, as opposed to making cuts, but the two approaches are equivalent.) Here's how the two-dimensional sequence begins:

# of cuts (n):	0	1	2	3	4	5	6	7	8	9	10
		+	+	+	+	+	+	+	+	+	+
Max # pieces from n cuts in 2 dimensions	1	2	4	7	11	16	22	29	37	46	56

To explain the plus signs, once you place a 1 at beginning of the bottom row, each of the following numbers in that row can be obtained by adding the number to its left to the number above it—in other words, you add along the diagonals and then drop. Let's try that same procedure, replacing the top row with the bottom row (except that we add a 0 in the first position) and again starting with a solitary 1 on the new bottom row:

0	1	2	4	7	11	16	22	29
+	+	+	+	+	+	+	+	
1								

In short order the table fills out as below.

# of cuts (n):	0	1	2	3	4	5	6	7	8
2-dim seq for (n-1)	0	1	2	4	7	11	16	22	29
		+	+	+	+	+	+	+	+
Max # of pieces from n cuts in 3 dimensions	1	2	4	8	15	26	42	64	93

Remarkably, the bottom row now consists of the maximum number of pieces that can be generated by n cuts in *three* dimensions, culminating with 93 pieces from 8 cuts. (Pizza is considered two-dimensional in this cutting exercise, whereas a cake represents a three-dimensional object.)

What makes the following 93 numbers special? And what is different about the ones in boldface? (See Answers.)

10301 10501 10601 11311 **11411 12421 12721 12821 13331** 13831 13931 14341 **14741**
15451 15551 16061 16361 16561 **16661** 17471 17971 18181 18481 19391 **19891** 19991
30103 30203 30403 **30703 30803 31013 31513 32323 32423** 33533 34543 34843
35053 35153 35353 35753 **36263** 36563 37273 37573 **38083 38183** 38783 39293
70207 **70507 70607** 71317 71917 **72227 72727** 73037 73237 73637 **74047 74747**
75557 **76367 76667 77377 77477 77977** 78487 78787 78887 79397 **79697 79997**

90709 91019 93139 **93239** 93739 94049 94349 **94649** 94849 **94949**
95959 96269 96469 **96769** 97379 97579 97879 98389 98689

The only hint you'll get is that these two questions, although juxtaposed, are on completely different wavelengths.

94 $[\,2 \times 47\,]$

THE factorization of 94 tells us at a glance that it is not divisible by 4. When the Winter Olympics were held in Lillehammer, Norway, in 1994, it marked the first time that the Modern Olympics, either summer or winter, were held on a year not divisible by 4. The idea introduced at that time was to stagger the winter and summer games, creating Olympic action every two years rather than a whole lot of action every four years. From this point forward, the Olympic Games will operate on two separate four-year cycles, with the summer games taking years divisible by 4 and the winter games the remaining even years: as a mathematician would say, those years that are congruent to 2, mod 4.

BOTH digits in 94 are perfect squares, as demonstrated by the diagram, which has nine dots altogether, four of which are white. But this diagram is the beginning of a very different route to the number 94. On the next page we see that there are plenty of other ways to choose four points so as to form a quadrilateral, from the trapezoid on the left to the parallelogram to the kite (yes, that's what the third figure is called) and finally to the nameless figure on the far right (and plenty more).

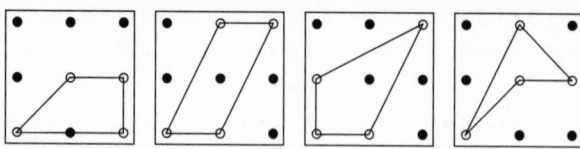

How many ways can four points be chosen so that their vertices form a quadrilateral? Altogether it is possible to form 6 squares, 4 rectangles, 12 parallelograms, 28 trapezoids, 8 kites, 16 other convex shapes, and 24 non-convex shapes, for a total of 94.

▼

CHECK out the measurements of the following old ships:

Ship	Launched	Tonnage	Crew
HMS *Speedy*	1782	208 8/94	90
HMS *Dart*	1796	386 16/94	140
HMS *Lively*	1804	1071 90/94	284
HMS *Surprise*	1794	578 73/94	200
HMS *Boadicea*	1797	1052 5/94	282

What's with the 94's in the denominators? They arise from the formula for Builder's Old Measurement, the prevailing standard for a ship's cargo-carrying capacity (tonnage) until the introduction of steam propulsion in the mid-nineteenth century. The precise formula is given by $T = (L - 3B/5)B^2/2/94$, where T = tonnage, L = length, and B = breadth. (Thames

Measurement, a predecessor formula for a ship's capacity, has a slightly different formula but was also characterized by a 94 in the denominator.)

Of course, all this still doesn't explain where the 94 in the formula comes from. Its origin turns out to depend on an old standard declaring that a ship's tax burden should be $\frac{3}{5}$ of its displacement. The formula for displacement is Length $\times$ Beam $\times$ Draft $\times$ Block Coefficient, all divided by 35 cubic feet per ton of seawater. The Beam is defined as the ship's widest point, while the Draft (the distance between the bottom of the ship and the water line, is estimated to be half the Beam. The Block Coefficient is estimated at 0.62; if you draw a box around the submerged portion of the ship, the block coefficient is the fraction of that box represented by the ship's volume. Multiplying $\frac{3}{5}$ by .62 and dividing by 35 gets us awfully close to $\frac{1}{94}$, hence the appearance of that fraction in the final formula.

I know. That was a lot of work just to track down a weird denominator, but there you have it.

95 $\left[\, 5 \times 19 \,\right]$

THE number 95 plays a time-honored role with respect to survey data and confidence intervals. When a poll is released indicating that, say, 57% of the respondents favor a certain political candidate, underlying this calculation is a margin of error and a confidence interval. If the poll has a margin of error of three percentage points and a confidence interval of 85%, that means that if the poll were to be conducted 100 times, you'd expect the percentage of respondents favoring that candidate would be between 54% and 60% on 85 occasions—three percentage points to either side of the announced figure. This delineation is not well understood, in part because most polls release a margin of error but not a confidence interval. The reason for this omission is that it's not really an omission at all. The vast majority of polls use a confidence interval of 95%.

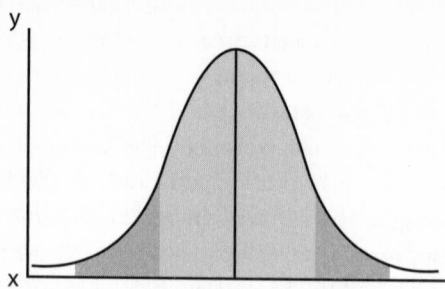

WHEN data follow a normal distribution (the bell curve shown above), the number 95 makes a more specific appearance. One nice thing about such distributions is that their means and standard deviations are either known or readily calculated. It turns out that when data follow a bell curve, 95% of all observations are within two standard deviations of the mean, as marked by the thick vertical bands to either side of the peak in the curve above.

▼

PERHAPS the most historically significant appearance of 95 came in 1517, when Martin Luther nailed his 95 Theses to the door of the Castle Church in Wittenberg, Germany. Space considerations don't permit a full listing of Luther's theses, so here is number 16, chosen for its relative lack of controversy: "Hell, purgatory, and heaven seem to differ as do despair, almost-despair, and the assurance of safety."

▼

IN computing, the list of displayable ASCII (American Standard Code for Information Interchange) characters comprises 26 uppercase letters, 26 lowercase letters, 10 digits, and 33 special characters, including punctuation. That's a grand total of 95.

96 $\left[\ 2^5 \times 3\ \right]$

FORMER major-league baseball player Bill Voiselle, a onetime pitcher for the New York Giants, Boston Braves, and Chicago Cubs, got special dispensation from the National League to wear the number 96, at the time the highest number ever worn by a major leaguer. Why? Because he grew up in the town of Ninety Six, South Carolina. The town was so named because it was thought to be 96 miles away from the Cherokee settlement Keowee (even though it really wasn't). Apparently a bill to change the name of Ninety Six to Cambridge once appeared before the state legislature, but a Ninety Six resident held up a sign with the number 96 on it, pointing out that it read the same right-side up as upside down, and so it should remain. And so it has.

$$96 = 2 + 5 + 7 + 10 + 30 + 42 \text{ and } \frac{1}{2} + \frac{1}{5} + \frac{1}{7} + \frac{1}{10} + \frac{1}{30} + \frac{1}{42} = 1$$

$$96 = 6 + 7 + 7 + 8 + 8 + 9 + 12 + 18 + 21 \text{ and } \frac{1}{6} + \frac{1}{7} + \frac{1}{7} + \frac{1}{8} + \frac{1}{8} + \frac{1}{9} + \frac{1}{12} + \frac{1}{18} + \frac{1}{21} = 1$$

ABOVE are two partitions of 96 whose reciprocals add to 1. Such a partition is called "exact." Believe it or not, there are precisely 96 exact partitions of 96.

THE game of Ishido is played on a board measuring 8 squares $\times$ 12 squares, for 96 squares altogether. Although it has the look of an ancient game, it was introduced in 1990.

97 $\left[\ \text{prime}\ \right]$

THE Gregorian calendar has a cycle of 400 years, during which time there are 97 leap years. In theory, you'd expect one leap year every four years, for a total of 100, but only one of the four "century years" in a 400-year span (the one that's divisible by 400) is a leap year.

▼

$\frac{1}{97}$ = 0.01030927 . . . Note that if you multiply the first pair of digits after the decimal point by 3, you get the second pair, and so on until you get to 27. No, this pattern doesn't continue, but it was nice while it lasted.

▼

WHEREAS a standard tarot deck consists of 78 cards, the Minchiate Tarot deck of the Renaissance contained 97. The extra cards were four Virtues (Prudence, Hope, Faith, and Charity), the four elements (Earth, Air, Fire, and Water), and the 12 signs of the zodiac. That's 20 extra cards, but for some reason the High Priestess of the standard tarot deck was not included in the Minchiate deck, so the final total was 97.

▼

WHEN written out, NINETY-SEVEN alternates consonants and vowels, and is the longest number to do so. Sort of. Can you come up with a longer one? (See Answers.)

▼

THERE are 97 ways of using the 10 digits 0 through 9 to form two fractions that add up to 1. On the assumption that you might not believe me, here they are:

$$\frac{3485}{6970} + \frac{1}{2} \qquad \frac{3548}{7096} + \frac{1}{2} \qquad \frac{3845}{7690} + \frac{1}{2} \qquad \frac{4538}{9076} + \frac{1}{2}$$

$$\frac{4685}{9370} + \frac{1}{2} \qquad \frac{4835}{9670} + \frac{1}{2} \qquad \frac{4853}{9706} + \frac{1}{2} \qquad \frac{4865}{9730} + \frac{1}{2}$$

$$\frac{7365}{9820} + \frac{1}{4} \qquad \frac{3079}{6158} + \frac{2}{4} \qquad \frac{1278}{6390} + \frac{4}{5} \qquad \frac{1872}{9360} + \frac{4}{5}$$

$$\frac{7835}{9402} + \frac{1}{6} \qquad \frac{3190}{4785} + \frac{2}{6} \qquad \frac{1485}{2970} + \frac{3}{6} \qquad \frac{2079}{4158} + \frac{3}{6}$$

$$\frac{2709}{5418} + \frac{3}{6} \qquad \frac{2907}{5814} + \frac{3}{6} \qquad \frac{4851}{9702} + \frac{3}{6} \qquad \frac{4362}{5089} + \frac{1}{7}$$

$$\frac{5940}{8316} + \frac{2}{7} \qquad \frac{6810}{9534} + \frac{2}{7} \qquad \frac{5803}{7461} + \frac{2}{9} \qquad \frac{1208}{5436} + \frac{7}{9}$$

$$\frac{1352}{6084} + \frac{7}{9} \qquad \frac{729}{3645} + \frac{8}{10} \qquad \frac{927}{4635} + \frac{8}{10} \qquad \frac{876}{3504} + \frac{9}{12}$$

$$\frac{485}{970} + \frac{13}{26} \qquad \frac{369}{574} + \frac{10}{28} \qquad \frac{486}{972} + \frac{15}{30} \qquad \frac{485}{970} + \frac{16}{32}$$

$$\frac{287}{369} + \frac{10}{45} \qquad \frac{728}{936} + \frac{10}{45} \qquad \frac{169}{507} + \frac{32}{48} \qquad \frac{269}{807} + \frac{34}{51}$$

$$\frac{204}{867} + \frac{39}{51} \qquad \frac{678}{904} + \frac{13}{52} \qquad \frac{893}{1026} + \frac{7}{54} \qquad \frac{609}{783} + \frac{12}{54}$$

$$\frac{309}{618} + \frac{27}{54} \qquad \frac{308}{462} + \frac{19}{57} \qquad \frac{273}{406} + \frac{19}{58} \qquad \frac{307}{614} + \frac{29}{58}$$

$$\frac{748}{935} + \frac{12}{60} \qquad \frac{207}{549} + \frac{38}{61} \qquad \frac{208}{793} + \frac{45}{61} \qquad \frac{485}{970} + \frac{31}{62}$$

$$\frac{507}{819} + \frac{24}{63} \qquad \frac{284}{710} + \frac{39}{65} \qquad \frac{148}{296} + \frac{35}{70} \qquad \frac{481}{962} + \frac{35}{70}$$

$$\frac{145}{290} + \frac{38}{76} \qquad \frac{451}{902} + \frac{38}{76} \qquad \frac{417}{695} + \frac{32}{80} \qquad \frac{306}{459} + \frac{27}{81}$$

$$\frac{630}{945} + \frac{27}{81} \qquad \frac{405}{729} + \frac{36}{81} \qquad \frac{540}{972} + \frac{36}{81} \qquad \frac{60}{1245} + \frac{79}{83}$$

$$\frac{109}{327} + \frac{56}{84} \qquad \frac{307}{921} + \frac{56}{84} \qquad \frac{310}{465} + \frac{29}{87} \qquad \frac{315}{609} + \frac{42}{87}$$

$$\frac{231}{609} + \frac{54}{87} \qquad \frac{504}{623} + \frac{17}{89} \qquad \frac{105}{623} + \frac{74}{89} \qquad \frac{276}{345} + \frac{18}{90}$$

$$\frac{372}{465} + \frac{18}{90} \qquad \frac{138}{276} + \frac{45}{90} \qquad \frac{186}{372} + \frac{45}{90} \qquad \frac{381}{762} + \frac{45}{90}$$

$$\frac{185}{370} + \frac{46}{92} \qquad \frac{140}{368} + \frac{57}{92} \qquad \frac{426}{710} + \frac{38}{95} \qquad \frac{473}{528} + \frac{10}{96}$$

$$\frac{357}{408} + \frac{12}{96} \qquad \frac{735}{840} + \frac{12}{96} \qquad \frac{375}{480} + \frac{21}{96} \qquad \frac{531}{708} + \frac{24}{96}$$

$$\frac{135}{270} + \frac{48}{96} \qquad \frac{351}{702} + \frac{48}{96} \qquad \frac{143}{528} + \frac{70}{96} \qquad \frac{34}{578} + \frac{96}{102}$$

$$\frac{693}{728} + \frac{5}{104} \qquad \frac{59}{236} + \frac{78}{104} \qquad \frac{63}{728} + \frac{95}{104} \qquad \frac{56}{832} + \frac{97}{104}$$

$$\frac{56}{428} + \frac{93}{107} \qquad \frac{87}{435} + \frac{96}{120} \qquad \frac{496}{508} + \frac{3}{127} \qquad \frac{57}{204} + \frac{98}{136}$$

$$\frac{795}{810} + \frac{6}{324} \qquad \frac{684}{702} + \frac{9}{351} \qquad \frac{792}{801} + \frac{4}{356} \qquad \frac{693}{704} + \frac{8}{512}$$

$$\frac{792}{801} + \frac{6}{534}$$

98 $\left[\, 2 \times 7^2 \,\right]$

THE number 98 makes a pivotal appearance in the "potato paradox." Specifically, suppose you start with 100 pounds of potatoes, which you understand to be 99% water. Over time, as the water in the potatoes evaporates, this percentage figure decreases. By the time the potatoes are 98% water, how much do they weigh? (See Answers.)

▼

PICTURED is one of 98 theoretical tic-tac-toe (noughts and crosses) patterns in which **X** has a win. However, not all of these positions are realizable in an actual game, because in some of those patterns **O** would also have a win. (See **62**.) Of course, any game of tic-tac-toe that is not a draw is pretty suspect to begin with, so you're more likely to encounter the above outcome in a game of *random* tic-tac-toe.

X	X	X
O	O	X
O	X	O

▼

AS of the year 2000, 98 is the highest number that can be worn by players in the National Hockey League. Of course, this has less to do with the number 98 than with the fact that (1) no player can wear a number with more than two digits, and (2) 2000 was the year in which the league permanently retired the 99 worn by Wayne Gretzky from 1978 to 1999. (Gretzky originally wanted Gordie Howe's number 9 back in his junior hockey days, but a teammate already had that number so he settled for 99.)

99 $\left[\ 3^2 \times 11\ \right]$

ACCORDING to Thomas Edison, who really should know, genius is 1% inspiration and 99% perspiration.

▼

IF you get a perfect score on a standardized exam, you're still "only" in the 99th percentile. In general, the percentile rank of a test score is the percentage of scores in the overall frequency distribution that are lower, and technically the highest integral value that this number can take on is 99. Of course, there's nothing preventing someone from being in the 99.99 percentile, depending on the nature of the distribution, but percentile ranks on standardized tests don't ordinarily include any decimal points. Even students who score in that rarefied territory should be humbled by another Edison quote: "We don't know a millionth of one percent about anything."

▼

POPULAR culture has seen its fair share of 99's throughout the world. Canada produced the greatest number 99 ever, hockey Hall of Famer Wayne Gretzky; America was home to Barbara Feldon, aka. Agent 99 of *Get Smart* fame; and the German rock group Nena had a smash 1983 hit with "99 Luftballons," a song that made it into English-speaking countries under the name "99 Red Balloons." The song was a Cold War protest in which a bunch of balloons got loose and crossed international borders, triggering a military overreaction.

▼

OF course, the Anglicized version of "99 Luftballons" wasn't the first song to have "99" in the title. That honor surely belongs to "99 Bottles of Beer on the Wall," which in turn derives from the British song "10 Green Bottles." The original version has presumably been sung from start to finish on many occasions, unlike its unwieldy successor.

▼

THE Muslim rosary theoretically has 99 grains, representing the 99 sacred names of Allah. The beads serve as a counting device for incantations in which these names are repeated, but in practice these grains often number 33, the same number as the beads found on Christian rosaries. Because 33 is a factor of 99, this smaller set of beads functions perfectly well as a counting mechanism.

▼

IN the original specifications for compact discs, CD Digital Audio, the CD commonly used in stereo systems, was capable of holding up to 99 tracks.

▼

IN Italian legend, there was once a king who had 99 elite bodyguards, giving the number 99 an association with quality and elegance. In modern legend, "Number 99" ice cream was allegedly so named by Italian expatriates who wanted to convey the notion of high quality. But neither legend holds up very well. Research has revealed that the bodyguards in question must have been the Vatican's Swiss Guard, a group that traditionally numbered 105. And the "99" ice cream—vanilla with a chocolate sliver—apparently was named by the Italian owners of a Scottish ice cream shop not because of any ties to ancient legend, but because the shop was located at 99 High Street. More evidence that you can't believe what you read.

100 $\left[\ 2^2 \times 5^2\ \right]$

$100 = (1 + 2 + 3 + 4)^2$ and $100 = 1 + 8 + 27 + 64 = 1^3 + 2^3 + 3^3 + 4^3$

IN general, the sum of the first n cubes equals the square of the sum of the first n integers.

▼

IN a base 10 world, it is not surprising that the number 100 shows up in some important places. For example, there are 100 cents in the dollar, the boiling point of water in the Celsius scale, aka centigrade, is 100 degrees, quite by design, and 100 is also the number of US senators, two from each of the 50 states.

THE prefix *cent-* means 100, as in century, centipede, and so forth. In French, *cent* is the word for 100 and is the biggest French number to be in alphabetical order. In fact, look what happens when you spell out the equation $2 \times 5 \times 10 = 100$ in French:

DEUX × CINQ × DIX = CENT

Each of the numbers is in alphabetical order!

PERHAPS my favorite use of the number 100 comes from China, where tradition holds that the naming of a newborn panda must wait until the cub is 100 days old.

100 equals 10 squared, and there are a couple of 10×10 squares worth noting. This 10×10 word square was sought after for many years. Although imperfect (it uses two obscure place names— Adaletabat and Dioumabana—and a hyphenated expression—nature-name), it is a remarkable accomplishment, perhaps a maximal one; the odds of someone coming along with an 11×11 square are slim indeed.

D	E	S	C	E	N	D	A	N	T
E	C	H	E	N	E	I	D	A	E
S	H	O	R	T	C	O	A	T	S
C	E	R	B	E	R	U	L	U	S
E	N	T	E	R	O	M	E	R	E
N	E	C	R	O	L	A	T	E	R
D	I	O	U	M	A	B	A	N	A
A	D	A	L	E	T	A	B	A	T
N	A	T	U	R	E	N	A	M	E
T	E	S	S	E	R	A	T	E	D

A different type of 10 × 10 square consists of 100 squares and another set of 100 smaller squares nested inside. Although we don't have the luxury of a 10-color presentation, suffice it to say that for both sets of 10 squares, each row and each column consists of 10 different colors.

This square was discovered in 1959 by E. T. Parker of Remington Rand and R. C. Bose and S. Shrikhande of the University of North Carolina. Their work put to rest a longstanding conjecture of Euler, who had posited over a century and three-quarters earlier that such a Graeco-Roman square was impossible if the side of the square was 2, 6, 10, 14 . . . and so on (in general terms, congruent to 2 modulo 4). All other sizes were known to work.

The appearance of the computer company Remington Rand (Univac) on Parker's resume suggests that the discovery was computer-aided, but in fact that wasn't the case. While it would have been possible to harness computer power to create Graeco-Roman squares of certain sizes, the work of Parker, Bose, and Shrikhande was more general, resulting in the proof of the astonishing fact that Graeco-Roman squares were in fact possible for any side lengths whatsoever other than 2 and 6. (See **36**.)

101 [prime]

DODIE Smith's 1956 novel *The Hundred and One Dalmatians* had a plotline that might seem too gruesome for younger audiences, but Walt Disney Productions made the book into a highly successful animated film in 1961 and then a live-action film in 1996.

AT age 20, Joseph Fourier asked if 17 lines could create precisely 101 points of intersection. The diagram to the right represents one of four possible families of solutions. Fourier later revolutionized algebraic and differential equations and even discovered (in 1824) the atmospheric phenomenon that would one day be known as the "greenhouse effect."

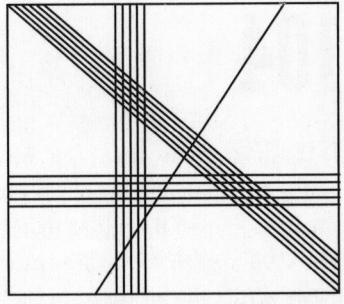

102 $\left[\, 2 \times 3 \times 17 \,\right]$

THE Empire State Building has a total of 102 stories. Upon its completion in 1931, it surpassed the Chrysler Building and 40 Wall Street to become the world's tallest building. It has its own ZIP code—10118.

103 $\left[\, \text{prime} \,\right]$

IN the play/movie *Proof*, the lead character is a mathematics professor who upon his death left 103 notebooks, the value of which would be explored by a graduate student in mathematics and his own daughter. The daughter, played by Gwyneth Paltrow in the film version, turned out to be the author of the one piece of groundbreaking mathematics contained in the notebooks.

104 $\left[\, 2^3 \times 13 \,\right]$

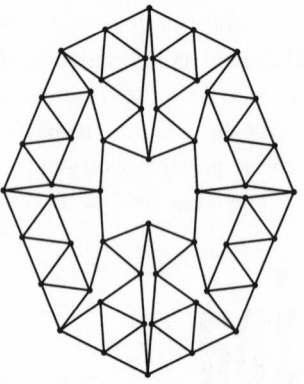

THIS diagram is the creation of German mathematician Heiko Harborth and is the smallest known 4-regular matchstick graph: The 104 matchsticks are arranged so that every vertex in the diagram has four matchsticks emanating from it.

It turns out to be impossible to create an arrangement in which *five* or more matchsticks meet at every vertex. For two matchsticks at each vertex, the answer is an equilateral triangle. Can you find the (12 matchstick) solution in which precisely three meet at each vertex? (See Answers.)

105 $\left[\, 3 \times 5 \times 7 \,\right]$

THE smallest number to have three distinct odd prime factors is 105. In advanced mathematics, this fact leads to a surprising result involving $\Phi_{105}(x)$—the so-called cyclotomic polynomial of degree 105. For any positive integer n, cyclotomic polynomials are the building blocks for the expression $x^n - 1$, and they take on some simple forms, as in

$\Phi_2(x) = x + 1$

$\Phi_4(x) = x^2 + 1$

$\Phi_7(x) = x^6 + x^5 + x^4 + x^3 + x^2 + x + 1$

Anyway, it's not much of a punch line, but $\Phi_{105}(x)$ is the first cyclotomic polynomial having any coefficients other than 1 and -1.

106 $\left[\, 2 \times 53 \,\right]$

THE New York Philharmonic, by the numbers:

Violin	33
Viola	12
Cello	11
Bass	9
Flute	4
Piccolo	1
Oboe	2
English horn	1
Clarinet	4
E-flat clarinet	1
Bass clarinet	1
Bassoon	4
Contrabassoon	1
Horn	6
Trumpet	3
Trombone	3
Bass trombone	1
Tuba	1
Timpani	1
Percussion	2
Harp	1
Harpsichord	1
Piano	2
Organ	1
TOTAL	**106**

107 [prime]

AM radio signals are assigned within a band between 535 and 1605 kilohertz (kHz). Since each frequency has a bandwidth of 10 kHz, there are $\frac{(1605 - 535)}{10}$ = 107 possible carrier frequencies in any given area.

108 [$2^2 \times 3^3$]

PERHAPS the best-known mathematical appearance of 108 comes from the regular pentagon, in which each of the five interior angles measures 108 degrees.

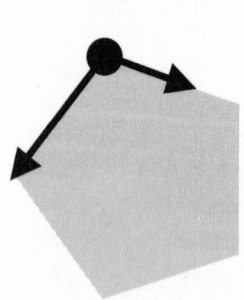

THIS particular pentagon is nested inside a pair of clock hands set at 3:36. Note that the product of the hours and minutes is 3 × 36 = 108 = the number of degrees between the two hands. Can you find the two other times that have this property? (See Answers.)

IN Homer's *Odyssey*, Penelope was wooed by 108 suitors during Odysseus's absence.

THERE are 108 double stitches on an official Major League baseball.

THE game of canasta uses 108 cards—two full decks plus 4 jokers.

109 [prime]

TWICE the sum of the first 109 integers equals 10,900 + 1090.

$\frac{1}{109}$ is a 108-digit repeating decimal that ends with 853211—the beginning of the Fibonacci sequence, only backward. Specifically, if you take the first 109 Fibonacci numbers and divide each by 10 raised to the power of 109 MINUS its position in the Fibonacci sequence (including 0), the sum of those 109 numbers is $\frac{1}{109}$. (See **89**.)

110 [$2 \times 5 \times 11$ $\quad$ $5^2 + 6^2 + 7^2$]

TO J.R.R. Tolkien, 110 was "eleventy." To readers of *Scientific American*, it was the number of regions in this William McGregor drawing, used by Martin Gardner as an April Fool's prank in 1975. Gardner claimed that this pattern could not be colored using only four colors, and many believed him. Just one year later, however, Appel and Haken proved that four colors were sufficient for any map. (See **4**.)

111 $\left[\, 3 \times 37 \,\right]$

ANY 6 × 6 magic square has the property that the sum of any row, column, or diagonal equals 111. (The general formula for the magic constant of an $n \times n$ square is $\frac{(n^3 + n)}{2}$, and $111 = \frac{(6^3 + 6)}{2}$.) The pictured square dates back to the Middle Ages, when magic squares were accorded mystical properties. Speaking of sixes, 111 is the smallest number requiring six syllables in English, although the British style ("and" included) brings the total to seven.

6	32	3	34	35	1
7	11	27	28	8	30
19	14	16	15	23	24
18	20	22	21	17	13
25	29	10	9	26	12
36	5	33	4	2	31

112 $\left[\, 2^4 \times 7 \,\right]$

WE saw in **21** that the smallest possible dissection of a square into squares with *distinct* integral sides requires that the large square be 112 units per side.

▼

IN 1945, the US Occupation Forces published "112 Gripes About the French" as a guide for troops stationed there. The title sounds like an effort to ridicule, but the actual purpose of the book was to promote cultural and historical understanding. As in:

6. We're always pulling the French out of a jam. Did they ever do anything for us?
The answer is yes, if you count the American Revolution, as in General Lafayette, 45,000 French army volunteers crossing the Atlantic in small boats, and over $6,000,000 in loans when a million dollars was a lot of money. And so on.

113 [prime]

$\frac{355}{113}$ is an extremely good approximation of π ($\frac{355}{113} = 3.1415929\ldots$, while $\pi = 3.1415926\ldots$). It was discovered in the fifth century AD by Chinese mathematician and astronomer Tsu Ch'ung-Chih.

114 [2 × 3 × 19]

THE number 114 apparently held special fascination for film director Stanley Kubrick, who brought us the CRM 114 radio in *Dr. Strangelove* and Serum 114, with which Alex was injected in *A Clockwork Orange*.

115 $\left[\, 5 \times 23 \,\right]$

THE Rule of 115 works just like the Rule of 72 (see **72**), except that it involves tripling instead of doubling. To find out how long it takes an investment to triple in value, divide the expected annual return into 115. For example, using the factorization of 115 above, an investment that returns 5% per year will triple in approximately 23 years. Just as the Rule of 72 works because 0.72 is close to the natural logarithm (base e) of 2, 1.15 is close to the natural logarithm of 3.

116 $\left[\, 2^2 \times 29 \,\right]$

THE Hundred Years' War between England and France was actually a series of conflicts between 1337 and 1453, a span of 116 years.

117 $\left[\, 3^2 \times 13 \,\right]$

THIS diagram shows a Heronian tetrahedron—a tetrahedron in which the sides (labeled in the diagram), faces, and volume are all rational numbers (fractions). The depicted figure is the *integral* Heronian tetrahedron whose largest side (117) is the smallest possible. (Yes, you read that right.) Its surface areas are 1170, 1800, 1890, and 2016 square units, and its volume is 18,144 cubic units.

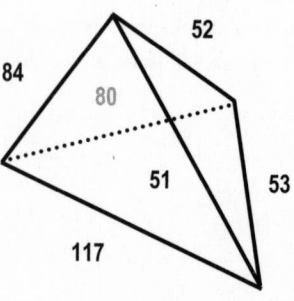

118 $\left[\, 2 \times 59 \,\right]$

THE shortest ribbon length that solves the Christmas Package Problem with $n = 4$ is 118: Find four packages of different sizes but with equal length ribbons and equal volumes.

$$\mathbf{118} = 14 + 50 + 54 \qquad 14 \times 50 \times 54 = \mathbf{37{,}800}$$
$$\mathbf{118} = 15 + 40 + 63 \qquad 15 \times 40 \times 63 = \mathbf{37{,}800}$$
$$\mathbf{118} = 18 + 30 + 70 \qquad 18 \times 30 \times 70 = \mathbf{37{,}800}$$
$$\mathbf{118} = 21 + 25 + 72 \qquad 21 \times 25 \times 72 = \mathbf{37{,}800}$$

A dime has 118 grooves on its side.

119 $\left[\, 7 \times 17 \,\right]$

AND a quarter has 119 grooves on its side.

A Pythagorean triple, the third smallest with consecutive legs, is **119–120**–169.

(The smallest and best known is 3–4–5, and the second is 20–21–29.)

120 $\left[2^3 \times 3 \times 5 \right]$

120 = 5! = 5 × 4 × 3 × 2 = the number of ways of arranging a five-card poker hand.

THE highest possible score for the first move in Scrabble using familiar words is 120: For *jukebox*, count a double letter score for X or J, plus a double word score and 50-point bonus. *Squeeze* and *quizzed* can also produce 120 points.

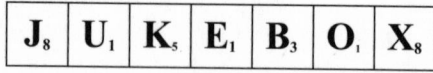

THE set {1, 3, 8, 120} has the unusual property that if you multiply any two of these numbers together and add 1, the result is a perfect square:

1+1×3	1+1×8	1+1×120	1+3×8	1+3×120	1+8×120
4	9	121	25	361	961

At each stage the number that is added to the sequence is the lowest possible. The next number in the sequence is 1680, followed by 23,408.

EACH of the interior angles of a hexagon measures 120 degrees.

121 $\left[\ 11^2 \qquad 3^0 + 3^1 + 3^2 + 3^3 + 3^4\ \right]$

THE number 121 is a palindrome and is also the square of a palindrome (11) and the square root of a palindrome (14641). There are infinitely many numbers of this type: Can you find the next one? (See Answers.)

CHINESE checkers is neither Chinese nor checkers, but a standard board has 121 holes.

IN math parlance, a number that is both a perfect square and a star number is called—no surprise here—a square star number. The next square star number after 121 is 11,881.

122 $\left[\ 2 \times 61\ \right]$

IN computing, a universally unique identifier, or UUID, is essentially a 128-bit construction of which 6 bits are claimed by version and variant, leaving 122 random bits. The total number of UUIDs is 2^{122}, a number with 37 digits.

Having a gigantic number of individual IDs is important because it makes the likelihood of an accidental repetition so small that it can be ignored.

123 [3 × 41]

THE sum of the digits of 123 equals the product of the digits.

▼

START with any number, say, 829,432,154. Count up the number of even digits (5) and odd digits (4) and create a number using those two digits as well as their sum: 549. If you repeat the process starting with 549, you get 123. No matter what number you start with, you'll end up with 123 after some finite number of steps.

▼

IN the United Kingdom, dialing 123 gets you to British Telecom's "speaking clock," said to be accurate to within five thousandths of a second.

▼

THE number 123 is best known not as a number but for its digits, as in "easy as 1-2-3," "Lotus 1-2-3" (surely intended to be easier than, say, Visicalc), and Len Barry's "1-2-3," which never hit number 1 on the Billboard charts but reached number 2 in the United States and number 3 in the United Kingdom upon its release in 1965.

124 $\left[\, 2^2 \times 31 \,\right]$

THE United Kingdom has 124 postcode areas, defined as the first two letters in the postcode.

125 $\left[\, 5^3 \,\right]$

THE number 125 is a Friedman number, the term given to numbers that can be expressed as an equation using only the digits in the number itself: Behold the equation $125 = 5^{(1+2)}$.

126 $\left[\, 2 \times 3^2 \times 7 \,\right]$

126 is the biggest of the six magic numbers of physics, so called because atomic nuclei with 2, 8, 20, 50, 82, or 126 nucleons are especially stable. In 1963, Maria Goeppert-Mayer, Eugene Wigner, and J. Hans D. Jensen shared the Nobel Prize in Physics for their work in the "shell" method that sought to explain some of the higher magic numbers.

▼

THE equation $126 = {}_9C_5 = \frac{9!}{5!4!}$ is a bit of math shorthand, seen in many other places in the book, to represent the fact that there are 126 ways of choosing 5 (or 4) objects from an original set of 9. Now, frankly, a whole lot of numbers can be represented in this fashion by letting 9 and 5 equal, well, anything else. But this particular "choice" function has a real-life representation, because it indicates the number of possible 5–4 decisions from the Supreme Court of the United States.

127 $\left[\text{prime} \qquad -1 + 2^7 \right]$

THERE are 127 matches required to determine the singles champion at Wimbledon—or any tournament with a full draw of 128. There are two ways to determine that 127 is the correct number. The first method begins by observing that the finals consists of one match, the semifinals two matches, and so on all the way back to the 64-match first round. The sum $1 + 2 + 4 + 8 + 16 + 32 + 64$ equals 127. (In general, the sum of the first n powers of two, including 2^0, equals one less than the *next* power of two.) The other way of counting the matches is to note that each match knocks out one participant. Only one person doesn't lose at all, so the total number of matches equals $128 - 1 = 127$. This shortcut applies to draws of any size: When the number of players or teams in a tournament is not a power of two, "byes" are given to ensure that the *second* round is a power of two.

128 $\left[2^7 \right]$

AS mentioned in **127**, the first round of any major tennis championship consists of 128 players. In general, a tournament with 2^n players will have n rounds. Not only is 128 the number of entrants in a grand slam singles event in tennis, it is the largest number that cannot be expressed as the sum of three distinct squares.

129 [3 × 43]

WHEREAS 128 cannot be written as the sum of three distinct squares, 129 can be expressed as the sum of three distinct squares in two different ways. $129 = 100 + 25 + 4 = 10^2 + 5^2 + 2^2$, and $129 = 64 + 49 + 16 = 8^2 + 7^2 + 4^2$. (The smallest number with this same property is 62.) Upon including the representations $64 + 64 + 1$ and $121 + 4 + 4$, in which two squares are repeated, there are altogether four representations of 129 as the sum of three squares, and 129 is the smallest number with four representations.

130 [2 × 5 × 13]

SPEAKING of sums of squares, the smallest divisors of 130 are 1, 2, 5, and 10, and $130 = 1^2 + 2^2 + 5^2 + 10^2$. No other number equals the sum of the squares of its first four divisors.

131 [prime]

THE number 131 is not only prime, it is a permutable prime, so called because the other numbers that can be obtained by permuting its digits, namely 113 and 311, are themselves prime. And, of course, 131 can be made by overlapping the primes 13 and 31.

132 $\left[\, 2^2 \times 3 \times 11 \,\right]$

$$132 = 12 + 13 + 21 + 23 + 31 + 32$$

IN other words, 132 is the sum of all the two-digit numbers that can be formed using its own digits. In particular, 132 is the smallest such number. Care to guess what the next one is? (See Answers.)

▼

THE sixth Catalan number is 132. Catalan numbers show up in a wide variety of contexts in the field of combinatorics. There are 132 ways of dividing an octagon into six triangles. Depicted below are two of 132 ways in which six rectangles can cover the same "step diagram."

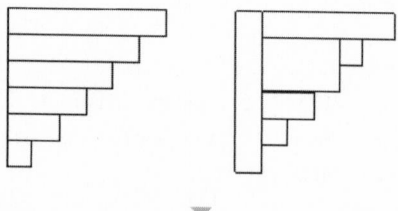

▼

THE general formula for the nth Catalan number is $\frac{2nCn}{(n+1)}$, which equals $\frac{(2n)!}{(n!)^2(n+1)}$.

133 $\left[\, 7 \times 19 \,\right]$

ACCORDING to a seminal classification by D. E. Wilson and D. M. Reeder in 1993, there are 133 families of mammals. The names of mammal families are readily detected because they end in -*idae*, as in Caenolestidae (shrew and rat opossums), Dasypodidae (anteaters), Odobenidae (walrus), Erethizontidae (New World porcupines), and Castoridae (beavers).

Surprisingly, 19 of these 133 families, fully one-seventh, are some form of bat.

134 $\left[\, 2 \times 67 \,\right]$

USING Roman numerals, 134 is a Friedman number: $CXXXIV = XV*(\frac{XC}{X}) - I$. (See **125**.)

135 $\left[\, 3^3 \times 5 \qquad 1^1 + 3^2 + 5^3 \,\right]$

EACH angle of a regular octagon is 135 degrees.

136 $\left[\, 2^3 \times 17 \,\right]$

ACCORDING to the standard Myers-Briggs personality classification scheme, there are 16 distinct personality types (see **16**). But if the psychotherapist who has to be familiar with all these types has it rough, the situation gets quite a bit worse for couples therapists. The number of ways you can choose two distinct types from a total of 16 equals $\frac{16(15)}{2}$, or 120. And if the two members of a couple are the same personality type, that's 16 more possibilities, for a grand total of 136.

IF you sum the cubes of the digits of 136, you get $1^3 + 3^3 + 6^3 = 244$. If you repeat the process, you get $2^3 + 4^3 + 4^3 = 136$. The only other pair of numbers that produces this same symmetry is (919,1459).

137 [prime]

PHYSICIST Wolfgang Pauli is said to have died in hospital room 137, this after spending a lifetime trying to demonstrate that 137 is the "fine-structure constant."

138 [2 × 3 × 23]

UNTIL the punk band the Misfits came out with their song "We Are 138" in 1982, there was absolutely nothing to say about this number. In some sense there still isn't.

139 [prime]

A multiyear computer study directed by master puzzle designer Bill Cutler demonstrated that the maximum number of pieces into which a six-piece burr puzzle can be maneuvered without falling apart is 139. The pictured puzzle is one of those that produces the maximum.

140 $\left[2^2 \times 5 \times 7 \right]$

A "knight's tour" on a chessboard is created by placing a knight on any one of the 64 squares and traversing a path that takes the knight to each of the other squares once and only once. A magic knight's tour adds the provision that if you number each position of the knight as it makes its way around the board, the resulting set of 64 numbers forms a magic square. A semi-magic knight's tour (history's first one, constructed by William Beverley in 1848, is shown below) is a tour that creates a semi-magic square—one whose rows and columns sum to a magic constant (260) but whose diagonals do not. (In this case they sum to 280 and 212.) A pure 8×8 magic knight's tour was shown to be impossible in 2003 by J. C. Meyrignac and Guenter Sterntenbrink, whose research also revealed 140 different geometric forms for a semi-magic tour.

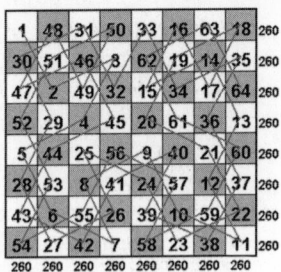

141 $\left[3 \times 47 \right]$

A Cullen number, named after Irish mathematician-turned-theologian Rev. James Cullen (1867–1933), is a number of the form $n \cdot 2^n + 1$. If $n = 1$ then $n \cdot 2^n + 1 = 3$, a prime number, but the next Cullen prime doesn't occur until $n = 141$. It is unknown whether an infinite number of Cullen primes exist.

142 [2×71]

A pound equals 453.59 grams. An ounce equals $\frac{1}{16}$ of a pound. A carat equals 200 milligrams. Put it all together and you find out that an ounce is slightly less than 142 carats.

143 [11×13]

THE number 143 is a factor of 1001 and therefore divides evenly into any number of the form abc,abc.

144 [$2^4 \times 3^2$ $(1 + 4 + 4)(1 \times 4 \times 4)$]

JUST as a group of 12 is called a dozen, a group of 144, or a dozen dozen, is called a gross. In particular, 144 is 12 squared. As luck would have it, 144 is also the twelfth Fibonacci number. The only other square in the Fibonacci sequence is 1.

▼

THE number 144 also played a role in a counterexample to Euler's "Sum of Powers Conjecture." Euler had conjectured that for $n > 2$, at least n nth powers are required to add to a number that is itself an nth power. (Sort of a cousin of Fermat's Last Theorem.) This conjecture went unresolved until 1967, when L. J. Lander and T. R. Parkin discovered the equation $144^5 = 27^5 + 84^5 + 110^5 + 133^5$, meaning that a fifth power could be the sum of only four fifth powers.

145 $\left[\ 2^2 \times 5 \times 7\ \right]$

$$145 = 1 + 24 + 120 = 1! + 4! + 5!$$

THE only other number (besides the trivial cases of 1 and 2) that equals the sum of the factorials of its digits is 40,585.

NOW start with any positive integer and add up the squares of its digits. For example, if you choose 769, you get $7^2 + 6^2 + 9^2 = 166$. Do the same again and you get $1^2 + 6^2 + 6^2 = 73$. Next you get $7^2 + 3^2 = 58$. Remarkably, if you keep going, one of two things will happen: (1) You'll get to 1 and stay there forever; (2) You'll arrive at a loop of eight numbers, the largest of which is 145, and you'll stay in that loop forever. In particular, if you start with 769 you'll get to 145 after just five steps. The full loop involving 145 is {145, 42, 20, 4, 16, 37, 58, 89, 145}.

146 $\left[\ 2 \times 73\ \right]$

$$146 = 1 + 4 + 9 + 16 + 25 + 36 + 25 + 16 + 9 + 4 + 1$$

THE above equation arises in calculating probabilities in the rolling of two pairs of dice. There is one way for the sums of both pairs to equal 2, four ways for the sums of both pairs to equal 3, and so on, with a "7" being the most common sum and with the other likelihoods being symmetric around 7.

IN probabilistic terms, the equation means that there are 146 ways (out of 1,296) to roll two pairs of dice so that the sum of the rolls is the same. So the probability of a greater sum from the first pair of dice equals $\frac{575}{1,296}$, the probability of the second sum being greater is also $\frac{575}{1,296}$, while the probability that the two sums are equal is $\frac{146}{1,296}$.

147 [prime]

IN the absence of fouls, 147 is the highest possible score that can be achieved on a snooker break.

148 [$2^2 \times 37$]

A vampire number is a number whose digits can be regrouped into two smaller numbers that multiply to the original. There are 148 six-digit vampire numbers (assuming you can't add extras by padding with zeroes), the smallest being $102{,}510 = 201 \times 510$ and the largest being $939{,}658 = 953 \times 986$.

149 [prime]

ALTHOUGH 149 is prime, its main properties revolve around perfect squares, as follows:

149 is the sum of two perfect squares (100 and 49).
149 is the concatenation of two squares (1 and 49).
149 is also the sum of three consecutive squares ($6^2 + 7^2 + 8^2$).
149 is also the concatenation of three squares (1, 4, and 9).

150 $\left[\, 2 \times 3 \times 5^2 \,\right]$

AUSTRALIA'S House of Representatives has 150 members, each representing a different electoral division. A sesquicentennial is a 150th anniversary. The Bible contains precisely 150 Psalms. All well and good, but the most interesting application of the number 150 can be traced to British anthropologist Robin Dunbar, whose research indicated that 150 is the maximum number of people that can maintain a social relationship. Dunbar's research is actually a formula that provides a maximum group size per species as a function of the size of the neocortex of that species. The mean figure for *Homo sapiens* was 147.8, which Dunbar conveniently rounded to 150, known as Dunbar's number.

▼

AS Malcolm Gladwell notes in *The Tipping Point*, Dunbar's research confirmed the role of 150 (or at least 150ish) in such groups as the Hutterites, who had kept their colonies limited to 150 long before the existence of social psychology. Armies from Roman times to present day have kept units small to improve cohesion. And the manufacturers of Gore-Tex have specifically kept the number of employees at a given plant under 150 for the same reason, discovering Dunbar's number purely through experience.

151 $\left[\, \text{prime} \,\right]$

A prime palindrome. Also the number of Pokémon figures.

152 $\left[\ 2^3 \times 19\ \right]$

AN American mah-jongg set consists of 152 tiles: 108 suit tiles, 16 wind tiles, 12 dragon tiles, 8 flower tiles, and 8 jokers.

153 $\left[\ 3^2 \times 17\ \right]$

153 $= 1^3 + 5^3 + 3^3$ and is the smallest of four integers with that same property (370, 371, and 407 are the only other numbers that equal the sum of the cubes of their digits, while *no number* is the sum of the squares of its digits). 153 also equals $1 + 2 + 3 + 4 + 5 + 6 + 7 + 8 + 9 + 10 + 11 + 12 + 13 + 14 + 15 + 16 + 17$, (making it the seventeenth triangular number), and equals $1! + 2! + 3! + 4! + 5!$ as well.

154 $\left[\ 2 \times 7 \times 11\ \right]$

BETWEEN 1904 and 1960 (with the exception of 1919), a baseball season consisted of 154 games: With eight teams in each league, each team played the other seven teams in its league 22 times apiece. (See **162**.)

$154! + 1$ (1 plus the product of the first 14 integers) is prime and for many years was the largest known prime number of that form. Primes of the form $n! \pm 1$ are known as *factorial primes*. It has been conjectured that there are infinitely many factorial primes. Note that if p is prime and $p < n$, then $n! + p$ can never be prime, because it is divisible by p.

155 $[\ 5 \times 31\ ]$

AS we saw in **148**, any number whose digits can be rearranged to form two numbers that multiply to the original is called a *vampire number*. There are a total of 155 six-digit vampire numbers if you include the seven lousy ones with zeroes at the end, as in $150 \times 930 = 139{,}500$. In 2003, the 100-digit vampire number 9754610579850632525872580399376108520048510982876394437067250691992046193141970418786383479631226428 was found. It equals 98765432109876543210987654321098765432108990776898 × 98765432109876543210987654321099765432110002523486.

156 $[\ 2^2 \times 3 \times 13\ ]$

SUPPOSE a clock strikes only on the hour. Over a 12-hour period, the total number of strikes equals the sum of 1 through 12, otherwise known as the twelfth triangular number, or 78. Therefore, the total number of strikes in a full day is $2 \times 78 = 156$.

157 $[\ \text{prime}\ ]$

$$157^2 = 24{,}649 \text{ and } 158^2 = 24{,}964$$

AT one time 157 was the largest known number whose square consists of the same digits as the square of its successor. Can you come up with the *smallest* pair of consecutive numbers whose squares use the same digits? And, for those who truly love a challenge, can you come up with a *bigger* pair of consecutive numbers with the same property? (See Answers.)

158 [2 × 79]

THE Greek national anthem is based on a 158-verse poem written by Dionysios Solomos. The poem "Hymn to the Freedom" was inspired by the Greek Revolution of 1821 against the Ottoman Empire. The anthem was officially adopted in 1864.

159 [3 × 53]

A barrel of oil contains 159 liters.

160 [2⁵ × 5]

$160 \quad [\; 2^5 \times 5 \;]$

DON'T believe this poster. We'll set you straight a few pages from now.

161 $\left[\, 7 \times 23 \,\right]$

ALL primes other than 2 and 3 are of the form $6n \pm 1$. Where 161 fits in is that all numbers greater than 161 can be expressed as the sum of distinct primes specifically of the form $6n - 1$. For example,

$$162 = 47 + 41 + 29 + 23 + 17 + 5$$
$$163 = 101 + 29 + 17 + 11 + 5$$
$$164 = 131 + 17 + 11 + 5$$
$$165 = 89 + 71 + 5$$
$$166 = 107 + 59$$

And so on. There's no particular pattern at work here, but the construction is apparently always possible from 162 on.

162 $\left[\, 2 \times 3^4 \,\right]$

SINCE 1961, the number of regular-season games in Major League Baseball has been 162 (see **154**).

But there's an interesting and forgotten wrinkle here. The 154-game schedule in effect before 1961 made sense because there were eight teams in each league. Each team therefore had seven opponents, and because $154 = 7 \times 22$, each team could play every other team precisely 22 times.

So far so good, but when the American League expanded to 10 teams in 1961 with the addition of the Los Angeles Angels and Minnesota Twins, that even divisibility would have been lost, but for the move to a 162-game schedule. Yet the National League still had only eight teams, because the New York Mets and Houston Colt .45s didn't arrive until 1962. So which league gave up its nice, clean schedule?

The answer is neither. While AL teams played 18 games against each of nine opponents for a total of 162 games, the NL kept to its 154-game schedule for one final season. That's one reason why Roger Maris's extra eight games in which to break Babe Ruth's home run record were so conspicuous.

Nowadays, with extra divisions and interleague play, the notion of divisibility feels antiquated and the rumor (yes, it was just a rumor) of an asterisk on Maris's 61 home runs wouldn't get any traction. But things were different in 1961.

163 [prime]

THE number $e^{\pi\sqrt{163}}$ is very close to being an integer. Its value is 262,537,412,640,768,743.99999999999925.

This number was the subject of a 1965 April Fool's joke played on the readers of *Scientific American* by its famous columnist Martin Gardner. Gardner not only claimed that $e^{\pi\sqrt{163}}$ was integral, he credited Indian mathematician Ramanujan with having conjectured this "fact" in a 1914 paper, even though French mathematician Charles Hermite knew otherwise as far back as 1859. Ever since, the number $e^{\pi\sqrt{163}}$ has gone by the whimsical name of Ramanujan's constant.

164 [$2^2 \times 41$]

REMINISCENT of 149, 164 is the sum of two squares (100 and 64) and can be expressed as the concatenation of squares in two different ways: 1 and 64 or 16 and 4.

165 $\left[\ 3 \times 5 \times 11\ \right]$

AS the sum of triangular numbers, 165 can be found along the third diagonal of Pascal's Triangle—in the eleventh row. Otherwise stated, the number of ways of choosing 3 objects from a set of 11 equals 165.

166 $\left[\ 2 \times 83\ \right]$

AN example of a Smith number is 166—the sum of its digits (1 + 6 + 6 = 13) equals the sum of the digits of its prime factors (166 = 2 × 83 and 2 + 8 + 3 = 13). By convention, the prime factors are summed in accordance with their multiplicity; therefore 4 (= 2 × 2 and 2 + 2) is the first Smith number, while 166 is the eighth. The first 14 Smith numbers all have digital sums of 4, 9, or 13.

Smith numbers came into being in 1982, when Lehigh University mathematician Albert Wilansky pondered his brother-in-law's phone number: 493-7775. As a seven-digit number, this factors into 3 × 5 × 5 × 65837, and 4 + 9 + 3 + 7 + 7 + 7 + 5 = 42 = 3 + 5 + 5 + 6 + 5 + 8 + 3 + 7. Wilansky was so amazed by his discovery that he named it after his brother-in-law, Harold Smith.

167 $\left[\ \text{prime}\ \right]$

COAXIAL cable has a bandwidth from 0 to 1 GHz, and can therefore accommodate 167 separate TV signals at 6 MHz each.

MARTINA Navratilova won 167 singles titles, a record for the Open Era.

▼

APPARENTLY the poster at **160** was just an approximation, because an actual count came up with 167 bullet holes (entrance and exit) in Bonnie and Clyde's car following the May 23, 1934, ambush that claimed the bank robbers' lives. Moral of the story: Don't believe round numbers.

168 $\left[\, 2^3 \times 3 \times 7 \,\right]$

IF an activity is literally done 24/7 for a full week, it is done for $24 \times 7 = 168$ hours.

▼

THERE are 168 possible knight's moves going up the chessboard. The number in each square to the right gives the possible upward knight moves starting from that square.

0	0	0	0	0	0	0	0
1	1	2	2	2	2	1	1
2	3	4	4	4	4	3	2
2	3	4	4	4	4	3	2
2	3	4	4	4	4	3	2
2	3	4	4	4	4	3	2
2	3	4	4	4	4	3	2
2	3	4	4	4	4	3	2

169 $\left[13^2 \right]$

WHILE $13 \times 13 = 169$, $31 \times 31 = 961$, the only such construction in which no number has repeated digits.

▼

THERE are 169 functionally distinct (two-card) starting hands in Texas hold 'em poker: 13 having the same rank, 78 of different ranks in the same suit, and 78 of different ranks in different suits.

170 $\left[2 \times 5 \times 17 \right]$

THE Athenian trireme was powered by 170 oarsmen on three tiers: 31 on each side of the top level, and 27 per side on each of the lower two levels.

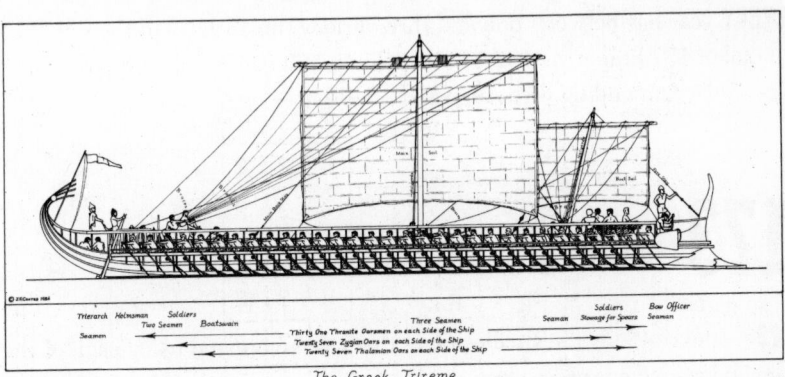

The Greek Trireme

171 $\left[\, 3^2 \times 19 \,\right]$

171 is triangular, being the sum of 1 through 18.

▼

HOW many Starbucks are there in Manhattan? The number changes, but on Friday, June 29, 2007, they totaled 171, and in a celebrated video, writer/comedian Mark Malkoff visited each and every one of them beginning that day at 5:30 a.m. and ending at 2:56 a.m. on Saturday the 30th.

172 $\left[\, 2^2 \times 43 \,\right]$

172 = $(4 \times 36) + (4 \times 6) + (4 \times 1)$, so $172 = 444$ in base 6.

▼

EVERY year has between one and three Friday the 13ths, and there will be a total of 172 Friday the 13ths in the twenty-first century, starting with April 13, 2001, and ending with August 13, 2100.

173 $\left[\, \text{prime} \,\right]$

173 + 286 = 459 is the smallest sum that can be created using each of the nine nonzero digits precisely once. The largest sum is 981, which can be created in two ways: $324 + 657 = 981$ and $235 + 746 = 981$.

▼

THE period between lunar eclipses is roughly 173 days—slightly less than six lunar months.

174 $\left[\, 2 \times 3 \times 29 \,\right]$

BY regrouping the factorization of 174 in two different ways, we come up with the side-by-side equations $58 \times 3 = \mathbf{174} = 29 \times 6$, which together use each of the nine nonzero digits exactly once.

175 $\left[\, 5^2 \times 7 \qquad 100 + 1^2 + 7^2 + 5^2 \qquad 1^1 + 7^2 + 5^3 \,\right]$

THE sum of the first 49 positive integers equals $\frac{49(50)}{2} = 1{,}225$. Dividing by 7 yields 175, so each row, column, and diagonal of a 7×7 magic square must add up to 175. In a superstition that dates back at least to the sixteenth century, magic squares have been assigned to various planets in the solar system. Seven planets were known at that time, and the magic square below is known as the Venus magic square.

22	47	16	41	10	35	4
5	23	48	17	42	11	29
30	6	24	49	18	36	12
13	31	7	25	43	19	37
38	14	32	1	26	44	20
21	39	8	33	2	27	45
46	15	40	9	34	3	28

176 [$2^4 \times 11$]

177 [3×59]

THE numbers 176 and 177 are linked by the diagram below, which creates a 176 × 177 rectangle—"almost" a square—by using using 11 smaller squares of distinct sizes. The minimum number of distinct squares needed to produce an actual square equals 21. (See **21**!)

Rectangles subdivided into squares have been used to model certain types of electrical networks. Within such a model, the sizes of the individual squares correspond to the currents and/or voltages of the network itself.

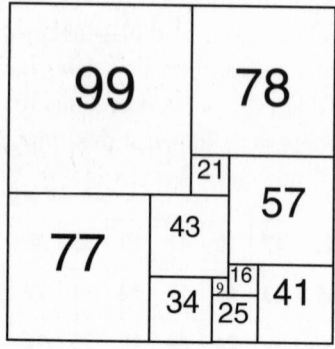

178 [2 × 89]

THERE are 220 4 × 4 magic squares before rotations. Of these 220 squares, 178 are "balanced," meaning that every row, column, and diagonal has two numbers between 1 and 8 and two numbers between 9 and 16.

179 [prime   17 × 9 + 17 + 9]

THE equation $179 = 11 × 15 + 14$ enables us to conclude that every year has 179 days whose day of the month is an even number. February has 14 even days whether or not it is a leap year.

180 [$2^2 × 3^2 × 5$ (10 − 1) (10 − 8) (10 − 0)]

IF you take the product of the first seven positive integers and divide it by their sum, you get 180.

▼

IN most areas of the United States, 180 is the standard number of days in the school year. Among other things, students learn that a semicircle consists of 180 degrees, and that the sum of the degrees in the three angles of a triangle also equals 180 degrees. These two statements are related, as shown by the standard proof of the triangle result:

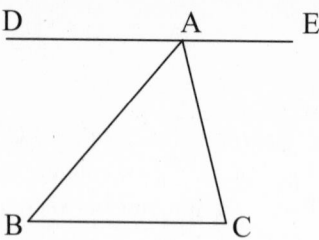

In the triangle ABC above, just draw a line through A that is parallel to the base BC. (Euclid's parallel postulate says that we can do this, and if it's okay by Euclid, it's okay by me.) From elementary geometry, the fact that DE and BC are parallel means that the angles ACB and EAC are equal, and likewise for DAB and ABC. Therefore, since the angle BAC is equal to itself, the sum of the angles in the triangle equals the number of degrees between points D and E, and that's obviously a half circle, or 180 degrees.

One corollary of this result is that the sum of the angles of a regular polygon with n sides equals 180 times $(n - 2)$, because such a figure can be divided into $(n - 2)$ triangles.

▼

BECAUSE 180 degrees is a half circle, *doing a 180* has come to mean "turning around," whether in a vehicle or in the sense of completely changing one's mind.

181 [prime]

ONCE major league baseball moved to a playoff system involving a five-game divisional playoff followed by a seven-game league championship series and, of course, a seven-game World Series, a team could theoretically play 162 + 5 + 7 + 7 = 181 games in a single season.

RECALL that the game of Go is played on a 19 × 19 grid. That gives 19^2, or 361 total intersections on which to place pieces. Since black goes first, there must be 181 black pieces and 180 white pieces to yield 361 in all.

182 $\left[\, 2 \times 7 \times 13 \,\right]$

THE number 182 made a brief, unwanted, and possibly apocryphal appearance in the construction of the Fahrenheit scale. According to one of many tales on the subject, Daniel Gabriel Fahrenheit (1686–1736) wanted the freezing points and boiling points of water to be separated by 180 degrees, as they are today, but he originally assigned 30 degrees as the freezing point of water, with 0 degrees the freezing point of a 50-50 salt/water combination. When, however, he measured the boiling point of water as 212°F, the undesirable 182-degree gap caused him to readjust the freezing point to 32°F.

183 $\left[\, 3 \times 61 \,\right]$

184 $\left[\, 2^3 \times 23 \,\right]$

THE numbers 183 and 184 are linked by more than just proximity. For starters, the number 183,184 is a perfect square (428^2), and is the smallest square obtained by concatenating two consecutive integers. (The only other six-digit numbers that work are $328{,}329 = 573^2$, $528{,}529 = 727^2$, and $715{,}716 = 846^2$.)

▼

THE two numbers also appear in the realm of "self-avoiding walks." Below, on the left, is one of 183 possible 7-step paths on a 7×7 grid such that the first step is to the right and no subsequent steps cross an existing path. Below, on the right, is one of 184 possible self-avoiding rook paths of order four, in which a rook goes from one corner of a 4×4 grid to the opposite corner, again without revisiting any spot along the tour.

Self-avoiding walks have been used in the study of polymers, solvents, and other chemical substances whose physical properties can be mimicked with a lattice-type structure.

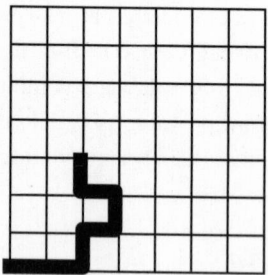 

185 [5 × 37]

THE number 12,421 is the first of 185 five-digit mountain primes, so called because the digital values peak in the middle.

186 $\left[\, 2 \times 3 \times 31 \,\right]$

THERE are 186 days between the spring and fall equinoxes. Note that this number easily exceeds half a year. The difference between those 186 days and the 179 days between the fall and spring equinoxes is explained by the fact that the Earth maintains an elliptical orbit around the sun, so the distance traveled between spring and fall is actually greater. Not only that, the Earth moves slightly faster when closer to the sun, and the closest point, the perihelion, comes in early January, close to the Winter Solstice. This is a special case of Kepler's Second Law, which states that the radius vector from the sun to the earth sweeps out equal areas in equal times.

SPEAKING of spheres, the diagram shows a so-called icosahedral tiling of the sphere by triangles. This particular tiling is called a $(2,3,5)$ tiling, for which the angles of each triangle are $\frac{180}{2}$, $\frac{180}{3}$, and $\frac{180}{5}$ degrees. Add those up and you get $90 + 60 + 36 = 186$ degrees, a reminder that the famous rule we proved in 180 that the sum of the angles of a triangle equals 180 degrees, well, that rule only applied in two dimensions.

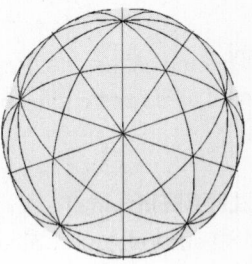

187 $\left[\, 11 \times 17 \,\right]$

AS an extension of the birthday paradox (see **23**), if you have 187 people in a room (not necessarily a good idea, but let's just suppose), the odds are greater than 50% that *four* of the people in the room share a birthday.

188 $\left[2^2 \times 47 \right]$

THE number $188 = 1 + 4 + 9 + 25 + 49 + 100$, the sum of six distinct squares. All numbers > 188 can be expressed as the sum of at most *five* distinct squares.

189 $\left[3^3 \times 7 \right]$

$$189 = 12 + 34 + 56 + 78 + 9$$

BY some counts, the English language contains 189 irregular verbs, starting with *abide* and ending with *write*.

ELSEWHERE in language, the Braille alphabet (Braille II) contains a total of 189 one-cell and two-cell contractions.

190 $\left[2 \times 5 \times 19 \right]$

IF you write out the factorization of 190 in Roman numerals, you get II × V × XIX. Each of these distinct prime factors is a palindrome, as is the product, CXC, and no number bigger than 190 has this property.

JUST as X's play a vital role in Roman numerals, they play a vital and especially desirable role in bowling, where an X denotes a strike. But if your X's are hard to come by, perhaps you should know that 190 is the highest score that can be achieved without rolling a single strike.

191 [prime]

IF you had one of every denomination of coin produced by the US Mint, you'd have a silver dollar, a half-dollar, a quarter, a dime, a nickel, and a penny, for a total of $100 + 50 + 25 + 10 + 5 + 1 = 191$ cents.

192 [$2^6 \times 3$]

NOTE that the factorization of 192 involves a bunch of 2's and a single 3. Numbers such as these have a lot of divisors, and in fact 192 is the smallest number with 14 divisors: 1, 2, 3, 4, 6, 8, 12, 16, 24, 32, 48, 64, 96, and 192 itself.

TAKE two sticks 20 inches in length and join them at one end. If you move the other ends until they are 24 inches apart, you will have created a triangle with an area of 192 square inches. If you keep spreading the sticks, the area will get bigger to a point, then fall. By the time the ends of the sticks are exactly 32 inches apart, the triangle they create will again be precisely 192 square inches. Somewhere in between a maximum area is obtained: Care to guess what that maximum is? (See Answers.)

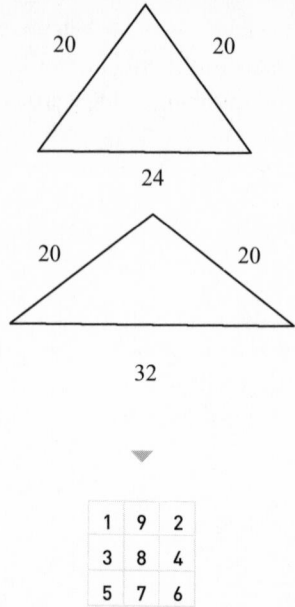

1	9	2
3	8	4
5	7	6

THE above 3 × 3 square is nothing more than the first three multiples of 192 stacked upon one another. What makes it special, of course, is that it uses each of the digits 1 through 9 precisely once.

193 [prime]

IN the words of zoologist Desmond Morris, "There are 193 species of monkeys and apes, 192 of them are covered with hair. The exception is a naked ape self-named Homo sapiens." Morris wrote about that exception in his revolutionary 1967 book, *The Naked Ape*.

194 $\left[\, 2 \times 97 \,\right]$

THE Roman Catholic Church has 194 dioceses within the United States, a number that becomes 195 upon the inclusion of the Archdiocese of the Military Services.

195 $\left[\, 3 \times 5 \times 13 \,\right]$

STEINWAY'S "Peace Piano," crafted in 2004, contained the flags of 195 nations around its perimeter, representing the number of countries in the United Nations at that time.

196 $\left[\, 2^2 \times 7^2 \,\right]$

MOST numbers become a palindrome by repeatedly reversing their digits and adding: For example, a starting number of 349 yields 349 + 943 = 1292, 1292 + 2921 = 4213, and 4213 + 3124 = 7337. The process isn't always this swift: Starting with 89 takes 24 steps before you arrive at a palindrome. Where does 196 fit in? Astonishingly, it is not known whether you *ever* get a palindrome starting with 196. It is the smallest number whose conversion is uncertain. Numbers that aren't known to ever convert are called Lychrel numbers, an amusing class of numbers in that by the nature of the definition of a Lychrel number, it's hard to be certain that a particular number is one!

197 [prime]

197 belongs to a restrictive club called the Keith numbers. The first Keith number is 14, as follows: If you begin a sequence with 1, 4 (in other words, the digits of 14), after which each new member of the sequence is obtained by adding the previous two (as in the Fibonacci numbers), the sequence proceeds 1, 4, 5, 9, **14**, reaching the starting number. With 197, the sequence begins with 1, 9, 7, and then adds the previous *three* numbers, forming 1, 9, 7, 17, 33, 57, 107, **197**. Keith numbers are extremely rare: Last we checked, the entire list of known Keith numbers consisted of only 95 numbers, from 14 all the way to the 29-digit whopper 70,267,375,510,207,885,242,218,837,404.

198 [$2 \times 3^2 \times 11$ $(1 + 9 + 8) \times 11$ $11 + 99 + 88$]

THERE are 198 palindromes under 10,000, as follows:

   9 – one digit: 1, 2, ... 9
   9 – two digits: 11,22, ... 99
  90 – three digits: 101, 111, ... 191, 202, 212, ... 292, ... 909, 919, ... 999
<u>+ 90</u> – four digits: 1001, 1111, 1991, 2002, 2112, ... 2992, ... 9009, 9119, ... 9999
  198

199 [prime]

THE number 199 is a permutable prime, meaning that it remains prime even when you rearrange its digits.

BECAUSE 199 has a repeated digit, all that means is that the numbers 919 and 991 are prime as well. On the other hand, 199 offers an extra flourish that it becomes 661 when viewed upside down, and that number is prime as well.

NOTE that 191, 193, 197, and 199 are all prime.

200 $\left[\, 2^3 \times 5^2 \,\right]$

OUR final entry, 200, has a little bit of everything, sort of like this book. First, we have a touch of mathematics:

In sharp contrast to 199, 200 is the smallest unprimable number: Not only is 200 composite, it remains composite if you change any one of its digits to any other number. Equivalently, the numbers 200, 201, 202, 203, 204, 205, 206, 207, 208, and 209 are all composite, the first such ten-number sequence.

There are $2^8 = 256$ subsets of the numbers $\{1, 2, 3, 4, 5, 6, 7, 8\}$. But only 200 of them are "weakly triple-free," meaning that they don't contain either $\{1, 2, 3\}$ or $\{2, 4, 6\}$ as a subset.

AND then we have some sports:

In bowling, if you alternate strikes and spares for an entire string, you will have attained a score of 200, sometimes called the Dutch 200. Even more surprising, fighters who weigh more than 200 pounds are considered heavyweights.

FINALLY, we have some approximations and lame tie-ins:

The human field of vision is said to be approximately 200 degrees. And there are approximately 200 seeds on a strawberry (just as there were 200 pounds on Darryl Strawberry when he entered the major leagues—however, no one was calling him a heavyweight, even though he certainly wasn't weakly triple-free).

If only this were Monopoly, you could now pass Go . . . and collect your $200.

ANSWERS

3 ▶

The ratio of odd numbers to even numbers in Pascal's Triangle approaches zero as the number of rows heads to infinity.

4 ▶

The proof that any number eventually gets to four after counting the letters in its English name (creating a new number, and continuing in this fashion) is far easier than you'd think. The first step is to notice that any number less than 4 has more letters than itself: ONE has 3 letters, TWO has 3, and THREE has 5. FOUR has 4 letters, and it is not hard to see that the number of letters in any number greater than FOUR is less than the number itself.

Starting with ONE and applying the letter-counting sequence produces the chain ONE-THREE-FIVE-FOUR. Starting with two produces TWO-THREE-FIVE-FOUR. Starting with THREE produces THREE-FIVE-FOUR. Now suppose you pick any number whatsoever. That's right, any number. If you count the letters in its English representation, you get a smaller number than you started with, so if you keep going, you'll eventually get to 1, 2, 3, or 4. But we've already seen that those numbers end up at FOUR, so we're done.

10 ▶

The letters in question are the last letters of the first ten positive integers.

The logarithm equation is actually easier than you think. The left hand side reduces to $\log_2(\log_9^{(\frac{1}{2^n})} 9)$, or $\log_2(2^n)$, which by definition equals n.

12 ▶

Suppose that a Buckyball has P pentagons and H hexagons. The total number of faces on the Buckyball is therefore $P + H$. The total number of edges is $\frac{(5P + 6H)}{2}$, the division by 2 accounting for the fact that every line in the Buckyball is a side of two figures. Similarly, the total number of vertices is $\frac{(5P + 6H)}{3}$. According to Euler's formula:

$$2 + \frac{(5P + 6H)}{2} = \frac{(5P + 6H)}{3} + (P + H)$$

Multiplying both sides by 6 yields:

$$12 + 3(5P + 6H) = 2(5P + 6H) + 6(P + H), \text{ which simplifies to}$$
$$12 + 15P + 18H = 16P + 18H$$

Miraculously, the H terms cancel and we are left with $P = 12$.

16 ▶

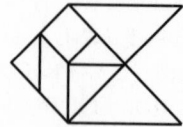

17 ▶

Here's the solution for the 17-clue Sudoku puzzle:

9	1	4	6	5	3	8	7	2
5	3	6	8	2	7	1	4	9
8	2	7	9	4	1	6	5	3
7	6	8	3	1	5	9	2	4
1	5	3	4	9	2	7	6	8
2	4	9	7	6	8	3	1	5
3	7	5	1	8	4	2	9	6
6	8	2	5	7	9	4	3	1
4	9	1	2	3	6	5	8	7

19 ▶

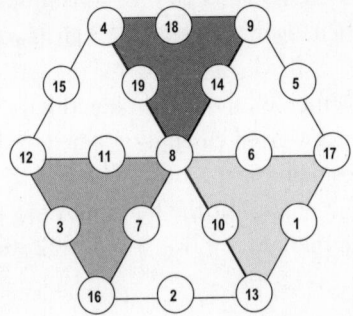

23 ▶

The 23-letter sequence gives you the alphabet, in order of appearance within the string ONE, TWO, THREE, FOUR, FIVE, and so on. The letter C doesn't appear until ONE OCTILLION, and J, K, and Z never appear at all.

24 ▶

The woodcut is from the second edition of *Geoffrey Chaucer's Canterbury Tales*, printed by William Caxton in 1483.

27 ▶

The number 15 has the same property, since $1 + 2 + 3 + 4 + 5 = 15$.

29 ▶

A rectangular block with sides of length a, b, and c will have volume equal to abc, a number with at least three prime factors (possibly repeated). But the combined volume of the 29 pentacubes is by definition 5×29, a number with only two prime factors. So, no matter how you combine the 29 pentacubes, they'll never form a perfect block.

31 ▶

At first glance this puzzle looks easy. Starting at the top, you subtract 72 from 99 to get 27. Then you subtract 27 from 45 to get 18, 18 from 39 to get 21, and so on. Placing 15 in the question mark continues the pattern perfectly, because $36 - 21 = 15$ and $28 - 15 = 13$. But this rule fails its final test at the bottom, when, agonizingly, $21 - 13$ gives you 8, not the 7 in the lowest circle.

Once you poke around a bit more you should have no trouble discovering that the number in any given circle is obtained by adding the individual digits in the two circles pointing toward it. Thus $7 + 2 + 9 + 9$ gives you 27, all the way to $1 + 3 + 2 + 1 = 7$ at the bottom. Along the way you see that replacing the question mark by $2 + 1 + 3 + 6 = 12$ works out just fine. So your answer is 12.

35 ▶

The diagram below is a 1930 creation of T. R. Dawson and demonstrates one way to move a knight 35 times without having it cross its own path.

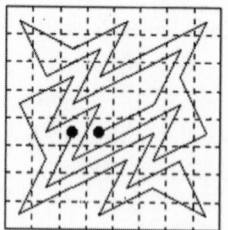

37 ▶

1. The number of hairs on a human head varies with hair color (blondes have more hair than brunettes, for example), but the upper limit is somewhere around 140,000. By contrast, more than 12 million people live in Tokyo. You can't put those 12 million people into 140,000 slots without at least two sharing a slot, and those two people by definition have the same number of hairs on their heads. Using a city as populous as Tokyo was, of course, overkill: The puzzle would have worked equally well using Stoke-on-Trent, England, or Huntsville, Alabama.

2. Divide the original equilateral triangle into four smaller equilateral triangles, as in the diagram. Each of the smaller triangles measures one inch on a side; in particular, any two points inside any of these triangles must be within an inch of one another. But if you had five points to place in these four triangles, the pigeonhole principle guarantees that (at least) two of the points must reside in the same triangle.

3. Choose any 10 numbers from the first 100 positive integers. The number of subsets of these 10 numbers is $2^{10} = 1,024$ (see the discussion in **4**). But the highest possible sum of 10 numbers in the range 1 through 100 equals $91 + 92 + 93 + \ldots + 100 = 955$. If there are more subsets than possible sums, at least two subsets must have the same sum. If those two sets are disjoint, you're done, and if not, just get rid of the common elements and the disjoint subsets that arise must also have the same sum, because all you've done is removed the repetitions.

39 ▶

There is one number smaller than 39 such that the sum of the primes in between the smallest and largest divisor equals the number itself. That number is 10: Its prime divisors are 2 and 5, and $2 + 3 + 5 = 10$.

48 ▶

A 5 × 12 rectangle also works. The interior uses $3 \times 10 = 30$ tiles and the border uses the remaining 30.

51 ▶

The 51 nations listed were the original 51 members of the United Nations in 1945.

59 ▶

The number 419 (= 60 × 7 − 1) leaves a remainder of $n − 1$ when divided by any of $n = 2, 3, 4, 5, 6,$ and 7.

62 ▶

This puzzle is often given using a chessboard, from which you extract diagonally opposite squares and ask if it can be covered using pieces that look like this:

The coloring of the squares makes it easier to reach the correct conclusion, which is no. Each of the 1 × 2 "dominoes" consists of a white square plus a black square, whereas the 62-square board obtained by removing two squares from the same diagonal must have 32 squares of one color (in this case black) and 30 squares of the other color. So no covering is possible.

69 ▶

The other number that equals the alphanumeric value of its Roman numeral representation is 63. (63 = LXIII = 12 + 24 + 9 + 9 + 9 = 63.)

72 ▶

List all possible sets of three positive integers whose product is 72. Here is the list, with the sum of the three numbers provided to the right of the equal sign:

1, 1, 72 = 74 ; 1, 2, 36 = 39 ; 1, 3, 24 = 28 ; 1, 4, 18 = 23 ; 1, 6, 12 = 19 ; 1, 8, 9 = 18 ;
2, 2, 18 = 22 ; 2, 3, 12 = 17 ; 2, 4, 9 = 15 ; 2, 6, 6 = 14 ; 3, 3, 8 = 14 ; 3, 4, 6 = 13

Had the number on the front door been anything but 14, there would be no ambiguity, so we can assume that the kids' ages are either 2, 6, and 6 or 3, 3, and 8. That's where the line "my youngest likes ice cream" comes in. Electing not to split hairs with the timing of the births of a set of twins, we conclude that the youngest is 2 and the other two kids each 6 years of age.

The next number after 72 that could work in this problem is 225, which can be represented as either $1 \times 15 \times 15$ or $3 \times 3 \times 25$, and both sets of three numbers add up to 31.

75 ▶

The missing possibilities are the six cases in which there are *two* ties:

[AB][CD]   [AC][BD]   [AD][BC]   [BC][AD]   [BD][AC]   [CD][AB]

79 ▶

The idea of the Coconut Problem is to work backward. Let x = the number of coconuts each thief took when they divvied up in the morning. Then the coconuts on hand after the third thief took his "share" (after giving one to the monkey) were $3x + 1$. The third thief took one-half of this number, so the amount left by the second thief was $(\frac{3}{2})(3x + 1) + 1$, which only makes sense if $3x + 1$ is an even number. Therefore x is odd. Okay, we've at least established something.

When you investigate the next level, you find that the conditions of the problem force $\frac{(3x+1)}{2}$ to be odd as well. And, whatever that number is, if you multiply by 3, add 1, and divide by 2, that number has to be odd, too.

This is getting confusing. Let's look at an actual example. If $x = 3$ there were 10 coconuts left in the morning, and therefore 11 prior to the third thief giving one to the monkey. That means the third thief took 5 coconuts (3 times 3, plus 1, divided by 2, as expected), so he must have encountered 16 originally (taking 5, leaving 10, and giving one to the monkey). That means that the second thief left 17 before giving one to the monkey, so he must have taken 8 ($\frac{(3\times5+1)}{2}$). But 8 is an even number, so we can't go up another level.

Similarly, if $x = 5$ we reach 8 even quicker, so that doesn't work. But if the final distribution was 7 coconuts apiece, the third thief must have taken 11 from a batch of 34, the second thief took 17 from a batch of 52, and the first thief took 26 from the original batch of 79. Since 26 is even, you can't go up another level, but you don't have to, as there were only three thieves.

81 ▶

It is possible to rewrite the expression as $(p + 1 + \frac{1}{p})\,(q + 1 + \frac{1}{q})\,(r + 1 + \frac{1}{r})\,(s + 1 + \frac{1}{s})$.

A little thought will reveal that each of the four bracketed expressions must be greater than 3, so the product must exceed $3^4 = 81$.

83 ▶

The 83 numbers listed are the five-digit numbers whose squares contain nine of the ten digits. The numbers to the left of each batch of numbers indicate the digit that does *not* appear in the corresponding squares.

For the second question on the page, if you write out the first 500,000,000 positive integers, you will use precisely 500,000,000 1's. There are a total of 83 positive numbers n such that writing out 1 through n uses precisely n 1's, with 500000000 being right in the middle.

92 ▶

Five queens are sufficient to attack any square on a chessboard. Four queens aren't enough.

93 ▶

The 93 listed numbers form the complete list of five-digit palindromic primes. Those in boldface are the five-digit sequences that at this writing are working ZIP codes in the United States.

97 ▶

Hope the wording of the problem gave you a hint, because the answer is a cute but cheesy "NEGATIVE NINETY-SEVEN."

98 ▶

At the outset, you have 100 pounds of potatoes, of which 99% is water, so basically you have 99 pounds of water and 1 pound of something solid. Because the solid part is assumed not to change, it becomes 2% of the whole when the water weighs 49 pounds. At that point the total weight of the potatoes is 1 + 49 = 50 pounds.

104 ▶

Voilà: Twelve identical matchsticks arranged so that precisely three meet at each vertex.

108 ▶

12:00 and 11:20 are the other two times of day in which the hour figure multiplied by the minutes figure equals the number of degrees between the two hands, but for 11:20 you have to take the long way around.

121 ▶

There's a bit of a trick to this one. The next number that is both the square and square root of a palindrome is 10201, which is 101 squared and the square root of 104060401.

132 ▶

The next number that equals the sum of all the two-digit numbers that can be formed from its digits is 264, which of course is two times 132. From that you should be able to figure out the third number with this same property!

157 ▶

The smallest pair of consecutive numbers whose squares use the same digits is the pair $\{13,14\}$, as $13^2 = 169$ and $14^2 = 196$.
The next pair to have this property is $\{157,158\}$, and the one after that is $\{913,914\}$, where we have $913^2 = 833,569$ and $914^2 = 835,396$.

192 ▶

The maximum area is obtained when the legs form a right triangle, at which point the area is 200 square inches. The result relies on the fact that the area increases to a point, then decreases, and that maximal point represents some sort of symmetry.

ACKNOWLEDGMENTS

THE cover and title page suggest that I wrote this book by myself, but don't think for an instant that I didn't have massive amounts of help along the way. Fortunately, I now have the space to acknowledge all those individuals who gave me a boost. Here goes:

Let me start by thanking my agents, Jennifer Griffin and Mary Clemmey, who represented the book in New York and London, respectively. I'm sure that this particular book wasn't the easiest task of their careers, but they never gave up on it, for which I'm grateful. My editors in London, first Caroline MacArthur and then Mary Morris, inherited this project and were able to manage it nicely from afar. Nick Webb, who was the first to sign on to the book and the one who put in countless hours tracking its intricacies, was a delight to work with. Finally, Marian Lizzi at Perigee was there to put everything together, ably assisted by Christina Lundy, Tiffany Estreicher, and many others who worked just outside my radar screen.

Lynne Emmons of Arness House saved the day with her conversions of web-based artwork to formats suitable for reproduction on paper.

I am grateful for the conversations I had with first-rate mathematicians whose specialties overlapped with some of my goals for the manuscript. I would especially like to thank Norton Starr, David Kelly, Ross Honsberger, Richard Stanley, Arthur Benjamin, Raymond Smullyan, Gordon Prichett, and Herbert Scarf for their accessibility and their time.

I was able to use dozens of images that I first located on the web, each with a helpful creator or web designer who gave me the requisite permission. Thanks to Ken Knowlton at www.knowltonmosaics.com, Professor Carsten

Thomassen for his Thomassen graph, Bill Harrah for his beautiful Lincoln Memorial drawing, Stephane Gires and Mathilde Spriet at Gigamic for their wonderful games, and likewise for Kate Jones at Kadon Enterprises. The list goes on: Professor Heiko Harborth, with the help of Jens P. Bode, provided his famous toothpick drawing; Galen Frysinger, his Pont du Gard artistry; Achim Flammenkamp, his remarkable 52-square creation; Jim Loy, his 17-gon representation; Michel Emery for the wonderful kissing number diagram in L'Ouvert; Michel Guntern for the map of France at www.1800-Countries.com; Thomas Green at Contra Costa College for his bridges of Konigsberg diagram; Lawrence Charters for his calendars; Ed Rosenberg for his flags; A. Chatterjee in Mumbai for his chess diagram software; Rebecca Clark-Smith for her Patolli image; Allen Broughton at the Rose-Hulman Institute of Technology for his sphere-tiling drawing; Bill Cutler for the images of his clever work with Burr puzzles; Dan Thomasson for his knight's tour diagrams; and Andrew Ruddle for his pictures of triremes.

I'd also like to thank those people whose images, alas, ended up on the cutting room floor. There were many more of these than I'd like, including Laura Pecci at Winning Moves; Stefan Goya at www.psychicteddybear.com; Kristin MacQuarrie at www.harpconnection.com; Christopher Monckton, Alex Selby, and Oliver Riordan for their extraordinary Eternity puzzle images; Danny Smythe for his coconut picture; Theodor Lauppert for his images of Ishido; David Phillips for his graphs on the Baskerville effect; Steve and Tim Sommars for their clever work with octagons; Marc Gilbert for his website's Yankee Stadium image; Dollie at Jerry Ohlinger's Movie Material Store for pulling out a few real oldies; David DeJean for his colorful Lotus palette; Michael Kroeger and Thomas Detrie for their drawings of the icosahedron; William Waite for his Knit Pagoda puzzle; Don Hodges for his Pac-Man images; and, finally, Kristin Hylek at McDonald's.

There were also several organizations that chipped in to the effort. Thanks to Heidi Dettinger at Steinway & Sons, Sarah Hart and Jessica Zadlo at ThinkFun, Chris Holmes and Peter Costa at Owl Engineering, and Andrea Phillips at Fotosearch. I contacted several museums and other such collections during my image hunt, and was greatly assisted by Amanda

Turner and Helen Statham at the Ashmolean Museum at Oxford, Calune Eustache at United Media, Catherine Howell at the Victoria and Albert Museum, and Meghan Mazella and Valentina at the British Museum. And where I would have been without Brian Blankenburg at Getty Images is just too sad to contemplate.

Individuals who rose to the occasion included my sister, Eliza Miller, who tracked down a fabulous picture of Balanchine's *Serenade* from the Maine State Ballet. Jerry Slocum generously provided an image of the original 15 puzzle from 1880. Pete Malaspina provided access to all sorts of academic references that would otherwise have eluded me. Joseph West at Abaris Books gave me some helpful counsel. Boots Hinton gave me more information about Bonnie and Clyde than I ever thought I'd know. I regretted that I didn't have more than a couple of paragraphs to allot to those infamous gangsters, who died just five months after Boots was born—with Boots's father a member of the posse. And if there were any details that eluded Boots, Frank Ballinger was there as backup.

Finally, I benefited from a variety of mathematically oriented websites: MathWorld was absolutely indispensable; www.primecurios.com was delightfully bizarre; Mudd Math Fun Facts had some nice puzzles and curiosities; Erich Friedman at Stetson University is a one-man mathematical show whose work I greatly admire; Kevin Brown's work at www.math pages.com was helpful on several occasions; Ed Pegg's www.mathpuzzles.com was a delight to return to; and finally, moving overseas, the French website www.pagesperso-orange.fr/yoda.guillaume was a pleasure to translate through, and I have Gerard Villemin et al. to thank for that.

There. I think I've demonstrated that I didn't write this book alone. Thanks again to all.

TOWER HAMLETS COLLEGE
POPLAR HIGH STREET
LONDON
E14 0AF

PHOTO CREDITS

page 3: Prisoners in a Lineup—Fotosearch

page 7: Three Legs of Man—Travel Ink/Gallo Images/Getty Images

page 12: Koch Snowflake—Wikimedia Commons

page 17: Map of England—Wikimedia Commons

page 19: Five Stones—The Ashmolean Museum at Oxford

page 22: Sand Dollar—Siede Preis/Photodisc/Getty Images

page 23: Blue Angels in Flight—Don Farrall/Photodisc/Getty Images

page 30: Bridges over Rivers—Thomas M. Green, Math Dept., Contra Costa College

page 33: Seven Circles Theorem—Stanley Rabinowitz

page 46: Susan B. Anthony Coin—Time Life Pictures/Getty Images

page 60: Backgammon Board—Jeffrey Coolidge/Iconica/Getty Images

page 60: Billiard Balls—Davies and Starr/The Image Bank/Getty Images

page 67: Bachet Square Cards—Gerard Michon

page 69: 17-gon diagram—Jim Loy

page 73: Volleyball—Siri Stafford/Digital Vision/Getty Images

page 81: Puzzle Pieces—Livio Zucca

page 92: People at Table—William Caxton/Wikimedia Commons

page 111: Thomassen Graph—Carsten Thomassen

page 117: Lincoln Memorial—Bill Harrah, Wolf Run Studio

page 118: 36 Cube—Peggy Malaspina

page 125: Roulette Wheel—www.clipart.com

page 150: Patolli Game—Rebecca Clark-Smith, Great Hall Games

page 160: Chinese Character—Erin Silversmith

page 171: Braille Mosaic—Ken Knowlton, www.knowltonmosaics.com

page 180: Gordian's Knot—ThinkFun, Inc.

page 185: 72-sided sphere—Pacioli, Luca. *De divina proportione* (English: *On the Divine Proportion*), Luca Paganinem de Paganinus de Brescia

page 185: Archery Target—Wikimedia Commons/Alberto Barbati

page 187: Water Clock—Time Life Pictures/Getty Images

page 188: Stacked Balls—Wikimedia Commons/Greg L

page 199: Dart Board—www.CKSinfo.com

page 202: How to Tie a Tie—Yong Mao

page 209: Sunflower—John Foxx/Stockbyte/Getty Images

page 210: Baseball Diamond—Fotosearch

page 210: Dried Mud—Mike Norman/National Geographic/Getty Images

page 212: Abacus—Red Chopsticks/Getty Images

page 218: Builder's Old Measurement—Wikipedia/L'enciclopedia libera/Edoardo

page 220: Bell Curve—Chris Holmes/Owl Engineering

page 230: Matchstick Graph—Heiko Harborth

page 238: Poker Hand—Poker Pundit

page 246: Wooden Burr—Bill Cutler

page 247: Knight's Tour—Dan Thomasson

page 254: Bonnie & Clyde Poster—Frank Ballinger

page 259: Ship—Andrew Ruddle, The Trireme Trust

page 267: Sphere—Allen Broughton